The MISSUS

ALSO BY E L JAMES

Fifty Shades of Grey
Fifty Shades Darker
Fifty Shades Freed

Grey
Darker
Freed

The Mister

The MISSUS

E L James

PENGUIN BOOKS

PENGUIN BOOKS

UK | USA | Canada | Ireland | Australia
India | New Zealand | South Africa

Penguin Books is part of the Penguin Random House group of companies whose addresses can be found at global.penguinrandomhouse.com

Penguin Random House UK

First published in the US in 2023 by Bloom Books, an imprint of Sourcebooks
First published in the UK by Penguin Books 2023
001

Printed and bound in Great Britain by Clays Ltd, Elcograf S.p.A.

The authorised representative in the EEA is Penguin Random House Ireland, Morrison Chambers, 32 Nassau Street, Dublin D02 YH68

A CIP catalogue record for this book is available from the British Library

ISBN: 978-1-80495-334-1

www.greenpenguin.co.uk

FSC www.fsc.org MIX Paper | Supporting responsible forestry FSC® C018179

Penguin Random House is committed to a sustainable future for our business, our readers and our planet. This book is made from Forest Stewardship Council® certified paper.

For D with love.

Chapter One

My footsteps echo an urgent beat on the hard reflective floor, and I squint beneath the unremitting light of the fluorescents.

'This way.' The A&E consultant stops, and she ushers me into a cool, stark room that is the hospital mortuary.

On a table, beneath a sheet is the fractured, lifeless body of my brother.

My shock is seismic, pressing on my chest and squeezing the last of my breath from my lungs. Nothing could have prepared me for this.

Kit, my big brother.

My touchstone.

Kit, the twelfth Earl of Trevethick.

Dead.

'Yes. This is him.' The words are like cotton in my mouth.

'Thank you, Lord Trevethick,' the doctor murmurs.

Shit. That's me now!

I look down at Kit.

Except it's not him. *I'm* on the table – lying bruised and broken . . . cold . . . dead.

Me? How?

From my prostrate position, I watch Kit lean over and kiss my forehead. 'Goodbye, you fucker,' he rasps, the strain of unshed tears heavy in his throat. 'You've got this. This is what you were born to do.' He smiles his crooked, sincere smile that's reserved for those rare moments when he's fucked up.

Kit! No! You've got this wrong.

Wait!

'You've got this, Spare,' he says. 'You're lucky number thirteen.' His smile slips, and he disappears. And I'm looking down at him once more, leaning over him while he sleeps. Except his battered body belies that – he's not asleep – he's . . . dead.

No! Kit! No! My words stay stuck in a throat that's crowded with too much sorrow.

No! No!

I wake, my heart pounding.

Where am I?

It takes a nanosecond to orientate myself as my eyes adjust to the half-light. Alessia is curled around me, her head on my chest, her hand splayed on my stomach. As I take a deep, cleansing breath, my panic recedes like the gentle wash of a tideless sea.

I'm in Kukës in Northern Albania, at her parents' place, and across the lake, dawn is a whisper in the sky.

Alessia's here. With me. She's safe, and she's fast asleep. Carefully, I tighten my arm around her shoulders and kiss her hair, breathing in her scent. The faint balm of lavender, roses, and my sweet, sweet girl soothes and stirs my senses.

My body rouses; desire, hot and heavy, flowing south.

I want her. Again.

This is new – this need, but it's become ingrained, a part of who I am, and it's heightened when I'm with her. She's so enticing and lovely that I crave her like an addict. But I resist waking her – she's been through nine circles of hell.

Again.

Fuck.

I bring my body under control and close my eyes as my anger and regret resurface. I let her slip through my fingers. I let that violent arsehole, her 'betrothed,' steal her away. What she's endured, I don't want to know, but her cuts and bruises tell their own awful tale.

I'm never going to let that happen again.

Thank God she's safe.

Let her sleep.

Gently, I toy with a strand of her hair, marvelling as ever at its softness. Drawing it to my mouth, I brush it against my lips in a tender kiss.

My love. My beautiful, brave girl.

She's overcome so much in such a short time: trafficking, homelessness, finding paid employment . . . and falling in love with me.

My sweet daily.

Soon to be my bride.

Closing my eyes once more, I snuggle closer, seeking her warmth, and doze.

I wake suddenly, prompted by – something, an external source.

What was that?

It's later – the light in the room is brighter.

'*Alessia!*'

Her mother is calling her.

Shit! We've overslept!

'Alessia! Wake up. Your mother's calling.' I kiss her forehead, and she grumbles as I extract myself from her arms and sit up. 'Alessia! Come on! If your dad finds us, he'll shoot us both.'

The memory of her father, and his pump-action shotgun from last night, rises unwelcome in my mind.

You're going to marry my daughter.

Her mother calls again, and Alessia opens her eyes, blinking the sleep away. She looks up at me, all tousled and sleepy and arousing, and beams her brightest smile. For a moment, I forget the grim threat of her father with his trigger finger on that shotgun.

'Good morning, beautiful.' I stroke her cheek, avoiding the scrape that's still there. Closing her eyes, she leans into my touch. 'Your mother is calling you.'

Her eyes spring open, and her smile disappears, replaced with an expression of wide-eyed alarm. She sits upright, wearing nothing but her little gold cross. 'O Zot! O Zot!'

'Yeah. O Zot!'

'My nightdress!'

There's a muffled but urgent knock on the door. 'Alessia!' Mrs Demachi hisses.

'Shit! Hide! I'll get this.' My heart is beating a frantic tattoo.

Alessia bounces out of bed, all naked limbs and loveliness, while I jump up and slide on my jeans. Honestly, I want to laugh – it's like we're in some ridiculous British farce. It's insane. We're both consenting adults, and we're soon to be married. With a quick glance at Alessia, who is wrestling into her gothic nightdress, I pad over to the door, open it a crack, and feign sleepiness. Her mother is on the other side. 'Mrs Demachi, good morning.'

'Good morning, Count Maxim. Alessia?' she asks.

'Has she gone again?' I try to look concerned.

'She is not in her bed.'

Alessia's feet patter over the cold tiled floor, and she slips her arms about my waist as she peeks around me. 'Mama, I'm here,' she whispers in English for my benefit, I think.

Bloody hell.

We've been discovered, and now I'm framed as a liar to my future mother-in-law. I give Shpresa an apologetic shrug, and she frowns without a trace of humour in her expression.

Shit.

'Alessia!' she hisses and looks nervously over her shoulder. 'Po të gjeti yt atë këtu!'

'E di. E di,' Alessia replies and in answer to my scowl, she gives me a sweet, contrite look and raises her lips to mine, offering me a chaste kiss. She slips out of the door, shrouded in her Victorian nightdress, and regards me with a heated over-the-shoulder look as she follows her mother up the stairs. I forgive her for outing me as a liar to her mother, and stand and listen as they hiss at each other in Albanian. I don't hear her father.

I think we got away with it.

Well, he did say she's my problem now. I shake my head as I shut the door, angered by the thought. Alessia is not *my problem*, for fuck's sake. She's a woman who knows her own mind. How could he even think that? It grinds my gears. Culturally, her dad and I are poles apart, and as much as I want to be respectful to him, he needs dragging into the twenty-first century. It's obvious why Alessia is wary of him. She obliquely alluded to his volatile nature when she mentioned him during our time in Cornwall. She said then that she didn't miss him – only her mother.

Hell. The sooner we leave here, the better.

How long will it take to get married?

Perhaps we should make a break for it.

Elope?

We could hole up at the Plaza Hotel in Tirana while we wait for her new passport and discover the delights of the capital together. How long will it take to get a passport anyway? Long enough for her father to come after us with his shotgun? I don't know, and somehow, I don't think Alessia would like the idea.

But this furtive running around like we're kids – it's crazy. It's as if we've travelled back several centuries, and I'm not sure I'll be able to tolerate this for long.

I check the time, and it's still early, so I strip out of my jeans and lie down. As I stare at the ceiling and reflect on the last few days, thoughts of my most recent dream drift into my consciousness.

What the hell was that about?

Kit?

He approves of me inheriting the earldom.

Is that it?

Would he approve of my hasty proposal and this shotgun wedding?

No, I don't think he would. Perhaps that's what it meant. Come to think of it – I'm not sure anyone in my family will approve. I close my eyes, imagining my mother's response to the news. Maybe she'll be happy to see me married . . . finally.

No. She'll be furious. I know it.

Perhaps my dream meant Kit is offering his solidarity.

Could be . . .

Yes.

That's what the dream was about.

Her mother is angry, and Alessia doesn't know what to say to pacify her.

'What do you think you were doing?' Shpresa growls.

Alessia raises a brow in answer.

'Alessia!' her mother snaps, knowing full well what Alessia is trying to convey. 'Just because that man has had a bite of your cherry doesn't mean you shouldn't wait until after you're married!'

Mama!

'If your father catches you!' She sighs. 'I think he's gone out, maybe to look for you. He would probably have a heart attack if he knew what you were doing.' She tuts in exasperation as they make their way down the hall, but her expression softens when they reach the living room. 'I suppose you're pregnant already, so . . .' She lifts her shoulders, resigned.

A slow flush creeps over Alessia's face. Should she tell her mother it was a lie?

'So, your handsome count, he's in good shape.' Shpresa eyes her daughter with a teasing smile.

'Mama!' Alessia exclaims.

'He has a tattoo.'

'Yes. It's his family's coat of arms.'

'I see.' She sounds disapproving and she purses her lips.

Alessia shrugs. She likes his tattoo.

Her mother smiles. 'He is good to you . . . in bed?'

'Mama!' Alessia's voice rises several octaves in shock.

'It's important. I want you to be happy, and you must keep him happy. And it won't be long before the child arrives, and, well . . .' Her mother huffs, her disappointment rolling off her in waves while Alessia stares back at her blankly.

What can she say? That she lied to her parents?

And is this how it was for her mother after Alessia was born?

Alessia doesn't want to think about that. Besides, it's too early in the morning to be having this conversation.

'I think he's happy,' she says eventually.

'Good. We can talk more on this.'

'I don't want to talk more on this,' Alessia retorts, mortified.

'Don't you have questions?'

Alessia pales at the thought. 'No!'

'I suppose it's a bit late for that now. But if you have questions, your father and I—'

'Mama! Stop!' Alessia puts her hands over her ears. 'I don't want to know.'

Her mother laughs good-naturedly. 'It is good to have you back, my heart. I have missed you so much.' Her laughter fades, and her eyes narrow, her expression shifting – becoming serious. 'Last night, I tossed and turned in bed. I was thinking about the ramifications of something that Lord Maxim said. I couldn't sleep with worry.' Her voice fades away.

'What is it, Mama?'

She takes a deep breath as if what she's about to say is particularly unpalatable. 'He said something about sex trafficking.'

Alessia gasps. 'Oh, Mama, I have so much to tell you, but first I'll have a shower.'

Her mother gathers her into her arms. 'Sweet child of my heart,' she says softly in her ear. 'I'm so glad you are home. And safe.'

'Me too, Mama. And no more Anatoli.'

Shpresa nods. 'And your fiancé, does he have a violent temper?'

'No. No. He doesn't. Quite the opposite.'

Her mother beams. 'You light up like summer when you talk about him.' She takes Alessia's hand and, raising a brow, admires the beautiful engagement ring. 'He has money and taste.'

Alessia nods and stares at the sparkling diamond on her finger.

This beautiful ring is now hers.

She can hardly believe it.

'Go shower. I will make bread and coffee.'

Alessia stands beneath the shower in the family bathroom, revelling in the hot water. It's not as fast flowing as the showers in Cornwall, but she welcomes the warmth as she scrubs her skin clean. This is the first moment she's allowed herself to reflect on all that's happened over the last few days.

Anatoli. Her kidnapping. The long journey here. His brutality.

She shudders. He's out of her life now, and for that, she's grateful.

And she was welcomed home; even her father admitted he missed her.

Alessia closes her eyes as she vigorously rubs the shampoo into her hair, trying to erase her guilt. She's lied to her parents, and her dishonesty chafes like a burr on her conscience.

She's not pregnant, but should she tell them the truth?

What would her father say if he knew? What would he do?

She raises her face to the cascade and lets it wash over her.

And then there's Maxim.

She grins into the stream of water. He crossed a continent to find her and brought a ring with him to propose. It's far more than she could ever have dreamed of or hoped for. Now, she needs to find out how Maxim really feels about having an Albanian wedding forced on him.

He didn't object last night.

But she wishes her father were less insistent.

Alessia would be happier back in London and worries Maxim will feel the same. How long will it be before he becomes bored of being in Kukës? He's used to a very different life, and there's not much to entertain him here. Perhaps they should flee Kukës together. They could marry in England.

Would Maxim consider this idea? Alessia rinses her hair and stops.

No. Mama!

Alessia cannot leave her mother at the mercy of her father. She must bring her mother with her. *Could she? Would Maxim object?* After all, Shpresa speaks fluent English. *Her* mother, Alessia's beloved grandmother Virginia, was English. She must have family in England. Alessia doesn't know. Her nana never spoke of her English family because they disapproved of her marriage to an Albanian man.

Will it be the same with Maxim's family?

Will they disapprove of her?

A shiver skitters down her spine. Maxim's marrying his cleaner, a penniless foreigner. Of course they won't approve. Alessia's mood sours.

What can she do?

Perhaps they shouldn't marry until she's met his family, and she'll know if they accept her, or not, because in the depths of her heart – she wants their blessing.

But first, she must navigate her father and his expectations, and he's a stubborn, temperamental, proud man. He said he wanted them married by the end of the week.

Is that even possible?

She scrubs her face. There is much to think about and much to be done.

When Alessia enters the kitchen, her mother looks up from kneading dough and studies her. 'You look different,' she says, setting the dough aside to rise.

'Is it the clothes?' Alessia does a twirl. She's wearing a skirt, top, and cardigan from the collection that Maxim bought her in Padstow.

'Yes, maybe. But you look more worldly.' Her mother moves to the sink to wash her hands.

'I am,' Alessia replies quietly. She's been trafficked through Europe, been homeless, lived in one of the busiest cities in the world, and she's fallen in love . . . then had that all snatched away from her as she was kidnapped, and nearly raped, by her betrothed. Alessia shudders.

Don't think of him.

'Coffee?' her mother asks.

'No sugar for me,' she says as she sits at the table.

Shpresa peers at her in surprise. 'It tastes okay?'

'You get used to it.'

Shpresa places a full cup on the table for Alessia and sits opposite her with a cup of her own. 'Tell me. What happened after I put you on that minibus on the road to Shkodër?'

'Oh, Mama.' Alessia's lip quivers as the enormity of what she's experienced since she left Albania rises in her chest like a tidal wave. Haltingly, between her tears, she tells her mother the whole story.

I wake feeling refreshed. The sun is higher in the sky, and when I check the time, it's 9:30 a.m. It's late. Hurriedly, I drag on my jeans, T-shirt, and jumper. At some point, I'll need to head back to the hotel and collect my stuff. But more importantly, I need to know what's happening with our shotgun wedding.

In the living room, I find Alessia and her mother quietly sobbing at the table.

What the hell?

'What's wrong?' I startle them both as my anxiety rockets.

Alessia dashes the tears from her eyes and leaps up from her chair into my arms.

'Hey. What is it?'

'Nothing. I'm glad you are here.' She hugs me.

I kiss the top of her head. 'So am I.'

Shpresa rises too and wipes her eyes. 'Good morning, Lord Maxim.'

'Good morning. Um . . . Maxim is fine. It's my name.'

She gives me a tight smile. 'Coffee?'

'Please.'

'No sugar, Mama,' Alessia interjects.

I tilt her chin up and gaze into sad, dark eyes that have seen and experienced too much. My heart clenches.

My love.

'Why are you so upset?'

'I was telling Mama about everything that happened after I left Kukës.'

I tighten my hold on her as a surge of protective energy constricts my chest. 'I see.' Kissing her hair, I cradle her against me, grateful once more that she's survived her harrowing ordeal. 'I've got you now, and I'm not going to let you out of my sight.'

Ever.

I frown, surprised at the ferocity of my feelings. I really *don't* want to let her out of my sight. She's been through too much already. 'I mean it,' I add. She runs her fingertips over my stubble, and her touch reverberates . . . everywhere. 'I need a shave.' I sound gruff.

She grins. 'I would like to watch.'

'Would you now?' I raise a brow.

Alessia's eyes are no longer despondent but sparkling with amusement and an emotion that speaks directly to my groin.

Mrs Demachi busies herself preparing coffee, noisily banging the small pot, so the spell between Alessia and me is broken. I kiss Alessia's nose, and grinning like a fool, I turn my attention to her mother. Alessia nuzzles my chest as I watch the elaborate process that includes a small tin pot, a long teaspoon, and studious stirring at the stove.

Mrs Demachi gives me a brief smile. 'Sit,' she says, so I release my fiancée and, with a glance at the shotgun on the wall, take a seat at the table.

Alessia retrieves a cup and saucer from the dresser. She's wearing the dark denim skirt we bought in Padstow, which clings enticingly to her perfectly formed arse.

She's gorgeous.

I shift in my chair, and Alessia fills my cup from the tin pot. 'Your coffee,' she says, her dark eyes gleaming with delight, and she places the cup in front of me. She knows I'm ogling her, and she likes it. I grin and, with my eyes on hers, purse my lips together to blow gently over the rim of the cup. Her lips part as she inhales sharply, and my grin widens.

Two can play this game.

Her mother clears her throat, and we're both brought back into the kitchen. Alessia laughs and says something in Albanian to Mrs Demachi, who nods in quiet disapproval at her daughter.

I attempt a sip of coffee. It's scalding hot, aromatic and bitter but warming. Alessia's mother lights the oven and then starts rolling out some dough. She's quick and efficient, and before long, she's cut them into strips, then squares. The speed is impressive. No wonder Alessia cooks so well. Alessia joins her, and I watch, fascinated, as they each form little round dough balls in their hands. Their ease in the kitchen reminds me of Jessie and Danny at Tresyllian Hall in Cornwall. Her mother arranges them close together on a baking tray, and Alessia paints them with milk using a little plastic brush. Their competence, their ease with each other – their domesticity is comforting to watch.

Hell. Where are my manners?

'Can I do anything to help?' Maxim asks.

Alessia carefully shakes her head while her mother nods.

'No, Mama. The nodding means yes.'

Shpresa laughs. 'We are not used to help from men in the kitchen.' Her eyes are alight with humour as she places the baking tray in the oven.

Alessia starts laying the table. 'I told you. Only women cook here.'

Breakfast is a delicious fresh-from-the-oven feast. I'm on my fourth bubble bread roll with butter and berry jam and my second coffee when we hear the front door slam. A few moments later, Mr Demachi appears wearing a sombre suit and matching expression that gives nothing away. Shpresa leaps up from the table and starts to fill the coffee pot with water.

Perhaps she needs a larger pot.

Alessia rises from the table, reaches for a plate, and lays it at the head of the table with a knife. Demachi sits down, and it's obvious this is normal – he's been waited on, hand and foot, for his entire life.

Um . . . So have I. But not by my mother – or my sister for that matter.

'Mirëmëngjes,' he grunts, looking directly at me as inscrutable as ever.

'My father is wishing you a good morning,' Alessia translates and looks amused.

Why does she find this funny?

'Good morning.' I give my future father-in-law a nod.

He starts speaking, and Alessia and her mother listen,

enthralled by his deep melodious voice as he explains something to them. I just wish I knew what he was saying.

Eventually, Alessia turns to me, her eyes wide as if she doesn't quite believe what she's about to tell me. 'My father, he has arranged our marriage.'

Already?

It's my turn to look incredulous. 'Tell me.'

'All you need is your passport.'

We gaze at each other, and I think the same thought runs through her head and mine.

This sounds too easy.

My eyes meet his, and he raises his chin in an arrogant don't-fuck-with-me glare as if he's daring me to argue.

'He met the clerk of the, um . . . civil status . . . office. I don't know the precise translation,' Alessia says. 'They met for coffee this morning. They agreed on everything.'

On a Sunday? Is it that simple?

'Okay. When?' I keep my voice measured, as I don't want to rile the old goat. He has a short fuse – almost as bad as my friend Tom's.

'Saturday.'

A frisson of doubt trickles down my spine. 'Okay,' I answer, and my hesitancy must give me away. Mrs Demachi glances anxiously from me to her husband, then to her daughter.

Alessia says something to her dad, and he shouts back at her, startling us all. She pales and hangs her head but peeks at me as I push back my chair.

He shouldn't speak to her like that.

'The clerk and he are good friends,' Alessia says hurriedly. 'Old friends. I think I know him. I've met him before. My father says it's all arranged.' She's obviously used to his outbursts, but she, too, seems uncertain.

As am I. This arrangement seems far too convenient.

Perplexed, I settle in my chair once more, not wanting to provoke him. 'What do I need to do?'

'We must meet with the clerk tomorrow at the bashkia – I mean, town hall – to answer some questions and complete some paperwork.' She shrugs, looking as troubled as I feel.

Okay. Let's talk to the clerk.

As I stand under the rather rudimentary shower and wash my hair, I have a complete crisis of conscience. A quick internet search on my phone has told me that it's far more complicated to marry as a foreign national in Albania than Alessia's father seems to think. There are forms to be completed, then translated and notarised – and that's just a quick and dirty glance of what's required.

What has her father organised?

How has he managed to circumvent the usual protocols?

If he has, are they legal?

And if they're not, how can I go ahead with a wedding that's probably not legal to appease a proud, impatient old man? I know he'll be my father-in-law, but what he's asking is too much. All his talk of honour yesterday accounts for nothing if he treats his daughter this way.

And I'm in a bind. I can't leave without Alessia, and I know the old bastard won't let me take her with me. She needs a passport and a visa to return to the UK, and I have no idea where or how we get one. Probably somewhere in Tirana. I don't know.

Though he did say she was my problem now.

Maybe I should take him at his word.

I switch off the shower, resentful and bewildered by the situation I've found myself in – and by the large puddle of water I've left on the bathroom floor. It does not speak well of Albanian plumbing. I snatch a towel and quickly dry myself, then drag on my clothes and open the door.

Alessia is standing outside, brandishing what looks like a high-tech shower-cleaning device. I laugh, surprised and pleased to see her, and I'm transported back to a time when she was in my flat, wearing her frightful nylon housecoat, and I was surreptitiously watching her . . . and falling in love.

She grins and places her fingers against her lips.

'Does he know you're here?' I whisper.

She shakes her head, places her hand squarely on my chest, and pushes me back into the bathroom. She drops the mop and promptly locks the door.

'Alessia,' I warn, but she cups my face and pulls my lips to hers. Her kiss is soft and sweet but demanding – surprisingly demanding. As her tongue finds mine, she presses her body against me, and I close my eyes and wrap my arms around her, delighting in her kiss. Her fingers slide into my wet hair, and her lips become more insistent as she tugs. It's a wake-up call to my impatient dick.

Hell. We're going to fuck.

In an Albanian bathroom with poor plumbing.

I pull away so we can catch our breath, and Alessia's eyes are dark and full of promise but also uncertainty.

'What is it?' I ask.

She shakes her head.

'No.' I clasp her face and gaze into her eyes. 'God, as much as I want you, we're not fucking in this bathroom. Your parents aren't far away, and I don't have a condom. Now tell me, what's wrong? Is it the wedding?'

'Yes.'

I blow out a breath in relief and release her. 'Yeah. What your father's arranged – I don't know if it's . . . legitimate.'

'I know. My parents want to discuss the, um . . . arrangements with us in the afternoon. I don't know what to do. I think it's because my father thinks I am with child. He's managed to pull the strings.'

An image of her dad as an evil puppet master with Alessia and me as his marionettes comes to mind, making me chuckle. 'We say "pull some strings."'

She repeats the saying and gives me a shy smirk.

'You still don't mind that I correct your English?'

'Never.'

Okay. Let's go with Plan A. Here goes.

'Let's leave. You don't have to stay here. You're an adult. You're not beholden to your father – whatever he thinks. We can go to Tirana. Get a passport for you and arrange a visa. Then we can fly back to the UK. We'll get married there. And your parents can join us for the wedding.'

Alessia's eyes widen as several emotions flit across her face. Hope seems to win, and I think she's been considering this possibility herself.

But then her face falls, so I draw her into my arms and hold her. 'We'll figure this out.' I kiss her hair.

She peers up at me, and I think she's inwardly debating whether to ask me something.

'What?'

'No. It's okay.'

'What?' I insist.

She swallows. 'My mother.'

'What about your mother?'

'I can't leave her here with him.'

'You want to bring her with you?'

'Yes.'

Fuck. 'Okay. If that's what you want.'

Alessia looks stunned. 'You are saying yes?'

'Yes.'

She lights up like Christmas, as if she's finally unburdened of all her woes. She flings her arms around my neck. 'Thank you. Thank you. Thank you,' she gasps between kisses and starts to laugh and cry.

Oh, baby.

'Don't cry. I'd do anything for you. You should know that. I love you.' I wipe her tears away with my thumbs as I caress her face. 'And like I said, we'll figure this out. We'll make a plan.'

Her eyes, dark with adoration, peek up at me as if I have all the answers to the eternal questions of the universe and a welcome warmth spreads through my chest. Her trust and faith in me are bewildering, but damn, it feels good.

And I know, for her, I'd do anything.

Chapter Two

It's dark outside as I stumble towards the bed and attempt to peel off my jumper, but it fights back and finally gets the better of me. 'Shit!' I fall on the bed and stare blindly at the blurred ceiling.

Oh God. Why did I drink so much?

After an afternoon of wedding planning and trying not to lose my temper, the raki was a mistake. The room swims, and I shut my eyes, praying for sleep.

I surface from a dreamless sleep. It's quiet. And bright.

No. Dazzling.

I scrunch my eyes closed, then open them cautiously as pain slices with a laser's precision through my brain. I shut them again quickly.

Hell. I feel like shit.

Pulling the covers over my head to shut out the light, I try to remember where I am, who I am, and what happened last night.

There was raki.

Shots and shots of raki.

Alessia's father was exceedingly generous with his lethal, local intoxicant. I groan and flex my fingers and toes and am pleased to find that they still work. I reach out beside me, but the bed is empty.

No Alessia.

Drawing down the covers, I slowly open my eyes and ignore the sharp jab to my frontal lobe as I survey the room. I'm on my own, but my tired gaze rests on the little dragon nightlight on the table beside the bed. Alessia must have brought it back from London. The thought is touching.

Also, was she here? Last night?

Vaguely, I remember her joining me, and maybe undressing me. I lift the covers. I'm naked except for my underwear. She must have undressed me.

Damn. I passed out and have no memory of her in here at all.

Why did I let him ply me with so much alcohol?

Was it his revenge because I've bedded his daughter?

And what happened?

Snippets from yesterday sneak past the pain in my head. Alessia and I had sat down and discussed wedding plans with her parents. I close my eyes and try to recall the details.

From what I understand, we're departing from the Albanian tradition by celebrating on one day only – rather than several days. Firstly, because I'm British and have no family or home here, and secondly, we're doing all this at such short notice as Alessia is 'with child.' Demachi gave me a sour look as he sputtered this, and Alessia, blushing furiously, had to translate.

I sigh. Perhaps we should confess to the lie. Maybe he'll back off.

Maybe he'll let me take her back to the UK and get married there.

The ceremony and celebration will be on Saturday and will start at lunchtime – not in the evening. It's another break with tradition, but because I'm staying with the bride's family, it makes sense, or so they told me. Besides, the registrar has another wedding to conduct in the evening.

The Demachis will host the wedding themselves, and Mr Demachi asked if my family would attend. I set him right on that score. My mother will no doubt be in New York, and she wouldn't get here in time, and my sister, as a doctor, won't be able to get the time off at such short notice. I reassured them that we will celebrate in London when we're back in the UK. My excuses seemed to pacify the old goat. I don't think my family will approve of a shotgun wedding, and I don't want to give them the opportunity to object, or question the legitimacy of our marriage. However, I'm hoping my sparring partner, Joe Diallo, will join us so I'll have him and Tom Alexander with me. They are my oldest friends.

That counts for something, surely.

I had offered to pay for everything but was shot down by my father-in-law, with his most wounded expression.

Boy, is he proud.

He would hear of no such thing. I suspect he likes a little drama; he's a melodramatic man. I suggested a compromise, and we agreed that I'll supply the alcohol. But it chafes that he'll be out of pocket if Alessia and I decide not to go through with it.

Hell. That's his problem.

There's also something about the rings, which I can't remember.

Rings! I need to buy rings.

Shall I buy them here?

I sit up and my head swims, but once it settles, I stagger out of bed and drag on my jeans to go in search of my future wife. What I do remember is that today we implement our plan. Alessia and I will visit the police station to apply for her new passport and then on to the town hall to keep our appointment with the clerk officiating the marriage and find out if what Demachi has organised is indeed legitimate.

Yeah. That's the plan.

I reach for my phone and notice a couple of texts from Caroline left last night.

Where are you? Did you find her?

Call me. I'm worried about you.

Surprised that my thumbs are cooperating, I send her a quick text, knowing she'll probably send out a search party if I don't respond.

All good. Found her. Will call later.

She'll lose her shit over this wedding; I know it in my bones. Perhaps I shouldn't tell her until I see her.

Coward.

My head throbs, and I rub my temples, trying to calm the squall that rages between them. If I tell Caroline, I'll have to tell Maryanne and my mother, and that's a conversation I'm actively avoiding, especially with a hangover. I'm not ready for that yet. I need to know where Alessia and I stand legally, then, maybe, I'll tell the Mothership, but perhaps I'll leave telling her until the day before we do the deed.

I drag on a T-shirt and pocket my phone. All that can wait; I need pain relief and coffee, preferably in that order.

Alessia and her mother are sitting at the dining table, drinking coffee.

'Mama, do you have my ID card?'

'Of course, my heart. I've treasured it since you left.'

Alessia is taken aback at her mother's words, and an aching void forms in her throat as she reaches across to squeeze Shpresa's hand. 'I thought of you often while I was gone,' she says, her voice husky with emotion. 'I didn't have any of my photographs or my phone. The men . . . They took everything. Including my passport. I'm glad I left my ID with you. I need to get another passport.'

'I'll fetch it for you shortly. I'm glad that the scrape on your face has almost healed. And the bruises. They look much better.'

Her mouth thins as she examines her daughter. 'I would like to box Anatoli Thaçi's ears.'

Alessia smiles. 'I would like to watch you do that.' She releases her and stares anxiously across at her mother. Alessia realises this is her opportunity. She's been trying to bring up this subject since she and Maxim discussed it yesterday. 'I have to ask you something.'

'Yes, child?'

Alessia swallows, and the thoughtful speech she'd rehearsed so many times in her head dries on her tongue.

'Alessia, what is it?'

'Come with us,' Alessia blurts, suddenly incapable of saying what she'd planned.

'What?'

'Come with me and Maxim to England. Please. You don't have to stay with him.'

Shpresa gasps, her dark eyes widening. 'Leave Jak?'

Alessia hears the dismay in her mother's voice. 'Yes.'

Her mother sits back in the chair and gapes at Alessia. 'He's my husband, child. I'm not going to leave him.'

This is not what Alessia is expecting to hear. 'But he's not kind to you,' she protests. 'He's violent. Like Anatoli. You cannot stay.'

'Alessia, he's not like Anatoli. I love your father.'

'What?' Alessia's world shifts on its axis.

'My place is with him,' Shpresa says with steel in her voice.

'But you told me love is for fools.'

Her mother's eyes soften, and she lifts her lips in a rueful smile. 'I am a fool, my heart. We have our ups and downs, I know. Like all couples—'

'I've seen the bruises, Mama! Please. Come with us.'

'My place is with him. This is my home. I have a life here. There's nothing for me in a land I don't know. Besides, since you left, he's been more considerate. Contrite, I think. He believes he drove you away. He was so relieved when we got word of you.'

Alessia is shocked. This is not how she viewed her father or, indeed, her parents' relationship at all.

'You see, my heart,' her mother continues, and she reaches across the table to grasp Alessia's hand. 'This is the life I know. Your father loves me. Baba loves you too. He may not show it like we see in the American television programmes – and I see it's different with your betrothed, but that's how it is in *our* house. This is my home, and he's my husband.' She shrugs and then squeezes Alessia's hand as if trying to convey the truth of her words through the pressure of her fingers, but Alessia is reeling. She'd always thought her mother was miserable with her father.

Was she wrong?

Did she misread the situation between them?

I stand unseen on the threshold of the family room and observe Alessia's mother speaking in urgent, hushed tones to her daughter. They're sitting at the dining table – the location of Mr Demachi's raki attack last night – and their conversation is intense. But the pounding in my brain needs therapeutic drugs, so I stagger in, surprising them both, and slump into one of the chairs.

Shpresa releases Alessia's hand. 'We can talk more on this later. But my mind is made up, sweet girl. I'm not leaving my husband. I love him. In my own way. And he loves and needs me.' She smiles benevolently at Alessia, then turns her attention to Maxim. 'Your count, he had too much to drink last night. Fetch him a couple of painkillers. I'll make him some coffee.'

Alessia looks anxiously at her mother, surprised and confused by her reaction. 'Yes, Mama. We'll talk later.' She's bewildered by her mother's response, but she turns to Maxim, who holds his head in his hands, and her stance softens. 'I don't think my fiancé is used to raki.'

'I understood raki,' Maxim groans, husky-voiced, and he peers at her, bleary-eyed.

Alessia smiles. 'I will fetch some tablets for your head.'

I lean towards her. 'Thank you for putting me to bed last night.' I keep my voice low as her mother busies herself with the coffee pot.

'It was interesting.' She stops and checks that Shpresa is out of hearing range. 'It was fun undressing you.'

I take a quick, sharp breath as she rises and retrieves a first-aid kit from the pantry, and when she turns back, her dark, provocative eyes dart to mine, her face illuminated with a shy, secret smile.

My heart lurches in my chest.

My girl undressed me, and I was unconscious with drink.

Hell. An opportunity wasted.

But more than the wasted opportunity, she's not judged me for being inebriated, and now she's taking care of me. It's a new and wholly enlightening experience, and I love her for it. I can't remember anyone doing that for me as an adult – except Alessia when she put me to bed after that crazy drive from Cornwall. She's kind, caring and . . . hot, especially in tight jeans.

I'm a lucky guy.

I attempt a broad smile but my head throbs, and I'm reminded that it was her father who inflicted this damage – and I was only drinking the ghastly beverage to be polite. Alessia places two tablets and a glass of water in front of me. 'It was my father who did this to you. I know. And it was our local raki. Made here in Kukës.'

'I see.' *It was his revenge!* 'Thank you,' I offer.

'You are most welcome.' She gives me a coquettish smile, and I wonder if she's talking about the tablets or undressing me. Grinning, I down the painkillers and wonder if Tom and Thanas will be in a similar state to me.

Following our lengthy discussions yesterday, and with the marriage formalities supposedly settled, Mrs Demachi and Alessia had prepared a lavish meal and kindly invited my friend Tom, our translator Thanas, and Drita, his girlfriend. While they prepared the meal, Alessia taught me some Albanian words – my pleases and thank yous.

She laughed.

A lot.

At my pronunciation.

But it's always a joy to hear her laugh.

Alessia's mother had been in her element, happy to have a house full of guests, even though she didn't say much. She left that to her husband, who regaled us with stories of the turbulent 1990s as Albania transitioned from Communism to a democratic republic. It was fascinating – his family was caught up in a terrible pyramid scheme, and they'd lost what money they had. It's how they'd found themselves in Kukës during those dark times. While he talked, his generous but heavy hand poured and poured the raki. Tom and Thanas matched me shot for shot, I'm sure. They'll be meeting us at the town hall, provided they've survived the Ordeal by Raki. I check my watch. I have an hour to get it together.

The town hall is a nondescript modern building a stone's throw from Hotel Amerika where Tom and Thanas are staying. Hand-in-hand, Alessia and I stand in the reception area waiting for them to join us, and despite the dull ache in my head from my hangover, I cannot help my smile. Alessia's so buoyant since our earlier stop at the police station that she lights up the dreary foyer. Her new passport will be ready to collect on Friday – I paid for it to be expedited – and one would think I'd lassoed the moon she's so jubilant, but Alessia having a passport gives us options.

'Just the sight of your joy is easing my hangover.' I try to contain my smile, but I fail. She *is* a joy.

'I think it is the tablets I gave you.'

'No. It's you.'

She laughs, peering at me through her lashes, and I lift her hand and skim her knuckles with my lips.

God, I wish I could whisk her away from this drab little town.

Soon, dude. Soon.

Tom and Thanas appear, Thanas looking how I feel – dishevelled and hungover.

'Well, Trevethick, you look like hell. What are we doing here?' Tom asks, bright as a fucking button. Raki appears to agree with him.

'I am sorry we're late,' Thanas mumbles. 'I took Drita to board the bus to Tirana. She has to get back to her studies.'

'We're here to visit the clerk who will officiate our wedding.'

'The registrar. I'll go check where we must go,' Thanas says and wanders towards the reception desk to wait in line. Alessia joins him.

'So,' Tom hisses, keeping his voice low and sounding conspiratorial. 'I never congratulated you about the baby.'

The baby?

It takes me a moment in my befuddled state to realise what he's talking about. I laugh and stop suddenly as my head throbs. 'Alessia's not pregnant. She told her father she was so she wouldn't be forced to marry that wanker Antonelli or whatever his name is.'

'Ah.' Tom looks relieved. 'Well, I suppose that's good. Too early in a relationship for sprogs.' He leans into me while watching Thanas and Alessia and hisses, 'But you know you don't have to marry her, old boy.'

For fuck's sake.

'Tom.' My voice warns him off the subject. 'We've had this conversation already. For the last time, I love Alessia and want her to be my wife. Understand?'

'Frankly, no. She's a beautiful girl, I'll give you that, but I can't imagine you've got much in common. But the heart wants what the heart wants.'

I'm in no mood for an argument, so when he holds a conciliatory hand up at my scowl, I blow out a breath. 'Should I humour the old goat, marry her here? Or wait until we return to the UK? I'm stuck here until she gets her passport and a visa, and I'm not leaving her on her own.' I glance over to where she's standing patiently beside Thanas, who's talking to the receptionist.

'Well,' Tom says. 'If it's what you want, I think you should go along with it. It's a civil ceremony at the town hall. You'll keep the old chap happy, and then you can abscond with his daughter and do it properly in London, Cornwall, or Oxfordshire. Wherever.' He frowns. 'If you can.'

'What do you mean?'

'I don't know if you can get married more than once to the same woman, old boy. I'm sure there are rules. What do you have to do here?'

'I have to show my passport, and apparently that's it, though that's not what the official government website says.'

Tom's brow furrows once more. 'You think something's off?'

I nod. 'But we'll find out with Thanas. Will you stick around until then? And . . . you know, help out?'

'Of course, Trevethick. Wouldn't miss this high drama for the world.'

'High drama?' My scalp itches. Has he guessed we might abscond?

'You've travelled to the back of beyond to save your lady. If that's not the definition of drama, I don't know what is.'

I laugh. He has a point. 'And, um . . . will you be my best man?'

Tom is momentarily speechless, and when he finds his voice, it's gruff. 'I'd be honoured, Maxim.' He pats me on the back, and we turn to find Thanas and Alessia heading over to us.

'This way,' Thanas says, and we follow him up the stairs to the next floor.

The brass nameplate on his desk reads F. TABAKU. He's the registrar who will officiate at our civil ceremony. He's a similar age to Demachi and wears the same dark suit and impenetrable expression. He rises as we enter his office, greets Alessia cordially, gives me a curt nod, then waves us to the small table where the five of us take our seats.

Thanas translates as we quickly establish that he needs to see a copy of Alessia's birth certificate and ID card, and my passport. I fish mine out of my coat and open it up to the correct page, realising that I, too, will have to get a new passport. At present, mine is in the name The Hon Maximillian John Frederick Xavier Trevelyan.

We hand over our documents, and he gives Alessia's a cursory glance. My passport receives a more thorough examination. Tabaku frowns and says something to Thanas. Alessia interjects. 'Vëllai i Maksimit ishte Konti. Ai vdiq në fillim të janarit. Maksimi trashëgoi titullin, po nuk ka pasur ende mundësi të ndryshojë pasaportën.'

Tabaku seems satisfied with whatever Alessia has said and rises from the table to a small desktop photocopier. While he makes copies, I ask Alessia, 'What did you say?'

'I told him that you have only recently . . . um . . . inherited your title.'

He turns and addresses us both. Thanas translates. 'Spouses, when entering into marriage, have the right to choose to keep one of their surnames as a common surname or you keep your own. You need to decide.'

I turn to Alessia. 'What do you want to do?'

'I would like to take your name.'

I smile, pleased. 'Good. For your purposes, Alessia's name is Alessia Trevelyan. Her formal title will be Lady Alessia, The Right Honourable the Countess of Trevethick.'

'Please write that down,' Thanas translates.

I oblige on the notepaper provided and hand my scribble to Tabaku.

Tabaku responds, and Thanas says, 'I will name Alessia as Alessia Demachi-Trevelyan; your passport says nothing about Trevethick.'

'That's fine,' I grumble and turn to Thanas. 'Ask him about the certificate of no-impediment that I'm supposed to provide.'

Thanas does, and Alessia glances anxiously at me.

The registrar's eyes widen, and he spits an answer back at Thanas, who turns to me as he reels off Tabaku's response. 'He says that because time is an issue,' his eyes dart to Alessia, 'he is expediting your marriage. He has the power to do so in special circumstances. Alessia's father is a close and trusted friend, and that's why he's offering this service.'

The registrar continues in his low voice, his eyes not leaving mine, and it dawns on me that he's doing Demachi, and thereby us, an enormous favour.

'He says the marriage will be legal. It's all you need,' Thanas translates. 'You will have a marriage certificate.'

'And if we want to do it with all the correct paperwork?' I ask.

Tabaku retakes his seat, hands our documents back, and responds to Thanas's question. 'That will take between two to three months.'

'Okay. I see. Thank you.' Even though he's doing us a favour, I'm still uncomfortable. It feels like a sham and that thought is unsettling.

The registrar says something to Alessia and Thanas. Alessia nods and starts speaking to him in Albanian. I look hopefully at Thanas. 'He's asking for your profession, place of residence, and where you'll live once you're married.'

Profession!

I give Thanas my address in Chelsea and tell him that's where we'll live when we're married. Alessia glances at me with a shy smile.

'And profession?' Thanas inquires as the words my father used to adopt when asked this drift conveniently into my head.

'Farmer and photographer,' I state quickly, though it's not the entire truth. Now, I'm a landowner and a landlord – the CEO of the Trevethick Estate.

'And DJ,' Tom interjects rather unhelpfully, and when I glare at him, adds, 'You know, spin the decks.' He mimes the action. 'And peer of the realm, of course. Heavy is the head and all that.'

'Thanks, Tom.' I ignore Alessia's stifled giggle while Tabaku finishes scribbling his notes. He places his biro on his notepad and, leaning back into his chair, says something to Alessia and me.

'He has all he needs to write the contract,' Alessia says.

Reaching over, I squeeze her hand. 'That's it?'

'Yes.'

'Good. Let's go back to the hotel and decide what to do next.'

She nods, and I rise from my seat and give Tabaku a brief nod. 'Thank you.'

Thanas translates his response. 'I will see you on Saturday in the afternoon. And you must choose two people to be witnesses.'

Witnesses? More like accomplices.

Alessia does not know how to gauge Maxim's mood – or what he'll do. He was quiet and brooding as he stalked back to the hotel. Is he angry? Does he still want to flee? They're sitting in the Hotel Amerika bar, a first for her in her home country, and she wonders what he's thinking.

Tom and Thanas have returned to their rooms, so she's alone with him. He looks pensive as he reaches over and takes her hand. 'I'm somewhat aggrieved that we're jumping through all these hoops to appease your father's ego.'

'I know. I am sorry.' She stares at the table, not knowing what to say and unable to escape the feeling that she's responsible for their predicament. If only she hadn't lied about the pregnancy. But then her father might have insisted she marry Anatoli.

'Hey. It's not *your* fault, for heaven's sake.' Maxim gives her hand a reassuring squeeze. She returns her gaze to his and is relieved to see nothing but his concern. 'I don't want to fight with your father, but I wish he hadn't put us in this position. I know he thinks he's doing the right thing.'

Alessia nods, surprised at how seriously he's taking their situation. He wants their marriage to be authentic. His jaw is tense, his expression serious, and his eyes a glowing green. She hates that he looks so troubled. 'What do you think we should do?' she asks.

Maxim shakes his head but then smiles; he's dazzling, stealing her breath away.

He really is the most attractive man.

'Well, we're stuck here until you get your passport and visa – I'm not leaving without you. So, if you have no objection, I think we should do it.'

Alessia considers his words. He's resigned to the wedding. Is that what she wants?

'Do you feel trapped?' she whispers.

'No. Yes. But not in the way you think. I came here to ask you to marry me. You said yes, and fundamentally your father is fulfilling that wish for me.'

Alessia nods. 'I see that. Also, I think it will help my mother if we stay here and go through with the wedding.'

'Oh?'

'She doesn't want to come to England with us. She wants to stay with him. I don't understand why. But I think he'll be angry if we leave, and he might –' She doesn't finish the sentence, too ashamed of what her father might do to her mother.

Maxim studies her, his expression full of resolve. 'That's a compelling argument to go through with it. For her sake as well as ours.'

Alessia breathes a sigh of relief. 'I agree.'

He smiles. 'That makes me feel better.'

'Yes. Me too. I think it's the right decision for her.'

'And the right decision for you?' he asks.

'Yes,' she answers emphatically. 'It will mean that my family will not lose . . . um . . . the face in the community.'

Maxim blows out a breath and looks relieved. 'Good. Okay. Decision made.'

And Alessia feels lighter – the weight of her father's expectation lifted. How easy it was for them to reach a consensus – her fiancé and her.

Is this what their marriage will be like?

She hopes so.

'And now, I have much to do,' Alessia says.

'Yeah. I'll grab the rest of my things from Tom's room, and let's head back. I have something for you.'

'Oh?'

He grins. 'Yes.'

There are several cars in the drive when we arrive at the house.

'O Zot,' Alessia says as she turns to me. 'My family. The women. They are here.'

'Ah . . .' It's all I can think of to say.

'Yes. They will all want to meet you.' She pouts. 'And I wanted to . . . um . . . set up this phone.' She holds up the iPhone box I handed her at the hotel, and I give her a sympathetic smile. She sighs. 'I'll do it later. The women gather. We always do when there's a wedding. And they will want to check you up.'

'Check me up?' I chuckle. 'Well, I hope I don't disappoint them.' But despite our levity, I feel a rising sense of panic, though I'm not sure why.

'Don't worry, you will not disappoint them.' Alessia's lips quirk in a shy grin.

'Oh yeah?'

'Yeah. And I'll protect you from them. I've got you.'

I laugh once more, and we climb out of the Dacia. Alessia takes my hand, and together we enter the house. I slip off my shoes, as does Alessia, and they join the many shoes scattered beside the shoe rack.

'Ready?' Alessia asks.

I nod and take a deep breath as we stride down the hall towards the buzz coming from the family room.

When she sees us in the doorway, Shpresa announces what I assume is our arrival rather loudly, and several pairs of eyes turn to stare at us as the noise level rises exponentially. There must be at least a dozen women, aged from fifteen to fifty, gathered in the room, and they surge towards us. The older women look a little like Mrs Demachi and are dressed more traditionally with scarves on their heads and full skirts. The younger women are in more casual contemporary clothes. Alessia squeezes my hand and starts to make introductions as her relatives kiss and hug her. She manages to keep hold of my hand throughout as they kiss and hug me too. By all accounts, they are delighted to meet me. None of the older women speak English, but the youngest two are pretty fluent.

After fifteen minutes of continuous smiling to the point I might get rictus in my cheeks, I manage to extricate myself with the excuse that I have calls to make, and I head down to the guest room.

Alessia is overwhelmed with the attention of her aunts and cousins. *He's so handsome. Where have you been? What happened to you? We thought you were marrying Anatoli Thaçi. He's a count! Let us see the ring. So European. Is he rich?* The questions come thick and fast, and Alessia fends them off with the help of her mother.

'I did not wish to marry Anatoli,' she says as the women hang on her every word.

There are gasps of dismay.

'But your father's besa?' Her father's sister tuts.

'He was not for me.' Alessia raises her chin in defiance.

'Alessia has captured the heart of a fine man. She's in love. She will be happy,' her mother declares. 'And what's more, he's come all the way from England to claim her.'

I place my luggage on the bed and withdraw my phone from my jacket, pleased to be out of the limelight and the rapt attention of so many curious women – though I can still hear them chattering and laughing above me through the ceiling. Ignoring them, I switch on the phone.

First, I call Oliver, the chief operating officer of the Trevethick Estate.

'My lord – I mean Maxim. How are you? Where are you?'

I quickly fill him in on all he needs to know. '. . . And we'll need to press on with a visa for Alessia. Let Rajah know. Alessia and I are getting married.'

'Oh! And, um – congratulations. When?'

'Thank you. Saturday.'

I hear Oliver's gasp and then his silence. It speaks volumes.

'Yes. Sudden, I know.' I break the awkward silence.

'Do you want to place an announcement in *The Times*?'

'People still do that?' I'm unable to keep the incredulity from my voice.

'Yes, my lord. Especially as a peer of the realm.' He sounds disapproving.

'I think under the circumstances, we'll draw a veil over that. No announcement. Can you give the keys to my flat to Joe Diallo? He'll come round and collect them from the office.'

Well, I hope he will.

'Of course,' Oliver breathes. I think he's still in shock. 'I'll chase Rajah about visas.'

'Thanks.'

'I've also had news today from the Met Police. Alessia's assailants have been charged with trafficking offences.'

Fuck. Good.

'They've not been granted bail. They're a flight risk, and I believe other individuals have been charged too.'

'I'm glad. That's a relief.' I hope Alessia's not called upon to be a witness in court. That could get tricky. But she'll be my wife by then.

Don't dwell, dude.

Cross that bridge as and when.

'Any estate business I need to know?' I ask to change the subject.

Oliver fills me in on what's been happening back home. Fortunately, not much. 'I've sent you a couple of emails that need attention, but nothing serious.'

'Thanks, Oliver.'

'My lord . . . um . . . is everything okay?'

I run a hand through my hair, feeling that same sense of panic

I felt when we arrived back at the house. I damp it down. I don't want to tell him that my marriage might be illegitimate. I'll deal with that later once we're back in the UK. 'Yes. Everything's fine.'

'Righto. I'll report back on where Rajah is with visas.'

Next, I call my friend and sparring partner Joe Diallo.

'Bruv,' he says. 'Where you at?'

'Albania. I'm getting married. On Saturday.'

'What the fuck! This Saturday?'

'Yeah. Can you come?'

'Mate. Wait. Really?'

'Yes.'

'Your daily?' he squeaks, several octaves above his normal voice and I roll my eyes.

'Yes,' I hiss with exasperation.

'You're sure. She's the one?'

I sigh. 'Yes, Joe.'

'Okay,' he says, his uncertainty ringing in his voice. 'I'll look into flights.'

'Can you be here on Friday? And bring one of my suits?'

He sighs. 'Only for you, mate.'

'I'm going to need you to go to Boodles too.'

There's a loud knock on the front door, and as Alessia is near the doorway, she extracts herself from the crowd to find out who's calling. She's delighted to see her relatives but is grateful for the distraction and a moment of peace as she strolls down the hall. She's forgotten what it's like to be surrounded by her noisy and inquisitive family.

She skips up to the door and opens it.

And stops. Shocked.

'Hello, Alessia.'

The blood drains from her face as she stares at the man standing on the doorstep. 'Anatoli,' she whispers as fear clogs her throat.

Chapter Three

Alessia cannot believe he's audacious enough to return to her father's home dressed in his fine Italian coat and expensive brogues. Yet Anatoli makes no move to come in. He just stares at her with eyes that blaze an icy blue. Then he swallows, as if he's going to say something, or from nerves; Alessia doesn't know. Instinctively, she takes a step back as her heart begins to pound and a shiver skitters up her spine, either from his presence or the chilly February air.

What does he want?

'Don't go. Please.' He puts his foot on the threshold so she cannot close the door, his eyes beseeching her.

'What do you want?' she snaps as her outrage fuels her courage.

How dare he show up here!

She doesn't want to engage with him on any level. She glances behind her to see if anyone has come to see what's going on – but there's no one. She's on her own.

'I want to talk to you.'

'We said all we needed to say on Saturday.'

'Alessia. Please. I came to . . . apologise. For everything.'

'What?' Alessia feels like the air's being sucked from her lungs. She's stunned.

'Can we talk? Please. You owe me that. I brought you back here.'

A surge of anger rises from deep within her chest. 'No, Anatoli! You kidnapped me,' she snarls. 'I was happy in London, and you took me away from all that. And put me in a difficult situation. You must go. I have nothing to say to you.'

'I mishandled everything. So badly. I see that. I have had time to think. Let me plead my case. Please. I won't touch you.'

'No! Go!'

'Alessia. We're betrothed! You are the most beautiful, maddening, and talented woman I have ever known. I love you.'

'No. No. No!' Alessia closes her eyes, trying to contain her shock and outrage. 'You don't know how to love. Please go.' She tries to close the door, but his foot prevents her, and he splays his hand on the door, holding it steady.

'How can you marry someone that will take you away from your homeland? Our homeland? You are an Albanian woman to your soul. You will miss your mother. You'll never belong in England. The English are such terrible snobs. They'll despise you. They'll look down on you. You'll never be accepted there.'

His words slice through her, their weight stirring her darkest fears.

Is he right? Will Maxim's family and friends despise her?

Anatoli's gaze intensifies as he senses her doubts. 'I speak your language, carissima. I understand you. I acted stupidly. Badly. I can change. You've been in the West. You expect more, and you deserve more. I get that, and I can give you more. So much more. I will accept your child. Treat him or her as my own. Alessia, please. I love you.' He steps forward and boldly takes her hand between each of his, imploring her and staring into her eyes. 'You will make me a better man. I need you,' he whispers, his desperation evident in every syllable.

Alessia tugs her hand free and meets his intense gaze. 'Let me go, Anatoli.' She takes a deep breath, her heart in her mouth, and finding a courage she didn't know she possessed, she reaches up and caresses his cheek. He leans his face into her hand as his eyes sear hers. 'If you love me, let me go. I won't make you happy. I'm not the woman for you.' He opens his mouth to speak – she suspects to contradict her – but she places her finger over his mouth. 'No, I'm not.'

'You are,' he whispers, his breath warm on her finger.

She drops her hand. 'No. You want to find someone who will light up when you walk into a room.'

'I have,' he whispers.

'No! That's not me.'

'You did once.'

'An age ago. But you . . . you hurt me. So much so, I had to get away. There's no coming back from that.'

He blanches.

'You're not that person for me,' Alessia continues. 'You'll never make me happy.'

'I could work at being that person.'

'I've already met him, Anatoli. I love him. We're to be married this week.'

'What?' His mouth drops open – he's stunned.

'Please. Go. There's nothing for you here,' Alessia whispers.

He steps back in disbelief, his expression desolate.

'I hope you find your person,' she says.

'Carissima . . .'

'Goodbye, Anatoli.' Alessia, her heart still in her mouth, closes the door as her mother calls her.

'Alessia? What's keeping you?' Shpresa appears in the hallway.

'It's okay. I'll be there in a minute.'

'Who was it?'

'Mama, I need a minute.'

Frowning, Shpresa studies her daughter, then nods and returns to the family room. Alessia blows out a breath, trying to expel the frenzied fear and emotion that's choking her. She peers through the spy hole in the door and watches as Anatoli trudges with long strides up the driveway to where his car is parked. His shoulders are squared, a picture of a man determined, not defeated. It's a chilling sight.

No!

Alessia turns and slumps against the door.

That was most unexpected. But his words – *they'll despise you* – have struck home. She clutches her throat as it seems to constrict against the truth, and she suddenly has an overwhelming urge to cry.

What if he's right?

I've unpacked the few belongings that I threw, panicked, into my duffle bag when I thought I'd never see Alessia again. I've arranged them, rearranged them, and I know I'm actively avoiding my next call.

Coward. Call her.

I stare out at the still, quiet waters of the lake, the grey skies reflected in its depths, the scene mirroring my mood. The women upstairs are still in conference, and by their loud laughter and chatter, I know they're enjoying themselves. Taking a deep breath and figuratively girding my loins, I press Call on my phone and wait for Caroline to answer.

Shall I tell her?

Shall I not?

'Maxim!' she exclaims, gushing and concerned at once. 'How are you? Where are you?'

'Caro. Hi. I'm in Kukës, staying at Alessia's parents' place.'

'You're still there? I don't get it. If you've found her, why aren't you either back here or on your way?'

'It's not that simple.'

'Her fiancé?'

The Arsehole. 'Um . . . no.'

She's silent for a moment, waiting for me to elucidate. She sighs. 'What are you not telling me?'

Inspiration hits me, and it's the truth. 'We have to wait for a passport for Alessia.'

'Ah. I see.' She sounds uncertain but continues, 'You don't want to come home and go back for her?'

'Definitely not. I'm not letting her out of my sight.'

'Oh, how protective!' she scoffs. 'Your white knight is showing.'

I chuckle, relieved she's her usual caustic self. 'Yes. It's been showing for a while, much to my surprise.'

'Surely she's safe with her parents.'

'It was her mother who handed her over to the traffickers, albeit unwittingly.'

She gasps. 'I didn't know. That's awful.'

'Yeah. Hence my need to be protective. Anyway – enough of this. What have you been doing?'

'Oh,' she breathes, and I almost hear her fold in on herself.

'What is it?'

'I've finally found the strength to go through Kit's things.'

My grief surfaces, unexpected, raw and vicious, winding me. *Kit*. My dear brother.

'I see,' I whisper.

'I have a few things of his that you might like.' Her tone is soft – laced with regret. 'The rest . . . I don't know what to do with yet.'

'We can go through it all when I'm home,' I offer.

'Yes. Let's do that. I'm going to tackle some of his papers tomorrow.'

'Good luck.'

'I miss him.' Her quiet sorrow is ingrained in her voice.

'I know. I do too.'

'When will you be back?'

'Next week, I hope.'

'Good. Okay. Thanks for calling. I'm glad you found her.'

Feeling guilty as hell, I hang up.

Guilty by omission.

I should have told her.

Hell!

I'm tempted to call her back and confess that I'm getting married, but she'd want to get on a plane and come here, and frankly, I don't want the hassle.

I decide not to tell my mother for precisely the same reason. The Mothership will lose her shit, and I'm not sure Kukës or the Demachis are ready for the *Dowager* Countess in all her glory because I'm certainly not.

Better to ask for forgiveness than permission. My father's oft-repeated phrase comes to mind. He'd say it with a twinkle in his eye as he caught me about to do something I shouldn't.

I brush off the thought, and there's a knock on my door. Before I can say anything, Alessia hurries in, closes the door, and leans against it. She raises anxious eyes to mine. She's ashen.

'What's happened?' I ask.

She takes a deep breath, moves forward, and surprises me by wrapping her arms around my waist. I fold her into my embrace, alarmed, and kiss her hair.

'Alessia, what is it?'

She tightens her hold on me. 'Anatoli. He was here.' Her voice is barely audible.

'What?' My world shifts, and I tense as anger flares in my gut.

She looks up, her eyes wide with fear. 'He came to the door.'

Horrified, I cup her head in my hands and study her face. 'That fucking animal. Why didn't you call me? Did he touch you? Are you okay?'

'I'm okay.' She places her palms on my chest. 'And no, he didn't. He wanted me to reconsider.'

My breath catches in my throat. 'And are you?'

That's why she didn't call me.

She frowns, not understanding.

'Are you reconsidering?'

'No!' she exclaims.

Thank God.

'Why would you think that?' She draws back, looking very much affronted, and I have no choice but to release her. 'Do you think like this because you are reconsidering?' she asks, lifting her chin in that haughty way she does, and I laugh at the absurdity. The absurdity of the two of us . . .

How could she think that?

'No. Of course not. Though I wish we were doing this at our own speed. But you know that. Why do you doubt me? I'm thoroughly, indubitably . . . muchly in love with you.' I open my arms, and after a beat, she steps back into them with a shy forgiving smile.

'That is many adverbs,' she says. 'Muchly?'

'My favourite word.' I smile. 'I want to marry you. Properly.' Feeling a little calmer, I kiss her hair once more. 'What did you say to him?'

'I told him no. I told him we were getting married. He left.'

'I hope that's the last we see of him.' Gently, I fist my hand in her hair, tugging her head back and planting a soft kiss on her lips. 'I'm sorry you had to deal with that arsehole. I'm glad you stood up to him, my courageous girl.'

Alessia stares into his glittering green eyes and sees her love reflected in the depths of his. She skims her hands up his muscled arms, his shoulders, his face, and into his chestnut hair. His scent is so achingly familiar – Maxim and sandalwood. She guides his mouth back to hers, driven by a desperate longing as she coaxes his lips with her own and opens her mouth to him. Maxim groans as her tongue pleads with his. She wants to climb inside his skin and obliterate the memory of her encounter with Anatoli. He tightens his hold on her, one hand travelling to and gripping her backside, the other grasping her hair at the nape and holding her fast as he takes what she so freely gives. He moves, steering them backwards while they consume each other until Alessia feels the wall at her back. Desire pulses through her body and pools deep inside her, feeding her need.

Maxim breaks the kiss, his breathing accelerated. 'Alessia, it's okay. I've got you.' He leans his forehead against hers. 'We can't do this right now.'

'Please,' she whispers. She wants him.

'With your extended family upstairs? Any one of whom could come looking for you?'

Alessia trails a finger down his throat to the collar of his sweater, making her intention clear.

'Baby, I don't think this is a good idea.' He places his hand over hers, his eyes dark emerald and, if she's not mistaken, conflicted . . . yet he's saying *no.*

Alessia doesn't understand. Her first instinct is to withdraw.

It is not her place to question him. But this is her future husband, and his words, spoken on a winter's afternoon at the big house in Cornwall, come back to her.

Talk to me. Ask me questions. About anything. I'm here. I'll listen. Argue with me. Shout at me. I'll argue with you. I'll shout at you. I'll get it wrong. You'll get it wrong. That's all okay. But to resolve our differences, we have to communicate.

What the hell, dude?

I'm having a crisis of conscience or something. I don't want to get caught *in flagrante delicto* by a member of the Demachi clan. Frankly, it's just so weird when I can hear the gaggle of women laughing and joking above us with her mother, and knowing that her mad dad isn't far away with his shotgun.

I've stepped into the wrong century, and it's messing with my head.

Alessia's eyes widen. 'You don't want to?'

'Oh, baby, nothing could be further from the truth. Here.' I take her hand and press it against my rigid dick.

'Oh,' she says, her cheeks pinking, and her fingers start exploring.

Fuck.

'Alessia,' I growl, not knowing if it's a warning or an entreaty.

She peeks at me, all dark, dark eyes full of longing, and I can take no more. I haul her into my arms and start kissing her. Properly. Fervently, like a starving man. My fingers are in her hair, holding her in place while our tongues explore. Desire, hot and molten, fires my blood, and I think I'll explode. She matches my passion, pushing me back towards the bed, yanking the hem of my shirt from my jeans and tugging at my sweater. I cradle the back of her head with one hand, my mouth on hers, revelling in the taste of her, my other hand on her fine, fine arse.

'*Alessia!*'

There's a knock at the door.

Fuck.

We spring apart – each of us breathless and dark-eyed and panting and slack-jawed.

I run my hands through my hair. 'Fuck!' I whisper, and Alessia giggles.

Blowing out a breath, I pull her into my arms and kiss the top of her head. 'Come in,' I call, my voice hoarse. 'We never have long together, do we?' I say to Alessia.

'Except at night.' Her eyes flash with a needy carnality.

Oh. It's like she's directly addressing my over-interested dick.

Shpresa comes into the room and frowns at Alessia in Maxim's embrace. 'There you are, my heart.' Her mother addresses her in Albanian. 'We have guests.'

'I know, Mama,' Alessia replies, sounding out of breath.

'Put that man down, and let's continue with our plans. They'll be going soon.'

Alessia smiles at Maxim.

'Are you going back to your relatives?' Maxim asks.

'Yes, I must. We were discussing food and decorations for the wedding,' Alessia responds with a sigh. 'Don't worry; they won't be here long. And then we start cleaning.' Alessia huffs out a breath.

'I have some emails that need my attention.'

'Mama. I will be a minute.'

Shpresa frowns, then holds up her forefinger. 'A minute. That's it.'

She turns and leaves Alessia and Maxim, both still trying to find their equilibrium.

I watch her mother leave, grateful we were still clothed when she interrupted us. I kiss the top of Alessia's head again. 'Baby, I will always want you. But let's wait until we're out of here.'

'But that is days away!'

Alessia's protests widen my smile.

'And I don't have any condoms,' I mutter into her hair.

'You should buy some.'

'I should. But don't you think it will be odd if people think you're pregnant and I'm buying condoms?'

'Oh.'

'I'll ask Tom to get me some.'

Alessia gasps, flushes beet red, and buries her face in my Aran sweater.

I grin and tighten my hold on her. 'I told him you're not pregnant.'

'I . . . I . . . um . . . could go to the clinic. And get the contraceptive pill,' she says, the sound muffled by my knitwear.

'That's a brilliant idea.'

She chances a cautious look at me, and I smile.

Sex without condoms will be a first!

'Okay. I will do that. I should tell my parents that I am not pregnant.'

'Yes. We should.'

'I have a plan.' Hesitantly, she looks up at me.

'You do?'

'Tomorrow.' She buries her head in my sweater once more. 'Is the date I bleed.'

Ah.

'Okay. So you'll tell your mother you're not pregnant?'

'Yes. I will find a time to tell her.' She can't look at me, and I think it's because she's embarrassed. Taking her head in my hands again, I stare into her beautiful dark eyes.

'We should be able to talk about this – you and your body. It's okay. I think it's a good plan.' I kiss her forehead. 'Maybe tell her Saturday.'

Reassured, I think, she nods. 'I'd better go.'

Reluctantly, I release her, and with a lingering, thirsty look at me, she exits the bedroom, leaving me with a hard-on and a severe case of blue balls.

Like I had when I first made her acquaintance.

I smirk at the memory and take a deep, cleansing breath. As predicted, her mother made an untimely appearance. And it's a fucking problem. The proximity and the constant monitoring from her parentals is driving me crazy. Being here has given me a valuable insight into Alessia's upbringing and makes me admire her all the more for escaping to London She's grown up and lived in this stifling atmosphere, controlled by her mother and father her whole life. I've been here two nights, and I'm missing my freedom. I feel like a teenager back in school.

I'm a grown man, for fuck's sake.

Well, most of the time.

But I'm not leaving here, especially if that arsehole thinks he can turn up and have another chance with her.

I snort at the irony. *Man, you're keeping an eye on her.*

I rub the last of my hangover away from my temples and make

a mental note of where her father keeps his shotgun . . . just in case Anatoli the Arsehole makes another unwelcome appearance. I'd be more than happy to put a bullet through him.

Hell.

The sooner we're out of here, the better; I'm contemplating murder.

Chapter Four

Under the glow of the little dragon nightlight, Alessia lies in bed staring at the ceiling while her fingers worry the gold cross at her neck. She's exhausted, but her mind refuses to settle as it churns through the day's events and her to-do list.

This morning, Tom had driven Alessia and her mother to Prizren in Kosovo to buy a wedding dress. Her mother wouldn't let her fiancé take them because it was 'bad luck' and would 'spoil the surprise,' so Maxim had insisted Tom drive. Her father had shrugged. 'Like I said, you're his problem now. If that's what Maxim wants, then so be it. Besides, he and I have work to do here.'

Alessia scowls in the dark and turns on her side towards the nightlight.

She is not a problem!

She directs her thoughts back to their trip. It had been a success. They'd been lucky to find a beautiful dress, and she'd discovered a softer side to Maxim's gruff friend. He'd been courteous, kind, and vigilant while with them. He'd also given his begrudging approval of her dress as he'd sat quietly and discreetly near the door of the bridal store.

'Yes. Yes. That's the one. Jolly nice. You look . . . um . . . lovely,' he'd blustered and flushed the same colour as his hair; then, to hide his embarrassment he'd turned to scan the passers-by through the shop window. Alessia had suspected he was looking for Anatoli.

On the drive to Kosovo, Tom had told her about the security company he owned where he could put the skills he'd learned in the British army to good use. He'd been delighted to have a captive and attentive audience. Alessia had been fascinated, asking questions about his work, and grateful that he was with them, as Maxim had been hypervigilant since Anatoli's untimely reappearance.

She shudders, still shaken by her encounter with Anatoli.

What had he been thinking?

While out in the streets of Prizren, she'd found herself glancing over her shoulder several times, a sense of unease settling in her stomach.

Was she being watched?

No. It was just her imagination.

She shuts down that idea, and her mind flits to happier thoughts – her fiancé, recalling him in his shirtsleeves earlier this afternoon. While she'd been in Kosovo, and much to her surprise, Maxim and Thanas had helped her father clear the garage where the Demachis were to host the wedding celebrations. Her dad, with Maxim's help, had driven the three Mercedes he usually kept locked in there to his repair shop in town. When he'd returned, he and Maxim and Thanas had continued to empty and tidy the garage in preparation for the tent that will arrive in the morning. The plan is to erect it in front of the garage, making a larger entertainment space.

When Alessia and her escort had returned from Kosovo, Tom had rolled up his sleeves too and joined the men. While they cleared the outside, Alessia and her mother had begun the mammoth task inside of cleaning, cleaning, and yet more cleaning.

Alessia had managed to slip out in the late afternoon to the local clinic. After a brief conversation, she had persuaded the doctor to prescribe the contraceptive pill. She'd only just made it to the pharmacy with her prescription before it closed, and she'd been relieved not to recognise anyone there. She'd rushed home to continue cleaning, and no one asked where she'd been. Later, when her period started, she'd been able to sneak upstairs and take her first pill.

Early evening, Maxim had appeared in the kitchen, his shirt-sleeves rolled up despite the cold; he was dirty, his colour heightened, and his hair damp with sweat. He looked . . . hot.

Manual work suits him.

He'd given her a quick kiss that made her long for more before heading to the shower.

Maxim in the shower.

Closing her eyes, Alessia turns onto her side, and her mind conjures a fantasy that she's in the shower with him. They're in Cornwall, at the Hideout, and Maxim is soaping her body while they stand beneath the cascade, getting wetter and wetter. Her hand travels down her body, becoming his in her thoughts as she hears his voice.

Do you want me to wash you all over?

Her breath quickens, and she tugs at her nightdress so the hem glides up her thighs. As her hand slips between them and starts to move, she rolls onto her back.

She remembers his skilled hands slick with soap on her breasts, then sliding over her belly and slipping down to the apex of her thighs. Her desire unfurls in a rush that stiffens her nipples against the soft cotton, but she imagines them hardening between his lips and against his stubble, then teased by his teeth.

She groans.

In her mind, he kisses her neck, a sound of approval resonating deep in his throat.

Mmm-hmm.

His words fill her head.

You're so beautiful.

She gasps as her hand picks up speed.

Faster. Faster.

You like?

And she's hanging.

Nearly there.

I want to try something new. Turn over, he purrs in her ear.

Alessia comes. Hard. Fast. And she gulps in a lungful of air.

And as her equilibrium returns, she thinks perhaps now she'll sleep. She curls up as her lingering sense of pleasure and well-being starts to fade, and her thoughts intrude once more.

Tomorrow the garage set-up will be finished, but there's more cleaning and cooking to be done. So much cooking. And the party favors to put together: sugared almonds in tiny cloth bags. Fortunately, her extended family are eager to help – the menu and who is making what were set when they visited yesterday. A chef will be on hand to assist them on the day.

Will Maxim be happy with the arrangements?

O Zot! She hopes so.

She knows this isn't the wedding he wants.

But he's still here, he hasn't left, and he's proceeding with the ceremony for her sake – but also for her mother's. Alessia opens her eyes and stares at the ceiling again, her fingers finding her gold cross once more as her anxiety flares like a flame.

Her mother, who wants to stay with her father.

Will she be okay?

Having observed them for the last few days, her mother and father seem to have reached some kind of accord. It's strange to witness. Maybe her mother was right – he seems . . . kinder. Maybe Alessia leaving was what they had needed. Perhaps she had been the object of strife between them.

After all, she's not a boy.

The thought brings a lump to her throat.

All this time, had she been the one who stood in the way of her mother's happiness?

She's your problem now . . .

A tear trickles down the side of her face and into her ear.

This idea is too much to bear alone.

She tosses her sheets aside and climbs out of bed. Hastily grabbing the little dragon, she makes her way to the door. She thinks it's about two in the morning, but she doesn't know for sure. She tiptoes out of the room, silently closes the door, and stands in the hallway where all is quiet, as her parents went to bed hours ago. She moves noiselessly to the stairs and heads down two floors. Alessia doesn't care that she might wake him when she steals into this room, because right now, all she wants, all she needs, is Maxim.

I cannot sleep, and yet I don't think I've ever laboured as hard as I did today. Well, not since my father had us helping with the harvests at the Home Farm on the Trevethick Estate. I was in my early teens then and had boundless energy.

Now? Not so much.

I didn't even begrudge the shot of raki I had this evening to ease my aching muscles. Tomorrow morning, I'm going for a run before I do anything else, and I'm grateful I packed my running gear.

Weirdly, it felt good helping my soon-to-be father-in-law. He's gruff and sullen, and I have no idea what he's thinking, but he's decisive, hard-working, and organised. He has a plan, which is a relief because I'm out of my depth here. And at the end of a long day, he'd clapped me on the back and given me the keys to one of his cars – an old Mercedes C Class. Thanas had translated. 'For you. When you are here. Your car. You can give the Dacia to your friend. Collect it later. And for now, park it up on the road.'

'Faleminderit,' I'd replied. *Thank you* in Albanian.

He'd grinned then, and it was the first time I'd seen him smile properly. His acceptance and generosity had lifted my spirits.

Perhaps he's not so bad.

He's only doing what he thinks is right for his daughter.

But now I'm finding it hard to sleep. Did I ever imagine I'd get married in a garage? In Albania? Did I ever imagine I'd get married before I was thirty? Thank God my mother doesn't know. But the thought does bring a wry smile to my face . . . if she knew, she'd flip.

Alessia and her mother went shopping with Tom. I was forbidden to go as they were buying The Dress. I'd just handed her my credit card and winked. And she'd accepted it with a quick word of thanks and a kiss on the cheek.

They returned triumphant, and Tom was quite enamoured of my wife-to-be.

'She's a gem, Trevethick. I get it,' he'd said when he joined us in our quest to clear the garage.

Alessia and her mother spent most of the afternoon cleaning. By this evening, the entire place was spotless. She must be exhausted, and I hope she's sleeping soundly and dreaming of me. When all this is over, and after all this hard work, we're going to need a holiday.

A honeymoon.

I could take Alessia somewhere beautiful. The Caribbean, maybe. We could sit on a quiet beach beneath swaying palms, drink cocktails and read books and make love beneath the stars. My body stirs at the thought.

Fuck. I was in Cuba and then Bequia at Christmas with my brother and Caroline, his wife.

That seems like yesterday.

It was only eight weeks ago.

Hell.

So much has happened since then.

Earlier this evening, I spoke with Oliver. As well as updating me on estate business, he's arranged for us to collect a visa for Alessia from the British embassy in Tirana. It's been expedited by the ambassador himself – because he knew my father – so at least Alessia will be able to come to the UK as a visitor until we can get her settled status or a spousal visa. The embassy will also organise a notary to apostille our marriage certificate, which makes everything official.

I'll be meeting a lawyer that Rajah has recommended on our return to London. He's warned me that we have much more work to do before Alessia can stay in the UK.

The door creaks open, startling me, and Alessia creeps inside, wearing her ridiculous nightgown and carrying the little night-light. My heart rate jumps.

She's here. My girl.

I grin into the darkness as she makes her way towards the bed.

'Hello,' I whisper in the dark, my joy ringing out loud in my greeting. I draw back the covers for her to join me.

'Hi,' she replies, and she sounds a little hoarse.

'You okay?'

In the glow of the little dragon, she nods once, places him on the bedside table, and climbs into bed beside me. I kiss her cheek, then wrap her in my arms and hold her close as she rests her head on my chest.

'I couldn't sleep. And I am so tired,' she mutters.

'Me too. You can sleep now.' I kiss her hair, inhale her fragrance, and shut my eyes. This is where she should be . . . with me.

Forever.

I drift.

Alessia closes her eyes in the arms of the man she loves. This is where she belongs. Being here, in his embrace, feels like home. She doesn't care if her father or mother catches her; she and Maxim are only sleeping. She sighs as her mind finally quiets, and she falls into a dreamless sleep.

It's early afternoon on Friday, and I can't stop checking my watch. Joe is due here around 3:20 p.m. Tom, who has done more than his fair share of driving over the last few days, has collected him from Tirana International Airport. Joe has texted me that they're on their way and he has a surprise for me.

I'm not sure I like surprises.

The front yard at the Demachis is pristine and wedding-worthy. There's a marquee of sorts up against the garage, and tables and chairs are arranged inside. The place has scrubbed up well. Yesterday, we'd all had a hand in putting up the white netting that was donated by one of Alessia's aunts. The ceiling of the garage is now swathed in gossamer and fairy lights. And it looks quite lovely. Romantic even. There are fairy lights on the walls and clusters of lights at each of the plastic tables, which are all covered in linen. The Demachis have done well – given the time. They've hired a few patio heaters for the marquee, and there's a sizeable wood-burning stove at one end of the garage, which I'm assured will be lit, so hopefully, our guests won't freeze.

The DJ, Kreshnik, one of Alessia's cousins, has set up a little booth in the corner of the garage. His gear is old school: a laptop and humble Numark Mixtrack pro DJ decks. I haven't seen one of those for years. He's plugged them into a couple of speakers, and the sound is surprisingly warm and crisp.

'Great sound.' I give him a thumbs-up and a broad smile. He grins back, and I know he hasn't understood a word I've said.

'Maxim!' Alessia calls.

I smile. She probably wants me to taste something delicious. The aroma from the kitchen has been enticing all day. Demachi turns from piling wood in the corner of the garage, ready for the wood-burning stove and flashes a quick grin. 'Ajo do të të shëndoshë!' he calls, laughing, but I have no idea what he's said.

Thanas joins me, chuckling. 'He says, "She's going to make you fat."'

Amused by the banter, I begin to jog backwards. 'Tell him "I hope so."' Turning, I hurry back into the house, take off my shoes, and head to the kitchen. I lean against the arch and quietly admire my future wife. She's standing over the stove, stirring a large pot and swaying her hips to the music blaring via a speaker from her new phone. Her hair is tied back in a swinging ponytail, and she's wearing tight jeans with one of the tops we bought in Padstow and a pretty, flowery apron. She looks young, beautiful, and in her element – every bit the domestic goddess. All trace of her trauma has disappeared. No bruises. No grazes, and I'm beyond grateful she looks so well.

Shpresa is also jigging about in time to the music and kneads a large mound of dough.

Man, she has such energy.

The song they're dancing to is Albanian pop. It's a *tune*. A female vocalist with a great voice.

Alessia grins when she sees me. 'Here.' She holds up a wooden spoon dripping with an aromatic meaty concoction. When I reach her, she flashes me a smouldering look and eases it between my lips, watching me closely – her eyes darkening as the spicy morsel melts in my mouth.

It's succulent and with a hint of garlic and something piquant.

Delicious.

'Mmm,' I respond as I swallow.

'You like?'

'You know I do. Very much. And I like you.'

She grins, and I give her a swift peck on her lips.

'Tavë kosi?'

'You remembered! My special recipe.' She's delighted and swings her hips in time to the music, her dark eyes full of promise as she stirs the pot.

Oh, baby.

Soon.

She now has a brand-new passport, so we can leave whenever we want.

Thank heavens.

'*Hey!*' There's a call from near the front door.

'Joe!' I exclaim to Alessia and dash in my socks out of the family room into the hallway.

Joe stands on the threshold, looking his usual dapper self in a tailored dark blue suit and navy overcoat. As soon as he sees me, he opens his arms. 'Trevelyan! Mate.'

I run into them and hug him.

Fuck, it's good to see him.

'Mate.' I sound hoarse as a sudden swell of emotion chokes my throat. He hugs me hard, then leans back, studying me.

'You okay?' he asks.

And I'm too emotional to do anything but nod.

Fuck. I do not want to break down right now. I'll never live it down.

'You look good, Maxim,' he says with a wide grin. 'Luggage is in the car. Brought your suits, the rings, and . . .' He turns, and behind him, standing by the car, is my sister.

Maryanne.

Shit.

Behind her, wearing an expression that may turn me to stone, is my brother's widow.

Caroline.

Fuck a duck.

Chapter Five

I glance at Joe, who shrugs apologetically as Maryanne steps over the threshold and throws her arms around me.

'Maxie,' she whispers. 'You found her then.'

'I did.'

'Something you want to tell us?' she adds, sarcasm dripping off every word as she cocks her head to the side – and I know she's apoplectic but keeping a taut rein on her temper.

Oh no.

Caroline waltzes in behind her and offers me a cheek to peck. No hug. 'We had to fly economy,' she snaps.

Shit.

I'm in more trouble than I thought Tom and Thanas follow her inside.

'Come and meet the family,' I say, ignoring her frostiness. 'And shoes off.'

Shpresa and Alessia are standing at the stove as I usher Joe and our surprise guests into the family room. They stare blankly at us as we crowd into the space. Alessia abandons the pot on the stove, wipes her hands on her apron, and switches off the music on her phone. I introduce Joe first, as we've been expecting him, and he's at the head of the queue. Ever the gentleman, he bounds forward, hand outstretched. 'Mrs Demachi, how do you do?' he says with a dazzling smile. 'I'm delighted to meet you.'

Smooth, mate. Smooth.

Shpresa, even in her state of shock, takes his hand. 'Hello. You are welcome here,' she says. He grins and turns to Alessia, who is wide-eyed and pale as if caught in the crosshairs.

Oh no.

'Alessia, how lovely to see you again.'

'Hello,' she responds. 'And this time, you are wearing clothes,' she adds.

He laughs out loud, and a little colour returns to her cheeks as she breaks into a smile. He hugs her and kisses her on both cheeks.

Both!

Mate!

Her mother frowns at their exchange but keeps her counsel.

'Mrs Demachi, this is my sister and my sister-in-law, Maryanne and Caroline.' They shake hands in turn.

'And this is my fiancée, Alessia. Caroline you've met.'

Caroline gives her a brief, but I think sincere, smile. 'Hello again,' she says.

Alessia offers her hand, and they shake. 'Hello . . . Caroline.' Her voice is tremulous, betraying her nerves, but before I can say anything, Maryanne offers her hand.

'How do you do?' she says. Alessia takes her hand and looks from her to me.

Yes. We look alike.

'How do you do?' she responds, and Maryanne's eyes widen slightly in surprise, and she smiles.

'I can see what all the fuss has been about,' she says in her no-nonsense way.

Alessia's brow creases, presumably not understanding that it's a compliment.

'Yes. Well.' I flounder for words.

This is awkward.

'Now we've all said hello –' I manage.

'Please sit.' Shpresa saves me and waves to the dining table. 'We are in preparations for the wedding.'

'Actually, before we sit,' Maryanne says, using her strident doctor's voice. 'Could I possibly have a word with my brother? In private.' Maryanne turns her brilliant green eyes on me, and I know I'm in deep, deep shit.

'You can use the front room,' Alessia says, eyeing me anxiously.

'Lead the way,' Maryanne says, and because I know what she's going to say, and I don't want her saying it in front of Alessia and her mother, I take her hand and practically drag her out of the room. In stiff silence, we stalk down the hallway.

Alessia watches Maxim leave with his sister. She thinks he's angry but doesn't understand why.

Does he not want his family here?

Is he ashamed of his relatives?

Or is he ashamed of her and her family?

Alessia doesn't dwell on this as she fears this may be the reason. She turns her attention to Tom and Thanas, who have walked into the room. She watches Tom fist bump Joe. 'I'm so glad you've joined us, old boy.' Joe flashes bright white teeth and slaps Tom on the back. It's obvious they're good friends. Tom offers Caroline a polite smile. He's more reserved with her. Alessia thinks Tom is happier in the company of men rather than women.

Like an Albanian man.

Tom introduces Thanas to Joe and Caroline.

'We were not expecting these women,' her mother says in their tongue, distracting her.

'I know. I don't think Maxim is pleased.'

'They will have to sleep in the room we had set aside for Maxim's friend.'

'Yes. We should offer them tea or something stronger.'

At that moment, her father enters, and the introductions begin again. He appears delighted to meet a beautiful, fragrant woman, and Alessia cannot blame him. She cannot take her eyes off Caroline. She's the most elegant woman Alessia has ever seen. In camel slacks and a cream sweater, a simple silk scarf with an understated camel-and-cream pattern at her neck, Caroline radiates wealth and good breeding. Even down to the pearls at her ears and her glossy hair, cut in a sleek bob.

Next to her, Alessia feels dowdy and unkempt in her jeans and soiled apron.

She looks every bit like Maxim's cleaner.

And the last time she saw Caroline, she was in Maxim's arms.

As I close the door, Maryanne whirls around, hair flying. 'What the hell do you think you're playing at? Marrying your daily? Really? What the fuck has got into you?'

I gape at her, stunned by her attack and momentarily lost for words at her ferocity.

'Well?' she demands.

'I didn't take you for a snob, Maryanne,' I respond, my anger rising.

'I'm not. I'm just being practical. What the hell can a slip of a girl from . . . here' – she waves her arms around the room – 'offer you?'

'Love, for starters.'

'Oh, for God's sake, Maxim. Have you lost your mind? What do you even have in common?'

'Music, for one thing.'

She ignores me; she's on a roll. 'And doing this just weeks after Kit's death? This is your grief – you know that, don't you? We've not had enough time to mourn. Have you no respect?'

'Well, the timing's not great, but—'

'Not great! Why the alacrity?' Her eyes widen. 'Oh no.' Her voice drops. 'Don't tell me she's preggers.'

I grit my teeth, barely holding on to my temper. 'No. She isn't. It's –' I sigh and run a hand through my hair as I struggle to find an explanation that will satisfy her.

'It's what!'

'It's complicated.'

She glares at me, and I swear if I were dry tinder, I'd be a pile of burnt ashes. She's livid, but suddenly her face falls. 'And to think you would go ahead with this farce without even inviting us!' Her voice cracks, and tears well in her eyes.

Shit. M.A.!

She's hurt.

'That's what's most wounding,' she whispers.

Her words are a gut punch.

Hell. I had no idea she'd feel this way.

'Is that the problem?' My tone is softer. 'My marrying Alessia, or you not getting an invite?'

'The problem is you thinking that we wouldn't want to be here. Even in the back of beyond! Or it's that you didn't want us here. Either of those options is hurtful. What's wrong with you, Maxie? I've already lost one brother this year. You're all I have. You are my family.' Her tears are flowing now. 'And that you'd go through this without us.' She sniffles and drags a handkerchief from her sleeve to wipe her nose.

Fuck.

'I'm sorry.' I open my arms, and she walks straight into them without hesitating and hugs me hard.

'And I had to find out from Caro,' she splutters.

'M.A., I didn't think,' I whisper into her hair. 'This has all happened so quickly. And we'll celebrate in London or Cornwall and do it again there. And just so you know, this isn't a fucking farce.

'I'm getting married because I've met a woman I'm passionately in love with, and I want to grow old with her. Alessia is everything to me, and I've come alive since I met her. She's supportive, caring and compassionate. She's amazing. I've never met anyone like her, and I've never felt like this about anyone. I need her, and what's more, she needs me.'

Dude, quite the speech.

She lets out a long, shaky breath and examines me with red-rimmed eyes. 'You have fallen hard, haven't you?'

I nod.

'You know it's going to be hard for her, stepping into the role that's expected of her.'

'I know. But she has us to help. Doesn't she?'

She studies me once more and sighs. 'If she makes you happy, because that's all I want for you, Maxim, then yes, she does.'

I smile. 'Thank you. She makes me more than happy. And I hope I do the same for her.'

'She's beautiful.'

'She is. And funny and sweet and loving.'

Maryanne's eyes soften.

'And she's extremely talented.'

'In what?' Maryanne cocks a brow.

I laugh. 'Alessia's a pianist.'

'Oh.' She's surprised and glances at the old upright piano that has pride of place in the drawing room. 'I can't wait to hear.'

'Um . . . did you tell the Mothership?'

Maryanne narrows her eyes. 'No. I didn't want to hurt her feelings.'

'She has feelings?'

'Maxim!'

'We should get back.'

Everyone, bar Shpresa, is seated at the table. Alessia glances at me as Maryanne and I enter. She frowns and looks down at her nails, even though I try to telepathically reassure her that everything is okay. Caroline's eyes narrow as I hold out a chair for Maryanne to sit upon, and I know that in the not-too-distant future, I will face the same conversation that I've just had with my sister, with my sister-in-law.

Shpresa is bringing over a pot of tea, some cups, and a bottle of raki with several glasses.

Raki. Already? Oh boy.

Alessia twists the apron between her fingers. Maxim's sister is as elegant as Caroline. She's tall and beautiful, with vibrant red hair, and she's dressed as smartly as her sister-in-law.

How can Alessia hope to fit in with these women?

The English are such terrible snobs. They'll despise you. They'll look down on you. Anatoli's words return to haunt her and put Alessia on her guard.

Shpresa offers the women tea and the men raki.

'These women must stay here,' her father says to her mother.

'Yes,' her mother agrees. 'Alessia, tell them.'

'I can help,' Thanas says as he sceptically eyes his glass of raki.

'It's okay,' Alessia says in English. 'Caroline, Maryanne, you are welcome to stay here. You will have to share a room.'

'That's very kind of you, Alessia. We had thought we'd check into a local hotel,' Caroline responds.

'You are welcome here,' Shpresa says.

'We'd be delighted to stay if it's not too much trouble,' Maryanne says.

'Great. That's settled,' says Tom, and he turns to Maxim. 'Now, as your best man, it is incumbent on me to organise your stag night. It's traditional.'

'What?' says Maxim as he sits beside Alessia and reaches for her hand. He gives it a reassuring squeeze.

'Trevethick, may I remind you: you're getting hitched tomorrow.'

'How could I forget?'

Maryanne and Caroline exchange glances.

'So tonight,' Tom continues, 'we're going to hit Kukës with all we've got.'

'Bruv,' Joe says. 'I'm game.'

'Thanas?' Tom asks.

'I wouldn't miss this for the world!'

'What is this?' Jak asks, looking towards his daughter for an explanation.

'The men are going out tonight in Kukës. I think it is a Western tradition,' Alessia informs him.

'Out where?'

'To the bars.'

'I must go with them. I know the best places.' Her father beams at Maxim.

'I will tell him.' Alessia looks uncertainly at Thanas, then at Maxim.

'Your father wants to join us,' Maxim guesses.

'Yes.'

'Oh boy.' Maxim smiles and shakes his head. 'Okay.'

'I will let my brothers know. And my cousins and uncles,' her father says.

'What about us? Maryanne and I?' Caroline asks, staring at Maxim with huge blue eyes. She cannot seem to tear her gaze away from him.

Oh.

'Stags only!' Tom insists.

'Maybe we should take Alessia out,' Maryanne offers.

'I have too much to do,' Alessia says quickly.

'Well, in that case, we'll help you. Won't we, Caro?'

'Oh, no. You are guests,' Alessia protests.

'We'd be honoured to help if we can,' Caroline responds, but she gives Maxim a lingering look of anxiety, or is it devotion? Then Alessia remembers she's not long lost her husband – and Maryanne, her brother; they are bonded in their grief.

Joe and I are now sharing the guest room. It's not the first time we've bunked together. We've done it at school and on school trips, and more recently when utterly hammered at the end of a good night.

He's unpacking his bag, and I'm hanging the two suits he brought with him.

'Mate, how have you been, really?' he asks.

'Okay. A little stir-crazy if you want the truth.'

'Maxim. I need to ask you. This marriage. Is it you? Is it what you want?'

'What do you mean?'

'You're a player. Are you ready to saddle yourself with one woman?'

I gape at him. 'I wouldn't be going through all this fucking grief if I wasn't!'

'Mate. I'm just asking.'

I blow out a breath, keeping a rein on my temper. 'It's what I want. It's what she wants. Why is that so hard to believe?'

He raises his hands. 'Okay, okay. I believe you.'

'But enough of that. What happened?'

'I thought I'd bring two suits. Give you a choice.'

'No. I mean about my family, whom you've brought along for a jolly.'

'Yeah. Sorry about that. I met Caro as I was coming out of your building. I had your suits.'

'Ah.'

'I was dead in the water. She wanted to know what the hell I was doing.'

'I see.'

'She's pissed, bro. At you.'

'I know. I didn't tell them. I didn't want the fuss. But I've managed to talk Maryanne down and round. Caro will have to wait.'

'Does Alessia know about you and her?'

'What do you mean?'

'Before Kit.'

'Um . . . No.' And, of course, there was the grief-fucking after Kit's death.

Hell.

'Do you think I should tell her?' I ask.

He shrugs. 'I have no idea.'

'We've not talked about . . . any of that.'

'Save it for the honeymoon.'

I laugh a little nervously. 'Yeah. Good idea.'

'Have you planned to go away?'

'Yeah. Arrangements have been made. It's a surprise for Alessia.'

'Cool. Here are the rings.' He hands me a small bag, within which are two pink gift-wrapped boxes.

'Great. Thanks.' I sit on the bed and start unravelling the ribbon.

Joe sits beside me. 'So tell me how a wedding works here.'

Later Maxim and Joe step into the kitchen. Alessia looks up from the worktop where she's beating eggs and inhales sharply, drinking in the sight of her fiancé. His green eyes gleam with a seductive promise and his hair shines, the golden highlights glinting beneath the overhead lights. She still finds it astonishing that this attractive man will be her husband. In his jacket, white shirt and jeans, he looks edible. His gaze finds hers, and he smiles and saunters over to her.

'How are you doing?' he asks so only she can hear.

'I'm good. You?'

'Good.' He kisses her forehead, and she inhales a trace of his scent – soap and shaving foam – and her favourite fragrance, Maxim. He tucks a stray hair behind her ear. 'You look delectable.'

She laughs, basking in his attention. 'I look like your cleaner.'

He takes her chin between his thumb and forefinger, gently tilts her head up, and drops a lingering kiss on her lips. 'No. You look like a countess.'

She gasps at his shimmering, intense expression, but her mother clears her throat, interrupting them both. He turns and grins at Shpresa, then at the two women sitting at the table.

'I see you've been set to work,' he says to Caroline and Maryanne, who are slicing spinach and sorrel at the table.

'We want to help,' says Maryanne with a bright smile.

'This is surprisingly therapeutic,' says Caroline, looking up at Maxim with her bluest of blue eyes.

'There's wine somewhere,' he says, ignoring her look. 'We bought a load for the celebration on Saturday. I think it's out back.'

'I could murder a glass of wine,' Caroline exclaims, and Alessia's not sure if she's expressing her desperation or relief.

'I will fetch a bottle,' Shpresa says, and she disappears into the utility room.

'So, how's the nightlife here, Alessia?' Joe asks.

She shrugs, a little embarrassed. 'I don't know. I've not been out at night much.' All the English turn to stare at her, and she flushes. 'My parents are protective,' she explains in a rush but notices Caroline glance at Maryanne with a furrowed brow. Her mother returns, brandishing a bottle of white wine.

'I'll open that,' Joe offers, and Shpresa hands him the bottle and a corkscrew and brings two glasses to the table.

'Two?' Joe says in consternation.

Alessia and her mother exchange a look. Then her mother's gaze passes over the English as they stare at the Albanians and lands back on Alessia, her eyes twinkling with a devilry that Alessia's not seen before. She grins and fetches two more glasses.

Mama!

Joe pours four glasses as Baba enters the room. He's freshly shaved and wearing a tie and a clean shirt. He looks quite dashing. 'Is everyone ready?' he asks Alessia in their tongue; his tone is buoyant.

'I think so, Babë.'

His eyes drift to his wife. 'Are you drinking?' he asks, shocked.

'Yes. We have all eaten. I should be fine.' She raises the glass to him. And Maryanne, Caroline, and Alessia follow suit.

'Gëzuar, Babë,' Alessia says.

He gapes at his wife and daughter and then glances at Maxim, nodding. 'Like I said, she's your problem now.' But Maxim doesn't understand.

'Gëzuar, Zonja,' he says to the women, then turns to Joe and Maxim. 'We go.'

What!

Alessia gapes at her equally awestruck mother. It's the first time they've ever heard her father speak English. She takes a quick gulp of wine and watches as the men file out of the room.

'What is it?' Maryanne asks Alessia.

'My father. He never speaks English.'

Maryanne laughs. 'There's always a first time. And this wine's not bad.'

'It is Albanian,' Alessia says and cannot keep the pride out of her voice.

'Cheers, Alessia, Mrs Demachi, and congratulations.' Maryanne raises her glass. Caroline follows suit, and they all take a sip. The wine is delicious, though not quite as tasty as the wine she had in the library in Cornwall. Still, Caroline and Maryanne seem to appreciate it, which, as a proud Albanian, pleases Alessia.

'That's the last of the spinach. What shall we do now?' Caroline asks.

Alessia has placed the two large dishes of Tavë kosi in the oven to bake, and she takes a seat beside her mother as the women make byrek rolls. Shpresa rolls out the dough while Alessia, Maryanne, and Caroline fill them with the spinach, sorrel and feta cheese mix, which Shpresa has prepared with eggs, onion and garlic. In between rolls, they each sip their wine.

The conversation ebbs and flows, but the banter between Caroline and Maryanne is entertaining.

'I can't believe you've fallen for an American,' Caroline teases Maryanne.

'Fallen?'

'Darling, you've had an uncharacteristic smitten look since he called you at the airport.'

'I have not!'

'Methinks she doth protest too much. When are we going to meet him?'

'I don't know. Ethan may come to the UK at Easter. We'll see. He's hard to read.' Maryanne gives her a pointed look, and Caroline purses her lips in feigned contempt.

'How long have the two of you known each other?' Alessia asks. She's feeling a little light-headed from the wine, especially as they're on their second bottle.

'I was friends with Maxim at school,' Caroline says. 'Well, more than friends. But that was a long time ago.' She frowns at the spinach mix, pats it down on the dough, then twists it efficiently into a roll.

More than friends!

'I think *we* met at one of Rowena's summer parties. The annual Trevethick cricket match at the Hall,' Caroline says to Maryanne.

'Yes. Back in the day. You came down from London with Maxim. I have to say, those are still so much fun. I do love a man in cricket whites.'

'Yes.' Caroline sounds wistful. 'Kit looked great in whites and was a skilled batsman too.' She stares down into her glass.

'He was,' Maryanne says, and the atmosphere among the women nosedives.

'I am sorry for your loss,' Alessia says quietly.

'Yes. Well. Thank you.' Caroline swallows and tosses her glossy hair as if shaking off a nasty thought. 'It will be down to you to host the annual village cricket match next summer, Alessia, among many other events.'

Alessia stares at her. She knows nothing of cricket.

'You really don't know what will be expected of you, do you?' Caroline states.

'Not now,' Maryanne warns Caroline.

'No,' Alessia whispers.

Caroline sighs. 'Well . . .' She gives Maryanne a reassuring glance. 'We'll be there to help you.'

'Let's get these byrek finished,' Maryanne chirps, and Alessia knows she's trying to lighten the mood.

The bar is crowded and noisy, but the atmosphere is sociable and celebratory, despite the spartan surroundings. This is the third bar we've been in, and it's as functional as the first two, though not quite as austere because there are several FK Kukësi football scarves and shirts on the walls. Football is big in Kukës. Tonight the men, all of whom seem to be related in some way to Jak Demachi, are drowning their sorrows as their team lost to Teuta, the team from Durrës.

Our love of football is an icebreaker – Joe and I, who are Arsenal and Chelsea supporters respectively, share their sorrow. Tom, on the other hand, is a rugby man, as are we – but he's no time or love for the beautiful game.

I'm on my fourth beer and feeling the buzz. I cannot remember anyone's name, but Tom and Joe are holding forth.

Joe, as a good-looking guy, is undoubtedly an attraction. I've not seen any Black people in Albania, though I'm sure they exist, so he's an object of curiosity. He doesn't seem uncomfortable – quite the opposite. He's lapping up the attention, and we're all treated as honoured guests. The Albanians are delighted that we're here.

Frankly, it's touching.

There are only two flies in the proverbial ointment: One is Caroline and facing her wrath at some point – I've not been lulled into a false sense of security about that. She's probably hurt too, and I need to make it up to her. The second is the uneasy feeling that I'm being watched. I know that we're curiosities here in this small town, but every so often, an unsettling itch skitters down my back as if someone has me in their sights.

Is it him?

Her '*betrothed*.'

Is he watching? I don't know.

It could be my overactive imagination.

'Urdhëro!' Jak hands me another beer. 'Më pas raki!' He clinks my bottle with his.

Oh God, raki. The devil's brew!

It's late. The food is cooling and ready to go into the refrigerators in the utility room. Alessia sits with Caroline and Maryanne at the table, and they're on their third bottle of wine. Alessia, feeling more light-headed than before, has stopped drinking. Her mother has been sensible and retired for the night. After all, they have a big day tomorrow.

She yawns. There is no sign of the men, and she suspects Maxim will be as drunk as he was that night of the raki. She'd like to go to bed, but Caroline and Maryanne are talking about men, and it's fascinating.

'Men are confounding,' Maryanne says.

'Emotionally unavailable more like,' Caroline responds. 'But, all they really want is someone to suck their dick.' She laughs, but her laughter sounds forced and hollow.

'Caro. Enough,' Maryanne scolds, glancing at Alessia, who is trying to absorb this arresting insight. She's shocked at the turn in the conversation but keeps her face neutral, she hopes, as she struggles with how to respond.

Is this how English women talk to each other?

Caroline turns her attention to Alessia, narrowing her eyes as if assessing her anew now that they're all tipsy. 'You really are very pretty,' she says, slurring her words slightly.

Alessia suspects she's more than a little tipsy.

'I'm not surprised he's fallen for you . . . but . . . I've not seen it before. Him. In love. You know, he's my best friend.'

Best friend, now.

Alessia seizes her chance.

The phrase *more than friends* has been rattling around her brain, tormenting her since Caroline blurted it out earlier. 'You and he were . . . lovers?' she asks.

'I should say so. We popped each other's cherries.' Caroline quirks her lips up as if it's a fond memory. 'He's a better fuck than my husband.'

'Oh.' Alessia is now completely lost for words, as a vision of Caroline wearing nothing but Maxim's shirt and making coffee in his kitchen comes unwelcome to mind.

'Caroline!' Maryanne exclaims, shocked.

'It's true. I know he's your brother. They're both your brothers,' she slurs. 'But you know Maxim's a complete player.' She turns her unfocused gaze on Alessia. 'Darling, he's slept with most of London.' Her face falls. 'And after Kit . . . Well, we – Ow!'

'Enough,' Maryanne growls, her voice much firmer, and Alessia suspects she's kicked Caroline under the table.

Caroline shrugs. 'It's true. Promiscuous doesn't cover it. He's proof of the adage: Practice makes perfect.'

'I think it's time we got you to bed, Caro.' Maryanne stands. 'Forgive her; she's grieving and had too much to drink,' Maryanne says to Alessia. 'Don't pay any attention.'

Caroline frowns as she stands as if she's just realised what she's said. 'Yes. Of course. I'm sorry. I don't know what I'm talking about. Do forgive me.'

'Good night, Alessia,' Maryanne says, and she drags a staggering Caroline out of the room, leaving Alessia reeling.

He's a better fuck than my husband.

Present tense.

Chapter Six

Mrs Demachi has cooked a monumental breakfast for us all. From her huge smile and the little song she's humming as she makes coffee and busies herself around the kitchen, I know she's in her element and loving every moment. It's heartening that we're not too much of a burden on her.

'Good morning, Maxim.' She greets me, radiating happiness.

I give her a quick kiss on the cheek.

'Good morning, Shpresa. Thank you for feeding my friends and family.'

'Dear boy.' She places her hand on my cheek. 'It is my pleasure. I know you bring great happiness to my Alessia.'

'And she to me.'

She grins. 'Sit. Eat. Big day, today. And the weather has been kind to us.' She directs my gaze to the window, and outside the sky is glorious – a bright February blue. I hope it's not too cold.

Maryanne and Joe are already seated at the table. They're in high spirits as they tuck into omelettes and Mama Demachi's delicious bubble bread. There is cheese, olives, local honey and stuffed vine leaves too. Jak sits at the head of the table, slathering butter and berry jam on his bubble bread. He is the definition of bright-eyed and bushy-tailed. He's been positively upbeat since last night. There's a smudge of soot on his hand, and I know he's been outside to light the stove in the garage to warm up our wedding venue.

The Demachis are the most excellent hosts.

Apart from the cockblocking, of course.

The only person not full of the joys of the day is Caroline, who sits quietly, looking pale and morose as she nurses a cup of coffee. I suspect she's hungover. Maryanne casts an occasional anxious glance at her and then at me.

What? What's happened?

Maryanne gives me a quick, subtle shake of her head.

Leave it, she's saying.

Of course, missing from the table is my beautiful bride. Alessia is being prepped for the wedding, and I've not seen her since we left for my stag night. And what a night it was – Kukës can party. Well, the men of Kukës can. And it ended happily – meaning I wasn't handcuffed to any street furniture without my trousers, which Tom threatened at one point during the night.

You don't have any handcuffs.

I'll improvise, old boy.

And I feel fine this morning. That's probably because I ditched the raki. Now, I'm excited and a little anxious to get on with the day, and I'll be glad when it's over.

'Can I talk to you?' Caroline asks as I take my seat. I glance at her, sensing she's on edge. And Maryanne is being evasive. Has something happened? If so, what?

My stomach churns.

'Of course.' My tone is brusque.

This is it. The moment of reckoning I've been dreading.

'In private?'

'After breakfast. You should eat something.'

She grimaces, and I know she has a Grade A hangover.

Alessia stares unseeing at her reflection in the bedroom mirror. She's seated at her dressing table as Agnesa, her cousin, who's a hairdresser and makeup artist, curls her hair with a styling iron. Agnesa chatters away, excited to be involved in all the preparations and eager to see Maxim, the handsome fiancé, again.

Alessia tunes her out. She's numb, and she's not sure if it's her nerves or if she's still reeling from Caroline's drunken revelations.

Darling, he's slept with most of London.

This is not news to Alessia. She used to empty his bin of condoms every time she cleaned for him. She wrinkles her nose in disgust at the recollection – sometimes, there were *many* discarded condoms.

And then they suddenly stopped appearing.

She rubs her forehead, trying to remember when that happened. So much has occurred since then, and her memory of the timeline is confused. She attempted to figure it out last night while trying to sleep but couldn't because Caroline's thoughtless words echoed through her brain, taunting her.

He's a better fuck than my husband.

So, they *were* together.

Maxim and Caroline.

But when? When did this *fucking* happen? It sounds recent, and an unwelcome image of Caroline in Maxim's arms in the street outside his apartment forms in her mind.

No.

Her imagination is choking her and making her doubt herself. Making her doubt him – her man. Her Mister. On her wedding day.

She feels like she's going to suffocate under the weight of these awful thoughts.

'I need a minute,' she says.

'Okay,' Agnesa responds, a little surprised, but she steps aside. As only half her hair is curled, Alessia finds a scarf and ties it around her head, concealing it all. She grabs a robe, hastily wraps it over the slip she's wearing, and leaves the room. She needs the one thing that will bring her solace.

She reaches the bottom of the stairs and hears everyone at breakfast. Ignoring them, she hurries to the front room and sits at the piano.

She takes a deep breath and places her fingers on the keys, feeling immediately more grounded as her fingers touch the cool ivory. She closes her eyes, then launches into Beethoven's *Moonlight Sonata*, the tricky third movement. In C-sharp minor. It's the most fitting piece, in the correct key to reflect her anger. The music flows. Loudly. Easily: Blistering off the walls, through the room. Her anger and resentment pour into the keys, emphasising the loud accents of the sonata in brilliant oranges and reds until there's nothing but her and the colours of the music.

The frantic, fast arpeggios of Beethoven's third movement echo furiously off the hallway into the family room with such ferocity and passion that the entire table is momentarily silenced and paralysed.

I look up at Shpresa, who looks anxiously at Jak. He shrugs.

'Alessia?' Maryanne asks, and I hear the breathless wonder in her voice.

I nod and turn to her parents. 'Has something happened?'

'I do not know,' Shpresa responds, and her eyes widen in astonishment. 'You know?'

'That she's angry. Yes. But I don't know why.' I frantically rack my brain, trying to think if I could have done something to upset her.

Hell. Is she having doubts about the wedding?

'That's Alessia?' asks Joe with a forkful of omelette raised mid-air.

'Yes.'

'Dude!'

'I know.'

'She's extraordinary,' Joe murmurs.

'Yeah. But she's pissed off. At something or someone.' I turn my attention to Maryanne and Caroline, who saw her last night. Maryanne's lips thin, and Caroline avoids my eyes, and I have my culprit. 'What did you do?' I ask quietly as my scalp tenses.

What the fuck? Did you say something?

'Caroline?'

She pales and shakes her head, still avoiding my gaze.

Shit.

'I'll go.' Shpresa wipes her hands on a dishcloth and heads out of the room.

'How do you know she's angry?' Maryanne asks.

'This is in C-sharp minor.'

She frowns.

'C-sharp minor. Angry music. In reds and oranges. She told me. Sad and angry. E flat.'

'Wow.'

'Yeah. Music. I told you.'

'She's brilliant.'

'Yes. She has synaesthesia. She's playing this from memory.' I can't hide the pride and awe in my voice.

'She's amazing.' Joe is stunned.

'She is,' I agree. 'In every way.'

Alessia reaches the end of the piece, and I listen acutely, wanting to hear if that's the end or if she'll play something else.

Alessia is breathing hard when she finishes. Her thoughts clear as the colours fade, and she takes a deep breath. She turns to find her mother in the room. She'd been so lost in the music she didn't hear her come in.

'That was beautiful, my heart. What's wrong?'

Alessia shakes her head. She doesn't want to admit her fears. If she speaks them aloud, she makes them more tangible – more real. She's at a crossroads. Does she believe the man she loves or . . . not?

'He knows,' Shpresa says.

'Knows what?'

'That you are upset.'

'He's heard me play.'

'Often, I think,' her mother says.

Alessia nods.

'He's so proud of you. I can tell.'

'I must go and get ready.' Alessia stands and faces her mother.

'He loves you.'

'I know.' But her voice wavers, betraying her true feelings.

Why is she so suddenly unsure? Of everything.

Shpresa's expression softens. 'Oh, my heart. Go and get ready. You're making the right decision. These past few days, I've never seen you so happy. And he's glowing.'

'Is he?' Alessia hears the breathless hope in her own voice.

'Of course he is.' She caresses her daughter's face. 'You have made us so proud, Alessia. Me and your father. Go conquer the world. Like you always wanted to. And with that man by your side, you won't fail.'

Alessia's spirits lift. This is the most robust affirmation she's ever heard from her mother. 'Thank you, Mama.' Alessia clasps her mother tightly, and they stand hugging each other in the front room.

'I know about the baby,' Mama whispers.

Alessia gasps.

'I know you're not pregnant.'

'How?'

'The number of painkillers you've been taking over the last few days. And I found your contraceptive pills while I was cleaning your dressing table.'

Alessia flushes. 'I'm sorry to . . . mislead you.'

'I understand. And I'll find a way to break it to your father. Does Maxim know?'

'Thank you. And yes, Maxim knew from the beginning.'

'And he still went along with all this?'

'Yes. For me . . . and for you.'

'For me?'

Alessia nods.

'I don't understand.'

Alessia kisses her mother's forehead. 'One day, I will tell you.'

Fuck this!

I've been stewing in my own juices, trying to figure out what's wrong with Alessia, and I can't bear it a moment longer. I leave the table, and disregarding the many pairs of eyes I feel burning into my back, I stalk down the corridor towards the front room.

'Alessia,' I call through the door and hold my breath.

'Yes,' she says eventually.

I exhale sharply. 'Are you okay?'

'Yes.' She sounds uncertain.

'Do you want to talk about anything?'

'No.'

It's not enough. I don't believe her.

'I don't care about this superstitious nonsense, but you and your mother do. That's why I'm staying out here. I don't know what's upsetting you, but I want you to know, I love you. I want to marry you. Today. If you need to speak to me . . . I'm here.'

Shpresa eyes her daughter.

'Mama, I need to talk to him,' Alessia says.

'I will leave you. It is your decision whether you invite him into this room or not. Nothing about this wedding is conventional . . . so . . .' Her mother waves her hand in resignation, kisses her forehead, and leaves.

'Can I come in?' Maxim asks from outside the room.

'Yes.'

Maxim peeks around the door and smiles when he sees her. It's impossible not to return his smile, and her heart rate spikes at the sight of him. She's missed him. He enters and comes to stand beside her, green eyes ablaze. He's in a T-shirt and jeans, the black ones with the rip at the knee . . . and he looks concerned and *hot*.

Especially hot.

'What's wrong?' he asks.

Alessia is wearing a blue scarf around her head that conceals her hair and a blue robe, reminding me of when she was in my flat.

What a time that was . . . Me lusting after her while she ignored me.

She's as lovely now as she was then. More so, and I'm still lusting after her. She gazes at me, a mountain of hurt in her eyes.

'What is it?'

She pales a little.

Shit. It's bad.

'Tell me, please.'

'It was . . . just words.'

'Tell me,' I insist.

'Your sister-in-law.' Her voice is barely audible.

'Caroline?'

She nods.

'Ah.' *I knew it.* 'What's she said?'

She seems to be debating whether to tell me. I watch her inner struggle play out on her expressive face. Finally, she swallows. 'She said that you are a better . . . *fuck*' – she whispers the word – 'than her husband.'

I inhale sharply as my temper flares. I've never heard Alessia use crude language before, and hearing that word come out of her mouth has shocked me more than it should.

What Caroline said is more shocking and *un-fucking-becoming*.

No wonder she's at breakfast, hanging her head in shame.

So she should be.

Caro's come here to cause trouble. And she's succeeded. I bridle my anger, knowing I can deal with her later. 'I'm sure she was drunk,' I mutter charitably.

'I could not stop thinking about that last night. As I was trying to sleep.'

Shit. We're having this discussion now – on the day of our wedding?

'Do you love her?' Alessia asks.

I gape at her, stunned into silence. *What? How can she think that?*

'You are not answering my question. In Cornwall, you said, "talk to me," "ask me questions." I am asking you now.'

'No, I don't love her like that.' I'm emphatic. 'I used to, a long time ago. But I was fifteen. She's family. My brother's wife.'

'And physically?'

I frown, not entirely understanding what she's trying to ask.

'Did you have sexual intercourse with your brother's wife?'

Hell.

'Um . . . no. But I had sex with his widow.'

Alessia winces and closes her eyes, and her expression slices me to the bone.

Shit. And I've never felt quite as ashamed as I do now.

'When I last saw her,' Alessia says as she opens dark, dark wounded eyes, 'she was in your arms, on the sidewalk outside your apartment building.'

'In my arms?' I frown, desperately trying to remember, feeling like I've been caught on the back foot.

'I was in Anatoli's Mercedes.'

A chill grips my heart, and I'm transported back to that dreadful night. 'Oh, yes. She was apologising, and she ran into me. We would have fallen had I not caught her.' I swallow. 'We had a fight. A big fight.'

'It makes sense. You and her. You are the same. The same class.' Her voice gets quieter and quieter.

'No! I don't want Caroline. I want you, Alessia. When I went to see her, I told her I was in love with you. She threw me out of the house and then came running to apologise. And it was just as Anatoli was getting into the car. I didn't listen to what Caroline was saying. I knew something was wrong. I recognised the Albanian plates on his car, and I cannot tell you how harrowing it was to watch in complete helplessness as it drove off into the distance.' I close my eyes and remember the feeling of utter impotence and despair as the Mercedes disappeared from view. 'It was one of the worst days of my life.'

Her fingers find mine, and I open my eyes as she squeezes my hand.

'What's going on, Alessia?' I return the squeeze.

'Are you sure you want to do this?' she asks. 'She loves you too.'

I pull her into my arms and hold her. 'It's you I love, not her. It's you I want to marry. Not her. Please don't let her ruin our day.'

I can't believe we're having this discussion.

Alessia lets out a sigh, her dark eyes on mine.

'Baby, let's do this.' I stroke my thumb over her lip. 'I want to grow old with you. And I don't want my family to be in any doubt about how I feel about you, Alessia Demachi – you are the love of my life.'

I hear her small gasp. 'You are the love of mine.' And she presses her lips against the pad of my thumb.

'Thank God.' I exhale with relief. 'I'm not going to kiss you. I want to save that for tonight.' As the words leave my mouth, a frisson of desire skates over my skin, lifting the hairs on my body.

Wow.

Alessia inhales sharply. 'Okay.' She sounds a little breathless.

'Okay.' I grin.

Her answering smile is shy, and I know I've won her back.

'That was a stunning piece you played. Knocked the socks off my friends and family.'

'I was angry.'

'I could tell. I'm sorry.'

She shuts her eyes and quickly shakes her head as if ridding herself of a terrible thought.

'Are you packed?'

She opens her eyes and nods. After the wedding, we are out of here.

'Good. Please, go and get ready.' I lean forward and kiss her forehead, closing my eyes.

I do not want to lose you. Again.

I return to the breakfast table, where the conversation is more muted, and I know all eyes are on me. I cannot bring myself to even look at Caro. She's really crossed a fucking line, and I'm furious.

No. Raging.

How dare she?

Right now, I don't trust my temper, and for fuck's sake – it's my wedding day.

There's a knock at the front door, and Jak springs up from the table as if he's expecting the caller.

'Okay, mate?' Joe asks me.

'Yeah.' I glance at my watch. I have time. 'I'm going for a run.'

When I come back upstairs in my running gear, it's a hive of activity. There are more people in the house, presumably to help with the catering and set up. I manage to avoid them; I'm glad I'm leaving for a run. I've left Joe in the room to shower, and I've no idea where M.A. or Caro are, and frankly, I don't want to know and I don't care. I need some time with my own thoughts to calm down.

I step outside into the bright but chilly day to see sunlight bouncing off the glittering green lake. But just at the bottom of the driveway, Demachi is in a full and intense conversation with *him*!

Demachi and the Arsehole turn to stare as I stand immobilised, glaring at them.

What the fuck is he *doing here?*

My hands fist, and I'm ready. Nothing would give me greater pleasure than beating this man to a pulp – especially the way I'm feeling at this minute.

'This is not what you think, Englishman,' Anatoli sneers.

Demachi holds up his hands. 'Po flasim për punë, asgjë më shumë.'

I have no idea what he says.

'Ha!' Anatoli says, his scorn evident in that one syllable. 'If you knew the language, you'd know what he's said. We're discussing business. Nothing more. Nothing to do with you.' The Arsehole's English is impeccable, which is bloody irritating. 'We're not discussing Alessia,' he continues, and his voice catches as he says her name.

What! Does he care for her?

'Mos e zër në gojë Alesian,' Demachi snaps at him.

'I'll be here, Englishman, waiting, in her homeland, with her family. When you fuck up,' Anatoli scoffs.

'You'll wait a long bloody time, mate,' I mutter, more to myself than to him. 'I hope.'

Fuck this.

'Farewell, Arsehole,' I call, knowing full well my father-in-law won't understand, and turn and sprint up the driveway, leaving them standing. To my great satisfaction, I see Anatoli's mouth pressed in a hard line, and I know my gibe has provoked him.

Yes!

Out on the road, I dodge past his Mercedes, stretch my legs, and run.

Run like I've never run before.

'You look great, mate,' Joe says as he straightens my tie.

'I'm glad you brought the Dior. It's my favourite.'

'French navy is your colour. Goes with your blood.'

'Very funny, Joe.'

'I'm pissed you didn't give me time to make you a bespoke suit.'

'You'll get a chance.'

'For a wedding?' Joe's brow furrows.

'We'll do this again in London, or Cornwall. Or Oxfordshire,' I reassure him.

'You and Alessia?'

I laugh. 'Yes. Don't look so alarmed. It's complicated. But I'll probably be in full morning dress.'

'Dove grey? Black? Stripes?' Joe's eyes light up.

'Mate. Let's get this wedding out of the way first.'

'Buttonhole,' he says and pins the white rose to my lapel. He places his hands on my biceps. 'You look like a groom.'

'Thanks, bro.' And I'm suddenly overwhelmed by all that's happened, by what I'm about to do. I hug him. Hard. 'I'm so glad you're here, mate.'

Joe slaps me on the back. 'Me too, Max. Me too.'

I clear my throat. 'Now. You know what we have to do.'

'Yep.'

Albanian tradition dictates that the groom should collect his bride and take her to his home for a feast. That's impossible for us as I don't have a home here. But I'm to escort Alessia from her front door to the wedding party. It's the closest we can get to this tradition.

Outside, by the front door, Joe, Tom, and I wait for my bride. Joe's also in a navy suit, and as ever, he looks sharp and stylish. Tom is in a black dinner suit with a black tie.

It's all I brought with me, Trevethick.

Both have buttonholes, and I'm relieved they're here with me. Their friendship and support over the last few years has been everything. And they scrub up well.

Wedding guests are milling around in the driveway, and some are coming out of the house. I think they're immediate family who have been greeting Alessia inside, as is traditional. Some are filing into the tent beside the garage as it's warmer in there, and I know the registrar is already inside and set up. Beside this stunning lake and mountain setting, there's a convivial, festive feeling of a community coming together.

It's moving and I swallow down my emotion.

I'm definitely not in Kansas any more.

The coloured lights on the fir trees that Jak hung yesterday add to the atmosphere, as do the few children running and laughing in the yard, holding and waving Albanian flags.

People greet me with a handshake or kisses. Many of the men I met on our impromptu stag do address me as '*Chelsea*' after my football team. It's a nickname I rather like – but I'm still finding it impossible to keep up with all their names.

A photographer is documenting our day with a Canon EOS. I think she's one of Alessia's cousins. But I'm not sure.

I'm a world away from home.

Maryanne and Caroline exit the house to make their way to the venue. They're both in winter wedding finery. Maryanne's in a navy trouser suit, and Caro, a navy velvet dress – and I know Joe has tipped them off as to what I'm wearing.

Maryanne hugs me. 'Maxie, you look splendid. So does your bride.' She sniffs and walks hastily away before I have a chance to say anything.

Caro still can't look me in the eye. 'You've been avoiding me,' she says quietly.

'What did you expect? This isn't the time, Caro. I'm still so fucking angry with you.'

'I'm sorry.'

'I'm not the one you need to apologise to.'

'I needed to tell you something.' And she peers at me, her blue eyes wide and a little teary. 'And you're going to be angry about this too, but I did it for you and her,' she whispers.

'What did you do?'

'I told your mother. She'll be here shortly.'

'What?' The word is almost inaudible, and I can hardly breathe.

Fuck.

Chapter Seven

'Darling, I'm here already,' a clipped, mid-Atlantic voice drawls over the light breeze towards us. We whirl around as my heart sinks, and my mother is making her way down the drive through the crowd. She's dressed in a heavy black coat – probably from Chanel's upcoming collection for next winter – oversized Chanel sunglasses, a faux fur hat, and Louboutin boots.

Accompanying her is a young man about my age, dressed in black Moncler. He has model-good looks, American teeth, and I suspect he's her latest fuck. Her hand rests in the crook of his arm.

'Mother, what a pleasant surprise,' I say, retreating into the detached persona I reserve exclusively for the woman who birthed me. 'You should have told me you were coming.'

'Maxim.' She offers her cheek, and I give her a quick peck, inhaling the expensive scent of Creed, her perfume of choice.

'Joe and Tom, you know. And Judas Iscariot, my sister-in-law.' I take a small amount of pleasure in Caroline's ashen face as she gives her mother-in-law a quick kiss.

'Thank you for letting me know, Caroline. Short notice, I know. But it looks like we made it here in time. This is my friend, Heath.' Rowena introduces the blond on her arm.

'How do you do?' I respond, plastering a smile on my face.

Before he can reply, she releases him. 'Might I have a word, darling?'

'I'm afraid it's not convenient at this time. I'm about to get married. Please make your way into the venue.' I wave her in the direction of the marquee. 'Judas will find a seat for you.'

Caro flushes and stares down at her Manolos.

'I'm not here to prevent your wedding, Maxim. That would be a little vulgar, don't you think? But we will talk afterwards. And you will explain to me why you are marrying the help and why the fuck you haven't invited your grieving mother to this . . . event. Are you ashamed of your bride and her family? Because, frankly, that's how this looks.'

I can't see her eyes, but she purses her scarlet lips, and I know that beneath her cool disdain, she's seething.

Well, that makes two of us.

No, I'm not seething. I'm apoplectic with rage.

But I hide it well. 'I didn't invite you, Rowena dearest' – I lean down and whisper in her ear – 'because you're doing exactly what I thought you'd do. Projecting your pretentious privileged shit onto my situation. Now, if you'll excuse me, I'm about to marry the woman I love.'

She stiffens. 'I know that marrying this girl is a way to get back at me, but let me warn you—'

'It's not about *you*, for fuck's sake,' I hiss. 'Not everything is about you, Rowena. I fell in love. Deal with it.'

Tom clears his throat, a flush at his neck – did he hear us? Behind him, Jak and Shpresa have appeared at the front door. I turn to greet them. Shpresa is almost unrecognisable. She's wearing a pale pink shift dress and a matching chiffon wrap. Her hair is coiffed and sleek and dark, like Alessia's. And she's wearing a little makeup.

She looks stunning.

'Mama Demachi, you look lovely,' I murmur, and she smiles, showing us where Alessia gets her looks.

Chin up, dude. Here goes.

I turn and make the introductions. 'Jak, Shpresa, my mother has decided to grace us with her presence. May I present Rowena, Dowager Countess of Trevethick.' I stress the word *dowager*, and Rowena's lips tighten – because it's rude and also incorrect – but she doesn't miss a beat, and graciously, she holds out her hand.

'Mr and Mrs Demachi, what a pleasure to meet you and under such happy circumstances.' She sounds sincere, but her statement is tinged with condescending sarcasm for my benefit, I'm sure.

It's infuriating, but I ignore it and wrap my arms around my in-laws as they shake hands with my mother. 'Jak and Shpresa have done an incredible job of pulling this event together at such short notice.' I kiss Shpresa's cheek, and she flushes and quickly translates everything for her husband.

'Konteshë?' Jak says.

'Yes.'

'How do you do?' Shpresa says. 'Please. Come.' Shpresa casts a curious glance at me and directs Jak to accompany my mother and her lover into the house.

'That was a bit rough.' Tom states the bloody obvious. 'You okay, old boy?' He pats me on the back as we fall into line behind them.

'Yes,' I hiss. But it's a lie. Taking a deep breath, I bury my anger and follow them into the house.

The Demachis have suspended their no-shoes policy for the day, and we stand in the hallway, which is frankly crowded now that my mother and *Heath* have joined us, and wait.

Jak squares his shoulders and, with a theatrical flourish, opens the door to the front room, and there in the centre stands Alessia Demachi.

She's a vision in lace, satin, and a soft diaphanous material, silhouetted by the light from the window. I stop and stare at the woman who will shortly become my wife and completely lose my train of thought. She's gorgeous. With dark expressive eyes ringed in kohl, she looks a little more sophisticated, a little more . . . knowing, but demure and sexy as hell.

She takes my breath away.

Her gown is the epitome of elegance: a tight white satin corset covered in lace – lace over her shoulders and arms, and from her waist a skirt that flares softly. There are tiny pearl buttons at the front. Her hair is curled in a delicate updo beneath a fine, gossamer veil.

I realise I'm gawking, saving this moment so I'll remember it for an eternity, and my throat has constricted in a knot of exhilaration, awe, and anticipation.

She looks every inch a goddess . . . no, a countess. My countess.

Dude, don't get emotional.

Suddenly, I no longer care that what we're doing may not be strictly legitimate. I'm just so glad and thankful that we're doing this today. Here. Now.

'Hello again, beautiful. I could look at you all day.'

'And I you,' she whispers; her dark eyes, framed with the darkest, longest lashes, are vivid and intense, and I want to drown in her gaze.

I step forward and kiss her cheek. 'You look stunning.' And I realise this is the first time I've seen her in makeup. She's beautiful.

She strokes my lapel and smiles up at me. 'So do you.'

'My mother's here.'

Her eyes widen in shock.

'Yeah. Brace yourself,' I warn, for her ears only, then call, 'Mother.' And Rowena enters the room. She's removed her sunglasses, so she squints slightly as she observes the exquisite vision in front of her. 'May I present Alessia Demachi.'

'Darling girl,' Rowena says and kisses her cheek, then stands back to scrutinise my fiancée in her usual myopic way.

'Lady Trevethick, how do you do?' Alessia responds.

'You speak English?' Rowena sounds surprised.

'Fluently,' Alessia replies, and I could fucking kiss her.

My girl has teeth.

Rowena nods and smiles. I think she's impressed. 'It's a pleasure to meet you on such an auspicious day.'

'And you.'

It's only then that I become aware of the others in the room. Alessia's cousins, I think. And maybe a couple of her aunts.

'We'll have plenty of time, after this expeditious wedding, to get to know each other. I look forward to it.' Rowena's tone is neutral but friendly enough. 'We'll go and take our seats.' She turns and exits the room. As she does, I notice Alessia blow out a quick breath. Probably from relief. I take her hand and whisper in her ear.

'You were wonderful. Well done!'

'I did not know she was coming,' she whispers back.

'Me neither. A bit of a shock, to be honest. We can talk about it later. Shall we go and get married?'

She grins. 'Yes.'

'Oh, I forgot. The tradition. I'm supposed to give you this.' From inside my jacket pocket, I remove a handkerchief. In it is a sugared almond. I hold it up to Alessia's lips.

Maxim is mesmerising, especially in his sharp, dark suit. She's never seen him dressed this elegantly before, and he looks born to it.

But, of course he is. He's an aristocrat.

His eyes shine a brilliant green as his gaze moves from her eyes to her mouth. His lips are slightly parted as Alessia licks, then presses her lips against the candy he's holding. 'Mmm,' she murmurs, and he shuts his eyes for a nanosecond, then pops the sweet in his mouth. The muscles deep in Alessia's belly tighten, and she inhales sharply. He gives her a wicked grin full of sensual promise. It gives her an idea . . . for later when they're finally alone together.

By then, he'll be hers.

She cannot believe he'll be hers to keep. Her own man.

She wants to strut about the house on his arm, so everyone can see, and shout *he's mine.*

Alessia laughs at herself, feeling a little foolish and giddy.

He loves her – he told her in no uncertain terms this morning – and his declaration has fortified her inner strength.

Since Caroline's shocking revelation, Alessia has realised that his family is challenging her. She squares her shoulders.

Challenge accepted.

Maxim is worth fighting for.

She's just stood up to his mother, and she'll remain vigilant. Maxim has always been circumspect about Rowena, so Alessia will be cautious too. She knows that she must build a bridge with Caroline. After all, she's Maxim's sister-in-law. But still, she's wary. Caroline has her own agenda, and Alessia suspects she's in love with Maxim.

'Alessia, here!' Agnesa calls and hands Alessia her bouquet of white roses.

'Thank you.' Alessia smiles as Maxim takes her hand, and she puts her thoughts aside as together they leave the house.

Alessia drops Maxim's hand as she steps out of the house and takes the handkerchief her mother has embroidered for her for this very occasion. As tradition dictates, she pretends to be sad that she's leaving her parents' house and dabs at her eyes, but inside she's dancing.

'Are you okay?' Maxim asks, concerned as he slips his hand over her elbow.

She flashes him a quick grin and winks at him.

His brow creases. He's puzzled but amused.

'It's tradition.'

'Oh?'

'There's no prettiness in a bride without tears,' she whispers.

Maxim shakes his head, not understanding, but they're soon distracted by the cheers and applause from family and friends as they make their way, flanked by Tom and Joe, towards the spacious tent. Her parents and Maxim's mother follow in their wake as they head into the venue, ready for the wedding ceremony.

We're seated in front of Ferid Tabaku, the registrar, at a small table – with the Demachis, their family and friends, and the scant members of my family sitting at the tables behind us – while he solemnly informs us of our obligations.

Tabaku stands and reads through the code for the family, explaining what is expected of us during our marriage. Thanas quietly translates everything for me.

'Spouses have the same rights and duties towards each other.' He peers at both of us, his dark eyes bright with sincerity. 'They should love and respect each other, maintain marital fidelity, assist each other in fulfilling all family and social obligations . . .'

I glance at Alessia, and she squeezes my hand as tears form in her eyes. I look away quickly as a knot forms in my throat.

Deep breaths, mate.

Tabaku goes on and on and on . . . and I think it takes longer because poor Thanas has to translate everything.

Behind us, the crowd, even though they are seated, begins to fidget. There are coughs and snickers, and a baby starts to cry. A child says something that causes some tittering in the congregation, but I have no idea what he's said. I think it's his mother that removes him from the room, and I suspect he needs the lavatory.

Finally, Tabaku asks if we agree to our obligations and consent to the marriage.

'I agree to all our obligations, and consent,' I respond.

The registrar nods, satisfied with my answer, and turns to Alessia, who answers him in Albanian, and I hope she agrees and consents too. She gives me a quick smile.

'I have your consent. I now declare you are married in the name of the law.' Tabaku smiles, and the Albanians erupt into applause. 'Congratulations,' he says. 'You may exchange rings.'

I wondered when we were going to do the rings.

I fish them from where I've secured them – my inside pocket, next to my heart.

'Lady Trevethick,' I say to Alessia, and she gives me her hand. I slide on the platinum ring, feeling a little weird that I don't have to say anything. It fits perfectly. Thank goodness. I raise her hand to my lips, my eyes on hers, and kiss the ring and her knuckle together.

Alessia's answering smile is crotch-tighteningly beautiful. I hand her my ring, and she slips it on my finger. 'Lord Trevethick,' she whispers, and taking my hand in both of hers, she kisses the ring and my knuckle, then leans forward and kisses me.

The Albanians applaud and cheer, and Tom leans down. 'Congratulations, Trevethick,' he says, and I stand and hug him. Joe is next.

'Gentlemen, you will need to witness the marriage contract. Maxim, Alessia, you need to sign them too,' Thanas tells us.

Maxim's family approaches them.

'Congratulations,' his mother says to Maxim in her clipped, crisp tone. She places her hand on his arm and offers her cheek.

'Thank you, Mother,' Maxim responds, equally clipped and crisp, and his lips barely graze her cheek.

She turns her steely, dry eyes on Alessia. 'You make a beautiful bride, Alessia. Welcome to the family.' She offers her cheek to Alessia, and taking her cue from Maxim, Alessia gives her a quick peck, mindful that she's wearing lipstick.

Maryanne throws her arms around Maxim, and he hugs her. 'Maxie,' she says, and she reaches out a hand to Alessia at the same time. 'Congratulations, you two. I hope you'll be very happy.' She releases Maxim and hugs Alessia. 'Reformed rakes make the best husbands,' she whispers, but before she can respond, Alessia is distracted by Caroline, who's touching Maxim's lapel, a beseeching look in her big blue eyes.

'Congratulations.' Caroline gives him a quick kiss on his cheek.

Stony-faced, he nods. 'Thank you.'

She flushes a little, and Alessia realises that Maxim is still mad at her, and Caroline doesn't know how to deal with his anger. She turns to Alessia, her expression cooler, and Alessia's heart starts to pound.

'Congratulations, Alessia. And I'm so sorry. For what I said last night. It was graceless and utterly uncalled for.'

Alessia, acting on pure instinct, hugs her before she can say anything else. 'Thank you,' she says and releases her.

Caroline, embarrassed, nods and moves on, leaving Alessia alone with Maxim.

'How was that?' he asks as he takes her hand.

'Okay,' she whispers, and he brings her hand to his lips.

'You coped admirably with my family. Congratulations, Lady Trevethick.'

She grins, blossoming under his praise. 'We have to sit over there.' Alessia points to two grey velvet chairs set up beneath a small arbour, before a table covered in white linen, white roses, and fairy lights. Once they've taken their seats, two children – Alessia's young cousins – present them with plates from the impressive buffet.

The party is in full swing. Alessia is giddy and a little tipsy from the wine. Maxim has removed his jacket and tie, his hair is tousled from all her female relatives ruffling it, and he looks so handsome. The men have started to dance, and her uncles are trying to persuade Maxim to join them.

'Vallja e Kukësit. Come! Chelsea!' her cousin Murkash goads Maxim. 'You are Albanian now!'

Maxim rolls his eyes and turns to Alessia. 'You didn't mention dancing. With a bunch of men.'

'This is the traditional dance from Kukës,' Alessia says, grinning at him.

He flashes her a smile as he gets up to join them.

Man. What fresh hell is this?

'Okay! Okay, I'm coming. Joe, Tom, join me,' I call over to them at their adjacent table, where they're sitting with my family.

Murkash puts his hand on my shoulder, then takes my hand, and several of his . . . no, *our* male relatives join us, linking hands, including Tom and Joe.

'This!' Murkash says, holding a red handkerchief aloft, signalling to Kreshnik, our DJ, and the music kicks in. A traditional ballad with a thumping techno beat, and a slightly off-key melee of strings accompanied by archaic voices, thunders through the room. It's not something I've heard before. But more men get up and join us. It's a real crowd-pleaser.

Murkash slowly shows me the steps, and I follow him step for step – it's not as challenging as it looks. Soon we are circling the room, and a couple of the younger boys have joined us too.

Joe is grinning at me. Tom is concentrating on his steps.

We circle the dance floor once, twice – the men cheering and smiling, enjoying their collective camaraderie and the energetic dance.

By the time the music ends, I'm a little winded.

My bride joins me, looking as radiant as she did when I saw her standing, silhouetted against the window in her front room.

'We dance now.' She takes her handkerchief, holds her arms up as the music starts, and begins to sway, her alluring dark eyes on mine. I'm not sure what I am supposed to do. Our wedding party leaves their tables, forming a circle around us, so seizing the initiative, I take her hands, and we dance together, but then I pull away and just watch her because she's entrancing.

My wife slowly twirls her wrists, handkerchief in hand, and turns in time to an ancient-sounding tune with a percussive beat. She's utterly captivating to me and the audience. She beckons me forward again, and I surrender willingly and take another few turns with her before the music ends.

Mr Demachi takes to the floor with his handkerchief, and the older men of his community join him. The DJ plays a different, traditional track, and Jak leads his fellow men around the venue.

I stand and watch with Joe and Tom. It's . . . affecting, this expression of male kinship, one that we don't choose to encourage in the UK. Vaguely, I wonder why that's the case. Demachi signals for us to join the throng, and we comply, as do some of the women.

After a couple of hours of exhausting carousing and more dancing, we finally cut the impressive, highly decorated wedding cake and eat it with a glass of champagne. Our guests will continue into the night, but I'm done. I want out. I want to be alone with my bride.

'Our cab should be here shortly,' I murmur to Alessia.

'I will go and change.'

'Don't take too long.' I give her a wolfish grin, and she has the grace to blush. She hurries out of the venue, followed by her mother, and I find Joe and Tom standing by the makeshift bar.

'Trevethick, as weddings go, this has been a good one. Different,' Tom says.

'Yeah. It's cool, bro.' Joe claps me on the back. 'You look happy. Don't let your mother kill your buzz.'

'I won't. Thanks for coming. May do this all again in the summer. I'll keep you posted.'

'Marrying the same woman twice in the same year? That must be some kind of record,' Joe observes drily.

I nod my agreement and turn my attention to my family. Rowena is in a deep conversation with Heath. He's looking intensely at her, his expression grave as she speaks. He nods as if in agreement and glances at me, a calculating look on his face. He flushes, embarrassed to be caught looking my way, and promptly turns his attention back to my mother. He laughs at something she says and strokes her cheek.

There are certain things a man shouldn't see. His mother canoodling with a man half her age is one of them.

In disgust, I focus on Maryanne, who is talking to one of Alessia's cousins. I think it's Agnesa, who did Alessia's hair and makeup. They're having an animated conversation. Caroline is staring at . . . me! She gets up.

Shit. I don't want or need any more drama from her.

She sidles up to me, and I know she's had too much to drink.

'Caro, s'up?' I ask, my heart sinking.

'Stop being an arse,' she snaps.

'What?'

'You know what!'

I stare at her, trying to convey how monumentally she fucked up disclosing our personal shenanigans to Alessia. Alessia didn't need to hear that from her.

She should have heard it from me.

But I'm tired of being pissed off with Caro.

'I'm leaving shortly. What is it?' I ask.

'You're leaving?'

'Yes. Honeymoon. It's traditional.'

'Where are you going?'

I make a face. *Like I'm going to tell you.*

She huffs but doesn't press me. 'I just wanted to say sorry. Again. Are you going to ignore me forever?'

I sigh. 'I'll see. You fucked up, Caro. You need to stop that.'

'I know,' she says quietly, and she nudges me with her shoulder in a most un-Caroline show of affection that it makes me chuckle. I put my arm around her and kiss her hair.

'Thanks for coming to my wedding.'

'Thank you for inviting me.' She makes a face . . . because I didn't. 'Am I forgiven?' she asks.

'Just.'

'Maxim, might I have a word?' It's my mother.

Hell.

She looks pointedly at Caro, who nods and moves off to give us some privacy.

'Rowena.'

'I'll be brief. I wish you every happiness.' My mother's smile doesn't reach her eyes. 'On the plus side, this young girl will inject new DNA into our gene pool, but she has no idea what she's signed up for. You could at least enroll her in some etiquette lessons, so she doesn't make a complete fool of herself or you when you're in company. Or perhaps send her to finishing school. She might have a hope then.'

'Thank you for your concern, Mother. I'm quite sure Alessia will hold her own.'

'I'd be happy to pay. My wedding present to the two of you.'

I manage, by some miracle, to hold on to my temper.

'It's a tempting offer, thank you, Mother. But we're good.'

'The offer stands and I'll see you in London when you're back from your honeymoon. I'll have more to say on this whole . . . debacle then.'

'I can't wait.' I smile – a smile so fake I think I'm going to crack wide open.

She raises her cheek to me, which I brush with the briefest of kisses, and she turns to Heath. 'Let's go, darling.'

Shpresa helps Alessia out of her dress and her veil. 'Darling girl, you looked so beautiful today.'

'Thank you, Mama. And thank you for all your hard work.' She hugs her tightly, trying to convey her gratitude for everything over the last few days.

'You will come and visit, yes?' her mother asks, a desperate tang to her voice.

'Of course, Mama,' Alessia says, trying to fight back her tears. 'And you know, my offer, our offer, if you want to come with us . . . and . . .'

Her mother holds up her hand. 'My heart, Jak and I will be delighted to visit you in England once you're settled.' She's adamant.

Alessia sighs and hugs her mother again. 'The invitation is still there. Whenever.'

'Thank you,' Shpresa responds. 'Now, let me help you into this new dress.'

Alessia reappears in our makeshift wedding venue looking radiant. She's changed into a simple emerald dress that clings . . . everywhere.

Fuck.

My body tightens.

Everywhere.

She's simply stunning. Her hair is in its elegant updo, although some tendrils now frame her beautiful face. She's clutching her bouquet when I reach her side and take her free hand. As I do, all the anger I'd been feeling at my remaining parent fades away. 'You look lovely,' I whisper. 'I can't wait to get you out of this dress.' It's then that I notice a slit up one side, and I catch a glimpse of her stockinged thigh and high-heeled shoes.

Oh, man.

'Let's go. Now.'

After a half-hour of tearful goodbyes, Alessia and Maxim are ready to leave. He drapes her coat over her shoulders as they make their way out of the tent.

There's a chill outside – the ground sparkles with an early

frost – as the waxing moon casts a glimmering path across the lake.

Alessia turns and throws her bouquet at the waiting crowd. It's caught by Agnesa, who jumps up and down in excitement, waving her prize above her head.

The guns begin; Alessia's cousins and uncles fire their pistols in the air, and at the same time, the women shower them with rice.

'Fuck!' shouts Maxim, ducking and clutching Alessia. He looks wildly around at her crazy compatriots.

'It's tradition,' Alessia shouts above the noise.

'Hell! Tom!' Maxim says, but Tom is standing calmly next to Joe, watching her relatives with their weapons and shaking his head.

We hurry up the drive, away from the volley of shots.

How the fuck is gunfire at a wedding a good idea?

The Mercedes C class is waiting, and our driver, one of Alessia's cousins, opens the passenger door. Alessia turns and gives the throng one last wave before climbing in. I dash around to the other side and clamber in beside her.

'You don't like the guns,' he says.

'No! I don't!'

'Welcome to Albania!' He laughs, then puts his foot down and speeds away from the revelry, the gunfire, and the best wedding a man could have hoped for, given the circumstances and the fact that it was organised within a week.

I take Alessia's hand. 'Thank you for becoming my wife, Alessia Demachi-Trevelyan.'

Alessia's eyes shine with unshed tears, and her heart, chest . . . her soul is suddenly too full. 'Maxim,' she whispers but her voice cracks as she's overcome with emotion. She turns and stares blankly out of the window over the dark waters of the Drin as they cross the bridge that will take them away from Kukës to a new life. A life with the man she loves with her very being. After all that he has given her, and all he's done for her, she only hopes she's enough for him.

'Hey,' he whispers.

And she turns to see his eyes shining in the darkness.

'I've got you. You've got me. We've got this. It's going to be great,' he says.

And Alessia's tears of joy slide down her cheeks, letting some of her emotion out into the world.

Chapter Eight

A manager shows us into the presidential suite at The Plaza in Tirana, which I've booked for two nights. Alessia eyes the massive vase of white roses that greets us in the small foyer. 'Uau!' she whispers. I squeeze her hand, and the porter deposits our bags in what I assume is our bedroom. He returns to the foyer, I hand him some lek as a tip, and he scurries out.

'Can I offer you assistance with the facilities?' the manager asks in accented English.

'I'm sure we'll figure it out.' With a practised smile, I give him several notes, hoping he'll leave. With a nod of gratitude, he exits, leaving Alessia and me alone for the first time in forever.

'Here. Come. Let me show you.' I stayed here with Tom when we first arrived in Albania – what feels like a lifetime ago – and I know what I want to show Alessia first. Taking her hand once more, I guide her into the drawing room, which has two seating areas, a dining area, and floor-to-ceiling windows. On one of the coffee tables, I spy a bottle of champagne in an elaborate ice bucket, with chocolate-dipped strawberries artfully arranged on a dish. But that's not what I want her to see. Over at the window, I draw back the nets, revealing the city illuminated in all its glory at our feet.

'Uau!' she says again.

'Your capital city. It's quite stunning from the twenty-second floor.'

Alessia drinks in the view. It's a patchwork of light and shade and darkness – tall buildings and small – and lit-up streets like threads woven through the patchwork flowing towards the distant mountains. She recalls telling Maxim she'd never visited Tirana – and here he is, making her dreams come true.

In so many ways.

'The dark over there.' Maxim points with his chin as he stands beside her. 'That's Skanderbeg Square. The National History Museum is beside it. We'll go tomorrow if you want.' He turns, flashes her a quick smile, and fetches the champagne from the cooler. 'Would you like a glass?'

'Yes. Please.'

Alessia notes that it has a copper top – it's the Laurent-Perrier rosé, the first champagne she ever drank, not so long ago, in the bathroom at the Hideout. Maxim's smile widens as if reading her thoughts, and his fingers make deft work of removing the cage and cork with a satisfying pop. He fills their flutes with pink, bubbling champagne and hands her a glass.

'To us. Gëzuar, my love.' In the soft light, his green eyes glitter with a warmth that stirs her blood.

'To us. Gëzuar, Maxim,' she responds, and they clink glasses. She takes a sip, enjoying the taste of a joyous summer and mellow fruits as it slips down her throat. She feels a little shy now that they're finally alone together.

Shy of my husband?

Husband.

She lets the word ring in her head, enjoying the sound of it there.

Maxim turns to the view once more. '"Had I the heavens' embroidered cloths,"' he whispers, almost to himself.

'"Enwrought with golden and silver light,"' Alessia answers.

Maxim turns his head to her in surprise. '"The blue and the dim and the dark cloths."'

'"Of night and light and the half-light."'

'"I would spread the cloths under your feet."' His eyes sear hers, his expression intense.

'"But I . . . being poor . . . have only my dreams,"' Alessia whispers, and her throat burns with unshed tears and the truth of the words.

Maxim smiles and traces her cheek with the back of his forefinger. '"I have spread my dreams under your feet. Tread softly,"' he murmurs.

'"Because you tread on my dreams."' Alessia blinks back a tear, and Maxim leans down and plants a gentle kiss on her lips.

'You never cease to amaze me,' he says.

Alessia swallows, searching for her equilibrium. At every turn, she's reminded of what he's done for her – and the difference between them, but she shakes off the idea. It's too complex and too overwhelming to contemplate now. 'My English grandmother. She loved her poets. Yeats and Wordsworth. We have books of their poetry. Scandalous in Albania a few decades ago.'

Nana.

What would she have made of her granddaughter, married to an English lord, sipping champagne in the presidential suite of a fine hotel in Tirana?

'I wish I'd met her,' Maxim says.

She smiles. 'You would have liked her. She would have loved you.'

'And I her. I know you've been through a great deal over the last couple of weeks. We have two items of business at the embassy tomorrow when we collect your visa. But that's it. We're on our honeymoon now. It's just us. Relax. Enjoy.' He slips his arm around her waist, pulls her to his side, and nuzzles her hair.

She rests her head against his shoulder as together they stand in an easy silence and stare out at Tirana and sip their champagne.

'More?' Maxim asks, looking at her glass.

'Please.'

He refills their flutes and replaces the bottle in the ice bucket. She watches as he slips off his jacket and drapes it over one of the sofas. At the console table, he connects his phone to a speaker and selects some music. A moment later, the strains of a guitar echo through the room and a man with an American accent starts to sing.

'Who is this?' Alessia asks as Maxim comes to stand beside her once more.

'It's an oldie, but goodie,' he murmurs and wraps his arms around her, her back pressed to his front. He rests his chin on her head and starts to sway. 'JJ Cale. "Magnolia." Hmm . . . You smell good.' He kisses the top of her head.

Alessia relaxes against him, swaying with him, placing a hand on top of his and sipping her champagne.

The song is soft and sensual – more so as Maxim sings a line quietly in her ear.

'Makes me think of my babe . . .'

She grins.

He can sing! Sweetly too.

'Let's go to bed.' His voice is husky and full of promise as he gently tugs her earlobe with his teeth.

Alessia's breath catches, and that sweet, delicious pull tightens deep in her belly. Then she remembers. 'Um . . .'

Maxim takes her glass and sets it on the table.

'Hmm?' he asks and tips her chin up, his eyes burning. He kisses the corner of her mouth. 'What did you say?'

'I–I . . .'

He kisses her again at the pulse point beneath her ear as she presses her hands against his shirt. Her fingers move of their own accord to the buttons.

Just a bit longer.

And she starts to undo them.

He cups her face between his hands and angles her head, bringing his lips to hers.

'Wife,' he whispers and gently teases her lips with his, the tip of his tongue seeking hers.

She sighs, and his tongue finds and caresses hers while his hands glide down her body, one pressing her to him while the other skims her backside. Alessia abandons his buttons and tugs at his shirt, freeing it from his pants. Her hands coast up his firm biceps and shoulders, and her fingers fist in his tousled, soft hair as they devour each other.

He groans and pulls back, winded. 'I've missed you,' he whispers. 'So much.'

'I've been here . . .' Her voice is a breathless whisper.

'Not like this.' He moves suddenly, scooping her up into his arms.

She smiles, her heart brimming with love, and folds her arms around his neck as he carries her through the suite into the bedroom, leaving behind the velvet timbre of JJ Cale.

The bedroom is decorated in muted creams, minimalist and modern, but Alessia hardly notices as Maxim slides her down his body and sets her on her feet. His fingers move to her hair, and he carefully removes the pins – freeing her hair lock by lock. She closes her eyes, relishing his tender care – and also surprised by it.

But her thoughts nag her.

Tell him.

No. She can't yet. She's enjoying this too much.

'There, that's the last of them, I think,' he murmurs, his eyes darkening with desire as he catches a strand and winds it around his fingers. 'So soft.' He tugs gently, bringing her closer, and kisses the lock before releasing it. 'Now, this sensational dress.' With a hand at her nape, the other on the zipper, he kisses her once more as he drags the zipper down.

Alessia gasps and crosses her hands over her chest so her dress doesn't fall to her feet.

Tell him.

'Maxim, I . . . I'm . . .'

He stops, his brow furrowing. 'What's wrong?'

She flushes and clutches her dress to her breasts while staring down at the brilliant diamond nestled next to her wedding ring on her finger. 'I'm bleeding.'

'Ah,' he says and tenderly tilts her chin up, and she's expecting him to be disappointed, or worse, disgusted, but all she sees is his relief, and concern. 'Do you feel okay?'

'Yes. I am fine.'

'We can wait, if you want . . .' He kisses the corner of her mouth, then murmurs against her lips, 'But just so you know, that doesn't bother me.'

'What?'

'I still want you.' He trails feather-light kisses along her jaw.

'Oh,' Alessia breathes, and she's momentarily stunned.

Can they? Even if . . .?

Maxim smiles and caresses her cheek with his fingertips. 'I've shocked you. Beautiful Alessia. I'm sorr—'

Before he can finish, Alessia lifts her hands, releasing her dress so it slides down to her waist, hitching at her hips, and she encloses his face between her palms and guides his lips to hers.

I catch a tantalising glimpse of a pretty, lacy bra. But Alessia's lips are on mine, her tongue insistent, and she's pressing her body against me. Closing my eyes, I surrender to her ardour, my fingers in her hair as I hold her to me. Any hesitancy she had about continuing seems a distant memory.

When she pulls away, we're once more breathless, and my dick is straining against my fly.

Fuck.

'What do we do?' Her voice is husky.

It takes me a nanosecond to realise what she's talking about as I step back to behold the vision that is my wife in pretty underwear. 'Take your dress off.'

She inhales sharply and considers me, her eyes straying from mine to my mouth and then down my body to the hardening bulge at my crotch. With a coy but victorious smile, she shimmies out of her dress so that it skates past her hips and down her thighs to reveal a tiny white lace thong and stockings.

My mouth is suddenly arid, and I'm sure it hangs open in awe as my trousers get tighter by the second.

'Now you,' she whispers while draping her dress over the chaise longue.

Quickly, I step out of my shoes and peel off my socks, then undo the remaining buttons of my shirt that Alessia abandoned. I make short work of my cufflinks, slide my shirt off, and discard it with the rest of our clothes on the chaise.

'Pants,' she prompts, her dark eyes shining and dropping below my waist.

My wife is demanding.

I like it.

With a deliberate leisurely pace, I undo my belt, and she laughs and steps forward to help.

Yes!

She undoes the button, unzips my fly, and drags my trousers down, kneeling at my feet.

Fuck.

A vision of my cock in her mouth while she's on her knees comes unbidden to my mind as we lock eyes. With huge, dark eyes, she reaches up to drag down my underwear . . . and I watch. Spellbound. And hard. Almost unbearably hard as she tugs down my pants and frees my enthusiastic dick.

Her eyes stray from mine to my cock.

'Alessia,' I whisper . . . and I know it sounds like a plea.

Alessia kneels up, grasps Maxim's erection, and tightens her fingers around him. He's velvet-smooth and rigid in her hand as he gasps and closes his eyes. Alessia knows this is what he wants . . . It's what she wants too. She's been too shy to do this until now, but she wants to please him, in every way. His lips part, but he seems to have stopped breathing, his body taut with anticipation as he stands over her. She slowly moves her hand up and down like he's shown her before, and gently he places his hand on her head. When he opens his eyes, they're green fire.

His reaction ignites her desire, tightening muscles in the pit of her belly. She loves turning him on. He's used his tongue and his lips on intimate parts of her body often enough, and she's wanted to do this for so long to him. *For him.* She leans in, her eyes still on his, and runs her tongue over her top lip, watching him closely. He's enthralled, his eyes searing hers. He's captivated and entirely at her mercy.

The power she feels. It's heady.

She leans forward and kisses the tip, and her tongue follows, sweeping over him. He tastes salty. Male. Of Maxim.

Mmm . . .

Maxim groans. And she sheaths him with her mouth, pushing him deeper and deeper.

'Fuck!' he exclaims.

I give myself one nanosecond to enjoy her lips around me – it's fucking heaven, and I want more than anything to push further into her mouth, but she takes control and does it anyway.

Oh, God.

Instinctively, I flex my arse, gently driving deeper into her mouth, and she clamps down a little harder on me.

Hell. Yes.

She pulls back and then forward again as if she's done this before. And my resolve not to let this continue is a distant memory as I let her take me. Over and over. In her hot, wet, tight, sweet mouth!

My legs begin to tremble as I strain to contain my climax.

Hell.

She's going to unman me.

Now.

On the bed.' He leans down. 'As much as I want to do this, I will come very quickly in your mouth if—'

Alessia swats his hands away, silencing him.

She wants him.

All of him.

In her mouth.

'Alessia!' He cradles her head. 'I'm going to come!'

She looks up at him from beneath her lashes as he tips his head back and lets go, his warm, salty seed spilling down her throat. She swallows, a little shocked but triumphant that she's done this. She eases back, releasing him, and wipes the back of her hand across her mouth.

As Maxim gasps for breath, he turns blazing eyes on her, reaches down, helps her to her feet, and folds her in his embrace. He kisses her hard and fast, his tongue exploring her mouth, taking all she has to give and surely tasting his seed.

'I love you so much,' he breathes.

'I love you,' she answers, feeling on top of the world.

She did it!

It!

Finally!

He grins. 'How was that?' he asks, and she hears his hesitancy.

'Good.' She bites her bottom lip. 'For you too?'

'Oh, baby. That was mind-blowing. We can do that anytime. Now you'd better go to the bathroom and . . . do what you need to do. Bring a towel back with you.'

She smiles.

I watch her sashay into the en suite. My cock – game once more – twitches in appreciation as her arse looks like fucking poetry in a thong.

Maybe Yeats or Wordsworth.

My wife is full of surprises.

Who knew she'd be able to quote Yeats?

Who knew she'd be up for giving head on her knees?

Sweet Alessia.

Grinning and giddy with delight, I draw back the duvet and, on a whim, return to the drawing room, gather up our glasses, and place them on the tray with the ice bucket, champagne, and strawberries. On my return to the bedroom, I place the tray on our bedside table as Alessia opens the en suite door and leans against the frame. She's naked except for a towel.

'More champagne?' I offer. She shakes her head, and I watch her gaze travel the length of my body.

My dick responds in greeting, ready and willing for more.

Wow! Quick recovery or what!

'All I want is you,' she whispers.

'I'm all yours.' I open my arms, and she strolls towards me, opening the towel as she does. I slip my arms around her, and she wraps us both in the soft material.

'Big towel,' I murmur.

She giggles. 'Big . . .'

'Room? Head? Dick? What?'

'Dick,' she whispers.

And I laugh. 'I love it when you talk dirty.'

She giggles once more, and my restless cock can wait no longer. Taking her head in my hands, I press my lips to hers, and she opens her mouth, seeking my tongue. I willingly oblige, and as I walk her back towards the bed, we kiss, all tongues and lips and breath, until I'm ready to explode again. I come up for air, and Alessia is breathless too.

'Bed,' I whisper, and together we fall onto the mattress.

Alessia tumbles onto the bed, the towel beneath her, and Maxim looms on top of her, but his hands support his weight.

'Now I've got you where I want you,' he whispers and nuzzles between her breasts. 'Are you sore?'

'No.'

'You're sure?'

'Yes!' she says. Emphatic.

I lean up on my arms and look at her. The last time we did this, she had grazes and bruises and God knows what covering her body. But now, she lies beneath me, her hair fanned in a dark mane across the pillow, her eyes shining with love and lust, and there's not a mark on her. She reaches for me, running her fingers through my hair and tugging, bringing me back to half-lie on the softness of her body – my dick cradled between us, against her belly.

But it, like me, is yearning to be inside her.

I kiss the underside of her breast and leave a trail of kisses up to its peak. She tugs on my hair, and I close my lips around her nipple and suck. Hard – feeling it firm and elongate beneath my lips and tongue. I tug gently, and Alessia groans and writhes beneath me, her hips rising and pressing against me. I repeat the action again and again and move to its twin.

'Please,' Alessia pleads.

I reach over to the bedside for a condom.

'No,' she says. 'I started the contraceptive pill.'

What?

'It's okay.' Her eyes sear mine.

And I can't wait any longer. I kiss her again, grab my dick, and guide it to where it wants to be . . . 'Ah!' I breathe as I ease myself inside her.

Skin against skin.

A delectable first.

She's tight and slick and wet with want, and she curls her

arms around me, her hands moving to my arse, her legs winding around my calves as I start to move and lose myself in the pleasure of her.

In the passion of her.

In the love of her.

My wife.

On and on.

Her fingernails etch her desire on my skin as she gasps and moans close to my ear. She's building, and climbing, as am I, and suddenly she's stiffening beneath me as she cries out, her orgasm pushing me over the edge.

I cry out as I come, and the world around us fades, and it's only me and my wife.

My love.

I lean over her, propped on an elbow, smoothing her hair off her face, as she stares intently at me. We're still intimately connected, and I don't want to move.

'How was that, Lady Trevethick?'

She smiles, lighting up the room and my heart. 'That was wonderful, Lord Trevethick. And for you?'

I move then, so she's lying on top of me, and kiss her hair.

'That was muchly.'

She giggles, and I kiss her hair again.

'In fact. I'd like to do it again very shortly. But perhaps you'd like some champagne and strawberries first?'

Alessia lies beside me, fast asleep. Her dragon nightlight is with us, a sweet sentinel watching over her, keeping her safe from the dark. I'm delighted that she's brought him with us. I snuggle closer, inhaling her soothing scent, and marvel at how much I enjoy just lying here beside her . . . just being. Is it because she doesn't make demands on me? Is it because she makes me feel needed? Loved? I don't know. Whatever it is, I've never felt as content as I do now. Content, yet excited. Tomorrow we get to explore her capital city and just be. Together.

Closing my eyes, I kiss her hair.

Until tomorrow, and the rest of our lives, my love.

Chapter Nine

The sun glints off the sparkling Caribbean in Endeavour Bay as my wife paddleboards over the turquoise sea. Her tongue is sticking out as she concentrates on staying atop the board. It's alluring, and I've seen a great deal of that tongue recently – teaching her to paddleboard, play poker, play pool, use chopsticks, give head . . .

Fuck.

The thought of my wife with her lips wrapped around my rigid dick fellating me has an immediate and significant effect on my body. I shift on the board trying to bring myself under control but lose my balance and fall into the Caribbean with a loud, undignified splash.

When I surface, Alessia is laughing. At me. At *me*.

She's wearing a skimpy, bright green bikini we bought at Pink House, the local store, and her body is beautifully bronzed all over. She looks gorgeous, but she's laughing at me.

Right! This is war.

I grab the paddle, vault back onto the board, and, grinning like a maniac, pursue her.

She screeches and turns her board to the shore and begins to paddle frantically.

The chase is on.

But she's no match for me, and I catch her just before the shallows, leap off my board, and grab her, throwing us both into the sea.

She screams, but the water silences her, and she surfaces coughing, spluttering and laughing. I reach for her as I'm within my depth and pull her into my arms and kiss her.

Properly.

She tastes of happiness and sunshine and crystal-clear seawater. She tastes of my beloved wife. 'That's better,' I murmur against her lips.

'Je trap fare!' She pushes at my shoulders but I refuse to let go.

'I take it that wasn't a compliment.' I nuzzle her nose, and she giggles.

'I said you are an arsehole.'

'Talking dirty again?'

'I am learning from you.'

'Hmm ... am I a good teacher?' I capture her bottom lip between my teeth and tug gently.

Her dark eyes shine, and her cheeks flush beneath her tan. 'You tell me,' she whispers.

I grin. 'No complaints here.'

'My grandmother said the best foreign dictionary is a lover.'

Of course, her English grandmother married an Albanian.

'Lover, eh? Does husband count?'

She wraps her limbs around me, cups my face, and kisses me – all tongue and lips and love – weaving her hands into my wet hair. I hold her fast against me. And we're skin on skin, and my body responds, hungry for her again.

Will I ever have my fill of my wife?

I am utterly in her thrall as I surrender myself to her kiss, her tongue ... her love.

When we come up for air, I'm aroused and ready for her. 'Shall we fuck in the sea?' I whisper breathlessly, half in jest. 'There's no one here.'

'Maxim!' Alessia is scandalised, but she scans the shoreline where there are a couple of villas, but there's no one in sight on the beach or in the sea. She gives me a coy smile, kisses me again, and grinds against me. Then reaching into my trunks, she grabs my more-than-ready dick.

Fuck . . . we're doing this!

Our paddleboards hover beside us as they're still attached by their lines to our ankles, providing us with a modicum of cover. Gently, I sweep aside her bikini and ease myself inside her. She pushes down on me, her teeth toying with my lower lip.

Ah!

The surf is gentle, keeping us buoyant as I slowly start to move, holding her to me. She starts tipping her hips towards me, rocking against me at an agile beat. And soon, we're lost in our rhythm. Together. Breath mingling, eyes closed, eyes open, and mouths slack and hungry as we consume each other.

Fuck, she's hot.

She tips her head back and groans as she comes, taking me with her, and I ride out my climax in the clear, blue waters of the Caribbean Sea.

~

It's our last night here, and the candles flicker in the gentle breeze as we sit in the airy gazebo enjoying another of Chef's incredible meals. Alessia sips her rosé and stares out at the sliver of pale sky that straddles the horizon. The sun has long set, but there's a whisper of the day left at the edge of the Earth. She's wearing a green silk dress, again courtesy of Pink House; her hair is tied back, but tendrils have escaped and frame her beautiful face. At her ears are the pearl earrings I bought her in Paris. She looks every bit a countess.

My countess.

I reach across the table and take her hand.

'How is it?'

She turns dark eyes that shimmer in the candlelight towards me.

'Beautiful,' she says, but there's an edge to her voice.

'What's wrong?'

'Do we have to go back?'

I laugh. 'Sadly, yes. I don't think my uncle's hospitality will extend beyond this week.'

My uncle Cameron, my father's brother, was the bête noire of his generation. After a monumental fall-out with my mother and father that happened before Kit was born, he fled to LA and established himself as an artist. During the late '80s, he took the American art world by storm, and these days he's mentioned in the same breath as David Salle and Jean-Michel Basquiat. He now resides in the Hollywood Hills and owns two properties on Mustique.

We are in one of them. An elegant two-bed, Oliver Messel–designed, beachfront villa named Turquoise Waters – it's stunning, and he was delighted when Alessia and I chose to spend our honeymoon here.

Congratulations, Maxim, my dear, dear boy. I'm delighted for you. Of course, you can use the villa. My wedding gift to you.

I haven't been here since my mid-teens when my mother reluctantly let Maryanne and me stay with Uncle Cameron after our father died. There is bad blood between them, so much so that Cameron only made a brief appearance at my father's funeral, and an equally fleeting appearance at Kit's. He didn't stay with us, and he and I only exchanged a few words afterwards. I can't decide if he doesn't like us, or if Rowena doesn't like him because he's so much like her – he shares her passion for young male lovers – or because he doesn't tolerate her bullshit. Either way – they don't talk. Ever.

It had been a pain in the arse to get to Mustique. I couldn't fly Alessia through Miami because she needed an American visa, and we didn't have time to apply for one. I didn't want to fly via London, so we'd come via Paris to Martinique, ferry to Castries, and then we flew to Mustique from there.

And Alessia had never been on a plane before.

Going home will be more straightforward.

'I love that your uncle has a place with a baby grand piano. This place is magical,' Alessia whispers.

I kiss her hand. 'It is, with you here.'

Bastian, our butler, appears. 'May I clear for you, my lord?' he asks.

'Thank you.'

'A digestif?' he offers.

'Alessia?' I ask.

'I'm happy with the wine; thank you, Bastian.'

'My lord?'

'Cognac, please.'

He nods and clears away our dessert plates.

'Tell me. Something's troubling you,' I ask once more.

'I'm not sure what will be expected of me. When we are home.'

I squeeze her hand and sigh. 'To be honest, I don't know.' I have no idea what Caroline, or my mother for that matter, used to do. I wish I'd taken more notice. 'But don't worry, we'll figure it out.'

She withdraws her hand and places it in her lap. 'I am . . . um . . . nervous that I will eat a meal with the wrong knife or I will say the wrong thing to one of your friends, and I will embarrass you.'

Shit.

'And there will be staff like here,' she says.

'You'll get used to it.'

'You are used to this because you have had staff all your life.'

'True.'

'I have not.'

'Hey, stop. You'll be fine. You have been fine here, with

Bastian, with Chef and the housekeeper. Just keep doing what you're doing.'

Alessia frowns. 'I am out of the depths.'

I smile. 'Out of your depth. And I don't think you are. You're going to be amazing. I saw how you and your parents pulled together a full-scale wedding in less than a week. All the skills you need are there.'

He reaches over and tugs Alessia's hand, and she moves willingly into his lap, where he folds his arms around her and nuzzles her hair. 'Besides,' he whispers. 'Who gives a fuck what other people think?'

Alessia chuckles. 'You say that word a lot.'

'I do, and your English is improving. I've really noticed on this holiday.'

'That's because I spend my time with someone who speaks it so well, apart from the cursing, of course.'

Maxim laughs. 'I know you love it when I talk dirty.'

He's wearing a loose white cotton shirt and linen trousers. His hair is sun-kissed, and his green eyes sparkle in the wavering candlelight.

He's delicious.

'Your cognac, my lord,' Bastian says, interrupting them.

'Thank you.'

'I've taken the liberty of moving two of the lawn chairs down to the beach and lighting the firepit.'

'Thanks, Bastian. We'll enjoy one more paddle in the moonlight.'

Alessia climbs off Maxim, and he takes her hand – and his cognac – and leads her down the garden steps onto the beach where Bastian has set up a little bower for them. Torches blaze at the four corners and the firepit flames flicker in the evening breeze.

The lawn chairs, as well as cushions, have blankets draped

over them. Alessia takes a seat in one, and Maxim settles in the other beside her. Taking her hand again, he brings it to his lips. 'Thank you for a wonderful honeymoon.'

She laughs. 'No, Maxim. Thank you. For everything.'

He kisses her palm, then her rings – then leans back, and they each gaze out across the dark water that glimmers in the light of the waning moon. They're serenaded by the song of the tree frogs, the crackle, hiss and spit of the fire in the iron pit, and the gentle wash of the Caribbean lapping at the shore. Alessia takes a deep breath, inhaling the scent of the tropics – the lush earthiness of the rainforest and the salty tang of the sea – and she tries to commit the scene to memory. Above them, there's a spectacular starscape.

'Uau, so many stars,' Alessia murmurs.

'Hmm . . .' Maxim replies, staring up at the sky.

'They look different here.'

'Hmm . . .' The sound of his contentment rumbles in his throat once more.

She gazes at the night sky, feeling that providence has provided the impressive light show above them solely to make amends for all that had befallen Maxim and her before their wedding.

Alessia's heart is full to overflowing.

This is her life now.

She has to pinch herself.

He's shown her the sights of Tirana, whisked her to Paris and then to this magical place.

What has she done to deserve all this good fortune?

She'd fallen in love with him. Her Mister . . . No, her lord.

'Dance with me?' Maxim says, interrupting her reverie, and he lays his phone on the arm of his chair and hands her an AirPod. He slips one in his ear, and she does the same. He presses Play, and the familiar strains of RY X fills her ear.

Maxim gazes down at her and opens his arms. She walks into his embrace, and together they sway slowly in the sand.

'Our first dance,' Maxim whispers.

And Alessia is thrilled that he remembers.

'The first of many,' she answers, and he moves his hands to caress her face and turns her lips to his.

They flow together. Taking and giving. Two as one. Alessia clutches the sheets, her body slick with sweat . . . her sweat . . . his sweat, and Maxim cries out and stills as he climaxes, triggering her orgasm, so she cries out too and rises and falls through her bliss. She folds her arms around his neck as he collapses on her, then moves them to the side.

'Fuck. Alessia,' he whispers and kisses her forehead as she comes back to sanity.

She opens her eyes and strokes his face as they stare at each other. Her finger tracing the outline of his lips. Lips that have been on her.

Everywhere.

'Is it always like this?' Alessia asks.

'No,' Maxim says and kisses her forehead again. He eases out of her, and she winces. 'Are you sore?' His voice rings with concern.

'No. I'm good.' She grins. 'More than good.'

'I'm more than good too.'

Their bedroom is all whitewashed wood, with distressed furniture and discreet art. A four-poster bed, sheathed in nets, dominates the room. Alessia loves the romance of the nets – when in bed, they're cocooned in their own small haven.

As her heart rate slows, a thought that has been nagging her since the wedding strays unfettered into her mind.

'What?' Maxim asks. He's naked and beautiful, his eyes bright in his tanned face, as he hugs his pillow facing her.

She stares at his tattoo of his coat of arms and, reaching over, traces the outline with her finger while she wonders how she should ask this question.

'What?' he presses her and smooths a stray strand of damp hair behind her ear.

'Um . . . it is something your sister said to me at the wedding.'

Oh shit. What could that be?

I tense, wondering what Maryanne has blurted to my dear, dear Alessia.

'She said, "Reformed rakes make the best husbands."' Alessia's dark eyes glimmer, full of questions in the soft light.

I blow out a breath, trying to think what to say.

'I have read Georgette Heyer. I know what a rake is . . .' she adds.

'And?'

'Is your sister saying that you are a rake?'

'Alessia, it's the twenty-first century, not the eighteenth.'

She stares at me for several seconds, her teeth toying with her upper lip as she assesses me.

Hell. Is she judging me?

Found me wanting?

I have no idea. I hold my breath.

'How many women?' she asks eventually.

Ah. My stomach sinks. This is where her thoughts are going. 'Why do you want to know?'

'I am curious.'

I reach out and caress her face. 'In all honesty, I don't know. I didn't keep count.'

'Many?'

'Many.'

'Tens. Hundreds. Thousands?'

I make a face. *Thousands! Sheesh.* I don't think so.

'Tens . . . or so. I don't know.' And it's a small white lie.

Hundreds more like, dude.

She stares back at me, and I hope to God she's not seeing through my untruth or seeing me in a sordid new light. It was just sex. 'Hey.' I shift closer to her. 'No one since I met you.'

'Not the widow?' she whispers.

And in those three words, I hear her anguish and distrust. I close my eyes as an ember of anger flares in my gut at my loose-lipped sister-in-law.

Bloody Caro!

'No. No one since I saw you clutching the broom in my hallway.'

When I open my eyes, she's studying me once more, and I have no idea what she's thinking. But Alessia nods, seemingly satisfied, and I blow out a breath.

Thank fuck for that.

'Here.' I draw her to me. 'There was before Alessia, and then there's the rest of my life with you. That's all that matters.' And I kiss her once more.

As dawn breaks over their little part of heaven, Alessia is curled up in one of the armchairs watching Maxim sleep. He's sprawled face-down and naked on the bed. His legs tangled in the sheets, like the first time she ever saw him . . . not so long ago.

She was shocked then but fascinated – drawn to the chiselled lines of his athletic body. Now she can appreciate every line and sinew. How sculpted he looks and how young and relaxed he seems in sleep. The tan line between his back and his muscular, curved behind is far more defined, and she'd like to sink her teeth into that butt. Shocked at her wayward thoughts, she sips her unsweetened black coffee, enjoying its bitter, strong taste and the enticing view of her husband.

Should she wake him?

A wake-up call?

He'd like that. The muscles deep in her belly tighten in pleasure at the thought.

Alessia! She can hear her mother's voice.

He's my husband, Mama.

Today, they head back to England.

Her new home.

And she'll have to face his family, his friends, his work colleagues, and she only hopes they won't find her lacking.

And she'll have to find something to do.

What's expected of her, she doesn't even know.

She suspects this is why she can't sleep. It's the excitement and the anxiety.

Maxim stirs and reaches out to her side of the bed, then looks up and around when he finds the bed empty, his green eyes bright in the soft pink light of dawn.

Alessia puts down her cup, lifts the net, and scrambles into bed beside him.

'There you are,' he murmurs, pulling her into his arms.

We touch down at Heathrow just after eight in the morning. Once we've disembarked the plane, we arrive at the top of the jetty, where an official from the VIP service greets us. She escorts us airside via a lift to ground level, and we exit the terminal beside the British Airways Boeing 777 that's brought us from St Lucia. There, a sleek black 7 series BMW awaits us. Our greeter opens the boot and places our hand luggage inside. Then she opens the rear passenger door, and we both climb in and sink into the leather seats.

'This is unexpected,' Alessia says, turning wide eyes in my direction.

I shrug. 'I'm not dealing with the scrum that is passport control.'

Our guide climbs into the car and drives us across the airport to the VIP building.

'You'll need your passport,' I tell Alessia as we're ushered out of the car.

The Border Force official gives my passport a cursory glance and a more thorough inspection of Alessia's.

I hold my breath.

He looks up and scrutinises her face, comparing it to her photograph, and then stamps her passport. 'Welcome to the UK, miss,' he says.

I blow out a breath.

She's here! Legally! Hurrah!

Alessia rewards him with a dazzling smile, and we follow our escort into one of the stylish and comfortable suites to await our luggage.

'Your butler will be with you shortly to take your breakfast order. We should have an update on your baggage in the next ten minutes. There's an en suite just behind you should you need it. Anything else, just press the call button.' She points to a red button on the coffee table.

'Thanks.'

With a bright, practised smile, she leaves us, and I offer Alessia the menu. 'Are you hungry?'

She shakes her head.

'Me neither. Did you sleep?'

Alessia nods, taking in our surroundings. 'I have never been anywhere like this. Do you always do this at Heathrow?'

'Yes.' I kiss her hair. 'Get used to it.'

She smiles. 'I think it will take a while.'

I shrug as there's a knock at the door and one of the butlers enters.

'Good morning, Lord Trevethick. May I bring you breakfast and a drink?'

They are back in the expensive black car, and a man in a smart suit is driving them into London. As they sit in traffic on the motorway, Alessia glances over the skyline and notices the towers at Brentford.

Magda! Michal!

She wonders how her friends are doing in Canada. She doesn't have a phone number for Magda, but maybe she can contact

Michal through Facebook. That part of her life seems so long ago, yet it was only weeks. And now here she is in a fancy car with her beloved husband, shooting into London after a holiday in beautiful Mustique.

What has she done to deserve such good fortune?

Maxim threads his fingers through hers. 'Seems an age since we were here,' he says, and he sounds a little wistful.

'Yes.' She returns his squeeze but doesn't know what else to say. She's feeling overwhelmed and a little untethered, as if she's in a dream and she'll wake at any moment to some dreadful reality.

He raises her hand to his lips and plants a sweet kiss. 'We'll be home soon. I'm going to need a nap.'

'Did you sleep?' They'd travelled first class where their seats converted into comfortable beds.

'Not much. The flight was noisy, but mostly because I'm too excited to get you home.'

Alessia smiles, and just like that, her misgivings disappear.

The black car pulls up outside Maxim's building on Chelsea Embankment, and the chauffeur opens Alessia's door. He removes the bags from the trunk and places them in the foyer. Maxim graciously tips him and, grabbing their bags, heads to the waiting elevator. Maxim ushers Alessia inside, and the doors close, leaving just the two of them and their luggage. Maxim presses the button for the top floor, and his emerald gaze moves to hers. Alessia's breath catches at his smouldering look.

He steps towards her and cups her face gently in his hands. 'You're safe. We're home,' he whispers and leans down to kiss her, a slow, sweet and grateful kiss, but as his coaxing, teasing tongue finds hers, desire blossoms deep inside Alessia. Her body has become so attuned to his that she wants him. Now. Here. Maxim presses her to the wall, his excitement hard against her belly, and it feeds her lust. She moans, her body moulding to his and kissing him back with a fervour that sears her soul.

The elevator stops, the door opens, and Maxim guides them out of the elevator while they are still locked in an embrace, still locked in each other.

Will she ever get enough of him?

'Maxim, how lovely to see you. Have you been away?'

The not-so-dulcet tones of Mrs Beckstrom interrupt our make-out session, which I'm hoping will lead to some pre-nap hot sex. Briefly, I lean my forehead in frustration against Alessia's, then peek down at her, and she looks as dazed as I feel. Taking a deep breath, I hold Alessia against me to hide my evident excitement.

'Mrs Beckstrom. And Heracles.' I bend and give her annoying lapdog a quick pat. He bares his teeth in disgust. 'How lovely to see you. How are you? May I introduce my wife? Alessia.'

'Oh, how lovely.' Mrs Beckstrom holds out her hand to Alessia, who's breathless.

'How do you do?' Alessia says as they shake hands.

'You are so pretty, my dear. Wife, did you say, Maxim?'

'Yes, Mrs B.'

'You finally got married. Well, congratulations. That was rather sudden. Are you in the family way, my dear?'

For fuck's sake! I daren't look at Alessia's face as I haul our luggage out of the lift.

'No, Mrs Beckstrom,' Alessia says quickly, and her cheeks are rosy despite her tan.

'But I'll see what I can do about that!' I wink at Mrs B, and Alessia's blush deepens.

'Well, you young people enjoy yourselves. Heracles and I are going for our morning stroll.' And she steps into the lift and presses Ground.

Once the doors close, I turn to Alessia, she bursts out laughing, and I join her. I pull her into my arms. 'I'm sorry about that.'

'She is, what did you say . . . oh, yes, eccentric.'

'Yes. She certainly is. Now, I have one duty to perform.' I lift her into my arms, and she squeals in surprise. Holding her against me, I slide the key into the front door, open it, and step across the threshold with her in my arms.

I set her on the floor and kiss her, hoping to continue what we started in the lift, when I realise the alarm isn't on. We both look up, and there's a 'Welcome Home' banner draped over the double doors at the end of the hallway.

Suddenly, Caroline, Tom, Joe, Maryanne and Henrietta appear at the doors. 'Surprise!' they yell.

Fuck a duck!

Chapter Ten

Alessia and I stand in the hall, bewildered and tired from our journey. Mrs Blake, Caroline's housekeeper, appears at the kitchen door holding a tray of drinks, and I'm struck dumb.

What the ever-fucking-hell is this?

'Welcome home, Maxim, Alessia.' With a smile plastered on her face, Caroline steps forward cautiously, holding out her arms in welcome.

Has she been drinking? Already?

This is very un-Caro-like behaviour.

'Hi,' I say, bemused, as she hugs me and then Alessia.

'Welcome back, Alessia,' she says, a little too brightly.

'Hello,' Alessia whispers, and I can tell from the waver in her voice that she's rattled too.

My friends surge forward to welcome us while Mrs Blake serves everyone drinks. Buck's Fizz, champagne or freshly squeezed orange juice.

'Well, this is a surprise. No, shock, actually. But thank you,' I mutter to Caro.

'I thought a celebratory brunch would be in order to welcome you home, and it's a sort of apology.' She shrugs impishly and grabs a glass of champagne. I suspect it's not her first.

Mrs Blake offers the tray to Alessia with what I can only describe as a hostile smile. 'My lady,' she says, her tone terse. Alessia thanks her and takes a glass of champagne.

Frowning at Mrs Blake – in the hope that I've misinterpreted her frosty expression – I take a glass of orange juice.

She flushes. 'Nice to have you back, my lord.'

'Thank you, Mrs Blake. I hope you and Mr Blake are well.' I give her a pointed look, and she gives me a sweet smile, so maybe I'm imagining her less than warm reception of my wife – though she didn't offer us congratulations.

Maryanne hooks her arms around us both and propels us towards the drawing room, where the table is set for brunch.

Okay. We're doing this.

And all I really want to do is take my wife to bed.

And fuck and then sleep.

But Henrietta, Tom's girlfriend, is there and it's great to see her. She is a beacon of light compared to his pugnacious darkness.

'Maxim, I'm so thrilled for you. Congratulations.' She hugs me.

'Henry, how lovely to see you. This is Alessia, my wife.'

The grease and grime from the journey stick to Alessia's skin, and here she is, in Maxim's apartment, with . . . guests. His friends. What she'd like to do is have a quick shower and change. Beneath the black tailored jacket, she's wearing her 'It's better at Basil's' T-shirt that Maxim bought for her at a bar on Mustique – and her jeans. She'd prefer to be a little more formal for his friends, but leaving them right now would be rude.

And these women, they all look impeccable.

Especially Caroline.

'Hello, Alessia. It's lovely to meet you,' Henry says. Her voice is melodic, measured and sweet, and she has the face of an angel framed by soft sepia-brown curls. Her tawny eyes are warm and brimming with sincerity.

'How do you do?' Alessia replies, feeling immediately at ease with her.

'There she is!' Tom says and engulfs Alessia in a huge hug. 'I do hope he's treating you well, Alessia. I'll horsewhip him if he's not.'

Alessia laughs. 'It's good to see you, Tom.'

'When was the last time you were near a horse?' Caroline scoffs. 'Your polo-playing days are long over.'

Henry frowns at Caroline, and there's a slight lull in the conversation, and Alessia notices Maxim and Joe are frowning too.

'Alessia,' Joe says after a beat and hugs her. 'You look so well. Did you have a great time? Where did you guys go? Maxim kept all the deets to himself.' He flashes bright white teeth in a broad contagious smile. He looks so smart in his suit – and Alessia realises he must always dress like this, even on a Saturday.

Maxim slips his arm around her and kisses her hair. 'We had a wonderful time. In Tirana and Mustique, if you must know.'

'We did,' Alessia agrees shyly. 'And Paris.'

'That sounds heavenly,' Caroline exclaims. 'I hope you're all hungry. Dear Mrs Blake has cooked up a storm.'

Once I've relaxed into what this is, it's actually rather lovely that Caroline has organised brunch. It's good to reconnect with my friends after our honeymoon and to introduce Alessia to everyone in such a casual setting. And it's a joy to see Henry. Alessia looks relaxed too, or maybe she's just tired. But she's tucking into her smoked salmon, eggs, and avocado toast and happily chatting with Henrietta, who has the rare ability to put everyone at ease.

Even Tom.

Maryanne tells me they all came home from Albania with Rowena on a private jet.

'Private?'

'Yes.'

'Hmm . . . I wonder who paid for that.'

'You did, probably,' Caro says as she picks at her food.

So, my mother is still charging her shit to the estate.

Well, not for long.

'Your parents did a splendid job at the wedding, Alessia. I have to say it was quite the highlight of this year so far.'

'It's only March, Tom,' Caro interjects.

He ignores her. 'It also inspired me.' He stands, looking his usual proud and pompous self. 'I'm very honoured to say that Henry, mad woman that she is, has consented to be my wife. We are officially engaged.' He beams at Henrietta, who smiles back at him and blushes prettily under our collective attention.

'Congratulations, bro,' Joe says and raises his glass. 'To Tom and Henry!'

A chorus of congratulations echoes around the room, and we take turns to hug and kiss them both.

'Of course, you'll have to time your wedding with Trevethick here for when he marries again,' Joe says and takes another sip of champagne.

'Again?' ask Caroline and Maryanne in unison.

Damn.

'Um . . . yeah.'

'Can you do that?' Henry asks with a slight crease on her forehead.

'I hope so. I'll have to find out. We want to get married here too. Don't we, Alessia?' I reach out, and she grasps my hand, a slight frown marring her brow as she digests my panicked expression. Maryanne or Caroline cannot know about the questionable circumstances of our marriage and that we haven't followed the usual protocols.

'Yes. Of course,' Alessia responds. 'This way all of Maxim's friends can join us,' she says sweetly. 'We have accom . . . accommodated . . .' She glances at me, and I think she's checking her

English. I nod and she continues. '. . . my friends and family, and now it's Maxim's turn. We want to honour his family and friends too.'

Alessia, you fucking goddess.

Caroline narrows her eyes and she takes another slug of champagne. 'Another wedding? Well, that will be lovely. In London, Cornwall, or Oxfordshire?'

'We've just got home from the last one, Caro. Give us a break,' I retort.

Her lips thin, but she doesn't respond. Instead, she turns to Alessia. 'Of course, all the staff at each of the estates are dying to meet you. Do you ride?' she asks.

Alessia gives me a quick, dark look, and an image of her naked, on top of me, breasts bouncing, head back, hair tumbling over her shoulders, mouth open celebrating her passion, comes unbidden to mind.

Fuck.

It's arousing.

My sweet, innocent wife. *She gave me that look deliberately.*

'No,' Alessia says, and I hide my smirk. Caro looks from her to me, and back to my wife, and I half expect Alessia to say, 'Only my husband,' but fortunately, she doesn't.

Mate. Grow up.

'We'll have to see what we can do about that,' Caro mutters.

'Caroline is a keen horsewoman, as am I. Maxim, not so much. But, of course, he and Kit used to play polo,' Maryanne says.

'You have horses?' Alessia turns her attention to me.

'We do. In Oxfordshire,' I respond. 'We'll do a tour, don't worry.'

A tour. What does he mean?

'Of the estates,' Maxim answers her unspoken question. 'You've been to Cornwall. We have another in Oxfordshire. And one in Northumberland, but that's rented to an American who's made his millions in tech. Why he doesn't buy his own estate, I don't know.'

Alessia nods as she absorbs this new information. During their entire honeymoon, he did not mention more estates.

More land. More property!

Just how rich is her husband?

'We should be going. Let you two get some shut-eye,' Tom announces. 'But I do have one request.'

All eyes turn to Tom.

'I missed your epic performance on the piano before the wedding, Alessia, as I was with Thanas at the hotel. Please, will you play for us? I've only heard good things.'

'Oh yes, please!' Henrietta claps. 'I'd love to hear you. Joe has raved about you.'

Oh.

'Are you up for this? You don't have to,' Maxim is quick to reassure her.

'No. It's okay. You know I love to play.' She smiles, delighted that she can do something for Tom after all his help in Albania. Rising from the table, she makes her way over to the piano. She feels everyone turn to watch her.

Why does she feel so nervous?

Opening the lid that covers the keys, she takes a deep breath and sits down on the stool. She decides what she wants to hear and the colours she wants to see, places her hands on the keys, and closes her eyes. She launches into Rachmaninoff's arrangement of Bach's Partita No. 3. Her fingers find every note as they blaze through her head in soft pinks and lilacs while the prelude echoes delicately through the room – comforting her and consuming her until she's part of the music and the colours.

I've not heard her play this piece before, and as ever, my girl . . . my wife, is lost in the music, delivering a stellar performance. Our guests are transfixed, as they should be. But what I love about her relationship with her music is that she's submerged in it. It totally absorbs her – no, it possesses her – so much so that I'm sure we've all disappeared, and it's just her and the piano and this delightful piece.

She comes to the final trilling note, and it hangs in the air, holding us all rapt before she lifts her fingers off the keys.

Our guests burst into applause and stand.

'*Alessia, that was amazing.*'

'*My goodness!*'

'*Brava! Brava!*'

Alessia smiles shyly at them as I approach her and place my hands on her shoulders. Her hand clasps mine. 'Ladies and gentlemen, my wife.' I lean down and kiss her quickly. 'And on that note! It's time for you to go home. We're both weary from our travels.'

'Yes. We'll be on our way,' Tom says.

'Thanks again,' Joe adds as he makes his way out of the drawing room.

Mrs Blake is clearing the kitchen, and I thank her before Alessia and I accompany our guests to the front door. It's then that I notice, much to my delight, that my photographic landscapes are reframed and back on the walls.

Caro hugs me goodbye. 'Take Alessia shopping for some clothes, for heaven's sake,' she hisses in my ear. 'Or let me!'

I release her. 'Okay. If you think I should.'

'Yes. She's a countess, for God's sake. Not a student. Take her to Harvey Nicks.'

Alessia frowns. 'What is it?' she asks.

'Let him take you shopping, darling.' She hugs Alessia, smiles sweetly, and exits with the rest of my family and friends while Alessia turns to me. But before she can say anything, I'm saved by Mrs Blake, who comes to the door.

'All the washing is done. The kitchen is clean and stocked with the groceries you requested. The dishwasher will need emptying.' She gives Alessia a sly glance. 'I know – I mean . . . I hope that shouldn't be a problem for *you* . . . my *lady*.' Mrs Blake purses her lips in what I assume is supposed to be a smile but is more of a sneer.

'That's enough, Mrs Blake,' I state in a brusque, rebuking tone, holding the door open for her. 'It's time for you to leave.'

Alessia places her hand on my arm, to stop me from saying more . . . I don't know. She draws herself upright and lifts her chin.

'Yes. Of course. Thank you for your help, Mrs Blake.'

'My lord. My lady.' She nods, her look uncertain because she's been called out, and she leaves.

Too bloody right.

Maxim's face is carved in stone as he bids the housekeeper good day, but Alessia is delighted that he noticed Mrs Blake's condescending tone. He turns to face her. 'I think Mrs Blake might need a talking to.'

Alessia wraps her arms around Maxim and hugs him.

He noticed and acted.

But Alessia would like to fight her own battles in future. She's sure there will be more. After all, Alessia was his cleaner, and she understands Mrs Blake's resentment.

She smiles at him. 'She is Caroline's servant.'

'We would say staff. Servant seems a little . . . feudal.'

'I was your servant,' she whispers.

Maxim leans down and runs his nose against hers. 'And now I'm yours.' His lips are on hers, and he presses her against the wall, kissing her until she wants to curl her toes. 'Let's go to bed,' he murmurs in a dark tone that speaks directly to her most intimate places.

'Yes,' she whispers.

Maxim dozes beside Alessia. His lips gently parted, his eyelashes feathered above his cheeks, his face tanned and relaxed in sleep – he really is beautiful. Alessia watches him, marvelling at how young he looks. She resists touching him and turns to survey the room. She has no idea what time it is, though it's still light outside. When she was last in this room, they'd made love, and then she left the apartment, and Anatoli was waiting for her.

Don't think about him!

She distracts herself by studying the room in a new light as Maxim's wife. It's a masculine space: clean lines, minimal furniture in muted silvers and greys. The only ornate piece of furniture is the substantial gilt mirror on the wall behind and above the bed's headboard. And on the wall opposite are the two photographs of naked women, their backs turned to the camera, so they're not too explicit. But still, they're erotic and sensual. And he said that all the photography in the apartment was his; he must have taken these pictures.

Darling, he's slept with most of London.

Alessia sighs. This she knows – she saw the evidence every week in his wastebasket. And there was that young woman in the pub in Cornwall. Alessia cannot remember her name.

But how many women in this bed?

She shudders.

Don't think about that!

Yet in these quiet moments, she wonders if she measures up to all who came before her. She snorts at the irony – all who literally came before her.

The thought is distasteful, and she doesn't want to brood on it or spend all day in bed. She's not tired, so she slips quietly out from under the covers and makes her way into his wet room to shower and clean off the last of their journey and the last of their fabulous honeymoon.

I wake to the sound of the shower in the wet room.

Alessia.

Wet and naked.

The thought is immediately arousing, and I bound out of bed to join her.

She's standing beneath the cascade of hot water, her back to me and washing her hair. Her hair hangs down to her waist above her fantastic arse as she lathers the shampoo on her head. I step in behind her and gently place my hands on her head to assist her by massaging the soap into her scalp.

'Hmm . . . that feels good,' she groans.

I stop.

'Oh!' Alessia steps back, pressing her body against mine, but more importantly, my erection is resting in the cleft of her backside. I grin, and she turns her head, flashes me a bright, playful smile, and wiggles her arse, teasing me.

Oh, man.

'You want me to continue?'

'Yes. Please.'

I return to the serious task of washing her hair, spreading soap through her long tresses and gently untangling the strands. She raises her face into the cascade to rinse off the soap, and I reach for the body wash, squirting some onto my hands and rubbing them together to work up a lather. Gently, I slather the soap just over the soft skin of her belly then under her breasts, brushing the peaks with the tips of my thumbs. Alessia gasps with pleasure and arches her back, pressing herself into my palms.

Fuck. She has gorgeous tits.

I skate a hand over her body, feeling the supple lines and planes of her skin while I soap her. My other hand continues to tease her hardening nipples, my hand spanning slightly more than an octave as I tantalise each one. As they lengthen under my fingers, my dick gets heavier and heavier.

'You have beautiful breasts, Alessia,' I whisper and tug at her earlobe with my teeth. Reaching down, I move my hand over her sex, my fingers skimming over her clitoris.

She groans, leaning back, and extends her hands around my

neck, her back against my chest. She twists her head and presses her lips on mine.

We kiss. Hot. Heavy. All tongue and desire – my cock still cradled in her arse.

Alessia keeps one hand tangled in my hair, moves the other behind her, and grasps my erection in her palm. She wraps her fingers around me, squeezing hard, and begins to slip them up and down slowly. Oh-so-fucking-slowly. Torturing me. My breath hisses between my teeth, and I walk her forward so her front presses against the dark slate tiles. 'Now you're clean. Let's make you dirty.'

She frees me, her mouth slack, her eyes dark, and places her hands on the slate tiles.

'Shall we do this? In here, like this?' I ask.

'Hmm . . .'

'Is that a yes?'

She wiggles her arse against me, and I grin. 'I'll take that as a yes.'

Carefully, I ease a finger inside her. She's wet. From earlier? From now? I don't care. She's ready. For me. I tug her hips back. 'Hold on.' And slow as slow, so she doesn't lose her balance, I ease myself into her as she pushes back against me.

Yes!

Holding her hips, I edge back and then slide into her again, relishing every fucking centimetre of my wife. She lets out a loud moan, pushing back against me, and I take that as my cue and pick up steam, building momentum.

Harder. Faster.

Repeatedly. Loving the feel of her around me. As we both climb higher. And higher still.

Suddenly, I feel her contracting inside, and I brace myself, with one hand over hers.

'Ah!' she cries and spirals into orgasm, taking me with her. I cry out her name and hold her as I come . . .

Then we sink together to the floor beneath the torrent of water.

How was that?' Maxim asks as he smooths wet hair off her face, then kisses her temple.

'Good. Very good.' Alessia grins.

'Yeah. For me too. I think making love to you is my new favourite pastime.'

'It is a . . . um . . . worthy . . . Is that the right word? A worthy pastime.'

He laughs. 'It works. Very worthy.' He folds his arms around her and pulls her close. 'I'm so glad you're here, safe with me.'

'I'm glad too.'

'When I think of what might have happened . . .' Maxim's voice trails off.

Alessia turns and kisses him. 'I'm here. I'm safe. I'm with you.'

He kisses her forehead. 'Good.'

Unbidden, an image of Bleriana, one of the girls trafficked with Alessia, comes to mind. They made friends in the back of the truck that brought them to the UK. They thought they were coming here to work.

O Zot. Bleriana was only seventeen.

Alessia frowns and tries to dampen her anxiety and guilt.

Did Bleriana escape too?

Did Dante and Ylli catch her?

The notion is terrifying.

'Hey, what's up?' Maxim says.

She shakes her head, trying to rid herself of the thought. She'll reflect on it later when she's on her own and not worry Maxim right now.

He's done enough.

'I think I am clean again.' She smiles.

He laughs. 'Are you hungry?'

She nods.

'Good. Let's go out to eat.'

Chapter Eleven

It's early on Sunday morning: the air is cool and crisp, the trees still dormant and leafless as I run through Battersea Park. It's that particular time of day when this place belongs solely to dogwalkers and runners. The sky is grey and threatening rain, but there's an energy in the chilly breeze – the park is waking up from the long winter, spring is on the horizon. As I find my rhythm, placing one foot in front of the other, my mind clears. It's great to be outside with upbeat lo-fi house bouncing off my eardrums while I take deep gulps of London air. I've missed it.

I left Alessia curled up asleep, and we have the whole day stretched before us to enjoy – all we have to do is unpack and settle back into the flat.

As I run, I realise that for the last few weeks, I haven't thought beyond finding Alessia, then the wedding, then our honeymoon. Now, I need to figure out what our married life looks like.

And I have no idea.

I don't think Alessia does either.

Do we stay in London?

We'll need to keep a base here. But we could move to Cornwall or Oxfordshire – though I'm not sure how Alessia will like Angwin, as the estate employs more staff there than at Tresyllian Hall because it's open to the public.

Maybe we should make babies.

An heir and a spare.

A little boy like Alessia?

A little girl like Alessia?

Fuck. Not yet.

We're both still young.

Tomorrow, we'll see the lawyer who will help us with our visa situation. Then we can make some decisions.

Yeah.

Tomorrow will be all about decisions. Let's just enjoy today.

Alessia wakes to find herself alone. There's a note on Maxim's pillow.

Gone for a run.
Back soon.
I love you. Mx

Alessia smiles, remembering how she would have to pick up his sweaty gym clothes from the floor after he'd been running. And then there were the notes she found screwed up on the floor. Usually phone numbers. From women?

O Zot. She frowns and tries to banish the thought.

Don't dwell, Alessia.

She stretches, feeling well rested, then rises from the bed. It's time to unpack and clean the apartment.

Same old, same old.

She grins, her good mood restored.

And she can cook Maxim some breakfast, maybe some bubble bread, provided Mrs Blake has been as good as her word and stocked up on the essentials they requested while on their honeymoon. Happy, she strolls into the wet room for a shower.

Maxim returns as she's unpacking her case in the spare bedroom. Grinning, because he's finally home, she stops to listen as he walks into his bedroom, and then she hears him jog up the hall with some urgency to check the kitchen, then the living room.

'Alessia!' he calls, panic evident in his voice.

O Zot! No!

'Maxim. I'm here!' She steps out of the spare room and stares at him standing at the end of the hallway. His shoulders drop in relief, and he runs a hand through his damp hair.

'Don't do that to me. I thought – I thought you were gone.' His voice fades as he strides towards her, a wary expression etched on his face.

'I . . .' Alessia is lost for words. She did not mean to worry him, and her heart melts that he would be so concerned for her. But why would he think she would leave? She's confused, but he doesn't wait for her explanation; he pulls her into a tight, sweaty hug.

'Don't do that to me again,' he repeats, each word a staccato, and he kisses the top of her head. 'Last time you weren't here, that fucker had kidnapped you.'

Oh!

He blows out a breath as if he's releasing his tension, but his lips are a thin line, so she suspects he's a little annoyed too. 'I'm going to shower,' he says sulkily, and stalks off in the direction of the bedroom, leaving Alessia wrestling with her guilt in the hallway.

O Zot. O Zot. O Zot.

The last thing she wants to do is upset him – but she didn't think.

'Fuck,' she says under her breath and decides to abandon her unpacking and heads into the kitchen.

Using a wine bottle because there's no rolling pin, she rolls out the dough she prepared earlier, then cuts it and forms small balls, placing them on the only baking tray she can find. They will need to shop for more culinary equipment if she's to cook in this kitchen. She frowns, unsure if Maxim will be willing to pay for such things. They haven't discussed money at all – she has her cleaning money, but that's it, and it's dwindling. During their honeymoon, Maxim paid for everything. She knows she'll need to raise the issue with him at some point, but she's unsure how to go about doing it.

Deep in thought, she slips the baking tray into the oven, washes and dries the bowl, and then sets the small round table for the two of them. When she returns to the oven to check on the bread, she's startled to find Maxim watching her. He's leaning against the doorjamb, dressed in a long-sleeved white T-shirt and his black jeans with the tear at the knee. Her favourite. His hair is tousled and wet, and against his tanned face, his eyes are a vibrant spring green. She inhales sharply, drinking in the sight of him.

He's stunning.

And hers.

He takes her breath away, but his expression is unreadable, and he remains mute as his eyes pin her to a standstill.

She swallows. 'Are you mad at me?'

'No. I'm angry at myself.'

'Why?'

'Because I overreacted.'

She moves forward, standing so close that she feels his heat bathing her skin. 'I should have told you I am in the spare room. I'm here. I'm safe.'

He tips her chin up as his eyes sear hers. 'I was . . . anxious.' He plants a soft kiss on her lips. 'It's not a feeling I like.'

'I'm sorry. I didn't think.' Gingerly she wraps her arms around him, placing her cheek against his chest. He rests his chin on her head, folding her into his embrace and breathing in her scent.

'You smell amazing,' he whispers.

'So do you. Clean.'

She senses his smile and relaxes as he kisses her hair. He grasps her face between his hands and raises her lips to his. 'I need to know you're safe.'

'I'm safe. With you.'

He kisses her – soft, sweet, wet, and warm, and she surrenders to his skilled tongue. He rests his forehead against hers and blows out a breath. 'Is that fresh bread I smell baking?'

She grins. 'It is. Bubble bread.'

His answering smile is dazzling. 'Your father warned me.'

'My father?'

'Yes. He said you'd make me fat.'

'I will only make this on Sundays.'

Maxim laughs, his good mood restored. 'Good plan.'

Alessia takes a deep breath. 'But I will need to go out sometime. Shop for food.'

'I know. I know. Of course. I'm being ridiculous.' From his back pocket, he produces the key he gave her not so long ago. 'Just let me know where you are. Please.'

Alessia takes the key. 'Thank you.' She examines the leather fob. 'What is this place . . . Angwin House?'

'It's our Oxfordshire estate. We'll go later this week if you like. Today even. We could take a quick trip there if you wish.'

He takes a seat at the table, and Alessia grabs a tea towel to remove the bread from the oven while she digests this piece of information.

'What were you doing in the spare room anyway?'

'I was unpacking. My clothes. There's no space in your closet.'

'Oh. I see.' His mouth flattens in a line. 'We should get a bigger place for the two of us.'

Alessia gapes at him.

'The estate owns a great deal of property,' he answers her unspoken question. 'I'll talk to Oliver and see what's coming available.'

Another home? Just like that? Alessia's brow furrows in consternation.

'What is it?'

'How much land . . . um . . . property do you own?'

'Personally, not much. All the Trevethick Estate property, and that includes the three great estates, and all its assets, are held in trust. The trust is the legal owner of the estate, and Kit, Maryanne, and I were trustees. Now, with Kit gone, it's just me and Maryanne – but as the earl, I'm the beneficial owner. Does that make sense?'

Alessia stares blankly at me.

'It's complicated,' I concede, knowing it's not easy to understand. 'Basically, the estate owns a great deal of property, and its income is made through rents and leases on all the residential, retail and business premises the estate owns.'

'Oh . . .' Alessia says. 'And your job is to . . . um . . . run this?'

'Oliver, whom you met through a car window, is the chief operating officer of the Trevethick Estate. He does the day-to-day running. I'm . . . his boss. It was my brother's job, and Kit had the business acumen for the role. Me, I'm still learning.' My mood heads south. This is the crux of the problem I have with assuming the title. I've not been trained to do it, while Kit was skilled at it. Not only that, but he was so economically astute that he increased the fortunes of our individual trusts too.

Hell. I don't want to think about this now.

'Look, it's the last day of our holiday,' I add. 'Let's enjoy it. We could take a drive up to Angwin. It's about two hours. Have a look around. Then tomorrow, the work will begin.' I reach for one of the bread buns Alessia has placed on the table. 'We need to find a new home. Organise a visa for you to stay here. Get back to work.'

Now, there's four words I never thought I'd utter.

Shaking my head in mock self-disgust, I spread some butter on the roll and watch it melt before I add some blackcurrant jam, then take a bite.

Good God. This stuff is delicious.

Alessia places a cup of coffee in front of me and takes a seat.

'Okay. I would love to see Angwin.'

I grin. 'I could get used to this, you know.' And I raise a piece of bubble bread in salute to my wife.

'You do not have a choice.' Alessia smirks.

'But *you* do. You know you don't have to do this. We could go out to eat, or we could hire some help.'

'I want to do it. For you. It is my job.'

And there it is, her upbringing and our cultural divide. I don't know any women like her. She's waited on the men in her life for years, and her expectations are limited by that. I never thought I'd marry such a domesticated woman. Will she ever get over this?

I mean, I like that she wants to care for me.

Mate.

Okay, I love that she wants to care for me.

But I want Alessia to have options. The sooner we move to somewhere bigger, the better. We can get some help, and she won't have to do this. Besides, there are houses to run, estates to oversee, and people to manage.

Mate. It's a lot.

'I do not know what I would do if I didn't cook and clean for you,' she adds as she takes a bite of bubble bread and butter.

'I'm sure you'll be busy once we've established you as countess.'

Alessia's eyes widen. 'What does that mean?'

'Staff to manage, houses to run, functions to organise and attend.'

She gasps, her dark eyes stricken with alarm.

'Sorry.' I shrug. 'It comes with the territory. Don't look so worried. You'll be fine.'

'I think I need lessons!' she exclaims.

'Lessons?' And my mother's contemptuous offer of 'finishing school' pops unwelcome into my mind.

'Yes. There must be something I can read, or . . . a school I can . . .' Her voice tails off.

'You're serious?'

'Yes,' she responds emphatically.

'Well, I'm sure we can find something. If you want. If it would give you confidence.'

She smiles. 'Yes. That is exactly what I need.'

'Are you sure?'

'Yes. I was not born into this . . . life. I don't want to let you down.'

I laugh. 'It's me that should be saying that to you. You are perfect the way you are, but we could look into lessons, if that's what you want.'

Alessia smiles, her eyes shining.

Etiquette lessons.

How did my mother know?

'I'll unpack.' I change the subject, irritated that my mother was right. 'Afterwards, we could go to Angwin. Go shopping, out for lunch, whatever you want to do.'

Alessia nods. 'Yes. I'd like that. And I have unpacked your clothes.'

'Oh, thank you.'

'I would like to go to the store. We need cooking . . . um . . . equipment.'

'I hadn't thought of that. Yes, I suppose we do. I am not much of a cook.'

'You make a good breakfast.'

I grin, remembering our time at the Hideout. 'I do. Okay. Peter Jones is probably the best place to go. I've never shopped for that stuff. We could look online. We could also get you some new clothes. That reminds me—'

Maxim stands and leaves the room only to return a few moments later with four envelopes addressed to Alessia Trevelyan. Alessia examines them, turning them in her hands.

What could these be?

'I arranged these while we were away. Bank cards. And their PINs. You'll need them. One's a debit card. The other is a credit card.'

'Money?' she says, staring at him. 'For me?' She's stunned.

'Yes. For you. Magic cards, you called them once. They're not magic; let me stress that. So don't go crazy.' He gives her a crooked smile.

And just like that, the issue of money is resolved.

'Thank you,' she says.

'You don't have to thank me.' Maxim frowns. 'You're my wife.'

And once more, Alessia tries to quell her rising panic at her good fortune . . . when she thinks of what might have been. An image of Bleriana crosses her mind again, and her thoughts take a darker turn.

Where is she?

Is she okay?

Could Alessia find her?

'I'll wash up,' Maxim says, interrupting her thoughts.

'No. No, you won't. I'll do it.'

Maxim laughs. 'This isn't up for discussion. I can wash up. And load a dishwasher. Let's do a surprise visit to Angwin when I'm done.' He rises, taking his breakfast plate and coffee cup with him.

Angwin is nestled in the Cotswold hills near Chipping Norton. In the Jag, I turn off the road and glide through the main gate and along the majestic beech-lined driveway towards the property.

'Uau,' Alessia breathes as she catches sight of the main house in all its Palladian splendour, with its four Corinthian columns and impressive pediment. Between the stark beeches, it dominates the groomed landscape in honeyed stone.

'Yes. That's Angwin.'

She grins at me with a suitable look of awe on her face.

I pull into the visitors' parking lot, which I'm pleased to see is busy. Normally, I would park around the back of the house near the stables, but I want to keep our visit low-key. I haven't warned anyone we're coming, and I don't want to overwhelm my new countess. 'Ready?' I ask as I switch off the engine. Alessia's smile is answer enough.

Once out of the car, I grab her hand, and we stroll down the driveway towards the main house. ‘See over there.’ I gesture to where the driveway forks left to the thriving garden centre built where the original, extensive kitchen gardens used to be and explain that beyond that is a children’s play gym and our small petting zoo, each hugely popular with the locals and their kids. And a destination for tourists during school holidays. One of our tenant farmers provides the sheep, cows and pigs for the small zoo, and they join our three resident alpacas and four donkeys – all rescues, and a passion of Maryanne’s.

‘No goats?’ Alessia asks, her eyes sparkling with mirth.

I laugh. ‘I don’t think so. We could go and check. Maybe we could get some just for you.’

We stop at the small ticket office, which is occupied by someone I don’t recognise. ‘Good afternoon,’ the young man offers.

‘Two for the house, please.’ It seems easier to buy the tickets rather than explain that I own the house.

The man hands me two tickets, and I tap my card on the card reader.

Alessia smiles. ‘You have to pay?’

I laugh. ‘Not usually. I don’t know that young man.’

We amble down the drive towards the great house. Through the trees we can see the shoreline of the first of our two lakes, and among the weeds, I spy two coots and some ducks paddling towards the shore.

‘Swans,’ Alessia exclaims with delight, spotting our resident pair of mute swans who are gliding majestically across the still waters, their snowy feathers curled like sails.

‘Yeah. This pair have been with us for about ten or so years. I think Kit called them Triumph and Herald, though which is which I don’t know.’

‘Grand names. They’re beautiful.’

‘They are. Kit was obsessed with cars, especially old classics. Hence the names.’ I laugh at myself. Alessia won’t have a clue about old British cars. ‘They mate for life, you know,’ I add, turning towards her with a broad grin.

She smiles and lifts her chin, amused but haughty. 'I know about swans.'

Of course she does.

'These two raise their new cygnets here each year.'

And one day maybe we will raise our children here too.

The thought surprises and pleases me.

One day.

She squeezes my hand and I wonder if she's thinking the same thing.

At the front of the house is the impressive lawn, which is about a hectare in size. The nearest half is neatly mowed in stripes. It's surrounded by ancient oaks, elms, beech trees and the lake. It is a stunning setting, now that I survey it.

'So, anyone can come here?' Alessia asks as she takes in the view from the steps of the main house.

'Yes, as long as they pay. It's not much if you just want to use the grounds. It's very popular in the summer. For picnics. Behind the house are the stables. We provide a livery for the locals with horses, and a friend of Caroline's runs a riding school from there. This is where Maryanne and Caroline keep their horses. Come, I'll show you inside.'

Alessia trails after Maxim as he bounces up the stone steps and through the double doors into an impressive reception hall. There are statues in little alcoves and ornate plasterwork over the entire room, even the ceiling. Alessia's chest constricts as she tries to take in the majesty of a room that is merely the entrance to this huge house.

Behind a reception desk, the younger of two women looks up in greeting.

'Hello there. Are you here for the tour?' she asks.

Maxim laughs, and the older woman raises her head. 'Oh my goodness! Maxim!' she exclaims. 'I mean, my lord.'

'Hello, Francine. How are you?'

'I'm doing well, my lord.' She bustles around the worktop, much to the surprise of her colleague.

'Please, Maxim will do. It's my name. I've said this already when I was last here.'

'I know, my lord, but I'm an old-fashioned woman.' Her affection for Maxim is obvious as she beams at him.

Maxim wraps his arm around Alessia and pulls her close. 'Francine, may I present my wife, Alessia.'

'Your wife!' Francine exclaims. 'Why, Lady Trevethick, what a pleasure to meet you.'

Alessia holds out her hand, and Francine shakes it vigorously.

'Lady Caroline said you'd married. Congratulations to you both, my lord.'

Caroline. She was here?

'Thank you.'

'I wish you'd told us you were coming—'

Maxim holds up his hand to stop Francine. 'We'll come and do a proper introduction later in the month. I just wanted to give my wife a quick and dirty look around the house. Give her an idea of what she's taken on.'

Francine laughs, good-natured, her eyes twinkling at Alessia. 'I've known his lordship since he was a young lad.'

Maxim quickly interrupts her. 'You're new,' he says, turning to the younger woman behind the desk.

'This is the earl. The owner,' Francine hisses at her. 'This is Jessica. She's been with us for about three weeks now.'

The younger woman stands, flustered. 'I'm sorry, sir. Maxim. Um . . . my lord.'

'Welcome to Angwin, Jessica.' Maxim extends his hand, and Alessia follows suit, taking Jessica's limp, clammy hand and giving it a reassuring squeeze.

Jessica bows her head in a brief salute, and Alessia's cheeks pink.

'We'll go look around,' Maxim says.

'You do that, sir,' Francine replies with a huge smile. 'I'll let Mrs Jenkins know you're here.'

They walk through a door at the side of the reception hall, into a corridor that's crowded with paintings.

'You didn't tell me he was so good-looking!' they hear Jessica hiss at Francine.

Alessia cocks a brow at Maxim, and he shrugs and laughs.

Alessia is quiet while I drive the Jag through Chipping Norton, heading home to London. Reaching over, I grasp her hand and cradle it in mine. 'It's a lot. I know.'

Alessia nods. 'I didn't realise it would be so . . . big. Bigger than . . . um . . . the Hall, in Cornwall.'

'Yes. It's the largest property we own in terms of the actual house and the land. Most of the land's farmed – organically, of course. My father was ahead of his time. An eco-warrior in the late '70s.'

My heart swells, and an aching knot forms in my throat. I miss him. *Father.*

And Kit.

I clear my throat. 'Angwin mostly takes care of itself because the staff who run it are excellent.'

'But you don't live there.'

'No. We stay occasionally. As you saw, we have an apartment in the main house. But that's it. I always think of Angwin as a historical document and an amenity for the community. It's open to the public, and they can roam the house and see how the landed gentry used to live. And browse the art collection . . .'

Alessia nods. 'So many rooms . . .'

'Yeah. I know. The upkeep for that house is astronomical. But we've managed to keep it going and not let it die.'

She offers me a slight smile, and my scalp tightens as I wonder what she's thinking.

Is she judging us? My family?

The wealth?

Shit.

'Are you okay?' I ask.

'Yes. Yes. Of course. I am a little . . . um . . . overwhelmed. But thank you for showing me your . . . other home. It is very clear that your staff admire you.'

What? Her words are unexpected. 'You think?'

Her smile warms. 'Yes. Everyone. They are . . . loyal. It's the right word?'

I snort. 'Yes. I suppose so, but I'm not sure I agree with you. I think the jury is out for them.'

'I think they want you to succeed.'

An unfamiliar warmth spreads through my chest – commendation from the staff, that's new. All praise was usually reserved for Kit.

'I was the family reprobate,' I mutter while I muse on Alessia's observation. 'Kit was the stable, mature, hard-working brother, but then he didn't have a choice.'

'Reprobate?' she asks.

'Definitely.' I flash her my most wicked grin in the hope of lightening the mood, and to my relief, it works.

She laughs.

'Put some music on.' I point my chin to the sound system, and Alessia scrolls through the tunes.

In the glow of the little dragon, Alessia watches Maxim sleep. He's more boyish when he sleeps. Gently, she smooths his hair off his forehead and plants a tender kiss there. She turns and lies on her back, staring at the dancing, watery reflections on the ceiling, and all she can think about is how one family can own so much property.

And now she's one of them.

She has so much when others . . . do not.

She closes her eyes to blot out the reflections wavering on the ceiling and to quell her pervading sense of guilt.

Chapter Twelve

Bleriana! Sweet, young Bleriana is outside the locked doors of the ornate reception hall at Angwin House. Trying to get in. She rattles the door.

Banging her fists on the glass of the double doors.

On the glass.

She'll break the glass.

She's screaming. But Alessia cannot hear a word.

Alessia tries and fails to open the doors.

And behind Bleriana . . . Dante and Ylli emerge from the darkness.

Black plastic bags open and ready.

Alessia is plunged into choking darkness.

Bleriana screams.

'Alessia! Alessia! Wake up!' Maxim's panicked voice penetrates Alessia's horror, dragging her towards the light from the depths of her nightmare. Heart pounding, she opens her eyes – her fear, a tight knot in her chest clawing its way into her throat and choking her.

Maxim.

Her saviour.

Again.

His bright green eyes stare into hers, his face etched in worry. 'Are you okay?'

'It was a dream, a bad dream,' Alessia mumbles and shudders as Maxim gathers her in his arms.

'I've got you,' he whispers, tightening his hold and folding his body protectively around her. He kisses her forehead.

Her thundering heartbeat slows as she clings to her dear, dear husband and inhales his comforting scent – body wash, sleep, and Maxim.

'Hmm,' she breathes.

'Hush now,' he murmurs in the semi-darkness and lies back with Alessia in his arms. 'Go to sleep, sweetheart.'

Alessia closes her eyes, and as her fear recedes, she drifts once more.

It's my first day in the office after the tumultuous events of the last few weeks. As the cab pulls up at the front door, I wonder what today will bring. I'm still unsettled by Alessia's plaintive wail in the depths of the night – her cry for help from her nightmare. She seemed fine this morning and couldn't remember her bad dream, but I'm worried her past trauma is catching up with her. She always seems so stoic but perhaps, now that she's safe, the shock of the numerous ordeals she's endured recently is finally taking its toll.

Dude. It's one nightmare.

Taking a deep breath, I push my thoughts aside, pay the driver, and stride up the steps into the office building.

The receptionist greets me with a cheery smile. 'Good morning, Lord Trevethick.'

'Good morning, Lisa.'

'And congratulations, my lord. On your wedding.'

'Thank you.'

I head through the outer office, knock on Oliver's door, and enter. He grins broadly; if I'm not mistaken, I think he's pleased to see me. 'Maxim. Welcome back, and congratulations.' He stands and holds out his hand.

'Thanks, Oliver.' We shake, and I'm grateful he's been holding the fort. 'And thank you for restoring the photography in my flat.'

'You noticed! It's a pleasure. You have a good eye. You had a relaxing and enjoyable honeymoon?'

I grin. 'I did, thank you.'

'We have a long agenda, so I wonder if we should get cracking.'

'Yes, of course. I want a moment, though. I've decided that it's time to move into Kit's office.'

'Very good, sir,' Oliver says gently and gestures towards the door of the hallowed room that was my brother's and my father's domain. 'If you need anything,' he adds, 'I'm here.'

'Thanks.'

I cross the floor, grab the brass handle, and open the door to the inner sanctum. Taking a deep, steadying breath, I step inside as a wave of nostalgia crashes over me. The smell, the ambience, the décor – it's all Kit.

It's a gut punch of memories.

One wall is lined with books and various curios: a polo ball and trophies, a model Bugatti Veyron, the family crest, and a few of his rallying trophies. The wall behind his desk has pictures, paintings, certificates, and photographs, including a large daguerreotype of Tresyllian House in Cornwall. Beside it is my photographic re-creation in black and white taken with my Leica. I reach out to straighten my print, and I'm reminded that Kit always supported my photography.

The desk is ornate, with intricate carvings and an embossed black leather top. On his desk are more portraits in gilt frames of us, Caroline, Jensen and Healey, his beloved red setters. I glide a finger over the cool, gleaming wood and then test the various drawers. They're all locked.

There's a knock at the door, and Oliver steps in. 'You'll need these.' He produces a set of keys, setting them down on the desk.

'Thank you.'

He looks around the office. 'I haven't been in here for a while either.' He glances at the photo of Kit shaking hands with some dignitary I don't recognise and then back at me.

'You miss him too.' It's a statement that causes a tightening in my chest.

'Yeah,' he says and clears his throat. 'Those keys should open the desk and the filing cabinet over there.'

'Shall we get on with our meeting? We can do it at the rather fine Queen Anne table in here.'

Oliver laughs. 'I'll fetch my notebook.'

I blow out a breath as I remove and hang my coat on the hatstand, thinking about how Kit's death has affected so many of us, even Oliver.

'What's first on the agenda?' I ask when he returns.

'Perhaps you should do a press release about your marriage. The tabloids are pestering our director of communications.'

'Really?'

Oliver nods.

I don't want the press delving into the minutiae of my marriage.

'I'll think about it. And can we get me a computer for here?'

'Of course. I'll get that sorted today.'

'What's next?'

Alessia is in the apartment sitting at Maxim's desk, using his iMac and trawling the internet. She's trying to find out how to track a trafficked person. It's an impossible task, especially as the intercom keeps buzzing. There are reporters outside, wanting to speak to Maxim. She's feigned ignorance and is now listening to Angela Hewitt's interpretation of Bach's preludes and fugues from the Well-Tempered Clavier through headphones. Alessia was surprised that only a few women artists were featured in the classical albums on Apple Music. The various colours that ring in her head keep her grounded as she reads report after report from victims who have escaped their traffickers and abusers and found safety in England through the work of various charities.

It's sobering reading.

In the back of her mind, she keeps returning to the mantra: *That could have been me.*

She shudders.

If she hadn't escaped from Dante's and Ylli's clutches, she'd have her own harrowing story to tell, and she would, in all probability, become another appalling statistic.

A fractured shard from her nightmare pierces her mind.

Bleriana hammering on the doors at Angwin.

Her face tear-stained. Her fear wild and disturbing in her eyes.

O Zot. O Zot. Poor Bleriana.

When Alessia looks up to check the time, she finds tears coursing down her cheeks. She dashes them away, more resolved to try to find her friend. Somehow.

Oliver and I are concluding our meeting. The Mayfair refurbishment is near completion, and it's time to hire an interior designer. I need Caro to decide if she wants the gig.

I've asked Oliver for a full rundown of the expenses my mother has made against the estate for the past year, which means I'll be privy to my parents' divorce settlement. And he'll prepare a list of all the larger houses belonging to the estate, that are or will be coming available for lease shortly.

That's on the agenda for tomorrow.

Throughout our discussions, I've ignored my phone. When I glance at the screen, I'm astonished to find it crowded with a ton of text messages and missed calls.

What the hell! You got married!!!!

When do we get to meet your WIFE?

What's this I hear about you getting married?

You're finally off the market.
My heart is broke!

Maxim. You're hitched!!!

WTF man? You wed!

Who's the lucky girl?

Can I get an interview with
you and your bride?

Shit! The last is from a journalist from one of the glossies. I fucked her back in the day.

How do all these people know?

'You were right about the world knowing about my nuptials,' I mutter to Oliver, who is gathering his papers together.

'It's not too late to put out a press release,' he says.

I roll my eyes, refusing to contemplate any interaction with the press as I scroll through a flurry of texts Caroline sent a couple of hours ago.

Can we meet today?
You need to see what I've unearthed.
It may affect you.

What fresh hell is this?

Can it wait?

No.

There's a knock on the office door as Oliver rises.

'Come in,' I call.

Lisa steps inside. 'I'm so sorry to interrupt you, my lord. Lady Trevethick is here.'

Alessia! My heart skips a beat, and I rise from the table, a broad smile plastered on my face ready to greet my wife. 'Show her in.'

Lisa steps aside, and Caroline enters and pockets her phone.

Oh.

'Expecting someone else?' Caroline snipes. 'Your face has fallen several floors, darling.'

'Hello, Caro.' Ignoring her jibe, I kiss her cheek. 'What a lovely surprise.'

'Oliver,' she acknowledges him, and he gives her a quick nod before exiting. Caroline watches him leave, her face impassive, and then she turns to survey the room. 'It's been a while since I was in here.' She turns her attention to me, her eyes welling with her sadness.

'Funny, Oliver said that,' I whisper.

Her nose pinks charmingly, and she shakes her head, steeling herself. 'I was in the area. I wondered if you might want lunch.'

'I've just got back and I'm busy, Caro.'

She laughs – a sad, sorry sound. 'You would never have said that back in the day.'

'True. What can I help you with?'

'May I sit? I have something to show you.'

'Of course.' I gesture towards the Queen Anne table and pull out the chair I've just vacated for her to sit down. While I take a seat beside her, she places her handbag on her lap and ferrets through it, avoiding eye contact.

'You know I've been going through Kit's belongings and his papers.'

'Yes.' *Where is she going with this?*

'Well, I found all sorts of things. It's amazing what can turn up.' She sounds nervous.

'What is it, Caro?'

'Well.' She swallows. 'This might concern both you and Maryanne.' She fishes a couple of letters out of her handbag and places them on the table in front of me.

I glance down at them, then back at her, cocking my head. 'What are these?'

'I think you should read them.' The haunted look in her eyes sends a frisson down my spine, and I grasp both letters and scan them. Every hair on my body stands to attention.

'Genetic . . . what?' My mouth dries as I look at her. 'Why would Kit be referred for genetic counselling?'

'Exactly,' she whispers.

'You don't know?'

She shakes her head, her eyes wide and luminous with doubt. 'No. These are a surprise for me too.'

What the hell is this?

Carefully, I re-read both letters and check the dates. His GP referral was in October last year, and the genetic counselling service wrote back with an appointment in November.

'Have you found any other letters? Results?'

Caroline shakes her head.

'Dates in his diary?'

'No.' Caro looks as bemused as I am.

'If Kit's been referred for genetic counselling, it'll be for a reason.'

Oh shit.

I feel the blood drain from my face.

If Kit was facing a genetic medical issue, then . . . I am too, surely.

And Maryanne.

Hell.

Could there be something wrong with me?

I rack my brain, trying to remember if there are any documented medical conditions in my predecessors. Nothing comes to mind. 'Maybe I should get tested too.'

'Tested for what? We don't have a clue,' Caroline says.

This is true.

'Maybe it was just a precautionary investigation,' Caro says. 'You know how thorough Dr Renton can be. He's always overzealous. It racks up the bill.'

'Was Kit ill?' I ask.

'Not as far as I know. He had headaches, which you know about.'

'He's always had those.'

Hell. What could this be? I have no idea. 'Did you call Renton's office?'

'Yes. They wouldn't divulge any information.' Caro sounds frustrated.

Double hell.

I wonder if my mother knows. 'Did you mention this to Rowena?'

'No. She flew back to New York as soon as we touched down from Tirana.'

'You knew about this at the wedding?' My voice has risen several octaves.

Caroline's eyes widen, and I have my answer.

And you didn't fucking tell me?

I glare at her, suddenly livid. I might have something wrong with me, and I've just got married!

Fuck. What have I saddled Alessia with?

But before I can get really fucking angry, we're interrupted by a knock at the door, and Lisa enters carrying a tray with coffee. It gives me a moment to rein in my temper.

'I took the liberty of making you some coffee,' Lisa says with a bright smile.

'Thanks,' I mutter as she places it on the table.

'Thank you, Lisa,' Caro says, and Lisa stands awkwardly, surveying us for a moment.

'That will be all. Thanks again.' I force a smile, and I'm relieved when she leaves.

'Did you call this place?' I ask, tapping the letter from the genetic counselling clinic.

'Yes. They wouldn't tell me anything either, even though I'm next of kin.'

Fucking hell.

'I don't think they'd talk to you either,' Caroline says gently.

'Well, maybe I can get some answers out of Renton. After all, he's my GP too. In fact, I need to sign Alessia up. Hell, I may even have to call Rowena.'

'Maxim, I'm sure it's nothing,' Caroline says.

'How the hell do you know?' I shout, rising from the table, and to my shame, Caro flinches.

Fuck. Fuck. Fuck.

I want to scream.

I'm as angry with her now as I was in Albania when I found out she told Alessia about us. I drag a hand through my hair and pace across the fucking antique Persian rug on the floor.

Dude. Get a grip.

'I'll do some digging before we tell Maryanne,' I mutter.

'She might be able to shed some light. After all, she is a doctor.'

'Let me find out what we're dealing with here.'

She's my sister, and it's my fucking job to protect her.

Caro blows out a breath. 'Okay. The other thing we need to discuss is Kit's memorial.'

'Not now.'

'Well, I've spoken with the Dean of Westminster's office.'

'And?'

'They're suggesting a date in April.'

'Isn't that a bit soon?'

'Is it?' Caroline says.

'Oh hell, Caro. I don't know. Let me think about it. This is . . . a lot.'

'It is,' she admits. 'Are you sure I can't take you to lunch?'

'I have to leave shortly. Alessia and I are meeting a lawyer. About her immigration status.'

'Oh?'

'Yeah.'

Caroline purses her lips, but her expression softens. 'I'm sorry,' she murmurs. 'For not telling you. At the wedding.'

I slump into the chair behind what is now my desk. 'Perhaps something here might shed some light on these letters.' Grabbing the keys, I try the first tiny brass key that looks most likely to fit. The fourth key works and I open the first of the drawers. It contains a rack of suspension files.

Caroline moves to sit in the chair opposite the desk, craning her neck to see if I find anything. I quickly scan through the files, but they seem to be personal – a collection of clippings from car magazines, a file with letters from the LSE, some CVs, and a weighty leather diary from last year. I drag it out, place it on the desk, and quickly leaf through it, checking the dates mentioned on the letters. Alas, the diary holds no clues.

Bugger.

'Anything?' Caroline asks.

I shake my head.

The other drawers don't yield any leads either. Just some cool stationary and some mementos from Kit's trips around the world. My search is fruitless, but a thought occurs to me.

'Where's Kit's laptop? Or his phone for that matter? Or even his journal?'

'I've no idea.'

'What do you mean? They're not with his possessions? Perhaps it's here. Or in the safe at Trevelyan House or the Hall?'

Caroline lifts her chin. 'I don't know.'

'Can you check?'

She shrugs in a noncommittal, un-Caro way.

'Really?'

She shakes her head looking abashed and a little sheepish. 'I can try,' she mutters.

'I'm going to call Renton, make an appointment, and also try the genetic counselling clinic.'

'I hope you have better luck than me.' She stands. 'I'd better go. I'm sure this is nothing, Maxim.'

I rise to my feet, and we gaze at each other, and I'm wondering once more what Kit was doing on his motorcycle racing through the Trevethick lanes in the depths of an icy winter. Is she thinking the same? Was the news so bad that he took his own life?

Fuck.

Neither of us says anything. Caroline's breath catches and her pupils grow darker and larger. I don't like what that telegraphs, but before I can be sure, she breaks eye contact, glancing towards the door. 'I'm sorry,' she whispers, and she exits the room, leaving me entirely at sea – alone, angry . . . and scared.

I check my watch and realise I've enough time to walk home and clear my head. Grabbing my coat, I head out of the office.

Oliver looks up and frowns. 'You okay, Maxim?'

'Yes. I've got to leave.'

'Did you mention interior design to Lady Trevethick?'

Damn!

'No. I will, though. Unless you'd like to?'

Oliver's face falls and he looks a little uncomfortable. 'I'd rather you did, Maxim,' he responds eventually.

'Okay. I'll do that. I'll see you tomorrow.'

Disheartened, I trudge through the backstreets of Chelsea back to the flat. So far, today has been exasperating. I feel like I've been thwarted at every turn. I've made a call to Kit's and my GP, Dr Renton, and have an appointment to see him tomorrow. Hopefully, I'll get some answers then. The genetic counselling clinic was not forthcoming at all and the clinician dealing with Kit is on holiday, but I have an appointment in a couple of weeks to see her. I've even called my mother and left a message for her to call me . . . all to no avail.

I cannot believe how bewildering this news has been.

There may be nothing wrong.

But on the other hand, something awful could befall me as I get older.

Hell.

It's the not knowing that's so frustrating.

As I round the corner of Tite Street onto the Embankment, I spy a few people – mainly men – hanging around the entrance to my building.

Wait. These are not people!

Three of the shambolic riffraff are holding cameras.

Paparazzi!

For a nanosecond, I wonder who they're waiting for, and then an older man wearing an Arsenal FC scarf spots me. 'There he is!' he shouts.

Fuck. They're after me!

Lord Trevethick! Lord Trevethick! Maxim!

Congratulations.

Care to comment on your marriage? Your bride? When do we meet her?

My mood slides from bad to worse as they swarm around me like cockroaches. I put my head down and walk through them, saying nothing.

This is all I fucking need.

I head into the safety of the building while a couple of the reporters shout questions at me. Leaving them on the doorstep, I vault up the stairs, cursing whoever informed the press about our marriage. Alessia is not going to appreciate the attention; this I know.

I've not been accosted by any journalists since I was with Charlotte, an ex-girlfriend. She loved attention – as an actor . . . sorry, no, an artist, as she liked to style herself – she lapped it up, especially from the press. I roll my eyes at the memory. She was socially ambitious and hideously pretentious. Thank God she moved on. Apart from my time with her, I've managed to avoid being tabloid fodder, but I'll get the occasional mention in the social diary columns of more discerning publications.

I unlock the front door, step into the hall, and stop.

Alessia is at the piano, and I recognise the melody immediately – *Clair de Lune*, a piece I can play myself but with nothing like her grace. As I listen in wonder, the last few frustrating hours slip away, and I'm transported to a more peaceful, hopeful state. I creep down the hall, peer into the drawing room, and watch her.

Eyes closed, head bent, she's wholly surrendered to the music as it flows effortlessly through and from her. Somehow, she senses my presence and turns and smiles, her face lighting up at the sight of me.

'Don't stop,' I say, walking towards her.

She shifts on the piano stool, not missing a note, and I settle beside her, wrapping my arm around her waist while the music caresses and holds the pair of us.

This is sublime.

And I have an idea – I hover my right hand over hers, and she immediately understands what I'm trying to do. She withdraws her hand, and I take over. We stumble over the first few notes, but I watch her left hand, following her lead, and we continue the piece.

Together.

I'm thrilled that I'm able to keep up with her without the composition in front of me. She makes it easy because she's so attuned to the music and its languid rhythm.

Following her lead makes me a better pianist.

It's humbling.

It's exhilarating.

As the final note drifts into the ether and disappears, we grin at each other like fools. 'That was amazing,' I whisper.

Alessia laughs, threading her arms around my neck and drawing my lips to hers. We kiss. Her mouth is warm, wet, welcoming, and arousing all at once. I tug her onto my lap, deepening our connection, our tongues celebrating each other so that we're breathless when we pull apart.

She rests her forehead against mine. Her eyes closed. 'I've missed you,' she whispers.

'Oh, baby. I've missed you. And I'd like nothing more than to take you to bed, but we have an appointment with the immigration lawyer.'

She pouts but stands, obviously reluctant to leave the safety of my lap. 'I am ready.' She hands me our passports, our marriage certificate and the apostille issued by the notary in Tirana confirming our marriage certificate is legitimate. I slip them all into my jacket pocket. Then frown.

'There's a slight problem. We've been besieged by the press outside.'

'I know.'

'You do?'

'They have been ringing the bell outside. Asking for you. Asking me questions.'

'What did you do?'

'I said I was your cleaner and that you weren't here. And then I stopped answering.' She bites her bottom lip looking impish.

I laugh out loud. 'Brilliant. Apparently, our marriage appears to be in the public interest.'

'Are they still outside the building?'

'Afraid so.'

'We can escape through the utility room and go that way.'

'Of course! Let's go.'

Standing outside on the fire escape, Maxim locks the utility room door and grins down at Alessia. 'I can't remember the last time I was out here!'

She laughs, then sobers. The last time she used it was to escape Dante and Ylli when they came to Maxim's apartment. And she's used it often to empty Maxim's trash.

'I'll follow you,' he says, and gingerly they make their way down the six flights to the side alley.

As they pass the bins, Alessia remembers throwing up beside them. Maxim grabs her hand and threads his fingers with hers. 'What is it?' he asks.

She shakes her head, reluctant to tell him and to rid herself of that awful recollection. An image of Bleriana's sweet face imprints on her mind. The poor child. Did she evade their captors? Did the others?

Maxim says nothing, letting her be, and together they make their way to the gate at the side alley. Maxim opens it and peers out. The street is empty.

'This is how you got out and away when those thugs showed up.'

'Yes.'

'You must have been so scared. Come on. Coast is clear. Let's grab a cab.'

Hand in hand, they walk briskly up the street, unhindered by the press, and Maxim hails the first cab he sees.

The offices of Lockhart, Waddell, Mulville, and Cavanagh are on Lincoln's Inn Fields. An office junior shows us into a conference room. 'May I fetch you tea or coffee?' he asks, blinking rapidly.

'I'm good. Alessia?'

'No, thank you.'

'Very good, Lord, Lady Trevethick. Ticia Cavanagh will be with you shortly.' He exits, and I usher Alessia to a seat at the table. Ms Cavanagh is a partner in the firm, and she comes highly recommended by Rajah – she's an expert in her field.

The door opens before I've sat down, and Ticia Cavanagh enters. She's wearing an expensive black suit and a white silk blouse. In her hand, she clutches a legal paper pad, her scarlet nails vivid against the canary yellow.

Oh, shit.

We stare at each other in instant recognition. The last time I saw her, I'd just untied her from my bed.

Could this day hold any more surprises?

I clear my throat. 'Leticia, how nice to see you again.'

Chapter Thirteen

'Lord Trevethick,' Leticia says in her soft Irish lilt, stressing my title. 'How do you do? And your wife' – she emphasises the word *wife* – 'Lady Trevethick.' She steps forward, her face etched in disdain as she holds out her hand in greeting, and as she grasps mine a little too tightly, I feel the need to defend myself.

'Recent. Wife. We married. Recently.'

Alessia frowns, her eyes darting to me and then back to Ticia Cavanagh as they shake hands. 'How do you do?' Alessia murmurs as if her throat is dry, and she casts another glance at me, her eyes wide with insight.

Damn. She knows.

My heart sinks, and I briefly close my eyes, summoning some resolve while realising I'll have to explain myself later.

Had I known . . . *hell.*

I'm confused by Leticia's use of a nickname. 'Ticia?'

'Here. Yes,' she says, her tone terse, and I realise she's not going to offer any other explanation, which is, of course, her prerogative. I wonder if she'll ask us to leave or hand our case to a colleague. 'Now, how can I help you and your . . . recent wife?' Her lips curl into a professional smile that's almost a snarl as she takes a seat at the head of the table, but her eyes remain arctic.

I take a seat beside Alessia. 'Alessia and I recently married in Albania, and she needs indefinite leave to stay here.'

Leticia taps scarlet nails on the table, and I remember her brandishing them as a weapon.

Mate! I banish that thought. Pronto.

'Tell me. How did the two of you meet? And when?'

I glance at Alessia with what I hope is a reassuring smile, but she doesn't return it. She swallows and stares down at her hands, which are knotted in her lap. With a sigh, I turn my attention back to Leticia.

'Alessia worked for me . . .'

While Maxim summarises the last few months' events to the attractive lawyer, Alessia is trying to stay afloat. She feels like a block of cement sinking beneath the weight of Maxim's past liaisons, and she's struggling to breathe.

Darling, he's slept with most of London.

It appears that Caroline was not exaggerating.

Ticia, Leticia – whatever her name is – is older, a mature, elegant woman with intelligent hazel eyes that give nothing away as she makes notes on the lined paper pad. Her voice is soft with an accent Alessia doesn't recognise. She seems to be a woman who does not suffer fools gladly and has something of her nana's spirit – an underlying grit – that's attractive.

Is that what led Maxim to her?

Alessia tries to shake off the thought. She would not want this woman as an adversary, but as an ally – who's slept with her husband, her crimson nails raking his back.

O Zot. Do not think of this.

Maxim tells the lawyer everything.

The trafficking.

The arrest of Dante and Ylli.

Anatoli. The kidnapping.

His trek to Albania.

The speed at which they were wed and the questionable legitimacy of their marriage.

Leticia holds up her hand, interrupting Maxim. 'Were you coerced into this marriage?' she asks Alessia directly. Maxim scowls and opens his mouth to speak, but she silences him with a look. 'Let your wife speak, Lord Trevethick.'

'No!' Alessia says. 'Not at all. If anything . . . it's the . . . um . . . other way.'

'You were coerced?' Leticia scoffs, looking at Maxim.

'No,' he says in a rush. 'Her father has an intimidating shotgun, but I went to Albania to marry Alessia. For love.'

Alessia raises her head and, much to my relief, offers me the ghost of a smile. Leticia notices and sits back in her chair, looking a tad more relaxed.

'So, you married within a week.'

'Yes.'

She raises her brows. 'I see. Do you have the marriage certificate?'

I fish the documents from my inside breast pocket. 'I do. And an apostille.'

Leticia gives them a cursory glance. 'Good,' she mutters. 'I'll need a copy of these so we can have them translated. Also, copies of your passports.'

I hand them over.

Leticia looks through her notes. 'To be clear,' she says, regarding Alessia, 'you were illegally trafficked into the country?'

'Yes. With other girls.'

'Others? Did they escape too?'

'I don't know,' Alessia says quietly, her voice laced with guilt.

'Lady Trevethick, this is not your fault,' Leticia says, her voice firm. 'Now, is there any evidence of the trafficking?'

'The men. They were arrested,' Alessia says.

'It's an ongoing case,' I add.

'Ah. In the press recently? Part of a ring?'

'Yes,' I reply.

'I've read about it.'

'They took everything. My passport . . .' Alessia's voice fades.

Leticia eyes her sympathetically. 'Well, that could be a fly in the ointment if your old passport surfaces, but we'll deal with that should it arise.'

'What's the worst-case scenario?' I ask.

'Well, I suppose there's a risk that Lady Trevethick could be deported.'

'What!' I glance at Alessia who's now ashen.

'Lord Trevethick, it's a slight risk, but I think we'd have a strong case to keep her here, and we're certainly not there yet.' She looks from me to Alessia, and she seems more predisposed to both of us. 'The validity of your marriage might be an issue if any bad actors discover that official protocols weren't followed.'

'That's why we'd like to get married again. Here. So there's no doubt,' I respond.

'That's not possible. Under English law, there's only one valid ceremony of marriage that creates the status of marriage, and you have what looks like a legitimate marriage certificate that has been certified with this apostille. If you marry again, your second marriage won't be legally recognised.'

'Oh, I didn't realise that.'

'You'll have to have the original marriage annulled to get married again. You could have a blessing here if it's that important to you. But' – she examines our marriage certificate and the apostille again – 'I think we need to trust the Albanian authorities and the certificate you've been given. This looks very much in order.'

'Okay.' The scepticism is clear in my tone – this isn't what I expected. 'My only issue is the considerable press interest,' I continue. 'I don't want any zealous reporters digging around and finding out about the speed at which we got married.'

'Is that likely?'

'There was a flock of press outside our building today.'

'Ah. I see. Okay, let's cross that bridge should we need to.' She turns to Alessia and addresses her directly. 'First, we need to switch you from your visitor's visa before we can contemplate applying for a family visa for you. Unless you'd consider returning to Albania and applying for the spousal visa from there?'

No,' Maxim says immediately.

Ticia's lips press together. 'Lord Trevethick, I was addressing your wife.'

Maxim scowls but clamps his mouth shut and remains silent.

'How long would I have to go for?' Alessia asks.

'Well, if it's fast-tracked, you can usually get a visa within thirty or so days. You'll have to do an English test, and Lord Trevethick has to meet a minimum income threshold.' Ticia glances at Maxim. 'I think we can safely assume that you do that and have adequate accommodation in the UK.'

'I do,' Maxim snaps.

'So, do you want to return to Albania?'

'No. I'd rather stay with Maxim.'

'Okay. Then the alternative might be studying in this country. Have you thought about that?'

Alessia is pensive in the cab back to Chelsea. She's not said a word since we left Leticia's offices. The traffic is sluggish at Westminster, and I check the time. It's 5:30 – the height of rush hour. I have more missed calls and texts, including one from Caro, that I'm ignoring. Joe has forwarded a short article from one of the London evening tabloids. It's speculation about our marriage and it's illustrated with a photograph of me entering my building from earlier today. Since when did I become so interesting? It's pissing me off.

And I still haven't had a response from my mother.

And I'm getting the silent treatment from Alessia.

Could this day get any worse?

'Do you want to go out to eat?' I ask, in the hope of getting her to talk.

Alessia is gazing up at Big Ben as we round the square. 'I'm not hungry,' she says.

'Alessia. Look at me.'

She turns dark, wounded eyes to me that slice through my soul. 'What is it? I don't know what you're thinking. It's driving me crazy.'

'You had a relationship with the lawyer?'

'No. She was a one-night stand. Just sex. Once.'

Well, more than once that night if we want pinpoint accuracy.

Alessia glances at the cabbie.

'He can't hear us.'

'Maxim, I am trying to . . . ugh . . . my English.' She closes her eyes in frustration.

'Tell me.'

She squares her shoulders and turns her dark gaze on me again. 'You have a . . . colourful past, with many lovers. And I don't know why that hurts me so much. I think . . . um . . . I am anxious that I am not enough for you. Or you will become bored with me.'

There. She said it. Her darkest fear out between them.

Maxim scoots across the cab's back seat and grasps her chin, so she's pinned by his intense green gaze. He leans in. 'Never,' he says with such conviction that Alessia feels a frisson of alarm. 'You own me. Body and soul. Fuck's sake, Alessia!' He releases her and leans forward, placing his head in his hands.

She blows out a breath, startled by his vehemence. 'You're angry with me.'

'No. I'm angry at myself, but I don't think it's deserved.'

'No,' she says quietly. 'It's not. I'm sorry.'

He looks up and gives her a crooked smile. 'You don't need to apologise. Like I said, I have a past. Look, let's just go home. It's been a shit day. A really shit day.'

Alessia places a hand on his arm. 'It's not so bad a day.'

'No?' Maxim sits back.

'This morning, I talked to my mother. She's . . . um . . . basking – is that the right word? – in the glow . . . afterglow of the wedding. It is the talk of Kukës. She's happy. My father is happy.'

'That's the right word. I'm glad your parents are happy. And it looks like we don't need to get married again, though I wouldn't mind. I would marry you over and over to the end of time if I could.'

Alessia blows out a breath in awe at his words and rewards him with a hesitant smile. 'I would marry you again too. But it is a relief not to organise another wedding so soon. We have done it once.'

Maxim takes her hand. 'We have. And it was a beautiful wedding. It's official. We're married. Our lawyer said so.'

'And this afternoon, we did a duet together.'

Maxim's lips curl into a dazzling smile. 'That was exhilarating. You're so talented and easy to follow.' He stops. 'You've had no formal musical training, yes?' He squeezes her hand and releases it.

'None. I learned at home. You know this.'

'Well, not that you need it. But have you ever thought of music school? Here. In London, to formalise everything you've learned?'

Alessia stares at him, nonplussed, as she tries to weigh his words.

'You could study. We could get you a student visa for that.'

Study. Music. In London.

Alessia's heart starts to pound with sudden excitement. 'That would be expensive.'

Maxim snorts. 'I think we can afford it,' he says drily.

'See. Not such a bad day.' She beams broadly at me, and her delight is infectious.

'No.' I grin back. 'Let's do some research when we get home. Etiquette and music. We'll find something.'

And just like that, my spirits lift and the atmosphere between us is transformed.

Only two shifty characters, both carrying cameras, are outside our building when we return home. I ask the cabbie to drop us in Tite Street, as I have a Cunning Plan.

Once the cab has left us, Alessia walks around the corner and heads into the building. Of course, the paps have no idea who she is, and they give her a cursory glance, although from my vantage point, I watch one of them ogle her as she walks past him in her tight, figure-hugging jeans.

Dirty bastard.

Once she's inside, I follow, head down, ignoring their questions. I walk briskly into the building and join Alessia inside the lift.

'You have no idea how much of a kick I got out of that.' I chuckle. 'They didn't have a clue that my mysterious wife walked right by them.'

The doors close behind us, and it's just us in the small space. Her eyes meet mine, peering up through her lashes, a smile teasing her lips, and everything tightens in my groin.

'Feeling happier?'

She nods and reaches for my jacket, tugging me towards her. Her hands snake around my head, and her lips meet mine. We kiss. Long. Hard. And I push her up against the wall, pressing my greedy dick against her belly while our tongues slip and slide against each other.

'Maxim,' she breathes and shifts, so she runs her fingers over my fly, tracing my erection through denim.

Ah!

The lift stops, the doors open, and I pick her up. 'Wrap your legs around me, baby.' She complies, her fingers tangled in my hair, our lips locked, as I carry her the short distance from the lift to our front door.

Alessia giggles as Maxim reaches around her thigh into his jeans pocket for the key to the front door. 'Not much room in my jeans,' he grumbles, retrieving his key and unlocking the door while holding her. The alarm beeps, but he disarms it, carries Alessia into the hallway, and sets her on her feet.

'As much as I want to take you to bed, let's look at music colleges.'

'No. Let's go to bed.'

He draws back, his expression blank in apparent surprise. 'But—'

'No. Bed.' Alessia is more insistent.

He frowns and grasps her head, lifting her face to his, his intense green gaze on hers. For a moment, he looks lost and confused, but he closes his eyes.

'What did I do to deserve you?' he breathes, and then his lips are on hers, his tongue taking hers as he walks her backwards into the bedroom. As their tongues wrestle, he keeps moving until Alessia feels the bed at her calves. He stops and, with a wicked carnal smile, gently pushes her onto it so she falls back flat on the bed, a strand of her hair settling on her face.

Maxim stands over her, removes his jacket, and tosses it on the floor. With blazing eyes, he yanks his shirt from his jeans and starts to undo the buttons. Slowly. One at a time. His lips are parted, soft and sensual, his breathing measured but increasing.

Alessia licks her lips in anticipation.

Once his shirt is flapping open, revealing the tanned and toned torso beneath, he raises a cuff of his sleeve and undoes that . . . then the other.

He's stripping for her.

At a wanton and leisurely pace.

Alessia watches. Captivated. Her gaze drinks him in: his broad chest, with its smattering of hair, the toned abs, the trail of hair from his belly that heads down beneath the waistband of his jeans.

His eyes don't leave hers. He's not even touching her and she's seduced, her arousal spreading between her legs and making her squirm. He draws off his shirt, in the way he does, over his head, so it ruffles his hair, messing it up just the way she likes it. Then he discards the garment on the floor without a care in the world.

He undoes the button of his jeans.

And stops.

No!

He leans forward and grabs her ankle – adroitly removing her ankle boot and sock. He then repeats the process with her other boot, running his thumb down her instep when her foot is naked and making her squirm.

He leans over and undoes her jeans. Deftly. He's so quick that he's grabbed the hems of her jeans and yanked them off before she can take a breath. He deposits them with his clothes on the floor.

'You. Your jeans.' She waves towards his groin.

Maxim grins and slowly unzips his fly, but he doesn't remove his pants. He steps out of his shoes and removes his socks. Then he sweeps off his jeans and underwear so he's free in all his glory.

Alessia gasps and Maxim moves onto the bed and plants a soft wet kiss at the juncture of her thighs through the soft cotton of her panties. The contact sends a jolt of electricity through her body so that she gasps once more, her fingers tangling in his hair. He strokes his nose up and down along her most precious seam, his stubble prickling her thighs.

'Your panties are wet, sweet Alessia. I like. I like that a lot.'

He nips the inside of her thigh, his lips sheathing his teeth, and Alessia tightens her hands in his hair and tugs.

He kneels up between her legs, pulls her into a sitting position, and quickly divests her of her jacket and her long-sleeved T-shirt. They go the way of the rest of their clothes, so Alessia's left in her bra and panties.

She reaches up and strokes his stubbled chin.

'Do you want me to shave?' he asks.

'No. I like. Muchly.' She gently rakes her fingernails across his cheek, and he closes his eyes.

'I have an idea,' he whispers, and grasping her head once

more, he kisses her. His tongue is insistent, dominating and subduing hers as he lies them both down. His fingers tug down the cup of her bra, freeing her aching breast, and abandoning her mouth, he leaves a trail of wet kisses down her throat, across her chest to the straining peak of her nipple.

Desire courses through her veins, and she turns dark eyes to blazing green as he strokes his chin across the sensitive bud.

Ah!

'Sure you don't want me to shave?' he teases, and he does it again, his eyes never leaving hers.

'No!' she cries out as her nipple hardens and lengthens beneath his assault.

'Feel good?'

'Yes.' Her pulse is racing, pumping blood to her breasts, swelling her nipples that ache for his touch, and also to the small powerhouse at the junction of her thighs. 'Please!'

He does it again, and she arches her back into his touch.

He grins, tugs down the bra cup shielding her other breast, and begins the same tortuous motion, brushing his stubble over her super-sensitised skin.

She clutches the duvet as his lips and stubble head south, and he nestles between her thighs. He kisses her, *there* . . .

Then slowly draws down her panties and kisses her *there*. *Again*.

This time, circling the swollen bud with his tongue.

O Zot!

Alessia closes her eyes and arches her back, and his tongue continues its leisurely assault. Round and round. Licking and sucking.

Ah!

He stops and draws his chin over that sensitive spot, his stubble wreaking havoc with her nerve endings.

'Të lutem!'

'English,' he warns. And he does it again.

'Please. Maxim.'

He sits up, drags off her panties, and flips her over and undoes her bra.

He lies down on top of her, his erection nestling in the cleft of her behind.

'Shall I take you this way?'

'Yes!'

'You sound like you're in need.'

'I am.'

She senses his smile at her ear, and gently he tugs her ear-lobe with his teeth. 'God, I love you, Alessia. Wife. Of mine.' He pushes her knees apart with his and tugs her backside towards him. He trails a finger down between her cheeks, and her muscles tighten as it trails over and past her arse.

'One day, Alessia,' he whispers and then his thumb is inside her, pushing at that sweet spot deep, deep within her. His fingers at her clitoris. Circling. Teasing. Tormenting.

She makes a strangled sound as her body convulses around his thumb. Her orgasm surprising her and spiralling through her limbs.

Maxim withdraws his thumb and flips her back over. With her dazed eyes on his, he slowly enters her, absorbing the last of her shock waves.

He groans his approval and starts to move. Hard. Fast. Taking her higher. So she doesn't have a chance to land. She's flying once more, driven by him. Pushed onward and upward by him. He looms over her. Sweat breaking on his brow. He's relentless. Taking her higher and higher. Her legs stiffen once more, and she cries out as she climaxes a second time. More intense and more draining. Alessia thinks she can see heaven.

'Thank God,' Maxim churns out between gritted teeth, and he comes and comes, collapsing on her and holding her close.

Alessia opens her eyes as Maxim eases out of her, leaving a silky, slick trail of his seed across her upper thigh. She doesn't care. She revels in it.

He kisses her brow and smooths damp strands from her forehead. 'Okay?' he asks.

'More than okay,' she whispers.

He strokes his knuckles down her cheek. 'Don't ever think you're not enough. Please. It breaks my heart to hear you say that. I love you. Don't forget it. This feeling is new for me too. I've only felt it since I met you.'

She leans up and kisses him. 'I know.'

'Do you?' He looks lost all of a sudden.

She nods quickly to reassure him.

Nothing's changed, Alessia.

He loves you.

Maxim's smile is cautious. 'Good. Look. I can span an Alessia. You're an octave.' He stretches his hand out, the tips of his thumb and little finger brushing her nipples. He grins, and she giggles, enjoying his boyishness. 'I could lie here and look at you all day, but I need the loo.' He gives her a quick peck, rises from the bed, and heads into the bathroom.

Alessia watches him move with his usual athletic grace, his muscular backside pale against his tan.

She sighs as she's still coming back to earth.

He is an exceptional lover.

Not that she has any experience and no one to compare him to . . . but Caroline's words haunt her. *Promiscuous doesn't cover it. He's proof of the adage: Practice makes perfect.*

Alessia wraps herself in the duvet.

Maxim is *her* lover. *Her* husband. And only *hers.*

He said so . . .

That should be enough.

But that nagging voice persists. *For how long?*

Chapter Fourteen

The Thames's reflections flicker on the ceiling, taunting me as they've done over the years. I can't sleep, though Alessia is comatose beside me. I envy her ability to sleep, but we've made love twice this evening – my desperation driving me to take my wife, so she's exhausted. I want her safe and happy, and I want her to know that I worship the ground she walks on.

Hell, if she knew about Kit, would she leave me?

As much as I've tried to quell the thoughts, my brain continues to chew on the information that Caro sprung on me today, and it won't leave me alone. Carefully, so as not to wake Alessia, I ease myself out of bed, grab my phone and sweatpants from the sofa, and head out to the drawing room. There, I pull them on and stand at the window, staring blankly out at the night.

I've called my mother. Again. And she's not answered.

The woman is fucking useless.

She's the only one who may be able to shed light on this situation. Perhaps Kit talked to her? Confided in her? She thought the sun rose and set with Kit. They were close.

Sadly, I couldn't find a way to please Rowena when I was young.

Dude. Move on.

I'm tempted to call Maryanne, but I don't want to worry her, and she mentioned she was on nights this week – so she'll be busy right now. The woman works too hard, considering she doesn't have to.

Placing my fist against the cold glass, I lean my forehead against it, stare out at the darkness, and reflect on the day, starting last night with Alessia's meltdown in her sleep. How can I burden her with Caroline's revelation when she's still having nightmares? She doesn't need to know this . . . not yet, anyway. Especially as she's having doubts about me and my – what did she call it – *colourful* past.

The women.

I hope to God I've reassured her. I don't know what else I can do.

Despite the silent treatment earlier, my sweet wife has been the saving grace of today – joining her while she played *Claire de Lune*. Making love. And her cooking. This evening she made a delicious lamb and aubergine concoction. She's a magician in the kitchen, but I think her father was right; she's going to make me fat – though we burnt off some calories tonight . . . so, there's that.

A vision of Alessia on top of me, grasping my wrists, tipping her head back and crying out in ecstasy invades my thoughts, arousing my libido, and leaving me hot and heavy with need. I contemplate returning to bed, waking her, and losing myself in her again.

Mate. Let her sleep.

But these fleeting feelings of joy evaporate quickly. As I stare across the glimmering dark river to Battersea Park, I feel numb as my mind gnaws at the news about Kit.

Health-wise I'm fine – in fact, I've never felt better.

But is something awful going to afflict me in later life? Or did this genetic issue, whatever it was, solely affect Kit?

I keep returning to the same depressing theory. Is this why he was riding his motorcycle through the icy lanes? Was the news so devastating that he thought *Fuck it* and let rip on his Ducati, the turbocharged beast that was his pride and joy?

I have no idea.

And if the news was that bad, does that mean I'll suffer horribly? Will Maryanne?

Fuck.

Thank God for contraception.

Until we find out what's happening, I can't contemplate kids. Can I?

Shit. This uncertainty. This ignorance. This powerlessness. It's torture.

Nothing's changed.

My rational self tries to reassure me.

But that's not true. The path I thought I was set on has altered entirely.

Mate, you don't know that yet.

Hell.

I open my texts and notice the one that Caroline sent earlier.

You look good, Maxim.

You always do.

I'm sure this is nothing to worry about.

I ignore her compliment.

Can't sleep.

Keep thinking about Kit.

Me too.

Sorry about today.

You don't need to apologise.

Where's the Albanian?

Fuck off, Caro.

You make that sound offensive.

My beloved wife Alessia is asleep.

FFS! Chill. She's Albanian!

Good night.

Maxim, don't be like that.
In spite of the why, it was
good seeing you today.
I miss you.
Cx

What does that mean? In disgust, I toss the phone on the sofa, not wanting to deal with Caro's shit and wondering why I even texted her in the first place. Returning to Alessia, I slip into bed.

As I do, she stirs. 'Maxim,' she whispers sleepily.

'Hush. Go back to sleep, baby.'

She shuffles over, so I'm forced to put my arm around her, and she lays her head on my chest. 'I've got you,' she murmurs, fighting sleep.

A tangled knot of emotion forms in my throat as I feel her slip away and settle back into her dreams, and I've never felt as grateful for my wife as I do now.

My love. I kiss her hair and close my eyes as a knot of fear and regret forms in my throat. Will we make it through this? Whatever it is?

I breathe in her fragrance, and it's a balm to my misery.

I've got you. Those words, in her accent, float through my brain, soothing me, and I drift.

The following crisp, chilly morning, I walk to my doctor's, which is a few streets away from our flat, for my appointment and hopefully some answers. The brisk, efficient receptionist ushers me into his consulting room as soon as I arrive.

Dr Renton is wearing his usual sharp suit and red bowtie. In his sixties, with lank, thinning hair, he stands when I enter his office and waves me to a chair in front of his desk. 'What can I do for you, Lord Trevethick?' He gives me his familiar avuncular smile as he resumes his seat.

'My brother. Genetic counselling. What do you know?'

'Ah.' His bushy grey eyebrows shoot up his forehead – he's taken aback. He leans forward in his chair, and his eyebrows make the return journey as he frowns. Propping his elbows on his desk, he rests his chin on his hands. 'I can't help you, my lord.'

'What?'

'Your brother, for whatever reason, has decided not to impart information to you, and as his doctor, I cannot breach his privacy. I have a duty of care to him.'

My mouth falls open in disbelief. Feeling winded, I watch dumbfounded as he folds his hands in his lap and sits patiently, waiting for me to say something. 'Your response is unacceptable. My brother is no longer with us.'

'I'm sorry, Maxim. There's nothing I can do. As part of his genetic counselling, prior to being tested, your brother will have discussed the implications and whether or not to tell his immediate relatives.'

'But surely—'

'My hands are tied.'

'I've just got married.'

'Congratulations.'

'For fuck's sake, Renton.'

His blue eyes narrow, and his voice hardens. 'There's no call for that kind of language, my lord.'

I huff in frustration, and in my mind, I'm back in my House Master's office at Eton, being admonished for some minor deed.

Renton sighs. 'Do you have any health concerns?' He's changing tack.

What? 'No.'

'That's your answer. I suggest you put all this behind you and respect your brother's decision.'

'Did Kit kill himself because of his diagnosis?'

Renton blanches. 'Maxim, the late Lord Trevethick died in a dreadful accident.'

'Exactly. He won't know that you've told me! And what about your duty of care to me? I'm your patient too.'

'But you're not sick,' he says gently.

I glare at him, hoping to intimidate him into changing his mind, but as he sits back with his benevolent smile, I realise he's not budging.

Well, how bloody inconvenient is this?

A part of me admires that he's not willing to breach my brother's confidence, so I place a tight lid on my temper and change the subject. 'I'll need to register my wife here.' I sound petulant.

'I can't wait to meet her,' Renton says kindly. 'Will that be all, my lord?'

I get up to leave. 'I'm disappointed you can't help me.'

'I'm sorry to disappoint you, Maxim.'

My mood is bleak as the black cab trundles through the traffic on the way to the office. I'm furious at Renton. Perhaps it's time to find someone new – someone a little younger.

Someone less ethical?

Hell.

My phone buzzes with a text. It's my mother. Finally!

Just touched down at LHR.
Need sleep.
I'll call you later.

Fuck! No. I press Dial, and her number goes straight to bloody voicemail. 'Rowena. Call me. This is not a fucking request.' I hang up and glare out of the cab window. The bright, sunny morning seems to mock my mood.

My mother is driving me insane.

Why won't she talk to me?

As the cab pulls up outside the office, I take a deep breath and bring my irritation under control. I pay the driver and stride up the steps into the building.

Oliver has forwarded details of three properties that are either vacant or soon to be vacant for Alessia and me to consider. I peruse them at my desk, welcoming the distraction as I sip black coffee. One is a mews house that's smaller than my flat – so I disregard that immediately.

The other two have potential as family homes.

Hell.

I want kids – one day. Part of my job is to protect the family's legacy. But if there's something wrong with me, how can I consider having a family?

Yet, Renton asked me how I was feeling.

Maybe that was his coded way of saying I don't have anything to worry about.

Mate. Get a grip.

I push my fears about children aside and decide to stay hopeful.

It's time to move. We need the space. My wild single days are over.

Who knew I'd be content to stay home, eat home-cooked food, and make love to my wife?

It'll be good for Alessia too.

In a new place, we'll be able to forge our own path where there are no memories of my colourful and dissolute past. It's an unsettling idea, mainly because it's accompanied by a pang of lingering guilt.

Why?

I've not done anything wrong.

Have I?

I shake off the thought.

Looking through the details of the properties, the house on Cheyne Walk has a distinct advantage. At the end of the back garden, there's a mews house with a garage that can house two cars. We could use it for staff. I've not raised the issue of having help with Alessia yet, but it will mean that *that* part of her life will be history. I'll always have fond recollections of pink knickers and blue housecoats, but she'll be busy with other things – music school, with any luck. The additional advantage of the Cheyne Walk house is it's between my flat and Trevelyan House, where Caroline lives.

Perhaps I should ask Caro to swap. She could take my flat or another, smaller property. Trevelyan House is mine, after all.

No. It's too soon since Kit's demise to broach that subject.

Picking up the phone, I press Caroline's number.

'Hello, Maxim.' She sounds sniffy and aloof. Maybe it's because I scolded her via text yesterday.

I feign ignorance. 'Hi, what's wrong?'

'You're all over the press. And they've been calling here. About you. And Alessia.'

'Shit. I'm sorry. Just ignore them.'

'I am. You should do something. Perhaps host a sort of "coming-out" party for your wife. Invite everyone, and then you'll be done with all this fevered interest.'

The last thing I want or need is the press digging into our hasty marriage.

But I can't let Caro know that!

'That's not a bad idea.' I throw her off the scent.

'I could organise it for you!' she says enthusiastically.

Hmm . . . not sure how Alessia would feel about that.

'Let me think about it. I'm calling because it's crunch time with the Mayfair mansion block refurbishment. Do you want to do the interior design?'

Caroline takes a deep breath. 'Yes. I do. It will give me something to focus on and put me back in that world. I've missed it.'

'Good. I'm glad.'

'Besides, I might need the money,' she adds, sounding more like her usual spirited self.

'Caro, you have a huge trust fund and the stipend from the estate.'

She snorts, unimpressed, but neither one of us mentions Kit's will, and how he left her out of it.

Dude, don't go there.

'I'll get Oliver to call and deal with the details.'

'Oliver!' she says as if she's surprised.

'Of course. He can put you in touch with the developer. Okay?' What is her problem with him?

'Yes. Yes. You're right. Have you told Alessia about the letters?'

'Not yet. Have you spoken to Rowena?'

'No. Why?'

'She's avoiding me. I've left her countless voice messages, and she's not returning my calls.'

'Rowena . . . is Rowena.'

'True enough. Any luck with Kit's laptop? I've drawn a complete blank.'

'Even with Dr Renton?'

'He wouldn't tell me.'

'The tight-lipped old bastard!'

'Exactly.'

'No luck with the laptop. Fact is, Kit never gave me any of the safe combinations. Not for here or for the Hall. Why do you think that is?' Her voice wavers as she finishes her question, and I realise she's upset.

'I don't know. Kit was Kit . . . a bit like his mother.'

'Yes. He was . . .' Caroline's voice has dropped to a barely audible whisper, and I want to kick myself.

'I'll think about the party idea.'

'Do,' she responds, brightening. 'You know, you should let me take Alessia shopping.'

Oh, I'm not sure that's a good idea.

'Maxim, I told you, she dresses like a student.'

'Funny you should say that. I'm hoping to get her into college. It will help with her visa. That reminds me. Your stepmother—'

'Stepsow,' she corrects me.

'Isn't she a patron of the Royal College?'

'Yes. Ah. Music. For Alessia?'

'Yes. What do you think?'

'I think it's a good idea. Alessia is obviously hugely talented.'

'Well, I may need to lean on the Stepsow.'

Caroline snorts. 'Good luck with that. I've never known her to be helpful or amenable. I don't know what my father sees in her.'

Caro is always complaining about her father's wife.

'Did you attend etiquette lessons?' I change the subject.

'Of course I did. Kit insisted. He was a bit of a bore about it, actually.'

I gasp, shocked. *Kit? A bore?*

'Yes. Just after we got married.'

Kit insisted his wife sign up for etiquette lessons!

What a snob. I had no idea.

'Alessia wants to go.'

'It's a good idea. It'll give her some confidence. It did for me. The one I went to was great. In Kensington. I'll send you the details.'

'Thanks. And to be clear, this is Alessia's idea, not mine.'

'You're so woke, Maxim,' Caro grumbles. 'My offer stands. I'd be happy to take her to Harvey Nicks. With your credit card.' She cackles.

And I find myself smiling reluctantly. 'I'll talk to her.'

'Good. I need to make amends.'

'Yes, you do.'

Oliver knocks on the door and enters.

'Gotta go.' I hang up and look directly at him. 'I've spoken to Caroline. She's up for the interior design.'

'I'm glad that's settled. Here are the details of your mother's expenditure against the estate.' He hands me a spreadsheet, and the bottom line leaps off the page in all its profligacy.

What the fuck!

I glance at him in shock.

'Yes.' His lips are a thin line of disapproval.

'Is this part of her divorce settlement?'

'Here.' He hands me another document. 'I've highlighted the figures you need.'

I scan it quickly.

Wow. A disquieting void lodges in my stomach as I intrude on my parents' private affairs. Their divorce killed my father. He died of a broken heart, and I've never forgiven my mother for his death. 'This is more than double her allowance.'

'Yes, my lord.'

'Okay. I'll deal with this.'

'Good luck with that, my lord.' He gives me a sympathetic smile and exits.

I call my mother and get her voicemail again. 'Rowena. I'm about to cut off your access to estate funds. Call me.' I hang up, then call the bank and have a quick word about my mother with my bank manager.

Next, I text Maryanne.

Please ask your mother to call me.

I have left numerous messages.

All to no avail.

I need answers. And I'm stunned that my own mother won't do me the courtesy of returning my call. Life as I knew it hangs in the balance – all my hopes and vague dreams on hold.

Hell.

If this tactic doesn't work, I don't know what will.

Alessia has unpacked, cleaned, and put away all the new cookware she and Maxim ordered online from John Lewis. She's cleaned. Polished. Washed. Everything. The place is spotless. She's prepped dinner. She's practised several pieces on the piano. She's now sitting at Maxim's desk, poring over the computer comparing music courses, and making notes. As she considers the merits of the Royal Academy versus the Royal College, her eyes stray to Ticia Cavanagh's business card perched on the desk. She recalls the lawyer's shocked statement yesterday.

Others? Did they escape too?

Bleriana's sweet face, laughing at one of Alessia's jokes while they were in the back of that awful, stinking truck, rises in her mind. Perhaps Ticia could help find her. She's a lawyer. She would know. Wouldn't she?

Ignoring her conflicted feelings – this woman has had carnal knowledge of her husband – she fishes out her phone and dials her number.

'Ticia Cavanagh's office,' a male voice answers.

'Hello. Um. This is Alessia Trevelyan. I wanted to speak to Ticia Cavanagh.'

'I'll see if she's available.'

The line goes quiet but a moment later, Ticia answers. 'Lady Trevethick, what can I do for you?'

'Please, call me Alessia. Um . . . I'm, er . . .'

'Is it about your husband?' Cavanagh asks in a stilted breathy rush.

'No. No. It's not. I think . . . um . . . your . . . acq . . . acquaintance predates me.' Alessia cannot believe that she's discussing Maxim in this way. There's an awkward moment of silence, where Alessia hears Ticia inhale sharply.

'I think so too,' she says eventually, and her response is a relief.

To the matter in hand, Alessia.

'I am calling about the other girls who were trafficked with me. I want to find them. Well, one of them at least. If I can find the others, that would be good too.'

'I see. I'm not sure I can help, but what can you tell me?'

Alessia sits back in Maxim's chair and stares down at her notes. Ticia has given her the number of a private investigator her firm uses. They're discreet but expensive. She wants to call them; after all, she now has the means. But should she ask Maxim first? By rights, it is his money. Would he approve of the plan? She doesn't know. Perhaps, like Ticia, he would think it's impossible as Bleriana and the other girls could be anywhere in the country.

But Alessia has to try.

Also, it will give her *something* to do.

As much as she enjoys being in the apartment, she's beginning to feel a little claustrophobic. She needs to get out.

But should she tell her husband?

Her phone buzzes, and it's as if she's conjured Maxim to call her just by thinking about him.

'Hi,' he says, and the warmth in his voice heats her heart.

'Hi. How is work?' He left early this morning, and he was preoccupied with something. Alessia assumed it was his work.

'It's okay. I have a surprise for you. I'm going to text you an address. It's a short walk from the flat. I'll meet you there in half an hour.' She suspects he's grinning. He's excited about something.

'Okay,' she says, grinning back.

'Thirty minutes.' He hangs up, and a text appears on her screen. It's an address on Cheyne Walk, meaning she has long enough to make a phone call and begin her mission to find Bleriana.

I pace outside the house on Cheyne Walk to keep warm and glance up the street to see if I can spot Alessia. Our potential new home is set back behind the greenery of Chelsea Embankment Gardens, which means – provided Alessia likes this place – I won't have to suffer the watery reflections that occasionally torment me on my bedroom ceiling. I hope she likes it; I think it will serve our needs well.

Through the shrubbery, I catch glimpses of the Thames. Pausing, I breathe in a lungful of air, detecting the muddy tang of the river that's so grounding and familiar.

It's home.

When I look, Alessia is heading towards me down the street. Her face lights up when she sees me, and I jog to meet her.

'Hi.' I grab her hand. 'Come. I'm excited to show you something.'

Her answering smile lifts my spirits, and I usher her towards an iron gate. She gives me a questioning look, her curiosity piqued as I tap the keycode into the electronic lock. The gate swings open with a creaky protest, and we walk across the flagstones to the gleaming black front door topped by a splendid fanlight.

Maxim fishes out some keys from his pocket and unlocks the door. 'This could be ours if you like it,' he says and waves Alessia inside.

The whole house?

It must be four stories high!

They're met by a wide sweeping hallway that opens onto a stylish dining room and beyond into an extensive modern kitchen that's similar to the glass kitchen in Maxim's apartment. Through the sliding French doors at the end of the room, there's a neat, manicured backyard, and at the other end of the yard, what looks like another house.

'Yes. Two houses. We could make that the staff quarters.' Maxim points outside.

Staff!

'Oh,' says Alessia.

Upstairs there's a sweeping reception room that spans the whole length of the house, tastefully decorated in muted cream, beige, and taupe.

'We can redecorate,' Maxim says, his brow furrowed with what Alessia thinks is concern.

'It's lovely,' she says automatically.

Alessia's intimidated by the sheer scale of the house. There are five bedrooms, all with their own en suites. The principal suite comprises a large bedroom, a bathroom with two sinks – in marble – an egg-shaped tub, a shower big enough for four people, and two walk-in closets that would more than serve her and Maxim's needs.

'What do you think?' Maxim eyes her anxiously.

'You want to move here?'

'Yes. We need the space.'

'Five bedrooms?'

'You'd prefer something smaller?' He frowns.

'I had not thought somewhere so big . . . I suppose one day, we'll have children.' She flushes at the thought, though she doesn't know why.

'Yes. One day,' he says quietly and closes his eyes as if this is a painful idea.

'One day,' Alessia responds, wondering why this should be a painful thought for him. 'You do want children. Yes?'

He nods, but his eyes say something else. He's fearful.

Why?

'Could we put a piano in here?' Alessia asks brightly to distract him.

He laughs. 'Of course. I'm not leaving the baby grand behind. Let me show you the basement.'

Hand in hand, we walk back to the flat.

'Have you lived there before?' Alessia asks.

'No. I've never even been inside until today.'

'Do you like it?'

'Yes.' I squeeze her hand. 'Do you? We can make our own memories there.'

Alessia regards me with – awe, relief – I don't know, but she offers me a beautiful smile. 'Yes. It will be just us.'

We round the corner, and I'm relieved to see no paparazzi lingering outside the front of the building. We're yesterday's news.

As we head into the flat, my phone buzzes.

It's my mother. *Finally*.

Chapter Fifteen

'It's Rowena. I need to take this,' I mutter, and leaving Alessia to close the front door, I head into the privacy of our bedroom and answer the phone. 'Rowena. Thank you *so much* for returning my call.' My sarcasm is heavily laced through every word.

'Maxim. Your messages are insufferably rude. Why would I want to talk to you? And what the fuck do you mean, you've cut me off?'

Swearing now! My mother is in a snit.

'Exactly what I said. I rang you days ago, and you've not replied. *That's* insufferably rude.'

'Once you've learned to be a little more gracious when leaving messages, you'll receive a quicker response. You'll catch more flies with honey than vinegar, Maxim. Surely a man of your appetites understands that.'

What!

'Lord help the estate with you barking down the phone at everyone,' she continues.

'That makes you the fly in this analogy,' I snap. 'And it's only you that elicits that response, Mother. And I don't think you're one to preach about appetites!'

She inhales sharply. 'So you've cut me off to bring me to heel?'

'No. I've cut you off because you're overspending the allowance you're entitled to under your divorce settlement.' She's silent on the other end of the phone, and I know she's seething. 'Did you think I wouldn't notice? Perhaps Kit let you get away with it.' Again I don't get a response – and this isn't helping my cause. I take a deep calming breath in an attempt to bring my temper under control. 'But this isn't why I called. Did you know that Kit was seeing a genetic counsellor?'

There's an audible gasp on the other end of the phone. 'What?' she whispers, and I know by her quiet tone that she's been shocked into next week.

'Yes. I was hoping you could enlighten me as to why.'

'No.' She chokes back a gut-wrenching exclamation that makes my scalp tingle and my entire attitude shift.

'What do you mean no? What do you know?' I sound breathless.

'This is nothing to do with you, Maxim. Nothing. Just forget it.' She's curt and panicked.

'What do you mean?'

'Forget about it!' she shouts, and the line goes dead.

She's hung up on me!

She's never done that before, and she was *shouting*, which is completely out of character – she's normally so cool and detached. I press Redial, and the call goes straight to voicemail. I do it again, with the same result.

Something's wrong. Seriously wrong. I stare at my phone in a chasm of confusion.

What the fuck?

I phone Maryanne and get her voicemail. 'M.A., call me. The Mothership is behaving more irrationally than usual.'

As I slip my phone into my pocket, it buzzes.

I glance at the screen and answer. 'M.A.'

'Maxie. What the hell did you say to your mother? She's just slammed the front door as she went out.'

Bugger. I have to come clean with my sister.

'My mother! She's your mother too. And I didn't want to bother you with this, Maryanne.' I give her a brief explanation about the letters that Caro found from Kit's GP and the genetic counselling place, Dr Renton's refusal to shed any light, and now our mother's refusal too.

'And you didn't think to tell the only medically qualified person in this family?' Maryanne spits.

'I didn't want to worry you. I know you're busy.'

'Maxim! You are such an arse sometimes. What exactly did your mother say?'

'Basically, your mother said it's none of my business.'

'That's weird.'

'Exactly.'

'Oh,' Maryanne whispers as if she's just had a rather unappealing thought.

'What?'

'I'll call you back.'

'Maryanne—'

She's hung up.

What the hell?

The female members of my family are driving me crazy.

Alessia tries to quell her anxiety but it expands in her chest, causing her heart to race. What's happened? Why is Maxim taking a call from his mother in private? He's not a secretive man generally. Is he? But what does he not want her to hear? What does he have to hide?

She heads into the kitchen so she's not tempted to press her ear to the door and listen. To divert her thoughts, she busies herself with final preparations for dinner. But her mind turns to how preoccupied Maxim has been over the last couple of days.

Except in bed.

She frowns at the thought. She figured his absentmindedness was due to the surprise meeting with Ticia Cavanagh and Alessia's subsequent reaction. But maybe not. While they explored music colleges last night on the internet, he'd been distracted by something, so much so that she'd asked him if he wanted to continue. He'd reassured her that he did, but something was bugging him. It still is. She can feel it.

Maxim is leaning against the doorjamb, watching her, when she looks up from grating parmesan. He looks anxious. Bewildered even.

Oh no.

'What is it?' Alessia asks.

Maxim moves into the room and rakes a hand through his hair, leaving it tousled and unkempt, just the way Alessia likes it. But his eyes are wide with disbelief and confusion as if he's wrestling with some inner turmoil.

'What did your mother say?' Alessia prompts.

'She hung up on me.' He raises his hands in dismay. 'And I need answers from her . . .' His voice tails off, but he steps forward and brushes his knuckles over her cheek, the contact reverberating enticingly through her body. 'It's nothing for you to worry about.'

'But you're worried,' she murmurs.

His stance changes, his jaw tensing, and he rakes a hand through his hair again, his frustration apparent.

'Do you want to go and see her?'

'It's tempting. Rowena lives with Maryanne when she's in London. They share a townhouse in Mayfair. She bounces between there and an apartment in Manhattan. She's here at the moment.' He glances at his watch. 'Perhaps I could go and confront her.' But his mouth turns down and he shakes his head.

'What answers do you need?'

He blows out a breath. 'Honestly, don't worry about it. It's something Caroline showed me on Monday—'

'Caroline?' Alessia's immediately on high alert.

Maxim frowns, and his eyes widen – as if caught in headlights. 'Yes. She came to the office with some letters concerning Kit.'

'Oh.'

Caroline.

Why is she going to see Maxim at his office when Alessia's never been to his office? And Alessia knows it isn't jealousy that's bothering her – she doesn't want her husband alone with his sister-in-law.

His ex-lover.

Because, deep down, she doesn't trust Caroline.

Does she trust her husband? Well, she's only hearing about this visit that took place yesterday.

Alessia ignores the nagging voice in her head while Maxim's lips press together in an angry line and he closes his eyes. When he opens them again, he looks irritated.

'Alessia,' he says. 'This is nothing for you to worry about. Let's go out. I need a change of scenery. We'll eat out.' He sounds exasperated.

'Okay,' Alessia capitulates immediately. She can cook the lasagne tomorrow. Or freeze it.

Maxim narrows his eyes. 'We can stay in if you want to. You need to tell me what you want to do. This is a partnership.' He waves a hand between them, his tone terse.

Is he angry with her?

Alessia suddenly feels they're on the edge of some precipice, and she doesn't know what to say or do.

Why is he so agitated? He didn't tell her about Caroline. Or letters concerning Kit.

How is she supposed to feel about that?

But she can tell he's distraught about something, and she doesn't think it has to do with Caroline, and Alessia doesn't want to add to his worries.

'We can discuss the house,' he adds in a gentler tone.

She nods and instinctively reaches out and grabs his hand. 'Whatever's going on, you'll figure it out. You always do.' She steps into his arms and holds him close.

I'm touched by Alessia's faith in me, though I think it's misplaced. Yet her caress and her words are soothing – the warmth of them spreading through my chest as I gradually relax in her embrace. Holding her close, I kiss her hair, grateful she's with me. 'Both my mother and my sister are behaving strangely.'

'That sounds . . . um . . . frustrating,' Alessia says. 'We can go out. I'll go and change my clothes.'

'You look fine in jeans.' I stop, grab her hands, and raise them in mid-air as if we're about to begin a folk dance. I let my gaze sweep over her body, ignoring the familiar tightening below my gut.

Caro's right.

Alessia needs clothes fit for a countess. Not a student. 'Let's go shopping. You need clothes. Proper clothes.'

Alessia gapes at him.

'Yeah. Let's do that.' I check the time. 'Harvey Nicks should be open for another couple of hours.'

'But . . . but . . . I don't know where we would start.'

'There's a personal shopping service. We'll start there.'

And it will be a wonderful distraction from all this genetic bollocks.

Alessia's head is spinning. In less than ninety minutes, she's become the proud owner of a 'capsule wardrobe' with 'key pieces' that will see her through the next few months. The cost is staggering, but Maxim seems delighted, and deep down, so is Alessia. She'll no longer feel like a cleaner when standing beside Caroline.

Maxim scrawls the delivery address on headed notepaper for the personal shopper.

'These will be with you tomorrow morning, Mr Trevelyan.'

The young woman bats her lashes at Maxim, but he ignores her – and doesn't correct her about his title.

'Shall we go eat?' Maxim takes Alessia's hand.

'Yes. And thank you. For all this.' Alessia eyes the bags containing her new clothes and shoes.

'You don't have to thank me.' He frowns as if a monumental thought has just occurred to him. 'I want to provide for you.' He leans in and kisses her quickly. 'We'll go across the road to the Mandarin Oriental and have dinner there.'

Alessia grabs her new Saint Laurent tote, and hand in hand they head out of the store, with Maxim's words ringing through her head.

I want to provide for you.

Alessia is not sure how she feels about this. She wants to be more than a chattel handed from her father to her husband. Her brief bid for freedom when she first came to the UK was an attempt to work for herself. Alas, that failed. But she found Maxim. Except now, she's a little at a loss.

He wants a partnership.

What can she do to contribute to a partnership?

Maxim tightens his hold on her hand, distracting her from her thoughts, and weaves them through the traffic as they cross the road to the magnificent building that is the Mandarin Oriental Hyde Park. 'This way,' he says, and they walk towards The Aubrey restaurant.

Alessia's tongue pokes out between her lips in studied determination as she grips her chopsticks, and I remember the first time she used them, in Mustique. Chef had prepared a sushi and sashimi extravaganza, and with her on my lap, I'd wrapped my hand around hers as I demonstrated how to use them. As ever, she was a quick learner.

'You've remembered how to use the chopsticks.'

She flashes me a quick hopeful smile as she reaches for some hamachi.

'So you like the house?'

'How could I not like the house, Maxim? It's beautiful.'

'Good. Then I'll make arrangements to have us move in. But if you want it redecorated, we should do that before we move.'

'I like it how it is now. Perhaps we should live there before we decide if it needs decorating.'

'That sounds sensible.'

My phone buzzes. It's a text from Maryanne.

Mama is at the airport.
She's heading back to New York.

I give Alessia an apologetic glance and text back.

What? Why?

She didn't say.
She texted from the gate.

That's it. No explanation?

None!

What the hell?

She's only just left New York, and now she's on her way back.

'Excuse me,' I murmur to Alessia. I leave the table and press my mother's number as I walk into the vestibule. As I feared, her phone goes to voicemail.

'Mama, please. What's going on? What do you know? Is this serious? I just got married. I–I . . . *we* want children. Call me. Please.'

I'm tempted to head out to Heathrow and follow her to Manhattan, but I know I've missed the last flight out tonight. Maybe my plea will ignite a modicum of maternal feeling if she has any left.

Mate.

My mother is not renowned for her sentiment or her maternal feelings.

Fuck.

Perhaps Alessia and I should fly out to see her together?

Bugger. Alessia will need a visa.

I head back to the table, and she looks up. 'Okay?'

'Yeah. I called Rowena again and left a voicemail. She's returned to New York, so I won't hear from her this evening. Let's enjoy ourselves.' I take a swig of sake, and Alessia raises her small porcelain cup.

'Gëzuar, Maxim,' she says.

'Your good health, my dear wife.'

'In Japan, there is sake; in Albania, raki. What do the English have?'

'Gin, I suppose. There are many new distilleries popping up to quench the nation's thirst for English gin.'

She smiles. 'I would like to try this.'

I don't have any meetings in the morning. 'Okay. We can do that.'

It's midnight, and my wife has had too much to drink. I've seen her tipsy before when we were in Cornwall, and she took a tumble into the sea, but she's never been like this.

And it's my fault.

Alessia is new to drinking, and I should have kept a better eye on her. I bet she'll have a hangover tomorrow.

'Come on, princess. I've got you.' I hold her tightly to my side as we stagger out of Loulou's to a hail of flash photography and clamber into the cab. In the back seat, I direct the cabbie to take us home and keep an arm wrapped around my wife.

Alessia gives me a crooked smile. 'Maxshim.'

'I think you've had too much sake and gin, baby.'

'Yesh. I like the gin. But it is fun. Was fun,' she corrects herself. 'S'good to meet your friends.'

'I think you dazzled them.'

'You have many friends. Women too. How many have you had sexual . . . intercourse with?'

Whoa! 'What?'

'How many?' She gazes at me, dark eyes hazy and unfocused. She closes one and squints, trying to look serious.

Two. I think.

'Let's talk about this when we get home.'

When we started our evening, I didn't know we would end up at Hertford Street. But after these last few shitty days, it seems we both wanted to let off steam.

This much steam?

I pull Alessia closer and kiss her forehead. She raises her face to mine and puckers her lips, looking adorable.

How can I resist?

I offer her a quick peck on the lips.

'Why so many lovers, Maxshim? I don't understand,' Alessia says.

'Can we talk about this when you're sober?'

She considers my response. 'Yesh. I will not forget.'

Oh, I hope you do.

I'm worried about her line of questioning. I thought we had settled this the other day. She seems obsessed with my sex life prior to meeting her, and I don't know why. I didn't behave inappropriately with any of the women we met tonight. Did I? I was friendly enough. But just that – friendly, even with Natasha and Sophie, two one-night stands. I sigh and nuzzle Alessia's hair, wondering how to reassure my wife.

Maxim sits Alessia on the edge of the bed. 'Let's get you undressed.' He sinks to his knees and removes her boots.

Alessia reaches out, running her fingers through his hair. 'So soft,' she whispers.

Maxim removes her socks, then stands up and wrestles her out of her jacket.

'The photographs in here,' Alessia says and sways as she turns towards the nudes. 'You know these women?'

'Yes.' He tosses her jacket on the sofa.

'In the . . . um . . . biblical sense.'

Fuck.

Maxim grasps her chin, forcing her gaze on him. She squints so that he's in focus. 'Alessia, you've got to let this go. For your sanity and mine. I'll take these photos down. It was thoughtless of me to leave them here. I'll do it tomorrow.' He leans down and kisses her, his tongue warm and wet, and Alessia wraps her arms around his neck, tugging him onto the bed. He falls to her side, still in her arms.

In the light from the bedside lamp, she studies him.

Her husband.

Her lover.

Her lothario.

His eyes gleam, a brilliant emerald, the pupils dilating. She runs her fingers over his stubble and traces the soft cushion of his lips, which part as he inhales.

'I love you,' she whispers. 'But I don't want to be a chattel.'

'Chattel?' His eyes cool. The fire in them doused with doubt.

'You want a partnership. What do I bring to our partnership?'

He gasps. 'Everything.' The word is a prayer.

Alessia cups his cheek – her throat suddenly raw.

'Hey. What's this about?' Maxim peers into her eyes, and his beloved, concerned face blurs through her tears. 'Alessia, what's wrong?'

She shakes her head as the question spirals through the drunken haze in her mind.

So many women.

'Tell me,' he pleads, and when she doesn't answer, he continues. 'Oh, my love, we'll figure this out. It's going to be okay. Have faith.' He kisses her forehead. 'I love you.' He tugs her into his arms and holds her.

The knot in her throat gradually dissolves, and her anxiety recedes as she falls into a drunken sleep.

Alessia's breathing settles, and I know she's fallen asleep, but I don't move. I don't want to disturb her. Instead, I stare at the ceiling, mystified. What's brought about her emotional outburst? Is it the drink talking? I thought she was happy. But have I been deluding myself? I've been so hung up on my own shit that I haven't thought about how she's been settling into her new life in London. She's been present and giving, consoling me while I deal with my mother and Kit's mystery genetic issue – even though she knows nothing about it. And I'm loath to tell her because it'll add to her anxiety.

And she might have second thoughts about us.

Dude. Don't go there.

Being cooped up in the flat may be affecting her. It's spotless – that hasn't gone unnoticed – but she needs more. She needs friends. She's here on her own, isolated, and only has me.

Fuck. Mate.

Tomorrow we'll start applying to the music conservatoires in London and find a finishing school for etiquette lessons. She'll be less isolated and have more to do. If that's what's bothering her, that should help.

It's you, dude. You're bothering her.

Your fucking fucking.

I sigh. Caroline spilling the beans didn't help. I understand why Alessia is sensitive about her. By revealing our sexual past, Caro sowed doubt in Alessia's mind about my fidelity, and then we met Leticia, which only worsened matters. I rub my face, trying to forget that awkward moment. Alessia has been confronted with my sexual antics since she's known me.

I blow out a breath, and a thought occurs to me. Maybe it's our cultural differences that she's finding difficult. One aspect I observed of life in Kukës was the casual segregation of men and women.

Maybe that's it. She doesn't understand that here people can fuck *and* be friends.

Why so many lovers?

It's a good question, and I think this is the answer. Sex, here, is a recreational activity for many, including me. It still is, but it's so much more satisfying with my wife.

Why is that?

Love?

Yes. Love.

Avoiding intimacy has been a way of life for me, and it was never an issue until I found Alessia and fell in love.

There. That's it. And she doesn't understand. I grin. Relieved. I think I've cracked the code to her anxiety.

Gently I untangle myself from my girl, stand, and strip.

Before I head into the bathroom, I remove the two photographs from my wall and place them in the walk-in wardrobe.

Shame. I like these photographs.

Some of my best work.

And yes, I knew them both in the biblical sense, or should I say recreational sense?

When I emerge from the bathroom, I feel much calmer. Carefully I undo Alessia's jeans and gently peel them off. I drape the duvet over her, clamber into bed, and snuggle up to her sleeping frame. 'What are you thinking about, baby?' I kiss her hair, and she mumbles my name.

Me?

The thought pleases me far more than it should.

Maybe she's overwhelmed by being here. A new life with an ex-player – a rake.

Maybe that's what this is about.

She needs to understand that all that is behind me.

Yeah. That's it.

I close my eyes, and with Alessia's scent invading my senses, I drift off to dream about my love.

Chapter Sixteen

The smell of fresh coffee rouses me from my beguiling dream.

Alessia.

Blue nylon housecoat.

SpongeBob pyjama bottoms.

Pink knickers.

Opening my eyes, I find her standing beside the bed dressed in cream silk, looking her usual beautiful self – except for her uncertain smile. 'Good morning,' she says as she sets a cup on the bedside table.

'Morning, my love. Thank you for the coffee.'

'It is after 9:30.'

'Oh dear, I've slept in.' I rub my face and haul myself to a sitting position, and she sits on the bed beside me. 'How are you feeling?'

'Okay. I had a headache.'

'Better now?'

She nods. 'I'm sorry. I did not mean to get so drunk. I hope I didn't embarrass you.'

'Sweetheart, you do not need to apologise. You were fine.' I'm horrified that she feels the need to express remorse. 'My friends adored you. How could they not?'

'It was good to meet them.'

'I hope you liked them. I have to confess that used to be me most nights – drunk in a club, somewhere. Meeting you has probably saved my liver.'

Her eyes soften. 'I liked your friends. They were entertaining. And I liked the gin. Maybe too muchly.' She looks down at her hands in her lap.

'You did? Good. Maybe friends and gin in moderation next time.' I run my fingers beneath her chin, turning her face to mine. 'You said some things last night. I've been consumed with my own problems, and I haven't asked you if everything's okay or if there's anything I can do to make settling into this new life easier for you.'

'We have only been back from our honeymoon for a few days.'

'I know. But still.'

She swallows and steels herself as if garnering some inner strength, and I don't know what she's going to say. From nowhere, my apprehension beats fast, furious wings in my gut.

'Maxim, I want to see if I can find one of the girls who was trafficked with me.'

My relief is instant. 'Oh. Okay,' I respond cautiously. 'But how the hell would you start to search for someone who could be anywhere?'

'I spoke to Ticia Cavanagh.'

Shit. The apprehension returns full force.

'And?'

She smiles, and I think she's reading me like the open book I am. 'We did not talk about you. Though maybe we should . . . um, compare notes?'

She's teasing me! 'Alessia!' I don't know if I'm warning her to back the fuck off or congratulating her on her gumption.

'She gave me a number of a private investigator,' Alessia says hurriedly, 'who might be able to help. I need to find her.'

I stare blankly back at her as my anxiety returns.

This seems an impossible task.

'Bleriana's only seventeen,' she says, her voice low.

'Oh, God. That's awful.' I close my eyes, not wanting to wrap my head around the horror that Alessia and her young friend have endured. 'Did she run when you did?'

'I think so. I ran for my life. I didn't have time to check . . .' The words trail off as if this is a failing.

No!

I haul her into my lap and wrap my arms around her. 'I didn't mean to imply – God, Alessia. I'm so glad you escaped. Heaven knows what would have . . .' My words die as horrific scenarios scroll through my head. 'Look, I don't think it's a good idea that you get involved in that gruesome world again. Even from a distance. I'd never forgive myself if something happened to you because of your search.'

She stiffens in my arms.

'I'm not going to lose you again.' I tighten my grip on her and bury my nose in her hair. 'Please.'

'But—'

'No. Alessia.' I breathe in her scent. 'The answer's no. It's too big a risk. I'll talk to Tom. His company does PI work too. I'm not sure if they locate missing persons, but perhaps he can help.'

She pulls away, her dark, dark eyes luminous, and I don't know if she'll fight me on this. 'Thank you,' she says and wraps her arms around my neck. 'If Tom can find her –' Her breath is warm against my throat, but her voice catches. 'I . . . I was lucky. And I feel guilty. I managed to escape.'

My blood curdles in my veins. 'Oh God. No. Never feel like that. Jesus, Alessia.' If those thugs had caught her. I close my eyes again, imagining all the circles of hell – and Alessia in the infernal heart of the worst of them. 'Don't ever feel like that, sweetheart. Ever. I'm not asking. I'm telling you. Those men were monsters.' I cradle her head in my hands, and she turns her eyes to mine.

'Okay,' she whispers, and after a beat, her fingers twist in my hair, and she draws my lips to hers.

'My coffee is cold.' I sweep my nose down Alessia's as I lie beside her, spent.

She giggles. 'I can make you some more. And some breakfast.'

'No. Don't go. I'll make it. And some for you.' I kiss her cheek.

'No!' Her fingers tighten in my hair, scraping my scalp. 'Don't go.' She presses her fantastic breasts into my chest and winds her leg around my hip.

Oh boy . . . again!

I stand beneath the shower and wash away my hangover, feeling more settled.

It's the sex.

Twice in one morning – I can get on board with that.

Alessia is voracious. *Who knew?* I grin into the water cascading over me.

She seems much happier today, and my mind turns to her emotional state last night. I think she's suffering from being cooped up, a lack of friends, and her survivor's guilt. Maybe it's reminders of my old life too.

Alessia and I are still getting to know each other. But she's usually so self-contained and stoic, so her outburst was a surprise.

I'm glad we talked, and I'll call Tom today and get the ball rolling on what's probably a futile search – but for Alessia's sake, and her friend's sake, we can try.

I turn off the shower, stagger out, and inspect my chin, ready to shave.

No. Not today.

I leave the stubble – my wife likes it – and head back into the bedroom with a towel wrapped around my waist. The bed is already made.

You can take the girl out of Albania . . . I smile.

I'm glad she's out of Albania.

With me.

But I'm not sure what to think of her mission. Is it wise? I imagine it'll be fruitless. How can you find a trafficked illegal immigrant?

We can try from a safe distance because there's no way I'm letting anyone pull her back into that hideous underworld.

I need to keep her safe.

Oliver is running through the monthly profit-and-loss accounts for each of the individual estates. We're in surprisingly good shape, and I know my instinct to leave everything well alone until I understood how it all works was a good one.

'So we're not making massive profits on any of the houses, but it's enough,' Oliver says.

'I've been thinking of a way to plough these profits back into each of the estates.'

Oliver raises a brow, surprised by my rare display of entrepreneurial spirit, so much so that I want to laugh. 'I'm thinking gin, Oliver. Trevethick gin.'

'Now, that is an interesting idea.'

'I'll talk to Abigail Chenoweth at Rosperran about her potato crop. And Michael at the Hall about the north pasture barn.'

Oliver nods. 'That could be a good place for a still.'

Alessia presses the intercom on the anonymous-looking door in a backstreet in Covent Garden that bears the discreet sign: MPPI. Maddox Peacock Private Investigators. 'Hello,' answers a gruff, disembodied voice.

'Hello. My name is Alessia Dem . . . Trevelyan. I have an appointment.' She didn't have the courage to tell Maxim she'd already made the appointment to see the private investigator.

What harm could it do?

Two companies searching for Bleriana might yield better results.

She knows she's acting in defiance of her husband, and she feels guilty, but as Maxim himself once told her – it's better to ask for forgiveness than permission.

She did ask for permission.

He said no.

An emphatic no.

O Zot. The door buzzes and Alessia steps into a grubby hallway and heads up the flight of stairs. At the top is a waiting area with cushioned armchairs and a coffee table. The door to one of the offices opens, and a tall, well-built man with a shock of blond hair comes out to greet her. 'Alessia Trevelyan, I'm Paul Maddox.' He has bright blue eyes that coolly assess her as his large hand engulfs hers in a firm handshake.

Alessia swallows, trying not to feel intimidated.

'Please, come this way.' He ushers her into a small, cluttered office that his broad shoulders seem to fill and directs her towards a chair in front of a wooden desk piled with papers. Alessia takes the seat and waits for him to sit down. 'What can I do for you, Mrs Trevelyan?' he asks as he glances at her wedding ring, and she knows he's appraising her. She's glad she's worn her new tailored trousers, cream silk blouse, black jacket, and Gucci loafers.

'I'm looking for a missing person and want to trace a family.'

'Are these related?'

'No. I'm trying to find a girl who was trafficked to England from Albania, and I'd like to trace the family of an English woman. Her name was Virginia Strickland.' From her purse, she pulls a small faded black-and-white picture of her grandmother as a young woman – in pearls, a dark sweater with short sleeves, her head cocked to one side, her smile lighting up the frame. She hands it to Maddox.

'I see, Mrs Trevelyan. Two cases. Let me take some notes.'

After my meeting with Oliver, I call Tom and ask him if Alessia's mission to track down her friend is a fool's errand or if it's possible to find someone after they've been trafficked into the country.

'Well, this is a challenge,' Tom says after I've explained the situation, and I can almost hear the cogs in his brain whirring. 'How many women?' he asks.

'I believe there were six, including Alessia.'

'Dreadful business.'

'Yes. Alessia tried to get the others to run when she did.'

'Where was this?'

'All I know is that it was a motorway service station.'

'It's possible we could track the girls down – tall order, mind. I need more information. I can make inquiries with the police. I have a contact. You know him. Remember Spaffer from school?'

'How could I forget him?' Charlie Spafford had been a fearsome bully. No wonder he joined the plod.

'He's a high-flyer at the Met. I'll call him. I think he's with the organised crime division. He may know something about the traffickers you apprehended in Cornwall. I'll see if there are any leads that may direct us to find the girls.'

'Sounds like a plan, but I don't want your inquiry to lead back to Alessia.' We don't need Sergeant Nancarrow breathing down our necks.

'I hear you, old boy. I had no idea that poor Alessia's experience was so traumatic.'

'She needs to be kept out of this. She was here illegally.'

'Understood. I want to talk to her, though. If she has any recollection of where she was, we could work out which service station and some of the girls may still be in that area.'

'I'll talk to her.'

'Roger that.'

I roll my eyes. You can take the man out of the army. 'Thanks, Tom.' I end the call and check my phone for the millionth time for any messages. There's still nothing from my mother.

What the hell is wrong with her?

And I know deep in my bones it's because she despises me. She always has. It was always Kit. Kit. Kit with her.

I used not to care, but now it cuts deep, and I wonder what I did when I was young to inspire such contempt.

Fuck it. To hell with her.

There are, however, texts from Caroline.

You went to Loulou's without me!

How do you know?

You're all over the Daily Fail.

WTF!!!

Yes. Staggering into the night.
Drunken Earl with Mystery Wife?

Hell.

Just ignore them.

They're still calling here.
Blake is deflecting.

Good.

I miss going out.
How long do I have to stay in purdah?

That's up to you.

I've had an invitation to
Dimitri Egonov's party.

It's on Saturday.

Are you going?

I've always thought he's a bit dubious.

His father is anyway.

Are you ready to face the world again?

My phone rings. It's Caro.

'What?' I ask.

'I think I'm ready. It's sweet of you to care.'

Shit. In a fraternal way, Caro! I don't want her to get the wrong idea.

'I'm not sure I could bear another night in,' she continues. 'And Dimitri knows how to throw a party. Everyone will be there.'

'I'll think about it.'

'In fact,' she says with the enthusiasm of a new idea, 'this might be the perfect place to launch Alessia.'

'She's not a boat!'

Caroline laughs. 'Listen, Maxim. Everyone will be there. It's perfect. And she'll need a new frock. Something ultra-glamorous. Please let me take her shopping!'

'Caro, I'm not about to unleash society on Alessia.'

'She'll be fine. Sink or swim, to keep your boat analogy.'

'Boats don't swim. They float.'

'She'll float. She'll fly! She is lovely. I'll give you that.'

That she is. It's not a bad idea. And Alessia needs friends – it's a perfect place to make connections. 'I'll talk to her.'

'You can't keep her hidden away forever. You're not ashamed of her, are you?'

'Fuck off, Caro. Of course not.'

'It will be fun. And I need some fun. And mention the shopping!'

'Well, I think she's lonely. So I'll think about it. I've got to go.'

Are you okay?' Alessia asks when Maxim leans oh-so-casually against the doorjamb of the kitchen. This is a habit of his that Alessia enjoys – he likes leaning there and watching her, and she can admire him; his hair is rumpled, his chin stubbled – he's a welcome sight. This evening, he's just returned from work, and his face is tense, his jaw strained.

'I'm fine. Just another day at the office.' He smiles, and Alessia snakes her arms around him and tilts her face up for a kiss. Maxim obliges willingly, his mouth firm and demanding against hers.

'That's better,' he whispers.

She grins. 'Dinner is in the oven.'

'How was your day?'

'It started very well. Very well indeed.'

'Why, Lady Trevethick, whatever do you mean?'

The heat rises in Alessia's cheeks, and she bats her eyelashes. 'I think you know.'

'I do.' Maxim kisses her again – longer this time, so they're both breathless when he pulls away. He rubs her nose with his. 'Seriously. How was your day?'

Tell him.

Alessia debates whether to tell him about Paul Maddox, but because he's brooding about something, and she's not sure how he'll react if he finds out she went against his wishes, she distracts him with a question. 'It was good. Did you hear from your mother?'

His face shutters immediately, and Alessia knows this is what's vexing him. 'No,' he says. He blows out a breath. 'But I did speak to Tom. He wants to talk to you. About your friend.'

'Bleriana?'

'Yes. Call him after dinner.'

'I can call him now.'

'I'll text you his number.'

It's just after 9:00 p.m., and Alessia and I are sitting at my desk, staring at the computer. I feel like I've taken my common entrance exams again, but it's been a welcome distraction. We've signed Alessia up for an intensive week-long social etiquette course at the academy that Caroline recommended.

'Caroline did this course too?'

Alessia was incredulous.

'Yeah. Kit insisted.' I'd shrugged, still shocked that Kit would insist on such a thing.

And we've completed four applications to music conservatoires in London. Her favourite is the Royal College of Music because it's within walking distance.

'I don't know if my English will be good enough,' Alessia says.

'You'll be fine. And let's hope you can start in the summer term, after Easter. You said your mother was going to send your exam certificates.'

She chuckles. 'Yes. My Matura Shtetërore. I should have packed them. I didn't know I'd need them.'

'You got top marks in English, which will help.' I blow out a breath, a rosy sense of achievement glowing in my chest. 'Now that this is done, what would you like to do?'

'It's late.'

'Not that late. I know what I want to do.'

He grins, boyish and breezy, and taking her hand as he rises from his desk, he moves towards the coffee table in front of the sofa and grabs one of the remotes. He's not been this upbeat since their honeymoon.

'Sit,' he says, and Alessia settles on the couch beside him.

We're going to watch TV?

Alessia is surprised. They've never watched television together, even in Kukës. The large flatscreen pops to life with an electronic hiss of static, but instead of a TV programme, there's a strange white logo on a black background.

'Here.' Maxim hands her a game console controller.

She frowns up at him.

'*Call of Duty*?' he prompts.

She smirks. 'I thought that's what we always do?'

Maxim laughs. 'Duty?' he scoffs in mock horror, then pounces on her so she's suddenly prone on the sofa, his weight pressing her into the soft cushions. He grins. 'Duty, Lady Trevethick?'

She giggles. 'Well, duty and pleasure.'

He kisses her quickly and sits up. 'Your English is getting so much better. No. I fancy playing a game that I know I can win. It's what my ego needs right now.'

Alessia laughs and sits up beside him. 'How do you know you can beat me?'

'I didn't see a PS4 in Kukës. And you're holding the console upside down. Here, I'll teach you.'

Games! He plays video games! This is a side of Maxim she's not seen before.

'Okay?' he asks, green eyes bright but less sure.

'Yes!' Alessia declares enthusiastically because she's never played computer games before.

'Right. Bring it!' Maxim means business.

'So, how's doing your duty going so far?' I whisper against the soft skin of her inner thigh.

'Maxim. Please.' She tugs my hair, trying to shift me from between her thighs.

I grab her hands and hold them fast against her. 'Oh, no.' I blow gently on her clitoris and follow with my tongue, provoking the greedy, swollen little bud between her thighs. She garbles my name in a cry, and it's a gratifying, cock-hardening sound. It's such a heady thrill to tease and tantalise my passionate wife. I stop because I think she's close and trail wet kisses over her plucked labia along the edge of her soft, warm belly.

'Please. Maxim.' It's a desperate cry.

I nip her hip bone, kiss the sweet well of her navel, and then skim my lips up her body, to her peaked breasts, where her nipples are hard and ready, begging for me.

'Oh, Alessia,' I whisper in awe as I take each in turn, sucking and tugging until they're straining for the ceiling, and she's squirming beneath me, her hips moving in a reckless counterpoint. I rear up over her, and her dazed eyes meet mine, full of longing and love. I release one of her hands and slowly sink two fingers inside her.

Ah! She's so wet and ready for me.

'Baby,' I murmur as she hungrily tilts her pelvis to meet my fingers. She's so close. I jerk my fingers free and quickly flip her over onto her stomach. Grabbing her hips, in one swift move, I tug her onto my straining cock.

'Ah!' she cries and pushes back against me, wanting and taking all of me.

Oh, my thirsty girl.

Doing her duty.

I lose myself, over and over in my wife, and time and space are suspended. It's just us. Now. In this moment of love. She lets free another garbled cry and stiffens beneath me as she peaks. Her body pulsing around me as she rides out her orgasm. I don't stop. I want it all. Onward. Rocking into her. Pulling her back against me. Driving onward and onward until I can't hold on any more.

I come. Loudly. Calling out her name and collapsing on top of her.

Engulfing her with my body.

Holding her fast as we both return to the present.

Duty done.

I'm slippery and sticky from our combined sweat. *Yes*. I'm also bone tired.

Fuck, that was good.

I kiss her cheek as she pants beneath me.

'Wow . . .' I whisper in her ear.

Her lips lift in a tired grin. 'Yes. Wow.'

'Duty done, baby.' I ease out of her, enjoying the slip and slide of it all. Her back. Her arse. Her sex.

Yeah.

Wow.

Alessia blows out a breath and gives me a sleepy smile. 'You have also fulfilled your duty.'

I nuzzle her ear. 'I'm glad to hear it. And I got to beat you at *Call of Duty*. I'd call that a good day.'

'Tomorrow, I will practice. Then we shall see.'

I laugh. 'God, I love you.' And in the light of the little dragon, she closes her eyes with a most satisfied smile on her face, and it makes me feel that I have some worth, after all.

Chapter Seventeen

Alessia's fingers rest on the keys, the last of Bach's fugue ringing through the room – the bold blues dissipating as the notes fade. If – and it's a big if – she gets an interview at one of the music colleges in London, she'll have to audition. She's been playing through her repertoire for the last two days and trying to decide what would be appropriate. Maxim thinks the Beethoven *Moonlight Sonata* third movement would *crush it*. She smiles, recalling how bright-eyed and sincere he looked as he uttered those words.

Alessia wants to crush it.

Completely.

The thought of studying in London is one she'd never contemplated before. She's excited, and her parents are thrilled, but she doesn't want to fail; she wants Maxim to be proud of her. Next week she'll start the etiquette course that Caroline recommended. It confounds Alessia that Caroline, who's so poised and elegant, had to attend such a course. She always imagined that her gentility was innate. Alessia hopes she'll learn such propriety too, enabling her to move seamlessly in the circles that Maxim inhabits.

Her smile fades.

She wishes she knew what she could do to help her husband. Maxim is still distracted and frustrated by his mother not returning his calls. He's reassured her that it's nothing for her to worry about, but she does. Alessia loves him and wants to help. She finds his relationship with his mother unfathomable. She's sure Maxim loves his mother, but does he like her? She thinks not. And her instinct is that Rowena feels the same antipathy towards Maxim.

Why?

Perhaps his mother will speak to him today and put him out of his misery.

Alessia checks her phone to see if Maxim has texted her – there's nothing, but an email from Paul Maddox appears in her inbox. Her scalp tingles, and butterflies flutter in her stomach.

He has information about her grandmother's family.

Already?

With trembling fingers, she dials his number.

Maxim. Max!'

'Sorry. What?' I look up from my desk to find Oliver standing in the doorway.

'May I come in?'

'Of course.'

Fuck. Dude. Pay attention.

'I have some brochures here for distilling equipment as requested. I have a favourite. Let me know what you think. There are many, many rules and regs to overcome, but nothing insurmountable. My second question relates to the Cheyne Walk property, and if you wanted it decorated before you move in?'

'It looked like it had been newly decorated.'

'It was. Ready for the next tenants.'

'Alessia's happy with it, though I think in time she might want something less . . . beige.'

Oliver laughs. 'True. Do you have a move-in date?'

'Not yet. Soon, I suppose.'

'Anytime is good, Maxim.'

'I'll talk to Alessia. I should bring her here to meet you all.'

'You should.' He nods. 'We'd all be delighted to meet the new Lady Trevethick. Incidentally, the press are still calling.'

'They'll get bored.'

'They've been at it every day.'

I shrug. 'I want to keep Alessia out of the limelight. I'm sure she'll be uncomfortable with any press scrutiny.'

'Hmm, perhaps. Or you could show her off to the world, and then the press might leave you alone.'

'Maybe,' I mutter, knowing that Caro is of the same opinion.

'Maxim, are you okay?' he asks as he places the brochures on my desk.

'Yes. Fine. Thanks, Oliver.'

He nods, but his brow creases with concern as he exits.

I glance at my phone. Still nothing from my mother. How can she be so callous?

I text her once more, switching to super-grovelling mode.

Mama, please.

Call me.

I'm begging you.

I'm not seeing the genetic counsellor who advised Kit for another week, and I need to know. *Am I a walking time bomb or not?*

'Virginia Strickland's remaining relative was easy to trace. She has a brother. He's still alive. I'll email you everything we have,' Paul Maddox says.

'Thank you,' Alessia replies, feeling a little light-headed. She hadn't expected this to be so fast. 'Do you have any information about Bleriana?'

'No, Mrs Trevelyan. Not yet. Finding her is far more tricky. But, as her traffickers are in custody and there's an ongoing criminal investigation, we're hopeful that we might get a lead from our contacts in the police.'

Alessia remembers Tom mentioning he also had a contact in the police. She shudders.

Dante and Ylli.

Still in custody.

Thank God.

She blows out a breath. 'Okay.'

'I'm going to close off the Virginia Strickland case. But we'll continue with the hunt for your friend. I'll send you an itemised invoice, but we have enough funds in the retainer you gave us to last for a week or two – depending on how our inquiries go.'

'Thank you.'

'I'll be in touch when I have further news.' He hangs up, and Alessia checks her email. Sure enough, there's one from Maddox with a PDF attachment. She clicks it open and reads. There's information about her nana's parents but, most importantly, her grandmother's older brother.

TOBIAS ANDREW STRICKLAND

Date of Birth:	4th September 1952
Age:	66
Address:	The Furze House, Kew Green, Kew, Surrey, TW9 3ZJ
Marital Status:	Single
Employment:	Emeritus Professor of Music. Worcester College. Oxford.

Alessia has a great-uncle who was a professor of music! Musical ability must run in her family. Virginia had taught Shpresa the piano, and they both taught her. Alessia quickly checks Google Maps and finds that Kew is only a few miles from Chelsea. As she studies the map, a frisson of recognition travels up her spine.

Kew is over the river from Brentford.

Where she had lived for a couple of months.

He was so close!

She's stunned.

All that time when she was worried about where she could live, and he was just across the river.

She should visit. Introduce herself. Tell him about his niece in Albania. Her mother will be delighted. Surely. She hugs her phone.

Should she tell Maxim?

Perhaps she should meet Tobias first.

Alessia skips over to the piano, sits down on the stool, and starts on her favourite prelude in celebration.

Caroline texts me when I'm in a cab on the way home.

I'm taking Alessia shopping tomorrow.

No ifs or buts.

Warn her.

She might not want to go shopping!

Maxim, she's female.

She'll want to go shopping.

And I'm not giving her a choice.

You are coming to Dimitri's.

Hell. Caro is not going to let this go. But on the other hand, Alessia needs to get out more and meet people, and frankly, after the past week, so do I. It would be a welcome distraction to see everyone. No doubt Tom and Joe will be there. Oliver suggested I show her off to the world. This would be one way of doing it.

Okay!
We'll come.

Great!
I'll be there in the morning.
Tell Alessia.

Caro is so bossy, and I don't know if Alessia will be up for this. After Caroline's behaviour before the wedding in Kukës, it could go either way. But Caro is a force of nature, so maybe she'll prevail. I need to warn my wife.

My phone buzzes again with a number I don't recognise. 'Trevethick,' I answer.

'Lord Trevethick. My name is Donovan Green. I'm a journalist for the *Weekend News*.'

'How did you get this number?'

'Lord Trevethick, is it true that you married your cleaner, Alessia Demachi?'

His question winds me as if his fist has slammed into my solar plexus. I hang up without making a comment. How the hell did the slimy bastard get my number? And how did he get Alessia's name?

My phone rings again, but I block the number.

Fuck a duck.

What am I to make of this? I'd better warn Alessia's parents that some stringer may turn up on their doorstep looking for a story. I know Shpresa will stay quiet, but my father-in-law, who, let's face it, likes a little drama and attention, might not be so taciturn.

Maybe I should throw these vultures a bone.

Tomorrow night, Alessia and I will be guests at Dimitri Egonov's annual spring bash, which will be attended by the great and the good and the not so good, so there'll be no doubt. The world will know that we're married, and the Grimy Slimy *Weekend News* can fuck off.

The cab stops outside my building, and it's a relief that there are no reporters or paparazzi outside. I pay the driver and hurry inside, anxious to see my wife.

Alessia wraps languid limbs around me as we both return to earth. I nuzzle the special pulse point beneath her ear and move over onto my side, taking her in my arms. 'You are the world to me,' I murmur as I hold her close. It's early Saturday morning, and I want to spend the whole morning getting lost in my wife.

The buzzer from the building intercom sounds.

'What the hell?' I grumble.

Is it the press?

'Can we ignore them?' Alessia whispers against my neck, her breath tickling the fine hairs there. The buzzer sounds again, and this time a garbled, disembodied voice echoes through the hallway from the intercom.

'Bugger.' I sit up.

Who the hell is that?

'Do you think it's that reporter?' Alessia is wide-eyed with alarm.

'I don't think so.'

The buzzer sounds again, and I clamber out of bed and wander naked into the hall to answer the intercom. 'Hello,' I grunt into the speaker.

'Hi. It's me.'

'Caro. What gives?' *Shit!* I forgot to mention Caroline's plan to Alessia last night. I'd been too distracted by the journalist.

'I'm here to take Alessia shopping. I told you. Let me in.'

Shit. I haven't broached this with Alessia. I press the door release and pad back into the bedroom, where Alessia is up and draped in the quilt.

'Caroline is on the way up,' I mutter as I hunt for my jeans. 'She wants to take you shopping. Do you want to go?'

'Shopping for what?'

'Clothes.'

'I have clothes.'

'For the party tonight?'

'Party?'

Hell. I'd forgotten this too! 'We're going to a party. An acquaintance. That's if you want to.'

'Okay,' she says, but her eyes are wide with uncertainty.

'It should be fun. Go shower. I'll entertain Caroline.' I zip up my jeans.

The front doorbell buzzes, and Alessia gives me a hesitant, unreadable look as she hurries into the bathroom. I pad out to the front door holding a T-shirt.

'Good morning, Maxim,' Caro says brightly, offering her cheek for a quick peck. I oblige, then drag on my T-shirt to stop her from checking out my torso. 'You're only just getting dressed? Did I interrupt you shagging?'

'Fuck off, Caro.'

'Yes. I'd love a coffee. I'll make it.' She breezes into the kitchen, leaving me standing barefoot in the hallway.

I follow her in.

'Where's Alessia?' she asks.

'Showering. And black. No sugar, please.'

'I know how you take your coffee,' she chides.

Alessia showers in record time. She doesn't trust Caroline, and doesn't want to leave her sister-in-law alone with Maxim, who happens to be Caroline's ex-lover. Caroline is still in love with him, or so Alessia thinks.

Draped in a towel, Alessia dashes into the spare room where all her clothes are kept, to dry herself and dress.

Maxim and Caroline are in the kitchen. She hears him laugh at something she says. And Alessia is spurred on to be quicker. Three minutes later, she's dressed in black trousers and a white long-sleeve T-shirt, with Gucci loafers.

'Good morning, Alessia,' Caroline says brightly when Alessia walks into the kitchen. 'You look nice.'

'Thank you,' Alessia responds, surprised at the compliment. 'So do you.' Caroline is dressed in dark jeans, knee-high boots, and a fitted tweed jacket. She gives Alessia a quick hug and peck on the cheek.

'Sorry to interrupt your morning shag,' Caroline says with a wink.

Alessia blushes and turns her attention to Maxim. He hands her a coffee. 'Here you go. Just ignore her.'

Alessia smiles and takes the coffee.

Why is this woman so brazen? Are all English women like this?

Or is this awkward because Caroline knows Maxim intimately, and they used to 'shag'?

'Do you want to go shopping?' Caroline asks, utterly unabashed by what she's just said. 'We can find you something gorgeous for this party. And for me too!'

'Sure,' Alessia responds.

'Great.' Caroline beams.

Caroline intimidates Alessia. On every level. But this friendly, happy Caroline is something new.

Alessia gulps down her coffee. 'I'll get my things.' She escapes into the spare bedroom to collect her jacket and handbag.

Spare room? Don't tell me you have separate beds already!' Caro scoffs. 'Because you being half-dressed is not what that looks like.'

I give her an exaggerated sigh, irritated by her teasing. 'No. Separate wardrobes.'

'Ah. Look, I get it. She's a tempting little morsel, isn't she?' She sounds wistful, and I cock my head in warning. 'Oh, relax, Maxim. You're newlyweds. You must be at it like rabbits.'

I rake a hand through my hair. 'This is none of your fucking business. Where are you taking her?'

'Knightsbridge or Bond Street. I'm not sure yet. But I was thinking about what you said.'

'Oh?'

'About her being lonely.' Caroline glances down, avoiding eye contact. 'I know how that feels. I have friends, but they were Kit's friends too, and it's extraordinary how grief has spirited them away.' Her face falls, and for a moment, she looks devastated.

'Oh, Caro. I'm sorry.' Without thinking, I reach out and hug her.

She gives me a watery, grateful smile. 'Maybe I can forge a friendship with your wife.'

'I'd like that. I hope you do.'

Alessia watches their exchange from the hall. He does love his brother's wife. His words are kind and sweet.

But not like he loves Alessia.

You are the world to me.

And he wants them to be friends. She sighs. For Maxim, she'll try.

Alessia shoulders her bag and steps into the kitchen doorway, and they break apart. Not guiltily, because right now, they don't have anything to feel guilty about, Alessia can see that, but still – she wishes that Caroline would keep her hands off her husband. 'Shall we go?' she asks.

'Yes!' Caroline exclaims with an overexuberant enthusiasm.

'Don't go crazy,' Maxim warns, and he leans down and kisses Alessia hard and fast on her lips.

'Of course we're going to go crazy. It's Dimitri's party.' Caroline winks at Alessia once more, grabs her hand, and together they set out the door.

Alessia with Caroline. I'm not sure how I feel about this. I don't want Caro upsetting Alessia again. Though she seemed genuinely remorseful after the last time, Caro is like the proverbial bull in a china shop regarding other people's feelings. I hadn't noticed before . . . before Alessia.

Hell.

Alessia can look after herself.

Can't she?

The apprehension that's become familiar since I lost Alessia reverberates in my chest, and I'm suddenly a little overwhelmed, standing in the echoing silence of my hallway. This is the first time I've been alone in the flat since Alessia went missing.

Shit. Mate.

Pull yourself together.

I drag out my phone and text Joe.

Bout?

Bro! The missus letting you out?

Mate!!!

My missus is shopping with Caro.

Sounds expensive!

I'll grab my blade.

See you at the club.

Alessia closes her eyes as Jimmy, one of the young men at the beauty salon, massages conditioner into her hair. She's shocked that most of the staff at the salon are men, and it's the first time a man has washed her hair. She smirks. Technically, Maxim was the first man to wash her hair. But they were naked together in the shower. This experience is entirely different, and the strong-fingered young man gives a good massage. The sensation is blissful, and after a hectic morning, it's a welcome respite from shopping with her full-on sister-in-law.

Caroline's been more than friendly, chattering nonstop and

offering her opinion on *everything*. She's encouraged Alessia to buy two dresses – no, gowns – that were outrageously expensive.

Darling, you'll have to get used to spending money. It's all about quality, not quantity. These pieces are classic and will last you for years, and you look fabulous in both.

Alessia loves them, and she hopes Maxim will too.

Darling. He'll love them!

She's also bought matching high-heeled shoes and a little black Chanel evening bag.

These are perfect accessories for those frocks.

Afterwards, they had a quick lunch at a champagne bar, where Caroline quizzed Alessia about her life in Albania.

Caroline was fascinated and continued her friendly interrogation at the salon while their finger and toenails were trimmed, shaped, and polished a bright scarlet.

But the truth is, Alessia feels indolent; this is not a life she ever aspired to – spending outrageous amounts on high-end fashion and grooming. But her apartment is spotless, Maxim's and Alessia's clothes clean and ironed . . . and now and again, a woman needs to spoil herself, or so says Caroline.

'Mmm.' She smiles, drifting off as Jimmy continues his massage and grateful for a few minutes' peace.

Mate, you are easy meat. Your game is way off. You okay?' Joe says as he tugs off his fencing mask, having scored the winning point.

I gape at him through the mesh of my mask. My mother is AWOL. My brother may have killed himself because of a genetic disorder that I may or may not have, and some scummy hack is digging into my nuptials. 'Just a lot of shit going on,' I mutter, breathless, as I pull off my mask. 'Besides, you're performing way too well for my liking.'

'Practice. That's all it is. What with you married, and Tom all loved up with Henry, I'm on my own.'

'My heart bleeds, bro.'

He laughs and claps my back. 'You going to Dimitri's tonight?'

'Yeah.'

'Let's have a swift drink, and then I'll let you go.'

'Okay. But it needs to be a swift one. I need to pick up some jewellery from the vault.'

'For your countess?'

'Yep.'

Joe grins. 'Need a hand selecting something?'

'Mate!'

'Just asking.'

Alessia and Caroline are in the back of a taxi cruising back to Chelsea from Knightsbridge. Alessia's phone buzzes. She has a text from Maxim.

What colour is your dress?
Mx

One is black.
The other is red.
Why?

You'll see!
Mx

'Is that Maxim?'

Alessia nods.

Caroline smiles. 'I think he'll be pleased with today's endeavours.'

'I hope so.'

'It's been fun.'

'It has,' Alessia acknowledges, surprised.

'Of course, this is my last hurrah for a while,' Caroline says.

'Last hurrah?'

'Yes. I start work on a project for Maxim next week.'

'Oh?' Alessia glances at Caroline, who seems oblivious to the alarm writ all over Alessia's face.

'In my old life,' she continues, 'I was an interior designer, and one of the Trevethick properties in Mayfair is being refurbished. He wants me to add my special sparkle to it.'

Special sparkle. What does that mean?

Caroline works for Maxim. This is news.

How closely do they work together? A chill grips Alessia's heart as she recalls them hugging this morning. 'And you enjoy it. Working?' she asks, trying to keep her voice level.

'Yes and no. Depends on the client. Maxim will be fine, but some can be a complete nightmare.' Caroline makes a face, and Alessia can't help but laugh because it's so unexpected. 'Yes. I've had some dreadful, demanding, delusional clients in the past. But I've missed being in the fray. And now, well, I need to get back out there since, since Kit . . .'

Caroline exudes a confidence that Alessia envies, but one mention of her deceased husband and her confidence crumbles – her shoulders droop, and her face clouds. Instinctively, Alessia reaches out and clutches her hand. Caroline turns raw blue eyes to her that shimmer with unshed tears and returns her squeeze. 'Thank you,' she whispers.

Alessia's compassion shines in her kind smile, and they continue their journey in silence for a few moments.

Alessia glances out of the cab window, wondering what it would be like to have a proper job. 'I'd like to work, but I can't because I don't have a visa,' she says, almost to herself.

'Oh?' Caroline is surprised.

'It's frustrating. I'd like to . . . um . . . contribute.'

'I see.' Caroline looks thoughtful. 'I'm sure you contribute in other ways.' She gives Alessia a quick smile, and Alessia wonders if she's referring to sex as she usually does, but there doesn't seem to be any malice or vulgarity in her expression.

'Yes. I may go a little crazy in the apartment.'

'Oh, you'll have enough to do once you've established yourself. There are two estates to oversee as countess. Incidentally, Maxim asked me about finishing school. I recommended the one I attended. It was just what I needed. It's a good idea that you go.'

'I was surprised you needed to go.'

Caroline scoffs. 'Kit wanted me to go. Darling, I'm not aristocracy. He was very particular in how things were done.'

'Oh.' Alessia is surprised.

'Yes. He was a bit of a snob, to be honest. Everything had to be just so. Maxim isn't like that.'

'No.' And Alessia is waiting for her to say – *he married you* – as an example of how he's not a snob.

But she doesn't.

'Once you're done, you'll have the confidence to assume your place, and then you should have a proper introduction to both the estates as Maxim's countess.'

'That's the reason for doing the course. My confidence.'

'You'll be fine.'

Astonished by Caroline's sincerity and kindness, Alessia fixes a smile on her face, which her sister-in-law returns.

Caroline cocks her head to one side as she scrutinises her. 'Your hair looks so pretty blow-dried in these soft waves, Alessia.' She sighs. 'I envy your thick hair. It looks so healthy. You should go twice a week and have Luis style your hair each time. They'll cover grooming during etiquette lessons. It's fun. Nails. Hair. Everything. Tonight you will stun, darling. You'll meet everyone, and they're all dying to meet you. Once tonight's over, the press should stop bothering you.'

Alessia is bewildered by Caroline's candour and that she envies Alessia, when it's the other way around – Alessia hopes to emulate Caroline's elegance, poise and confidence. She's her only role model as to how Alessia should look and behave. The fact that Alessia will be attending the same finishing school gives her hope that she will.

'I know very little about the party we are attending.'

'Has Maxim not told you about Dimitri?'

Alessia shakes her head. 'Who is Dimitri?'

'He's some Russian oligarch's son. Bit of a player. Likes to throw lavish parties. Spends oodles of money. You'll see. Kit knew him well, Maxim less so. Dimitri likes to surround himself with the influential and the glamorous, beautiful people.'

Uau. Of course Maxim would be invited to such a party.

And Caroline.

Alessia can only hope that she won't let Maxim down.

'He's ingratiating himself into society. Everyone can see that, and rumour has it that his father is ex-KGB. Exciting stuff. And he knows how to party. It will be fun.' She smiles at Alessia, unaware that her nerves are now on edge.

The party sounds totally intimidating to Alessia.

'You really are very pretty.' Caroline changes the subject and pauses for a moment while Alessia flounders for what to say in response to such a statement. 'He's different with you. Protective. You know.' Caroline's tone softens, her fondness for Maxim apparent. 'He's head over heels. Must be nice.'

It's such a gear change from what they were discussing. 'It is,' Alessia replies quickly and firmly. She knows she's staking a claim on her own husband.

'It's admirable what you've done. He's avoided intimacy all his life – you've achieved the impossible.'

Alessia squirms in her seat, uncomfortable with the direction of their conversation. 'Thank you,' she mutters, because she doesn't know what else to say – but inside, she wants to shout from the rooftops.

He's mine. Keep your hands off him.

'Do you want to stop for anything else?' Caroline asks.

'I should get home. Though I've enjoyed today, thank you.'

Alessia is surprised that she means what she says, in spite of all of Caroline's intimate observations and personal questions. It has been fun to get out of the apartment and spend time with her sister-in-law.

Perhaps she's not a rival.

Perhaps.

'I have to prepare dinner,' Alessia adds.

'What? You cook? For him?'

'Yes.'

'Wow.' Caroline is stunned. 'I suppose it's not surprising. I saw you cooking up a storm with your mother in Albania. That was nice. Intimate. You have a good relationship with her.'

'I do. Do you have a good relationship with your mother?'

Caroline scoffs. 'My mother lives in the South of France. I don't see her very often.' She tucks her hair behind her ear as if she's distracting herself from an unpleasant thought and continues, 'And the food at your wedding was delicious. I don't cook. But then I have Mrs Blake.' She lowers her voice as if her sadness has returned, and Alessia remembers overhearing her conversation with Maxim.

Caroline is lonely too.

'You are welcome to join us for an evening meal. I'll cook something light.'

Caroline laughs. 'Normally, I would love to, but I must get ready for this evening. And so do you. And can I ask, may I come with you and Maxim to the party? I don't want to go on my own.'

'Of course,' Alessia says automatically, knowing Maxim won't mind.

'Thank you,' Caroline gushes. 'I'm looking forward to it. I haven't been out since your wedding. And I need some excitement. In fact, why don't you two come over for a pre-party cocktail?'

'Sure.' Alessia smiles, but her nerves flare again. She's excited about this party, though she's terrified too. Supposing she puts a foot wrong . . . or says the wrong thing . . . or . . . or . . . She swallows her rising panic and clasps her hands together.

Alessia, calm down. It will be fun.

What could possibly go wrong?

Chapter Eighteen

My mouth dries. Beneath the hall chandelier, the light burnishing her dark hair, Alessia is a screen siren. She's wearing an ankle-length soft silk dress fitted at the waist and fastened at her neck, exposing shapely shoulders. The skirt sculpts her hips, tapers to her knees, and then falls in swathes of ruby red to her feet. Her dark eyes are framed in kohl, her lips are as scarlet as her dress, and her hair falls in soft, gentle waves around her. She is a goddess. Aphrodite. And she's mine. I clear my throat. 'You look stunning.' My voice is hoarse.

She smiles, knowing and shy and sweet at once, and I feel it in my dick.

Fuck.

'You look edible,' she says.

I laugh. 'This old thing; it's my lucky suit.'

'You could get lucky,' Alessia purrs, teasing me.

I reach up and take a strand of her hair between my fingers. 'I hope so, but only with you. Your hair looks lovely.'

'We went to a salon at the store where a man washed it, and another man gave me a blowout.'

A momentary pang of what I can only assume is jealousy slices through me. 'Did they now?' I pull her into my arms. 'I'm not sure how I feel about that.'

Alessia giggles. 'It was a first for me too.'

Tenderly, I clasp her face between my palms and press my lips lightly against hers. 'Then I don't approve.'

'Of my hair?'

'No. The men. But whoever it was, they did a great job. Come, let me show you something.'

On the dining table, I've laid out three velvet boxes. I open them all, revealing their sparkling secrets. Alessia inhales in wonder.

'Yes. Trevethick booty. Part of a substantial collection.'

Alessia is awestruck. On the table, nestled in velvet, is some of the most exquisite jewellery she's ever seen.

Diamonds.

Diamonds winking in the soft light of the chandelier.

'I think these,' Maxim breathes eventually, and he reaches for a pair of starburst cluster diamond earrings. 'Let's see what they look like.' Gently he tucks her hair behind her ears and inserts first one, then the other earring. 'You're beautiful. You don't need any embellishments, but these earrings are fit for a goddess. And in that dress, that's what you are. Do you like?'

Alessia stares in the gilt mirror on the wall at the unrecognisable woman gazing back at her. She looks and feels . . . different. Confident. Potent. 'I love them,' she whispers, her eyes shifting to her husband's in the mirror and she drinks in his beauty. His emerald eyes glint, and his sculptured lips part as he inhales. He's in a fitted black suit, with a white shirt.

He looks virile. Elegant. Gorgeous.

He gives her a dazzling smile. 'Good. Let me put these back in the safe.'

'You have a safe?'

'*We* have a safe. It's in my wardrobe.'

Hand in hand, Alessia and Maxim walk up Cheyne Walk towards Trevelyan House. Alessia tries to stifle her nerves, remembering Mrs Blake's less than enthusiastic welcome last weekend.

What kind of reception will she receive today?

'This house has been in my family for generations. In fact, since it was new,' Maxim says as he opens an iron gate that leads down a short stone path in a neat garden. They stop outside an impressive old building with a gleaming black front door that looks remarkably like the door at the house on Cheyne Walk. 'I grew up here.'

Alessia smiles. 'Are there photographs of you as a boy here?'

Maxim laughs. 'Yes. Many.' He reaches up and pushes the bell, which rings shrilly somewhere inside the house. 'You've met Mrs Blake.' Maxim's mouth flattens into a bleak line. 'She's been with the family for years, since my father was earl. Mr Blake, her husband, is the family butler.'

'Okay.' Alessia inwardly girds herself.

A stout, balding man in a pristine black suit answers the door. He turns his shrewd brown eyes on Alessia, then Maxim. 'Lord Trevethick,' he says and, bowing his head, holds open the door.

'Blake.' Maxim is tight-lipped as he takes Alessia's hand and guides her into the hall. 'This is my wife, Lady Trevethick.'

'Congratulations to you both,' he says kindly. 'Lady Trevethick, welcome to Trevelyan House. May I take your coats?'

'Caroline is expecting us,' Maxim informs him as he hands over his coat. Following his lead, Alessia removes hers too.

'Lady Trevethick,' he murmurs as he takes it, his eyes bright with admiration. Alessia returns his smile. 'Lady Trevethick is in the drawing room, my lord. Brace yourselves. I believe cosmopolitans are on the menu.'

Maxim chuckles. 'Thanks.'

Blake gives them both a nod, turns on his shiny black shoes, and paces down the long black-and-white tiled hall. Alessia's gaze follows him. The walls are adorned with photographs and paintings. Two large chandeliers are hanging from the ceiling, much like those in Maxim's apartment, but these are bigger. An ornate gilt mirror sits above an old wooden console table where two elaborate lamps with golden lampshades cast a gilded light over the hall.

'The drawing room is upstairs,' Maxim says, smiling at her.

Their footsteps clatter up a broad staircase made of rich, russet-brown wood. Above them, on the walls, are more paintings and photographs. Alessia catches sight of one with Maxim. He looks younger, and he's posing with a blond, curly-haired man who seems a little older than him. They're in a uniform: white britches, long leather boots, and darker T-shirts with LAURENT PERRIER emblazoned on the front. A long mallet is casually propped on Maxim's shoulder, while the other man, who has an arrogant, imposing air, is resting his hand on a similar mallet.

'That's Kit and me in our polo gear. It's from about five years ago.'

'You both look very handsome.'

Maxim grins, looking boyish and pleased at once. 'Thank you.' He leads her through a door on the landing into a large drawing room where Caroline is waiting. She's impeccably dressed in a floor-length black gown with a plunging neckline, single pearls at her ears, and a long, knotted pearl necklace that falls between her breasts. She steps forward and grasps both Maxim's and Alessia's hands.

'Welcome, Alessia, you look stunning. Maxim.' She kisses Alessia's cheek and offers her own to Maxim.

'Caro. You look lovely.' Maxim gives her a brief peck.

'I do so hope you're both in need of a cosmo.' She squeezes their hands, then turns and presses a button on the wall. 'Do take a seat.'

Alessia glances around the room, taking in its opulence and antiquity. It's comfortable yet imposing. A marble fireplace with impressive columns dominates the room, and there are several overstuffed red-patterned couches. There are paintings of landscapes and still-lifes but also photographs of Caroline and her husband, several of an older man who Alessia recognises from the portrait in Cornwall as Maxim's father, and a few of Maxim, Kit, and Maryanne as children.

'May I look at the photographs?'

'Of course, Alessia,' Caroline responds. 'Please, be my guest.'

There's a brisk knock at the door, and Blake enters, making his way over to a silver bar cart that's laden with bottles of alcohol, sparkling crystal glasses, and a cocktail shaker.

'That dress does suit you,' Caroline says. 'Do you approve, Maxim?'

'I do. Very much.' Maxim's expression heats as he stares at Alessia.

Alessia smiles. 'Thank you,' she whispers, warmed by his gaze. She turns, flushing a little, to examine one of the family photographs. Maxim must be nine or ten, handsome even as a child, his father's hand cupping his shoulder. Maryanne stands between Maxim and his brother – who's taller with a mass of blond curls – while Rowena stands behind Kit, her arm draped around her eldest son. There's a steely glaze in her eyes as if she's daring the photographer to reveal the truth.

What truth?

'I have those items of Kit's,' Caroline says to Maxim and gestures to an elegant wooden box on the coffee table.

'Oh.' Maxim eyes the box, eyes suddenly wide with doubt. 'Um . . .'

'Now might not be the right time,' she adds quietly.

The atmosphere in the room cools, only to be revived by the loud rattle of a cocktail shaker. All eyes turn to Blake, who holds the silver shaker aloft with a flourish. He smirks, enjoying himself. Maxim grins while Caroline laughs and joins Blake at the drinks tray. 'Let me help.'

Deftly Blake pours alcohol into three cocktail glasses, and

Caroline adds a slice of fresh orange zest to each. 'There we go,' she says, handing a glass to Alessia then Maxim. 'This is a cosmopolitan. Or, as we say, a cosmo.'

'Cosmo,' Alessia repeats.

'Cheers,' Caroline says, smiling at Maxim.

'Gëzuar,' Alessia and Maxim say in unison, and Caroline laughs in response. Alessia takes a sip. The tangy, sharp taste is delicious. 'Mmm . . . what is in this?'

'Vodka, a dash of Cointreau, lime juice, cranberry,' Maxim responds, his voice husky as his eyes meet Alessia's.

'Oh, for God's sake, get a room, you two!' Caroline says. Maxim winks at Alessia, and Caroline continues, 'I thought a vodka-based cocktail might set us up for Dimitri's.'

Maxim nods. 'Yes. The vodka will be flowing this evening. Let's drink up and make a move.'

Dimitri lives in a newly renovated pile in Mayfair. The house is redbrick, squat, and furnished by the interior designer du jour. I've been a couple of times. The décor, the furnishings, and the art are on point and utterly soulless. I've never felt fully comfortable in his company – not that I've met him often – but his is the place to be seen, and if I'm going to out Alessia as my wife, there's no better way to go public. We'll be plastered over all the tabloids in the morning.

'Are you ready for this?' I ask Alessia as our cab stops close to his house. She nods, her eyes dark and shimmering from the streetlight. 'Caro?'

'Yes. Time to get back on the horse,' Caroline says.

'Okay. Let's go. Don't answer any questions.'

As we climb out of the taxi, I see there's a steady stream of the well-heeled already entering the property. The paparazzi step forward with shouts and cameras poised.

Lord Trevethick!

Maxim!

Look this way!

I wrap my arm around Alessia and grab Caroline's hand, and we walk through a sea of flashing cameras and shouted questions. It feels like forever, but it's probably seconds later that we're through the shining black door and into the relative safety of the courtyard.

Though it's still early, the place is already heaving.

An attractive young woman with slicked-back hair, dressed entirely in black, takes our coats, and we head into the courtyard proper. As we do, we're given a shot of vodka each from a waitress who looks the spit of the cloakroom attendant.

'Thank you.' Alessia looks dubiously at the concoction.

'Welcome to Dimitri's,' I mutter in as reassuring a voice as I can manage and down the shot. I'll say one thing for him – he does good vodka. Alessia downs hers as does Caroline.

'Uau! Ah! That's strong!' Alessia splutters.

'Yeah . . . maybe not too much, eh? Let's find Joe and Tom. They should be here.'

'Trevethick!' The booming voice of Dimitri Egonov interrupts us. 'I am so glad you could make it. And who is this beautiful young lady?' His accent is faint, but it's there. Could he sound any more oily? And he's wearing a white dinner jacket like he's Gatsby or Bogart.

'This is my wife, Alessia Trevethick. Alessia, our host, Dimitri Egonov.'

He takes her hand and brings it to his lips, his dark eyes searing hers. 'The rumors are true,' he murmurs. 'My dear Lady Trevethick, you are exquisite.'

'Mr Egonov.' Alessia smiles, but even I notice that her smile doesn't reach her eyes.

'You'll need to be careful of this one,' Egonov warns me. 'She's a rare diamond.'

'She is,' I agree, wanting him to drop her hand.

Get your hands off my wife.

I've never felt as territorial as I do now.

'Please enjoy my hospitality. There's all manner of entertainments to delight here. Maybe next time you'll DJ for me.'

Never.

'I think my DJ days are over, Dimitri.' My smile is polite, but I want him to release my wife. Finally, he does and turns to Caroline.

'Lady Trevethick, how lovely you look this evening.'

'Dimitri, darling.' She air kisses him on each cheek, but he pulls her into a tight hug.

'I am so sorry for your loss,' he says, holding her close.

Caro turns a panicked look towards me, but it's Alessia who takes her hand.

'Caro, please show me around,' Alessia asks sweetly.

'Thank you, Dimitri,' Caro purrs, and with a dazzling, knowing smile, he releases her and moves on.

Fuck.

'Are you okay?' I ask Caro, whose hand is still clasped in Alessia's.

'Yes. He is . . . extra.'

'He is. Let's go grab a drink.'

Alessia is dazzled by the spectacle of the event laid out before her. The courtyard is covered by a black silk canopy festooned with tiny, twinkling fairy lights. In the centre, on a black plinth, there's an ice sculpture of tall carved flames that branch in all directions. It's lit with red and orange flickering lights, so the flames look real. Three bartenders stand before it, serving shots from the vodka that's pouring through its icy flames.

How does that work?

'Vodka luge,' mutters Maxim. 'Let's avoid that and find some champagne.'

'I'll have another shot,' says Caro, and leaving them, she saunters up to the bar and greets a tall young woman standing there. Maxim turns abruptly away from them as if he's avoiding the other woman, grabs two glasses of champagne from a passing waiter, and passes a flute to Alessia.

'Let's move over there, and we can hold court and people-watch,' he says.

The area is crowded with men and women all dressed in their finery. Alessia recognises a few movie actors, celebrities, and a couple of British politicians that she remembers from the free newspaper she read on the train to and from Brentford. On the fringes of the throng, several conspicuous, burly men in dark suits, wearing earpieces, watch over everyone.

Security? For what? Alessia doesn't know.

Various people accost Maxim to offer their condolences at his brother's passing and to meet Alessia. She shakes hand after hand, aware that a few beautiful women she meets are eyeing her with ill-concealed envy. She wonders if they know Maxim intimately.

Alessia, don't go there.

She tightens her grip on her husband's arm.

A photographer asks for a picture, and Maxim pulls her closer. 'Smile,' he whispers. 'This will be all over the tabloids tomorrow, and I want the world to see that you're mine.'

Alessia beams at him, her doubts erased, and the photographer snaps a few shots, thanks them, and moves on.

'Trevelyan!' There's a shout, and Tom, in black tie, strides towards them, dragging Henrietta behind him through the crowd. 'Dear Alessia, you look stunning. Maxim, my goodness, what an extraordinary turnout. Of course, everyone here wants to meet your new bride!'

Henrietta lights up when she sees Alessia. 'You look lovely,' she gushes.

Alessia beams back. 'Thank you, so do you!'

Maxim and Tom begin an intense discussion. Alessia picks up the words *prying journalists*, *security*, and *kompromat* – whatever that might be.

'I've never been here before. Shall we go and explore?' Henry's brown eyes sparkle with curious delight and a little mischief.

'Okay,' Alessia replies, inspired by Henry's infectious enthusiasm and of course, Alessia is curious too. She's never been to a mansion owned by a Russian oligarch.

'Where are you going?' Maxim asks as soon as they move away.

'Exploring.' Henry smiles, and Maxim casts bright eyes that widen with concern at Alessia.

'Be careful,' he murmurs, and Alessia knows he disapproves, but he's not going to stop her.

'We will,' she says with a sweet smile. He nods in response, and Henrietta takes two glasses of champagne from another passing waiter, and they walk through the affluent crowd and into the house.

The residence is impressive, decorated in beige and browns and creams with touches of gold everywhere. It's opulent; the furnishings are in satin and silk. Abstract and figurative art hangs on every wall. It's stylish but a little sterile for Alessia's taste. Guests mingle, talking, laughing, and drinking in each room. In the first – a sitting room – a couple of close-up magicians entertain the milling folk. One produces a gold coin from behind Henry's ear. What's more, to her utter delight, he lets her keep it.

They move on through a dining room set with a lavish banquet. Alessia recognises the caviar and pink salmon roe, but there are dumplings and little pasties. *Pirozhok*, Henry informs her. The table, which must seat twenty people, is laden with food. Tall, attractive male servers with slicked-down hair dressed in their uniform black stand at points ready to serve. Henry and Alessia choose caviar with blinis, the little dumplings, and pasties.

'This will fortify us,' Henry declares, and they move with their plates into the next room, another sterile space crammed with beautiful people. Henrietta introduces Alessia to all who approach. A thin young woman in black accosts them – her flowing dress appears a little big for her. 'So you're the woman who snared Maxim Trevelyan,' she drawls as her brown eyes sweep over Alessia.

'Maxim is my husband,' Alessia responds stiffly, aware that she's been the subject of speculation and the occasional side-eye as she and Henry have wandered through the gathering. No one's been as overt as this woman.

'Pretty little thing, aren't you?' she says, and Alessia suspects she's had too much to drink.

'And you are?'

'Arabella Watts. Maxim and I used to date. Many moons ago. I must congratulate you on snaring one of the UK's most eligible—'

'Thanks, Arabella,' Henry interrupts. 'We have to find Maxim.' She grabs Alessia's hand, and they move through to another room. She whispers, 'Maxim's ex. A complete addict and a nasty piece of work too. Though I'm not sure if the two things are related.'

'Oh. Ex-girlfriend?'

'Yes. Has he not told you?'

'Briefly. But not . . . um . . . with . . . details.'

'Probably wise,' Henry adds. 'I mean, we don't want to hear about our partner's ex-lovers, do we?'

Alessia shakes her head and doesn't want to dwell on Maxim's exes at all.

There are too many.

Henry stops by a window so they can finish their food. When they're not being interrupted for introductions, Henry chats about her day. She's a nurse who met Tom while working at the veterans' hospital in London. Alessia listens attentively, feeling more relaxed and oh-so-comfortable in Henrietta's presence. She wonders vaguely where Maxim might be.

Once they've eaten, and with more champagne in hand, they wander through the hallway. The atmosphere among the revellers has heated up – the chatter louder and freer. They pass a magnificent wooden staircase that leads to the floor above and down to the basement, from where coloured lights flicker up the walls and thumping music can be heard.

Henry makes a face. 'We don't want to go down there,' she warns, and they move on into the main sitting room.

It's another opulent room, furnished as the others, though this has a modern gas fireplace where flames flicker, adding a little colour and life to the space. There's an excited buzz from the well-off crowd that hangs over the spacious room, accompanied by the chink of champagne and shot glasses.

Above them is a mezzanine floor. 'Look,' Henry says when she spots the grand piano on display above them. She grins. 'Let's go up there.' Henry downs her champagne, grabs another two glasses from a waiter, and leads the way to the spiral staircase. Alessia is keenly aware that their journey is followed by the curious eyes of the partygoers mingling in the room. Alessia downs one of her glasses of champagne and follows Henry up the staircase to the mezzanine. It houses an impressive library, the hardbacks sorted by colour and size, and the gleaming black piano. Alessia inhales sharply. It's a Bechstein.

'Well, hello there. Do you play?' A young man with black hair, tousled a little like Maxim's, steps out from behind one of the library shelves. His accent echoes Dimitri's.

'Not me,' Henry responds. 'But Alessia here does.'

He steps forward; his clear blue eyes scan Alessia's face, then skim down her body, so that she raises her chin to meet his challenge.

He smirks at her attempt to intimidate him and holds out his hand. 'Grisha Egonov, and you are?'

Alessia shakes his hand, alarm bells ringing in her head. His grip is too tight, his smile too warm. She withdraws her hand and resists the urge to wipe it against her dress. 'Egonov. Dimitri's . . .?' Alessia asks.

'Brother. Well, half-brother. Same father.'

'Alessia Trevethick.'

'Ah! The new countess.' He bows quite formally, takes her hand once more, and kisses her knuckles. 'My lady.'

A shiver runs up her spine.

'This is my friend Henrietta Gordon.' Alessia removes her hand and introduces Henry, who is watching Grisha with the same wariness as Alessia.

He gives a nod to Henrietta and turns his attention back to Alessia. 'Your accent. Like me, you are not from around here.'

'I am Albanian.'

'Ah. Interesting. Please.' He gestures towards the piano. 'Be my guest.'

'I wouldn't want to . . . um . . . disrupt the party.'

His eyes glow with an unwelcome intensity. 'Maybe it's exactly what this party needs. Or perhaps your friend's claim that you can play is . . . overstated?'

Henry laughs – at him, not with him – and Alessia glances at her friend. 'Show him,' Henry mouths. Grisha's gaze slides between the two of them, arrogant and amused.

'Please.' He gestures once more to the piano, and because Alessia doesn't know if she'll ever have the opportunity to play a Bechstein again, she concedes with a graceful nod. She sits on the stool, rests her fingers on her lap, and stares at the beauty before her. The piano gleams beneath the inset lights, and the golden words C. BECHSTEIN glint irresistibly on the fallboard, enticing her to play. Alessia presses middle C, and the note rings out, the tone deep, rich, and more golden than their surroundings.

Perfect.

Alessia glances up at Grisha, who's holding his phone and eyeing her speculatively.

She'll show him, arrogant arsehole.

Alessia smiles and winks at Henry. Turning to the keyboard, she places her hands on the keys and launches into Bach's prelude number 2 in C minor . . . her angry music.

The music rings through the room in oranges and reds, warmer and hotter than the colours of the ice-fire in the vodka luge outside, and Alessia loves it. And because she's had a little to drink, she's free and fast, letting the music overtake her and blotting out the arrogant fool beside her.

I've left Tom and Joe deep in conversation about the merits of rugby over football, to try to find Alessia. Ignoring the rising panic in my chest, I move through each room as Dimitri's guests offer me condolences or congratulate me on my marriage to my beautiful wife whom they've just met!

Where the hell is she?

Then I hear it. The sounds of Bach wafting over the hum of conversation.

Alessia.

She's in the main drawing room. I follow the sound, and with the crowd gathered in the room, I look up and spy her with Henry and Dimitri's arsehole younger brother Grisha on the mezzanine.

Now that I have her in my sight, I relax and listen. I know this is her angry music and I wonder what Grisha's said to piss her off.

'Maxim!' I turn and find Charlotte staggering towards me.

My ex.

Shit.

They're both here, though I've managed to avoid Arabella. Caroline was talking with Charlotte earlier, and I wonder what about.

'Hello, Charlotte.' I place my index finger on my lips to silence her because I want to listen to my wife's exquisite take on Bach. Charlotte glances up at Alessia in full flow.

'I've missed you.' She grasps my hand. 'Do you want to come and join me downstairs?' Charlotte's invitation is clear, but her eyes are unfocused as she weaves on her high heels at my eyeline.

She's drunk or high, or both, and I'm a little stunned.

Does she not know I'm married?

Alessia finishes the prelude, and as the final notes fade in the room, the gathered crowd erupts into applause. I extract my hand from Charlotte to applaud with them, but Charlotte grabs my lapels, surprising me, and plants her lips firmly on mine, pressing her wet tongue into my mouth. I'm vaguely aware of a flash of light.

What. The. Fuck.

I twist my head and grab her hands, pushing her gently back, escaping from her clutches. 'Charlotte! What the hell are you doing?'

Alessia hears the applause coming at her from what feels like the far end of the room.

'Brava, Lady Trevethick,' Grisha says. 'I was doubtful, but that was impressive.'

'Thank you,' Alessia says and grins at a smiling Henry before glancing down at the audience in the living room, her eyes straying to her husband.

He's kissing another woman.

And Alessia's world crashes to a halt.

What?

Chapter Nineteen

Alessia looks away, the sight too painful to endure as her head spins and bile rises in her throat. She swallows down the bitter taste, feeling light-headed. The room is suddenly too warm and too small for her to remain. The notion that she's intruding on her husband crystalises in her mind.

Perhaps he always behaves this way.

Alessia wouldn't know, as they've not been in a large social setting like this before.

This is him. This is what he does. Caroline warned her.

Alessia stands, swaying slightly from the shock of what she's witnessed, and refusing to glance in *his* direction again. She turns to Grisha. 'I need to get out of here.'

'Are you okay?' Henry asks.

Alessia shakes her head.

Grisha's brows knit together, his concern almost tangible. 'Do you feel faint?'

Alessia nods. She just wants to get away. *Now*. 'I need air.'

Frowning, Henry turns to view the now-disinterested congregation below. 'I'll get help,' she says, stepping to the balcony rail to scan the crowd.

'Here.' Grisha grabs Alessia's hand and leads her to the bookshelves, where he presses an unseen button, and one of the bookcases swings open, revealing a hidden passageway. 'Follow me.'

Alessia stumbles after him and hears the click of the bookshelf closing behind her.

Sit down, Charlotte. You're drunk. And haven't you heard, I'm married.' Shocked at Charlotte's behaviour, I guide her to sit in a vacant armchair, so she'll have less chance of falling flat on her face. She peers up at me, her expression scornful.

'I hear you married your daily.'

'I married the woman I love.'

She snorts. 'Is she up the duff? How very eighteenth century of you, Maxim.'

'Fuck off, Charlotte,' I mutter and turn to go.

She grabs my hand. 'I can't believe you're finally married,' she says.

'Believe it.' I raise my left hand, fingers spread so she can see my wedding ring. She's never behaved like this. I wonder if she's here alone or with her boyfriend. I look around but can't see anyone paying attention to her. 'Are you here on your own?'

'With a friend.'

'Where are they?'

She waves towards the crowd in the courtyard. 'Caroline said . . .'

'What?' My scalp crawls. 'What did Caroline say?'

Charlotte shakes her head. 'That you'll fuck any woman with a pulse.'

Fucking Caro.

'Even me. He's dumped me,' she wails.

'Charlotte, show some bloody dignity. Plenty more fish and

all that bollocks. Now, if you'll excuse me, I'm going to find my wife.' I leave her, feeling a little tarnished after our encounter. Glancing up at the mezzanine, I can see Henry looking at one of the bookcases. Alarm skitters down my spine.

Where's Alessia?

And where's Grisha?

I work my way through the crowd, ignoring the curious looks and the odd offer of condolences and congratulations, and vault up the spiral staircase.

'Henry! Where's Alessia?' I snap.

'Maxim. Hi. She disappeared with Grisha through this bookcase.'

What? Why?

I start feeling around the bookcase and find the hidden button. I press it, and the bookcase swings open.

'I was looking for that!' Henry exclaims.

'Come on. Let's find her.'

The passageway is lit by a couple of inset LEDs, and it ends in a door that opens onto a spacious open-air terrace above the drawing room. A couple in a dark corner among the lush pot plants are having sex against the wall. I catch a glimpse of blond hair, and I'm relieved it's not my wife. But I'm distracted by a shift in the light. A curtain closes in a room across from the terrace.

Has Grisha taken my wife in there?

Suddenly furious, I bolt through the terrace door, turn right, and burst through the bedroom door. Three men in various states of undress and arousal turn to face me in all their glory. A fourth is snorting a line of coke.

Shit.

'I'm so sorry.' I back up immediately, almost knocking over Henry, who's hot on my heels. 'Don't go in there. It's Ganymede central.'

There's a muffled cry from inside the room. 'I thought you'd locked the bloody door!'

'Dimitri's parties never disappoint,' Henry says breathlessly.

'I think one of them was a cabinet minister. Come on. Alessia must have gone downstairs.'

Grisha leads Alessia into the kitchen, where he barks at one of the staff in what Alessia assumes is Russian. The young woman scurries off to fetch a glass of water and returns to Grisha moments later. 'Here you go.' He hands Alessia the cut crystal tumbler, and she gratefully takes a long draught.

Perhaps Grisha is not so bad.

'Do you want to come down to the basement and let off some steam?' he asks, a gleam in his eye.

'No. I'd like to go home now,' Alessia responds, still wary.

'I'll summon my driver.' He takes out his mobile and makes a call. 'Where to?'

Alessia gives him the address on Chelsea Embankment, and he snaps the orders in the same foreign language into his phone, then hangs up. 'My driver will be outside in a moment. You can leave out the back, the way we do, and avoid the cameras out front.' From his pocket, he fishes out a card. 'Call me. When you're home.'

'Why are you being so kind?' Alessia responds.

Grisha cracks a smile. 'It would be very ungallant of me not to help such a talented and beautiful woman.'

'Thank you,' she whispers, but she can't believe her luck . . . in fact, she *can't* believe her luck, and a frisson of fear sends shivers up her spine.

Perhaps she's been too hasty.

Maxim will be furious.

She lifts her chin.

Well, *she* is furious. How dare he bring her to this opulent event to 'announce' their marriage and then kiss someone else?

'The car's here. Let me see you out,' Grisha says and offers her his arm.

I cannot find my wife. I've been in the basement, where the fun is heating up. Several people are naked in the swimming pool, and writhing bodies cover the floor of the softly lit studio. A woman flings herself at me, throwing her arms around my neck, cocaine dust on her upper lip. And I gently set her aside. 'I'm looking for my wife,' I growl. A quick scan of the bacchanalian horde in the studio tells me that Alessia's not a participant.

Not that I'd expect her to be here – not my sweet, innocent wife.

But these people. *It's like they're teenagers again.*

And they're probably being recorded.

Fuck. Where is she?

I head back upstairs, pull out my phone, and call Alessia once more. 'Where are you?' I snap when I get her voicemail again, and I try to think what would make her run.

Someone from her recent past?

Maybe the traffickers.

Perhaps they have her. Again.

This is my darkest fear.

Hell. I find Tom and Joe. 'Joe, please find Caroline and make sure she gets home in one piece. Tom, I can't find Alessia.'

'Henry told me. She's gone off to look for her in the other rooms. We'll mount a search.' He grabs my upper arm and gives it a brief squeeze. 'We'll find her. Don't fret, Trevethick.'

Fret! I'm going out of my fucking mind.

I nod in gratitude, unable to speak because there's a slight risk I might lose it. Last time she disappeared – she'd been fucking kidnapped.

My phone rings and hope swells in my chest.

Fuck, it's Oliver. I ignore the call.

Alessia sinks into the sumptuous leather of the Bentley SUV. The rear passenger door is super heavy, and she suspects the car is bulletproof. The driver gives her a cursory glance in the rear-view mirror and, without saying a word, sets off into the night.

Only now, in the privacy of the vehicle, does Alessia allow herself to replay what she witnessed.

Maxim kissing another woman.

Kissing. Another. Woman.

Tears well in her eyes.

Caroline had warned her.

Darling, he's slept with most of London.

Maryanne had tried to reassure her.

Reformed rakes make the best husbands.

Do they, though? Maybe they'll always be rakes. But does this mean he loves her less?

I want the world to see that you're mine.

Does it not work both ways?

Spouses have the same rights and duties towards each other. They should love and respect each other, maintain marital fidelity.

Their vows haunt her. Did they mean nothing to him?

O Zot. Was this inevitable? Her husband is just too promiscuous. Too handsome. Too charming.

A lump swells in her throat.

Her Mister. Her man.

She knew deep in her bones it would come to this.

She was never enough.

Alessia, you have been deluding yourself.

What will she do? Accept this? Leave? Alessia stares unseeing out of the window at the darkness between the lights of London.

Was it always going to come to this? A decision to stay or go? And for a moment, Alessia thinks of her mother and how her mother decided to stay . . . and her father is far worse than Maxim. Perhaps this is the lot of women as it has been for all time. The Albanian saying from the *Kanun of Lekë Dukagjini* springs to her mind: 'Gruaja është një thes, e bërë për të duruar.'

A woman is a sack, made to endure.

I spot Grisha coming out of one of the sitting rooms and make my way towards him. 'My wife? Where is she?'

'She's gone home, Trevethick. You should take better care of her.'

What the hell? And I want to ask him why she left, but it's none of his fucking business, though he seems to have made it so.

'What do you mean home?'

'She wanted to go home. I sent my car for her.' His simpering swagger makes me want to punch his stupid, arrogant face. 'She was feeling unwell. You really need to—'

I walk away before I deck him and find Tom. 'She's gone home. Tell Joe to watch Caro. Last time I saw her, she was three sheets to the wind.'

'Will do, old boy. Glad you tracked down Alessia. I'll check out that journalist you mentioned.'

'Thanks.'

In the cloakroom, I hand in my ticket and collect not just my coat but Alessia's too. She's left without her fucking coat. And she couldn't be bothered to tell me.

What the hell?

What did I do?

Maybe she's having second thoughts. I brought her to this den of iniquity and depravity, and she's disgusted. Let's face it, Alessia has not seen how the over-affluent can behave.

Fuck. I didn't think of this.

I storm outside, past a blaze of flashlights from the paparazzi, and make my way down the road to grab a cab.

Much to Alessia's relief, the Bentley draws up outside Maxim's building. The driver climbs out and opens her door, holding his hand out for her.

'Thank you,' Alessia says as she takes it.

He nods and walks with her to the building. From her evening bag, she extracts the keys and unlocks the front door.

Once she's inside, the driver turns and clambers back into his vehicle.

It's only as she calls for the elevator that she realises that there are no paparazzi outside. They're probably all still at Dimitri and Grisha's.

Thank goodness.

In the elevator, she finds her phone and texts Grisha her thanks and to tell him that she's arrived safely. There are a couple of missed calls from Maxim. She listens to his message as the elevator travels to the sixth floor.

Where are you? He sounds angry. Hurt. Confused.

The man doesn't even know he's behaved badly!

Maybe he doesn't think he has!

Alessia storms out of the elevator and, using her key, opens the apartment door, slamming the door behind her.

The alarm is off.

Did they not set it when they left?

The familiar cloying scent of expensive perfume hangs in the air, and the hairs on Alessia's neck stand to attention. The click, click of high heels alerts her to the end of the hallway, and standing in the doorway of the living room is Maxim's mother.

Rowena.

In the back of the cab, my anger mounts. What the hell was she thinking? Abandoning me at a party? But why? I don't understand what's happened. Did Grisha say something? Did Caroline?

I check my phone. There's the missed call from Oliver, but still nothing from Alessia.

Did she meet Arabella or Charlotte?

My scalp tingles.

Fucking Charlotte. That kiss.

Alessia must have seen us. That's the only reason I can think of that could explain why she left without so much as a goodbye.

My relief is monumental.

That's it. I lean back in the cab, feeling I finally have a handle on what's going on.

But wait. Charlotte kissed *me.* Not the other way around. I have zero designs on my ex. I have zero designs on any other women. Surely Alessia should know that . . . Why would she doubt me? And the fact that she does doubt me grinds my gears. She's punishing me for something that's not my fault – and punishing me with the worst of my fears.

It's aggravating.

Actually. I'm fucking furious.

Why the hell would she think I'd be interested in anyone else?

And from nowhere, loud and clear, the thought rings like a klaxon through my head.

Because of your past.

Your reputation.

Fuck.

My mood plummets even further. I'm going to have to convince my wife – *again* – that my past is in the past.

Alessia's reeling and stands immobilised in the hallway while Rowena gawks at her.

Why is she here? How *is she here?*

Her mother-in-law purses her lips. 'On your own, in Trevethick diamonds, I see. You've not wasted any time getting your little hands on our trinkets. Those earrings were one of my favourites back in the day. They're a little de trop, now, don't you think?'

Alessia finds her voice. 'Hello, Rowena. May I help you? If you're looking for Maxim, he's out.'

Maxim's mother folds her arms, remaining in the doorway, unmoving, unwavering, unwelcoming.

Hostile.

O Zot.

'You look very . . . nice, dear. But you'll never make a countess.

There's a saying that we have in this country – you can't make a silk purse from a sow's ear. How much money do you want to walk out of my son's life?'

Alessia feels like she's been gut-punched. 'What?'

'You heard.' Rowena slowly advances on Alessia. 'My friend Heath has been doing a little investigation. Turns out you haven't followed the correct procedure in this farce of a marriage to my son. It can easily be annulled.'

Not for the first time this evening, Alessia feels a little light-headed.

Heath? Her mother-in-law's lover?

Rowena smiles. A smile so chilling that a shiver runs down Alessia's back. 'I'll write you a cheque, and you can go. Lead the life you were meant to lead. Not this one – it's not for you. And it's not for Maxim either. He'll need someone with a gentility and refinement that you couldn't possibly achieve. Someone with breeding who won't bring scorn and embarrassment to the Trevethick legacy. He needs someone worthy. Someone who can offer him more. And that's not you, my dear. What could you possibly give him?

'He's only married you to spite me. He's a man who likes a good time; I'm sure you're aware of what I mean by that. It won't be long until he strays. He doesn't want the job of the earldom, and he's set himself up to fail by marrying you. You can see that, can't you?

'So, how much?'

'I want nothing from you,' Alessia whispers, her heart beating a frantic tattoo. 'And maybe, if you'd been a better mother, your son might have a better respect for women, and chosen someone with all the qualities you wish for in a daughter-in-law. But maybe, because *you* are his mother, he didn't. He chose me. And I am glad to say I am nothing like you.'

Rowena gasps, shocked.

Alessia walks to the door. 'I think it's time you left.'

The key rattles in the lock, and Maxim appears on the threshold.

When I open my front door, I'm met by my mother and my wife facing off in the hall, in an atmosphere so frigid, it might freeze my nuts off. My relief that Alessia's home and safe is tempered by my anxiety.

What in the name of hell is going on here?

Chapter Twenty

Rowena and Alessia stare at me – my mother cold and brittle in black Chanel, my wife magnificent in red Alaïa – and I know in my soul they've exchanged heated words. Alessia's eyes shine with unshed tears, and I suspect my mother has been a complete and utter bitch.

But, magnificent or not, I'm also really fucking angry with Alessia right now. Angrier than I've ever been. 'We'll talk later,' I mutter to her, holding up a finger in warning. 'Though, I'm glad you're home. Safe.'

And what I really want to do is grab her and kiss her and fuck her until she forgets everything but me, but now is not the time. I turn to Rowena. 'Mother, to what do we owe the pleasure?'

She purses her scarlet lips and squints at me in her myopic way, radiating tension and irritation. The doorbell rings, startling us all, and because I'm right beside it, I open the door, wondering who in the hell is calling at midnight. Maryanne stands on the threshold, wilting and wrung out in her scrubs. She casts a tired, wary, I-may-know-what's-going-on-but-I'm-not-sure look at me and shuffles in as I step aside.

'A family reunion. Past midnight. How quaint.' My sarcasm hides the fact that I'm completely blindsided by them both being here. It's after fucking midnight, I'm about to have a massive row with my wife, and I thought my mother was in New York avoiding me.

Maryanne follows in our mother's expensive-perfumed wake, and they head down the hallway to the drawing room.

'Please. Come in. Make yourselves at home,' I offer to their backs, altogether bemused that they're both here. The Mothership has come all the way from Manhattan. I just wanted her to return my call. Not turn up on my bloody doorstep.

I hang up the coats and turn to find Alessia eyeing me warily. She's said nothing. I reach for her hand, and she snatches hers away.

Okay. She's pissed off. 'We'll talk about whatever's bugging you and why you fled without telling me once I've dealt with the Mothership.'

Alessia raises her head, her eyes flashing.

Okay, she's really fucking pissed off.

'She was here when I arrived home,' she says.

'In the flat?'

'Yes.'

How the hell did she get in?

'Let's see what she wants.' Icily formal, I motion for my wife to proceed me and walk towards the drawing room. 'After you.' I'm relieved when she does as she's asked. I'm anxious to hear what my mother has to say because she's felt the need to make a personal appearance.

This is very out of character.

Rowena stands in the centre of the room, and from the disdain on her face, I suspect she's appraising it and finding it lacking. She scans me from head to toe and reaches the same conclusion. 'Hello, Maxim.' Her tone is clipped and, if I'm not mistaken, weary.

No niceties.

No cheek for me to grace with a kiss.

Not even her usual nasty sarcasm.

'You had a fine evening out, with or without your . . . wife?' The word *wife* is a sneer.

Ah. There she is. The Rowena I know. What the hell has she said to Alessia?

I glance at Alessia, who's frozen beside me, her dark eyes obsidian as she stares at my mother with thinly veiled hostility.

'What I've been doing with my wife is none of your concern. And how did you get into my flat?'

'I bullied Oliver into giving me a key and the code for your alarm. He said he'd send you an email.'

Ah. I remember his missed call. I'll have words with him on Monday, but I can only imagine the altercation they had for him to surrender my keys. Maryanne, who's said nothing, shrugs, her face a picture of tired bemusement, and she flops onto the sofa.

'You and your dubious marriage are all over the press.' Rowena purses her lips in disgust.

'Mother, you are the fucking press!' I retort.

Is this why she's here? My marriage? Or is it Kit?

She peers down her nose in that annoying, haughty way she has. 'I'm the editor and proprietor of one of the UK's leading women's lifestyle magazines. Not the gutter press.'

Alessia moves, recovering some of her composure. 'May I take your jacket? And would you like some coffee?' she interjects quickly.

'Please,' Maryanne half sighs, half gasps from the sofa. She's obviously exhausted. 'Then we can get this masquerade over, and I can get some sleep.'

'Really, Maryanne,' Rowena scolds, her lips pinched. 'I'll keep my jacket. And yes. I'd like some coffee. Real coffee.' Her tone is that of a woman in charge, but it's only now that I notice she's clutching a dainty handkerchief like her life depends on it.

Alessia squares her shoulders and lifts her chin. 'It's all we have.' And she gives her mother-in-law a slight smile she doesn't mean, turns on her Jimmy Choo heels, and struts out of the room in her sensational dress.

'So, to what do we owe this honour, Rowena?'

She turns bright blue eyes to me, and in them, I see . . . raw pain and uncertainty. It's completely confounding. All the animosity I usually feel in her presence evaporates, leaving me defenceless.

A torn white flag in a storm.

Fuck. Mate.

'Please. Sit,' I whisper, gesturing feebly towards the sofa.

She takes a deep breath. 'No. You sit. You'll need to.'

Like an automaton, I do exactly as she asks and perch on the sofa, waiting for whatever devastating news she has to give Maryanne and me.

Because something's wrong.

Seriously wrong.

She gathers herself, in that way she does – as editor, former countess, former It-girl – and raises her chin, just like my wife. 'I felt your last text message regarding Kit and his condition needed a personal reply.' She starts to pace while clutching her monogrammed handkerchief – and Maryanne and I watch wide-eyed, not chancing a glance at each other as our mother continues to act entirely out of character. 'In answer to your message, you have nothing to worry about, Maxim. Neither of you have anything to worry about. Nothing.'

Maryanne nods as if she's confirming a diagnosis.

What the hell does she know that I don't?

'Mama, please. I just got married. We want children.'

Her lips thin. 'You figure it out. I repeat. It's nothing to do with you or Maryanne.'

I frown as I fail to make any connection with what she's saying and what could possibly have been wrong with Kit, and why that has nothing to do with me or my sister.

'Oh, for fuck's sake, you're so obtuse, Maxie!' Maryanne explodes.

What?

'Daddy was not Kit's father.' Each word is a staccato expletive from Maryanne's mouth.

There are times when the world tips on its axis and starts to spin at a different and untried trajectory. When the world that you knew stops being and begins anew.

Like when my mother left my father.

Like when my father died.

Like when Kit died.

And, more hopefully, when I met Alessia.

And now, all that I knew and took for granted from my childhood has disappeared in five devastating words.

'So, you see. You have nothing to worry about,' Rowena says, her quiet tone tinged with the grief of a mother who's lost her favourite child.

Not a child of the family.

Her own boy.

Her own blue-eyed boy.

Alessia appears in the doorway, bearing a tray with delicate espresso cups and saucers and an elegant cafetiere that I didn't know we had. She places it on the coffee table in front of the sofa and looks warily at me before sitting at my side.

No one moves.

'Did Daddy know?' Maryanne's question echoes with righteous indignation through the oppressive atmosphere within the drawing room.

'Yes.' My mother fists her hands.

'And he took your shame to his grave,' Maryanne continues in the same vein.

Rowena closes her eyes. 'Yes.'

She turns to me, a tear sliding down her cheek.

Fuck. I have never seen my mother cry, and my emotions crowd into my throat and stay there. Expanding and smothering me.

'Say something,' she hisses.

But I'm hollow. Lost for words at her treachery and betrayal – a mere casual observer to a family tragedy.

My poor father.

My champion.

It all makes sense now.

'So, to be clear,' Maryanne says as she stands, 'it was Kit's biological father who had an issue.'

'Yes. He died last year from his condition.'

Fuck.

What I should feel . . . is relief. But there's nothing.

Except perhaps a bottomless rage on behalf of my father.

On behalf of Kit.

'Did Kit know?' The words are out of my mouth.

Rowena makes a strange, strangled noise.

'Did he find out over New Year?' Maryanne's voice is quiet with recrimination as tears pool in her eyes. My faithless mother closes her eyes once more, grasps her handkerchief, and emits an unearthly, spine-tingling cry as if she's being disembowelled.

Fuck. He knew.

That's why he was out on his motorcycle, haring through Trevethick's wintry lanes.

Maryanne lets out a similar sounding sob, her green eyes blazing with the ugliness of this tragic news; she stands and storms out of the room, down the hallway, and leaves, slamming the front door.

'Does Caroline know?' I ask.

My mother shakes her head.

'Good. We should leave it that way. Thank you for clearing that up. I think perhaps you should leave now.' I'm back – the detached persona I've cultivated over the years to deal with my mother restored.

She nods, unable to speak.

'May I get you anything?' Alessia asks.

Rowena seems to recover and peers down her nose at my beautiful, compassionate wife. 'No. I don't need anything from the likes of you.'

My detachment evaporates, and behind it is a seething cauldron of rage. 'Rowena, don't you dare speak to my wife like that,' I warn between gritted teeth.

'Maxim. Now you know. You are your father's son. A knight in shining armour – a sucker for a damsel in distress. Well, this damsel' – she points an elegant scarlet fingernail at herself – 'was up to the task of the Trevethick legacy. I doubt your . . . *daily* will be. You need someone of your own class, someone English who understands the pressures of the title and your position in society. Someone who can help you fulfil the role you were born to and help protect our legacy. Besides, it's not as if your marriage was legal. Heath has done some research.'

Alessia flinches as if she's been physically assaulted.

What the hell! Heath? Heath!

'Get out. Get out now.' Maxim is on his feet, and Alessia stands too.

They're a show of force. Together.

His mother casts a superior, scornful eye over them both, but Alessia sees through her veil of detachment as Rowena swallows, her jaw strained; she's wounded and hurt – rejected by both of her children – and she's lashing out, especially at Alessia who's an easy target. She's already been at the bitter end of Rowena's vicious tongue this evening.

'And you finally addressed me as Mama,' Rowena whispers as she regards her son. 'It was too much to hope that you might find some compassion for me.' She turns and waltzes out of the room, her heels clicking on the hardwood floor, echoing down the hallway until she exits quietly through the front door.

Compassion? For her?

And she knows! About our marriage because of Heath! Her fuckboy! *Shit!*

Alessia turns her elfin face to me, her eyes impossibly large, and I blow out a breath I didn't know I was holding. 'You okay?' I ask, my heart beating at a furious pace, pumping adrenaline through my body, so I'm ready to fight or flee.

I'm ready to fight. But Rowena's gone. Is Alessia going to fight?

She nods. 'You?'

'I don't know how I'm supposed to feel after that . . . bombshell. I'm so sorry that you had to witness that and bear the brunt of her meltdown.' I drag a hand through my hair, trying to assimilate what's just happened.

Kit was my half-brother.

Hell.

'I heard what she said. Did you know?'

'No. I'm stunned. My mother, a pillar of the establishment.' I take Alessia's hand and pull her into my arms.

We stand dazed and confused in each other's clutches for seconds . . . minutes – I don't know – as I try to recalibrate my life from within this new prism. All I have is questions that I was too stunned to ask before she left.

Did my father know when they married?

Who was Kit's father?

Shit.

Alessia pulls away, and I remember that she and I have yet to clear the air.

Is this why you have been distracted?' Alessia asks as she tries to find some equilibrium.

'Yes. Caroline came to the office with the letters from Kit's GP and a genetic counselling service.'

Alessia's hackles rise, equilibrium lost, and she stiffens. For the life of her, Alessia does not trust Caroline. Even after the pleasant time they spent together today. She knows Caroline is in love with Maxim. Maybe she was always in love with him but married his brother for the title, wealth, and social standing.

Maxim regards her warily. 'She needed to show me the letters. I told you.'

'She said she's working with you. You didn't tell me that.'

Maxim frowns. 'No, not with me. For me, I suppose. Well, for the estate. Honestly, Alessia,' he huffs in frustration, 'Caroline isn't important. She's the least of our issues right now. What is important was I thought that I might have a debilitating condition. I texted my mother to see if she knew anything about Kit. She wouldn't talk to me. Until now.'

'And you didn't tell me that either.'

Maxim closes his eyes and rubs his forehead. 'No. I thought you'd leave me.'

It's the third time this evening that Alessia's felt winded. *Uau. How could he think that?* 'I would never leave you—'

'You did fucking leave!' I almost shout. 'At the party, tonight. Without even a goodbye. Why?'

Her eyes cloud, and her face falls, her heartache writ large in the tension at her jaw. 'But you . . . you . . .' she whispers, unable or unwilling to say it out loud.

My chest constricts. 'The kiss?' Deep down, I know that's what she's trying to say. Alessia meets my gaze and gives me the same haughty look my mother gave us before she left. She's hiding behind that look, protecting herself. I see that now, and it cuts me to the quick. 'Charlotte was drunk,' I state. 'She's an ex-girlfriend, and for some bizarre reason, she threw herself at me. I was taken by surprise. *She* kissed *me* – not the other way round. I peeled her off me, sat her down, and came to find you. And you'd disappeared with fucking Grisha! Grisha!' Anger infuses my veins once more with heat. I step further away from her and run a hand through my hair, trying to hold on to my temper.

Fucking Grisha Egonov. Renowned arsehole. Possible underworld criminal.

'I saw the kiss,' Alessia says quietly. 'I had to leave. Grisha helped me. He sent me home. He was kind.'

'He is not kind! You cannot trust him,' I snap and reaching out, I grab her and pull her into my arms. I want to shake her, but I don't. 'You put yourself in what could have been a dangerous situation. Why do you do this? Why do you run? You have to learn to confront me. I didn't do anything wrong. And we could have sorted this out there and then.'

'I thought . . . I thought perhaps this was how you always behave,' she says quickly.

What? No.

'There are so many,' Alessia whispers, and in those four words, there's a world of hurt that I don't really understand, and can't do anything about.

'Alessia. We're married. I have a past. You know this. But I only want you. No one else. I don't care what my mother says. I don't care what the world says. The press . . . fuck them. I just want you. And you fucking left me when you know how anxious I am about your safety.' I rest my forehead against hers and close my eyes.

Fuck. This night.

'Look, it's really late. We've had enough drama tonight. Let's just go to bed.' I kiss her forehead.

Alessia feels like a scolded child. She wishes she hadn't looked away when she was on the mezzanine, just to verify Maxim's story. It sounds so plausible that it's probably true. She wants to believe that it's true. Then she finds out he's been wrestling with all these issues, which he hadn't shared with her.

Does he think she's incapable of handling this news?

Does he think she's a child?

She's young and inexperienced. But she's no child.

'What?' he asks, bright green eyes burning into hers.

'You should have told me about your brother.' She sounds sulky even to her own ears.

'I didn't want to worry you until I knew for certain what I was dealing with. Please. I'm tired. It's been a shitty few hours. Let's go to bed.' He releases her, steps back once more, and they stare at each other.

They're raw. And sad. And on either side of a huge divide that Alessia doesn't really understand.

Was it always there, or did the divide suddenly appear?

Maxim closes his eyes, and when he opens them, they're dim with defeat. 'You look beautiful. Every inch a countess, no matter what my mother may have said to you. And I know she said something else and for that I'm sorry. I'm here. I love you, but if that's not enough, I don't know what more I can do. I'm tired, and I'm going to bed.' He turns and walks from the room, his footsteps echoing down the hall towards his bedroom, leaving Alessia reeling and utterly alone.

Chapter Twenty-One

In our bedroom, I strip off my jacket and toss it on the sofa. So much for my lucky suit. I think I'll burn it. Like an idiot, I turn towards the closed door and *will* Alessia to join me. If she doesn't, I don't know where we go from here, and if she does, she can remove my cufflinks and undress me, and we'll go to bed and fuck and spoon and hold each other. The little dragon catches my eye, unlit and spiritless. He looks how I feel – dim and glum. But wherever Alessia sleeps, she'll need him, so perhaps she'll come and fetch him.

Hopefully.

I don't know how long I stand there dazed and confused, staring at a small piece of moulded plastic, but there's no sign of my wife. She's abandoned both my dragon friend and me.

I remove each cufflink and start on the buttons, fatigue wrapping round me like a shroud. Sinking onto the bed, I sit with my head in my hands and try to process the last couple of hours.

This evening has been . . . *intense*.

I've dealt with a drunken ex, my missing wife, my faithless mother and her revelations, and her meddling fuck toy. I wonder if Heath was the one who tipped off the press. He has the connections.

Fucker.

And then there's Kit. *My half-brother.*

Did he know? Rowena didn't answer the question. I cast my mind back to the New Year when we were at the Hall. '*Not now, Maxim!*' he'd snapped as he stormed out of the kitchen back door into the dark, icy night. And I'd turned and watched my mother stalk down the corridor, her heels tapping their brisk percussive beat, as she walked stiffly away from Kit's office.

Had they been talking? Fighting? I don't remember hearing any raised voices.

But maybe I was my usual oblivious self.

If she *had* told him – he'd have known he was an impostor, and he might lose everything. He would have been shocked and dumbfounded and furious, and that's probably what spurred him onto his Ducati.

Anger. At Rowena.

And now she has to carry that guilt.

His death is on her.

He'd lost everything. Except he hadn't. Not really – only he and Rowena knew.

Fuck a duck.

That's it. She feels responsible for his death. Her favourite child. The eerie sound she made this evening – the half-sob, half-cry – was proof enough. I'd not seen her shed a tear for him until tonight when the truth was finally aired.

Perhaps, before then, she grieved in private.

I'll never know.

Unless she and I talk.

And that's not going to happen anytime soon.

How the hell do we come back from this?

Alessia slumps onto the couch, tears welling in her eyes.

What has she done?

Somehow, during their fight, she's been made to feel like the villain.

How? She'd watched her husband kiss another woman, and she left because she didn't want to witness his betrayal. Is that so unreasonable? Then she arrived back at his apartment, and she'd been berated and found thoroughly wanting by her mother-in-law.

And insulted too!

As if Alessia is motivated by money!

It had taken all her resolve not to rip the earrings from her ears and toss them at Rowena.

All Alessia wants is Maxim's love.

You have that! The still, small voice of her conscience reminds her. He's told her often enough. And again! Just now.

What has he done to make her think he doesn't love her?

He's explained the kiss. He can't help how women react to him. He's probably had to contend with that kind of attention since he was in his teens. And what hot-blooded male wouldn't take advantage?

He only changed when he met Alessia.

She saw the proof . . . or lack, in the wastebasket in his bedroom.

No one since I saw you clutching the broom in my hallway.

I've only felt it since I met you.

Her ire dissipates, leaving a burning hole in her chest.

He didn't have to marry her. He could have left. He stood up to his mother on her behalf, and that's not something an Albanian man would generally do.

Maxim's given her the world.

Is that not enough?

Why is she so insecure?

The other women.

All of them. Including the ones she's met. Caroline. Ticia. Arabella.

Alessia. Alessia. Alessia.

Enough!

She must stop comparing herself to all the women he's bedded.

She has to learn to trust him. And now he's explained about that kiss – he's given her no reason not to. And if she does doubt him, she has his permission to question him. He's asked for that . . . *Confront me. Talk to me.*

It's not the first time he's said that . . . *You need to tell me what you want to do. This is a partnership.*

The hole in her chest deepens and darkens. He'd received such troubling news, and he didn't think he could share it with her because he thought she might leave

Does he think she's so faithless and lacking in compassion?

Where's the sense of partnership in her reaction?

Guilt slices like a scythe through her heart. She's been so absorbed in her own misgivings that she missed all these clues to Maxim's state of mind.

Maxim's in a new, demanding role that he wasn't expecting; he's fallen in love, he's rescued her from kidnappers, he's newly married, and he's been harbouring the news that he might have a potentially life-altering illness.

He's protected her from this.

And Alessia's just consumed by the number of women he's slept with and his ex-girlfriends. Remorse follows the scythe through her heart, filling the gaping hole and almost choking her.

O Zot. Fool! Go to him!

And I have my wife's insecurities to deal with. My beautiful, stoic, talented wife who thinks she's less than the women who came before. Rowena can be a complete bitch sometimes. Did she say something that's making Alessia reassess our relationship?

I hope not.

But I'm not giving up. I just need a moment to get my head together.

My sweet, sad wife.

Emotion gathers in my throat. Maybe she'll never get beyond my past. It preoccupies her in ways I don't understand. Perhaps it *is* our cultural divide, and in my defence, I can categorically say I've never looked at another woman since I met her and I'm as obsessed with her now as I was then.

But I didn't expect to feel this . . . vulnerable.

Or this . . . miserable.

What if she leaves?

Fuck! It's unthinkable.

I'll be crushed.

I remember when the Arsehole spirited her away and how devastating that was. I rub my face, trying to scrub the feeling away, and catch a whisper of her scent and hear the rustle of silk. An ember of hope lights up the cavern that is my heart, and I open my eyes. On the floor beneath my gaze are her bare feet, her toes painted scarlet. I look up, and she's standing in front of me, and the sight of her tear-stained face rips through my soul.

'Oh, love,' I murmur and stand in one swift movement.

'I'm sorry.' Her voice is barely audible.

'Oh, baby, so am I.' I pull her into my arms, breathing in her scent and holding her fast and hard against my body. As she nestles against me, her tears dampen my neck. 'Hey, love, please don't cry.'

She tightens her arms around me and starts weeping.

Hell. This is my fault. I've done this, and I remember her sobbing in the room next to mine at the Hideout. She was overwhelmed then and maybe now.

Frankly, so am I. I tighten my hold on her and let her cry. Perhaps that's what she needs. Sitting back on the bed, I cradle her in my lap, rocking gently, and it's soothing. Perhaps this is what we both need – an outward expression of the frustrations of the last few hours.

It's cathartic.

I calm just holding her close. My beautiful, stoic wife needing me. *Me.*

My mother was right.

I am a sucker for a damsel in distress, or maybe – it's just Alessia.

Eventually, she quiets, and I reach over to the bedside and grab a tissue. 'Here. Better?' I ask.

She nods and wipes her nose and eyes, which are all smudged kohl and running mascara and even like this . . . she's gorgeous.

More so.

'Good. Me too.' I kiss her forehead. 'Let me get you out of this dress, and we can go to bed.' Lifting her off my lap and onto the floor, I stand behind her, brush her hair over her shoulder, and unfasten her dress at the neck. Leaning down, I press my lips to her nape, inhaling her scent, and then turn to undress myself.

She wanders into the bathroom while I strip and clamber into bed. When she emerges a few minutes later, she's fresh-faced and wearing one of my T-shirts. She switches on the little dragon nightlight while I flip back the quilt, and she climbs in beside me and snuggles up, her head on my chest, her arm across my body.

'I love you,' she whispers, and her words unfurl inside my heart, filling the void left by my treacherous mother.

'I know. I love you too.'

I kiss the top of her head, close my eyes, and fall into an exhausted sleep.

> My footsteps echo an urgent beat on the hard reflective floor, and I squint beneath the unremitting light of the fluorescents.
>
> *I've been here before.*
>
> 'This way.' The A&E consultant stops and opens the door to a cool, stark room that is the hospital mortuary.
>
> *I don't want to go in. I don't want to see.*

The A&E consultant stares. Scarlet lips pursed.

Rowena?

'In you go,' she says in a clipped tone that's not to be contradicted.

Inside, on a table, beneath a sheet, is my brother.

Kit.

No! That's not him.

It's *me* – lying bruised and broken . . . cold . . . dead.

What?

From my prone position on the table, I watch Kit lean over and kiss my forehead. 'Goodbye, you fucker,' he rasps, the strain of unshed tears heavy in his throat. 'You've got this. This is what you were born to do.' He smiles, his crooked, sincere smile that's reserved for those rare moments when he's fucked up.

Kit! No! You've got this wrong.

Wait!

'You've got this, Spare,' he says again, then disappears. And I'm looking down at him once more, leaning over him while he sleeps. Except his battered body belies that . . . he's not asleep – he's dead.

No! Kit! No! The words stay stuck in my throat. I can't speak. This is all wrong.

And I'm outside the room watching my mother walk stiffly away, her heels beating a terse tattoo on the tiled floor as she moves further and further away.

Rowena! Mother! Mama!

I wake drenched in sweat, my heart thumping a furious rhythm, my blood pumping frantically through my veins, and I'm sure I'm shaking the bed. I take a deep, cleansing breath and my heartbeat gradually slows.

It's quiet and dark. Even the shimmers on the ceiling are absent.

Alessia mumbles something unintelligible but settles back to sleep.

Thank God she's here.

I turn over to face her, resting my head on my arm and watching her slumber, her features delicate and lovely in the soft glow of the little dragon.

It's just a dream.

No. A nightmare. A prophetic nightmare.

I rub my face and lie on my back, trying to drive out the images of Kit and me on the cold slab.

Was my mother's revelation such a shock to me? Did I know? Maryanne and I share similar colouring – a straightforward blend of our parents. Kit did not. He was blond and blue-eyed, driven and imperious. He was harder, more arrogant and meaner, maybe, than both Maryanne and me. It's been a revelation that he made Caro attend etiquette classes. He was always a bit of a snob, and I wonder if he knew deep down.

Hell. This changes nothing. No one need ever know.

I should contact Maryanne and find out how she's doing.

We can keep this within the family – provided my mother hasn't blurted all to *Heath*.

When I turn back to Alessia, she's watching me, her dark eyes gleaming in the soft light from the little dragon.

'Did I wake you?'

'No,' she whispers, placing her palm on my cheek and steadying me in the storm. I close my eyes, cherishing her touch and grateful that it distracts me from my fevered thoughts. 'Are you okay?' she asks. 'Is there anything I can do?'

With my eyes intent on hers, I try to articulate how I feel, but I'm lost in my own turmoil.

Alessia nods as if she understands and brushes her lips against mine. 'You will figure this out. And until then, I've got you. I'm sorry I wasn't here for you early . . . um . . . earlier.' She snuggles closer, resting her head on my chest, and I wrap an arm around her, holding on tight.

'It's okay, baby,' I murmur. 'I should have told you.'

When she's not angry with me, she's my guiding light, and with her so close, her scent fills my senses, soothing me.

As Alessia's breathing settles into the rhythm of sleep, I close my eyes and join her.

Chapter Twenty-Two

I wake with a start. It's a bright spring morning, and a glance to my side tells me I'm on my own.

Hell! Is she here?

I leap out of bed, grab my jeans, slip them on, and stalk out of the bedroom. Alessia is in the kitchen making bread, her face etched in furious concentration. She's bent over the worktop kneading the dough like it's deeply offended her, or her life depends on it – I'm not sure which. She's barefoot but not pregnant, I think idly and watch as a tendril from her ponytail escapes and curls down her cheek and under her chin. She shakes it loose, peers up, and freezes when she sees me.

'Good morning.' My voice is a whisper.

'Hi,' she says and stands upright. She's in tight jeans and a tighter T-shirt, and it's stirring as hell, but her dark eyes are wary.

Is this a hangover from yesterday's debacle? 'You okay?'

She presses her lips together, quickly rinses her hands, and grabs her phone from the countertop. 'My mother. She sent me this. She has the Google alert.'

My heart sinks as she hands me her phone, and sure enough, she reveals a tabloid article titled 'The Earl, the Ex and the Wife.' A series of photographs from last night accompany it – Alessia, Caroline, and me arriving at the party, together at the party, and there's a photograph of Charlotte kissing me. In it, I'm obviously taken aback and not a willing participant. I'm vindicated, though I'm sure that's not what the picture editor who chose the photo intended. I slide my gaze to Alessia's. 'I love the one of you and me.' I hand her phone back. 'Your mother sent that?'

Alessia nods and sets her phone on the worktop. 'She worries.'

'Did you reassure her?'

'I did.'

'Good. Are you reassured?'

She bites her lip, her eyes shining with unshed tears – and I have my answer. Reaching up, I run my thumb over her trembling bottom lip. 'You didn't sign up for any of this, did you?'

She inhales sharply, and I dread what she's going to say. But she skims her tongue across my thumb, then purses her lips and kisses the tip. The jolt travels like lightning to my groin, heating everything in its path, and I suppress a groan, taken completely by surprise.

Alessia's eyes, intent on me, widen a fraction.

Not from fear or anger.

From the same jolt of desire.

Her sharply exhaled breath dries the spot on my thumb moistened by her kiss, sending my blood racing.

South.

Her eyes follow, and my dick rejoices as I drop my hand.

'Alessia,' I whisper, and I don't know if it's a plea or a warning. Her darkening eyes lift, pinning mine. Gone are the unshed tears; there's just her burning gaze full of carnal promise. I step closer so I'm bathed in her scent and the warmth of her body. I want nothing more than to grab her, strip off her jeans, and fuck her on the kitchen worktop. But I want her to make the first move. 'What do you want, my love?'

Tentatively, she raises her hand and traces my bottom lip with her thumb. 'No, I didn't sign up for this. But I did sign up for you.'

The words are softly spoken.

And in them. There's hope. For us.

My senses heightened, I feel the air thicken between us, full of lush anticipation.

And heat.

And expectation.

It's heady and addictive.

I've never felt like this with anyone else. My sweet, siren wife. She has no idea about the potency of the magic she weaves and the spell she casts over me.

Or maybe she does.

'What do you want, Alessia?'

'You,' she whispers, and using one hand, she runs the tips of her fingers down my sternum, firing synapses throughout my body. Then across my chest, so my nipples pucker at her touch, and down my stomach, my belly, and my happy trail to the button on the waistband of my jeans. Keeping her eyes on mine, she undoes the button in one nimble move. And her fingers skirt lower, cradling my heavy erection through the denim.

'You have me.' I tilt my pelvis, finding some friction against her palm, and close my eyes, fisting my hands to stop myself from wrapping her in my arms.

Alessia regards her husband through heavy-lidded eyes.

You'll have to fight for him. Her mother's words from their call this morning ring through her head. And fight, she will. Using every available weapon she has.

She loves him.

She knows this.

She wants him.

And she wants him to want her. She skirts her fingers over his unyielding erection once more. The rigid proof at her fingertips means she's succeeded.

It's an intoxicating feeling. Seducing her husband.

Or maybe he's seducing her . . .

She doesn't care.

She didn't sign up for all the other women.

But they are out of his life. He said so, and she's chosen to believe him. Even though there's questionable evidence splashed all over the papers. She can see he's the reluctant party in the photograph.

And now she wants him. But he hasn't touched her since his thumb skirted her lip.

It's frustrating.

Confront me. Talk to me.

Those were his words. 'Take me,' she says, because that's what she wants. Here. Right now.

Maxim groans and steps forward, bringing his body flush against hers and clasping her face between his palms and bringing her lips to his. His tongue unleashed, he searches and finds and provokes her own. Her hands fist in his hair as she revels in his kiss – wanting and giving more. When they're both breathless, he pulls sharply away and drops to his knees. Deftly, he makes fast work of her jeans, unfastening them and sliding them and her panties down her legs and off. He grabs her thighs and tugs her against his waiting nose and mouth.

'Ah!' she groans and grabs the countertop for balance. Maxim's tongue is on her.

Big time.

Teasing.

Circling.

Coaxing her higher.

Making her wetter and wetter.

Alessia tilts her head back, one hand tugging his hair, the other gripping the worktop, and she moans, surrendering to his masterful ministrations.

I think I'm going to burst. Standing ready to bury myself in my wife, I grab her glorious behind and lift her onto the worktop. 'I've never done it here,' I mutter as I unzip my jeans, freeing my straining dick. Alessia approves and wraps her legs around me, hauling me closer, digging her heels in my arse. She rests her arms on my shoulders, and we both pause, our breath mingling, eyes on each other. She kisses me. And pulls away.

'I taste me,' she whispers.

'Best flavour in the world.'

She grins, her whole face lighting up like a blissful spring day, and she cups my face, bringing my mouth to hers and we kiss, our lips covered in a heady combination of her arousal and my saliva.

It's slippery and wet.

And wonderful.

And oh-so-slowly, I sink into my wife.

'Ah,' she cries, tipping back her head and hitting it on the cupboard behind. 'Ow!'

She laughs, and I cup her head, knowing she's not hurt – and thrust harder and deeper inside her. She clings to me as I set a punishing, forget-everything-else pace. She bites my earlobe, her breathing hot and harsh in my ear as I lose myself in her.

And I feel her. Climbing. Higher and higher.

I keep going, banishing all thoughts from last night, so it's only her and me in the now.

Alessia.

She's rising and soaring, taking me with her.

'Maxim,' she cries as she comes, and the power of her orgasm pushes me over the edge, and I climax hard and fast, buried in my beautiful wife.

I have flour on my backside,' Alessia mumbles.

Maxim raises his face from the crook of her neck and grins. 'There's a sentence I never thought I'd hear.' He runs his nose down hers and kisses her sweetly. They're still intimately joined, and neither of them seem to want to move.

'I love you, Lady Trevethick.'

'I love you, Lord Trevethick,' she responds.

'Good.'

She tightens her hold on him, keeping him anchored inside her. 'If you kiss anyone else, I will remove this organ,' she says, digging her heels into his naked butt.

Maxim laughs and eases out of her. 'Understood, my lady.'

Alessia smiles. 'I will fight for you,' she says as he tugs up his jeans.

He caresses her face with both his hands, his thumbs tracing the outline of her lips and his green eyes blazing. 'Oh my love, you don't have to fight for me. I'm yours. Always. I'll be yours for as long as you'll have me.'

Alessia is winded by his quiet but passionate entreaty.

He studies her as he stands between her legs. 'What can I do to convince you?'

She frowns. Where is he going with this?

'I know,' he says, his face lighting up with sudden inspiration. 'Let's have a baby.'

Chapter Twenty-Three

Alessia gasps and stares back into bright green eyes, totally blindsided. 'A baby?' she squeaks.

He plants a soft kiss at the corner of her mouth. 'Yes. A boy.' He kisses her again. 'Then a girl.' Kiss. 'Then another boy.' Kiss. 'And another girl.' He kisses the other side of her mouth.

Alessia giggles. 'Four children! I'm not sure it works like that.'

'I know how it works,' he growls, amused.

'*Call of Duty*?'

Maxim laughs. 'Oh, my love. Funny and talented. Never change.' He nuzzles her nose with his.

'My backside is covered in flour, and you want babies.'

He nods.

'Can I shower first?'

He grins and looks at the worktop beside her, where the dough lies neglected but rising. 'I was rather hoping for breakfast.' He kisses her again, and she swats him away.

'Help me down, and I will make you breakfast.'

'Only if you promise not to put your jeans or knickers back on.' He gently lifts her from the worktop and slides her down his body until her feet touch the floor. He cradles her head in his hands. 'I want babies – lots of them. I thought –' He swallows. 'I thought that maybe with Kit . . . and his . . . condition. That . . .'

'Oh, Maxim,' Alessia whispers, realising that this is another reason he's been so preoccupied. She leans in, bringing her lips to his, and kisses him, a sweet, remorseful kiss.

All the worry, and she never knew.

'Let's have breakfast and talk about it.'

'We could go out,' Maxim offers.

'I like making breakfast for you, Maxim. I want to take care of you, like you want to provide for me. That's a partnership.'

Alessia's fingers make patterns in my hair as we lie in bed. Spent. Replete. Together. My head on her stomach, I turn and kiss the soft skin of her belly and allow myself a little fantasy that it's swollen with our child.

Alessia doesn't have the same sense of urgency as I do. She doesn't realise that I'm trying to bind her to me in any way I can, but we've talked, and she's right. She's young and wants to see a little of the world before we embark on babies.

Mate. What were you thinking?

I wonder what my mother would make of being a grandmother.

I sigh. I have no idea how I'll repair that relationship.

Do I want to?

'What is it?' Alessia asks.

'I'm just thinking about my mother.'

Alessia stiffens beneath me.

Shit. 'Did she say something horribly dreadful to you?'

Alessia is quiet, and her fingers have stopped fiddling with my hair, so I look up.

Eyes gleaming, she swallows. 'She wanted to know how much money I wanted to leave you.'

What. The. Fuck?

Sitting up, I lean against the pillows and gather my wife in my arms. 'I'm so sorry.'

'I was hurt and angry, but she was only acting in what she thinks is your . . . um . . . best . . . um . . .'

'Interests?'

'Yes. That.'

'It's not in my best interests at all. The woman wouldn't know my best interests if she tripped over them and they smacked her bloody arse. You don't deserve to be spoken to like that. If anything –' I stop because what I'm about to say about my own mother is . . . *un-fucking-becoming*. 'Who the hell does she think she is?' I shake my head in disbelief and kiss the top of Alessia's head.

'She did come here and had the courage to tell you and your sister face to the face about your brother.'

'Well, that's putting a positive slant on what happened. But I suppose you're right.' I offer her a smile. 'And it's "face-to-face."'

Alessia grins. 'There he is – my English teacher.'

'For as long as you need me.'

'I will always need you.' Alessia's burning sincerity and love is in every syllable of her soft-spoken statement, and it feeds my soul. Curling my fingers around hers, I bring them to my lips. And to think we were at loggerheads last night – and I wonder what would have happened if my mother hadn't put in her untimely appearance. 'I wonder why she came all the way from Manhattan to tell us in such a hostile way.'

'Perhaps she is punishing herself?' Alessia offers.

Wow. 'That's insightful. Do you think so?'

She shakes her head, and it's plain that this is just Alessia's hypothesis, but it's credible. Perhaps my mother is filled with shame.

Who knows? Is she capable of shame?

'Shall we go out for lunch?' I ask, and Alessia grins. 'We'll probably have to dodge the press after that sordid article,' I add.

Alessia shrugs. 'We say nothing.'

I grin. 'Exactly.'

~

On Monday morning, Alessia and Maxim leave via the fire escape to avoid the cluster of reporters outside the building. Maxim hails a cab, and together, feeling pleased with themselves, they settle into the back seat and head to the London Academy of Social Etiquette and Graces.

'What's that place?' Alessia asks, pointing with her chin at an enormous, ornate, gothic building.

'That's the Natural History Museum. We should go. Beside it is the Science Museum. Many a Saturday afternoon was spent there. Our nanny at the time had a passion for science. But it has a great place for kids to play and explore.'

Alessia grins. 'One day, we will take our children.'

Maxim glances at her. 'Or the nanny will.' He finds and fondles her knee.

'Nanny?' Alessia had not thought that they might have help with childcare.

'Just a thought. I had one. Well, several, actually. And look how I turned out.'

Alessia laughs. And Maxim scowls, pretending to be offended. 'What are you implying? Am I not the epitome of well-bred manhood?'

'Of course you are.' She giggles. 'You have the best manners. And after this week, so shall I.' She pats his knee, suppressing her laughter.

The cab pulls up outside an impressive white building in Queen's Gate, South Kensington. 'We're here.' Maxim opens the taxi door and steps out while the cab idles. Alessia follows him, staring up at yet more imposing architecture. 'Do you want me to come in with you?' Maxim asks.

Alessia tries to suppress her smile. He's been fussing like a mother hen all morning, and it's a side of him she's not seen before. 'I'll be okay.'

'Text me if you need anything.' He kisses her quickly and

climbs back in the cab, and Alessia strides up the stone steps to the glossy black door.

So many shiny black doors in London.

She rings the brass bell, ignoring the fluttering of nerves in her stomach, and the door buzzes open. Alessia steps inside a wide hallway painted a brilliant white, and from behind a reception desk, a young woman in a grey suit looks up, an open, expectant expression on her face.

'London Academy—' Alessia asks.

'Up to the first floor. Registration is through the door on the left.'

'Thank you,' Alessia says, surprised to be interrupted. She heads up the wide staircase that creaks beneath each footfall to the first floor and turns left towards a door with a discreet sign that reads: L A S E G. Inside the white, high-ceilinged room, she's greeted by an older, smartly dressed woman with pearls at her ears and her neck, carrying a clipboard.

'Good morning,' the woman says pleasantly, her smile reaching her bright brown eyes.

'Hello,' Alessia replies.

'My name is Belinda Donaldson, I'm the administrator, and I'll be checking you in. We use first or given names for our delegates here at the Academy to protect everyone's identity.'

'Alessia,' Alessia replies.

'Excellent. Welcome, Alessia. You're the first to arrive. Punctuality is the politeness of kings . . . and queens. Please help yourself to tea or coffee, and do take a seat.'

Alessia pours coffee into one of the delicate cups and takes a seat. She watches as women arrive and are greeted in a similar fashion by Belinda. They're all elegant, some in dresses, some in pants like her, and most are young, like Alessia, but there's one older lady who must be in her fifties. Alessia is grateful to be wearing her new black pants, white shirt, and tailored jacket; knowing she's well-dressed has boosted her confidence. For the first time, she feels like she belongs with these women.

A breathless young woman with flowing red hair stumbles

into the room. 'Hello,' she says, gasping for air. 'I thought I was going to be late.'

Belinda regards her coolly. 'Good morning. Take a moment. You have time.'

'Great. Thanks. My name's Tabitha, Lady—'

'I'll stop you right there, Tabitha. We operate on a first-name basis only. Please. Come and sit down and help yourself to tea or coffee. We will begin shortly.'

After a delicious pub lunch yesterday afternoon, Alessia and Maxim had attended an exhibition of pre-Raphaelite art at Tate Britain, a gallery not far from their apartment. With her long red hair and flowing chiffon dress, Tabitha reminds Alessia of one of the subjects in the paintings.

The assembled women resume their quiet chatter among themselves as Tabitha sits down beside Alessia. 'Hi, I'm Tabitha,' she introduces herself. 'I thought I'd be late!' She makes a face, and Alessia smiles, feeling a little more relaxed as she introduces herself. She's drawn to Tabitha's bright grin.

'I was too early,' Alessia confesses. 'I am nervous.'

Tabitha beams as if she's met a long-lost friend. 'You'll be fine,' she says and Alessia feels lighter, buoyed by Tabitha's warmth.

On Sunday, my phone had blown up with texts about Dimitri's party and the photos of Alessia and bloody Charlotte. I'd ignored the messages, choosing to spend quality time with my wife. And what a wonderful day we had – we seem to have turned a corner. We've survived our first major argument, my mother's interference and her revelations, and some extremely unwelcome press attention.

And Alessia *finally* seems to be standing up for herself.

If you kiss anyone else, I will remove this organ.

I shake my head, smiling at my possessive, jealous wife.

But as I sit at my desk and try to read up on the rules for

distilling alcohol in the UK, I'm finding it impossible to concentrate. My brain continues to pick over my mother's disclosure like it's carrion. I've called and left messages for Maryanne so we can compare notes on the drama, but she's not returned either.

Is she angry with me?

I suppose I prompted the fallout and didn't tell Maryanne about Kit's genetic counselling.

Hell.

And I'm not sure how I'm supposed to feel after Rowena's shocking news.

Numb?

Distracted?

Angry?

Yeah, all those feelings.

Dude, get a grip.

My second meeting of the day is at the Mayfair mansion block refurbishment with Oliver and Caroline. We're going through design and décor plans for the foyers, the common areas, and the show apartment. Caroline and Oliver are already in the foyer, making what sounds like awkward small talk. Oliver, for some reason, looks a little flustered while Caroline observes him with cool detachment.

'Maxim!' Caro brightens, greeting me with a quick peck on my cheek.

'So, what do you think?' I ask.

'This is a light, airy space, and we can do a great deal with it. What, is up to you. What do you want this space to say? What do you want to achieve?'

I'm not sure if she's mocking me or not – we've never had a professional conversation before. 'What I want is something classic that doesn't date and doesn't need redecorating every year.'

Oliver smiles in approval. 'Yes. Pragmatic,' he pipes up.

'You sound just like Kit,' Caroline huffs, and a tangle of conflicted emotions fill my throat. Kit. My half-brother.

And Caro doesn't know. 'Thank you,' I mutter. 'I'm going to take that as a compliment.'

She smiles. 'It was meant as such.'

'Let's see the common areas so you can have an idea of the extent of the work required,' Oliver says, his gaze intent on Caroline.

She offers him a polite, cool smile. 'I can sketch some plans and take a few photos as we walk through.'

Alessia is paying attention to Jennifer Knight, their social etiquette instructor and the owner of the school. 'And our mission is to empower all of you to present your best selves. You'll have the confidence to walk into any room and know exactly how to behave. From the boardroom to the banqueting hall, you'll be equipped to handle any work and social situation. We'll start with the basics: introductions – both formal and informal – what forms of address you should use, and while mainly focusing on British etiquette, we'll touch on cultural differences that you should be aware of to make those you meet and greet feel respected and comfortable in your presence.' Jennifer gives the class a broad smile. 'If you'll turn to the first page in your workbook, we can begin.'

Alessia does exactly that, while Tabitha is trying and failing not to look bored.

'I think I have all I need,' Caroline says.

'Excellent.' Oliver gives us a rare, relieved smile.

'Do you have a budget in mind?' Caro looks to me.

'Do the designs and give us options,' I state, and Oliver nods with approval again – I think – which is heartening.

'Okay. That shouldn't be too difficult. If we're done, can we grab a coffee, Maxim?'

'Sure. There's a café across the road. Oliver, I'll see you back at the office.'

'Of course. I'll wait to hear from you, Caroline,' he says stiffly.

What is it with these two?

'Something troubling you?' I ask, watching Caroline slide into the banquette.

'Yes. Rowena. Have you managed to track her down and ask her?'

I take the chair opposite Caro as I struggle to find something to say. 'Ask her what?'

'About Kit! The genetic stuff.'

I clear my throat. 'Yes. Of course. I did. And she said there was nothing to worry about.'

Caro narrows her eyes, pinning me with her most intrusive gaze. Inside, I'm flailing. This is not a conversation I expected to have just yet. I'm still coming to terms with my mother's bombshell.

'What are you not telling me?' Caro's tone is terse. She's irritated.

'Nothing.'

'Maxim, you're lying. I can always tell. Your whole face becomes completely immobile while your brain frantically works out what to say.'

'It does not! And I told you. She said there's nothing to worry about.'

'It was all a false alarm?'

I make a noise in my throat that I hope passes for agreement. I don't want to lie to her.

'I'm trying to organise Kit's memorial service, and you won't confirm the date, and Rowena is not taking my calls.'

'Oh.' *Hell.* Kit's memorial had slipped my mind.

'It's not like her,' Caro continues. 'I don't know if I've offended her. But it must be something. Can you talk to her?'

'She's not talking to me either.'

'Really? Why? Do you think she's okay?'

'I don't know.'

'When did you talk to her?'

'Over the weekend.'

Caroline huffs. 'Maryanne's disappeared too. Perhaps they've found some late winter sun together.'

'Maybe. Do you have a guest list for the memorial service?'

'Yes. I'll send it over, and you can add people. I'm waiting for your mother's additions.'

'I told Rowena I'd write the eulogy.'

'Can we discuss readings?'

'Of course. Whenever. We're around. Alessia is on that etiquette course this week.'

'Good. She'll feel a lot more confident afterwards. And she should make some friends.'

'Yeah.'

'Are you worried?' Caroline scoffs. 'For heaven's sake, Maxim. She's a grown woman.'

'I know. I know. But the kidnapping. I . . . I . . .' I shrug. *What can I say?* Alessia's safety is my priority.

'Of course. But she's here now. With you. She'll be fine.'

'Incidentally, what did you say to Charlotte Hampshire at Dimitri's party?'

'Nothing!' she says far too quickly and holds my gaze, but I'm not sure I believe her.

'Caro?' I arch a brow in warning.

What did you say?

'Is this about the photograph? It's everywhere. Are you in trouble?'

'Was that your intention? To cause trouble between Alessia and me?' I glare at her, and the temperature between us drops to below zero.

Caroline's eyes widen. 'No! Why would I do that?' she says in a gush of faux indignation. 'Is that what you think?'

'Caro, I don't know what to think. But Alessia and I are fine. Stop inter-fucking-fering, or there will be consequences.'

She bristles but stays silent, and I know she said something to Charlotte.

'And what's with you and Oliver?' I ask to change the subject.

'What do you mean?' she snaps.

'I don't know, but there's some weird energy between you.'

'Oh, for goodness' sake. You're coming across all woo-woo. I'd better go and get on with this work.' She stands. 'Let me know if you hear from Rowena.'

And that's a wrap for today, ladies,' Jennifer says. 'Tomorrow, we'll be covering communication. Everything from texting to writing letters. Thank you for your time and attention today.' She smiles, and Alessia almost sags with relief but stops herself as she's endured a whole afternoon of deportment lessons and learned about correct posture.

'I am desperate for a drink,' Tabitha hisses beside her. 'Please say you'll come.'

'Um . . .' Alessia is hesitant. This is a first for her – a stranger asking her to come for a drink. But she likes Tabitha. A woman her own age. Maxim won't mind.

Will he?

'Don't tell me you have to get back to your husband, Alessia.'

'How did . . .?'

'Your ring. I assumed you were married. But you seem awfully young to be wed.'

Alessia smiles. 'In my country, it is normal to marry young.'

'Tell me all over a drink! Please.'

My phone buzzes. It's a text from Maryanne. *Finally*.

I'm in Seattle.

Will text when home.

Are you okay?

No. Still reeling from dear
Mama's revelations.
Here for some R&R.

How did you get the time off?

Skillz!

What! Her response makes me laugh. It's a most un-Maryanne text. But I'm glad that she's still speaking to me and that she's getting some rest. Has she gone to see that guy she met when she went skiing? I daren't ask.

Enjoy yourself.

Oh. I am.
Are you okay?

Of course.

Maxie, it was you all along.
Not Kit.

What?

The earldom.
It was yours.

My scalp prickles.

It was me all along.

I was the viscount. Then the earl.

Not Kit.

That's hard to hear.

I know ♥
But it was you, Maxie.
It was always you.
Remember that.
Poor Kit. Finding out like that.
He must have been furious.

Yes. I can't stop thinking about that.

I wonder what he had.

What he had?

His genetic condition.

Something awful, I suspect.
I don't want to know.
Poor man.

Yes. Maybe you're right.
We loved him.

We did.

I'll be back later this week.
We can talk then.
I've got to get up.
We're going sailing on a super-
duper catamaran.

Be safe.
Mx

I blow out a breath. Maryanne is still speaking to me, unlike my mother. And she's focused on something that I've not thought about. My family has been obsessed with bloodlines since the earldom was created in the 1600s. My mother was driven by legacy too. It was drummed into all of us.

Kit most of all.

How ironic.

And with his death, my mother's secret has died. And no one need ever know.

She didn't have to tell us.

She could have claimed that Kit's genetic issues were all a false alarm. Perhaps Alessia's right. She's atoning for her sins.

Her lies.

Hell. I need to talk to her. But after what she said to my dear wife, I'm not sure I want her in our lives.

My phone buzzes again, and I think it might be Maryanne with more pearls of wisdom. But it's Alessia.

I am going to a bar with a woman
I met on my course.
I will try not to be late.

Alarm tightens my chest. I'm not sure how I feel about Alessia on the loose in London with a stranger. Caroline's words from earlier come back to me.

For heaven's sake, Maxim. She's a grown woman.

Yes. But she's led a sheltered, claustrophobic life. I've seen it. I lived it for a week.

Sounds great. I'm finished here.
May I join you?

Yes!! 😁
We are at the Gore.
xxxx

Alessia is fascinated by Tabitha. As they sip gin and tonics, Tabitha divulges that she lives in a castle in Scotland, though Alessia can't discern a Scottish accent. Tabitha finished her History of Art degree last year at Bristol University and has been on a gap year trekking through Kenya and Tanzania with a friend. It sounds exciting and beyond anything that Alessia's experienced. Apart from her harrowing journey to England – but Alessia decides to keep that story to herself.

'Oh look, Maxim Trevelyan just arrived, or should I say Maxim Trevethick, now.'

'Oh.' Alessia turns to see Maxim scanning the room.

'I've not met him. But my sisters *know* him. You know. In the biblical sense.'

Alessia's spirits sink.

'They're twins.'

Twins!

'I heard he's married, though I know nothing about the lucky woman who bagged him.'

Maxim spies Alessia, and his face lights up with what she suspects is relief.

'Oh my God, he's coming over here!'

Alessia turns to Tabitha. 'Maxim Trevethick is my husband.'

Tabitha chokes on her gin. 'Oh my God.'

'I'm the lucky woman who . . . um . . . bagged him.'

'Oh no. I'm so sorry. About what I said.'

Alessia gives her a reassuring smile. 'His reputation is . . . extra.'

'Yes. It is!' Tabitha says quickly, her face flushed.

Alessia stands as Maxim approaches them, and he gives her a sweet, chaste kiss, suitable for public consumption. 'Hello, darling. How are you? How was the first day?' Maxim's husky tone suggests he's asking her something indecent.

'Good. Thank you.' Alessia is a little breathless. 'May I introduce Lady Tabitha.'

'How do you do,' Maxim says.

'Lord Trevethick.' Tabitha offers her hand, and Maxim takes it. 'I'm so sorry to hear about your brother.'

'He's sorely missed. May I join you?'

'Of course.' Tabitha summons the waiter, and Maxim orders an old-fashioned.

'So, what did you learn today?' Maxim turns his intense gaze on Alessia, his expression glowing with curiosity.

'How to sit. Walk. And how to say hello.' Alessia grins.

'Ah. The basics.' He grins back, and he's breathtaking, a licentious gleam in his eyes.

'I really should be going,' Tabitha says.

'Please don't leave on my account,' Maxim says.

'I should be getting back to the flat.'

Maxim stands when Tabitha does, and Alessia knows he doesn't need any lessons; his manners are innate. 'I'll pick up the tab,' he says.

'Thank you. Alessia, I'll see you tomorrow.' Tabitha gives her an embarrassed wave.

'I look forward to it,' Alessia says.

He sits back down.

'Twins?' Alessia asks.

He frowns, then glances at Tabitha's retreating figure. 'Ah. That Tabitha.' He looks back at Alessia. 'Do you really want to know?'

Alessia feels her cheeks warm but rolls her eyes. 'No.'

He laughs. 'Now, that is an appropriate reaction. A good eye roll.'

Alessia smiles, despite her misgivings, and leans forward and kisses him once more.

She's learning. This is growth. His past is his past.

'Shall we go out to eat?' he asks. 'We could eat here if you'd like?'

In the back of the cab, Alessia studies me. 'How are you?'

I blow out a breath. 'Honestly? A little numb. Dinner this

evening was a welcome distraction. And Maryanne has finally texted me back. She's in Seattle but says we'll compare notes when she's back.'

'And have you heard from your mother?'

I snort. 'I think that's unlikely for a while.'

Alessia reaches out and takes my hand. 'She is your mother . . .'

'I know.' I swallow. 'It will take time.'

She nods sympathetically. 'Do you want to talk about it?'

'What's there to talk about that we haven't already said? My mother has proved to be as duplicitous as I thought she was, and mean. And a terrible snob.'

'She is . . . human.'

I laugh, and it's a hollow sound. 'That may be the first time anyone has accused Rowena of being human.'

Alessia smiles. 'What do you want to do?'

'Well, I should read up on stills.'

'Stills? More landscape photography?'

I chuckle. 'No. Still. For distilling gin.'

Alessia's expression brightens.

'Yeah. I want to make gin. My wife likes it.'

The cab pulls up outside our building and it's besieged by photographers.

'Fuck,' I growl under my breath. 'Ready?'

Alessia nods.

'Say nothing. Let me clamber out first, and I'll open your door.'

'Okay.'

I do exactly that and tuck Alessia under my arm as we make our way into the building.

Trevethick! Trevethick!

What about your relationship with Miss Charlotte Hampshire?

What does your wife have to say?

We ignore them, but Alessia stops us at the front door of the building. 'What?' I ask.

She grabs my lapels, then slides her hands around the nape

of my neck, dragging my lips to hers. To a blaze of flash photography, she presses her body to mine and kisses me properly, her tongue insistent and possessive.

It's . . . hot.

And takes me by surprise.

When we move apart, we're both winded. She pushes open the door, and without a glance at the cheered crowd, she ushers me into the building.

Wow.

In the lift, I pounce, hungry for her, and we kiss all the way to the sixth floor.

'You know, we could play *Call of Duty* again,' I murmur against the corner of her mouth.

She tips her head back and laughs.

Alessia toys with Maxim's hair as they lie in bed, fresh from their lovemaking. Her limbs are boneless as her heart rate settles into a satiated, steady rhythm. Maxim rests his head on her stomach, his favourite post-lovemaking position, and draws a faint circle around her navel. It almost tickles, and she knows he's preoccupied.

'My father was always my champion,' Maxim interrupts their easy silence. 'Now it makes sense.'

Alessia stills her fingers, and he turns gleaming green eyes to her. 'I'm wondering if my mother overcompensated with Kit because of my father's . . . indifference to him. No, indifference is too strong a word. I didn't notice it then. I was too caught up in my own world, but now, looking back, perhaps he favoured me more.'

'No one suspected?'

'No. I don't think so . . .' He trails off. 'No. Wait. My mother and father had a huge falling-out with my uncle Cameron. Perhaps he knew.'

'He's never said anything?'

'No. Never.' Maxim rests his head on her belly once more.

'He escaped to LA in the late '80s. But now I think of it, Kit never felt comfortable with Cameron. We didn't visit him when we were in the Caribbean last Christmas. Now, I know why.'

They're quiet as they each digest this titbit of information. Alessia realises that the only person who can shed any light is Rowena.

'Are you going to talk to your mother?' Alessia asks.

Maxim snorts. 'We had a fractured relationship already. I don't see us coming back from this.'

Alessia says nothing but teases his hair once more. She wants to tell him that, in spite of how he and Alessia feel about Rowena, maybe he should listen to his mother's side of the story. They don't know all the details, but she doesn't think Maxim is ready to hear that yet.

One day.

Soon.

After all, Rowena is still his mother.

Chapter Twenty-Four

Tabitha makes a beeline for Alessia as soon as she walks into their classroom. 'Good morning, Alessia. I'm so sorry about yesterday.'

Alessia shakes her head. 'Don't worry.'

'Did you know you've gone viral?' Tabitha gushes.

'No. What? Where?'

'Here. I Googled you last night after my dreadful faux pas. And look. This is what I found.' She holds up her phone, and there's a video of Alessia playing the piano at Dimitri's party. It's an Instagram reel in the name of GrishaEgonov.

'You're very good,' Tabitha says.

'Thank you,' Alessia says automatically. She's staggered. She doesn't remember him filming her – she was too caught up in the music. The post has over eighty thousand likes and thousands of comments. The caption reads *Lady Alessia, Countess of Trevethick. Beautiful and talented.*

She gapes at Tabitha, who grins. 'Grisha's not wrong.'

'Good morning, everyone.' Jennifer Knight brings the room

to attention, ending their conversation. 'Today, we'll be discussing written communication and the correct forms of address, whether by email or snail mail.'

Abigail Chenoweth, our tenant farmer from Rosperran farm, and Michael Harris, Tresyllian Hall's estate manager, are beyond excited at the prospect of making gin. I conclude my conference call with them, pleased that, if we get this project right, we might bring some welcome revenue to the estate and provide employment for the locals from the surrounding villages. There's a great deal of work to be done to obtain the necessary licenses, planning, and all that bollocks, but I've got to say, I'm stoked: my first project for the estate – and all inspired by my wife.

My phone buzzes. It's Caroline. 'Caro.'

'Hi, have you seen that video of Alessia?'

What now?

'Video? No?'

'She's on Grisha's Instagram.'

'Well, I'd look at it, but I'm talking to you. What's she doing?'

'What do you think she's doing? She's playing his grand piano – and don't worry, darling, that's not a euphemism.' Caro cackles at her tasteless joke.

'And?' I know about the piano playing. I was there!

'The Stepsow has seen it. She wants to know if Alessia has applied to the Royal College of Music.'

Whoa!

'Yes. She has applied.'

'What name did she use?'

'Alessia Trevelyan.'

'Good. I'll let her know.'

'You two are on speaking terms?'

'She called. I thought Daddy might be ill or worse, so I took the call. But no, she wanted to know about Alessia, and she was sounding me out about you DJing?'

'Why?'

'The Demon Spawn is eighteen this year, and she wants a rave in the grounds at Horston.'

'Your little sister is eighteen! How the hell did that happen?'

'Stepsister!' she snaps. 'And yes. Cordelia's of age to spread her demon spawn-ness. The world should tremble.'

'Caro, my DJ days are over, unless your stepmother gets Alessia into the school. In which case, I might reconsider. It's the only way I can get her a visa without her returning to Albania.'

'Ah. I see. No more spinning the decks for you?' Caro sounds surprised.

'I don't have the time. Besides, the arseholes who trafficked Alessia stole my decks, and I haven't found a minute to replace them.'

'Oh.' Caro is momentarily silenced, but before I can say anything, she continues. 'I'll let her know. Although the Demon Spawn will be terribly disappointed. You know she has a huge crush on you.'

'Does she now?' *What the hell am I supposed to say to that?*

Caroline sighs, and I'm not sure why.

'Anyway,' she says. 'I should have some ideas sketched out for you by the middle of next week.'

'Great. Thanks, Caro.' I hang up, relieved that she changed the subject from Cordelia's crush, and open my Instagram app.

Alessia! Viral.

Does she know?

I search for Grisha and find his profile. There are several photos from the party – he's posing, of course, with many of the famous actors, TV personalities and models who were present at the party, but on his reels, there's my wife playing Bach as if that's what she was born to do.

Wow. The video has a hundred thousand likes.

Grisha's right, though it pains me to say – Alessia is gorgeous and talented.

And mine.

I take a moment out of my day and watch the video again. Then again. The fourth time, a movement in the background catches my eye.

I grin. Something to show my wife.

Their lessons finish early, and Tabitha invites Alessia to take tea. But Alessia politely declines and asks for a rain check; she has plans. She eyes her watch: 3:30 p.m. She has time – she's researched the journey a few times on the internet. Out on the street, she bids goodbye to Tabitha and hails a passing cab, just like Maxim, and clambers inside.

'Where to, love?' the cabbie asks.

'Kew Green, please.' Alessia sits back in her seat and takes out her phone. She texts Maxim.

Hello My Lord
We finished today early.
I am going out.
Axx

Alessia wants to see where her great-uncle lives. Maybe even meet him. During her lessons today, she'd written him a letter, and she hopes to post it through his door. Once they've made contact, she'll tell her husband that she's tracked him down, and only then. After all, Maxim didn't want her to contact the private detective.

And she did.

Her phone chimes.

It's a text from her husband.

Good afternoon, My Lady.
I love when you text me.
Out where? Curious minds need to know.
I'll come and join you if you wish.
Mx

Oh no.

I am going to Kew.
I will not be long.
See you later.
xxxx

What the hell is Alessia doing in Kew? The last time I was near that part of the world was when I drove out to Brentford after those arseholes showed up at my flat, and Alessia fled. *You are your father's son. A knight in shining armour – a sucker for a damsel in distress.*

The memory of my mother's words sours my mood and my concern for Alessia mushrooms.

What are you doing in Kew?

Alessia huffs. Her husband worries too much – she can tell by the brusque tone of his text. She thought she would reassure him by letting him know she was going out, but it appears to have added to his anxiety. She texts back.

It is a surprise.
Do not worry!!! 😃
xxxx

Alessia's text is moderately reassuring.

For heaven's sake, Maxim. She's a grown woman.

Okay.
Stay safe.
Text when you're coming home.

Mx

PS: Not sure I like surprises! 😑

Alessia sighs with relief. This is more like it. He seems to have recovered his sense of humour. Feeling reassured, Alessia stares out the cab window and spots a mother pushing a stroller. She wonders what Maxim would be like if she was with child. He'd probably be a great deal worse.

Maxim's child.

She loves the idea.

Just not yet. She was shocked when he mentioned it at the weekend, and she's glad he's eager for children. But the temptation to study at one of the best music schools in the country is too great a lure.

Parenthood can wait.

But if he insisted, she would capitulate. She wants children too.

Yes. She could see herself doing this.

Her parents would be thrilled, and so would Maxim.

But he agreed to wait. He wants to show her some of the world too.

My phone rings, and it's a number I don't recognise. 'Trevethick.'

'Lord Trevethick, it's Ticia Cavanagh.'

'Hello, Ticia. Please call me Maxim.' *Jesus, we've bumped uglies, for heaven's sake.* 'What gives?'

'I'm calling to let you know that, as we thought, all your marriage documents are completely bona fide. We've done the research. You are legally married.'

I laugh, more from relief than anything else. 'That is good news.'

After all that, Demachi and Tabaku's plan worked.

'I wondered if you'd made any movement on finding a place for Lady Trevethick—'

'Alessia, please.'

'For Alessia to study. I'm concerned about the rabid press interest you're attracting.'

'Oh. You've seen it?'

'Yes. "Oh" is right. You realise that if the Home Office finds out Alessia was here illegally earlier this year, they could refuse her a family visa. And *you* may also be in trouble, as you breached immigration rules, given that she was working for you and didn't have the correct visa in place.'

'Oh, shit.'

'Exactly. I'll follow up with a colleague to find out how the police investigation into her traffickers is progressing and if they have anything that might connect your wife to the crime. This will all be done anonymously, but the cost will come out of your retainer. So, I'm asking if—'

'Go ahead. By all means. And if the retainer doesn't cover it, let me know.'

'Okay. Good.'

'I'm hoping we'll secure a place for Alessia at one of the music conservatoires in London.'

'I've seen the video. She's very talented.'

I smile but shake my head. My wife has gone viral! 'She is, and she wants to study at the Royal College.'

'Good luck with that. In the meantime, it might be helpful if you could be a little more under the radar.'

'Point taken. We may go to Cornwall. We'll be off the grid there. Thanks for the warning.'

'You're welcome . . . Maxim.' She hangs up, and my brain feverishly starts processing this information. Perhaps going to Dimitri's was a mistake.

Of all the times to go viral!

Alessia fingers her grandmother's cross at her neck. Butterflies are forming in her stomach the closer she gets to Kew. The cab stops at a red light, and Alessia can see Kew Bridge before her and the road to Brentford off to her right. She remembers how happy she was living with Magda and her son for those few precious weeks. Michal has told her via Facebook that he and Magda are doing well in Canada. He has a bunch of new friends and is learning to skate. He has ambitions to play ice hockey like his new stepfather, Logan. From his posts, he looks happy, as does Magda.

Idly she wonders about grumpy Mrs Kingsbury, and Mrs Goode too. Her old clients. Do they have new cleaners?

Alessia shakes her head. She's come a long way since then.

The lights turn green, and the cab moves on, crossing Kew Bridge before stopping and turning into a side road. It draws up outside a large old house that would not look out of place on Cheyne Walk. It's one of several surrounding a pretty green pasture, flanked by enormous sycamore trees. Alessia pays the exorbitant fare with her credit card and climbs out of the cab.

It moves off, leaving her facing her great-uncle's house. The house is immaculate. There's a neatly trimmed tree at the front, and through the bay window, Alessia can see a baby grand piano.

A piano!

He plays too?

Her heart starts pumping with excitement, anticipation, and also, a little fear, but in that moment, she decides to call on him.

He might tell her to go away.

She grips the little gold cross that had belonged to her nana, *his* sister, and with her mind made up, she walks the short driveway to the gleaming black door and pushes the doorbell. It rings faintly inside, and seconds later, an older woman, her hair in a tidy bun, answers the door.

'Hello. Can I help you?' she asks.

'I am here to see Tobias Strickland.'

'Do you have an appointment?' she asks sternly.

'No. I was hoping he'd see me. I am his sister's granddaughter. Um . . . his great-niece.'

Given that Leticia Cavanagh is concerned, I call Tom Alexander to see if he's made any headway with finding Alessia's young friend and if he has an update on the police investigation.

'Trevethick. How goes it? I take it you found your wife.'

'I did. Grisha offered her his driver, and he took her home.'

'What? Why?'

'Don't you read the press, Tom?'

'Are you joking? Of course not. I told you. Never bother with that nonsense, unless I have a client who makes headlines. Suggest you do the same. Ignore the arseholes.'

'You're right. But if you happen across a lurid headline, Charlotte, my ex—'

'The actress? Not very good? Always plays herself?'

I chuckle despite myself at Tom's bluntness. 'Yes. That's the one. She jumped me.' There's an awkward pause in the conversation, so I continue, 'Alessia witnessed that and got the wrong idea. Anyway, I'm not here to dredge up recent history. I want to know if you've made any headway with the police investigation and finding Alessia's young friend.'

'Certainly nothing on the girl. But the details that Alessia gave us were so vague, I'd be surprised if we tracked her down. I spoke to Spaffer – he's actually working the case. They're still gathering evidence. He says he's getting inquiries from a private detective about the same case.'

A frisson of alarm runs down my back.

'Journalists?' I ask.

'He doesn't know. But there was a recent raid on a place in South London; they found four young women there.'

'Shit. Really?'

'Yes. They're now in the care of the Salvation Army.'

'Any of them Albanian? Any of them Bleriana?'

'I don't think so. But without speaking to them directly, we can't be sure.'

'What will happen to them?'

'To be honest. I don't know.'

'It's fucking grim.'

'It is, old boy. It is. We'll keep working. See if we can trace these women.'

'Good luck with that.'

'Oh, and while I remember, you don't need to worry about that journalist who called you.'

'Really?'

'No. He's got nothing.' Tom sounds definitive.

Okay then.

'Thanks for the update.'

The lady with the tidy bun must be in her fifties. She peers behind Alessia to see if she's shielding anyone and then casts a critical eye over her, and Alessia is relieved when the woman steps aside; she seems to have passed inspection. 'I'm not aware that Professor Strickland has a niece. Let alone a great-niece. You'd better come in.' She allows Alessia into the hallway.

The hall is much like Trevelyan House, where Caroline lives, and Alessia concludes they must have been built around the same time. 'Follow me,' the woman says, and she leads Alessia down the hall into an airy room with a prominent fireplace, an impressive mantelpiece, and French windows that look out onto a lush back garden. Seated at a desk, in front of a laptop, is a man with a full mane of blondish grey hair, an outrageously curled moustache, and a beard. He looks up with polite interest. His eyes are the same baby blue as her beloved nana's, his mouth the same shape and creased from his readiness to smile – it's her grandmother in male form. Alessia is blindsided; a well of emotion rises from her chest into her throat, and she's unable to speak.

'Well, my dear,' he says. 'What can I do for you?' When she doesn't reply, he frowns in confusion, looking from Alessia to the woman who, Alessia suspects, is a servant of some kind. No. Staff. Not servant.

'She says she's your great-niece, Professor.'

He pales and turns luminous wide eyes back to her. 'Alessia?' he whispers.

What! He knows her!

Tears well in her eyes, and she nods, still unable to speak.

'Oh, my dear!' he exclaims, rising from his chair. He steps around the desk and takes both of her hands in his. 'I never thought . . .' His voice trails off as he chokes up, and they stare at each other, holding each other's hands. She takes in the smile lines around his eyes and his ridiculous moustache that peaks at each end. His neat beard. His impressive mane of hair just like her grandmother.

'Virginia?' he whispers.

He doesn't know.

Alessia shakes her head.

'Oh no,' he says and tears pool in his eyes. He squeezes her hands while they face each other for several seconds, and myriad emotions flit across his face as he absorbs the sad news. Finally, Alessia's tears fall, streaming down her face as she remembers her dear, dear nana. Tobias pulls a cotton handkerchief from his pants pocket and wipes his eyes.

'My dear, you have quite undone me. My dear, dear sister. I wondered. I hadn't heard from her for a long while. I hoped . . .' He takes a breath. 'Mrs Smith. Tea. Please. You'll take tea, won't you, my dear?'

Alessia nods, and she reaches for a tissue from her handbag. Mrs Smith, whose gentle smile reveals her demeanour has transformed from suspicious to solicitous, hurries out of the room.

'That gold cross. It looks familiar. Was it hers?'

'Yes!' Alessia says. 'It was.' Automatically, Alessia's fingers fly to her throat, and she fiddles with the cross. 'It's very precious. I loved her dearly.'

He smiles. A sad smile. 'I remember it. My parents were

terribly religious. Ginny too. That's why she went to Albania, to spread the Word during the Communist era.' He shakes his head as if to rid himself of some unpleasant memory. 'Let's move to the drawing room.' He ushers Alessia towards the door.

'So, I never had an address for Ginny, but she would write to me very occasionally. That's how I know about you. I think she was concerned that my parents would go and "rescue" her from the depths of Albania. They did not approve of her marriage at all.' Toby sighs. 'Dreadful business. They lost a daughter.'

'She married well. She was very much in love with her husband. He was a fine man. Her daughter, my mother, was less lucky, though that seems to have changed.'

'Your mother. Shpresa?'

'Yes.'

'So, Alessia, tell me about yourself. How do you happen to be in England? Tell me all.'

'Honey, I'm home,' I call as I close the front door. It's deathly quiet, and the unsettled anxiety I've felt since Alessia announced she was going *out* rears its ugly head. 'Alessia!' I shout, just in case she's deep in a wardrobe or one of the bathrooms. But the flat has a ringing emptiness that I never noticed until Alessia moved in.

Hell. We forgot to set the alarm.

And she said she'd text. Scowling, I take out my phone and call. But it rings through to voicemail. 'Where are you?' I ask and hang up, blowing out a breath in frustration.

Alessia can look after herself.

Can't she?

She handled my mother. She handled Grisha.

The apprehension that's become familiar since Alessia was kidnapped flutters in my chest. I text her, keeping it light.

Where are you?

The flat is cold and lonely without you.

Mx

Also, I'm hungry. That isn't helping my mood. Feeling miserable, I drift into the kitchen, where the fridge is stacked with goodies.

No. I change my mind, head into the bedroom, and put on my running gear. A run will clear my head, and she'll be back when I'm done.

'I cannot believe that you were living across the river. That's extraordinary,' Toby says.

'Yes. I was happy there,' Alessia replies.

'West is best, I think the saying goes.' He smiles kindly.

Alessia glances at the time. It's after six! 'The time. I must go. My husband will be anxious.'

'I'm sure he will. Maxim, you say?'

'Yes. That's his name.' Alessia hasn't told Toby about Maxim's heritage. She's going to save that for their next meeting. 'I can't wait for you to meet him. He's a good man.' She stands and glances at the piano.

'Do you play?'

'Yes. I do. Nana taught my mother. Nana and my mother taught me. Do you?'

He chuckles. 'Musicality runs in the family. Sadly, I don't play as much as I used to.' He holds up his hands and waggles his fingers. 'These aren't what they were, but I've studied music all my life. It's more a science to me now than an art, yet it started in a blaze of colour for me.'

'You have synaesthesia?'

'I do, my dear. I do.' He's stunned. 'But I call it chromesthesia.'

Alessia grins. 'Chromesthesia. I have not heard this.'

'It's specific. Sound to colour synaesthesia.'

'I have this!'

'Ha!' he hoots, and he takes her hands. 'I have never met another synesthete! And when I do, we're related! How do you see the colours?'

'They match a key. You?'

'Mine are less defined, but listen, we can discuss this at another time. I know you need to go. I'll order you an Uber, and while we wait for it to arrive, will you play something for me?'

Alessia is giddy with joy as she climbs into the vehicle. Toby waves her off from the doorstep, and she waves frantically back until she can no longer see him. She hugs herself as the car turns and slowly eases into the traffic on the bridge. Toby is thoughtful, kind, musical and super-smart, but most of all, he's interested in her and her life in a way that her male relatives at home were not, and he cannot wait to meet her husband. She digs her phone out of her handbag to call Maxim and apologise for not texting. But it's dead.

O Zot!

Well, there's nothing she can do until she gets home. So she sits back and replays her entire conversation with Toby. Her great-uncle. Synesthete.

'Honey, I'm home!' I announce to an empty flat when I'm back from my exercise. The endorphins conjured by my run disappear as I head into the shower.

Where the hell is she?

By 7:00 p.m., I'm climbing the walls. I've left more messages but received no word from my wife. There's no one I can call, nothing I can do. I'm powerless.

I hate not knowing where or how she is.

I pace the drawing room, and every time I pass the double doors that open onto the hallway, I glance at the front door, willing Alessia to appear.

I. Am. Going. Crazy.

Hell.

I step into the echoing silence of my hallway. And I'm suddenly overwhelmed. I don't know where my wife is, and for some unknown reason, the memory of my mother's Louboutins clicking across the hardwood as she left springs to mind – reminding me that I've already lost another family member this week.

Was that the last I'll ever see of her?

And as much as Rowena annoys the hell out of me, that thought is depressing.

She's my mother.

Mama.

Fuck.

How do we come back from this?

I shake off the bleak feeling and text her.

We need to discuss Kit's memorial service.
When you're over your snit,
perhaps you can give me a call.

And I want to add *you faithless whore*, but I don't. She's my mother. Next, I text my absent wife. Again.

I am going crazy here!
Call me.
Please.
M

Suddenly the key sounds in the door, and it opens to reveal Alessia. She looks fine. When we lock eyes, her warm smile lights up the darkened hallway and my heart. My relief and anger seize the day in equal measure.

Thank fuck she's safe.

But as she steps into the hall, the anger triumphs, and my cry echoes off the walls. 'Where the fuck have you been?'

Chapter Twenty-Five

Alessia freezes as I stride towards her, wanting to vent my spleen. I'm overwhelmed with fury, but as I step up to her, she raises her face to mine, all innocence and beauty and beguiling dark eyes. 'I'm sorry. My phone died,' she whispers.

'Oh.' This is not what I thought she'd say. I'm expecting a spirited argument that will help me offload some of my frustration and fear. Her simple apology and admission steal the wind from my sails, and in a nanosecond my temper softens.

'I was worried,' I grumble.

Tentatively, as if she's about to beard a lion, she reaches up and strokes my cheek. 'I know. I'm sorry.'

Sighing, I rest my forehead against hers and close my eyes, taking a moment to calm the fuck down. Slowly, I circle my arms around her, drawing her close so she moulds herself against my body, bathing me in her reassuring warmth. She kisses my cheek. 'I am sorry. I lost track of the time.'

'Where were you?'

She grins. 'If you promise not to be mad, I'll tell you.'

'No. No, I don't promise. Not at all. I'm mad already. You have a disturbing tendency to put yourself in perilous situations. Tell me.'

'I met my grandmother's brother, my great-uncle.'

Maxim steps back, releasing Alessia. 'Uncle? You have family here?'

She nods, still radiating from the joy of finding her relative.

'Why would I be upset about that? Does he live in Kew? How did you find him?'

Alessia takes Maxim's hand and leads him into the kitchen. 'Sit,' she says and points to the kitchen chair.

He frowns, confused, but obliges and looks expectantly up at her, his hair tousled and green eyes no longer flashing with anger but bright with curiosity.

'Remember when I asked you about finding Bleriana?'

Maxim stills, and Alessia doesn't know how he'll react.

'I went to see the detective.'

'I see. And?'

'I asked him to find my grandmother's family.'

'Ah.'

'And Bleriana,' she whispers as if she's confessing a great evil.

'Even though I asked you not to.' Maxim's mouth flattens, his eyes frost, and she knows he's irritated. She nods, trying and failing to feel guilty. He shakes his head and, taking her hand, hauls her into his lap. 'What the hell, Alessia? I don't want you involved in that world, even from a distance. Tom's on it. Admittedly he hasn't got very far. Call the private investigator and ask him to stop. Let Tom deal with it. Someone I trust. Please.'

'Okay,' she says quickly. 'I'm sorry. I'm just anxious to find her.'

Maxim sighs. 'I understand. But why didn't you tell me you were going to meet your great-uncle? I would have come with you.'

'I didn't plan to meet him. I was going to deliver a letter. We learned about correspondence and letter writing today in class. But I saw the baby grand in his living room through the window, and once I saw that . . . It was . . . um . . . fate.' She shrugs, trying to convey that she felt compelled to knock on the door after seeing the piano.

Maxim sighs again. 'I see. Well, if you have any other hidden relatives, I'd be happy to take you to meet them. Let me. Please?'

'Okay.'

'Tell me about him.'

Alessia kisses his cheek. 'Thank you for not being too mad at me.'

'I am still a little mad at you. And we say "angry." "Mad" is American. And I was fucking incandescent earlier. With worry more than anything.'

'I know. I'm sorry. Shall I cook? Are you hungry?'

Maxim sits back, a reluctant smile tugging at the corners of his mouth. 'Yes. I'm famished.'

She smiles and caresses his face. Her husband is *hangry*. 'I'll cook and tell you all about him.'

So he was just across the river when you lived in Brentford?' I ask as I watch Alessia stir a tomato sauce. 'So near, and yet so far.'

'Yes. It is a grand house. He is a musician too, but he was a teacher. At Oxford. A professor in music. He has synaesthesia like me, but calls it, um . . . chrom . . . chromesthesia.'

'Wow.' *What are the odds?* 'Is it genetic?'

'I think so!' She beams as she stirs in some capers. Whatever she's concocting, it smells delicious. It smells so good – it deserves a glass of full-bodied red.

'Wine?' I ask Alessia.

'Please. He wants to meet you. And my mother!'

'Has he not met your mother?' I grab a bottle from the rack.

'No. He's never been to Albania. And my mother doesn't know he exists. My grandmother was shun . . . shunned by her family for marrying an Albanian.' Alessia's voice fades, and she stirs the sauce.

Shit.

My family haven't shunned her.

Have they? My mother – 'That's awful,' I mutter, immediately shutting that thought down.

'But he knew about me. She would write occasional letters to him.'

'He should go and meet your family. I can recommend it, in spite of your scary father. Have you told Shpresa?' I uncork the wine and, giving it zero time to breathe, pour two glasses.

'No. But I will after dinner.' She drains the spaghetti and adds it to the sauce, stirring it in. 'This is ready.'

Alessia places the last of their plates in the dishwasher, wipes down the countertop, and retrieves her phone from her purse. Setting it down, she plugs in the charger. Maxim is in the living room at the piano. She hasn't heard him play since he duetted with her. She leans against the doorjamb, unseen by him, and listens for a moment. He's improvising a melody in A minor. The notes sparkle across the room and through her head in a vibrant blue, sounding upbeat and full of warmth and hope, unusual for a minor key.

He sounds . . . happy.

Alessia smiles. The theme is a complete contrast to his melancholy composition that she played for him not so long ago in the Hideout in Cornwall. He turns, noticing her, and she sidles over and sits beside him at the piano.

'This is a happier tune.'

'I wonder why that is?' Maxim smirks, and she smiles. 'It's from *Interstellar*.'

Alessia frowns.

'The film?' he asks.

'I don't know it.'

'Oh. We'll have to watch it. Amazing movie. Great soundtrack by Hans Zimmer.' He stops and puts his arm around her. 'That reminds me. I spoke to Leticia today.'

Alessia tenses – despite the fact that she likes Ticia, she doesn't like him talking to women he's bedded.

Alessia! Stop.

Maxim continues either because he doesn't notice her tension or chooses not to. 'She says we should keep a low profile and avoid the press. So when you've finished your course, I think we should go to Cornwall. I have work to do at the Hall anyway. I know we were going to pack the flat up this weekend so we can move. But maybe we can get someone to do that for us. Or we can wait.'

Alessia's heart skips a beat. 'I love Cornwall,' she says breathlessly. 'Especially the sea.'

'Me too.' Maxim kisses her hair. 'That's settled then. We can go on Friday evening. And between then and now we can stay at home and watch films. You know, Netflix and chill.'

'I thought that was another way of saying sex on the couch.'

Maxim laughs. 'We can do that too.' He kisses her quickly.

'Play some more *Interstellar*.'

'I feel a little self-conscious playing for you.'

She laughs. 'Why? Don't, please. I love your compositions.'

'Well, this isn't mine. But if you listen, you'll probably be able to play it better than me.'

'Maxim. Play.'

He grins. 'Yes. My lady.'

With the music from Maxim's performance still ringing in her head, Alessia fetches her phone to FaceTime her mother. There are several messages from Maxim; he sounds more frantic and annoyed with each one, and she swallows down her guilt. She didn't mean to worry him.

There are emails from four of the colleges she sent applications to – the one she reads first is from the Royal College of Music.

She has an audition!

They are keen to see her.

Uau! She runs back into the living room. Maxim looks up. 'I have an audition at the Royal College of Music!'

He grins and applauds, rising slowly to his feet. 'My talented wife. That's fantastic news!'

Alessia opens the other emails and finds they all want to see her.

She gapes at Maxim. 'All of them want me to audition!'

'Of course they do! They'd be fools not to.' He cups her head in his hands. 'You're beautiful. Talented. And I'm so glad you're my wife.' He brushes his lips against her. 'Go. Tell your mother.'

Alessia beams and heads back into the kitchen to FaceTime Shpresa with the good news.

Maybe I worry too much. Alessia's fine. She came back in one piece. She's a functioning adult, for heaven's sake.

Who has been abducted.

Twice.

Fuck.

I thought . . . What did I think? She'd left? She'd been abducted again?

Mate. Let it go.

She's fine. She's here.

I take a sip of the extremely satisfying Bordeaux, which has had a chance to breathe now, and I briefly wonder if I should raid the cellar at Trevelyan House before Caroline drinks it all.

The doorbell rings. From outside the front door rather than the outside of the building.

Who the hell is that?

Rowena?

A dark shadow looms outside the front door. It's a man, not a woman. I open the door.

Fuck. It's him.

All slicked-back hair and expensive camel coat and brogues.

Ana-fucking-toli. Arsehole.

'Hello, Englishman,' Anatoli says, with an arrogance and swagger that makes me want to deck him.

'What the hell are you doing here?'

'I've come to see you.'

Me! 'Why?'

'Aren't you going to invite me in?'

'No. I'm going to tell you to fuck off.'

'And they say the English are so polite.' He steps in, and contrary to how I feel, I let him.

What the hell?

In the hallway, he stops and turns to address me. 'Where's your wife – the woman who should be my wife? Has she had enough of the upper-class snobbery and left you yet?'

'Do you mean the woman you abused and kidnapped and dragged across Europe?'

Alessia appears in the hallway and pales when she sees the Arsehole.

'I got her out of the country in one piece. She's back here legally. I did you both a favour,' Anatoli scoffs, eyes like flint.

Anatoli,' Alessia whispers. 'What are you doing here?'

His expression changes, his pale blue eyes warming as he studies her. 'I'm here on business,' he answers in her own language. 'It's good to see you, carissima. You look well. Your father says a journalist called at their home. He sent them away. The press don't approve of you here, like I told you. The English are such snobs. They say your marriage is not legal.'

'But we know that's not true!' Alessia exclaims.

Anatoli makes a face. 'Jak also told me that you're not with child. You lie well.'

Alessia flushes.

'Is the Englishman taking good care of you?' he murmurs.

'Enough!' Maxim snaps. 'You two speak in English, or I will throw him out.' Maxim glares at Alessia as if it's her fault that Anatoli is standing in his hallway.

Alessia frowns and moves to Maxim's side. He slides his arm around her and pulls her close.

'Don't get your panties in a wad, Englishman. It is you I came to see.'

'Me. What the fuck do you want with me? And why would I want to see you?'

'Such language. From an aristocrat too.'

Maxim tenses, and Alessia worries he might explode and hit Anatoli like he did before. She grips his shirt.

'Why are you here?' she pipes up.

'Your father sent me.'

'Baba? Why?'

'I told you. I have a message for the Englishman.'

'And my esteemed father-in-law can't send a message through his daughter?' Maxim scoffs.

'Jak is not proficient in English. Unlike my good self.' Anatoli's smug grin is annoying, his mockery unmistakable. 'And this is private. For you. Not for his beloved daughter.'

Maxim scowls. 'You turn up. Barge into my home. Chat up my wife at some unseemly hour. What is it you want?'

'I need to talk to you. It's a matter for men. And only men.' Anatoli looks pointedly at Alessia.

'I am not going anywhere,' Alessia exclaims. 'If you have something to say to my husband, you can say it to me. I'm not in Kukës any more.'

'No, carissima. This is for your husband's ears only.'

Alessia turns her bewildered gaze to me. It's obvious she has no idea why the Arsehole has appeared on our doorstep. I blow out a breath. 'Her name is Alessia. Or Lady Trevethick, to you. Now, say what you have to say, and then you can leave.' I give him a frosty, fuck-off smile, and Anatoli narrows his eyes.

'Is there somewhere private we could go?'

Fuck's sake.

'Not really. Unless we step outside. This is Alessia's home too.'

'Maxim, why don't you go into the living room, and I'll bring you another glass of wine.'

'There she is!' Anatoli grins. 'Alessia, you are an Albanian woman to your soul.' His face lights up. He's still smitten with my wife.

It's sickening.

'No. Arsehole, you're not welcome in this house. You took Alessia from here against her will. You threatened and abused her. And you have the fucking nerve to turn up here and expect us to invite you into our home—'

'I am an associate of Lady Trevethick's father. And he has a message for you, asshole.'

Alessia is tempted to step between them as they glower at each other.

'Let's take this outside,' Maxim says through gritted teeth.

Alessia looks up at him, eyes wide and her face etched in panic. He gives her a reassuring smile and turns his attention to Anatoli.

The Arsehole's icy glare doesn't intimidate me.

'Are you armed?' Alessia asks him suddenly, the words coming from her mouth in a distraught, breathless rush.

What the fuck?

He shakes his head. 'Not this time.' And he smirks. 'I came by air. Okay, Englishman, have it your way.'

I don't even want to think about the implications of Alessia's question. No wonder it was easy for him to take her – the monster was fucking armed. I scowl at him, trying to keep a rein on my temper. He brought a fucking gun into my home and threatened my wife.

Or me.

That's how he was able to whisk her away.

Fucking monster.

'Well, Englishman?' he says.

My blood boils, but I grab my jacket and head out, not bothering to wait for him. I don't take the lift – I bolt down the stairs, buoyed by my anger, and quickly reach the small foyer on the ground floor.

We'll do this. And then he's gone.

For good. Hopefully.

He follows me down the stairs, and I know he didn't expect me to move so fast because he's breathless when we reach the bottom.

It's hugely satisfying.

Fucking bastard brought a gun into my home.

'Here,' he shouts when he reaches the foyer before I can leave the building. 'There's light.'

I stop, and he pulls out a newspaper clipping from the inside of his coat and hands it to me. It's from an Albanian newspaper, so I don't understand the headlines, but there are grimy photographs of two men.

The hairs on the back of my neck rise in recognition.

Those fuckers!

The traffickers.

I shoot my gaze to him.

'This them?' he asks.

I nod. 'Why?'

He says nothing and then produces another newspaper cutting. It's the photograph of Charlotte kissing me.

Oh shit. 'This reached Albania?'

'It did. It made the papers. Jak thinks you should be more discreet with your affairs.'

'Whoa!' I hold up my hand. 'This is not what it looks like.'

'No?'

'No. For the record, I'm not having an affair. Also, it's none of Jak's or your fucking business.'

'Alessia has seen this?'

'Of course she's seen it. She was there.'

'Oh.' He looks crestfallen – so much so that I feel a nanoparticle of pity for him. He still holds a torch that shines brightly for my wife. He loves her. In his own way.

What an idiot.

'You know,' he growls. 'You fuck this up between you and her – I'm here. Waiting. It's obvious your gutter press, they don't approve. The snobbery and disdain is in every word they write about her. I'll be in her home country where we love her. I love her.'

'No, you don't. And keep away from my wife. If you hadn't mistreated her, she might be with you now. But you did. *You* fucked up. And she's mine now. In every way. And I don't give a flying fuck about the press. Leave Alessia alone. Now, you can see yourself out.'

Without looking back at him, I vault up the stairs, and when I reach the top floor, I've expended enough energy to calm down.

Alessia is still in the hallway. 'Where is he? What did he want?' she asks.

'Nothing important.'

She puts her hands on her hips. 'Maxim. Tell me.'

And suddenly, I want to laugh. She runs off to meet her uncle without saying a word. And here she is, demanding answers. 'You really want to know?'

'Yes. And why are you smiling?'

'Because you're making me smile.'

'Tell me!'

'Your father wants me to handle my mistresses more discreetly.'

Alessia pales, gaping at me as if I'd just slapped her.

Shit. I was joking!

'Hey. It's nonsense. Anatoli had a clipping from an Albanian newspaper with Charlotte.' And I'm suddenly inspired. Reaching out, I take Alessia's hand. 'Let me show you something.'

I guide her into the drawing room, sit at my desk, and seat Alessia on my lap. Grasping my iMac's mouse, I wake the computer. On Instagram, I find Grisha Egonov's reel of Alessia at the piano. 'Watch,' I say, and switching on the sound, I listen to my wife's exquisite performance of Bach. She squirms on my lap, unused to watching herself. 'It's good, don't worry,' I murmur.

Alessia watches the recording, noting her finger work and the sound from the piano. It's good. The tone is mellow yet bright. As she finishes the piece, there's a burst of applause from the audience. Maxim pauses the video. 'See?' he says, and with the cursor, he circles some blurred figures in the background, then presses Play. Alessia's scalp tightens. There's Maxim, leaning back from Charlotte as she kisses him. He twists his head, grabs her hands, and eases her gently away from him.

He stopped her.

Alessia slides her gaze to him. 'She kissed you.'

'I told you. *She* kissed *me*.'

'I believed you.'

'Did you, though?' he says, with a sideways look, his lips curved into a teasing smile.

Alessia laughs and throws her arms around his neck. 'Yes. A thousand times, yes. Of course I believed you.'

'So you should. Shall we Netflix and chill?' He kisses her, his hands in her hair, his tongue invading her mouth, stealing away her breath and making her heart sing.

Chapter Twenty-Six

'That was a good meeting. You're getting a handle on all of it, Maxim.' Oliver's smile is benevolent as he gathers his papers, so I don't think he's being sarcastic – just sincere. It's humbling and heart-warming at the same time. We've just concluded a discussion with the managing agents for the residential and commercial property divisions, and I'm pleased that all is well, though they're keeping a watchful eye on the retail sector – online shopping has much to answer for – and the churn on our retail property is up.

'I felt it went well. In fact, so much so, I might bunk off and walk home right now.'

'Good plan. You're off to Cornwall, yes?'

'Hoping to throw off the press.'

'Good luck with that.'

'Have a good weekend. And thanks, Oliver. For everything.'

'I'm just doing my job, my lord. Have a great weekend.'

He exits my office, and I remember when I thought he might

not have my best interests at heart. Well, I was wrong. He's an asset to me and the estate.

I bounce down the steps into a brisk March afternoon. I've decided to walk home, as I have plenty of time and I want to stretch my legs. I've only managed two runs this week, and I resolve to do better in Cornwall.

Alessia will conclude her course today and mentioned going for drinks afterwards with her classmates. I'm tempted to join her, but I haven't been invited, and I have to drive this evening.

Mate. Let her be.

As I walk through Berkeley Square, a nagging, skittering itch travels up my spine, and I find myself glancing behind me.

Am I being followed?

Reporters? Paparazzi?

I can't see anyone acting suspiciously, but I quicken my pace.

Mate. Get a grip.

I hurry on, tempted to grab a cab – but I need the exercise.

The uneasy feeling follows me to Chelsea Embankment, and I'm relieved that my building is press-free when I arrive home. I stride through the doorway and jog up the stairs, grateful to be home.

Alessia is seated beside Tabitha and two of her course colleagues at the bar in The Gore, enjoying a glass of champagne. The atmosphere among them is fizzing with celebration.

'I think my father will find my manners vastly improved. He'll be pleased. I hope,' Tabitha purrs. 'He wants me married off as soon as possible, like my sisters. You wouldn't think we're in the twenty-first century. Did your husband send you on this course?'

Alessia smiles. 'No. It was my decision. I'm thankful. I've learned so much. And the first banquet that we host, you must come.'

'Complete with minstrels? I'll be there!'

Alessia giggles. 'I am not sure about minstrels, but Maxim

has guitars, though I've never heard him play. We are moving to a new place soon. I hope we entertain there.'

'Oh! A housewarming party. That would be splendid. When and where are you moving? Tell me all.'

I'm about to head into the shower when the external buzzer sounds.

What now?

It better not be a reporter.

In the hall, I answer the intercom. 'Hello?'

'Hello. Alessia. Please,' a soft, hesitant feminine voice rasps.

'Who is this?'

'Friend. Alessia friend. Please.' A quiet desperation in her tone raises the hairs on my neck. English is not her first language. 'Sixth floor. Use the lift.' I buzz her in.

We'll see who this is.

Tabitha hugs Alessia. 'It's been such a pleasure to get to know you these last few days,' she gushes. 'Please, please stay in touch.'

Alessia returns her hug. 'I will. And yes, it's been lovely. I feel I have made a friend.'

'And we both know how to sit correctly. Deportment is important,' Tabitha mimics their tutor and Alessia laughs.

'And I know the difference between a salad and dinner fork. My life is now, um . . . complete.'

Tabitha grins.

'I have to go. Maxim will be waiting.'

'Don't stay in Cornwall forever. Please keep in touch.'

'I will. Goodbye.'

Alessia gives quick farewells and handshakes to her other classmates, and she's out the door and onto the street. There she waves down a cab and gives the cabbie her address.

I open the front door and wait for the lift to arrive. When it does, a young, slight woman steps out onto the landing. She has long, dark hair and dark eyes that regard me warily, and I suspect they've seen too much of the world.

'Hello,' I offer cautiously. 'Can I help you?'

'Alessia?' She's a little breathless. From nerves? I don't know. She's pretty in an understated way, but stands awkwardly in mismatched clothes at a distance from where I am, and I recognise the same reticence that Alessia used to have with me . . . with men.

Christ, where did that thought come from?

'She's not here, but she's on her way home.'

She frowns, and I step aside and gesture towards the inside and the hallway. 'You can wait in here. What is your name?'

'Me?' she asks.

'Yes. Your name. I am Maxim.' I place my hand on my chest.

'Bleriana,' she says.

'Bleriana!' I exclaim, beaming. 'Alessia has been looking for you. Come in.'

She tightens her fists as if she's steeling herself and regards me with dark eyes that hint at harrowing secrets beneath their sheen.

Fuck.

I offer her a reassuring smile because I don't know what else I can do while she takes a moment to decide whether or not to come in, and whether or not to trust me. Nervously, she licks her lips, and it's either curiosity or desperation that wins, and she steps past me and into the flat. I stand well back, not wanting to freak her out in any way, and close the door. In the hallway, I fish out my phone and call Alessia. Her phone rings and rings, then goes to voicemail.

Damn.

I text her under Bleriana's watchful gaze.

I have a surprise for you.
Come home.
Mx
PS – A good surprise.

'I think Alessia is on her way home. She shouldn't be too long.'

Bleriana stares with dark, haunted eyes, a little like my wife used to.

What has this young woman been through?

'Do you speak English?'

She nods, then shakes her head in response.

'Okay. Do you want a drink?' With my hand, I motion a cup at my lips.

'No. Thank you.' Her voice is hesitant and soft, and her arms are crossed in front of her – I suspect to try to make her already slight frame look smaller. She's trying to be invisible.

Oh, sweetheart. I see you.

'Come. You can wait in here.' I head down the hall, hoping that she'll follow, which she does, and I motion her into the drawing room. 'Sit.'

Bleriana perches on the edge of the sofa, stiff and scared, radiating a tension that I can't even imagine. She clutches her hands in her lap while her wide eyes dart everywhere, taking in her environs. I wonder if she's looking for an escape route.

I stand in the doorway, wondering what the hell to do or say.

'Um. Are you hungry?' With my hands, I motion eating.

She frowns, then nods, and then shakes her head.

Of course – she's Albanian.

'Yes. No?'

'No.'

I check my watch. 'Alessia. Here soon.'

The cab pulls up outside the building, and Alessia steps out and pays the cabbie. In the foyer, she has to wait for the elevator, and Alessia suspects that Mrs Beckstrom has returned from walking Heracles, judging by the time it takes to come from the top floor. While she waits, she fishes her phone from her bag. There's a missed call and text from Maxim.

A surprise?

Alessia smiles to herself, intrigued, as she finally steps into the elevator. She's excited to get to the Hall. Perhaps the surprise is something to do with Cornwall.

She opens the front door, and Maxim is standing at the end of the hallway, dressed in suit pants and a white shirt. His hair is tousled, his eyes bright green, and he smiles, relieved to see her.

'There you are. You have a friend here!' he says.

'Alessia!' Her name echoes with such hope down the hall, and a young woman comes to stand in the living room doorway. They gape at each other, neither quite believing what they are seeing.

Bleriana!

'O Zot! O Zot! O Zot!' A well of emotion bubbles from Alessia's chest into her throat, and she dashes down the hall, scooping Bleriana into her arms. 'You're here. How are you here? Are you okay? Did you escape?'

Bleriana starts to cry, and Alessia's tears push past the hope and joy and incredulity that's knotted in her throat, as they hug and sob, together.

Hell. Weeping women. Weeping women chattering fast and furious in Albanian.

Their emotional reunion chokes me for a moment.

Alessia turns a teary face to mine. 'How?'

I shake my head. 'I don't know. She found me. I think she might have followed me from my office. Ask her.'

Alessia poses the question to Bleriana, who turns a now teary but more hopeful face to me and answers her.

'Yes. She did,' Alessia says.

'I thought I was being followed. Look, I'm going to have a shower. I'll be a few minutes. I'll let you two reconnect.'

Alessia reaches out and takes my hand. 'Thank you,' she mouths.

'As much as I'd like to take the credit, this is not me. She found us.'

Alessia turns back to Bleriana. 'Tell me. How did you find us? We have been looking for you. Did you escape?' She takes Bleriana's hand, and they sit on the sofa, hands clasped tightly together.

'They caught me.' Bleriana whispers the words like she's confessing a terrible sin and with a fear and horror so deep that Alessia's revulsion rises with the bile in her throat.

She wraps her arms around Bleriana and holds her like she'll never let go. 'You're here now. You're safe.'

Bleriana sobs – a dam bursting within her – and holds on to Alessia like she's her life raft in a sea of awfulness, horror, and terrible abuse. Alessia rocks her gently, as Maxim has done for her, and they both shed tears and more tears. And more. And yet more.

'You're safe. I've got you,' Alessia repeatedly murmurs, comforting herself and Bleriana at the same time.

This could have been her.

Eventually, Bleriana quiets and wipes her nose and eyes on the tissue Alessia hands her.

'If you want to tell me, I am here. I will listen.'

Bleriana's bottom lip trembles, and she tells her story in a slow, halting voice while Alessia listens and dies a little inside.

From the safety of the doorway, I watch them talk quietly but intensely. I don't understand what they're saying, but Alessia's calm compassion for this stricken young woman resonates through her entire body. The way she gently holds her hands, strokes her back, her eyes warm with concern. Her concentration is utterly centred on Bleriana and nothing else.

It's . . . affecting.

Whatever Bleriana's telling her, it's distressing for both of them. I turn away, it's too painful to watch, and my morbid imagination kicks into overdrive.

Fuck. Fuck. Fuck.

'How did you find us? We had men looking for you,' Alessia asks.

'We were . . . rescued. By the English police. I am staying with an English family in a safe house. It's part of a charitable organisation. They are kind. And I must wait to find out if I can stay in England. Anyway, I saw the newspapers. And I recognised you.'

'Ah!' And for a brief moment, Alessia forgives the British press for hounding her and her husband.

'The daughter of the family who is hosting me. Her name is Monifa – she is very kind. She went online. And we found your husband and where he worked. And today, I came to London to find you.'

'And you succeeded.' Alessia beams and Bleriana's answering smile is radiant, even on her tear-stained face.

'So tell me. Alessia, Lady Trevethick. How did this happen to you?' Bleriana's eyes are alight with her curiosity, the dark shadows momentarily hidden behind her joy in her friend's good fortune.

'It is a long story.'

I return to the doorway when I hear laughter. Under Alessia's tender, calm care, Bleriana has relaxed and no longer looks like the harrowed young woman I met on the doorstep. Her face has softened, and there's a trace of the young, pretty girl she is, despite the unimaginable horrors she's endured.

My only hope is that she doesn't trigger Alessia's trauma – her nightmares. I didn't want her back in that awful world. Yet here we are.

Hell. I'm standing in the shadows as a bystander, feeling utterly useless.

What can I do?

And it dawns on me that this used to be my norm.

This was how I felt all the time. *Useless.*

It's only since I met Alessia that I've felt worthy and purposeful.

Fuck. I shake off the notion as it's a little disturbing.

There's no way we're going to the Hall this evening, so I head into the kitchen and call Danny to let her know.

'Oh, my lord. That is a shame. We are so looking forward to seeing you and our new countess.'

'We'll be down tomorrow. Something's cropped up here. I'll let you know.'

'Very good, Maxim.'

Next, I call Tom and tell him to call off the search for Bleriana.

'She's turned up here.'

'I say, Trevethick. What are the odds!'

'I know.'

When I'm off the phone, I wander back into the drawing room.

'Ladies. Shall we eat?'

Alessia jumps to her feet. 'Maxim! I'm sorry. The time has flown away.'

'It's okay. Talk to your friend. I'll order us a takeaway.'

'No. No. I'll cook. We are not going to Cornwall this evening?'

'We'll go tomorrow.'

Alessia turns to Bleriana. 'Can you stay? Are you hungry?'

Bleriana's slight smile signals her agreement.

Alessia makes quick work of preparing some lamb chops with olive oil, garlic and rosemary for grilling. Then she starts making a salad with feta cheese, onions, tomatoes and various types of lettuce from a bag. Bleriana helps chop the onions and tomatoes with Alessia. Maxim opens a bottle of red wine for them all to share.

'Alessia, ask Bleriana where she's staying,' Maxim says, pouring the wine.

'Reading,' Bleriana replies to Alessia's question.

'Can she stay here tonight?' Alessia asks.

'Darling, you don't need my permission. This is your home, too, and she's your friend.'

'I wanted to check you do not object.'

'Why would I?' His forehead creases with a frown. 'What I would say – is it okay with Bleriana? Does she need to get back to Reading this evening? Does she need to let anyone know where she is?'

'Good points.' Alessia beams at her husband.

He's so capable.

And asks the right questions.

Alessia quizzes Bleriana, who tells her that she can stay the night but must call the family she lives with to tell them. 'I have a phone. They will be anxious if I don't call them. I'll do it now.'

She steps into the hallway to make her call, leaving Alessia and Maxim alone for the first time since she arrived. Maxim folds his arms around Alessia and nuzzles beneath her ear. 'Can I tell you how much I love you,' he whispers.

His lips against her skin, the soft words in the shell of her ear send tingles down her spine. 'I am very lucky to have you.' He kisses, then nips her earlobe, taking Alessia by surprise and making her yelp. She turns in his arms.

'I am lucky to have you. Thank you for being so understanding about Bleriana.' She leans up and kisses him.

'Why wouldn't I be? She's been through hell. If she lives in Reading, we can take her back tomorrow on our way to Cornwall.'

'Okay.' Alessia wants to ask if Bleriana can come to Cornwall with them, but she'll bide her time and wait for the right moment.

How is Bleriana settling down in the spare bedroom?' I ask when Alessia eventually glides into bed beneath the covers.

'She is okay now that she has the little dragon.' Alessia snuggles up to me and slips her hand over my torso and belly, bringing it to rest just beneath the waistband of my PJs. 'You are dressed,' she murmurs, as her fingers skim the edges of my pubic hair, waking my dick.

'I am. We have a guest. I don't want to frighten her during the night.'

She removes her hand, much to my disappointment, and trails it over my body up to my chin, where she cups my face. Leaning over me, she whispers, 'Thank you.' And she offers me a quick, sweet kiss.

'Oh, no. I want so much more than that.' Pulling her into my arms, I turn us both, so she's lying beneath me, her dark hair splayed out over the pillow, her dark eyes gazing up at me, her body cradling mine.

I pause, drinking her in.

But something's off.

'Thank you,' she says once more, but this time it's with a breathy, quiet plea that's sobering. She cups my face with her hands, and tears pool in her eyes.

My breath catches in my throat.

Oh, God.

No.

Her soft entreaty almost undoes me and kills my desire. I gather her in my arms and roll back, holding her hard and fast on top of me.

It could have been her.

That's where she's gone.

It could have been her.

But she got away.

My girl. My wife. My sweet, sweet wife.

She lets out a gulping sob and starts to cry, and I hold her while she grieves for her dear, young friend and maybe for herself and all she's endured too.

I kiss her hair and murmur, 'I've got you. Let it all out. You're here. You're safe.' While my own tears stay lodged like a breeze block in my throat.

Chapter Twenty-Seven

When I stir, Alessia is pressed against me, her arse against my groin as we spoon. My arms are wrapped around her, and my nostrils fill with her delicious, arousing scent.

My dick, thwarted last night for compassionate reasons, is raring to go. Without opening my eyes, I kiss her hair. 'Good morning, my love,' I murmur and hear a gasp that doesn't emanate from my wife.

What the hell!

Opening my eyes, I raise my head, and Bleriana is staring at me all wide-eyed and pink-cheeked while she's lying next to my wife from the other side of our super-king.

I'm momentarily stunned.

I mean, it wouldn't be the first time I've woken up with more than one woman in bed, but never in this situation.

'Good morning,' I say because I can't think of anything else, and I'm conscious of the slow flush that heats my cheeks while my boner dies.

Alessia squirms as she rouses beside me, brushing my dick and bringing it instantly back to life. She reaches out and places a hand on Bleriana's cheek.

Wait a minute! What about me?

'Good morning. Did you sleep okay?' Alessia asks, her voice soft and welcoming.

Bleriana blinks a couple of times. 'Yes. Very well. Your husband is awake. Is he mad?'

Alessia smiles. 'No, why would he be?' and with a smirk, she continues, 'I think he's woken up to more than one woman in his bed before.'

Bleriana gasps once more, scandalised but amused by her friend's candour, then lets out a bubble of laughter and Alessia giggles too.

'I shouldn't tell you that. It's a good thing he doesn't understand Albanian.' Alessia turns over to face her husband.

My wife is tousled and sleepy and giggly and utterly beautiful. 'Good morning, Lady Trevethick. Something you want to tell me? We seem to have acquired a stowaway during the night.'

Alessia's gaze is alight with mischief and love, and to my relief, the anguish from last night seems a distant memory. Her dark eyes are focused on me, and all I see in them is her adoration – and I yearn for her. In every way, even with our audience present.

But I can't fuck her right now – though I'd like to – because . . . Bleriana.

'I hope you don't mind. Bleriana was afraid in the night. She came in here. I moved over, and we didn't wake you. There is more room in this bed than in the spare room; more important than that, *you* are here, keeping us safe from our bad dreams.'

'I thought the little dragon did that.'

'He does. But you do too. You always do.' She strokes my cheek, her fingers brushing my stubble, and the contact of her skin on mine and her sweet words lead directly to my dick.

'Oh, Alessia,' I murmur and kiss her lightly on the lips, though I want to do so much more.

Damn cockblocker!

To indicate my need, I tilt my hips forward, prodding her with my erection. 'I'd get out of bed, but this gives the game away.'

'Maxim!'

I grin. And plant a swift kiss on her forehead. 'This will take a moment.'

'We'll make coffee.' Alessia grins, turns, and ushers Bleriana out of bed.

Does he make you get up every day and make coffee?' Bleriana asks when they're in the kitchen, her disapproval apparent in her frown.

Alessia laughs. 'No. He makes coffee, even breakfast sometimes, but I like to do these things for him. He's a good man. I love him so much.'

'I can see that. You are lucky.'

'I am.' Alessia beams.

After her shower, Alessia quickly pulls on jeans and a sweater while Bleriana showers in the spare room en suite.

Maxim is already freshly washed, dressed and sitting at his computer in the living room when Alessia interrupts him. 'My lord, I have a request.'

He turns his attention from the screen to her. 'Why are you standing so far away?' He reaches for her and tugs her onto his lap. 'What is it, my lady?' He nuzzles her ear. 'And if it's about Bleriana joining us in Cornwall, I would rather she didn't.'

'Oh.' Alessia slumps against him, disappointed.

'Love, it's not what you think,' he says quickly. 'When Leticia rang earlier this week, she said that the Home Office might refuse you a family visa if they find out you've been in the country illegally. You were trafficked with Bleriana, and she's known to the police.' A crease forms between his brows. 'I'm worried that someone will make the connection between you two, and if the press get hold of that . . .'

'Oh.' Alessia pales.

'Exactly. But I suggest we ask Leticia to expedite whatever's happening with Bleriana's case for asylum. It's Leticia's area of expertise, and Bleriana might get a visa before you do.'

'Okay,' Alessia says, but she's still ambivalent about Maxim dealing with Ticia.

Alessia! Ticia is an expert.

'That is a good plan. You will ask Ticia?'

He smiles. 'I'll email her now. And when this is all sorted, Bleriana can come to Cornwall anytime. Though I would prefer it if she slept in her own bed.'

'She's . . . um . . . trauma . . . traumatised,' Alessia says quietly.

'I know.' He brushes her hair behind her ear. 'But it's not appropriate.' Maxim shrugs, his smile rueful.

Alessia nods in understanding. *If the staff find out, they will assume the worst.*

'She's very young,' he says. 'Does she want to go back to Albania?'

'No. She will be shunned. The stigma . . .' Alessia's voice trails off.

'Wow. That's awful. Her parents?'

Alessia shakes her head in answer to his unspoken question.

'Okay. Let's take her back to Reading and put her in touch with Leticia.'

Bleriana is quiet. She's seated with Alessia in the rear of Maxim's bigger car, the Discovery. They hold hands and make occasional small talk, but Alessia can sense her friend's growing anxiety as they get closer to their destination. Maxim, following the route guidance, comes off the motorway, and they head towards Reading town centre.

'I wish I could come with you,' Bleriana says quietly.

'I know.' Alessia squeezes her hand and glances at Maxim. Their eyes meet in the rear-view mirror, and she wonders if she should press Maxim to change his mind.

'I have to be here because of meetings,' Bleriana says.

'You do?' This news slightly consoles Alessia. 'Meetings?' she asks.

'Yes. A counsellor. And a social worker.'

Bleriana can't come to Cornwall. 'I see. I am glad you are seeing a counsellor.'

'When will I see you again?'

'Soon. I promise. You have my mobile number. Call me. Whenever.'

We pull up outside a modest terraced house in the backstreets near Reading station. I climb out and join Bleriana and Alessia on the small driveway. The front door opens, and a middle-aged woman steps out. She has a friendly, open face, and her teeth are dazzling against the darkness of her skin when she smiles. 'Bleriana, welcome back.'

A pale, portly, balding man, who must be in his early fifties, appears behind her, wearing a Reading FC shirt and jeans. His smile is as warm and friendly as his wife's. Well, I assume they're married, and these are Bleriana's foster parents. Alessia introduces herself as Alessia Trevelyan and me as her husband. I like that she doesn't flaunt her title. Sometimes, it's just not the done thing.

And she gets it.

Mr and Mrs Evans seem like lovely people, but when they ask us to join them for tea, I politely refuse. I'd like to get on our way.

Bleriana turns, hugs Alessia, and murmurs a teary goodbye

in Albanian, then offers me a goodbye, with a nod, from a safe distance.

'Come.' I hold out my hand to my wife, and we head back to the car.

From the passenger seat, Alessia gives them a wave, her eyes shining, and I know she's tearful. I put the Discovery in drive, head down the street, and reach over to grab her hand.

'She's going to be okay. They seem like good people.'

'They are. Bleriana is overwhelmed by their kindness.'

'You'll see her soon.'

Alessia nods and turns to stare out of the window.

'Do you mind if I put some music on?' I ask.

'No.'

'Any requests?'

She turns dark, sad eyes to me and shakes her head.

'Oh, baby. Do you want me to turn around and pick her up?'

'No. No. We can't do that. She has to see her social worker and her counsellor.'

I blow out a breath. Relieved. 'I'm glad she has support. She's going to be okay. She's like you. Self-sufficient. She came to find you through me. That was courageous on her part.'

Alessia gives me a slight smile. And I'm tempted to remind her she was crying the last time we headed to Cornwall but decide against it. Instead, I switch BBC Radio 6 on the sound system and let the music wash over me from an old timer, Roy Harper, his song 'North Country' from 1974.

Hmm. I'd like to learn to play this on guitar.

'Do you want to stop for lunch?' Maxim asks.

'I'm not hungry.' Alessia's heart is heavy.

'I can't tempt you with a panini?'

She smiles, albeit reluctantly. 'That seems so long ago.'

Maxim laughs. 'It was. A world away. I'm hungry. Please, can we stop?'

Alessia's smile broadens. 'Of course. I don't want you to be hungry.'

Alessia stays glued to my side, her hand in mine, as we make our way through the motorway services building at Sedgemoor. We buy ham-and-cheese toasties and coffee at Costa Coffee but decide to eat and drink on the road.

'One day, you won't think twice about being in a service station,' I try to reassure Alessia when I open her car door.

'I hope so,' she replies, but her eyes follow me as I walk around to my side of the Discovery, and I know she doesn't feel safe. The thought is depressing. I knew this might happen if she was exposed to her recent past and that awful underworld again.

It will take time, mate.

Time.

Once inside, I place the coffee cup in a holder, remove my sandwich from its wrapping, and take a big bite. I start the car and pull out of our space. 'You didn't get to tell me about your last day on the course. How was it?' I ask, with my mouth full and some butter dribbling down my chin.

She laughs at the state of me before passing me a napkin, and the sound warms my heart. 'The course was very . . . um . . . informative. We shall see. And I made some friends. Especially Tabitha.'

'That's great.' Out of the corner of my eye, I watch her take a delicate bite of her toastie as she deliberates over something. Her napkin is neatly laid on her lap, pointing the correct way, and it makes me smile. She's every inch a lady.

'I think they will help.'

'The lessons?'

'Yes. I want to prove to your mother and people like her that I am worthy of you and your . . . your legacy.'

Her softly spoken statement is a gut punch, sending shock waves to my soul.

Fuck a duck.

Rowena must have said something truly nasty and scathing last week, and my poor wife has taken my mother's poison to heart. I remember what she said when we were both with her in our drawing room, which was bad enough.

You need someone of your own class, someone English who understands the pressures of the title and your position in society. Someone who can help you fulfil the role you were born to and help protect our legacy.

The antagonism that I've come to associate with Rowena – that's been a part of my life since she walked out on us so long ago – simmers in my chest, and I grip the steering wheel harder. The resentment is my familiar – never really far away.

'You are more than worthy of me. If anything . . .' I mutter, trying to keep a handle on my temper. 'You are worthy of everything. Never think anything less than that, please.' I offer her an apologetic smile. 'You were on the receiving end of some dreadful diatribe from Rowena. I can only apologise.'

Alessia sighs. 'She was upset, Maxim. She thinks you married beneath you . . . a foreigner, a woman with nothing, and she was there to confess her . . . um . . .'

'Sins?' I sneer.

'She was there to put your mind . . . um . . . at ease. You should hear her side of Kit's story. Sometimes women find themselves in' – she swallows – 'difficult situations.'

I inhale sharply. My sweet, compassionate wife reminding me of the brutal truth of the world. *And she would know. Her awful travails brought her to me.*

It blows my mind.

My sweet girl. Defending my mother.

I clear my crowded throat. 'How's your toastie?' I ask because we're in difficult territory. I don't want to feel any compassion for my mother.

She left us.

She was cruel to my wife.

'Delicious,' she whispers, and another glance at her tells me she knows exactly what I'm doing.

Deflecting. Away from the sore spot that is my mama.

Mate.

'You are too kind to my mother. But I'll think about it,' I mutter, and because I don't want to discuss the Mothership, I turn on the sound system.

At just after five in the evening, the sun low in the sky, I turn right at the North Gatehouse and drive over the cattle grid and onto the northern driveway of the estate. Alessia leans forward to take in the rolling north pasture on our right. We've not been this way before.

'You have cows!'

'Cattle. Yes. Organic.'

'They are so pretty!'

I laugh. 'They're Devons.'

Alessia casts a look at me, her brow furrowed.

'The breed. Of cattle.'

'Oh.'

'You can meet them later.'

Alessia grins. 'Still no goats.'

I laugh. 'No goats.'

She looks ahead, and gasps as Tresyllian Hall comes into view. The magnificence of this house never fails to impress. It's always a moment for me as well. There's a sudden tightness in my chest. I'm bringing my wife to what will be a home for her, for our children, and hopefully for their children.

Fuck.

Dude. Steady.

That's a weighty thought.

Accompanied by weighty emotions.

Enough.

I shake it off. This place has been my haven, and I hope that Alessia will be happy here too.

I round the drive, run over the second cattle grid that rattles our teeth, and steer us around the old stables to the kitchen door where I park the Discovery.

I switch off the ignition and turn to Alessia.

'Welcome home, wife.'

Her smile lights up her face. 'Welcome home, my lord.'

The kitchen door opens, and Danny stands on the threshold, clasping her hands in excitement, her joy writ large in her sparkling blue eyes and beaming smile. Behind her, Jensen and Healey, Kit's beloved red setters, come barrelling out onto the gravel, curious to see who's arrived.

I clamber out of the car, and the dogs jump up, delighted to see me, insisting on some attention. 'Hello, boys. Hello!' I ruffle them both behind the ears. And they turn their enthusiastic attention and demands on Alessia when she comes to stand beside me. She pats them both, a little more reticent than me.

'Welcome home, my lord and my lady!' Danny gushes.

Danny gushing. It doesn't happen often.

She grabs Alessia's hand. 'I am so pleased to see you again, my lady.'

'Thank you, Danny,' Alessia says. 'Please, call me Alessia.'

'Alessia is fine, Danny. For heaven's sake.' And I give her a quick kiss in welcome. 'It's good to see you.'

'And you too, my lord.' She pats my face, and if I'm not mistaken, she's a little teary.

Oh, this will never do. 'Maxim. Please,' I instruct her. 'But wait, I have an important duty to perform.' I take Alessia's hand and lift her into my arms, making her squeal in surprise. The dogs jump up in encouragement and start barking. And rather than go in through the kitchen door, I hold Alessia to my chest and trudge over the gravel towards the front of the house.

'What are you doing?' Alessia laughs as she puts her arms around my neck.

'I'm taking you through the front door, which we rarely use. We should go through the boot room, but everyone uses the kitchen door, as it's the most welcoming part of the house.

However, as the new countess, I think you should go through the front door.'

The dogs are with us when I glance behind me, but Danny has disappeared. I know she's heading to the front door through the house. I round the corner and follow the path, lined with ancient yews, towards the old front door inset in the spacious stone porch. It's a quicker journey for Danny, who opens the old oak door. Beside her, Jessie, our cook, and Brody, one of the estate hands, stand ready to welcome us.

I carry Alessia inside and set her down in the hallway in front of my family coat of arms and our staff. 'Welcome, Countess Trevethick.' I cup her face, bring her lips to mine, and give her a sweet kiss that stirs my soul.

My wife.

Here. At last.

'Aww.' There's a collective sound of approval from the team, and I must remember we're not alone.

'Welcome home, both of you. And congratulations,' Jessie offers.

'Thank you. Danny, Jessie, Brody, may I present Alessia, Countess of Trevethick.'

Alessia is overwhelmed by the unexpected and warm welcome. The staff – even the dogs – are delighted to see her. Danny and Jessie have left to make a 'wee spot of tea,' and Brody has gone to replace some light bulbs somewhere. The dogs, sensing food might be forthcoming, have followed in Danny's and Jessie's footsteps.

Maxim and Alessia are alone in the front hall as they gaze at each other. From nearby, a rhythmic tick from an old clock beats a sensual, relentless pulse.

'How is it?' Maxim asks, his eyes searing hers, and he tucks a wayward lock of hair behind her ear.

His gentle touch echoes through her body, waking her up.

'It's good. Very good,' she whispers, unable to avert her gaze from his striking green eyes that darken as he stares at her.

'It's not so long since we were here.'

'No. But it was another lifetime.'

'It was,' he whispers and brushes his thumb along her bottom lip, sending a bolt of delicious electricity south through her muscle, sinew and bone and all the soft tissue in between. It's arousing.

'I know that look,' he breathes, his words barely audible.

'I know your look.' She can feel it. Their desire. Coursing between them. Electrical. Magical. Their own special alchemy.

'Let's go to bed,' Maxim whispers, eyes dark with carnal appreciation and bold promises.

How could she resist? Why would she want to?

'I'd like that very much.'

He grins, grabs her hand, and leads her towards the considerable staircase with its two-headed eagle newel posts.

'Race you?' he challenges with a wicked grin and bolts up the stairs taking two at a time. Alessia follows, trying not to laugh at his boyishness.

He waits at the top of the stairs, all tousled hair and licentious smile.

'Eager?' Alessia teases, a little breathless, and he laughs and dips suddenly, grabbing her around her thighs and hauling her over his shoulder so that she squeals and giggles in equal measure.

'You bet!' he exclaims and smacks her backside before striding down the corridor towards his bedroom with Alessia bouncing on his shoulder.

Fortunately, it's not far. In his bedroom, he sets her on her feet, and they regard each other, drinking each other in – all eyes and smiles and desire.

'I love you,' he breathes and leans forward, catching her lips with his, slowly snaking his arms around her and pulling her against his body. They kiss. And kiss. Tasting and teasing one another. Losing each other in their tongues and lips and teeth.

Her hands fist in his burnished chestnut hair while his are at her nape, cradling her head, and skimming her body to her behind, and squeezing hard, so she's flush against his growing erection.

'You taste so good,' Alessia breathes when they come up for air.

'So do you, baby. So do you. I want you so much. But for a moment, I just want to hold you. Here. Now.' He tightens his arms around her and rests his forehead against hers.

She smiles to herself and for him as she catches her breath, and they stand in each other's arms, at peace in the eye of their passionate storm.

Together, they hold each other.

Own each other.

'Oh, Maxim. I love you,' she whispers. 'More than you'll ever know.'

'I *do* know.'

But her love, her gratitude, her desire can't wait for long. 'I want you,' she whispers, reaching for Maxim's sweater and tugging it over his head. She jerks his shirt out of his jeans and starts to undo the buttons.

I stand as placidly as I can, given I want to jump my wife.

Now.

And I let her undress me. She's as driven by her longing as I am. My fingers are itching to undress her, but I'm happy to stoke the heat in my blood just watching her.

She slips her hand into the waistband of my jeans and undoes the button.

'Your turn,' I say, halting her, and I sweep off her sweater. Then I kneel at her feet, slipping her boots off one by one and peeling off her socks. I stand, and under her unremitting gaze, I remove my shoes and socks.

There. Ready.

So ready.

'Take your jeans off. Now,' I whisper.

Alessia gasps, and with her darkening eyes on mine, she steps back, slowly undoes her jeans, and lowers the fly at a glacial speed.

Tease!

Then she shimmies, swinging her fine arse to and fro, tugging her jeans down and stepping out of them.

My beautiful wife stands before me in a pretty lacy bra and panties.

And I take a moment to admire the fucking view.

She is gorgeous.

She reaches behind her back, undoes her bra, tosses it at me, and laughs when I catch it. Then she shimmies out of her panties.

'You are so beautiful, Alessia.'

'Now you,' she says with an imperious look that's hot as hell.

'Yes. My lady.' I make quick work of my jeans and underwear, so my ready, ready dick springs free, enthusiastic for her.

Alessia smirks and steps forward, taking me in hand.

It's my turn to gasp.

Her fingers are cold!

'Ah!'

Alessia laughs, and I join her. 'Enough!' I grab her around the waist and lift her. 'Wrap your legs around me, baby.' She obliges, and holding her, I walk to our bed and lower us onto it, so I'm lying cradled between her thighs.

'First time. As man and wife. Here,' I whisper, suddenly beset by a sense of history or legacy or something that's more than the two of us. She gazes at me and gently pushes my hair off my forehead.

'Husband,' she whispers, and the word echoes in my groin.

Fuck.

I want to be inside her. I run a hand down her body, skimming her nipple, so it stands to sweet attention, and continue, my hand celebrating the dips and shallows of her skin down to her belly and over her sex. Slowly, I insert a finger into her warm, welcoming wetness, and her hips rise, meeting my finger, and pushing against my hand, wanting relief.

Oh, baby.

I withdraw my finger and slowly ease myself into her and take her mouth with mine, my tongue mirroring my cock. Her body rises to meet mine, and she wraps her arms and legs around me. Holding me fast. It's intoxicating.

And I can resist no more.

And start to move.

Hard.

Swift.

Claiming the woman who is my wife.

Taking her higher as her nails etch my back.

Vaguely, as I lose myself in her, I hope she leaves marks on me.

I'm hers.

She's mine.

For all time.

'Maxim,' she cries as she comes, and I let go, finding release inside the only woman I've ever truly loved.

My wife.

Chapter Twenty-Eight

Alessia takes a break from practising her audition pieces and watches Maxim from the mullioned windows of the great music room. He's trudging up the driveway with Michael, the estate manager. Maxim is dressed in his long coat and wellingtons, holding what looks like a walking staff as he paces the ground. They are deep in discussion, probably about the still, Maxim's passion project. He's excited to get it up and running.

Behind him, Healey and Jensen are bouncing along the lane, stopping to sniff and mark their territory like dogs do. Even from here, Alessia can tell that the dogs are delighted to be with her husband. They adore him.

Like she adores him.

Maxim and Michael laugh at something Michael says, and it warms Alessia's heart to see him so happy. This is where Maxim belongs. He looks every centimetre the lord of the manor and so much more relaxed here in Cornwall than in London. And who could blame him? The pace of life is easier, and it reminds her more and more of her homeland.

In the pasture beside them, the deer congregate around the water trough. Maxim stops to admire the herd with Michael.

Alessia is distracted by the sound of footsteps. 'Ah, what a pleasure it is to listen to you play, my lady,' Danny says. 'I've brought you some refreshment.' She places a tray with a small coffee pot, cup and saucer on the console table beside her.

'Thank you.'

'His lordship has always had a fondness for the herd,' she murmurs as she glances out of the window.

Alessia nods. 'When I was here last time, we saw one on the road. A great stag. It stopped in front of us.'

'You did! Well, I never.' Danny looks shocked.

'Why is that a surprise?'

'Did Maxim not tell you?'

'No.'

'About the legend?'

Alessia shakes her head.

'Och, that boy,' Danny scoffs. 'Legend has it that the first countess, Isabel, encountered a stag out in the forest shortly after her wedding to the first earl. The stag spoke to her and told her that if her family cared for the wild herd, then she would be blessed with a long life and many children. And that's exactly what happened. The Trevethick estate has long been a haven for the deer. They're seen as a sign of good luck. That's why the two stags are the support in the family coat of arms. They symbolise protection for the earldom, the estate and the family, my lady.'

'I did not know this. They are not . . . um . . . hunted?'

Danny shakes her head. 'No. Not for centuries. They're humanely culled every other year to keep their numbers sustainable. And the venison is much coveted around here. Keeps the herd strong, and while the herd stands strong, so will the Trevelyans and the Earls of Trevethick.'

Alessia doesn't know what to say, but a frisson of hope for the future – a future for her and her husband skitters over her skin.

After all, the stag they saw when Maxim took them shooting seemed to be welcoming her. She grins at Danny.

'It's a good omen, my lady. The Trevelyan family is responsible for the well-being of the estate, the village, forests, fields, and pastures surrounding it. Their land extends many thousand acres. And they and their kin have kept it together and thriving since the 1600s. Long may they continue.' Danny's smile reflects her own. 'Now, once you've had your coffee, I was wondering if you wanted to see the private apartments and the attic – though that floor is mainly for staff and storage.'

'Yes. I'd love that. Thank you, Danny.' Alessia has cherished the housekeeper's thorough tours of the house. She's given Alessia a detailed history of each room that's open – not all are – and its place within the great house. She's introduced Alessia to most of the staff, who, so far, have been kind and accommodating. Alessia is increasingly in awe of the woman that keeps the entire house running smoothly. And she feels safe in her hands – after all, it was Danny who cared for her after Dante and Ylli's kidnap attempt.

And it's obvious she dotes on Maxim, and he on her. She seems more maternal than his own mother . . .

Alessia!

She tries not to think uncharitably about Rowena, but sometimes it's impossible. Perhaps, to make up for her unkind thoughts, she can do something to help repair the fissure between her mother-in-law and her husband.

But what?

'And then there's the all-important decision of moving his lordship into the earl's bedroom and you into the countess's room.' Danny distracts Alessia from her thoughts.

'Countess's room?'

'Yes. You each have your own apartments here.'

Separate bedrooms! Separate apartments!

'Sometimes it's good to have a bolt hole, my lady,' Danny says as if reading her thoughts.

Bolt hole? Alessia doesn't understand what that means and does not like the sound of it or the idea of sleeping elsewhere.

Is this what Maxim wants? To sleep without her?

Like the ancient Gheg custom! The thought depresses her immediately.

'Ach, my lady. It'll not be like that,' Danny says. 'I'll show you once you've had your coffee.'

Michael and I survey the motors in the old stables – these vintage and classic cars were Kit's pride and joy. I can almost see him, walking towards me in his filthy overalls, his hands covered in grease and smelling of oil and Swarfega. He'd have his cloth cap on, an oily rag protruding from his pocket, and he'd be so fucking happy.

Well, Spare, fancy a spin in this Ferrari?

He loved it here.

He loved his cars.

Me, not so much. However, I didn't mind the odd spin around the grounds in one of these beasts.

And now I have to decide what to do with them.

'You're right, Michael. This building would be a much better place for a still. It's more secure, closer to the house, there's room for expansion, and these old stables are in better condition than the north pasture barn.'

'Only problem is the cars.'

'I'm going to have to sell them. I have no need for all of these.'

Michael gives me a rueful smile. I know selling them would have broken Kit's heart, but he's not here. 'I'll keep the Morgan, and everything else can go. I'll ask Caroline if she wants any of them, but I doubt it. Cars were Kit's passion, not hers.'

'Yes, my lord.'

I head back into the house via the boot room while Michael returns to his office. We've had a good morning, and I'm ready for lunch. Michael was extolling the virtues of regenerative farming.

Apparently, it's the next step in green agriculture. I've vowed to read up on it, to see what the fuss is about.

I find Alessia in the small sitting room, seated at a table set for lunch. She looks up from the Daphne Du Maurier that she's reading, anxiety etched on her face.

'What is it?' I ask as I take a seat opposite her.

'Do you want me to sleep somewhere else?'

'What? No. What's this about?'

'Danny was talking to me about moving rooms.'

'Ah.' The penny drops. 'I'm not sure I want to move rooms. Do you?'

'No. I want to stay with you.'

I laugh. 'I'm glad to hear it. We can sleep where we like. The earl's room has been my father's and my brother's.' I shrug. I'm in no mood to move in there. 'And as for the countess's rooms, that's up to you. They're not far from my bedroom, and there's a dressing room there that might come in handy. You don't have to sleep there. I'd rather you slept with me. Unless I snore.'

She exhales and laughs. 'Good. That's what I thought. And you do not snore.'

'I have an idea of what we can do this afternoon.' I change the subject.

'Oh?' Alessia tilts her head to one side with a coquettish look, and I know she's thinking about sex.

I laugh. 'No. I'm going to teach you to drive.'

'Drive! Me?'

'Yes. You don't need a licence on private land. We can take the Defender, or maybe another, smaller vehicle, and I'll teach you.'

Danny enters, holding two plates. 'Lunch, my lord.'

I roll my eyes. 'Maxim. That's my name.'

'Maxim, my lord,' Danny concedes, and she places two plates on the table. 'Salad Niçoise with a Cornish twist.'

'Cornish twist?' I ask, intrigued, examining the plate in front of me.

'Pilchards, sir, instead of anchovies.'

I laugh. 'Okay then.'

'Steady, a little more gas, and slowly ease the clutch up,' I direct Alessia. We're in the Defender that Danny normally drives around the estate. It's battered but quite serviceable.

Alessia is grasping the steering wheel like her life depends on it, and her tongue peeks out between her lips because she's concentrating so hard. The car suddenly jerks forward and stalls, and Alessia stamps on the brakes.

I'm thrown forward, my seat belt cutting into my chest. 'Whoa!'

Alessia lets out a string of invective in her mother tongue, which I've never heard her do before.

She's not happy.

'It's okay,' I reassure her. 'It's about finding the biting point on the clutch when the engine engages. You just need a little more gas. Take it steady. We have all afternoon. And it's okay – driving can take a while to learn.'

She gives me a quick, determined scowl and starts the car again.

My girl is not going to give up.

'Take it slow. Put it into gear,' I murmur.

She fights the gear stick to put it back into first, and I wonder if we should have chosen an easier car.

Hell, if she can drive this, she can drive anything.

'Okay. Deep breaths. You can do this.'

The gears grind as she thrusts it into first and revs the engine once more.

'Easy does it. Not too much gas.'

She scowls at me again, and I shut up because if I don't, I suspect she'll be tempted to remove one of my limbs. I've never taught anyone to drive, and I learned here on the estate when I was fifteen. It was one of the last duties my father fulfilled before he died. He was calm and reassuring, his best self . . . and I hold that memory dear. He was a great teacher.

I want to be the same for Alessia.

At a snail's pace, we roll forward.

Yes! I let out a silent, internal cheer so as not to distract Alessia, and we inch across the gravel behind the stables.

'Okay, now into second. Clutch. Second gear. Ease up on the clutch.'

Her tongue appears again, and she shifts smoothly into second gear, letting the Defender pick up a little speed.

'Well done! Okay. Take it steady. Head straight towards the gates. Yes. Good!'

Alessia gingerly drives towards the gateposts where the cattle grid lies.

'We're going into the lane. Keep it going.'

She steers – successfully – between the gateposts and heads down the lane. A wild grin erupts on her face, and it's infectious.

'You're doing it. Keep your eyes on the road.'

She continues to drive slowly but solidly down the lane, concentrating hard; her tongue makes the occasional foray, peeking from her mouth.

It's sexy as hell.

But now is not the time to tell her. Or to think about that – it's distracting.

'You're doing so well. But beware, there might be deer in the lane. They should get out of the way when they hear this crate coming. You don't want to hit one. Kit did. Once . . .'

Shit.

And look what happened to him.

Hell.

I clear my throat, pushing my grief away, though I'm reminded that there's a mythical story about the deer that ties them to the estate, which I've forgotten. I must try to remember to tell Alessia. 'At the end of the lane by the north gatehouse, let's take the left fork. Take that, and we'll do a crisscross tour of the estate.'

Alessia is giddy with delight. She cannot believe she's managed to move the tank she is driving. But most of all, she's thrilled because she doesn't want to let Maxim down. He seems to think that she should be able to do this.

And so she has.

His faith in her is touching.

As they round a bend in the lane, she spots the gatehouse and the cattle grid and the road forks in three directions.

She panics for a moment.

Which is left?

O Zot!

Rather than turn at all, she slams on the brakes, throwing them both forward and stalling the car.

'Sorry!' she says quickly.

'It's okay. You don't need to apologise. You remembered the brakes and stopped the car. That's the most important thing. Not sure of your left?'

Alessia laughs, and she suspects it's more in catharsis than amusement. 'No. I was confused.'

'It's okay. You could have gone either way. This is all estate land. Turn the ignition off. Car into neutral. Brake on.'

Alessia follows Maxim's instructions and takes a deep breath.

She can do this!

'Do you want to try again?'

She nods.

Maxim sweeps his hand forward. 'Go ahead.'

She turns on the ignition, and the engine grumbles into life. She stamps on the clutch, wanting to show it who's in charge, and she slides, then pushes the stick into first. The gears make an awful grinding noise. Alessia chances a glance at Maxim, who's wincing, so she quickly looks back at the road and revs the engine, easing her foot on the clutch, releasing the handbrake . . . and they're off once more.

No stalling!

Alessia wants to cheer from the rooftops.

She turns the heavy steering wheel, and the car moves slowly to the left and continues along the lane

'Second gear?' Maxim says gently.

She nods and changes gear, keeping the car going. They pass one of the fields, and Alessia catches a glimpse of Jenkins on a tractor pulling a trailer. He gives them a wave, which Maxim returns, but Alessia keeps her hands firmly gripped on the steering wheel. As they head down the lane, Maxim continues to offer his support with sweet words.

He's pleased.

Alessia catches sight of another gatehouse and slows down as she approaches it. From beyond the gate, a small motorbike shoots in and across their path, the driver wearing black trousers and boots, and fastened to the rear, there's a carrier holding what looks like a small furry passenger. Alessia slams on the brakes as the motorbike continues at a pace up the driveway and doesn't stall the car!

Go, Alessia!

'Shit. It's Father Trewin,' Maxim exclaims. 'Driving much too fast. It must be God's will that he's still in one piece. Better follow him.'

Alessia does and speeds up to see if she can catch him.

'Steady,' warns Maxim, and she slows down again. 'We'll see him at the house. He's probably here to congratulate us. Or he's going to berate me for not coming to church yesterday. Probably both.'

Alessia stops beside Father Trewin while he's unfastening his Norfolk terrier, Boris, from his carrier on the back of his moped. Jensen and Healey are eagerly waiting to play, their tails frenetic flags.

I clamber out of the car, walk around to open Alessia's door, and turn to greet Father Trewin.

'Maxim, my lord. Congratulations on your marriage. How are you?' He offers his hand and gives me a firm handshake.

'Good. Thank you, Father. May I present my wife, Alessia, the Countess of Trevethick?'

'Lady Trevethick, what a pleasure to meet you again.'

'Father Trewin, how do you do?' Alessia shakes hands with him. 'Would you like to join us for tea?'

'I'd be delighted.' He gives us both a broad, benevolent, reserved-for-parishioners smile.

We make our way through the boot room and out into the west corridor, where we're met by Danny. 'Good afternoon, everyone,' Danny greets us. 'How was the car, my lady?'

'It was a tank!' Alessia beams. 'But I got it going.'

'I'm glad to hear it.'

'May we have some tea?' Alessia asks.

Danny smiles. 'Yes, my lady. The west drawing room?'

Alessia glances at me. I nod.

'Please.'

'We didn't see you at our service this Sunday,' Father Trewin says once we've sat down.

Bugger. I knew it. I'm going to get a lecture. 'Yes. I had to catch up here,' I mutter, desperate to change the subject. I lean down and scratch Boris behind his ears, wondering where Jensen and Healey are. 'And I was showing my wife around the estate.'

'Well, my lord, as I've said before, we lead by example. Perhaps next Sunday, you could do a reading.'

What?

I clear my throat. 'Sure. I'd be delighted.'

Liar.

'Your brother was a keen supporter of the church.'

Trust Kit. The nerd! I smile, my heart sinking.

That was Kit – the perfect earl. It's not me.

Mate. The irony.

'Will you choose a reading?' I ask.

'Of course. And might we expect to see Lady Trevethick there?' He casts his beady eyes at my wife.

Alessia smiles, but her eyes dart to mine in a silent plea for help.

'Alessia is Albanian, where religion was outlawed for many years. But her people are Catholic. As high Anglicans, I'm sure that won't be an issue.'

'We are a broad church, my lord, and welcoming of all faiths.'

'Of course, I'll be there,' Alessia says.

Danny enters and places a tray with cups and saucers on the table in front of Alessia. She gives her a nod and then leaves.

'Tea, Father Trewin?' Alessia asks.

'Yes, please, Countess.'

If the use of her title disconcerts Alessia, she gives nothing away. She takes the teapot and pours a cup, using the tea strainer that Danny has provided, and hands the cup and saucer with a small teaspoon to Father Trewin. She offers him milk and sugar, pours some for me, and gives me the cup and saucer.

Hiding my smile, I accept it. She's learned how to serve tea. Properly. 'Thank you, my love.' She gives me an impish smile before serving herself, and I know, that she knows, that I know that she's putting her social etiquette training into full force.

She's not put a foot wrong.

Would I expect anything less?

She's amazing. And adorable.

Even more so because I know she's done this for me.

And maybe for herself.

I turn my attention to our guest, who is fully conscious of Alessia and me grinning inanely at each other. His cheeks become rosier as he looks from me to my wife.

Yeah. We're in love.

Deal with it.

Which reminds me . . . 'Father Trewin, I had hoped that Alessia and I could marry again in the UK as we're now back home, but I've been reliably informed that it's not possible. Therefore, I was hoping we could have a blessing at the church. Give us a chance to celebrate here. Preferably in the summer?'

'That's a splendid idea. Of course we can do that. I'd be delighted.'

Alessia escorts Father Trewin back to his moped. He is positively blossoming under her attention, and I think she has a new fan. I head to the study to make some notes on the gin project, to find someone to sell Kit's car collection, and to read up on Michael's new passion – regenerative farming.

It's dusk when I look up from the computer. My head is buzzing from what I've learned about sustainable agriculture. Leaning back in my chair, I take in my surroundings to ease the strain on my eyes.

I've not really sat here since Kit died. There was that time when Oliver talked me through the burglary at Chelsea Embankment, and before then, when I visited the Hall for the first time in my capacity as earl, I sat here and mostly talked to the estate workers in turn.

A faint melody drifts through the hallways from the music room; Alessia is at the piano, no doubt practising her audition pieces. As I try to make out what she's playing, my gaze wanders over the desk that was once my brother's and once my father's. There are mementos that belonged to both of them: my father's Georgian tea caddy where he kept paper clips and such nonsense, two vintage Matchbox Bugattis from the 1960s – they were my father's, but I remember he used to let Kit play with them. He and Kit shared a passion for cars.

They *were* close.

And here I am, selling his prized collection.

Kit. I'm sorry, mate.

I open the tea caddy, more out of nostalgia than curiosity, trying to capture some essence of my beloved father.

There is a small set of keys sitting on top of a slightly larger key, which I know is for the safe.

The safe!

Maybe this is where Kit's missing laptop, phone and journal might be.

Grabbing the key, I stand and open the large wooden built-in cupboard that once served as the serving platter closet, where the old Cartwright & Sons safe is situated. The larger key fits the lock, and I open it, revealing Kit's laptop.

But no phone or journal.

There are also various papers that I don't have the energy to explore right now. I take out his laptop and place it on the desk.

Perhaps his journal is in a drawer.

I try one of the drawers, but it's locked.

A key from the small bunch opens it, and as I slowly tug the drawer open – there, in all its glory, is Kit's battered, brown leather journal and his dead iPhone.

I ignore the phone and laptop because they're probably password protected, so I'll need expert help to hack them.

It's the journal that will answer my questions.

My scalp tenses as I take it out – clasped with reverence between both hands – and place it on top of his laptop. I stare at it for a full minute before I decide to invade his privacy. Slowly, with a slight tremor in my hand, I unwind the leather tie ragged from overuse and pull the covers apart. It opens on the last entry.

2nd January 2019

Fuck! Fuck! Fuck!
A thousand times fuck!
I'm fucked!
Fucking Rowena!!!
First my wife, now my mother!!!

Chapter Twenty-Nine

Every hair on my body rises in shock as I pore over the entry time and time again.

First my wife, now my mother.

The words ring through my brain, a loud klaxon of wrongdoing.

My wife? Caroline?

And guilt surges like a tsunami through my chest.

But. But . . . we . . . we – Kit was dead when Caro and I fucked that first time. I never touched her while they were together.

Not once.

Before they were together. Yes. But . . . not while *they* were a couple.

First my wife!

Was she having an affair? And he found out?

Is this why he left her nothing in his will?

That makes sense. It always seemed such a shockingly cold-blooded move. And Caroline was angry . . . but she accepted the exclusion readily.

Was she aware that he knew?

Did he confront her?

He must have – his will was changed in September last year.

But an affair with whom? One person? Two people? More?

Fuck. Poor Kit.

I think back to Christmas in the Caribbean. There was no hint of marital un-bliss between them. Or maybe I didn't notice because I was too busy fucking my way through the American tourists.

Oh hell.

The answer is probably chronicled within these pages.

Dare I look?

Do I even want to know?

There's a knock on the door that startles me. I close the book and instinctively lean over the journal to hide it from view. Danny enters, and I must look as guilty as sin because she doesn't tell me why she's there. 'Are you okay, my lord?'

'Yeah. Yeah. What is it, Danny?'

'The countess has gone out with Jenkins to the sheep. She didn't want to disturb you. But she wanted to help. We have twenty-seven ewes lambing right now.'

'That many!'

'Yes, my lord.'

'But it's just the beginning of the season!' I frown – that's a lot at once. 'I'd better go and help too.' I rise from the desk, taking Kit's journal with me. I don't want any prying eyes seeing this, and on a whim, I grab the Leica M6 I brought from London and automatically check that it has film in it.

'I'll hold dinner, my lord.'

'Okay, thank you. I have no idea what time we'll be back.'

Alessia rides with Jenkins in the Defender as it bumps down one of the lanes in the dark. The high verges, covered with brambles and grass, seem to loom out of the night, so Alessia's grateful she's not driving. Jenkins glances at her, his brow etched in concern.

'My lady,' Jenkins almost shouts above the noise of the engine.

'Alessia.'

'Yes. I have to ask . . .' His words trail off as if he's reluctant to say more.

'What is it, Jenkins?'

He clears his throat. 'Are you . . . are you in the family way?'

Alessia frowns. *Family way? What does that mean?*

Jenkins tugs his ear. 'Might you be . . . might you be pregnant, my lady?'

Alessia's blush warms her cheeks, and she hopes it's not visible in the darkness of the car. 'No!' she exclaims. 'Why . . . why would you ask me such a thing?'

His shoulders fall as Jenkins visibly relaxes. 'No. 'Tis a good thing, my lady. We don't want pregnant women around lambing.'

'Oh. Oh yes. I understand. I am sorry.'

'No need to apologise, ma'am. I forgot to ask earlier.'

Alessia flashes him a smile. 'I know pregnant women should not be around lambs and goats.'

'Goats?'

Alessia laughs. 'Yes. Where I am from, we have goats.'

He turns by a large structure that Alessia realises is a substantial barn. He parks next to a steel door, where three other cars are stationed.

'We're here,' he says. 'You'll be glad you wrapped up warm.'

The barn is cavernous and chilly, and there must be a hundred or more ewes inside. Several are bleating loudly, in the throes of labour – these have been separated into smaller pens away from the pregnant flock. Among the pens, a few newborn lambs are already being nuzzled and licked by their mothers as they root for milk from swollen udders. A couple of the estate workers are busy with lambing among the pens.

They're just in time to watch one of the farmhands, whom Alessia has not yet met, help deliver a lamb. Wearing surgical gloves, he cleans the lamb's nose to help it breathe and places it in front of its mother to be licked clean. He grabs a bottle and dabs a little of the ointment, which Alessia notices is iodine, on the lamb's navel.

'Good evening.' He nods a greeting to Alessia. 'Oh, there's another,' the young man says, and he sits back while the ewe delivers that lamb on her own. 'Good girl. Easy there,' he says in a soothing voice to the ewe and repeats the same clean-up process with her lamb.

'Where are the gloves?' Alessia asks Jenkins.

'The workstation over there.' Jenkins points with his chin. His eyes are on the ewes and who's going to pop next. 'We try to let them do this themselves. New Zealand Suffolk rams tup the sheep. Means they should have narrow shoulders and finer heads. Makes them easier to deliver. But some of them need help, my lady. It's good we keep an eye. We don't usually have them all lamb at once.'

Alessia smiles at the young farmhand, who is now trying to get both lambs to feed. 'Colostrum. Very good for new lambs.' He grins.

Alessia heads to the workstation, spreads the disinfectant over her palms – paying particular attention to between her fingers – then slips on some disposable gloves. Jenkins joins her. 'It's all hands on deck. It's just observing. Checking they're not in distress.'

Alessia nods. 'I have done this. But with goats. And not with this many.'

Jenkins gives her a broad smile. 'You're going to fit right in, m'lady.'

I pull up at the Home Farm barn and, grabbing my camera, leap out of the car. I've stowed Kit's journal in the glove box and locked it. It should be safe there. Inside the barn, I scan the interior for my wife, but I can't see her. There are about thirty ewes in the birthing pens. I spot Jenkins, who's in the nearest pen attending a ewe. I squat down to talk to him.

'My lord.'

'All at once? What did we do to deserve this?'

'Maybe it's the moon,' he says as he pulls a lamb into the world. Its mother is very keen to get it cleaned up. Jenkins sits back.

I laugh. 'What can I do? And where's my wife?'

'She's in the thick of it, somewhere in here. She wants to help.'

I frown. *Does she know what she's doing?* But I keep that thought to myself.

'Okay, I'll get ready.' I head to the workstation, disinfect my hands, and pull on some blue gloves. From there, I spot Alessia, her hair snaking down her back in a long braid. She's in a pen, clearing the nose of a newborn lamb and placing it in front of its mother. As I approach her, I hear her cooing in her own language. 'Hej, mama. Hej, mami, ja ku është qengji yt. Hej, mami, ja qengji yt.' Gently, she strokes the ewe's nose and repeats whatever she's just said in her soothing tone, then sits back to see if the ewe will produce another.

I'm suddenly overwhelmed with a swell of emotion that mushrooms in my chest and stops me in my tracks. My heart is full. Full to bursting – just watching my sweet wife interact with a sheep. A Trevethick sheep.

One of ours.

I have never seen Caro, or my mother, help like this on the estate.

And in that moment, I know Alessia is the best thing that's ever happened to me.

To us.

All of us. Here. Now.

I clear my crowded throat as I kneel beside the pen. 'Hi,' I whisper, my voice hoarse.

'Hello.' She grins, and it's obvious she's pleased to see me, and she's in her element. She's thoroughly filthy, with blood, mucus, and heaven knows what all over her gloves, jeans and jumper, but she's radiant.

'You okay?'

She nods. 'And so is this little one.' She rubs the lamb's head. 'The mama did good. She may have another.'

'This is not your first rodeo?' I ask.

She frowns.

'Not the first time,' I clarify.

'No. Our neighbours. They came to our wedding. They have goats. I have helped when they are in kid. Often.'

'Alessia, you never fail to amaze me. We're lucky to have you.'

She waves off the compliment with a dismissive flutter of her hand. 'You do this too?'

I laugh. 'It's not my first rodeo either. I'll go see where I'm needed. But first . . .' I raise my camera and peer at my beautiful, dishevelled wife through the lens as she smiles back at me, and I press the shutter. 'I'm going to take more if I can. I don't have enough of you. And right now, you're absolutely fucking beautiful. I'd better go.'

She grins, a dazzling smile just for me, and I'm reluctant to leave her, but needs must.

It's three o'clock in the morning when I guide Alessia into the shower to clean her up from the evening's exertions. We're exhausted and squalid from a full shift in the sheep shed. But we have seventy-two new lambs. I don't think I've ever, ever worked as hard in my life, but I'm thrilled. Only one stillborn, no rejections, and all the ewes are in good condition. That's an epic start to lambing. And I am so glad that we were here to help.

Now, I need to get my wife clean and into bed.

Alessia leans against me under the welcome warm water, her eyes closed.

My love.

She's nothing short of amazing.

She's scooped her braid into a gravity-defying knot and manages to keep it out of the cascade of water. I grab a cloth and soap and gently start to wash her hands, her arms, and her face. Then hold her up, while I wash myself.

Maxim towel-dries Alessia. She can barely keep her eyes open and thinks even her hair is exhausted. But she's exhilarated too. Finally, she feels that she's helped and given back to Maxim, and to the estate workers who have welcomed her so warmly.

'Can we just go to bed?' she mumbles.

Maxim gently clasps her chin and tips her head back so Alessia opens her eyes. 'Your wish is my command, Lady Trevethick. Thank you for this evening and tonight. You were spectacular. You must be starving too.' He brushes her lips with his.

'No. Just tired. So tired.' She gives him a sleepy smile, and he drops the towel, scoops her up off the floor, then places her on the bed.

Alessia is asleep before I step back and cover her in the duvet. I move a stray strand of hair off her face, and she doesn't move. 'My brave, strong girl. Thank you,' I whisper and kiss her forehead.

I finish drying myself, drag on my PJs, and crawl into bed beside my wife, where I snuggle up to her and inhale her scent . . .

It's the rattle of cups that wakes me. Danny has entered our room with a very welcome tray of coffee and breakfast. The smell is tantalising, and my mouth pools with saliva.

I am fucking famished.

'Good morning, your lordship. I hear you had quite the night.'

'Good morning,' I mumble, not wanting to wake up. I open my eyes, and Alessia's eyes flutter open but close again.

Danny places a tray at the end of our bed. 'It's after eleven, my lord. I thought you might need some breakfast,' she says, and I cannot remember the last time she brought me breakfast in bed.

I must be in her good books.

Or maybe it's Alessia.

It's probably Alessia.

'Thank you, Danny.' I sit up, and Alessia is still fast asleep beside me.

Danny looks down at my sleeping wife, her face soft and sweet with a fondness I don't think I've seen before. 'Oh my lord, you chose well,' she says, and with that, she seems to come to her senses. She straightens, clears her throat, gathers our filthy clothes from the floor, and leaves.

Breakfast smells enticing.

Bacon, eggs, mushrooms, toast.

I pull the tray towards me, and Alessia rouses.

'I smell food,' she says sleepily.

'Hungry?' I ask.

She offers me a sleepy grin. 'Starving.'

Alessia is becoming familiar with the rhythm of the house. In the morning, after they've washed and dressed and maybe made love, she and Maxim have breakfast with the staff in the large kitchen – usually, it's the second sitting. Afterwards, she and Danny meet to discuss the day's menu, bookings and requirements for the holiday houses, which includes the Hideout, and any household issues or tasks that need to be completed. When that's all done, Alessia has been going to the great barn to help with the lambing and moving ewes with their progeny to the bonding pens.

She's even driven herself.

Without Maxim.

He was anxious, but he let her go.

And she succeeded.

She needs to apply for a driver's licence. And take a test.

All in good time, Alessia!

During the week, the Home Farm has welcomed 197 lambs and counting.

Alessia has done two more night shifts to help. And she loves it.

She loves it here.

She loves that she feels . . . useful.

She now knows all the estate workers by name, who lives-in, who lives nearby in Trevethick village, and who lives further afield. They are all delighted that she's there to share the workload.

And she is m'lady.

To everyone.

In the early evenings, she enjoys a walk with Jensen, Healey, and her husband. The dogs adore her husband almost as much as she does . . . though he assures her the dogs were Kit's. The four of them have roamed the estate, and Maxim has regaled her with stories of his youth and his many, many misdemeanours, and she's built a mental picture of an idyllic life led by Maxim and his siblings here on the estate.

No wonder he loves it so much.

They've taken a couple of walks along Trevethick beach, and she's breathed in the fresh, salty air by the sea.

He has given her the sea . . . again.

And she loves it.

But tomorrow will be different. Tomorrow, after church, they're returning to London for Alessia's audition that will take place on Monday. She's been studying for that in the afternoons. Losing herself in the colours of her music in the great music room.

Maxim, too, has been busy. As well as the new still idea, he's been preoccupied with the concept of regenerative farming. He's holding a meeting of all the tenant farmers at the Hall this evening, with a farmer who's come from a place called Worcestershire – which she finds impossible to pronounce – to share ideas. Snacks and drinks are being provided – Danny, Jessie, and Melanie, one of the part-time staff who helps Danny, are serving, but Alessia will also be on hand. She's looking forward to it, as it's the first time they've entertained at the Hall, and she, too, wants to learn about these new farming practices.

Alessia's only concern is Maxim. He seems a little distracted sometimes. And she's not sure if it's the estrangement with his mother or something else. She's asked him about it, but he says he's fine. In fact, he says he's never been happier.

It's all good.

We're here together.

And I'm loving life right now.

Thanks to you. I love you.

Alessia feels the same, but she wishes he'd reconcile with Rowena because, deep down, she suspects he's hurting.

Sitting at my desk, I read through my notes for the meeting this evening. I'm excited. Michael, our estate manager who's in charge of the Home Farm, has lit a fire under me. My father was ahead of his time when he went organic. Michael's father, Philip, who ran the Home Farm back then, helped persuade all our tenants to go the organic route too. Today, with Michael's help, I hope to convince our local tenant farmers that regenerative farming is the next step in our ecological journey. Sustainable, regenerative farming is the way forward – it helps the estate, our producers, our land, the locale and the planet. It feeds and repairs the soil, sequesters carbon and increases biodiversity. Through all my research, I've become a passionate fan. We have an advocate in a farmer from Worcestershire, Jem Gladwell, who will join us this evening. His substantial farm uses the latest regenerative techniques, and he's enough of a convert that he wants to spread the word and talk to fellow farmers using language that they understand.

I'm looking forward to meeting him, and he'll stay the night.

Our first guest!

And if tonight is a success, I hope we can repeat this process at Angwin and Tyok.

Once I finish my notes, I check my emails, and my thoughts turn to Caroline, and from her to Kit's journal. I have squirrelled it into the safe and pocketed the key. I haven't read any more pages, but I'm torn. I don't know if I want to find out more or if I should leave Kit to his secrets. After all, he's no longer with us.

I should let him rest.

But it gnaws at me . . . Caroline, faithless.

Is it any wonder we fucked when he died? I thought it was some grieving alchemy that got us together. It probably was, but as I look back, there was no restraint from either of us.

Hell.

Was she faithless throughout their marriage?

She said she loved him.

She was devastated when he died.

Devastated enough to sleep with me?

Fuck.

I hate that these thoughts plague me. Neither one of us behaved well.

Caro's sent me her interior design ideas for the mansion blocks. There are three options, all of them good. But I haven't picked up the phone to discuss them with her. Oliver wants the cheapest option, but that's no surprise. We'll be back in London for a few days from tomorrow evening – I'll arrange to speak to her then.

There's a soft tap on the door, and Melanie, one of Danny's protégés from the village, peeks around the door.

'Good afternoon, your lordship. Sergeant Nancarrow is here to see you.'

What! Shit!

Anxiety rises like the tide in my chest. What does he want? To interview Alessia? On a Saturday? I thought we'd avoided all that.

'Offer him some refreshment and show him into the main drawing room. I'll be with him shortly.'

'Yes, milord.'

I blow out a breath. What could he possibly want?

When I enter the room, Nancarrow is sipping a cup of tea and examining the family photographs displayed on one of the Queen Anne tables. Notes drift from the music room, where Alessia is at the piano.

Keep it together, dude.

'Sergeant Nancarrow. Good afternoon.'

He turns, and I extend my hand.

'My lord. It's good to see you.' We shake, and I usher him over to where Melanie's set up tea, and we both take a seat.

'Congratulations on your recent marriage,' he says and offers me a kind smile.

So far, so good.

'Thank you. What can I do for you?'

He blows out a quick breath and sets down his teacup, his expression now grim. 'I've brought news, my lord. Unfortunate news. Earlier this week, the two men we apprehended at your rental property were murdered while on remand.'

My scalp tightens, and I'm suddenly a little dizzy; I'm sure all the blood is draining from my head.

What the fuck? 'How?'

'Details haven't yet been released,' he mutters, watching my expression intently.

I sit back, utterly stunned . . . and a memory of the Arsehole showing me the newspaper clipping looms large and ugly in my head.

'I thought I should come and inform you. The case against them will lie on file but neither you nor Lady Trevethick will need to testify in court.'

'Yes,' I breathe as my mind goes into overdrive.

Did Anatoli *murder* them?

Does he have that kind of capability?

Was it someone else at his behest?

Fucking hell. Should I tell Nancarrow?

'So I wanted to return this.' His voice has softened, and he hands me a large Tesco's shopping bag. In it are my laptop and sound mixers.

'How did you come by these?'

'The gear was in the back of their car. The BMW. We were holding the car and these as evidence – but now the case is defunct.' He shrugs. 'The serial numbers match those of your missing items. I thought I'd return them.'

'Thank you.'

His eyes darken, and I don't know what that heralds. 'And there was this too.' He reaches into a pocket, pulls out a brown envelope, and hands it to me. 'We were waiting for the Met to ask for all the evidence, but they hadn't got around to it. And now, well, there's not much point.'

Intrigued, I open the envelope. Inside is a passport – Alessia's old one.

Shit.

My eyes meet his, and I have no idea what he's going to say or what my response should be.

'I thought Lady Trevethick might want this back, my lord.'

I'm stunned into complete silence.

He smiles at my expression. 'And let that be the end of it.'

I gape at him, not sure if I quite believe what he's implying. 'Thank you,' I blurt.

'I hear she's made quite the impression here, my lord.'

'Maxim. Please.'

He grins. 'Maxim.'

'She has. On all of us. That's her, playing now.'

'The piano?'

'Yes.'

'I do love a bit of Beethoven.'

'Come and meet her. She doesn't mind an audience.'

'I wouldn't want to intrude.'

'It's fine. Come.'

'Goodbye, Sargent Nancarrow,' Alessia says as they shake hands.

'My lady, such a pleasure.' His face flushes, and I know my wife has captured yet another heart.

'My lord. Maxim,' he corrects himself, and with a nod, he heads out towards his police car.

I blow out a breath. He didn't mention the death of the traffickers to my wife, and I decide to keep that information to myself for now – I know how unsettling it is for her to hear about that part of her life.

'He seems very nice,' she says but sounds uncertain. 'Why did he come here?'

'He was returning some of the gear that the arseholes who were arrested at the Hideout stole from my flat and also to return this.' I retrieve Alessia's old passport from my pocket.

'O Zot! He knows!' She bites down on her bottom lip, her eyes wide with worry.

'He does, but he's chosen to give us both the benefit of the doubt. He's not going to pursue it.'

Alessia frowns. 'But when Dante and Ylli go to trial . . .' Her voice fades, and I shift my focus to Nancarrow's car as it disappears down the lane. 'Maxim. What is it?'

Fuck.

'Tell me!'

I turn to face her, and her jaw is set in grim determination.

Hell.

'They died in custody.'

'What? Dante and Ylli? Both of them?' Her voice is barely audible.

I nod. 'That's the main reason Nancarrow came to see me . . . us.'

'They're dead,' she whispers again as if she can't quite believe it.

'It would appear so.'

'Murdered?'

'Yes.'

Her gaze scans my face, and I watch as a dozen emotions cloud her eyes, until they harden. Frigid. Callous. Unlike my girl. 'Good,' Alessia says, with such passion that I'm a little shocked. 'I hope they rot in hell.'

Whoa. But yeah. I hope so too.

'It also means there'll be no trial. We're free from all that,' I whisper.

Tears well in her dark eyes.

Shit. No.

'Please don't cry. Not for them.' I circle her in my arms, pulling her close and kissing her hair.

'No. Not for them,' she responds. 'For their victims. But I am relieved. We are free.'

'We are.'

She exhales, and her body relaxes in my arms as if a great weight's been lifted. 'It is a relief.' She tilts her head up, offering her lips, and I kiss her, falling under her spell as her fingers twist and tug my hair.

She pulls back, rewarding me with her sweet smile. 'Now. We just need you to talk to your mother.'

I scoff and shake my head. 'What? That's a change of subject. And it's my mother who needs to talk to me. I have texted her.'

'You have? Good. She will. She loves you. She wasn't ready to tell her story. Only the shocking . . . um . . . headlines. And you weren't ready to listen.'

I stiffen. 'I don't know if I'll ever be ready to listen, and I don't know if she ever loved me. She loved Kit.'

Alessia caresses my face. 'Of course she loves you.' She draws my lips to hers. 'How could she not? You're her son . . . and I love you,' she whispers.

There's a cough in the corridor behind us, and we straighten up and release each other.

'Danny?'

'My lord. Jem Gladwell is here to see you.'

'Great. Show him into the main drawing room.'

We're stretched out on our bed when we should be sleeping. 'Can we come back here?' Alessia asks, her head resting on her pillow, and I face her as she traces the outline of my tattoo with her finger. It tickles . . . but I love the attention.

'Of course we'll come back here. It's our home.'

'But soon.' Her hand cups my face.

'Once you've done your auditions. Sure.'

'Good. I love it here.'

'Me too. I feel hopeful in this place. And now more hopeful for the future of it and for the estate as a whole. I thought Gladwell was inspiring.'

'Yes. And funny too. He is good . . . um . . . company?'

'Yes. That works. He is good company. I look forward to seeing him again when he comes to Angwin.' I haul her into my arms. 'I think he liked you.' I nuzzle that pulse point beneath her ear.

Alessia squirms and giggles in my arms. 'That tickles.'

I stop torturing her and gaze at her beautiful face. 'We should sleep. I have to do my reading in church tomorrow morning, and then there's the long drive back to London.'

'Are you nervous about your reading?'

I lean against the pillows while considering my response, and Alessia snuggles against me. 'No. I'm not nervous at all. I feel a little hypocritical, to be honest. I'm not religious. Never have been. But Trewin is right. He's here for the community, and I need to step up and be here for the community, too, whether I like it or not.

'Tonight, listening and watching all our tenants and estate workers, I realised that all of us bind together to make a cohesive whole. We all work for the good of the community. And you and me, we're a part of that. I never thought about it before . . . when Kit was in charge here.

'Now, I want to be part of it more than ever. It's important to keep this place together and thriving for us and everyone who lives in and around Trevethick. We are its beating heart.'

Alessia's dark eyes are luminous. In them, I see her hope and . . . dare I say it, admiration. 'I want to be part of it too,' she whispers.

'Oh, baby, you are. More than you know already.'

'I have loved our time here. I can't believe that this is my life now. It is like a dream. Thank you.'

I skim my fingers over her cheek. 'No, my love. It's I who should thank you. This place has come alive with you here.'

Alessia shakes her head as if she doesn't believe what I'm saying and kisses me. Properly, her hand skimming down my body . . . waking everything.

Again? Oh boy!

Chapter Thirty

'Do you want me to wait?' Maxim asks. They're standing on an ornate mosaic floor in the impressive foyer of the Royal College of Music, and Alessia's audition is in forty minutes.

'I don't know how long this will take. But I'll be okay.' Alessia ignores her racing heart to reassure him. 'You have work to do. I'll come to your office afterwards.'

He frowns, unsure, and she places her hand on his chest, feeling the heat from his body through his shirt.

Comforted by his warmth, her heart rate slows to something approximating its usual rhythm. 'I'll be okay,' she repeats and tilts her head back for a kiss.

'Okay. I'll see you at the office. Good luck,' he says and brushes his lips against hers. 'As we say here, break a leg.'

Alessia's brow creases and she looks down at her feet.

Break a leg?

Maxim cups her chin with his thumb and forefinger, and lifts her gaze to bright green eyes that sparkle with humour. 'It's just an expression of good luck.'

'Oh.' Alessia returns his smile.

'Go. Warm up. You've got this.'

Alessia takes her bag, and with a final glance at her handsome husband, she follows the young student who's been patiently waiting for her.

They head up two flights of stairs and along a corridor. The student introduces himself as Paolo and welcomes her to the college. He's casually dressed in jeans and a sweater, and Alessia hopes she's not too smart in her black trouser suit. He stops and opens one of the doors to a small rehearsal room. 'You can warm up here. I'll be back to take you to the audition in about twenty minutes.'

'Thank you,' Alessia says, looking around the intimate space but, more importantly, at the upright Steinway and stool. They're the only pieces of furniture in the room. Paolo closes the door, and Alessia places her bag on the floor and sits on the stool.

This is it. She's here. She's practised and practised and practised some more. She knows her pieces backwards. She's watched YouTube video after YouTube video on audition techniques and what to expect. She's ready.

Taking a deep breath, she places her hands on the keys and launches into her warm-up . . . loving that the piano's tone is warm and immediate in this soundproofed cocoon.

In the cab on the way to the office, my phone buzzes, and I think it might be Alessia. No. It's another text from Caroline. She's sent me a few over the last few days begging for feedback on her designs.

For heaven's sake, we're meeting later this morning. I didn't know she was professionally so needy! Now she's trying a different tack.

How was Cornwall?

A303 or M5/M4?

In spite of myself, her text makes me laugh.

You know I hate the A303
It's for pensioners!
See you later

My eyes stray to the battered briefcase beside me on the seat. Within it are my notes from our meeting with Jem Gladwell, which I want to share with Oliver, and also Kit's journal – its mere existence searing a hole in my conscience and nagging me.

Should I read it?

Fuck.

Maybe I should burn it?

Alessia dampens down her nerves and steps into the audition room to meet a flank of the faculty, two men and a woman, sitting behind a long table. This room is airier than the last – big enough to house the Steinway grand piano in the centre of the room – and there's a large sash window that looks out over the Royal Albert Hall.

The older man rises from behind the table. 'Alessia Trevelyan. Welcome. I'm Professor Laithwaite, and I'm joined by Professors Carusi and Stells.'

Alessia takes his offered hand. 'Good morning, Professor. Good morning,' she says to the other staff, who offer her smiles in greeting.

'Do you have your music?'

'Yes.' From her bag, she retrieves all the scores and places them on the table in front of the tutors.

'Please take a seat at the piano.'

'Thank you.'

'Oh. What's this?' Professor Carusi asks as she looks at one of the scores. 'Valle e Vogël?'

'Yes. By an Albanian composer. Feim Ibrahimi.'

'Please. It's short. Let's hear it. And then move onto the Liszt.'

Alessia nods, pleased that they want to hear from one of her country's leading composers. She takes a deep breath and places her fingers on the keys, the familiarity of the ivories calming her, and starts to play. The music is bright and expressive, an homage to an Albanian folk song darting through the room in shades of purples and blues, morphing into paler blue colours. Once the final notes fade, Alessia places her hands on her lap, takes another deep breath, and begins the Liszt . . . the notes taking her back to the apartment in Chelsea, with the snow swirling through the window as she played for Maxim that first time.

'That's enough, thank you,' Professor Laithwaite interrupts at the beginning of the penultimate crescendo.

'Oh.'

'The Beethoven. I'd like to hear that from the thirty-seventh bar,' Stells says.

'Okay,' Alessia says, feeling a little shaken. *Did they hate it? Is she bad?*

She blows out a breath while her mind zips through the hues of the score to the thirty-seventh bar. She settles her hands on the keys once more, then starts pouring her heart and soul into the rest of the piece while the colours flare in angry reds and oranges around her.

Oliver's beaming smile and hearty handshake imply that he's delighted to see me. 'What did you think of Gladwell?' he asks.

'I thought he was fantastic. What's more, so did our tenants.'

Oliver claps his hands together in an unusual and spontaneous act of delight. 'Michael has been trying to get this regenerative farming idea off the ground for over a year.'

'He didn't tell me that.'

'Yes. Kit just wasn't interested.' Oliver shakes his head and looks away as if he's embarrassed or he's said too much, and I realise he doesn't want to be disloyal to his friend, my brother.

'Well, I think Kit missed a trick. I'm excited about it. Our next move is to galvanise the tenants at Angwin and Tyok. Gladwell's up for it. And we should talk in more depth about purchasing or leasing some capital equipment. It's going to be pricey.'

'We can budget for it. I'll talk to each of the estate managers and get a date in.'

'Great. Anything pressing?'

'Just the interior design for the mansion block.'

'Caro?'

'Yes.' And I don't think I've ever heard him say that word with such weariness.

'Is there a problem?'

'No. Of course not.' Oliver clears his throat, and I make my way into my office.

That was weird.

My first task is to call Leticia and tell her about Sergeant Nancarrow's news.

'And why do you want to study at the Royal College of Music?' Professor Carusi asks, her shrewd eyes assessing Alessia.

'I need a backbone to my music. My musical education so far has been . . . um . . . quite local. No, parochial, and I know I can take it further with the right tuition.'

'Where do you think you need help?'

'With my technique. I want to develop my voice, my playing. And my musical vocabulary.'

'To what end?' asks Professor Stells.

'I would love to perform. All over the world.'

Alessia cannot believe she's said that out loud.

They nod as if this might be a possibility, and Alessia is thrilled at the thought. She doesn't want to tell them that the other reason she needs to be there is because she needs a student visa.

'Well, thank you for coming to see us. Are you auditioning for other conservatoires?'

'I am.'

Professor Laithwaite nods. 'You'll be hearing from us.'

Alessia has no idea if it went well, but she's relieved it's over. She knows she played well . . . but was it good enough? In the cab, on a whim, she calls her great-uncle on FaceTime.

'Alessia, my darling. How are you?'

She fills him in on the past week in Cornwall and tells him about her audition.

'Who did you see?'

'What do you mean?'

'Who auditioned you?'

Alessia tells him.

'Hmm . . . All good people. You'll do fine. I know it. Have you told your mother? She'll be thrilled. We've spoken often, though her English is not as good as yours.'

Alessia grins, thrilled that they have been in touch with each other. 'No. I will call her now.'

'Well, good luck, my dear. Let me know how you get on and when I can see you again.'

Next, she calls her mother to share her news.

At my conference table, Caroline talks Oliver and me through her moodboards and designs, and it's clear she's put a great deal of thought into her process. The first option is opulent but elegant; the second, upscale, warm but airy; the third, bold but minimalist. I have to admit, they're all quite different but clever. Caro has excellent taste.

'I think I prefer the second option.' It's not the most expensive, but not the cheapest either. I glance at Oliver to see if he's on the same page.

'I concur,' Oliver says, nodding.

'Good. Let's do it. I'll crack on.' Caroline preens.

'Great. If you'll excuse me.' Oliver rises from the table and leaves.

Caroline watches him go with a frown. She turns back to me. 'So, how was Cornwall? How did Alessia fit in?'

'Great. Thanks. It was cool to be back. Alessia was and is amazing. Helped with the lambing.'

'Hmm . . . really?' Caro frowns.

Ignoring her reaction, I continue, 'Yes. She knew exactly what to do. In fact, she wants to return to Cornwall as soon as possible. I think she's more comfortable at the Hall.'

'Why wouldn't she be? She's waited on hand and foot, and it's very rural.'

'Actually, she's not waited on hand and foot,' I snap. 'And what do you mean by that?'

'Oh, for goodness' sake, Maxim. Give your hackles a rest. I think she's a little daunted by London life, that's all. And who wouldn't be? She does seem to attract a great deal of attention when she's here. It's not a surprise,' Caroline mutters and begins to pack her portfolio away.

Rather than provoke an argument, I change the subject. 'I'm going to sell Kit's car collection. Are there any that you'd like to keep?'

She pauses mid-packing as if considering the option, then shakes her head. 'No. That was Kit's thing. Not mine.'

'You're sure?'

She nods. 'I should move out of the countess's rooms,' she adds, a little sadly.

'There's no hurry. We've not moved from my room.'

'Oh.' She raises her eyebrows.

See, Alessia's not the mercenary little social-climbing, point-scorer you think, Caro!

'So, what's on the agenda while you're here?'

'I don't know how long we're going to stay. Alessia has

auditions at the RCM, RAM, Guildhall, and somewhere else. I can't remember.'

'All of them!'

'Yes. She's talented. And she needs to be offered a place so I can secure her a visa. Otherwise, she'll have to return to Albania for a month or so. And neither of us want that.'

Caroline rolls her eyes. 'For heaven's sake. It's not like she's going to be sponging off the state. I don't know why it's so difficult.'

I sigh. 'Me neither. It's the Hostile Environment that our government thinks we need. It's extremely bloody irritating.'

'Agreed.' She grabs her portfolio and rounds the table, only to stop in her tracks as she spies Kit's journal on my desk.

Hell. I should have put it away.

She pales instantly. Her cheeks ashen. 'You found it,' she says in a small voice that speaks volumes.

'Yes. It was in a locked drawer in Kit's desk at the Hall.'

She turns her face to mine, her eyes wide and fearful, and growing larger and darker as the seconds tick by – and we gaze at each other as the air is slowly sucked from the room by the weight of this small battered leather tome. By the weight of Kit's final written words.

'Say something,' she whispers.

'What is there to say, Caro?' I shrug. This is none of my business.

'You've read it?'

I open my mouth and close it again.

'Maxim. Tell me!'

And I know she'll hound me until she has the truth.

'You did. I can tell. I can always read you.'

Fuck. 'The last entry.'

She swallows. 'What did it say?' Her words are barely audible.

There's a knock at the door, and Oliver opens it, radiating polite smiles and fucking good cheer as he ushers Alessia inside. My spirits soar as she walks into the room. My wife is the cavalry, saving me from a beyond-awkward conversation.

'Am I interrupting?' Alessia asks, not unkindly.

'No. Of course not.' Delighted, I step towards her and kiss her lightly on her lips. Everyone else disappears. 'How was it?'

She shrugs but smiles. 'I don't know. We shall see. I like your office.' She looks around me. 'Hello, Caroline,' she says sweetly.

'Alessia, darling. How are you?' Caroline seems to recover her fortitude and steps forward to give my wife a kiss on each cheek.

Oliver has left the room.

'Caroline was just showing Oliver and me the designs for the mansion block refurbishment I've been telling you about.'

Alessia casts dark eyes at me and nods, but there's a question in her expression.

Fuck. She knows something's going down

I haven't mentioned Kit's last written words to Alessia, partly because it's none of my business, let alone my wife's, and partly because I don't know what she'd think of me invading Kit's privacy. But mainly because Alessia's opinion of Caroline is tentative at best – I've worked that out for myself – and I don't want to damage it any further.

'I'd better go. Oh, I meant to tell you,' Caroline says, her voice clipped, and she tosses her hair to one side, having reverted to her usual cool persona. 'Your mother's finally been in touch.'

Oh! 'She has?'

'She wants to postpone Kit's memorial until the autumn.'

'How do you feel about that?'

'I think it's a bit late. You know, it's a form of closure. A way to say a final goodbye.' She looks away, probably to hide her emotion or her shame, I don't know.

'Yes, of course. We should talk to her. I wonder what Maryanne thinks?'

Caro nods. Her lips clamp together as if containing her grief. And I have to remember that Kit found out Caro was unfaithful – because she sure puts on a good show of the grieving widow.

'Is Rowena in London?' Alessia asks.

'She is.'

Alessia looks from Caro to me. 'You should talk to her. And maybe persuade her that . . . um . . . more soon. No. Sooner is better.'

'She's coming over this evening. Maybe you'd like to join us for dinner,' Caro offers.

'We'd like that very much,' Alessia says without hesitation, taking hold of my hand so I can't object.

What?

Chapter Thirty-One

My wife has been quietly campaigning for me to reconcile with the Mothership since Rowena's midnight meltdown. Alessia thinks I haven't noticed, but for her to seize the moment to meet my mother with such enthusiasm is surprising, given how awful she's been to Alessia.

You should hear her side of Kit's story. Sometimes women find themselves in . . . difficult situations.

That she would volunteer to spend any time with the Mothership is either foolhardy or courageous.

Mate. Who are you kidding?

Alessia is beyond courageous.

She steps out of the spare bedroom to where I wait in the hall.

'Is this okay?' she asks, raising her chin, her dark eyes on me. She's dressed in her Jimmy Choos, elegant black trousers, and a cream silk blouse. Her hair is brushed and swept back in a chic fancy braid, and the pearls I bought her in Paris nestle at her ears. Her makeup is discreet, her perfume an expensive whisper of Chanel, and her engagement ring sparkles beneath the light from the chandelier.

She's every inch a peeress.

And for a split second, I'm transported back to a time when a timid young woman with the darkest of dark eyes clutched a broom and hesitantly told me her name in my hallway.

The headscarf.

The blue nylon housecoat.

The scuffed trainers.

A lump threatens to form in my throat.

My wife fucking rocks countessing.

I cough to clear my emotion. 'You're perfect.'

With a flick of her hand, she swats my compliment away, but I know from the lift of her lips that she's pleased. '*You* look perfect. Muchly.'

'This old thing?' I grin and tug on the lapels of my Dior jacket. 'Let's go and get this over with. You happy to walk in those heels?'

'Yes.'

I help her into her jacket and set the alarm, and we leave the flat hand in hand.

Our time away in Cornwall has done the trick. There are no press to hound us when we leave the building, and it's a mild evening; the dusk air is still warmed by a gloriously bright day that heralded the coming spring.

'We should move to the new house,' Alessia says as we approach what will be our home on Cheyne Walk.

'We should.'

'I can organise that.'

'Okay.' I grin. 'I'll leave it to you. We can move at anytime.'

'The most important piece of furniture is the piano.'

'We'll probably need to crane it out of the flat.'

She stops outside the house. 'A crane!'

'There are specialists. I think that's how we got it in there.'

'O Zot!'

'Yeah. O Zot. All manner of shenanigans. I'd buy a new one,

but I'm very fond of that piano.'

'As am I,' she says dreamily. 'It has such a rich tone. You know, when I was cleaning your apartment, it was my escape. I used to play when you were out. It was wonderful.'

I bring her hand to my lips and kiss her knuckles. 'I'm glad you had an escape.'

Reaching up, she cups my face. 'In so many ways,' she whispers, and her fingertips stroke the stubble on my cheek, stirring my desire.

Enough.

'Come. Let's get this over with before I decide to take you home and muss your makeup and ravish you.'

She grins. 'That would be fine. But we should see your mother.'

I ring the doorbell at Trevelyan House, and Blake answers almost immediately.

'Good evening, Lord Trevethick.'

'Blake.'

'Lady Trevethick,' he greets Alessia with a genial smile.

'Is my mother here?'

'Not yet, my lord.'

'Good. Caroline in the drawing room?'

'Yes, indeed, with Lady Maryanne.'

With Alessia's hand in mine, we head upstairs and along the open landing towards the drawing room. Before I open the door, I take a deep breath. I know Caroline will want to finish the conversation we started in my office.

Alessia mentally braces herself as Maxim opens the door. They enter to find Caroline in an animated conversation with Maryanne as they stand beside the bar cart holding drinks. Three hefty candles, each with three wicks, burn brightly on the coffee table, and a fire blazes in the grate, giving the drawing room a welcome, warm glow.

'M.A.' Maxim's voice caresses her nickname, betraying his fondness for his sister as he steps forward and kisses her cheek. 'How was Seattle?'

'It was fabulous, Maxie.' Maryanne hugs him and closes her eyes as she briefly holds him. Of course, they've not seen each other since their mother spilled her secrets in such an obnoxious fashion in Maxim's apartment.

Maryanne turns to Alessia and beams. 'Alessia, darling. How are you? I hear you were quite the hit during lambing at the Hall.' She hugs Alessia, long and hard, surprising her.

'Hi, Maryanne. Who have you been talking to at the Hall?'

'Gin and tonics for you two?' Caroline calls. 'Hello again, Maxim,' she says stiffly and offers her cheek, which he graces with a kiss.

Maryanne pulls back, her smile bright and sincere. 'I have my sources. You look lovely.'

'Thank you, as do you,' Alessia responds. 'And yes, please, Caroline.'

Both women are impeccably dressed, as usual – Maryanne in a navy trouser suit, Caroline in a belted charcoal silk shirt dress – but this time, Alessia feels she is too.

Caroline busies herself with fixing drinks, and Maxim offers his help.

'You look happy, Alessia,' Maryanne observes.

Alessia smiles. 'So do you. You went to see your friend in Seattle?'

Maryanne barks with laughter. 'He's more than a friend. I did. We had a great deal of fun, and I'm hoping you'll all get to meet Ethan at Easter.'

'I look forward to that.'

'Tell me about Cornwall. I miss it so.' Maryanne gestures to one of the couches and Alessia perches on it while Maryanne sits beside her, all eyes and bright smiles as if she's genuinely pleased to see her and interested in what she has to say. Alessia relaxes a little and regales Maryanne with her exploits.

Caroline hands me a gin and tonic. 'We were interrupted earlier. You never answered my question.'

'Caro. I don't think this is the time or the place.'

'Please,' she whispers, her plea so heartfelt it confounds me. Sensing my weakness, she persists. 'I *need* to know.'

'Maxim!' Maryanne exclaims. 'Tell me you didn't teach Alessia to drive in the Defender. What kind of sadist are you?'

I turn my attention to her and my wife, who's eyeing Caroline and me warily.

She knows something's going on.

'I did. And as ever, my wife did not let me down.' I give Alessia a sweet, and what I hope is reassuring, smile.

'The Defender?' Caroline scoffs, eyeing me from beneath her lashes. 'Really? You are a sadist.'

'Alessia can drive that, so she can drive anything.' I shrug and take a sip of my gin and tonic, pleased that both Caro and Maryanne are calling me out, albeit unnecessarily, on behalf of my wife.

Caroline's lips press into a hard line, and she moves to hand Alessia a drink, saving me from our awkward conversation about the contents of Kit's journal.

The door opens, and Rowena strides into the room. Stark in a flowing black jumpsuit, no doubt by Chanel, she halts as soon as she sets her myopic gaze on me.

'Hello, Mother,' I greet her brightly and step forward to kiss her cheek. She remains utterly frozen, blinking into the distance like she's desperately trying to wish herself anywhere but here. Ignoring her reaction, I kiss her anyway, and as I do, it dawns on me that she's terrified.

My mother? Terrified?

I'm horrified. But, what upsets me more, is that I recognise that look because I've seen it before . . . on my wife.

Something twists and turns and breaks inside me.

And before I can stop myself, I gather Rowena's thin frame in my arms, holding her close as my heartbeat races. 'It's okay,' I whisper as she stands unyielding in my embrace. 'It's okay. I've got you.'

Breathing in her expensive perfume, I just hold her, probably for the first time in my life – I don't remember ever clutching her like this, even as a child – and I don't want to let go.

As we stand in the middle of the drawing room, my heart rate settles into a calmer rhythm, and I become aware that the conversation behind us has ceased and that all eyes are on us, though neither of us can see anyone.

Rowena does . . . nothing. Just stands there. In shock, probably, and I think she might have stopped breathing altogether, but finally, she shudders, and with a half-sigh or silent sob, she raises her face to mine and kisses my cheek.

'My boy,' she whispers and cups my face, her eyes brimming with tears.

'Oh, Mama,' I mutter and kiss her forehead.

'I'm sorry,' she says almost inaudibly.

'I know. Me too.'

Alessia watches the mother-and-son exchange that unfolds before her, and tears prick her eyes. And even though she can't hear what they're saying, it's more than she could have hoped for . . .

She glances at her sisters-in-law. Maryanne is stunned into silence as she gapes at her mother and brother while Caroline stares at them, frowning in utter confusion. Finally, she scowls.

'What the hell is going on?' Caroline exclaims.

You haven't told her?' Rowena asks me.

I shake my head. 'No.'

She nods, a trace of, dare I say, admiration teasing her lips. 'You are just like your father. I think you are the best of him.'

'That's the nicest thing you've ever said to me.'

She half smiles, then rolls her eyes. 'All these . . . feelings. This is frightfully bourgeois.'

I chuckle. 'I know.'

She steps out of my embrace, taking the weight of my anger with her.

'Will somebody please explain what's happening here?' Caroline says.

'Caroline, darling. I think I have some explaining to do,' Rowena says. 'But first, Alessia.'

Alessia's heart starts pumping as Maxim's mother faces her and raises her chin.

What is this?

'I owe you an apology.'

Alessia's scalp tingles – she is not expecting this.

'What I said to you the last time we met was unforgivable. Heath had been interfering, as you know. But I brought him to heel. I didn't want him going to the press. Anyway, I hope you can find it within yourself to forgive me all the same.'

Alessia rises from her seat and moves towards Rowena. 'Of course,' she says.

Rowena holds out a hand, and Alessia takes it, surprised at the chilliness of her mother-in-law's fingers. 'You have a generous spirit, my dear. Don't lose that.'

'My husband has lost one parent, and you have lost a child . . . Neither one of you needs to lose another.'

Rowena blinks a couple of times, her surprise obvious. 'Yes. That's exactly right.' She squeezes Alessia's hand. 'You've had quite the effect on my son.'

'And he on me.'

Maxim wraps his arm around Alessia's shoulders and kisses her temple.

'I hear great things from the Hall about you, my dear,' Rowena adds kindly.

'Could someone please tell me what the fuck is going on?' Caroline snaps.

'Let me fix you a drink, Mother,' Maxim says.

'Wine. Please, darling.' She sits in one of the armchairs facing the fireplace, and Alessia takes a seat on the couch.

'Are you ready to hear this?' She's addressing her children.

'Yes,' Maryanne and Maxim say simultaneously.

'Hear what?' Caroline asks, still bewildered.

Maryanne turns to Caroline. 'Daddy was not Kit's father.'

'What?' Caroline pales and looks from Maryanne to Maxim, but he's busy pouring wine.

'It's true,' Rowena says, frowning at Maryanne, probably because she's just blurted out Rowena's secret so rudely.

'I'm just catching Caro up on events,' Maryanne says in her defence.

Caroline's lips part, but it's not from surprise – more like recognition.

'I didn't mean to spring this on you, Caro darling. I thought I might be able to tell you privately. I didn't expect the rest of the family would be here. Apologies for that.'

Caroline nods as if she understands . . . or she's in shock. Alessia's not sure.

I put a glass of chilled Chablis on the coffee table in front of my mother and take my place beside Alessia.

'Do you want to hear this?' Rowena is addressing Caroline.

'I do,' Caro responds quietly.

'Okay. I'll keep this brief,' she says in her clipped mid-Atlantic tone. She folds her hands in her lap and stares into the waning fire. 'When I first came down to London, I was naive and stupid. I wasn't interested in taking the university place that I had secured; I wanted to have fun. My parents had been terribly strict, but they seemed to abandon all parental control once I moved out. I was lucky, I was living in Kensington with friends from school, and one of them had a job as a model. She dragged me along to her agency. They signed me up, and the rest, as they say . . . I became what was known as an It-girl.' She says the final two words with disdain.

'It was the '80s. Greed was good. And I was greedy. I embraced the scene, parties, shoulder pads, big hair . . . and one day, I met a man who I thought was a good sort, a musician with a good head on his shoulders.

'Well, he was unattainable, and I became obsessed. But one night, after a great deal of alcohol . . . well, I attained him. I won't go into the sordid details, and he wanted nothing to do with me after that.

'Around the same time, I was doing a great deal of work with John, your father. As you know, he was such a talented photographer – at the peak of his career. He was the top pick for all the glossies . . . so we did many shoots together. And our relationship was . . . more than professional, shall we say. I knew he doted on me.'

Rowena pauses and takes a sip of her drink.

'By the time I found out I was pregnant, the musician had disappeared. When I finally tracked him down, he told me that the child was my problem. And that was that.

'It was . . .' She frowns. 'It was too late for me to . . . well . . . Your father took pity on me. He was good and kind like that. We married. He embraced Kit as his own. And it became our secret.

'Cameron guessed, of course.' She glances at Alessia. 'That's John's brother, Maxim's uncle. He was furious.' She turns to Maryanne. 'But your father loved me . . .' Her voice fades, and her eyes grow more luminous, and she stares into the fire. The crackle of the flames and the tick of the old Georgian clock accentuate the rapt silence.

She shakes her head as if erasing the memory. 'Anyway, Kit's father moved to the U.S. and became a hugely successful entrepreneur, and very publicly gay, which probably explains his dismissal of me and my child. I never heard from him again, and I pushed him to the back of my mind. Until he died last year. It was on the news, and that's when I learned of his genetic condition.' She pauses and takes a sip of wine. 'That was a dark day.

'It coincided with Kit seeking help for his recurring headaches. So I encouraged him to find medical help without informing him about his biological father. Just after the new year, Kit told me he had an issue, and he wanted to tell you two.' She glances at me and then at Maryanne. 'And that's when I confessed to him.' Her lower lip quivers, but she swallows and maintains her composure. 'He was furious, of course. And afterwards, he went out on his motorbike –' Her voice cracks, and from inside her sleeve, she produces a cotton handkerchief.

'Well, we know the rest,' I mutter gently.

'Our argument was the last exchange he had with anyone,' she whispers. 'He was so angry with me . . .' She sounds almost childlike.

The room falls silent again, the quiet only disrupted by the clock striking the half-hour, startling Alessia. The sound galvanises Caroline, who rises and comes to sit beside my mother, taking the other armchair and reaching for her hand. 'He wasn't just angry with you. We both let him down,' she murmurs, and I think only I can hear them.

Rowena casts her a sympathetic look. 'I know,' she says quietly.

'He told you?'

Rowena nods. 'I am in no position to judge, darling. Kit could be . . . difficult.'

Difficult? Kit?

Caroline glances at me and promptly averts her eyes.

What the hell is that about?

What other secrets has my family been keeping from me?

'It's time to give him a proper goodbye, Mama. For all our sakes,' Maryanne pipes up.

'Yes,' Caro and I say in unison.

'You're right,' Rowena concedes and dabs the corners of each eye with her dainty handkerchief.

'Good,' Caroline says. 'We'll go ahead with his memorial service as planned.'

There's a knock on the door, and Blake enters. 'Dinner is served,' he announces, seemingly oblivious as ever to the bombshells that have been dropped in this room. But I'm pleased to see him. All these secrets are making me hungry.

'You okay?' I ask Alessia.

'Yes. You?'

'I'm fine. Much better, in fact. You were right.' I reach for her hand and we follow Caro out of the drawing room. 'I needed to hear her story.'

'You . . . um . . . reconciled before you heard her story.'

'A wise young woman reminded me that Rowena's my one remaining parent.'

Alessia's cheeks flush a lovely shade of pink, and she smiles at my compliment as we head downstairs into the dining room that has been lavishly set for dinner.

The grand mahogany table is a spectacle, laid with delicate white-and-gold china with matching gold cutlery and candelabras. Alessia gasps when she sees it. But she also spies the Yamaha ebony upright piano at one end of the room.

Caroline insists that Maxim sit at the head of the table. On either side of him, Caroline and his mother take their seats, with Maryanne beside Caro and Alessia sitting beside Rowena. Alessia is pleased not to be fazed by the layout of the impressive cutlery, and once again, she's grateful for the etiquette course.

Dinner is a convivial affair. It's like everyone has taken a deep breath and exhaled. Maxim is charming and inclusive. He talks at length to his mother about his plans for Cornwall: The distillery. Regenerative farming. And Maryanne and Rowena plague him with questions, and Maxim answers them with informed ease.

His mother seems like a different person. Like she's broken out of a cage and is feeling the sun on her face for the first time in a long while. Alessia is fascinated.

Maryanne talks more about Seattle and Ethan and her exploits there. Alessia speaks of her audition at the RCM and her auditions to come.

The only person who doesn't seem at ease is Caroline. She glances continually at Maxim as if trying to convey something.

Finally, during dessert, Caroline rises. Maxim automatically does too.

'Darling,' she says to Maxim. 'I need to speak to you and give you those items that belonged to Kit. Please. Can we do it now?'

Maxim's gaze slides to Alessia's, and his eyes are wide, with what – panic?

Why?

Alessia decides this is something between him and his ex-mistress. Nothing to do with her. So she gives him a reassuring smile and offers a slight shrug of her shoulder.

'Of course,' he says to Caroline and follows her out of the room, leaving Alessia with her in-laws.

'Alessia, darling,' Rowena says. 'I've heard a great deal about your musical talent. I'd love to witness it. Would you do us the honour?'

'Of course. I'd love to.' Alessia rises from the table and heads to the upright. She lifts the lid and tries the middle C. It has a rich, robust tone that echoes in pure gold through the room. 'It's tuned,' she says, almost to herself, and takes a seat on the stool.

With a sinking heart, I follow Caro into the dark shrine that was Kit's study. I've not been in here since he died. It's a little oppressive, with navy blue walls, large paintings, and a shelf crammed with his curios, photographs and trophies. I think I detect a faint hint of his cologne, and a vision from a long-forgotten dream or nightmare pops unbidden into my head. He's leaning over me. *You've got this. This is what you were born to do.* And he's smiling his crooked, sincere smile that's reserved for those rare moments – well, I thought they were rare – when he'd fucked up.

I'm suddenly thrown.

Perhaps they weren't so rare where Caro was concerned.

Hell. I'd always looked up to Kit and envied him.

He got the girl. He got the title. He was gifted at his work in the City.

From the dining room, I hear the piano. The piano on which I learned to play.

Alessia.

She's playing 'Clair de Lune', and I remember the last time she played that, I did too – and what a life-affirming experience that was. It's calming, knowing she's close by, and it pulls me from my gloomy thoughts to the matter in hand. The last thing I want to do is betray his confidences. His journal was exactly that. It contains his private thoughts, and I don't want to intrude on those, and I don't want Caro to do the same.

I decide to grasp the bull by the horns. 'I heard what you said to Rowena.'

Caro leans against Kit's antique desk and crosses her arms. 'You know, then.'

I sigh. 'I know that Kit knew you had been or were playing away.'

Caro's gaze stays steady on mine. 'What did he write in his journal?'

'He was angry with you and Rowena. That's all. That's the last entry. I don't think he meant to kill himself. He was just angry. Angry at the shitty hand he'd been dealt.'

'Are you including me in that shitty hand?'

For fuck's sake.

I slump into one of the tartan armchairs facing his desk.

'I don't know, Caro. It wasn't me who wrote it. And I'm in no position to judge. Neither is Rowena, as she's said. Was it one person? Several people? That was between you and Kit and your conscience.'

She peers down at her fingernails, then turns and slumps into the chair beside me. 'I did love him.'

'I know you did. What did Rowena mean about him being difficult?'

Caroline sits up straight and peers at her fingernails again. She sighs. 'He was aloof and demanding. Controlling. Occasionally violent.'

What the fuck!

'With you?' I ask, sitting up properly as shock reverberates through every cell in my body.

She nods and looks from her nails to the ceiling. 'Not often.'

'That's awful. Why didn't you tell us?'

'I couldn't. I was too ashamed. And to spite him, I sought companionship elsewhere. I didn't think he'd mind. He did.'

'Oh, Caro, I'm so sorry.'

'Maryanne noticed. She told your mother. I think Rowena had words with him.'

She stops . . . and we listen to the faint strains of the piano that Alessia plays with such finesse, but all I can dwell on is that my family has been utterly shite, and I was completely unaware.

'I knew I'd made the wrong choice,' she whispers.

'Caro. Don't. We're not going there. What's done is done.'

'It was so hard for me, watching you aimlessly dipping your wick in anything with a short skirt and a pulse.'

I make a face. 'Like mother like son.'

She has the grace to laugh.

'But not any more,' I add, relieved that she still has her sense of humour.

She rolls her eyes. 'Yes. I've seen it. You light up like fucking Christmas when she walks into a room. It's nauseating.'

'No, Caro. It's love.'

'You were never like that with me.'

'No.'

'She's a lucky girl.'

'I'm a lucky man.'

'Are you going to give me the journal?'

'Do you really want to know what it says?'

'No. I just hope he didn't hate me.'

'I never got the impression he hated you, Caro. You two had a fine time in Havana and Bequia last Christmas.'

'We were making an effort. Don't get me wrong. There were good times too.'

'Dwell on those, darling.'

She nods sadly. 'I try.'

'We should get back.'

'Yes.' She rises, and I rise too. She leans over his desk and grasps a wooden box. 'These are some of his things I thought you might like.' She hands it to me.

'I'll check this out when I'm home.'

'Okay.'

With the box in one hand, I give her a one-armed hug. 'I'm sorry, Caro.'

'I know.'

'And well done for not crying.'

She laughs. 'Let's get back to the family.'

Family. Yes. My family. My fucked-up family.

Sheesh.

Thank God for Alessia.

Chapter Thirty-Two

We walk hand in hand back to the flat, with the wooden box tucked under my arm, as I refused Mrs Blake's offer of a Waitrose bag.

'We survived the evening,' I mutter to Alessia.

'It was . . . extra.'

I laugh. 'It was!'

'Your mother was kind to me over dinner.'

'My mother has seen the error of her ways. She seemed like a different person at dinner after she'd aired all her dirty laundry to the family.'

Alessia makes a strangled noise of disapproval.

'Sorry, was my mother's laundry an analogy too far?'

She shakes her head and laughs. 'What did you discuss with Caroline?'

'Kit.'

Alessia nods. 'I worry because I think Caroline is still in love with you.'

'I'm not so sure. Caroline and I were never a good match. We were good friends. Are good friends. And that's where she belongs. In the friend zone. She knows I only have eyes for you. I've never loved anyone like I love you.'

Alessia grins. 'I've never loved anyone but you.'

'Not even the Arsehole?'

She laughs, horrified. 'Especially not the Arsehole!'

'I wonder if he murdered those men. Your traffickers.'

'I have wondered the same thing.'

'Does he have that kind of . . . reach?'

'I don't know,' Alessia says.

'It's best not to know.'

'Yes. Like you say . . . I don't want to be mixed up in that world.'

'No. But we should do something. To help women like Bleriana. I'm going to discuss it with Maryanne. In fact, you should join our board of trustees for the charitable trust. And we can find a charity that helps women like your friend.'

'I would like that.' She squeezes my hand, and we walk in companionable silence along the Embankment. Alessia is not one of those women that needs to fill all the spaces with chatter.

And I love her all the more for it.

'What's in the box?' she asks eventually.

'Some of Kit's things. I'll have a look tomorrow. Right now, I'm having to re-evaluate my opinion of him.'

'Why? Because he's only your half-brother?'

'No. That's not the reason. He'll always be my brother. It's because of how he treated Caro. And me, actually . . . He wasn't a kind man, and he had a dark side that he kept well hidden. But not so much from Caroline.'

'Oh.'

'Yeah. Caro and I talked about that too. But that's her story to tell, not mine.'

We reach the building, where Alessia unlocks the front door, and we head inside.

'I will miss this place,' I mutter as we wait for the lift.

'So will I. I found happiness here.' Alessia leans up and kisses my cheek.

It's not enough. I snake my free arm around her waist and haul her against me, walking us into the lift when the doors open. 'So did I. I found you.' My lips meet hers, and I lean her into the wall as we kiss all the way to the sixth floor. Tongues and teeth and lips and love. It's all there – in our kiss. We're breathless when the doors open.

'Take me to bed, my lord,' Alessia whispers, her sweet breath mingling with mine.

'You read my mind, my lady.'

Once I've switched off the alarm and placed the wooden box on the console table, my wife takes my hand and leads me into the bedroom. Her dark eyes on mine, she removes my jacket and places it on the sofa.

She stands beside it and removes her jacket, laying it on top of mine – keeping her dark eyes on me the whole time. Her fingers move to her blouse, and she starts to unbutton it as she watches me.

Oh. I can play this game.

I raise my hand, remove one cufflink and then the other, place them on the bedside table, and shake my cuffs loose.

Alessia licks her upper lip, and it might as well be my dick.

Fuck.

She peels off her shirt and lets it fall free onto the sofa, so she's in her lacy cream bra, her dusky nipples straining against the gossamer material. She stalks towards me, tall in her heels, and swats my fingers away where they've frozen at my shirt buttons while I gawk at her.

'Let me,' she says, eyeing me from beneath her lashes.

'Be my guest,' I whisper.

Who is this siren?

She gently tugs my shirt from my trousers and continues to unbutton it.

Bloody slowly.

Each button.

From the top. It's driving me crazy, my dick extending and hardening with each unfastening. When she's reached the bottom, with a flourish, she pulls my shirt apart, leans forward, and plants a soft, wet kiss on my chest.

Fuck this.

I clasp her face between my palms and bring her lips to mine.

Oh, baby.

Her lips taste sweet, and they're eager. Eager to please me. And it's hot as hell. Our tongues caress each other, consuming and stoking our desire as I walk her back towards our bed. She comes up for air, runs her hands across my shoulders, and pushes my shirt off, so it falls to the floor. She runs her fingers down my stomach, through my happy trail, to the waistband of my trousers.

My girl is impatient.

I like.

And as she undoes the button on my waistband, I'm breathless, my dick hot and heavy. Pining. For her.

Alessia wants to taste him.

All. Of. Him.

She lowers the zipper on his pants and slips her hand inside. He hisses with satisfaction when she palms his thick erection.

She steps back. 'Take them off.'

He grins in obvious delight that she's taking the lead. 'As you wish, wife,' he growls and slides off his shoes and socks, then removes his trousers and underwear in one swift move – so he's standing gloriously naked . . . and ready.

Very ready. For her.

'You're wearing too many clothes,' he whispers and drops to his knees, gently unfastening her shoes and slipping them off. He gazes up at her and unzips her pants, removing them with a gentle tug, leaving her in her bra and panties.

Slowly, like a green-eyed panther, he rises to his feet and kisses her once more, his tongue wet and demanding. Alessia breaks free and moves them around so he's standing by the bed.

'You're still wearing too many clothes,' he murmurs.

'Let's see what I can do about that.'

She grins, and planting her hands on the warm skin of his chest, she pushes him onto the bed. He laughs as he falls, startled by her sudden move, but props himself up on his elbows to enjoy the floorshow. She stares down at him and takes a moment to appreciate the beauty that is her naked husband sprawled before her. From his broad shoulders to the smattering of hair at his chest and his tight, taut stomach, to the hair lining his belly that she wants to lick. He looks delectable, his skin still sporting a faded tan. And he's all hers.

His erection swells under her overt admiration.

Slowly, she shimmies out of her lace panties. Then, without taking her gaze off his glittering green eyes, she carefully removes her bra, one strap at a time.

'Tease,' he mouths, his eyes growing darker with desire.

Alessia relishes the effect she has on him.

She drops her bra to the floor and runs her hands over her breasts, still pinning him with her gaze. His mouth drops open, slack with needy lust, and she cannot resist a sensual smile of triumph. He's panting when she crawls onto the bed, over and above his body. She grabs his wrists, holds them to the bed, beside his head, and peers down at him so they are almost nose to nose. 'You are mine. I want you.'

'Back at you, baby,' Maxim breathes, and as she bends to taste his lips, she releases him.

His hands skim down her back, to her waist and then her backside, where he grabs and kneads her flesh with strong hands while they consume each other.

'Lady Trevethick, you have a fantastic arse,' he whispers, and she grins, nipping his chin before trailing kisses down his sternum, his stomach, over his navel and belly. His breathing shallows, and he tenses with anticipation when she sheaths her hand around his rigid erection.

With her eyes on his, she runs her tongue around him before drawing him into her mouth.

He closes his eyes and falls back on the bed, his breath hissing between his teeth in sheer pleasure. Gently, he places a hand on her head as she takes him. Up. Down. Again. Her lips sheath her teeth while he eases himself further into her mouth with a groan.

She's relentless.

Taking him. Higher.

'Enough,' he breathes. 'I want to come inside you.' He's hoarse. With want.

Alessia moves to straddle him, guiding him inside her in one swift move.

'Ah!' she cries out, relishing the fullness of his invasion.

And she starts to move up and down, cradling her husband and picking up her rhythm, in perfect counterpoint to Maxim as he meets her rise and fall. She leans forward, resting her hands on his chest. His eyes blaze a fiery forest green, the pupils large and dark. Full of love. Full of lust. Full of need.

'I love you.' Alessia's lips hover over his.

He jerks his hips up, craving more. 'I want you.' And he moves suddenly, surprising her and twisting them both, still linked, so he's on top of her – his weight pressing her into the mattress as he drives into her.

He folds his arms around her head, cocooning her as he moves with an intensity and passion that leaves Alessia breathless and near . . . near . . .

She cries out as she comes, and Maxim buries his head in the crook of her neck and follows, calling her name as he climaxes.

Alessia returns to earth, surprised at the speed and intensity of her orgasm. She holds him tight against her, loving that they are still intimately connected. Her heart overflows with emotion as she nuzzles his hair.

She cannot believe that this is her life now, as she lies with the man she loves.

Her loving husband.

Her reformed rake.

Will it always be like this?

This intense.

This passionate.

She hopes so . . . forever and ever. Feeling beyond replete, she takes Maxim's left hand and threads her fingers with his and raises his hand to her lips.

'This is the sexy thing . . . sexiest thing,' she whispers, correcting herself.

'What? My hand?' Maxim grins, his eyes reflecting her love.

'No.' She kisses the shining platinum ring. 'This means you're mine.'

'Always,' he murmurs against the corner of her mouth. He tightens his arms around her and they lie together, entwined, skin against skin. 'I just want to hold you. Until the end of time.'

'Will that be long enough?' Alessia whispers and kisses his chest.

'Never . . .'

When Alessia wakes, she's alone. It's Saturday morning, and she's had a busy week. Lying back on the soft silk, she revels in the quiet but listens to see where Maxim might be – but the apartment is silent. She calls out his name, and there's no reply. Perhaps he's gone for a run or maybe to fence with Joe.

She smiles, remembering their evening. They'd been out with Tom, Henry, Caroline, and Joe to celebrate her acceptance into the Royal College of Music. Their evening had started at a new restaurant in Mayfair, where Maxim and Caroline knew the chef – the Mediterranean food was terrific – and they'd ended the night in the small hours at Maxim's club. It had been a relaxing, cheerful evening – a perfect way for Alessia and Maxim to decompress after the stress of Rowena's revelations earlier in the week and Alessia's taxing auditions.

Today she'll start packing up the apartment, as they hope to move within a week. She'll need to go shopping for food because her great-uncle and Bleriana are joining them for lunch tomorrow, and she wants to cook her favourite Albanian dish for them. She checks the time, and it's after ten. It's not like her to sleep in. She climbs out of bed and heads into the wet room.

Fifteen minutes later, dressed in tight jeans and a white T-shirt, she enters the hallway and notices the red light.

Oh.

Maxim is in his dark room. She's never known him to use it. The only time she's been in there was the first time he kissed her. Walking up to the door, she presses her ear to it and hears him humming tunelessly to himself and moving around inside. Tentatively she knocks on the door.

'Don't come in!' he shouts.

She smiles. She had no intention of going in. 'Coffee?' she calls.

'Please. I should be finished in about five minutes.'

'Have you had breakfast?'

'No.'

She grins and heads into the kitchen, deciding that avocado on toast will be on the menu, one of Maxim's favorites. Maybe with some smoked salmon.

I have been waiting all week to develop my photographs from our time in Cornwall, and I'm thrilled with the results. I pin the last of the pictures to dry and admire my work.

It's my wife. Smiling. Beautiful. Tresyllian House is a stunning backdrop behind her. Next, Jensen and Healey gambolling up the lane, Alessia in the background, the evening light at magic hour. And the photograph is just that . . . magic. Alessia on the beach, staring out to sea.

Man, she's beautiful.

Then one of the deer on the horizon – this might be print-worthy, and it can be added to the collection of my prints we sell in the gallery in Trevethick.

But my favourite is the photograph I took in the lambing shed. Alessia's hair is escaping her braid, tendrils framing her beautiful face, and her eyes are shining with pure excitement – but it's her smile of joy, her smile at *me* that would light up the world if we let it, that I love. I grin back like an idiot at her infectious, intoxicating smile, pleased with my handiwork. I want this framed, and on every desk I own.

My stomach rumbles, and I switch off the red light and step out into the hallway.

I lean against the doorjamb and watch Alessia move gracefully through the kitchen as she makes breakfast.

Avocado on toast.

I approve.

Finally, she looks up and rewards me with that same smile that I'm blessed to have captured on film.

'Good morning, husband.'

'Good morning, wife.'

Alessia abandons the avocado mix she's spreading on toast, circles her arms around my waist, and offers me a brief kiss.

I run my nose along hers as I hold her. 'I'm feeling very virtuous.' I kiss her. 'I've been for a run.' I kiss her. 'I've showered.' I kiss her again. 'And developed the film I had in my camera when we were in Cornwall. I can't wait to show you the prints. I feel I deserve my breakfast.' I kiss the corner of her lips.

'You do and so much more,' she whispers, her arms sliding over my chest as she peeks up at me from beneath her lashes with a coy, provocative look.

Oh . . . like that, is it?

My body responds, and I fold her more tightly in my embrace and continue to kiss her, tugging her lips gently with my teeth. Her hands are in my hair, pulling me closer as she slides her tongue into my mouth, challenging me with hers. Closing my eyes, I groan and deepen the kiss, tasting her sweet, sweet mouth, my tongue meeting her challenge. I move one hand to her nape, cradling her head, the other cupping a cheek of her well-formed, denim-clad arse. Her hands are in my hair, pulling me closer, and I turn and press her against the wall, pushing my hips to hers to find some friction for my hardening dick.

Fuck breakfast.

'God, what you do to me, my lady,' I breathe against her jaw.

'What you do to me, my lord.'

'Shall we skip—'

The doorbell rings twice, and I place my forehead against hers. 'Fuck.'

'Not right now, it would seem.' Alessia giggles and wriggles out of my embrace to answer the intercom phone in the kitchen.

'Hello?'

'Alessia! Good morning. Let me in!'

'It's Caroline,' Alessia says.

Damned cockblocker.

'Hi. Okay!' Alessia answers with an apologetic smile at me.

I grin. 'Rain check.' I kiss her nose.

She glances at the front of my jeans. I laugh. 'Yeah. Yeah. I'll deal with this.'

Giggling, she leaves me to get a handle on myself and my erection while she opens the front door to welcome Caroline.

Good morning, Alessia,' Caroline says, giving her a quick hug and a kiss on each cheek in greeting. 'I hope I'm not interrupting anything.'

'No. Come in. We're about to have breakfast. Are you hungry?'

Caroline is wearing jeans, brown leather boots, and her tweed jacket over a cream cashmere sweater. She looks as elegant as ever, but Alessia is no longer intimidated by her, even though she's barefoot and in her softest, most worn jeans.

'Sounds great.' Caroline smiles a genuine smile. Alessia reflects that Caroline has been much friendlier and more relaxed since dinner earlier in the week, and she wonders if what she and Maxim talked about after dinner is the reason.

'We are having avocado on toast.'

'Yum. Hello, Maxim,' Caroline says as they join Maxim in the kitchen.

'Caro.' He kisses her upturned cheek. 'Coffee?'

'Please.'

'Sit,' Alessia says, directing her to the kitchen table she's already laid for two.

'You two are so domestic. Are you getting any staff?'

Maxim glances at Alessia, and before she can say anything, 'When we move, yes,' he says.

Alessia frowns. She's not sure they need staff in London, but she doesn't contradict him, and she retrieves a place setting and arranges it on the table, followed by coffee cups and saucers.

'When do you move?' Caroline asks.

'End of this week.'

'We are starting to pack today,' Alessia says, principally to remind Maxim that he needs to think about what he wants to take. She pops another slice of sourdough bread into the toaster and continues to spread the avocado-and-smoked-salmon mix onto the toast that's done.

Caroline's forehead creases with doubt. 'Isn't your removal company doing that?'

'Yes. But personal items. And we may have an opportunity to . . . what is the word. Declutter.'

Caroline laughs while Maxim eyes Alessia with alarm.

'Good luck with that!' Caroline says as Maxim joins her at the table with a cafetiere full of strong coffee. 'That smells good.'

Alessia places breakfast in front of Caroline and Maxim and waits for the toaster to pop up with her slice of toast.

'Hmm . . . this looks great, Alessia. Thank you. And I have some good news for you two.'

'Oh? What?' Maxim asks.

'I spoke to my father about Alessia and her visa.'

Alessia's scalp prickles and Maxim's head jerks up. 'Now that Alessia's been accepted into RCM, she can get a student visa . . . and we can go from there,' he says.

'But Daddy will expedite indefinite leave. He just needs the forms.'

'What?' Alessia breathes.

'He's a senior mandarin at the Home Office. This is within his gift. I had dinner with him and the Stepsow on Thursday – oh, sorry, my stepmother – and told him that you needed to jump through all these ridiculous hoops. For God's sake – you're married to a peer of the realm. He agreed with me. That doesn't happen often. Anyway, he called me this morning, with a plan.'

'Caro, that's . . .' Words fail me. On the one hand, it would be great to stop worrying about Alessia's legal status in the UK. On the other hand, this feels like . . . cheating.

'Darling, title has its privileges.' Caroline correctly interprets my frown. 'Wealth too. Of course,' she adds.

'It does,' I mutter, and turn to my wife, who's spreading avocado and salmon on her toast.

'That's great. Thank you, Caroline,' Alessia says with enthusiasm, and it's obvious she has no reservations at all.

'I'll talk to our immigration lawyer about it.' *And also my wife.* I'm not sure I want to cheat our way to citizenship for Alessia. After all, deep down, that's how I feel about our wedding. We didn't follow the rules, which led to awkward press questions, and I don't want to end up in the press because we circumvented the visa system. I'd like to do this properly, but perhaps keep Caro's father in reserve.

'This is really tasty, Alessia,' Caroline says. 'No wonder you don't go out as much as you used to!'

Alessia joins them at the table. 'Lime juice and ricotta. My secret ingredients.'

The beauty of launching my wife at Dimitri Egonov's party is that we are plagued with invitations for social engagements. I mean, I used to get my fair share of invites, but now we're inundated. Everyone wants to meet my wife.

I put the correspondence aside. I'll go through it with Alessia when she returns from her shopping expedition. Tobias Strickland, young Bleriana, and now Caroline are joining us tomorrow for Sunday lunch, and she's out somewhere on the hunt for ingredients – to say she's excited about this is an understatement.

I have offered to take us out, but she wants to cook.

And far be it for me to get between an Albanian woman and her cooking.

I sit back in my chair and eye the wooden box Caroline gave me at the beginning of the week, standing unopened on my desk. I don't know what's stopping me.

Dude. Open the box.

Reaching for it, I set it in front of me and lift the hinged lid. Neatly coiled on the top of a scrap of blue velvet is Kit's old Iron Maiden belt. I laugh out loud – Caroline knows I loathed Kit's taste in music.

Petrol Head.

Metal Head.

He loved, loved, loved his heavy metal bands.

I pick up the weighty belt. The leather has seen better days. The buckle, on the other hand, is as fearsome as the day Kit acquired it. Made of pewter, it depicts a beast's head, with one red jewelled eye over a skull and crossbones, with *1980* and *1990* carved on small plaques on either side. Between the dates, EDDIE is engraved on a scroll. Kit was fourteen when he bought this, and it was his pride and joy. I remember at ten years old being so envious . . . Odd to think I spent so much of my early life envying my big brother.

I put it to one side, reach into the wooden box, and pull out another box – this one clad in green leather. It looks vaguely familiar . . . The crown on the front should be a clue, but I can't place it. Opening it up, I find my father's Rolex.

It's a gut punch.

Daddy.

I ease it out of the box. It's chunky. A manly man's watch made from stainless steel.

My dad's watch.

ROLEX OYSTER COSMOGRAPH is written on the face above three dials.

The word DAYTONA appears in red above the third dial.

Fuck. I tear up examining it. I remember as a child – I used to fiddle with the crown and the two pushers while he wore it. I was fascinated by it and loved that he let me mess with it. He seemed to enjoy it. *Time is precious, my boy*, he used to say, and he was right.

I flip it over, and there's an inscription on the back.

Thank you.
For everything.
Always your Row.

Whoa. I had no idea this was a present from my mother. He wore it every single day, I imagine, as a testament to her. I shake my head, knowing what I know now.

She was lucky.

He loved her very much.

He gave her respectability and a title, and her son an earldom.

And on the back of this watch, there's only gratitude. She admitted she was obsessed with another man. A man who didn't want her or her child.

Maybe this was why I didn't want to open the wooden box. I knew there would be . . . *feelings.* I have to reconcile myself with the fact that my mother married for convenience, not love, and that my father didn't have the love of a good woman.

Like I do . . .

But he had her respect. So there's that. Maybe that was enough for him. I have to take comfort in that.

I place the Rolex back in its case and pull out another dark green velvet box.

Inside, nestled on velvet, are a pair of silver cufflinks with the Trevethick coat of arms. These are very Kit, and I'm trying to remember if he had them made or if they were a gift. If they are a gift, they'll be from Caroline. I'm heartened that she's decided I should have them, and what's more, it's appropriate.

Finally, at the bottom of the wooden box, I find a silver-framed photograph of Kit, Maryanne and me as children. Kit stands proudly between us, taller than us because he's about twelve and Maryanne and I are seven and eight, respectively. My father took the photograph among the dunes on Trevethick beach in Cornwall. Kit's arms are draped possessively over us, and he's beaming with pride. He was always king of the castle. His blond curls shimmer in the Cornish sunlight that burnishes our tawny hair, and we stand in dark contrast to our golden elder brother. I remember our father encouraging us to smile, and he must have said something funny, because Maryanne and I are both laughing – even though we'd probably just been playing a game that Kit devised, where we were at his capricious mercy.

The light is wonderful. Hold still, progeny.

That was Dad's collective noun for the three of us.

And his love is clear to see in the frame.

I don't remember seeing this photograph anywhere in Kit's house, but it must have meant something to him if he had it framed. And that gives me a warm but melancholy feeling of homesickness.

Kit. Kit. Kit.

I'm so sorry.

I trace my finger over his image . . .

You bastard. You let your anger get the better of you.

A lump forms in my throat.

Even though you were sometimes an arsehole, I loved you and I miss you.

I hear the rattle of a key in the front door, and I abandon the box to help my wife.

Alessia shuts the door behind her using her foot, as she's laden with shopping bags – only to put them down as Maxim comes barrelling towards her.

'Hey,' she says as he wraps his arms around her and holds her tight. 'What's wrong?' she asks, folding him in her arms.

'Nothing. I missed you. That's all.' He holds her for several seconds, his nose buried in her hair.

'I am back. In one piece.'

'I know. I know. I'm glad you're back.'

I release her and remember that I have a duty to perform. 'I need to show you something.'

'Okay. Can I put the shopping away first?'

I laugh. 'Of course. Let me help you.'

'So this is the safe, which you know. But this is the number.' I hand her a piece of paper. 'Memorise that and eat it afterwards.' I raise my brows.

She laughs. 'Tasty.'

We're in my walk-in wardrobe, and since I found out that Kit didn't give Caro access to any of the safes, I thought I'd need to make sure my wife isn't ever put in that position. I twist the dial to the numbers: 11.14.2.63. Then I turn the handle and open it. Alessia peers inside, fascinated.

'See?'

'Yes. What's in there?'

Kit's journal. 'Important documents. My birth certificate. Passport. You should give me yours. The jewellery you wore when we went to Egonov's, which I should take back to the bank.'

'The bank?'

'Yes. The good stuff is stored there. We have a vault, and we should go and look. There might be something you like.'

'Why are you showing me this?'

'If something happens to me.'

Alessia eyes widen in alarm. 'What's going to happen to you?'

I chuckle. 'Nothing, I hope. I just think it's important for you to know where everything is. There's also one at Angwin and the Hall. And when we're there, I'll show you those. You need to know what's in them and where they are.'

'Okay.'

'Good.' I grin, feeling . . . relieved.

'Now that we're in here. Are there any clothes in here that you'd like to donate to charity?'

'I like my clothes.'

'Maxim, nobody needs this many clothes. I'll fetch a black plastic bag.'

I sigh, examining my overstuffed wardrobe. Maybe Alessia has a point, but this wasn't how I wanted to spend the afternoon.

'There, I've filled one bag.' I step out of my wardrobe, feeling inordinately pleased with myself.

Alessia looks up. She's on the floor beside my bedside drawers, with a cardboard box and a black plastic sack. She holds up a pair of handcuffs and swings them around her finger. 'Yours?'

'Ah.'

'Ah,' she repeats and grins as I feel a fucking flush creep up my cheeks.

Why am I embarrassed?

I laugh, because I can't think what else to do, and sidle up to her.

'I thought you would have been through that drawer when you were cleaning.'

'No. But I've seen these before. Once. And this ribbon was tied to the headboard.' She holds up the ribbon.

Damn. That was to restrain Leticia and her talons.

'You know all my dirty secrets.'

Alessia nimbly gets to her feet. 'Do I?'

'Maybe not all of them.' I step closer and stroke her cheek. 'But we could make our own.'

'Dirty secrets?' Her eyes light up and she skates her fingers down my chest to the waistband of my jeans. 'How about the rain check?' She glances up at me through her lashes with her most come-hither look.

Fuck, yes.

Epilogue

February. The following year.
Cheyne Walk

'How is this?' Alessia steps out of her dressing room and slides her hands down the black satin of the long, body-skimming skirt she's wearing. She gazes intently at me – and I know she's looking for my approval.

She doesn't need my approval.

She's a fucking goddess.

'Wow.'

'You like?'

The fitted bustier is leather and strappy, so I can see skin beneath the bodice before it meets the skirt. I motion with my finger that she do a twirl, and she laughs and obliges. The back is held together by three separate straps that are unfastened. 'Would you like me to strap you into this stunning dress?'

Alessia giggles, and I suspect it's with nerves. 'Please.'

'You look sensational.' I kiss the soft, fragrant skin of her naked shoulder. 'Has your father seen this dress?'

'No. Is it too much?'

'No. It's perfect. You look like you could conquer the world in this.'

'That's what I thought. It's Alaïa.'

'It suits you.'

'Caroline thought so. She's a djinn to shop with.'

Deftly I strap my wife into her dress, and when she turns to face me, I notice she's wearing her gold cross, and Trevethick diamonds at her ears.

'I'm a very lucky man, Lady Trevethick. Now, let's go and shock your parents.'

Alessia is thrilled that her parents are visiting for this special occasion. They're staying with us in Cheyne Walk, and they love it. Especially Alessia's mother, who has blossomed in Chelsea. Her English has improved, and she's beyond grateful to see her mother's brother, Toby, again.

We've settled into our new home. After a great deal of negotiation between Alessia and me, we have a cook-cum-housekeeper who likes to be called Cook, and whose husband lives with us and works part-time as a driver and a handyman.

And then there's Bleriana, who is staying with us for another two months. Alessia is delighted to have her with us.

Me, I'm not so sure.

But, while she's studying English, she's earning her keep by helping Cook around the house.

Like Alessia used to do.

I just haven't told Oliver because I know he'd want her on the payroll.

And Bleriana prefers cash.

She's still nervous around me, and that makes *me* nervous, but she's making progress with her therapy, so we're hopeful that Bleriana will, one day, be less anxious. Alessia has been instrumental in restoring Bleriana's relationship with her parents. She hopes to return to Albania and teach, but in the interim she's been helpful in setting up our charitable trust for women who have escaped trafficking. Personally, I think her skills will lend themselves to this line of work once her English improves.

Jak and Shpresa will leave tomorrow, and Alessia and I will be heading down to Cornwall. Our wedding anniversary is on Sunday, and I've booked the Hideout for the weekend where we can celebrate, just the two of us.

It's a surprise for my wife and I can't wait.

I have plans.

I follow her down the stairs to the drawing room on the first floor.

'My darling, you look beautiful,' Shpresa says when Alessia enters the drawing room. She hugs her daughter. 'I am so happy for you,' she whispers against Alessia's ear, speaking in Albanian.

'Thank you, Mama. You look lovely too.' Alessia kisses her cheek.

Alessia's father frowns and looks at Maxim. 'You think this is acceptable?' He waves in Alessia's direction, and it's obvious he disapproves of her dress.

'She looks stunning,' Maxim says, even though he's not understood a word her father has said. Maxim's eyes heat as he stares at her, and his lips lift, either amused by her father or with a wicked, salacious thought.

Alessia grins at him.

'Like I keep saying, my daughter is your problem,' Jak mutters, and Alessia grasps her father's hand. He gives her a reluctant smile, and Alessia notices the ill-concealed pride reflected in his eyes. 'Your husband doesn't seem to mind you are half-dressed.' He shrugs and gives her a quick peck on her cheek.

'Baba, it's not up to my husband what I wear. It's up to me.'

Maxim intervenes. 'Are you ready? We have to go. The cars should be here.'

The Trevelyan family have had a grand tier box on level one of the Albert Hall since it was built, or so I'm told. I usher in our guests, and I'm delighted to find Tom and Henry, glowing with newlywed happiness, in situ with Caroline, Joe, and Alessia's friend Tabitha. I introduce them all to Alessia's parents, and I'm pleased Bleriana is with us, as she can help translate for Jak.

Her English is definitely improving.

I offer champagne to everyone.

'I say, Trevethick, I bet you never envisaged this when you first met Alessia?' Tom says as we look down at the stage where the orchestra has started to assemble.

I laugh. 'No. I did not. Who would have thought?'

'We're thrilled for her,' Henry adds.

'Is she wearing the Alaïa?' Caroline interjects.

'She is. She looks sensational.'

Caroline's smile is smug. 'It was perfect. I'm so glad. She's going to rock this concert.'

'Mate,' says Joe.

'Yep. Who knew?' I swallow down my nerves. My wife is performing at the Royal Albert Hall.

From our box I survey the great hall as it fills with patrons and wonder if I ever foresaw this moment. I'm transported back to that day when I first heard her play.

Bach.

And I tiptoed up my hallway to peer around the drawing room door and spy on her.

Maybe I did foresee this. I knew then that her playing was concert standard, and since enrolling at the Royal College of Music, Alessia's skill and technique has grown exponentially.

She's a classical rock star.

She's also a draw for the press. Her rags-to-riches story is irresistible to tabloid editors – we're occasionally hounded by paparazzi on a slow news day. I suspect that's one reason why the seats below us are filling up and the Hall is almost sold out.

I shake my head in awe and wonder, and there's a knock on the box door. Joe opens it and welcomes my mother, who enters with Maryanne and Tobias.

'Hello, darling,' she says, and offers me her cheek.

'Mother.' I give her and Maryanne a quick peck, then shake Toby's hand, delighted to see him again. His palms are clammy, and I suspect he's nervous for his great-niece too.

Alessia is performing as part of the RCM's special programme.

There are three other performers, but Alessia will be last – she's the highlight of the entire evening.

I can't wait.

But that's not the only reason I'm so nervous. I don't want her to be stressed in any way . . . but she's probably stressed right now. This morning – she told me she's pregnant. And I'm giddy with joy, but we have to keep it quiet for a few more weeks.

I'm going to be a father.

Me. A dad.

I'm fucking thrilled.

I take a gulp of champagne and blow out a breath, and in the distance, a bell rings.

The performance is about to begin.

AEDH WISHES FOR THE CLOTHS OF HEAVEN

Had I the heavens' embroidered cloths,
Enwrought with golden and silver light,
The blue and the dim and the dark cloths
Of night and light and the half-light,
I would spread the cloths under your feet:
But I, being poor, have only my dreams;
I have spread my dreams under your feet;
Tread softly because you tread on my dreams.

William Butler Yeats, *The Wind Among the Reeds*
1865–1939

MUSIC OF *THE MISSUS*

CHAPTER FOUR
'Delicious' – Dafina Rexhepi

CHAPTER SIX
Piano Sonata No. 14, in C-Sharp Minor, Op. 27 No. 2, Movement Three (*Moonlight Sonata*) – Ludwig van Beethoven

CHAPTER SEVEN
'Vallja E Kukesit' – StrinGirls, Jeris
'Vallja E Rugoves Shota' – Valle
'Vallja E Kuksit' – Ilir Xhambazi

CHAPTER EIGHT
'Magnolia' – JJ Cale

CHAPTER NINE
'Only' – RY X

CHAPTER TEN

Violin Partita No. 3 in E Major, BWV 1006: I. Preludio – Johann Sebastian Bach (Arrangement for Piano by Sergei Rachmaninoff)

CHAPTER ELEVEN

'Lo-Fi House Is Dead' – Broosnica

'Only Love' – Ben Howard

CHAPTER TWELVE

'Claire de Lune' – Claude Debussy

CHAPTER SEVENTEEN

Fugue No. 15 in G Major, BWV 884 – Johann Sebastian Bach

CHAPTER EIGHTEEN

'Runaway (feat. Candace Sosa)' – Armin van Buuren

Prelude No. 2 in C minor, BWV 847 – Johann Sebastian Bach

CHAPTER TWENTY-FIVE

'Cornfield Chase (from *Interstellar*)' – Hans Zimmer

CHAPTER TWENTY-SEVEN

'North Country' (John Peel Session 1974) – Roy Harper

CHAPTER THIRTY

'Valle e Vogël' – Feim Ibrahimi

'Années de Pèlerinage, 3ème année, S. 163 IV, 'Les jeux d'eaux à la Villa d'Este' – Franz Liszt

Piano Sonata No. 14, in C-Sharp Minor, Op. 27 No. 2, Movement Three (*Moonlight Sonata*) – Ludwig van Beethoven

CHAPTER THIRTY-ONE

'Claire de Lune' – Claude Debussy

ACKNOWLEDGEMENTS

Writing *The Missus* would have been a lot more challenging without the help, advice and support of the following lovely people, to whom I owe a huge debt of thanks:

My Albanian publisher, Manushaqe Bako of Dritan Editions, for her invaluable advice on Albanian wedding etiquette, and of course all her Albanian translations.

Kathleen Blandino for her web-mistress skills and for being a most trusted beta reader.

Ben Leonard, Chelsea Miller, Fergal Leonard and Lee Woodford for explaining the tortuous labyrinth of visa applications for those who wish to live with their loved ones in the UK.

James Leonard for all the posh-boy terminology – okay yah?

Vicky Edwards for her advice on foreign marriages and UK law.

Chris Brewin for his hard-won insights into British police procedure.

My beloved 'Major' for his expertise in music and DJ equipment.

My agent, Valerie Hoskins, for her constant emotional and moral support, her bad jokes, and her priceless insights on the challenges of farming in today's UK.

Kristie Taylor Beighley from Silk City, distillers of distinction, for her expert advice on creating fine spirits.

And my dear friend Ros Goode for all the tips about handling a Land Rover Defender!

Huge thanks to my talented editor Christa Désir, for buffing my grammar with great humour and finesse, and for the handholding.

To all my wonderful, industrious colleagues at Bloom Books and Sourcebooks – thank you for your hard work, professionalism, and for having my back.

Thank you to my author friends for your broad shoulders, the inspiration, and fun times – you know who you are . . . There are far too many of you to name, and I might miss someone off this extensive list and I'd be devastated if I did!

Thanks to the Ladies in the Bunker for your support, laughs and hilarious memes.

Thanks to all the authors from the Author Conference on Clubhouse, from whom I've learned so much.

Massive thanks to the ladies of the *I Do Crew* – your support means everything to me.

And thank you to all those social media goddesses for their continued friendship, including Vanessa, Zoya, Emma, Philippa, Gitte, Nic et al.

Thank you to my PA, Julie McQueen, for wrangling me and the Ladies in the Bunker.

As ever, thanks and much love to my husband, Niall Leonard, for tutting over my grammar, for listening (sometimes!), and for the constant supply of tea.

And to my boys, Major and Minor – thanks for being you! You both shine so brightly and bring me such joy. Love you, unconditionally, always.

And finally – to all my readers.
Thank you doesn't seem enough . . .
but thank you for reading.
Thank you for everything.

ABOUT THE AUTHOR

E L James is an incurable romantic and a self-confessed fangirl. After twenty-five years of working in television, she decided to pursue a childhood dream and write stories that readers could take to their hearts. The result was the controversial and sensuous romance *Fifty Shades of Grey* and its two sequels, *Fifty Shades Darker* and *Fifty Shades Freed.* In 2015, she published the No. 1 bestseller *Grey*, the story of *Fifty Shades of Grey* from the perspective of Christian Grey, and in 2017, the chart-topping *Darker*, the second part of the Fifty Shades story from Christian's point of view. She followed with the No. 1 *Sunday Times* and *New York Times* bestseller *The Mister* in 2019. In 2021, she released the No. 1 *Sunday Times* and *New York Times* bestseller *Freed*, the third novel in the As Told by Christian trilogy. Her books have been published in fifty languages and have sold more than 165 million copies worldwide.

E L James has been recognised as one of *Time* magazine's Most Influential People in the World and *Publishers Weekly*'s Person of the Year. *Fifty Shades of Grey* stayed on the *New York Times* bestseller list for 133 consecutive weeks. *Fifty Shades Freed* won the Goodreads Choice Award (2012), and *Fifty Shades of Grey* was selected as one of the 100 Great Reads, as voted by readers, in PBS's The Great American Read (2018). *Darker* was longlisted for the 2019 International DUBLIN Literary Award.

She was a producer on each of the three Fifty Shades movies, which made more than a billion dollars at the box office. The third instalment, *Fifty Shades Freed*, won the People's Choice Award for Drama in 2018.

E L James is blessed with two wonderful sons and lives with her husband, the novelist and screenwriter Niall Leonard, and their beloved dogs in the leafy suburbs of West London.

THE MISTER

ALSO BY E L JAMES

Fifty Shades of Grey
Fifty Shades Darker
Fifty Shades Freed
Grey
Darker

THE MISTER

E L James

arrow books

7 9 10 8 6

Arrow Books
20 Vauxhall Bridge Road
London SW1V 2SA

Arrow Books is part of the Penguin Random House group of companies whose addresses can be found at global.penguinrandomhouse.com.

Penguin Random House UK

First published in Great Britain by Arrow Books in 2019.
Simultaneously published in the United States by Vintage Books, a division of Penguin Random House LLC.

www.penguin.co.uk

A CIP catalogue record for this book is available from the British Library.

Typeset in 11/14pt Electra LH by Jouve (UK), Milton Keynes
Printed and bound in Great Britain by Clays Ltd, Elcograf S.p.A.

FSC MIX Paper | Supporting responsible forestry FSC® C018179 www.fsc.org

Penguin Random House is committed to a sustainable future for our business, our readers and our planet. This book is made from Forest Stewardship Council® certified paper.

For Tia Elba.
Thank you for your wisdom, strength,
good humour and sanity, but most of all for your love.

THE MISTER

daily
/ˈdeɪli/
noun
informal

1. a newspaper published every day except Sunday
   'The trial was reported in all the popular *dailies.*'
2. (BRITISH *dated*) a woman who is employed to clean someone else's house on a regular basis
   'My *daily* comes every day . . .'

Prologue

No. No. No. Not the black. Not the choking dark. Not the plastic bag. Panic overwhelms her, forcing the air from her lungs. *I can't breathe. I can't breathe.* The metallic taste of fear rises in her throat. *I need to do this. It's the only way. Be still. Be calm. Breathe slow. Breathe shallow. Just like he said. This will be over soon. It will be over, and then I will be free. Free. Free.*

Go. Now. Run. Run. Run. Go. She runs hard and fast but doesn't look back. Fear drives her forward as she dodges a few late-night shoppers in her quest to flee. Luck is with her: the automatic doors are open. She flies under the gaudy Christmas decorations and through the entrance into the parking lot. On and on she runs. Between the parked cars and into the woods. She runs for her life, down a small dirt path, through brambles, small branches slapping her face. She runs until her lungs are bursting. *Go. Go. Go. Don't stop.*

Cold. Cold. Too cold. Fatigue fogs her brain. Fatigue and the cold. The wind howls through the trees, through her clothes, and into her bones. She huddles beneath a bush and gathers the fallen leaves to build a nest with numb hands. *Sleep.* She needs sleep. She lies down on the cold, hard ground, too tired to be afraid and too tired to weep. *The others. Did they get away?* She closes her eyes. *Did they escape? Let them be free. Let them be warm . . . How did it come to this?*

She wakes. She's lying between trash cans, wrapped in newspapers and cardboard. She's shivering. She's so cold. But she needs to move on. She has an address. She thanks her nana's God for the address. With shaking fingers she unfurls the paper. This is where she needs to go. Now. Now. *Now.*

One foot in front of the other. Walk. It's all she can do. Walk. Walk. *Walk.* Sleep in a doorway. Wake and walk on. Walk. She drinks water from the sink at the McDonald's. The food smells enticing.

She's cold. Hunger claws at her stomach. And she walks and walks, following the map. A stolen map. Stolen from a store. A store with twinkling lights and festive music. She holds the scrap of paper with what little strength she has left. It's worn and torn from so many days hidden in her boot. *Tired.* So tired. *Dirty.* So dirty and cold and frightened. This place is her only hope. She raises her trembling hand and presses the doorbell.

Magda is expecting her. Her mother wrote and told her. She welcomes her with open arms. And then backs away quickly. *Jesus, child. What's happened to you? I was expecting you last week!*

Chapter One

Mindless sex – there's a lot to be said for it. No commitments, no expectations, and no disappointments; I just have to remember their names. Who was it last time? Jojo? Jeanne? Jody? Whatever. She was some nameless fuck who moaned a great deal both in and out of bed. I lie staring at the rippling reflections from the Thames on my ceiling, unable to sleep. Too restless to sleep.

Tonight it's Caroline. She doesn't fit the nameless-fuck category. She'll never fit. What the hell was I thinking? Closing my eyes, I try to silence the still, small voice that is questioning the wisdom of bedding my best friend . . . again. She slumbers beside me, her sleek body bathed in the silver light of the January moon, her long legs entwined with mine, and her head on my chest.

This is wrong, so wrong. I rub my face, trying to erase my self-loathing, and she stirs and shifts, waking from her doze. One manicured fingernail skims down my stomach and over my abdominal muscles, then circles my navel. I sense her sleepy smile as her fingers slip towards my pubic hair. Catching her hand, I bring it to my lips. 'Haven't we done enough damage for one night, Caro?' I kiss each finger in turn to take the sting out of the rejection. I'm tired and disheartened by the nagging, unwelcome guilt that gnaws at my gut. This is Caroline, for heaven's sake, my best friend and my brother's wife. Ex-wife.

No. Not ex-wife. His widow.

It's a sad, lonely word for a sad, lonely circumstance.

'Oh, Maxim, please. Make me forget,' she whispers, and plants a warm wet kiss on my chest. Tossing her fair hair away from her face, she gazes up at me through long lashes, her eyes shining with need and grief.

I cup her lovely face and shake my head. 'We shouldn't.'

'Don't.' She places her fingers on my lips, silencing me. 'Please. I need it.'

I groan. I'm going to hell.

'Please,' she begs.

Shit, this is *hell.*

And because I'm hurting, too – because I miss him, too – and Caroline is my connection to him, my lips find hers and I ease her onto her back.

When I wake, the room is flooded with bright winter sunshine that makes me squint. Turning over, I'm relieved to see that Caroline has gone, leaving behind a lingering trace of regret – and a note on my pillow:

> *Dinner Tonight with Daddy & the Stepsow?*
> *Please come.*
> *They are mourning, too.*
>
> *ILY x*

Fuck.

This is not what I want. I close my eyes, grateful to be alone in my own bed and glad, despite our nocturnal activities, that we decided to come back to London two days after the funeral.

How the hell did this get so out of hand?

Just a nightcap, she'd said, and I'd gazed into her big blue eyes, brimming with sorrow, and known what she wanted. It was the same look she'd given me the night we learned of Kit's accident and untimely death. A look I couldn't resist then. We'd almost danced the dance so many times, but that night I resigned myself to fate, and with an unerring inevitability I fucked my brother's wife.

And now we'd done it again, with Kit laid to rest only two days ago.

I scowl at the ceiling. I am, without doubt, a pathetic excuse for a human. But then so is Caroline. At least she has an excuse: she's in mourning, scared for her future, and I'm her best friend. Who else could she turn to in her hour of need? I'd just pushed the envelope on *comforting* the grieving widow.

Frowning, I crumple her note and toss it to the wooden floor, where it skitters to a stop under the sofa that's piled with my clothes. The watery shadows float above me, the light and dark seeming to taunt me. I close my eyes to shut them out.

Kit was a good man.

Kit. Dear Kit. Everyone's favourite – even Caroline's; she did choose him, after all. A vision of Kit's desolate, broken body lying beneath a sheet at the hospital mortuary appears unbidden in my mind. I take a deep breath, trying to dispel the memory, as a knot forms in my throat. He deserved better than dear Caro and me – his wastrel brother. He didn't deserve this . . . betrayal.

Fuck.

Who am I kidding?

Caroline and I deserve each other. She scratched my itch, and I scratched hers. We're both consenting and *technically* free adults. She likes it. I like it, and it's what I do best, fucking some eager, attractive woman into the small hours of the morning. It's my favourite recreational activity and gives me something to do – someone to do. Fucking keeps me fit, and in the throes of passion I learn all I need to know about a woman – how to make her sweat and if she screams or cries when she comes.

Caroline is a crier.

Caroline has just lost her husband.

Shit.

And I've lost my big brother, my only guiding light for the last few years.

Shit.

Closing my eyes, I see Kit's pale, dead face once more, and his loss is a yawning space within me.

An irreplaceable loss.

Why the hell was he riding his motorcycle on that bleak and icy night? It's beyond comprehension. Kit is – *was* – the sane one, the safe pair of hands, Lord Reliable himself. Between the two of us, it was Kit who brought honour to our family name, upheld its reputation, and behaved responsibly. He held down a job in the City and managed the substantial family business as well. He didn't make rash decisions, he didn't drive like a madman. He was the sensible brother. He stepped up, not down. He was not the prodigal mess that I am. No, I'm the other side of Kit's coin. My speciality is being the black sheep of the family. No one has any expectations of me, I make sure of that. Always.

I sit up, my mood grim in the harsh morning light. It's time to hit the basement gym. Running, fucking and fencing, they all keep me in shape.

With dance music hammering in my ears and sweat rolling down my back, I drag air into my lungs. The pounding of my feet on the treadmill clears my mind as I concentrate on pushing my body to its limits. Usually when I run, I'm focused and grateful that at last I feel *something* – even if it's just the pain of bursting lungs and limbs. Today I don't want to feel anything, not after this fuck-awful week. All I want is the physical pain of exertion and endurance. Not the pain of loss.

Run. Breathe. Run. Breathe.

Don't think about Kit. Don't think about Caroline.

Run. Run. Run.

As I cool down, the treadmill slows, and I jog through the final stretch of my five-mile marathon, allowing my feverish thoughts to return. For the first time in a long time, I have a great deal to do.

Before Kit's demise my days were spent recovering from the night before and planning the next night's entertainment. And that was about it. That was my life. I don't like to shine a light on the vacuity of my existence. But deep down I know how bloody useless I am. Access to a healthy trust fund since I turned twenty-one means I've never done a serious day's work in my life. Unlike my older brother. He worked hard, but then again he had no choice.

Today, however, will be different. I'm the executor of Kit's will, which is a joke. Choosing *me* was his last laugh, I'm sure – but now that he's interred in the family vault, the will has to be read and . . . well, executed.

And Kit died leaving no heirs.

I shudder as the treadmill comes to a stop. I don't want to think about the implications. I'm not ready.

Grabbing my iPhone, I swing a towel around my neck and jog back upstairs to my flat on the sixth floor.

Stripping off my clothes, I discard them in the bedroom and head into the en suite bathroom. Beneath the shower, as I wash my hair, I consider how to deal with Caroline. We've known each other since our early schooldays. We each recognised a kindred spirit, and it drew us together, two thirteen-year-old boarders with divorced parents. I was the new boy and she took me under her wing. We became inseparable. She is and always will be my first love, my first fuck . . . my disastrous first fuck. And years later she'd chosen my brother, not me. But in spite of all that, we managed to remain good friends and keep our hands off each other – until Kit's death.

Shit. It has to stop. I don't want or need the complication. As I shave, solemn green eyes blaze back at me. *Don't fuck it up with Caroline. She's one of your few friends. She's your best friend. Talk to her. Reason with her. She knows we're incompatible.* I nod at my reflection, feeling more resolved about her, and wipe my face free of foam. Tossing the towel onto the floor, I head into the dressing room. There I gather up my black jeans, which are embedded in a pile on one of the shelves, and I'm relieved to find hanging a newly pressed white shirt and a dry-cleaned black blazer. Today I have lunch with the family solicitors. I slip on my boots and grab a coat to defend myself from the cold outside.

Shit, it's Monday.

I remember that Krystyna, my ancient Polish daily, is due later this morning to clean. Taking out my wallet, I deposit some cash on the console table in the hall, set the alarm, then stroll out of the front door. Locking up behind me, I forgo the lift and take the stairs.

Once I'm outside on Chelsea Embankment, the air is clear and crisp, marred only by the vapour of my frozen breath. I stare beyond the gloomy, grey Thames on the other side of the street to the Peace Pagoda on the opposite bank. That's what I want, some peace, but that may be a long time coming. I hope to have some questions answered over lunch. Raising an arm, I hail a cab and order the driver to take me to Mayfair.

Housed in the Georgian splendour of Brook Street, the firm of Pavel, Marmont and Hoffman has been the family's solicitors since 1775. 'Time to be a grown-up,' I mutter to myself as I push open the ornate wooden door.

'Good afternoon, sir.' The young receptionist beams, a flush staining her olive skin. She's pretty, in an understated way. If these were normal circumstances I'd have her number within five minutes of conversation, but that's not why I'm here.

'I have an appointment to see Mr Rajah.'

'Your name?'

'Maxim Trevelyan.'

Her eyes scan her computer screen, and she shakes her head and frowns. 'Please take a seat.' She waves towards two brown leather chesterfields that are situated in the panelled hall, and I slump into the nearer one, picking up that morning's edition of the *Financial Times*. The receptionist is talking on the phone with some urgency while I peruse the front page of the paper but take nothing in. When I glance up, Rajah is coming to greet me himself, striding through the double doors with an outstretched hand.

I stand.

'Lord Trevethick, may I offer you my sincere condolences for your loss,' Rajah says as we shake hands.

'Trevethick, please,' I reply. 'I've yet to get used to my brother's title.'

My title . . . now.

'Of course.' Mr Rajah nods with a polite deference that I find irritating. 'Would you like to come with me? We're having lunch in the partners' dining room, and I must say we have one of the finest cellars in London.'

Mesmerised, I stare at the dancing flames of the fire at my club in Mayfair.

Earl of Trevethick.

That's me. Now.

It's inconceivable. It's devastating.

How I envied my brother's title and his position in the family when I was younger. Kit had been the favoured child since birth, especially with my mother, but then he was the heir, not the spare. Known as Viscount Porthtowan since he was born, Kit had become the twelfth Earl of Trevethick at the age of twenty upon our father's sudden death. At twenty-eight I'm lucky number thirteen. And though I've coveted the title and all that goes with it, now that it's mine, I feel like I'm intruding on my brother's domain.

You fucked his countess last night. That's more than intruding.

I take a slug of the Glenrothes I'm drinking and raise my glass. 'A toast to the Ghost,' I whisper, and smile at the irony. The Glenrothes was my father's whisky of choice, and my brother's – and from today this 1992 vintage will be mine.

I can't pinpoint the moment I made peace with Kit's inheritance and with Kit himself, but it happened sometime in my late teens. He had the title, he'd won the girl, and I had to accept that. But now everything is mine. Everything.

Even your wife. Well, for last night at least.

But the irony is that Kit has made no provision for Caroline in his will.

Nothing.

This is what she feared.

How could he have been so remiss? He'd drawn a new will four months ago, but he hadn't made provisions for her. They'd only been married for two years . . .

What was he thinking?

Of course, she may challenge it. And who would blame her?

I rub my face.

What am I going to do?

My phone buzzes.

WHERE ARE YOU?

It's a text from Caroline.

I switch off my phone and order another drink. I don't

want to see her tonight. I want to lose myself in someone else. Someone new. Someone with no strings attached, and I think I'll score some blow, too. I pull out my phone and open Tinder.

'Maxim, this is a stunning flat.' She gazes out over the murky water of the Thames that glimmers with light from the Peace Pagoda. I take her jacket and drape it over the back of the sofa.

'Drink or something stronger?' I offer. We are not going to be in the drawing room for long. On cue she flicks her shining black hair over her shoulder. Her hazel eyes, framed with kohl, are intent on me.

Licking painted lips, she arches a brow and asks, 'Something stronger?' Her tone is seductive. 'What are you drinking?'

Ah . . . she's not taking the hint, so no coke, then, but she's way ahead of me. I step closer so that she has to angle her head to look up at me. I'm careful not to touch her.

'I'm not thirsty, Heather.' I pitch my voice low, pleased that I've remembered her name. She swallows, and her lips part.

'Me neither,' she whispers, and her provocative smile reaches her eyes.

'What do you want?' I watch as her gaze moves to my mouth. It's an invitation. I pause for a moment, just to make sure I'm reading her correctly, then lean down and kiss her. It's the briefest touch: lips on lips, then nothing.

'I think you know what I want.' She reaches up to run her fingers through my hair and pull me back to her warm and willing mouth. She tastes of brandy with a faint hint of cigarettes. The taste is distracting. I don't remember seeing her smoke at the club. I pull her hard against me, one hand at her waist while the other travels down over her lush curves. She has a small waist and large, firm breasts, which she presses enticingly against me. I wonder if they'll taste as good as they feel. My hand skims down to her backside as I deepen the kiss, exploring her eager mouth.

'What do *you* want?' I whisper against her lips.

'You.' Her voice is breathy and urgent. She's turned on. Big time. She begins to unbutton my shirt. I hold still as she eases it off my shoulders and lets it fall to the floor.

Do I take her here or in my bed? Comfort wins and I grab her hand. 'Come with me.' I tug her gently, and she follows me out of the drawing room and down the hall, into the bedroom.

The room is tidy, as I knew it would be.

God bless Krystyna.

I switch the bedside lights on from the wall and walk her to the bed. 'Turn around.'

Heather does as she's told but sways a little in her high heels. 'Steady.' I clasp her shoulders and pull her tight against me, then turn her head towards me so I can see her eyes. They're intent on my lips, but she looks up at me. Eyes bright. Clear. Focused. Sober enough. I nuzzle her neck, tasting her soft, fragrant skin with my tongue. 'I think it's time to lie down.' I unzip her short red dress and peel it over her shoulders, pausing as I expose the tops of her breasts concealed by a red bra. I skim my thumbs across the surface of the lacy fabric. She groans and arches her back, pushing her breasts into my hands.

Oh, yes.

My thumbs dip beneath the delicate material and circle her hardening nipples as she gropes behind her for the button on my jeans. 'We have all night,' I murmur, and release her before stepping back so that her dress slides down her body and pools at her feet.

A red thong reveals her shapely behind.

'Turn around. I want to see you.'

Heather tosses her hair over her shoulder as she turns and gives me a searing look from beneath her lashes. She has the most magnificent breasts.

I smile. She smiles.

This is going to be fun.

Reaching forward, she grabs the waistband of my jeans and tugs sharply so her glorious tits are once more pressed against my chest. 'Kiss me,' she growls, her voice low and demanding. She runs her tongue over her top teeth, and my body responds, my groin tightening.

'Only too happy to oblige, madam.'

I clasp her head, my fingers in her silky hair, and kiss her more roughly this time. She responds, her hands grabbing fistfuls of my hair as our tongues lock. She stops and looks up at me with a salacious glint in her eyes, as if finally seeing me and liking what she sees. Then her lips are once more feverish against mine.

Man, she really wants this.

Nimble fingers find the top button of my jeans, and she pulls. Laughing, I grab her hands and push her gently so we both fall onto the bed.

Heather. Her name is Heather, and she's fast asleep beside me. I glance at my bedside clock; it's 5:15 a.m. She's a good fuck, no doubt about it. But now I want her gone. How long will I have to lie here listening to the soft sound of her breathing? Perhaps I should have gone to her flat instead, so then I could leave. But my place was nearer – and we were both impatient. As I stare at the ceiling, I mentally run through our evening, trying to remember what, if any, details I've learned about her. She works in television – or 'telly', as she calls it – and she has to be at work in the morning, which means she has to leave soon, surely? She lives in Putney. She's hot. And willing. Yes, very willing. She likes to be on her front during intercourse, she's quiet when she comes, and she has a talented mouth that knows exactly how to revive a spent man. My cock stirs at the memory, and I contemplate waking her up for more. Her dark hair is fanned out on the pillow, and her expression is serene in sleep. I ignore the pang of envy that her serenity inspires and wonder if I got to know her better, would I find the same peace?

Oh, for fuck's sake. I want her gone.

You have intimacy issues. Caroline's nagging voice reverberates through my mind.

Caroline. Shit.

Three whining texts and several missed calls from Caroline have pissed me off. My jeans lie on the floor in a crumpled heap. From the back pocket, I retrieve my phone. Checking on the sleeping form beside me – no, she hasn't stirred – I read my messages from Caroline.

WHERE RU?

CALL ME!

POUTING

What is her problem?

She knows the deal; she's known me long enough. A quick tumble between the sheets isn't going to change how I feel about her. I love her . . . in my own way, but as a friend, a good friend.

I scowl. I haven't called her. I don't want to. I don't know what to say.

Coward. The voice of my conscience whispers. I need to put this right. Above me the shimmers from the Thames bob and weave, free and easy. Taunting me. Reminding me of what I've lost.

Freedom.

And what I have now.

Responsibility.

Shit.

Guilt overwhelms me. It's an unfamiliar and unwelcome

feeling – Kit has bequeathed everything to me. *Everything*. And Caroline has nothing from his estate. She's my brother's wife. And we fucked. No wonder I feel guilty. And deep down I know she feels it, too. That's why she left in the middle of the night without waking me, without saying goodbye. If only the girl beside me would do the same.

I quickly type out a text to Caro.

Busy today. You OK?

It's five in the morning. Caroline will be asleep. I'm safe. I'll deal with her later today . . . or tomorrow.

Heather stirs, and her eyelids flitter open.

'Hi.' She gives me a tentative smile. I reciprocate, but her smile fades. 'I should go,' she says.

'Go?' Hope swells in my chest. 'You don't have to go.' I manage not to sound disingenuous.

'I do. I have to work, and I don't think my red dress will cut it in the office.' She sits up, clutching the silk quilt to conceal her curves. 'That was . . . good, Maxim. If I leave my number, will you call me? I'd rather speak on the phone than message on Tinder.'

'Of course,' I lie smoothly. I pull her face to mine and kiss her tenderly. Her smile is bashful. Rising, she wraps the quilt securely around her body and starts to gather her clothes from the floor.

'Shall I call you a cab?' I ask.

'I can Uber.'

'I'll do it.'

'Okay, thank you. I'm going to Putney.'

She tells me her address, I get up, slip on my discarded jeans and, taking my phone, leave the bedroom to give her some privacy. It's strange how some women behave the morning after: shy and quiet. She's no longer the lascivious, demanding siren of the night before.

Once I've ordered a car I wait, staring out across the dark Thames. When she finally appears, she hands me a scrap of paper. 'My number.'

'Thanks.' I slip it into the back pocket of my jeans. 'Your car will be here in five minutes.'

She stands awkwardly, her post-coital shyness taking hold. As the silence stretches between us, she surveys the room, looking anywhere but at me.

'This is a lovely flat. Airy,' she says, and I know that we've resorted to chit-chat to fill the awkwardness. She spots my guitar and the piano. 'You play?' She walks over to the baby grand.

'Yes.'

'That's why you're so good with your hands,' she says. Then frowns as if she's realised that she's spoken aloud, and her cheeks flush a fetching pink.

'Do you play?' I ask, ignoring her comment.

'No – I never made it further than recorder group in year two.' Relief softens her features, probably because I ignored her comment about my hands. 'And all that?' She points to my decks and the iMac on a desk in the corner of the room.

'I DJ.'

'Oh?'

'Yes. Couple of times a month at a club in Hoxton.'

'Hence all the vinyl.' She glances at the shelved wall housing my record collection.

I nod.

'And the photography?' She waves a hand at the black-and-white landscapes that hang on large canvases in the drawing room.

'Yes. And occasionally on the other side of the camera.'

She looks confused.

'Modelling. Editorial, mainly.'

'Oh, that makes sense. You really are a man of many parts.'

She grins, feeling a little more confident. She should. She's a goddess.

'Jack of all trades,' I reply with a self-deprecating smile, and her grin vanishes, replaced by a puzzled frown.

'Is something wrong?' she asks.

Wrong? What the hell is she talking about? 'No. Nothing.' My phone buzzes, and it's a text to let me know her car has arrived. 'I'll call you,' I say as I pick up her jacket and hold it open for her to shrug on.

'No you won't. But don't worry. That's Tinder for you. I had fun.'

'Me, too.' I'm not about to contradict her.

I follow her to the front door. 'Do you want me to walk you down?'

'No, thanks. I'm a big girl. Goodbye, Maxim. It was nice knowing you.'

'Same here . . . Heather.'

'Well done.' She beams, pleased that I've remembered her name, and it's impossible not to return her smile. 'That's better,' she says. 'I hope you find what you're looking for.' Reaching up, she gives me a chaste kiss on the cheek. She turns and teeters on her high heels towards the lifts. I frown at her departing figure, watching her fine arse move beneath her red dress.

Find what I'm looking for? What the hell does that mean?

I've got all this. I've just had you. It will be someone else tomorrow. What more do I need?

For some unknown reason, her words irritate me, but I shake them off and head back to bed, relieved that she's gone. As I strip off my jeans and slip between the sheets, her challenging parting words echo through my mind.

I hope you find what you're looking for.

Where the fuck did that come from?

I've just inherited a vast estate in Cornwall, an estate in

Oxfordshire, another in Northumberland, and a small portion of London – but at what cost?

Kit's pale, lifeless face surfaces in my imagination.

Shit.

So many people are now relying on me, too many, far too many: tenant farmers, estate workers, household staff in four houses, the developers in Mayfair . . .

Hell.

Fuck you, Kit. Fuck you for dying.

I close my eyes as I fight back unshed tears, and with Heather's parting words ringing in my head I fall into a stupor.

Chapter Two

Alessia digs her hands further into the pockets of Michal's old anorak in a vain attempt to warm her cold fingers. Huddled in her scarf, she trudges through the freezing winter drizzle towards the apartment block on Chelsea Embankment. Today is Wednesday, her second day here without Krystyna, and she is heading back to the big apartment with the piano.

In spite of the weather, she's feeling a sense of achievement because she's survived the cramped and crowded train journey without her usual anxiety. She's beginning to understand that this is what London is like. There are too many people, too much noise, and too much traffic. But worst of all, no one speaks to anyone else, except to say 'Excuse me' if they jostle her or 'Move down the carriage, please'. Everyone hides behind their free newspapers or listens to music on headphones or stares at their phones or electronic books, avoiding all eye contact.

That morning Alessia had been lucky enough to find a seat on the train, but the woman beside her had spent much of the journey shrieking into her phone about her unsuccessful date the night before. Alessia had ignored her and read the free newspaper to improve her English, but she'd wished she could listen to music through headphones and not this woman's loud whining. Once she finished the paper, she'd closed her eyes and daydreamed of majestic mountains dotted with snow and pastures where the air was scented with thyme and filled with the hum of honeybees. She misses home. She misses the peace and quiet. She misses her mother, and she misses her piano.

Her fingers flex in her pockets as she recalls her warm-up piece, hearing the notes loud and clear in her mind and seeing them in blazing colour. How long has it been since she played? Her excitement builds as she thinks of the piano waiting for her in the apartment.

She makes her way through the entrance of the old building towards the elevator, barely able to contain her enthusiasm, and then up to the top-floor apartment. For a few hours on Mondays, Wednesdays and Fridays, this wonderful place with its large airy rooms, dark wooden floors, and baby grand piano, is all hers. She unlocks the door, poised to switch off the alarm, but to her surprise there's no warning tone. Perhaps the system's broken or it's not been set. Or . . . *No.* She realises to her horror that the owner must be at home. Listening hard, trying to detect any signs of life, she stands in the wide hallway that's hung with black-and-white photographic landscapes. She hears nothing.

Mirë.

No. 'Good.' English. Think in English. Whoever lives here must have gone to work and forgotten to set the alarm. She's never met the man, but she knows he has a good job, because the apartment is huge. How else can he afford it? She sighs. He might be rich, but he's a complete slob. She's been here three times already, twice with Krystyna, and each time the apartment is a mess and requires hours of tidying and cleaning.

The grey day is seeping through the skylight at the end of the hall, so Alessia flicks the switch and the crystal chandelier above her bursts into life, illuminating the hallway. She peels off her woollen scarf and hangs it up with her anorak in the closet beside the front door. From her plastic shopping bag, she pulls out the old trainers that Magda has given her, and after taking off her wet boots and socks she slips them on, grateful that they are dry so her frozen feet can warm up. Her thin jersey top and T-shirt are no match for the cold. She rubs her arms briskly to bring some life back into them as she makes her way through the kitchen into the utility room. There she dumps her shopping bag on the counter. Out of it she pulls the ill-fitting nylon housecoat that Krystyna bequeathed her and puts it on, then fastens a pale blue scarf around her head in an effort to keep her thick, plaited hair in check. From the cupboard beneath the sink, she takes out the cleaning caddy, and from the top of the washing machine she grabs the laundry basket and heads straight to *his* bedroom. If she hurries, she can finish the apartment before it's time to leave and the piano will be hers for a short while.

She opens the door but freezes on the threshold of the room.

He's here.

The man!

Fast asleep face-down and sprawled naked across the large bed. She stands, shocked and fascinated at once, her feet rooted to the wooden floor as she stares. He's stretched across the length of the bed, tangled in his duvet but naked . . . very naked. His face is turned towards her but covered by unkempt brown hair. One arm is beneath the pillow that supports his head, the other extended towards her. He has broad, defined shoulders, and on his biceps is an elaborate tattoo that is partially hidden by the bedding. His back is sun-kissed with a tan that fades as his hips narrow to dimples and to a pale, taut backside.

Backside.

He's naked!

Lakuriq!

Zot!

His long, muscular legs disappear beneath a knot of grey duvet and silver silk bedspread, though his foot sticks out over the edge of the mattress. He stirs, the muscles in his back rippling, and his eyelids flicker open to reveal unfocused but brilliant green eyes. Alessia stops breathing, convinced he'll be angry that she's woken him. Their eyes meet, but he shifts and turns his face away. He settles down and goes back to sleep. Relieved, she exhales a deep breath.

Shyqyr Zotit!

Flushed with mortification, she tiptoes out of his bedroom and bolts up the long hall and into the living room, where she sets the cleaning caddy on the floor and begins to gather his discarded clothes.

He's here? How can he still be in bed? At this hour?

Surely he's late for work.

She glances at the piano, feeling cheated. Today was the day she was going to play. She didn't have the nerve on Monday, and she longs to play. Today would have been the first time! In her head she hears Bach's Prelude in C Minor. Her fingers tap out the notes in anger, and the melody resonates inside her head, in bright reds, yellows and oranges, a perfect accompaniment to her resentment. The piece reaches its climax and then diminishes to a close as she throws a discarded T-shirt into the laundry basket.

Why does he have to be here?

She knows that her disappointment is irrational. This is his home. But focusing on her disappointment distracts her from thinking about *him.* He's the first naked man she's ever seen, a naked man with vivid green eyes – eyes the colour of the still, deep waters of the Drin on a summer's day. She frowns, not wanting the reminder of home. He had looked directly at her.

Thank God he didn't wake. Taking the laundry basket, she tiptoes to his half-open bedroom door and pauses to see if he's still asleep. She hears the sound of the shower in the bathroom.

He's awake!

She contemplates leaving the apartment but dismisses the idea. She needs this job, and if she were to leave, he might fire her.

Cautiously she opens the door and listens to the tuneless humming that echoes from his en suite bathroom. Heart racing, she ducks into the bedroom to collect his clothes that are scattered over the floor, then hurries back to the safety of the utility room wondering why her heart is pounding.

She takes a deep, calming breath. It was a surprise finding him here asleep. Yes. That's it. That's all. It has nothing to do with the fact that she has seen him naked. It has nothing to do with a fine face, a straight nose, full lips, broad shoulders . . . muscular arms. Nothing. It was a shock. She never expected to encounter the owner of the apartment, and to see him like that is unsettling.

Yes. He's handsome.

All of him. His hair, his hands, his legs, his backside . . .

Really handsome. And he had looked directly at her with such clear green eyes.

A darker memory surfaces in her mind. A memory from home: ice-blue eyes flinty with anger, fury raining down on her.

No. Don't think of him*!*

She puts her head in her hands and rubs her forehead.

No. No. No.

She fled. She's here. She's in London. She's safe. She will never see *him* again.

Kneeling down, she loads the dirty clothes from the laundry basket into the washing machine, as Krystyna showed her. She goes through the pockets of his black jeans and pulls out the loose change and the customary condom that he seems to carry in all his trousers. In the back pocket, she finds a scrap of paper with a phone number and the name Heather scrawled on it. She slips it with the change and the condom into her pocket, tosses one of the detergent capsules into the wash, and switches on the machine.

Next she unloads the dryer and sets up the iron. Today she'll start with the ironing and stay hidden in the utility room until he's gone.

What if he doesn't go?

And why is she hiding from him? He's her employer. Perhaps she should introduce herself. She's met all her other employers, and they aren't a problem, apart from Mrs Kingsbury, who follows her around critiquing her cleaning methods. She sighs. The truth is, all the people she works for are women – except him, and she's wary of men.

'Bye, Krystyna!' he calls, startling her from her thoughts and the shirt collar she's ironing. The front door closes with a muffled bang, and all is quiet. He's gone. She is on her own, and she sags with relief against the ironing board.

Krystyna? Doesn't he know that she's taken Krystyna's place? Magda's friend Agatha organised this job. Hasn't Agatha told him about the change of staff? Alessia resolves to check this evening if the owner of this apartment has been informed. She finishes another shirt, hangs it on a clothes hanger, then goes to check the console table in the hall and finds he has left her money. Surely that means he won't be returning?

Her day brightens immediately, and with renewed purpose she runs back to the utility room and grabs the pile of freshly ironed clothes and his shirts and heads to his bedroom.

The master suite is the only non-white room in the apartment: all grey walls and dark wood. A large gilt mirror hangs above the biggest wooden bed that Alessia has ever seen. And on the wall facing the bed, there are two large black-and-white photographs of women, their naked backs to camera. Turning away from the photography, she assesses the room. It is in complete disarray. Quickly she hangs his shirts in the closet – a closet that is bigger than her bedroom – and places the folded items on one of the shelves. The closet is still a mess, and it's been like this since she started here with Krystyna last week. Krystyna always ignored the mess, and though Alessia wants to fold and put away all the clothes, it's a big project, and she doesn't have time now, not if she wants to play the piano.

Back in his room, she opens the curtains and glances through the floor-to-ceiling windows at the Thames. It's stopped raining, but the day is grey; the street, the river, the trees in the park beyond are all muted greys, so unlike her home.

No. Home is here now. She ignores the sadness that rises like a tide within her and places the items that she retrieved from his pockets into a dish on the bedside table. She then begins to clean and tidy his room.

The last job in the bedroom is emptying the wastebasket. She tries to avoid looking at the used condoms as she dumps the contents into a black plastic bag. It was a shock the first time she did this, and it's still a shock now. How can one man use so many?

Ugh!

Alessia moves through the rest of the apartment, cleaning, dusting and polishing, but avoiding the one room she's not allowed to enter. Fleetingly she wonders what's behind the closed door, but she doesn't try to open it. Krystyna was very clear that the room is off-limits.

She finishes mopping the floors with half an hour to spare. She puts the cleaning caddy away in the utility room and transfers the washed clothes into the dryer. She removes her housecoat and undoes her blue scarf, stuffing it into the back pocket of her jeans.

Carrying the black bag full of trash, she deposits it by the front door. She'll take it to the bins in the designated area in the alley beside the apartment block when she leaves. Anxiously, she opens the front door and checks up and down the hallway. There's no sign of him. She can do this. She wasn't brave enough the first time she cleaned here alone. She was afraid he might return. But since he left and said goodbye, she'll take the risk.

She rushes down the hallway into the living room and sits at the piano, pausing to enjoy the moment. Black and shiny, it's lit up by the impressive chandelier that hangs above it. Her fingers trace the golden lyre logo and the words beneath.

STEINWAY & SONS

On the rest there's a pencil and the same half-finished composition that has been sitting there since the first day she came to the apartment with Krystyna. As she studies the pages, the notes sound through her head, a sad lament, lonely and full of melancholy, unresolved and unfinished in hues of pale blue and grey. She tries to connect the profound and reflective tune to the indolent but handsome naked man she saw that morning. Perhaps he's a composer. She glances across the wide room to the antique desk in the corner cluttered with his computer, a synthesizer, and what might be a couple of sound mixers. Yes, they look like they belong to a composer. And then there's the wall of old records that she has to dust; he's certainly an avid music collector.

She pushes these thoughts aside as she stares down at the keys. How long has it been since she last played? Weeks? Months? A sudden, acute feeling of anguish steals the air from her lungs, making her gasp, and tears form in her eyes.

No. Not here. She will not break down here. She clutches the piano in an effort to fight off her heartache and her homesickness, realising it's been more than a month since she last played. So much has happened since then.

She shudders and takes a deep breath, forcing a feeling of calm. She stretches her fingers and strokes the keys.

White. Black.

The mere touch soothes her. She wants to savour this precious moment and lose herself in her music. Gently, she pushes down the keys, sounding an E-minor chord. The sound rings clear and strong, a bold and verdant green, the colour of the Mister's eyes, and Alessia's heart fills with hope. The Steinway is tuned to perfection. She launches into her warm-up piece, 'Le Coucou'; the keys move with ease and a smooth, fluid action. Her fingers fly across the keyboard vivace, and the stress, fear and sorrow of the last few weeks fade and finally mute as she loses herself in the colours of the music.

One of the Trevelyan London homes is on Cheyne Walk, a brisk stroll from my flat. Built in 1771 by Robert Adam, Trevelyan House had been Kit's home since our father died. For me it holds many childhood memories – some happy, some less so – and now it's mine to do with as I wish. Well, it's held in trust for me. Faced once more with my new reality, I shake my head and pull the collar of my coat up to fight the biting cold, cold that seems to emanate not from outside but from within me.

What the hell am I supposed to do with this house?

It's been two days since I saw Caroline, and I know she's furious with me, but I will have to face her sooner or later. Standing on the doorstep, I contemplate whether or not to use my key. I've always had a key to the house, but to burst in unannounced feels like an intrusion.

Taking a deep breath, I knock twice. After a few moments, the front door opens and Blake, the family's butler since before I was born, answers the door.

'Lord Trevethick,' he says, bowing his balding head and holding open the door.

'Is that really necessary, Blake?' I ask as I stride into the entrance hall. Blake remains mute as he takes my coat. 'How's Mrs Blake?'

'She's well, my lord. Greatly saddened by recent events, though.'

'As are we all. Is Caroline at home?'

'Yes, my lord. I believe Lady Trevethick is in the drawing room.'

'Thank you. I'll see myself up.'

'Of course. Would you like some coffee?'

'Yes, please. Oh, and, Blake, as I said last week, "sir" will suffice.'

Blake pauses, then gives me a nod. 'Yes, sir. Thank you, sir.'

I want to roll my eyes. I was the Honourable Maxim Trevelyan and referred to as 'Master Maxim' here. 'Lord' applied only to my father, then my brother. It will take me some time to get accustomed to my new title.

I bound up the wide staircase and along the landing into the drawing room. It's empty except for the overstuffed sofas and elegant Queen Anne furniture that has been in the family for generations. The drawing room opens onto a conservatory that has a spectacular view of the Thames, Cadogan Pier and Albert Bridge. There I find Caroline, nestled in an armchair, wrapped in a cashmere shawl, and staring out of the windows. She clutches a small blue handkerchief.

'Hi,' I say as I stride in. Caroline turns a tear-stained face towards me, her eyes red and puffy.

Shit.

'Where the fuck have you been?' she snaps.

'Caro,' I begin, ready to placate her.

'Don't Caro me, you wanker,' she snarls as she stands up, fists clenched.

Shit. She is really angry.

'What have I done now?'

'You know what you've done. Why haven't you answered my calls? It's been two days!'

'I've had a lot to think about, and I've been busy.'

'You? Busy? Maxim, you wouldn't know busy if you tripped and stuck your dick in it.'

I blanch and then laugh at the image.

Caroline relaxes a little. 'Don't make me laugh when I'm angry with you.' Her lips form a pout.

'You have a way with words.' I open my arms, and she walks into my embrace.

'Why didn't you call?' she asks as she hugs me back, her anger dissipating.

'It's a lot to take on board,' I whisper as I hold her. 'I needed time to think.'

'Alone?'

I don't answer. I don't want to lie. Monday night I was with, um . . . Heather, and last night it was . . . What was her name? Dawn.

Caroline sniffs and steps out of my arms. 'I thought as much. I know you too well, Maxim. What was she like?'

I shrug as an image of Heather's lips around my cock comes to mind.

Caroline sighs. 'You're such a whore,' she says with her usual disdain.

How can I deny it?

Caroline of all people knows about my nocturnal pursuits. She has a collection of choice epithets to describe me and regularly berates me for my promiscuity.

Yet she still went to bed with me.

'You're whoring your way through your grief while I had to endure dinner with Daddy and the Stepsow alone. It was awful,' she quips. 'And last night I was lonely.'

'I'm sorry,' I answer, because I can't think of what else to say.

'You saw the lawyers?' She changes the subject, giving me a direct look.

I nod, and I have to acknowledge that this is another reason I've been avoiding her.

'Oh, no.' She whimpers. 'You look so grave. I've got nothing, have I?' Her eyes are wide with fear and grief.

I place my hands on her shoulders and break it to her gently. 'Everything is in trust for me as heir.'

Caroline lets out a sob and covers her mouth as tears fill her eyes. 'Damn him,' she whispers.

'Don't worry, we'll work something out,' I murmur, and hold her once more.

'I loved him,' she says, her voice small and quiet, like a child's.

'I know. We both did.' Though I know she also loved Kit's title and his wealth.

'You're not going to evict me?'

I take the handkerchief from her hand and wipe each of her eyes. 'No, of course not. You're my brother's widow and my best friend.'

'But that's all?' She gives me a watery but bitter smile, and I kiss her forehead in lieu of answering her question.

'Your coffee, sir,' Blake says from the entrance to the conservatory.

Immediately I drop my arms and step away from Caroline. Blake enters, his face expressionless, and he's holding a tray laden with cups, milk, a silver coffee-pot, and my favourite biscuits – plain chocolate digestives.

'Thank you, Blake,' I respond, trying to ignore the slow flush I feel creeping up my neck.

Brazen this out.

Blake places the tray on the table beside the sofa. 'Will that be all, sir?'

'For now, thank you.' My tone is sharper than I intended.

Blake exits the room, and Caroline pours the coffee. My shoulders slump with relief at Blake's departure. And I hear my mother's voice ringing in my head: *Not in front of the staff.*

I'm still holding Caroline's damp handkerchief. I stare at it and frown, recalling a fragment from a dream I had last night – or was it this morning? A young woman, an angel? Possibly the Virgin Mary or a nun in blue standing in my bedroom doorway watching over me as I slept.

What the hell does that mean?

I'm not religious.

'What?' asks Caroline.

I shake my head. 'Nothing,' I murmur, taking the cup of coffee she offers and giving her back her handkerchief.

'Well, I might be pregnant,' she says.

What? I blanch.

'Kit. Not you. You're too bloody careful.'

Damn right. The ground seems to shift beneath my feet.

Kit's heir!

Could this be any more complicated?

'Well, if you are, we'll figure out what to do,' I reply, feeling at once a moment of relief that all this responsibility might pass to Kit's child, but also a sudden and overwhelming sense of loss.

The earldom is mine. For now.

Shit. Could this be any more confusing?

Chapter Three

My phone buzzes as I'm in the back of a black cab on my way to the office. It's Joe.

'Mate,' he says. 'How's it going?' He sounds sombre, and I know he's referring to my frame of mind since Kit's death. I've not seen him since the funeral.

'I'm surviving.'

'Fancy a bout?'

'I'd love to. But I can't. I have meetings all day.'

'Earl shit?'

I laugh. 'Yes. Earl shit.'

'Maybe later in the week? My épée is getting rusty.'

'Yes. I'd like that. Or perhaps a drink.'

'Yeah, I'll see if Tom's around.'

'Cool. Thanks, Joe.'

'No worries, mate.'

I hang up. My mood morose. I miss being able to do what the fuck I like. If I wanted to fence in the middle of the day, I could. Joe is my sparring partner and one of my closest friends. Instead I have to go into the office and do some bloody work for a change.

Kit. I blame you.

The music is pounding at Loulou's. The bass reverberates through my chest. I like it this way. The noise level cuts down on unnecessary conversation. I make my way through the crowd to the bar. I need a drink and a warm, willing body.

I have spent the last day and a half in tedious meetings with the two fund managers who oversee the considerable Trevethick investment portfolio and the charitable trust; the estate managers from Cornwall, Oxfordshire and Northumberland; the managing agent who handles the London properties; and with the developer who's remodelling the three mansion blocks in Mayfair. Oliver Macmillan, Kit's chief operating officer and his right-hand man, has attended all of them with me. Oliver and Kit had been friends since Eton; they'd both gone to the London School of Economics, until Kit dropped out to fulfil his aristocratic duty following the death of our father.

Oliver is slight, with a shock of unruly blond hair and eyes of an indeterminate colour that miss nothing. I have never warmed to him. He's ruthless and ambitious, but he knows his way around a balance sheet and can deal with the numerous personnel who answer to the Earl of Trevethick. I don't know how Kit managed it all and held down a fund-manager job in the City. But he was a smart, slick bastard.

Funny, too.

I miss him.

I order a Grey Goose and tonic. Maybe he succeeded because Macmillan had his back, and I wonder if Oliver's loyalty will extend to me or if he might take advantage of my naivety while

I try to come to terms with all my new responsibilities. I just don't know. But the fact is, I don't trust him, and I make a mental note to stay circumspect in my dealings with him.

The one bright spot in the last couple of days was a call from my agent telling me I have a job next week. I'd taken a great deal of pleasure in telling the old gorgon that for the foreseeable future I would no longer be available for modelling work.

Would I miss it?

I wasn't sure. Modelling could be mind-numbingly boring, but after I was sent down from Oxford, the work had gotten me out of bed and given me an excuse to stay in shape. I also got to meet hot, skinny women.

I take a slug of my drink and scan the room. That's what I want now: a hot, willing woman, skinny or otherwise.

It's Let's Fuck Thursday.

Her raucous laugh catches my attention, and our eyes meet. I see the appreciation and challenge in her gaze, and my cock stirs in anticipation. She has pretty hazel eyes, long brown glossy hair, and she's drinking shots. What's more, she looks sensational in the leather minidress and her thigh-high stiletto boots.

Yes. She'll do.

It's two in the morning when I let us both into my flat. I take Leticia's coat, and she turns immediately and wraps her arms around my neck. 'Let's go to bed, Posh Boy,' she whispers, and kisses me. Hard. No preliminaries. Her coat is still in my hands, and I have to steady myself against the wall to stop us both from falling. Her attack takes me by surprise. Perhaps she's more pissed than I thought. She tastes of lipstick and Jägermeister – an intriguing combination. I thread my fingers through her hair and tug, freeing my mouth.

'All good things, sweetheart,' I chide against her lips. 'Let me put your coat down.'

'Fuck my coat,' she says, and kisses me again. All tongue.

I'd rather fuck you.

'We're not going to make it to the bedroom at this rate.' I put my hands on her shoulders and gently push her away.

'Let me see your place, then, model-slash-photographer-slash-DJ,' she teases, her soft Irish accent a complete contrast to her direct manner. I wonder if she'll be as forthright in bed as I follow her down the hallway into the drawing room, her heels clicking on the wooden floor.

'Do you act, too? Great view, by the way,' she says as she glances through the wall of glass that looks out over the Thames. 'Nice piano,' she adds, and turns to face me, her eyes alight with excitement. 'Have you fucked on it?'

Lord, she has a foul mouth.

'Not recently.' I dump her coat on the sofa. 'Not sure I want to right now. I'd rather bed you.' I ignore her jibe about my current lack of a stable career. I haven't told her I have an empire to run. She smiles, her lipstick smudged and no doubt smeared over my mouth. The thought displeases me, and I run my fingers over my lips. She saunters towards me and tugs the lapels of my jacket, forcing me forward.

'Okay, Posh Boy, show me what you can do.' She puts her hands on my chest and rakes her nails over my sternum to the edge of my jacket.

Shit! It's almost painful. She has scarlet talons, not nails, talons that match her lipstick. She slides my jacket off my shoulders, letting it fall to the floor, and starts undoing the buttons on my shirt. The mood she's in, I'm relieved that she takes her time and doesn't just rip my shirt open – I like this shirt! Slipping it off me, she lets it fall to my feet and digs her nails into my shoulders. Deliberately.

'Ah!' I hiss in pain.

'Cool ink,' she says as her hands travel from my shoulders

down my arms and towards the waistband of my jeans, her nails leaving tracks across my stomach.

Ow! Boy, she's aggressive.

I grab her hand and tug her into my arms, kissing her roughly. 'Let's go to bed,' I say against her mouth, and before she can answer, I take her hand and haul her after me to the bedroom. There she pushes me towards the bed and again rakes her nails over my belly as her fingers find the top button of my jeans.

Fuck! She likes it rough.

I flinch and catch her hands in front of her in a vice-like grip, but in reality I'm avoiding her nails.

You want to play rough? I can, too.

'Play nice,' I warn. 'And you first!' I release her, moving her away so I have a good view. 'Strip. Now,' I order.

Tossing her hair over her shoulder, she puts her hands on her hips, her mouth set in an amused challenge.

'Go on,' I urge.

Leticia's eyes darken, and she pauses. 'Say please,' she whispers.

I smirk. 'Please.'

She laughs. 'I love your posh accent.'

'It's just an accident of birth, sweetheart. Keep your boots on,' I add.

She returns my smirk, reaches behind her, and casually unzips her tight leather dress. Wriggling her hips from side to side, she shimmies out of the dress and lets it slip down the length of her boots. I smile. She looks incredible. Slim, with small, firm breasts, she's wearing black French knickers and a matching bra and the thigh-high boots. Stepping out of her dress, she sashays towards me with a beckoning, sexy smile and grabs my hand. With surprising force she tugs me to the bed, then places her hands on my chest and pushes me hard so that I sprawl on top of the quilt.

'Take them off,' she commands, and points to my trousers as she stands over me, placing her feet wide apart.

'You do it,' I mouth.

She needs no further prompting and crawls up the bed to sit astride me, grinding down on my crotch. She drags her nails down my abdomen towards my flies.

Ow!

Fuck this! She's dangerous.

I sit up suddenly, taking her by surprise, and flip her onto her back, straddling her and pinning her arms down on either side of her head. She struggles beneath me, attempting to buck me off.

'Hey!' she protests, glaring up at me.

'I think you need to be restrained. You're dangerous.' My voice is soft as I gauge her reaction.

This could go either way.

Her eyes widen, and I'm not sure if it's fear or excitement.

'Are you?' she whispers.

'Dangerous? Me? No. Not nearly as much as you.' Releasing her, I reach over to the bedside cabinet and from a drawer take out a long silk restraint and a pair of leather cuffs. 'Do you want to play?' I ask, holding up both implements. 'Your choice.'

She gazes up at me, pupils large with lust and anxiety.

'I won't hurt you,' I reassure her. That's not my scene. 'I'll just keep you in line.' But the truth is, I'm worried she's going to hurt me.

A teasing, seductive smile tugs at her mouth. 'The silk,' she says.

I smile and toss the cuffs onto the floor: dominance as a form of self-defence. 'Pick a safe word.'

'Chelsea.'

'Good choice.'

I tie the silk around her left wrist and thread it through the slats of the bed's headboard, and then, taking her right hand, I deftly tie her right wrist to the other end of the restraint. With her arms outstretched, her nails are rendered harmless, and she looks fantastic.

'If you really misbehave, I'll blindfold you, too,' I murmur.

She squirms. 'Will you spank me?' Her voice is less than a whisper.

'If you play nice.'

Oh, this is going to be fun.

She comes quickly and loudly. Screaming and straining against the silken straps.

I sit up between her thighs, my mouth slick and wet, and I flip her over and slap her arse.

'Hang in there,' I mutter, and slip on a condom.

'Hurry up!'

Fuck, is she demanding!

'As you wish,' I growl, and thrust inside her.

I watch the rise and fall of her breasts as she sleeps. Out of habit I go through my ritual of recalling everything I know about the woman I've just fucked. Twice. Leticia. Human-rights lawyer, sexually aggressive. Older than me. Likes to be restrained. Likes it a lot. But forthright, assertive women typically do, in my experience. She's a biter, screams on orgasm. Vocal. Diverting . . . Exhausting.

I wake with a start. In my dream I'd been searching for something elusive, a vision that kept appearing and disappearing, an ethereal vision in blue. Then, just as I'd glimpsed it, I'd fallen into a wide, deep abyss. I shudder.

What the hell was that about?

The pallid winter sun seeps through the windows as reflections from the Thames play on the ceiling. What has woken me?

Leticia.

Boy, she's an animal. She isn't asleep beside me, and I can't hear anyone in the shower. Perhaps she's left already. I listen carefully for any noise within the flat.

It's quiet. I grin. No awkward small talk. The day is looking up until I remember I have a lunch appointment with my mother and my sister. I groan and pull the covers over my head. They'll want to discuss the will.

Bloody hell.

'The Dowager', as Kit referred to her, is a formidable woman. Why the fuck she hasn't gone back to New York, I don't know. Her life is based there, not here.

Something clatters to the floor somewhere in the apartment. I sit up.

Shit. Leticia is still here.

That means conversation. Reluctantly I haul myself out of bed, drag on my nearest pair of jeans, and go to find out if she's as wild in broad daylight as she is in the dark.

I pad down the hallway in my bare feet, but there's no one in the drawing room or the kitchen.

What the fuck?

I turn around at the kitchen entrance and halt. I'm expecting to see Leticia, but a slight young woman stands in the hallway staring at me. Her eyes are large and dark, reminding me of a startled doe, but she's dressed in a ghastly blue housecoat, cheap overwashed jeans, old trainers, and a blue headscarf that conceals her hair.

She says nothing.

'Hi. Who the hell are you?' I ask.

Chapter Four

Zot! He is here, and he is mad.

Alessia freezes as his blazing green eyes meet hers. Tall, lean and half naked, he towers over her. His hair is an unruly chestnut mess with gold highlights that glint beneath the chandelier in the hallway. He is as broad-shouldered as she remembers, but the tattoo on his upper arm is far more intricate than she recalls; all she can distinguish is a wing. A smattering of hair on his chest tapers down over a toned stomach. Then resumes beneath his navel and travels further down into his jeans. The tight black denim is ripped at the knee. But it's the hard line of his full lips and his eyes, the colour of spring, in a handsome, unshaven face that make her look away. Her mouth dries, and she doesn't know if it's from nerves or . . . or . . . from the look of him.

He is so attractive!

Too attractive.

And he's half naked! But why is he so mad? Did she wake him?

No!

He will send her away from the piano.

Panicked, she drops her gaze to the floor as she flounders for something to say and clutches the handle of the broom to keep her upright.

Who the hell is this timid creature standing in my hallway? I'm completely bemused. Have I seen her before? An image from a forgotten dream develops like a Polaroid in my memory, an angel in blue hovering at my bedside. But that was days ago. Could it have been her? And now she's here, rooted to the hallway floor, her impish face pale, her eyes downcast. Her knuckles grow whiter as she clasps the broom handle tighter and tighter, as if it's anchoring her to the Earth. The headscarf conceals her hair, and an oversize, old-fashioned nylon housecoat swamps her small frame. She looks totally out of place.

'Who are you?' I ask again, but in a softer tone, not wanting to alarm her. Wide eyes, the colour of a fine espresso and framed by the longest lashes I've ever seen, look up at me, then back at the floor.

Shit!

One peek from her dark, fathomless eyes and I'm . . . unsettled. She's at least a head shorter than me, perhaps five feet five to my six feet two. Her features are delicate: high cheekbones, an upturned nose, clear fair skin, and pale lips. She looks like she needs a few days in the sun and a good hearty meal.

It's obvious that she's cleaning. But why her? Why here? Has she replaced my old daily? 'Where's Krystyna?' I ask, growing a little frustrated at her silence. Perhaps she's Krystyna's daughter – or granddaughter.

She continues to stare at the floor, her brow furrowed. Her even white teeth chew at her upper lip as she refuses to meet my gaze.

Look at me, I will her. I want to reach forward and tilt her chin up, but as if she reads my mind, she raises her head. Her eyes meet mine, and her tongue darts out, and nervously she licks her upper lip. My whole body tightens in a hot, heavy rush as desire hits me like a demolition ball.

Fuck a duck!

I narrow my eyes as annoyance swiftly follows my desire. What the hell is wrong with me? Why does a woman I've never met have such an effect on me? It's irritating. Beneath fine arched brows, her eyes grow wider, and she takes a step back, fumbling with the broom so that it falls from her hands and clatters onto the floor. She bends with easy, economic grace to pick it up, and when she's standing once more, she fixates on the handle, a slow flush staining her cheeks as she mumbles something unintelligible.

Bloody hell! Am I intimidating the poor girl?

I don't mean to.

I'm annoyed at myself. Not her.

Or maybe it's another reason. 'Perhaps you don't understand me,' I say, more to myself, and I run a hand through my hair as I bring my body to heel. Krystyna's mastery of English extended to the words 'yes' and 'here', which often meant lots of gesticulating on my part when I needed her to undertake tasks that went beyond her usual cleaning routine. This girl is probably Polish, too.

'I am cleaner, Mister,' she whispers, her eyes still downcast and her eyelashes fanned out above her luminous cheeks.

'Where's Krystyna?'

'She has returned to Poland.'

'When?'

'Since last week.'

This is news. Why the hell did I not know this? I liked Krystyna. She'd cleaned for me for three years and knew all my dirty little secrets. And I never got to say goodbye.

Maybe it's temporary. 'Is she coming back?' I ask. The lines in the girl's forehead deepen, but she says nothing, though her eyes flick to my feet. For some unknown reason, this makes me feel self-conscious. Placing both hands on my hips, I step backwards as my bewilderment grows. 'How long have you been here?'

She responds in a breathless, barely audible voice. 'In England?'

'Look at me, please,' I ask. Why is she so reluctant to look up?

Her slim fingers tighten around the broom again, as if she might brandish it as a weapon, then she swallows and raises her head, regarding me with large, liquid brown eyes. Eyes I could drown in. My mouth dries as my body comes to attention again.

Fuck!

'I have been in England since three weeks.' Her voice is clearer and stronger, with an accent I don't recognise, and as she speaks, she pushes her small chin towards me in defiance. Her lips are now rosy, her bottom lip plumper than her top, and she licks the upper one again.

Hell!

I'm aroused once more. I take another step away from her. 'Three weeks?' I mumble, baffled by my reaction to her.

Why is this happening to me?

What is it about her?

She's fucking exquisite, the still, small voice roars in my head.

Yes. For a woman dressed in a nylon housecoat, she's hot.

Concentrate. She hasn't answered my question. 'No. I meant how long have you been here in my flat.'

Where does this girl come from? I rack my brain. Mrs Blake had organised Krystyna through some contact she had. But Krystyna's replacement remains silent.

'You speak English?' I ask, willing her to speak. 'What's your name?'

She frowns, looking at me like I'm an idiot. 'Yes. I speak English. My name is Alessia Demachi. I have been in your apartment since ten o'clock this morning.'

Wow. She really does speak English.

'Right. Well. How do you do, Alessia Demachi. My name is . . .'

What should I say? Trevethick? Trevelyan?

'Maxim.'

She gives me a brief nod, and for a moment I think she might curtsy, but she stands still, grasping the broom and stripping me naked with her anxious gaze.

Suddenly I feel like the walls of the hallway are closing in and suffocating me. I want to flee from this stranger and her soul-searching eyes. 'Well, good to meet you, Alessia. You'd better get on and clean, then.' As an afterthought, I add, 'In fact, you can change the sheets on my bed.' I wave in the general direction of my bedroom. 'You know where the linen is kept, don't you?'

She nods again but still doesn't move.

'I'm going to the gym,' I mutter, though why I'm explaining myself to her I don't know.

As he stalks back down the hallway towards his bedroom, Alessia wilts against the broom and takes a deep, relieved breath. She watches the flex and pull of the muscles on his back – right down to the two dimples that show just above the waistband of his jeans. It's a distracting sight . . . very distracting. He's even more distracting upright than he was lying down. He disappears into his room, and she closes her eyes, her heart sinking.

He didn't ask her to leave, but he may call Magda's friend Agatha and ask her to find someone else to clean his place. He seemed so cross that she had disturbed him, and then he became angrier still.

Why?

Alessia frowns and tries to quell her rising panic as she glances into the living room at the piano.

No. That cannot happen. She will beg him to let her stay if she must. She doesn't want to leave. She can't leave. The piano is her one source of escape. Her only happiness.

And then there's the Mister himself. His honed stomach, his bare feet and his intense eyes sear her imagination. He has the face of an angel, the body of . . . well . . . She blushes. She should not think of such things.

He's so handsome.

No. Stop. Concentrate.

With frantic strokes she continues to sweep the wooden floor of non-existent dirt. She will have to be the best cleaner he's ever had, so he won't want to replace her. With her mind resolved, she goes into the living room to sweep, tidy and polish.

Ten minutes later she hears the front door slam as she finishes plumping the black cushions on the L-shaped couch.

Good. He has gone.

She goes straight to his bedroom to strip the bed. The room is untidy as usual – clothes and strange cuffs on the floor, curtains half open, and the bedding a tangled mess – but she collects all the clothes and strips the bed quickly. She wonders why there's a wide silk ribbon tied to the headboard but unwinds it and places it on his nightstand next to the cuffs. As she throws a clean white sheet on the bed, she wonders what these items are for. She has no idea and doesn't want to hazard a guess. She makes the rest of the bed, then ventures into his bathroom to clean.

I run like I've never run before. I complete my five miles on the treadmill in record time, but I can't stop playing the conversation with the new daily in my mind.

Bugger. Bugger. Bugger.

I bend down and place my hands on my knees, trying to catch my breath. I am running from my fucking daily – cleaner, whatever she calls herself – escaping from her big brown eyes.

No. I'm running from my reaction to her.

Those eyes are going to haunt me for the rest of the day. Standing, I wipe the sweat from my brow, and a vision of her in that headscarf on her knees in front of me comes unwelcome to my mind.

My body clenches.

Again.

And this is just at the thought of her.

Fuck.

Angrily, I rub the sweat off my face with a towel and decide to do some weights. Yes. That should get her out of my mind. I pick up two of the heavier dumbbells and start my routine.

Of course, doing weights gives me space to think. In all honesty, I'm confused by my reaction to her. I can't remember meeting anyone who's had that kind of effect on me.

Perhaps it's stress.

Yes. That's the most logical explanation. I'm grieving Kit's loss and dealing with the aftermath.

Kit, you're a bastard for leaving me with all this responsibility.

It's overwhelming. *Fucking overwhelming.*

I push all thoughts of Kit and *her* out of my mind as I concentrate on my workout and count through my biceps curls.

And I've got lunch with my mother in two hours.

Shit.

Alessia is in the utility room moving wet clothes into the dryer when she hears the front door slam again.

No! He is back.

Glad that she's hidden away in the smallest room in the apartment, she sets up the ironing board and starts ironing the few garments that are ready. Surely he will not come in here. When she finishes the fifth shirt, she hears the door slam again, and she knows that she's on her own once more. It irks her that he's not shouted a goodbye like he did when he thought she was Krystyna, but she shakes off the feeling and finishes the ironing as quickly as she can.

Once done, she goes to check his bedroom to see if he has left it in a mess. Sure enough, his gym clothes are scattered on the floor. Gingerly, she picks up each item. They are all damp with his sweat, but to her surprise she doesn't find this as repellent as she did before she met him. She places the items in his laundry basket and checks the bathroom. The fresh, clean scent of his soap hangs in the air. Closing her eyes, she inhales, and suddenly she's transported back to the tall evergreens that surround her parents' house in Kukës. She savours the fragrance, ignoring her pang of homesickness. London is her home now.

She wipes down the sink and is finished with half an hour to spare. She runs straight to the living room and sits down in front of the piano. As her fingers caress the keys, the strains of Bach's Prelude in C-sharp Major fill the apartment, the notes dancing in vibrant colours into the corners of the room and soothing her troubled soul.

I stride into my mother's favourite restaurant on Aldwych. I'm early, but I don't give a fuck. I need a drink, not only to forget my brush with the new daily but I need some liquid fortification to face my mother.

'Maxim!' I turn, and behind me is the one woman in the world I adore. Maryanne, my younger sister by a year, is walking through the foyer. Her eyes, the same shade as mine, light up when I turn to face her, and she throws her arms around my neck, her red hair flying into my face because she's only a few inches shorter than me.

'Hey, M.A., I've missed you,' I say as I hug her.

'Maxie.' Her voice catches in her throat.

Shit. Not here.

I hug her harder, willing her not to cry, and I'm surprised by the raw emotion that burns my throat. She sniffles, and her eyes are red-rimmed when I release her. This is not like her. She usually takes after our mother, who keeps her emotions under ruthless control. 'I still can't believe he's gone,' she says as she clutches a tissue.

'I know, me neither. Let's sit and get a drink.' I take her elbow, and we follow the hostess into the large wood-panelled restaurant. The place has a classic old-fashioned feel: brass lamps, dark green leather upholstery, crisp white linen and sparkling crystal glasses. The atmosphere buzzes with the chatter of businessmen and women and the clatter of cutlery on fine china. I focus on the sight of the hostess's shapely backside swathed in a tight pencil skirt and the sound of her stiletto heels clicking on the polished tiled floor as she shows us to our table. I hold out Maryanne's chair, and we sit down.

'Two Bloody Marys,' I say to the hostess as she hands us each a menu and gives me a coy look, which I don't return. She might have a fine arse and a cute smile, but I'm not in the mood to play. I'm preoccupied by my encounter with my daily and the memory of anxious dark eyes. I frown, dismissing the thought, and turn my full attention to my sister as the hostess leaves with a disappointed pout.

'When did you get back from Cornwall?' I ask.

'Yesterday.'

'How's the Dowager?'

'Maxim! You know she hates that term.'

I give her an exaggerated sigh. 'Okay, how's the Mothership?'

Maryanne glares at me for a moment, but then her face falls.

Shit.

'Sorry,' I mumble, chastened.

'She's really shaken up, but it's hard to tell. You know what she's like.' Maryanne's eyes cloud, and she looks troubled. 'I think there's something she's not telling us.'

I nod. I know only too well. My mother rarely reveals a chink in her polished armour. She hadn't wept at Kit's funeral; she'd been the epitome of grace under fire. Brittle but gracious, as always. I hadn't wept either. I'd been too busy nursing one hell of a hangover.

I swallow and change the subject. 'When do you go back to work?'

'Monday,' Maryanne answers with a small, sad twist of her mouth.

Of all the Trevelyan children, it's Maryanne who has excelled academically. From Wycombe Abbey School, she'd gone up to read medicine at Corpus Christi, Oxford, and is now a junior doctor at the Royal Brompton Hospital, specialising in cardiothoracic medicine. She had followed her vocation, a calling that was born the day our father suffered a massive coronary and died from a heart attack. She was fifteen years old – and she wanted to save him. Our father's death rocked each of us differently, and Kit most of all, given that he'd had to drop out of college and assume the earldom. Me, I lost my only parental ally.

'How's Caro?' she asks.

'Grieving. Pissed off that Kit didn't leave her anything in his will, stupid bastard,' I growl.

'Who's a stupid bastard?' A clipped mid-Atlantic voice demands. Rowena, Dowager Countess of Trevethick, towers above us, auburn-haired, groomed, and composed in her immaculate navy Chanel suit and pearls.

I stand. 'Rowena,' I say, and give her a detached peck on her upturned cheek, then hold out her chair for her to sit.

'Is that any way to greet your grieving mother, Maxim?' Rowena scolds as she sits down and places her Birkin handbag on the floor beside her. She reaches across the table and clasps Maryanne's hand. 'Hello, darling, I didn't hear you go out.'

'I just needed some fresh air, Mother,' Maryanne replies as she returns our mother's squeeze.

Rowena, Countess of Trevethick, kept her title in spite of her divorce from our father. She spends most of her time between New York, where she lives and likes to play, and London, where she edits *Dernier Cri*, the glossy women's magazine.

'I'll have a glass of the Chablis,' she says to the waiter as he delivers two Bloody Marys to the table. She arches a brow in disapproval as we both take long sips.

She is still impossibly slim and impossibly beautiful, especially through a lens. She was the 'It Girl' of her generation and had become the muse of many a photographer, including my father, the Eleventh Earl of Trevethick. He was devoted to her; his title and money had seduced her into marriage, but when she left him, he never recovered. Four years after their divorce, he died of a broken heart.

I study her through hooded eyes. Her face is baby-smooth – no doubt as a result of her latest chemical peel. The woman is obsessed with maintaining her youth, and she only deviates from her rigorous diet of vegetable juices or whatever her latest food fad is with the odd glass of wine. There is no doubting that my mother is beautiful, but she's as duplicitous as she is stunning – and my poor father paid the price.

'I understand you've met with Rajah,' she says directly to me.

'Yes.'

'And?' She glares at me in her slightly myopic way, because she's far too vain to wear glasses.

'It's all in trust to me.'

'And Caroline?'

'Nothing.'

'I see. Well, we can't let the poor girl starve.'

'We?' I ask.

Rowena flushes. 'You,' she says, her voice frigid. 'You can't let the poor girl starve. On the other hand, she has her trust fund, and when her father shuffles off his mortal coil, she'll inherit a fortune. Kit chose wisely in that regard.'

'Unless her stepmother disinherits her,' I retort, and take another much-needed sip of Bloody Mary.

My mother purses her lips. 'Why don't you set her to work – maybe the Mayfair development? She has a good eye for interior design, and she'll need the distraction.'

'I think we should let Caroline decide what she wants to do.' I fail to keep the resentment out of my voice. This is my mother's usual high-handed manner in dealing with the family that she deserted many years ago.

'Are you happy with her staying at Trevelyan House?' she asks, ignoring my tone.

'Rowena, I'm not about to make her homeless.'

'Maximilian, would you mind addressing me as "Mother"!'

'When you start behaving like one, I'll take it into consideration.'

'Maxim,' Maryanne warns, and her eyes flash a fiery green. Feeling like a rebuked child, I clamp my mouth shut and scrutinise the menu before I say something I'll regret.

Rowena continues, ignoring my rudeness, 'We'll need to finalise all the details for the memorial service. I was thinking we could do this just before Easter. I'll get one of my lead writers to do Kit's eulogy, unless—' She pauses as her voice cracks, causing both me and Maryanne to look up from our menus in surprise. Her eyes grow moist, and for the first time since she buried her eldest child, she looks her age. She clutches a monogrammed handkerchief and brings it to her lips as she composes herself.

Bugger.

I feel like a shit. She's lost her eldest son . . . her favourite child.

'Unless?' I prompt.

'You or Maryanne could write it,' she whispers with an uncharacteristic, beseeching look at both of us.

'Sure,' Maryanne says. 'I'll do it.'

'No. I should do it. I'll expand on the eulogy I did for his funeral. Shall we order lunch?' I ask, wanting to change the subject and feeling uncomfortable at my mother's unusual display of emotion.

Rowena picks at her salad while Maryanne chases the last of her omelette around her plate with her knife and fork.

'Caroline said she might be pregnant,' I announce as I take another mouthful of chateaubriand.

Rowena's head comes up quickly, and she narrows her eyes.

'She did say they were trying,' Maryanne adds.

'Well, if she is, it might be the only chance I get to have a grandchild and for this family to secure the earldom for another generation.' Rowena casts an accusing look at both of us.

'That would make you a grandmother,' I say drily, disregarding the rest of her comment. 'How will that go down with your latest cute conquest in New York?'

Rowena's propensity for young men, sometimes younger than her youngest son, is renowned. She glowers at me as I take another bite of my steak, but I hold her glare, daring her to say anything. Strangely, for the first time ever, I feel as though I have the upper hand with my mother. It's a novelty; so much of my adolescence was spent striving and failing to gain her approval.

Maryanne scowls at me. I shrug and slice another piece of delicious steak and pop it into my mouth.

'Neither you nor Maryanne shows any sign of settling down, and God forbid that the estates should pass to your father's brother. Cameron's a lost cause,' Rowena grumbles, choosing to ignore my insolence. My encounter with Alessia Demachi springs unbidden into my head, and I frown. I glance at Maryanne, and she's frowning, too, and staring at her uneaten food.

Oh?

'What about the young man you met when you were skiing in Whistler?' Rowena asks Maryanne.

It's dusk when I return to my flat. Drained and a little drunk, I have endured a forensic cross-examination from my mother on the status of all the estates, the London leasehold and rental properties, and the apartment refurbishment in Mayfair, not to mention the value of the Trevethick portfolio. I wanted to remind her that it's none of her fucking business, but I feel a novel sense of pride that I was able to answer each of her questions in detail. Even Maryanne was impressed. Oliver Macmillan had briefed me well.

As I flop down on the sofa in front of the large TV in my spotless, empty flat, my mind wanders as it has all day, back to the conversation I had this morning with the dark-eyed daily.

Where is she now?

How long will she be in the UK?

What does she look like without the shapeless housecoat on?

What colour is her hair? Dark like her eyebrows?

How old is she? She looks young. Too young, maybe.

Too young for what?

I shift uncomfortably in my seat and click through the TV

channels. Perhaps my reaction to her was a one-off. I mean, she looked like a nun. Maybe I have a thing for nuns. I laugh to myself at the ridiculous thought. My phone buzzes, and it's a text from Caroline.

How was lunch?

Tiring. The Dowager
was her usual self.

I'll be the dowager
if you get married! ☹

Why is she telling me this? Besides, I have no interest in marrying anyone. Well . . . not at the moment. My mother's tirade about grandchildren comes to mind, and I shake my head. Kids. No. Just no. Not yet anyway.

That's not happening
anytime soon!

Good.
What are you doing?

Home watching TV.

Are you OK?
Can I come over?

The last thing I want or need is Caroline messing with my head or any other part of my anatomy.

I'm not alone.

It's a small white lie.

You're still whoring, I see. :P

You know me well.

Good night, Caro.

I stare at the phone waiting for her response, but it remains silent so I turn my attention back to the television, only to find there's nothing I want to watch. I switch it off.

Restless, I sit down at my desk and open Mail on the iMac. There are a few emails from Oliver about various estate issues that I don't want to deal with on a Friday evening. They can wait until Monday. I check the time, and I'm surprised that it's only 8:00 p.m., too early to go out, and the thought of a crowded club doesn't appeal to me right now.

Feeling cooped up but reluctant to leave my flat, I wander over to the piano and take a seat. A composition I'd started weeks and weeks ago sits neglected on the rest. I follow the notes, the melody sounding in my head, and before I know it, my fingers are pressing the keys and playing the tune. The image of a young girl in blue with dark, dark eyes that strip me bare pops into my head. New notes form in a flurry, and I continue to improvise, playing beyond where my composition had stalled.

Bloody hell!

In a rare rush of excitement, I stop, fish my phone out of my pocket, and find the voice-memo app. Hitting the RECORD button, I begin again. The notes ring out through the room. Evocative. Melancholic. Stirring me. Inspiring me.

I am cleaner, Mister.

Yes. I speak English. My name is Alessia Demachi.

Alessia.

When I look at my watch, it's after midnight. Stretching my arms above my head, I examine the manuscript in front of me. It's complete. I've written a whole piece, and I am overwhelmed with a sense of achievement. How long have I been trying to do this? And all it took was meeting my new daily. I shake my head, and for once I go to bed early and alone.

Chapter Five

It's with trepidation that Alessia unlocks the door to the apartment with the piano. Her heart sinks when she's met with the unnerving silence of the alarm. The hush means that the confusing, green-eyed Mister is in residence. He has invaded her dreams ever since she'd seen him sprawled naked on his bed. But during her weekend, in quiet moments, all she'd been able to think about was him. She doesn't understand why, though perhaps it's the brief, penetrating stare he gave her when he towered over her in the hallway or because he's handsome and tall and lean, with dimples on his back, above his muscled, athletic behind—

Stop!

Her wayward thoughts are out of control.

Quietly, she slips off her wet boots and socks, then scampers in her bare feet down the hallway through the kitchen. The counter is littered with beer bottles and take-away boxes, but Alessia scuttles into the safety of the utility room. She props her boots on the radiator along with her socks in the hope they might dry out before she leaves.

Peeling off her wet hat and gloves, she hangs them on the hook beside the boiler, then removes the anorak that Magda gave her. She places it on the same hook and frowns as water drips onto the tiled floor. Her jeans are soaked from the torrential rain, too. She shivers as she removes them and struggles into her housecoat, grateful that the plastic bag has kept it dry. The hem falls to below her knees, so that she's not immodest without her jeans. Peeking into the kitchen, she checks that he's not there. He's probably still asleep, so she pops her sodden jeans into the dryer and switches it on. At least they'll be dry when she goes home. Her feet are red and itch with cold, so she grabs a dry towel from the pile of clean laundry and rubs them both vigorously, massaging life back into her toes. Once they're warm, she slips on her sneakers.

'Alessia?'

Zot!

The Mister is awake! What does he want?

As quickly as her chilled fingers will let her, she pulls her scarf from the plastic bag and ties it around her head, conscious that her plaited hair is also wet. Taking a deep breath, she exits the utility room to find him standing in the kitchen. She wraps her arms around herself, trying to find some warmth.

'Hi,' he says, and smiles.

Alessia glances at him. His smile is dazzling, lighting up his handsome face and his emerald eyes. She looks away, blinded by his good looks and embarrassed by her creeping blush.

But she feels a little warmer.

He had been so cross the last time she saw him – what has brought about this change of heart?

'Alessia?' he says again.

'Yes, Mister,' she answers, keeping her eyes lowered. At least he is dressed this time.

'I just wanted to say hi.'

She peeks up at him but doesn't understand what he wants. His smile isn't as broad this time, and his brow is furrowed.

'Hi,' she says, uncertain what's expected of her.

He nods and shuffles from one foot to the other, hesitant. She thinks he might say something further, but he turns and leaves the kitchen.

What an idiot I am! I mimic 'Hi' to myself in ridicule. I've thought of nothing but this girl all weekend, and the best I can come up with is, 'I just wanted to say hi'?

What the fuck is wrong with me?

I wander back to my bedroom and notice a trail of wet footprints on the hallway floor.

Did she walk barefoot in the rain? Surely not!

My room is gloomy, and the view across the Thames is drab and uninspiring. The rain is lashing down outside. It had been pelting against the window early this morning and the noise had woken me. *Shit.* She must have walked through this atrocious weather. Again I wonder where she lives and how far she has to come. I had hoped to engage her in some conversation this morning to find out these details, but I can tell I make her uncomfortable.

Is it me or is it men in general?

It's a troubling thought. Maybe *I'm* the one who's uncomfortable. After all, she chased me out of the flat last week and the idea that I fled to avoid her is disconcerting. I resolve not to let it happen again.

The fact is, she's inspired me. The whole weekend I've immersed myself in my music. It's provided a distraction from all my new-found and unwanted responsibility and a respite from my grief – or maybe I've found a way to channel my grief . . . I don't know. I have three pieces completed, sketchy ideas for two more, and I'm tempted to put lyrics to one of them. I've ignored my phone, my email – everyone – and for once in my life I've found solace in my own company. It's been a revelation. Who knew I could be so productive? What I don't understand is why she's affected me like this when we've only exchanged a few words. It doesn't make sense to me, but I don't want to overthink it.

I pick up my phone from the bedside table and look down at the bed. The bedding is in complete disarray.

Bloody hell, I'm a slob.

Hastily, I make the bed. From the pile of clothes discarded on my sofa, I grab a black-hooded sweatshirt and slip it on over my T-shirt. It's chilly. With wet feet she's probably cold, too. In the hallway I stop and turn the thermostat up by a few degrees. I don't like the idea of her feeling the cold.

She comes out of the kitchen carrying an empty laundry basket and a plastic caddy full of cleaning fluids and cloths. Head down, she walks right past me towards my bedroom. I regard her retreating figure in the shapeless housecoat: long pale legs, a gentle sway of slim hips . . . are those bright pink pants I can see through the nylon? From beneath the headscarf a rich brunette plait snakes down her back to just above the line of her pink underwear, and it swings from side to side as she walks. I know I should look away, but I'm distracted by her underwear. They cover her backside and come up to her waist. They are possibly the largest knickers I've seen on a woman. And my body stirs like I'm a thirteen-year-old boy.

Fuck! I groan inwardly, feeling like a pervert, and resist the urge to follow her. Instead I head into the drawing room, where I sit down at my computer to work through my emails from Oliver and ignore my lust and my daily, Alessia Demachi.

Alessia is surprised to find that his bed has been made. Every time she's been to his apartment, this room has always been a mess. There is still a pile of clothes on the sofa, but it looks tidier than she's ever seen it. She opens the curtains fully and stares out at the river. 'Thames.' She whispers the word aloud, her voice wavering a little.

It's dark and grey like the naked trees on the opposite bank . . . not like the Drin. Not like home. Here it's urban and crowded, so crowded. Back at home she was surrounded by fertile countryside and snow-capped mountains. She sweeps away the painful thought of home. She is here to do a job – a job she wants because it comes with the added bonus of the piano. She wonders if he's going to be here all day, and the thought that he might bothers her. His presence will keep her from playing her favourite pieces.

But on the plus side, she gets to see him.

The man who's been dominating her dreams.

She has to stop thinking about him. *Now.* With a heavy heart, she begins to hang some of the scattered clothes in his walk-in closet. Those that she thinks need washing she places in the laundry basket.

The aroma of evergreen and sandalwood lingers in his bathroom. It's a pleasant, masculine scent. She takes a moment to inhale deeply and savour it like she did before. His striking eyes come to mind . . . and his broad shoulders . . . and flat belly. She sprays the bathroom mirror with Windolene and rubs energetically.

Stop! Stop! Stop!

He's her employer, and he would never be interested in her. After all, she's just his cleaner.

Her last job in his bedroom is to empty the bin. To her disbelief she finds the basket empty. There are no used condoms. She places it back beside his nightstand, and for some inexplicable reason the empty basket makes her smile.

Gathering up the laundry and her cleaning materials, she gazes for a moment at the two monochrome photographs on the wall. Both are nudes. In one a woman is kneeling, her skin pale and translucent. The soles of her feet, her behind and the graceful curve of her back are all visible, and she holds her blond hair piled up on her head; a few stray tresses kiss her neck. The model, from this angle anyway, is beautiful. The second photograph is a close-up and shows the contour of a woman's neck, her hair swept aside, and the arch of her spine from the first few vertebrae down to her backside. Her ebony skin is luminous, caressed by the light. She's stunning. Alessia sighs. Judging by these photographs, he must like women, and she wonders if he is the photographer. Maybe one day he might take her photograph. She shakes her head at her fanciful thoughts and returns to the kitchen to tackle the chaos of take-away boxes, empty beer bottles, and washing-up.

I've set aside all the condolence letters and emails to answer at a later date – I cannot face them yet. And how the fuck did Kit manage to get his head around farming subsidies and animal husbandry and all the other crap that goes with cultivating and grazing thousands of acres of land? For a fleeting moment, I wish I'd taken farm management or business studies at university, rather than fine art and music.

Kit had been reading economics at the LSE when our father died. Ever the dutiful son, he'd dropped out of the LSE and enrolled in the Duchy of Cornwall's university to study farming and estate management. With thirty thousand acres to oversee, I now understand that it was a sensible decision. Kit was always sensible, except when it came to riding his motorbike in the middle of winter through Trevethick's freezing lanes. I put my head in my hands as I remember his broken body lying in the mortuary.

Why, Kit, why? I ask for the thousandth time.

The worsening weather through the glass wall reflects my mood. I stand and walk over to look at the view. On the river there are a couple of barges heading in opposite directions, a police launch cruising east, and the river bus heading to Cadogan Pier. I scowl at the scene. During all the time I've lived this close to the pier, I've never taken the river bus. As a child I'd always hoped my mother would take me and Maryanne, but it never happened. She was always too busy. Always. And she never instructed our various nannies to take us. That's another grievance I have against Rowena. Of course, Kit wasn't with us then – he was already at boarding school.

Shaking my head, I walk around the piano and spy the sheet music I've been working on all weekend. The sight of the pages lifts my mood, and to take a break from my computer, I sit down to play.

Of the three kitchens Alessia cleans, this is her favourite. The wall, base cupboards and worktops are made of pale blue glass which is easy to wipe down. It's sleek and uncluttered – so different from the haphazard rural kitchen of her parents' home. She checks the oven, just in case the Mister has baked something, but she finds it's still pristine. Alessia suspects it has never been used.

She is drying the last plate when the music begins. She stops, recognising the melody immediately. It's from the manuscript she's seen so many times on his piano, but the melody goes further than she's read, the notes soft and sad, falling in mournful blues and greys around her.

This she has to see.

With quiet care she places the plate on the worktop and sneaks out of the kitchen towards the living room. She peers in and sees him at the piano. Eyes closed, he's feeling the music, every note expressed on his face. As she watches him – his brow furrowed, head tilted, lips parted – he takes her breath away.

She's captivated.

By him.

By the music.

He's talented.

The piece is sad, full of longing and grief, and the notes echo through her head in subtler tones of blue and grey now that she's watching him. He really is the most handsome man she's ever seen. He's even more handsome than— *No!*

Ice-blue eyes stare at me. Furious.

No. Stop thinking about that monstrous man!

She halts the memory. It's too painful. And she concentrates on the Mister as the melancholic melody draws to its end. Before he spots her, Alessia tiptoes back to the kitchen – she doesn't want to make him cross again by being caught peeking and not working.

As she finishes washing the worktop, she replays his composition in her head. And now the only room she has left to clean is the living room – where he is.

Plucking up her courage, she grabs some polish and a cloth, ready to face him. She hovers at the entrance while he stares at his computer. He glances up and sees her, his face registering pleased surprise.

'It is okay, Mister?' she asks, and waves the can of polish in the direction of the room.

'Sure. Come in. Do what you need to do, Alessia. And my name's Maxim.'

She gives him a quick smile and starts with the sofa, plumping the cushions and sweeping the odd crumb onto the floor with her hand.

Well, this is distracting . . .

How can I possibly concentrate with her moving about in such close proximity? I pretend to read the revised cost-to-complete for the remodelling of the Mayfair mansion blocks, but really I'm watching her. She moves with such easy, sensuous grace; bending over the sofa, lithe, toned arms reaching out and delicate, long-fingered hands cupping the crumbs from the seat cushions and brushing them off. A frisson runs through me, and my whole body is suddenly humming with a delicious tension, attuned to her presence in the room.

Could this be any more illicit? She's so close but so unattainable. She moves to plump the black scatter cushions on the couch, and her housecoat swings forward and stretches out across her backside, betraying the pink underwear beneath.

My breathing shallows, and I have to suppress a groan.

I'm a fucking pervert.

She finishes with the sofa, and her eyes stray towards me. I endeavour to look engrossed in the spreadsheet in my hand while the hairs on the back of my neck rise to attention. Taking the can of polish, she sprays some onto the cloth she's holding and heads to the piano. With another quick, anxious glance at me, she begins the slow process of buffing it to a brilliant shine. She stretches across it, the housecoat rising above the backs of her knees.

Oh, God!

With a deliberate and even pace, she works her way around the piano, buffing and polishing, her breathing becoming faster and harder with the exertion. It's agonising. I close my eyes and imagine how I could elicit the same response from her.

Shit. I cross my legs to hide my body's natural reaction. This is getting farcical. She's just cleaning my fucking piano.

She continues to dust the keyboard, though the keys make no sound. Her eyes shoot to me again, and I quickly look at the figures on the spreadsheet, which swim on the page, making no sense. When I dare to peer up at her, she's bending down, her face pensive, and she seems to be appraising the manuscript that sits on the music rest. She's looking at my composition, and her brow creases as if she's concentrating hard.

Can she read music?

Is she reading my score?

She looks up and meets my gaze. Her eyes widen with embarrassment, and her tongue escapes from her mouth to lick her upper lip as a rosy flush stains her cheeks.

Fuck.

Averting her eyes, she bobs down behind the piano, presumably to dust the legs or the stool.

I cannot bear it.

My phone rings, startling me. It's Oliver.

'Hi,' I say into the phone, my voice hoarse, and I've never been so grateful for the interruption. I have to get out of the drawing room.

Hell, I promised myself that I wouldn't let her chase me out again.

'Trevethick?'

'Yes. Oliver. What is it?'

'We have a planning issue which I think is going to need your attention.'

I stalk into the hallway as Oliver drones on about soffits and load-bearing walls within the Mayfair development.

When he leaves the room, it's as if a storm has passed overhead to wreak havoc elsewhere – in the hallway, perhaps. Alessia breathes a sigh of relief, grateful that he's gone. She hears him on the phone, his voice deep but melodious. She doesn't think she's ever been so acutely aware of someone else before.

She must stop thinking about him and concentrate on cleaning! She finishes dusting the piano, though she can't shake the uncanny feeling that he'd been watching her while she cleaned.

No. That's impossible.

Why would he be watching me?

Maybe he's checking on her cleaning capabilities like Mrs Kingsbury. Alessia smiles at the silly idea and realises she feels a great deal warmer than she did when she arrived. She isn't sure if the heat is within the room or within herself.

Warmed by his presence.

Her ludicrous train of thought elicits another smile. As he's out of the room, she seizes the opportunity to run and fetch the vacuum cleaner. The Mister is at the end of the hall leaning against the wall, all long legs and restless foot-tapping. He is talking into the phone in a low tone, but he watches her as she goes into the kitchen. She carries the vacuum cleaner into the living room to find him back at his desk but still talking on the phone. He rises when he sees her. 'Hold on a minute, Oliver. Go ahead,' he says to her, and he waves in the direction of the room, granting Alessia permission to vacuum as he leaves once more. He's undone the black hoodie he's wearing. Underneath she sees a grey V-neck T-shirt that has a black winged coronet and LA 1781 written on it. She flushes as she notices a little chest hair peeking through the top of the V. In her mind she hears her mother's voice scolding her in that tone she has: *Alessia! What are you doing?*

I am looking at a man, Mama.

A man I find attractive.

A man who makes my blood run hotter.

She imagines her mother's scandalised expression, and it makes her smile.

Oh, Mama, it's so different here in England. Men. Women. How they behave. Their interaction.

Alessia's mind goes to a darker place. To *him.*

No. Do not think of that man.

She's safe now, here in London with the Mister. And she must concentrate on keeping her job.

The vacuum cleaner is a make called Henry. Painted on his red cylinder are two big eyes and a smile. Whenever she sees Henry, she can't help but smile. She plugs him into the wall and begins to vacuum the rug and the wooden floor. Fifteen minutes later she's finished.

The Mister is not in the hallway as she pulls Henry back to his sleeping place in the utility-room cupboard. Alessia gives him a friendly pat before shutting the cupboard door and heading into the kitchen.

'Hi,' the Mister says as he comes into the kitchen. 'I have to go out. Your money is on the console table. You can lock up and set the alarm?'

She nods, so blinded by his broad smile that she has to stare down at the floor. But inside her, joy unfurls like a morning glory because he's leaving and she'll be able to play the piano.

He hesitates for a moment before holding out a large black umbrella.

'You're welcome to borrow this. It's still raining cats and dogs outside.'

Cats and dogs?

Alessia is stunned. She glances quickly at his face, and her heart skips a beat at his warm smile and this generous gesture. She takes it from him. 'Thank you,' she whispers.

'You're welcome. Until Wednesday, Alessia,' he says, and he leaves her alone in the kitchen. A few moments later, she hears the front door close.

Alessia stares at the umbrella. It's old-fashioned, with a wooden handle and a gold collar. It is exactly what she needs. Marvelling at the Mister's generosity, she wanders into the living room and sits down at the piano. She props the umbrella up against the end of the keyboard and in honour of the terrible weather begins to play Chopin's 'Raindrop' Prelude.

I positively bask and glow in the wake of Alessia's whispered 'Thank you'. I am ridiculously pleased with myself. I'm finally able to help her with this small gesture. I'm not accustomed to doing good deeds – though I probably have an ulterior motive for my kindness, a motive I don't want to analyse too deeply right now, as it might confirm I'm the shallow fucking bastard I think I am. Still, I feel good about this gesture, and it's a novel feeling.

With renewed energy I bypass the lift and fly down the main staircase to the ground floor. I'm reluctant to leave, but I have a meeting with Oliver and various contractors at the Mayfair development. Glancing down at my clothes, I hope they don't expect me to arrive in a suit. That's just not my style.

No. That was Kit's thing, and he had a wardrobe full of bespoke Savile Row suits to prove it.

Outside, I dodge the raindrops and hail a cab.

'I think that went well,' says Oliver. I nod as we walk through the new limestone atrium of one of the rebuilt mansion blocks. Workmen in high-vis jackets and yellow hard hats go about their business around us as we make our way to the boarded front of the building. The dust in the air claws at my throat. I need a drink.

'You've got a flair for this, Trevethick. I think the contractor liked your suggestions.'

'Oliver. It's Maxim. Please use my name. You used to. Before.'

'Very good, my lord.'

'For fuck's sake.'

'Maxim.' Oliver gives me a brief smile. 'We'll need to get an interior designer to source everything for the show apartment, probably within the next month. I've compiled a list of three that Kit liked to use.'

Kit? Kit was Kit. Why can't I be Maxim?

'Caroline might be a good idea,' I say.

'Oh? Lady Trevethick?'

'My mother suggested her.'

Oliver bristles.

Oh? What does Oliver have against Caroline? Or is he bridling against Rowena? She often has that effect on people.

'I'll talk to Caroline, but send me the names of the others and some examples of their work,' I respond.

Oliver nods, and I remove my hard hat and hand it to him.

'Until tomorrow,' he says, and pushes open the rickety door of the temporary wooden hoarding that hides the facade of the building.

The rain has finally stopped, but it's dark. I pull up the collar of my coat and wait for a cab while I decide whether to go to my club or go home.

Walking around the baby grand piano, I think about Alessia stretched across it while she was buffing the ebony to a glossy shine. It gleams under the chandelier. Who would have thought I'd be so attracted to a woman in a nylon housecoat and large pink panties?

How could she have worked her way under my skin in such a short time? I know nothing about her, except she's unlike any woman I've ever met. The women in my life are bold and confident and know what they want and how to ask for it. She's not like that. Demure and totally focused on her job, Alessia seems reluctant to engage with me . . . almost as if she wants to be invisible. She confounds me. Her shy acceptance of the umbrella comes to mind and makes me smile. She was so surprised and appreciative, and I wonder what her life must be like that she's so grateful for such a simple gesture.

I sit on the piano stool and read through my first manuscript, recalling her face as she pored over the score. Perhaps she reads music. Maybe she even plays. And part of me wants to know what she thinks of my composition. But I realise I'm just speculating. My only certainty right now is the dull ache in my groin.

Fuck it. Go out and get laid.

But instead I stay at the piano, playing each song over and over in turn.

Alessia lies on the small fold-out bed in the box room in Magda's house. Her mind is churning, she has so much to do – but her thoughts return once again to the green-eyed Mister. She sees him at the piano. His eyes closed, his brow furrowed, and his mouth slack as he feels the music – and later his warm expression as he hands her the umbrella. His hair rumpled and his full lips curved in an inviting smile. She wonders what they would be like to kiss.

Her hand moves down her body, over her breast.

He could kiss her here.

She gasps, embracing her fantasy, and her hand moves further down, and she imagines that it's his hand on her.

Touching her.

Here.

She starts to caress herself, stifling her moans, mindful of the thin walls of her room.

She thinks of him as her body builds.

Climbing.

Higher.

His face.

His back.

His long legs.

She climbs further.

His taut behind.

His flat stomach.

She groans as she comes, and, exhausted, she falls asleep.
Only to dream of him.

I toss and turn in my sleep.

She stands in the doorway. A vision in blue.
Come in. Lie with me. I want you.
But she turns, and she's in my drawing room. Polishing the piano.
She's wearing nothing but pink panties.
I reach over to touch her, but she disappears.

And I wake.

Fuck.

I'm hard. Painfully so.

Hell. I need to get out more.

I take quick care of myself.

When was the last time I did this? I need to get laid. Tomorrow. That's what I'll do. I turn over and fall into a fitful sleep.

The following afternoon Oliver is taking me through the accounts for each of the estates. Our offices are just off Berkeley Square in a Georgian house that was converted into offices during the 1980s by my father. The building is owned by the Trevethick estate and houses two other companies on the upper floors.

I'm trying to concentrate on the numbers we're discussing, but I'm conscious that the door to Kit's office is ajar. It's distracting. I cannot bring myself to work in there yet. I can almost hear him talking on the phone or laughing at one of my poor jokes or berating Oliver about some transgression. I half expect him to bound in off the street. He was so at ease in this world and in charge of his domain. He made it look effortless.

But I know he envied my freedom.

It's okay for you fucking your way through London, Spare. Some of us have to work for a living.

I stand over Kit's lifeless, fractured body with the A&E consultant.

Yes. This is him, I confirm.

Thank you, Lord Trevethick, she murmurs.

It was the first time anyone had used the title . . .

'So I think we can leave things as they are for the next quarter and then review,' Oliver says, dragging me back into the present. 'Though you should really go and visit the estates.'

'Yes. I should.'

At some point . . .

I am only vaguely aware of the recent history of the three estates, but I know that through the good stewardship of my grandfather, my father and my brother, all of them are profitable. Unlike many of our peers, the Trevelyans are not struggling for money.

Angwin House, set in the Cotswolds in Oxfordshire, is thriving. Open to the public, it has a vast garden centre, a children's jungle gym and petting zoo, a tearoom, and open pastures for the general public to enjoy. Tyok in Northumberland is rented out lock, stock and barrel to a rich American who fancies himself a lord. Kit and Oliver often speculated as to why he hadn't bought his own stately home, and now I'm wondering the same. Tresyllian Hall in Cornwall, on the other hand, is one of the largest organic farms in the United Kingdom. John, my father, the eleventh Earl of Trevethick, had pioneered organic farming while all his contemporaries had sneered at his initiative. More recently, to diversify the Trevethick portfolio and increase revenues, Kit had conceived and built a development of luxury holiday houses on the edge of the estate. They are in demand, especially in the summer.

'Now, we need to discuss how *you* intend to use the estates going forward and the level of staffing you'll need.'

'Oh?'

My heart sinks, and I struggle to remain engaged as Oliver drones on. My mind wanders. Tomorrow Alessia will be back. She's the only staff member I'm interested in at the moment, and for all the wrong reasons. This morning's punishing workout in the gym has done little to lessen my fascination with her.

I'm enthralled, and I don't even know the girl.

My phone buzzes, and I have a text from Caroline. As I read her words, my scalp tingles and my throat tightens.

I'm not pregnant. :'(

I have nothing of Kit's.

Not even his child.

Shit! My grief rises from nowhere, ambushing me.

'Oliver, we're going to have to call it a day. Something's come up.'

'Yes, sir,' Oliver responds. 'Tomorrow?'

'Yeah. Why don't you come to the flat tomorrow, mid-morning?'

'Will do, my— Maxim.'

'Good. Thank you.'

I type out a reply to Caroline.

I'm coming over.

No. I want to go out.

Let's get drunk.

OK. Where?

Are you home?

No. At the office.

Okay. I'll join you in town.

Loulou's?

No. Soho House.
Greek Street.
I'll know fewer people.

I'll see you there.

The private members' club is crowded, but I manage to find a table on the second floor near the blazing fire. I prefer the intimacy of 5 Hertford Street, which I consider my club – but I'm a member of Soho House too, as is Caroline. I take a seat, and I don't have to wait long before she appears. She looks tired, and sad, and thin. Her mouth is turned down and her eyes clouded and puffy. Her blond bob is dull and unkempt, and she's dressed in jeans and a sweater. Kit's sweater. This is not the effervescent Caroline I know. My heart aches as she approaches. I see my own grief engraved on her face.

I stand but say nothing as she walks into my arms, and I hold her close.

She sniffles.

'Hey,' I whisper against her hair.

'Life's shit,' she murmurs.

'I know.' I hope my tone is soothing. 'Do you want to sit? If you sit facing me, no one will see that you're upset.'

'Do I look that bad?' She sounds offended, though a little amused. It's a glimpse of the Caroline I know. I kiss her forehead.

'Never, darling Caro.'

She shrugs out of my hold. 'You charmer,' she grumbles, though I can tell she isn't angry. She sits down in the velvet chair facing me.

'What would you like to drink?'

'A Soho Mule.'

'Good choice.'

I signal the waiter and order.

'You've been a recluse this weekend,' Caroline says.

'I've been busy.'

'On your own.'

'Yes,' I say, and it feels good not to lie.

'What is it, Maxim?'

'What do you mean?' I give her a level I-don't-know-what-you're-talking-about stare.

'Have you met someone?' she asks.

What the hell!

I blink as an image of Alessia stretching over my piano and wearing nothing but pink panties comes to mind.

'You have!' Caroline says, startled.

I shift in my seat and shake my head. 'No.' My denial is emphatic.

Caroline raises a brow. 'You're lying.'

Fuck. Not emphatic enough.

'How can you tell?' I ask, as ever daunted by her ability to cut through my bullshit.

'I couldn't, but you always cave so easily. Tell me.'

Damn!

'There's nothing to tell. I spent the weekend alone.'

'That speaks volumes in itself.'

'Caro, we're each dealing with Kit's absence in our own way.'

'And . . . what are you not telling me?'

I sigh. 'Do you really want me to talk about this?'

'Yes,' she says, and I notice the wicked gleam in her eye, reminding me that the real Caroline is not far away.

'There is someone. But she doesn't know I exist.'

'Seriously?'

'Yes. Seriously. It's nothing. Just a flight of fancy.'

Caroline frowns. 'This is not like you. You're never distracted by one of your, um . . . conquests.'

I can't help my hollow laugh. 'She's not a conquest – not by any stretch of my imagination.'

She can barely look at me!

The waiter arrives with our drinks.

'When did you last eat?' I ask.

Caroline shrugs, and I shake my head. 'You must be driving Mrs Blake crazy. Let's eat. May we have the menu?' I ask the waiter, who nods and scuttles away.

I raise my glass to hers. 'To absent loved ones.' I hope we can change the subject.

'To Kit,' she whispers, and we smile sadly at each other, bonded by our love for the same man.

It is two o'clock in the morning when we return, inebriated, to my flat. Caroline is reluctant to go home. *I don't* want *to go. It's not home without Kit.*

I cannot argue with her.

We both stagger into the hallway, and I enter the code into the alarm, silencing the incessant beeping.

'Do you have any blow?' Caroline slurs.

'No. Not today.'

'What have you got to drink?'

'I think you've had enough.'

She gives me a crooked, drunken smile. 'Are you taking care of me?'

'I'll always take care of you, Caro. You know that.'

'Then take me to bed, Maxim.' She throws her arms around my neck, her face raised with blurry expectation and her unfocused eyes intent on my mouth.

Fuck. I grab her shoulders to hold her back. 'No. I'll put you to bed.'

'What do you mean?' Caroline scowls.

'You're intoxicated.'

'And?'

'Caroline. This has to stop.' I kiss her forehead.

'Why?'

'You know why.'

Her face crumples, and tears well in her eyes as she staggers out of my hold.

I groan. 'Don't. Please don't cry.' I pull her back into my embrace. 'We can't do this any more.'

Since when have scruples stopped me fucking?

I was supposed to go out tonight and find a willing hot woman.

'Is this because you've met someone?'

'No.'

Yes.

Maybe.

I don't know.

'Come on, I'll put you to bed.' I curl my arm around her shoulders and lead her into my seldom-used spare bedroom.

At some point in the night, the mattress dips as Caroline climbs in beside me. Relieved that I remembered to put on pyjama bottoms, I pull her into my arms.

'Maxim,' she whispers, and I hear the invitation in her voice.

'Go to sleep,' I grumble, and close my eyes.

It doesn't matter to me that she was my brother's wife. She's my best friend and the woman who knows me best. She's also a warm body and a comfort, and I'm grieving, too – but I'm not going to fuck her again.

No. That's done.

She rests her head on my chest, and I kiss her hair and promptly fall asleep.

Chapter Six

Alessia cannot contain her excitement. She clutches the umbrella and enters *his* apartment. Today she's pleased to note that the alarm doesn't sound.

He's here!

Last night in her narrow bed, she'd dreamed of him again – malachite-green eyes, shining smile, and that expressive face – engrossed in his music as he played the piano. She'd woken breathless and full of desire. And last time she'd seen him, he'd been kind enough to lend her his umbrella, and it had kept her dry on the way home and all day yesterday. She'd not received much kindness since she came to London, except from Magda, of course, so his gesture meant that much more. Pulling off her boots and leaving the umbrella in the hall, she hurries through to the kitchen. She is excited to see him.

She stops on the threshold.

Oh, no!

A blond woman wearing nothing but a man's shirt, *his* shirt, is standing in the kitchen making coffee. She looks up and gives

Alessia a polite but warm smile. Alessia recovers her capacity to move and walks through the kitchen towards the utility room with her head bowed, in shock.

'Good morning,' the woman says. She looks as though she's just climbed out of bed.

His bed?

'Good morning, missus,' Alessia mumbles as she walks past her. Once in the utility room, she stands for a moment to process this crushing turn of events.

Who is this woman with big blue eyes?

Why is she wearing his shirt?

A shirt Alessia had ironed for him only last week.

This woman is *with* him. She must be. Why else is she wandering around wearing *his* shirt? She must know *him* intimately.

Intimately.

Of course he has someone. Someone beautiful.

Like him.

Alessia's dreams lie in shards at her feet. Her face clouds as disappointment constricts her heart. Sighing, she removes her hat, gloves and anorak and slips on her housecoat.

What did she expect? He will never be interested in her – she is just his cleaner. Why would he want her?

The small bubble of joy she'd felt this morning – the first in a long time – has burst. She puts on her sneakers and sets up the ironing board. Her earlier excitement is a distant memory as she's forced to face reality. From the dryer she fishes out his clean laundry, transferring it into the ironing basket. This is her place. This is what she was raised to do: keep house and look after a man.

She can still admire him from afar as she's done since she saw him naked on his bed. There is nothing to stop her from doing that.

Feeling discouraged, she exhales as she fills the iron with more water.

Alessia stands in the doorway. A vision in blue. Slowly she removes her scarf and lets her plait swing free.

Shake your hair out for me.

She smiles.

Come in. Lie with me. I want you.

But she turns, and she's in my drawing room. Polishing the piano. Studying my score.

She's wearing nothing but pink panties.

I reach over to touch her, but she disappears.

She's standing in the hall. Eyes wide. Clutching a broom.

Naked.

She has long legs. I want them wrapped around my waist.

'I made you some coffee,' Caroline whispers.

I groan, reluctant to wake. A large part of my anatomy is also enjoying my dream. Fortunately, I'm on my front, so my erection is pressing against the mattress, hidden from my sister-in-law.

'You have no food. Shall we go out for breakfast, or shall I have Blake bring us something?'

I groan again, which is my way of saying fuck off and leave me alone. But Caroline is persistent.

'I met your new daily. She's very young. What happened to Krystyna?'

Shit! Alessia is here?

I roll over to find Caroline sitting on the side of the bed. 'Do you want me to get back in?' she asks with a coy smile, her head nodding towards the pillow.

'No,' I answer, gazing at her lovely but dishevelled state. 'You made coffee dressed like that?'

'Yes.' She frowns. 'Why? Does my body offend you? Or are you pissed off I'm wearing one of your shirts?'

I have the grace to laugh, and I reach out and squeeze her hand. 'Your body would never offend anyone, Caro. You know that.'

But Alessia will get the wrong idea . . .

Fuck. Why do I care?

Caroline twists her mouth in an ironic smile.

'But you don't want it,' she says, her voice suddenly quiet. 'Is this because you've met someone?'

'Caro. Please. Let's not go over that again. We can't. Besides, you said you were on.'

'Surfing the crimson tide has never been an issue for you,' she scoffs.

'Good God, when did I tell you that?' I put my hands on my head and stare in horror up at the ceiling.

'Years ago.'

'Well, I apologise for oversharing.'

Women! They fucking remember everything.

'And why the hell did you have to remind me?' Her face loses all semblance of humour as her sorrow resurfaces. She stares unseeing out of the windows, and her voice is soft and raw and anguished. 'We tried for two years for a child. Two whole years. It's what we both wanted.' Her tears begin to slip down her cheeks. 'And now he's gone, and I've lost everything. I have nothing.' She puts her head in her hands and begins to weep.

Fuck. I'm an idiot. Sitting up, I pull her into my arms and let her cry. I grab a tissue from the box on the bedside table.

'Here.' I hand it to her. She clutches it as if it holds the meaning of life, and I continue, my voice low, tender and sad, 'We can't keep doing this while we're both grieving. It's not fair on either of us, or to Kit. And you haven't lost everything. You have your own money. And you still have the house. We'll sort out a stipend for you from the estate if you need it. In fact, Rowena thinks you should do the interior design for the Mayfair apartments.' I kiss her hair. 'You'll always have me, but not as a diversion, Caro – as a friend and brother-in-law.'

Caroline sniffs and wipes her nose. She leans back and gazes at me with heartbreaking, watery blue eyes.

'It's because I chose him, isn't it?'

My heart sinks. 'Let's not go through that again.'

'Is it because you've found someone else? Who is she?'

I do not want to have this conversation. 'Let's go out for breakfast.'

I shower and dress in record time, and I'm relieved to find that Caroline is still in the spare room en suite when I take my empty coffee cup into the kitchen. My heartbeat rockets at the thought of seeing Alessia.

Why am I nervous? Or am I excited?

Much to my disappointment, she isn't in the kitchen, so I venture to the scullery, where she's ironing one of my shirts. Unobserved, I watch her. She irons with the same sensuous grace I noticed the other day, in long, easy strokes, her brow furrowed in concentration. She finishes the shirt and suddenly looks up. Her eyes widen when she sees me, her cheeks flushing with a rosy glow.

Man, she is lovely.

'Good morning,' I say. 'I didn't mean to startle you.'

She places the iron on the rest and stares at it, rather than at me, her brow more furrowed than before.

What? Why won't she look at me?

'I'm just taking my sister-in-law out for breakfast.' *Why am I telling her this?*

But her eyelashes flutter as she blinks, and I know she's processing this information. In a rush I continue, 'If you could change the sheets in the spare room, that would be great.'

She stills, then nods, avoiding my gaze, while her teeth worry her upper lip.

Oh . . . I want to feel those teeth on me.

'I'll leave the money as usual—'

Her face tilts up, and she gives me a dark glance with her beautiful, expressive eyes, and my words dry in my throat.

'Thank you, Mister,' she whispers.

'My name's Maxim.' I want to hear her say my name in her seductive accent, but she stands mute in her awful housecoat and gives me a tight smile.

'Maxim!' Caroline calls, then walks into the now-cramped scullery. 'Hello again,' she says to Alessia.

'Alessia, this is my friend and sister-in-law . . . um . . . Caroline. Caroline, Alessia.'

This is awkward. I'm surprised how self-conscious I feel making the introductions.

Caroline gives me a puzzled look, which I ignore, but she directs a kind smile at Alessia.

'Alessia, lovely name. Is it Polish?' Caroline asks.

'No, missus. It is from Italy.'

'Oh, you're Italian.'

'No, I am from Albania.' She takes a step back and begins to fiddle with a stray thread on her housecoat.

Albania?

She doesn't want to talk about this, but I'm so curious that I press on. 'You're a long way from home. Are you studying here?'

She shakes her head and starts to pull at the thread, more evasive than ever. It's clear she isn't going to elaborate.

'Maxim. Let's go,' Caroline says, tugging at my arm while maintaining her quizzical look. 'Lovely to meet you, Alessia,' she adds.

I hesitate. 'Bye,' I say, reluctant to leave her.

Bye,' Alessia whispers, and she watches him follow Caroline out of the kitchen.

Sister-in-law?

She hears the front door close.

Sister-in-law.

Kunata.

As she returns to the ironing, she says the words out loud in English and Albanian, and the sound and meaning make her smile. But it's odd that his sister-in-law should be here, wearing his clothes. Alessia shrugs. She's seen enough American TV shows to know that relationships between men and women are different in the West.

Later she strips the bed in the spare room. It's modern and chic and white like the rest of the apartment, but the most pleasing aspect of it is that it's been used. With a relieved grin, she collects more white bedding from the linen closet and remakes the bed.

Since meeting Caroline, one thought has plagued Alessia. In the Mister's bedroom, she has the chance to satisfy her curiosity. She wraps her arms around herself and approaches the wastebasket with caution. Taking a deep breath, she peeks in.

She grins.

No condoms.

Alessia goes about cleaning and tidying his bedroom with a little of the joy she'd felt earlier that morning.

'Is it her?' Caroline asks.

'What?' I scoff as we sit in a cab on the way to the King's Road.

'Your daily.'

Shit.

'What about my daily?'

'Is it her?'

'Don't be ridiculous.'

Caroline crosses her arms. 'That's not a no.'

'I'm not going to dignify that with a response.' I stare out at the drab Chelsea streets through the cab's steamed-up window as I feel a flush creep up my neck, betraying me.

How did I give myself away?

'I've never seen you so solicitous with your staff.'

I scowl at her. 'Speaking of staff,' I say, 'was it Mrs Blake who organised Krystyna for me?'

'I think it was. Why?'

'Well, I was a little surprised that she upped and left without so much as a goodbye and Miss Albania took her place. No one told me.'

'Maxim, if you don't like the girl, get rid of her.'

'That's not what I'm saying.'

'Well, you're acting pretty bloody weird about her.'

'No I'm not.'

'Whatever, Maxim.' Caroline's mouth presses into a hard line as she folds her arms and stares out of the misting cab window, leaving me to my own thoughts.

What I really want is information about Alessia Demachi. I process what I know. Fact one, she's Albanian, not Polish. I know very little about Albania. What brings her to the UK? How old is she? Where does she live? Does she travel far each morning? Does she live alone?

I could follow her home.

Stalker!

I could ask her.

Fact two, Alessia is reluctant to talk. Or is she reluctant to talk to *me*? The thought is depressing, and I stare at the rain-lashed streets, sulking like a needy adolescent.

Why does this woman confound me?

Is it that she's so mysterious?

That she's from a completely different background to me?

The fact that she works for me?

That makes her off-limits.

Fuck.

The truth is, I want to bed her. There. I admit it to myself. That's what I want, and I have a severe case of blue balls to prove it. What's more, I don't know how to make that happen, especially as she won't talk to me. She won't even look at me.

Does she find me repellent?

Maybe that's it. She just doesn't like me.

Hell, I don't know *what* she thinks of me. I'm very much at a disadvantage. For all I know, she could be rummaging through my belongings right now, learning more about me. Figuring me out. I grimace. Maybe that's why she dislikes me.

'She seems terrified of you,' Caroline observes.

'Who?' I ask, though I know full well who she's talking about.

'Alessia.'

'I'm her boss.'

'You're awfully touchy about her. I think she's terrified because she's crazy about you.'

'What? Now you're hallucinating. She can barely stand to be in the same room as me.'

'QED.' Caroline shrugs.

I frown at her.

She sighs. 'She can't be in the same room as you because she likes you and doesn't want to give herself away.'

'Caro, she's my daily. That's all.' I'm emphatic, and it's an effort to throw Caroline off the scent, though this gives me hope. She smirks as the cab pulls up outside Bluebird. I hand the cab driver a twenty, ignoring Caroline's look.

'Keep the change,' I tell him as we climb out of the cab.

'That's an excessive tip,' Caroline grumbles. I say nothing, too lost in thoughts of Alessia Demachi, and hold the door of the café open for her.

'So your mother thinks I should pick myself up by my bootstraps and get back to work?' Caroline says as we're led to our table.

'She thinks you're very talented and that working on the Mayfair development will be a welcome diversion.'

Caroline presses her lips together. 'I think I need time,' she whispers, and her eyes dim with sadness.

'I understand.'

'We only buried him two weeks ago.' She pulls Kit's sweater up to her nose and inhales.

'I know, I know,' I say, and wonder if his scent is still on the sweater.

I miss him, too. And actually, it's thirteen days since his burial. Twenty-two days since he died.

I swallow the harsh, hard knot that forms in my throat.

I missed my workout this morning, so I vault up the stairs to my flat. Breakfast has taken longer than I intended, and I'm expecting Oliver at any minute. Part of me also hopes that Alessia will still be there. As I approach my front door, I hear music coming from the flat.

Music? What's going on?

I slide my key into the lock and cautiously open the door. It's Bach, one of his preludes in G Major. Perhaps Alessia is playing music through my computer. But how can she? She doesn't know the password. Does she? Maybe she's playing her phone through the sound system, though from the look of her tatty anorak she doesn't strike me as someone who has a smartphone. I've never seen her with one. The music rings through my flat, lighting up its darkest corners.

Who knew that my daily likes classical?

This is a tiny piece of the Alessia Demachi puzzle. Quietly I close the door, but as I stand in the hallway, it becomes apparent that the music is not coming from the sound system. It's from my piano. Bach. Fluid and light, played with a deftness and understanding I've only heard from concert-standard performers.

Alessia?

I've never managed to make my piano sing like this. Taking off my shoes, I creep down the hallway and peer around the door into the drawing room.

She is seated at the piano in her housecoat and scarf, swaying a little, completely lost in the music, her eyes closed in concentration as her hands move with graceful dexterity across the keys. The music flows through her, echoing off the walls and ceiling in a flawless performance worthy of any concert pianist. I watch her in awe as she plays, her head bowed.

She is brilliant.

In every way.

And I'm completely spellbound.

She finishes the prelude, and I step back into the hall, flattening myself against the wall in case she looks up, not daring to breathe. However, without missing a beat she goes straight into the fugue. I lean against the wall and close my eyes, marvelling at her artistry and the feeling that she puts into each phrase. I'm carried away by the music, and as I listen, I realise that she wasn't reading the music. She's playing from memory.

Good God. She's a fucking virtuoso.

And I remember her intense focus when she examined my score while she was dusting the piano. Clearly she was reading the music.

Shit. She plays at this standard and she was reading *my* composition?

The fugue ends, and seamlessly she launches into another piece. Again Bach, Prelude in C-sharp Major, I think.

What the fuck is she doing cleaning when she plays like this?

The front doorbell sounds, and suddenly the music ceases.

Shit.

I hear the loud scrape of the piano stool on the floor and, not wanting to be caught eavesdropping, I barrel down the hallway in my socks and open the door.

'Good afternoon, sir.' It's Oliver.

'Come in,' I say, a little breathless.

'I let myself in downstairs. I hope you don't mind. Are you okay?' Oliver asks as he enters. He stops and stares at Alessia, who is now standing in the hall silhouetted against the light from the drawing-room doorway. As I open my mouth to say something to her, she scoots into the kitchen.

'Yes. I'm fine. Go on through. I just need a word with my daily.'

Oliver frowns in confusion but makes his way to the drawing room.

I take a deep breath and run both my hands through my hair, trying to contain my . . . wonder.

What the hell?

I stride into the kitchen, where I find a panicked Alessia struggling into her anorak.

'So sorry. So sorry. I am so sorry,' she mumbles, unable to look at me. Her face is pale and strained, as if she's fighting back tears.

Shit.

'Hey, it's okay. Here, let me help you with that.' My tone is gentle as I take hold of her coat. It's every bit as cheap, thin and nasty as it looks. The name MICHAL JANECZEK is sewn into the collar. Michal Janeczek? Her boyfriend? My scalp prickles as all the little hairs on the back of my neck rise. Maybe this is why she doesn't want to talk to me. She has a boyfriend.

Fuck. The disappointment is real.

I slip her jacket over her arms and shoulders.

Or maybe she simply doesn't like me.

Pulling the anorak more tightly around her body, she steps out of my reach while she fumbles with her housecoat and stuffs it into a plastic shopping bag.

'I am sorry, Mister,' she says once more. 'I will not do it again. I will not.' And her voice cracks.

'Alessia, for heaven's sake. It was a pleasure to hear you play. You can play anytime.'

Even if you do have a boyfriend.

She stares at the floor, and I can't resist. Stepping forward, I reach out and gently tilt her chin so that I can see her face.

'I mean it,' I say. 'Anytime. You play so well.' And before I can stop myself, I let my thumb trace her full bottom lip.

Oh, God. So soft.

Touching her is a mistake.

My body responds immediately. *Fuck.*

She draws in a sharp breath, and her eyes grow impossibly large.

I drop my hand. 'I'm sorry,' I whisper, appalled that I'm pawing the girl. Though Caroline's words come back to me.

She likes you and doesn't want to give herself away.

'I must go,' Alessia says, and not bothering to remove the scarf from her head, she scoots around me and bolts for the front door. As I hear it close, I notice that she's left her boots. I reach for them and rush to the front door and open it. But she's disappeared. Looking at her boots in my hand I turn them over and I'm distressed to see that they're so old the soles are worn thin.

Hence the wet footprints.

She must be penniless if this is what she's wearing. Scowling, I take them back to the kitchen and glance through the glass door that leads out onto the fire escape. The weather is fine today, so even in her trainers, her feet won't get wet.

What on earth possessed me to touch her? That was a mistake. I rub my thumb and forefinger together, recalling the softness of her lip. Groaning, I shake my head. I'm shocked and embarrassed that I've overstepped the mark with her. Taking a deep breath, I go to join Oliver in the drawing room.

'Who was that?' Oliver asks.

'My daily.'

'I don't have her on the roster of employees.'

'Is that a problem?'

'Yes. How do you pay her? With cash?'

What the fuck is he implying?

'Yes. Cash,' I snap.

Oliver shakes his head. 'You're the Earl of Trevethick now. She'll need to go on the payroll.'

'Why?'

'Because Her Majesty's Revenue and Customs will take a dim view of you paying cash to anyone. Trust me, they're all over our accounts.'

'I don't understand.'

'All employees have to go through the books. Did you organise her?'

'No. Mrs Blake did.'

'I'm sure it won't be a problem. I just need her details. She's from the UK, yes?'

'Well, no. She says she's Albanian.'

'Oh. Then she may need a work permit to be here – unless she's studying, of course.'

Oh, shit.

'I'll get the details for you. Shall we discuss the rest of the staff?' I ask.

'By all means. Shall we start with those who work at Trevelyan House?'

Alessia runs to the bus stop, unsure why she's running or from whom. How could she have been stupid enough to get caught? He said he didn't mind her playing the piano, but she doesn't know whether to believe him. He may be calling Magda's friend right now to have her fired! Her heart pounding, feeling confused, she sits on the bench to wait for the bus that will take her to Queenstown Road station. She isn't sure if her increased heart rate is from her mad dash along Chelsea Embankment or from what happened in the Mister's apartment.

She caresses her lower lip with her fingertips. Closing her eyes, she recalls the delicious jolt that went through her when he touched her. Her heart somersaults once more, making her gasp.

He touched her.

Like he does in her dreams.

Like he does in her imagination.

So gentle.

And tender.

Isn't that what she wants?

Perhaps he likes her . . .

She gasps once more.

No. She cannot think like this.

It's impossible.

How could he like her? She's just his cleaner.

But he helped her into her coat. No one has ever done that before. She stares down at her feet.

Zot!

She realises that she's left her boots in the apartment. Should she go back and retrieve them? She has no shoes except the pair she's wearing, and her pair of boots, which are one of the few possessions she retains from home.

She can't go back. He's meeting with someone. If she angered him by playing the piano, he is sure to be angrier still if she interrupts him. She sees the bus in the distance and resolves to collect her boots on Friday – if she still has a job.

Her teeth toy with her upper lip. She needs this job. If she gets fired, Magda might turn her out on the street.

No, that will not happen.

Magda wouldn't be that cruel, and Alessia still has Mrs Kingsbury's and Mrs Goode's houses to clean, though neither of them has a piano. However, it's not just the piano that Alessia needs – she needs the money. Magda and her son, Michal, are emigrating to Canada soon. They will join Magda's fiancé, Logan, who lives and works in Toronto. Alessia will have to find somewhere to live. Magda charges her a pittance of a hundred pounds a week for the tiny box room, and from her research on Michal's computer she knows this is a bargain. Finding other lodgings in London for so little is going to be a challenge.

Her heart warms when she thinks about Michal. He is generous with his time and his computer. Alessia's knowledge of the cyber world is limited, as her father was strict with the use of the old computer at home. But Michal's is not. He is all over social media. Facebook, Instagram, Tumblr, Snapchat – Michal loves them all. She smiles thinking of the selfie he took yesterday of the two of them. He likes to take the selfies.

The bus arrives, and still feeling giddy from the Mister's touch, she climbs aboard.

'Well, that's a run-through of all the staff. I need your daily's details so I can add her to the payroll,' Oliver says. We're seated at the small dining table in my drawing room, and I had hoped we'd concluded our meeting.

'Now I have a proposition for you,' he continues.

'What?'

'I think it's best if you take a thorough tour and inspect both the estates that are in your direct control. Tyok we can do when the tenant vacates.'

'Oliver, I've lived on these estates at various points in my life. Why do I need to inspect them?'

'Because you're the boss now, Maxim. It will show the staff you care and that you're committed to them and to the estates' longevity.'

What? My mother would have my head on a plate if I felt anything less. For her it's always been about the earldom, the bloodline and the family – which is ironic, considering she abandoned them. But not before she'd imparted to Kit her passion for our family's history and legacy. She'd schooled him well. He knew his duties. And like the good man he was, he rose to the challenge.

As did Maryanne. She knew our history, too.

Me. Not so much.

Maryanne had learned by osmosis; she was a curious child.

I was always too distracted and lost in my own world.

'Of course I'm committed to the staff and the estates,' I growl.

'They don't know that, sir,' Oliver says calmly. 'And . . . well, your behaviour there the last time . . .' His voice trails off. I know he's referring to the night before Kit's funeral, when I'd drunk my way through a portion of Kit's cellar at Tresyllian Hall. I was angry. I knew what his death signified for me. And I didn't want the responsibility.

And I was in shock.

I missed him.

I still miss him.

'I was in fucking mourning,' I mutter, feeling defensive. 'I still am. I didn't ask for all this.'

I'm not ready for this huge obligation.

Why didn't my parents foresee this?

My mother never made me feel as though I was going to be good at anything. She concentrated on my brother. She had tolerated her two younger children. Loved us, even, in her own way.

But she adored Kit.

Everyone adored Kit. My blond, blue-eyed, smart, confident, over-indulged elder brother.

The heir.

Oliver holds up his hands in a conciliatory gesture. 'I know. I know. But you have some bridges to mend.'

'Well, maybe we should schedule a trip in the next few weeks.'

'I think sooner rather than later.'

I don't want to leave London. I've made a little headway with Alessia, and the thought of not seeing her for a few days is . . . displeasing.

'When, then?' I snap.

'No time like the present.'

'You're kidding.'

Oliver shakes his head.

Fuck.

'Let me think about it,' I mutter, and I know I'm pouting like a spoiled child.

I am the definition of a spoiled child.

Gone are the days when I could do what the hell I wanted.

And I shouldn't take my anger out on Oliver.

'Very good, sir. I've cleared my diary for the next few days to come with you.'

Oh, great.

'Fine,' I grumble.

'Tomorrow, then?'

'Sure. Why not. We'll make it a royal progress.' I grit my teeth.

'Maxim, I know there's a great deal to take on board, but having all your staff well motivated will make a significant difference. They only know a certain side of you.' He pauses, and I understand that he's referring to my less-than-spotless reputation. 'Just talking to the estate managers on their home turf will mean so much to them. Your meeting with them last week was too brief.'

'Okay, okay, you've made your point. I've agreed, haven't I?' I know I'm being petulant, but deep down I don't want to leave.

Well, I don't want to leave Alessia.

My daily.

Chapter Seven

It's a cold and gloomy Tuesday afternoon. Exhausted, I lean against the chimney stack of the old tin mine and stare out towards the sea. The sky is dark and ominous, and a bitter Cornish wind slices through me. A storm is brewing, and the sea rages and crashes against the cliffs beneath, the sound booming and echoing through the ruined building. The first freezing spots of sleet from the coming storm spatter on my face.

As children, Kit, Maryanne and I used to play in and around the ruin of this tin mine that stands on the edge of the Trevethick estate. Kit and Maryanne had always played the heroes, and I was always the villain. *How apt.* It was typecasting, even then. I smile at the memory.

A considerable fortune had been made from these mines, and the profits swelled the Trevelyan coffers over the centuries. But they were closed in the late 1800s as they became less profitable, and the workers emigrated to places like Australia and South Africa, where the mining industry was flourishing. I spread my hand over the worn stone of the chimney stack, cold and rough to the touch but still standing after all these centuries.

Like the earls of Trevethick . . .

My visit has been a success. Oliver had made a good call insisting I visit both estates. And I'm beginning to re-evaluate my doubts about him. He's done nothing but steer me in the right direction. Perhaps he does have the Trevethick earldom and its continuing prosperity in his heart. The staff now know I'm behind them and that I don't want to make radical changes. I've discovered that I'm very much an 'if it ain't broke, don't fix it' devotee. My smile is rueful . . . I'm also too lazy to be anything else, for now. But the truth is, under Kit's authority and shrewd management the Trevelyan estates have been thriving. I hope I can keep them that way.

I'm weary from being encouraging and upbeat for the past few days and from listening to everyone. I'm not used to expending such positive energy. I've met so many people here and at Angwin in Oxfordshire, people I'd never met before who work on each estate. I've been coming to both of these places since I was a child, and I never had an inkling how many people work behind the scenes. Meeting everyone has been draining. All that talking, listening, reassuring, smiling – especially when I don't feel like smiling.

I gaze at the path that leads down to the sea and think of Kit and me as two young boys racing to the soft, sandy beach below. Kit always won . . . always. But then he was four years older than me. And then in late August, armed with bowls and buckets and anything else that would hold them, we three children would pick blackberries from the brambles that lined the path, and our cook, Jessie, would make blackberry-and-apple crumble for supper, Kit's favourite.

Kit. Kit. Kit.

It was always Kit.

The heir. Not the spare.

Fuck.

Why race through the icy lanes on a freezing night?

Why? Why? Why?

And now he lies beneath cold, hard slate in the Trevelyan family crypt.

Grief tightens my throat.

Kit.

Enough.

I whistle for Kit's gun dogs. On command, Jensen and Healey, two Irish setters, return from their romp along the path and come bounding towards me. They are named after cars. Kit was obsessed with all four-wheeled vehicles, especially fast ones. From an early age, he could strip an engine and put it back together in no time.

He was a true all-rounder.

The dogs jump up at me, and I rumple both sets of ears. They live at Tresyllian Hall on the Trevethick estate, cared for by Danny, Kit's housekeeper. No. *My* housekeeper, for fuck's sake. I've contemplated taking them back to London, but my apartment is no place for two working dogs used to roaming the Cornish countryside and the thrill of game shoots. Kit adored them, even though they are useless gun dogs. And Kit loved a shoot, too.

I wrinkle my nose in distaste. Shooting is big business, which means the holiday homes are booked out year-round. Bankers and hedge-fund managers seek their thrills at the wrong end of a gun during the open season. Affluent surfers and their families rent from spring through to autumn. Surfing I enjoy. Clay shooting I enjoy. But I am not a fan of killing helpless birds. My father, on the other hand, like my brother, loved the sport. He taught me how to shoot, and I do understand that the sport helps to keep the estate profitable.

I pull up my collar, push my hands deeper into the pockets of my overcoat, and turn to trek back up to the great house. Feeling glum and restless, I trudge through the wet grass, the dogs following close behind.

I want to be back in London.

I want to be back near *her.*

My thoughts keep returning to my sweet daily, with her dark eyes, her beautiful face, and her extraordinary musical talent.

Friday, I'll see her Friday, provided I haven't scared her away.

Alessia shakes the umbrella free of the snowflakes that had started falling fast and furious on her way to the Mister's apartment. She is not expecting him to be at home – after all, he'd left money for her last week that included payment for today. But she is ever hopeful. She has missed his brooding presence. She's missed his smile. She has thought of him. Constantly. Taking a deep breath, she opens the door. The silence that greets her is nearly her undoing.

No alarm noise.

He is here.

He is back.

Early.

The abandoned leather duffel bag in the hallway also confirms his presence, and so do muddy footprints in the hall. Her heart rockets into overdrive. She is thrilled; she is going to see him again.

Carefully she places his umbrella in the stand by the door so it won't drop and wake him if he's asleep. She'd borrowed it on Monday night. She hadn't asked, but she didn't think he would mind, and it had kept her dry from the freezing rain as she'd made her way home.

Home?

Yes . . . Magda's house is home now. Not Kukës. She tries not to think of her old home.

She removes her boots and tiptoes along the hallway, through the kitchen and into the utility room. Changing into her sneakers and housecoat, she dons her scarf and decides what to clean first. He has been absent since Friday, so everything is clean. The ironing and washing are up to date, and his closet is finally neat and organised, but it's packed. The kitchen still looks as spotless and tidy as she had left it on Monday afternoon; nothing has been touched. She has to mop up the hall, but first she will dust the shelves with all the records, then wash the windows in the living room. The balcony has a glass wall that looks out over the Thames and to Battersea Park beyond. Grabbing the window-cleaning spray and a cloth from the cupboard, Alessia heads into the living room.

She halts in her tracks.

The Mister is here. Propped up on the L-shaped couch. Eyes closed, lips parted, hair mussed and standing on end, he's fast asleep. He is fully dressed and still wearing his overcoat, though it's open, revealing his sweater and jeans. His filthy boots are planted firmly on the rug. In the white light that swirls through the glass wall, Alessia spies the telltale trail of dried mud all the way back to the door.

She stares at him, enthralled, and moves closer, drinking him in. His face is relaxed but a little pale, his jaw is rough with stubble, and his full lips quiver with each breath. He looks younger and not quite as unattainable as he sleeps. If she dared, she could reach down and stroke the stubble on his cheek. Would it be soft or prickly? She smiles at her silliness. She isn't that brave, and though it's tempting, she doesn't want to anger him by waking him.

What concerns her most is that he looks uncomfortable. Briefly she wonders whether she should wake him so that he can go to bed, but at that moment he stirs and his eyelids open and bleary eyes meet hers. Alessia's breath hitches.

His dark lashes flutter over drowsy eyes, and he smiles and holds out his hand. 'There you are,' he mumbles, and his sleepy smile galvanises her into action. She thinks he wants help to come to his feet, so she steps forward and takes his hand. All at once he tugs her down onto the sofa, kissing her quickly and curling his arm around her so that she's resting on top of him, her head on his chest. He mutters something unintelligible, and she realises he must still be asleep. 'I missed you,' he murmurs, and his hand grazes her waist, then rests on her hip, holding her to him.

Is he asleep?

She lies paralysed on top of him, her legs between his, her heart beating an insane rhythm, one hand still clutching the window-cleaning fluid and the cloth.

'You smell so good.' His voice is barely audible. He takes a deep breath, his body relaxing beneath her, and his breathing mellows into the rhythm of sleep.

He's dreaming!

Zot! What should she do? She lies stiff and unyielding on top of him, terrified and fascinated at the same time. But what if . . . ? What if he . . . ? All manner of horrible scenarios suddenly run through her mind, and she closes her eyes to bring her anxiety under control. Isn't this what she wants? What she has been longing for in her dreams? What she secretly desires in her private moments? She listens to his breathing. In. Out. In. Out. It's steady. It's slow. He really is asleep. She rests against him, gathering her thoughts, and as time ticks by, she relaxes a little. She spies a smattering of his chest hair in the V of his T-shirt and sweater. It's provocative. She lays her cheek on his chest and closes her eyes and inhales his familiar scent.

It's soothing.

He smells of sandalwood and the fir trees in Kukës. He smells of wind and rain and exhaustion.

Poor man.

He is so tired.

She purses her lips and leaves a shadow of a kiss against his skin.

And her heartbeat spikes.

I've kissed him!

She wants nothing more than to remain where she is, to enjoy this new and thrilling experience. But she cannot. She knows it's wrong. She knows he's dreaming.

Closing her eyes for one more minute, she delights in the rise and fall of his chest beneath her. She yearns to wrap her arms around him and curl up on top of him. But she can't. She lets go of the cleaning fluid and the cloth, depositing them on the sofa, then reaches for his shoulders and shakes him gently.

'Please, Mister,' she whispers.

'Hmm,' he grunts.

She pushes a little harder. 'Please. Mister. Move.'

He raises his head and opens his tired eyes, confused. His expression turns from confusion to horror.

'Please. Move,' she says again.

His hands fall away, releasing her. 'Shit!' He sits up immediately and gapes at her in utter dismay as she scrambles off him. But before she can run, he grabs her hand.

'Alessia!'

'No!' she shouts.

And he lets go immediately.

'I'm so sorry,' he says. 'I thought . . . I thought . . . I was . . . I must have been dreaming.' Slowly he stands, his face full of remorse, holding his hands up in submission. 'I'm sorry. I didn't mean to frighten you.' He drags his hands through his hair and rubs his face as if trying to rouse himself. Alessia stays out of his reach but scrutinises him and sees how strained and tired he looks.

He shakes his head to clear it. 'I'm so sorry,' he says again. 'I've been driving all night. I got in at four this morning. I must have fallen asleep when I sat down to undo my laces.' They both look at his boots and at the clumps of dried mud he's left in his wake.

'Oops. Sorry,' he says with a sheepish shrug.

From deep inside, her compassion for this man blossoms. He's exhausted, and he's apologising for making a mess in his own home? That's not right. He has shown her nothing but kindness, giving her his umbrella, helping her into her coat, and when he caught her at the piano, he was complimentary and generous in his offer to let her play.

'Sit,' she says, spurred on by her compassion.

'What?'

'Sit down,' she says more forcefully, and he does as he's told. She kneels at his feet and begins to untie his bootlaces.

'No,' he says. 'You don't have to do that.' Alessia bats his hand away, ignoring him, and undoes his boots, pulling each off in turn. Then she stands, feeling more confident that this is the right thing to do.

'You sleep now,' she says, and grasping his boots in one hand, she holds out the other to help him up.

He glances from her eyes to her fingers, his hesitation unmistakable. After a beat he takes her hand, and she hauls him off the sofa. Gently she leads him down the hallway and into his bedroom. There she releases him, draws back the duvet from his bed, and points. 'You sleep,' she says, and walks around him to the door.

'Alessia,' he calls before she leaves his room. He looks despondent and uncertain. 'Thank you,' he says.

She nods and exits, still holding his filthy boots. She closes the door behind her and leans against it, her hand at her throat in an effort to contain her emotions. She takes a deep cleansing breath. She's gone from uncertainty and confusion to delight and wonder to compassion and assertiveness in the space of a few minutes.

And he kissed her.

And she kissed him.

She touches her fingers to her lips. It was brief but not unpleasant.

Not unpleasant at all.

I missed you.

She takes another deep breath to calm her pounding heart. She has to get a grip on reality. He'd been asleep. He'd been dreaming. He hadn't known what he was saying or what he was doing. She could have been anybody. She shakes off her disappointment. She is just his cleaner. What could he possibly see in her? Feeling a little deflated, but with her equilibrium restored, she picks up the Mister's leather duffel bag and heads back to the utility room to clean his boots and sort his clothes for washing.

I stare at the closed bedroom door, feeling every shade of stupid known to man. How could I have been so fucking idiotic? I frightened her.

Shit.

I have no hope with her.

She'd appeared in my dream, a vision in blue – even in that ugly housecoat – and I'd welcomed her.

I rub my face in frustration. I'd left Cornwall at eleven the previous night, and the five-hour drive had been exhausting. It was a stupid thing to do. I nearly fell asleep several times. I had to open my car windows even though it was freezing and sing along to the radio to stay awake. And the real irony is that I drove home to see her. The weather forecast threatened a rare blizzard, and I didn't want to be stuck in Cornwall for a week . . . so I came home early.

Fuck.

I've blown it.

But she knelt at my feet and undid my shoes and led me to bed as if I were a child. Led me to bed to sleep. I snort. To sleep!

When was the last time anyone did that for me?

I don't remember any woman putting me to bed and leaving me . . .

And I frightened her.

Shaking my head in self-disgust, I peel off my clothes and leave them on the floor where they fall. I'm too tired to do anything but crawl into bed. As I shut my eyes, I find myself wishing she had undressed me completely and joined me . . . here. I groan as I recall her sweet, wholesome scent, roses and lavender, and how soft she felt in my arms. Feeling simultaneously morose and aroused, I fall fast asleep and surrender to her in my dreams.

I wake with a start and an odd feeling of guilt. My phone is buzzing on my bedside table. I didn't leave it there. I pick it up, but I'm too late. It's a missed call from Caroline. I place it back on my bedside table, noting that my wallet, spare change and a condom are also there. I frown, and then I remember.

Oh, God. Alessia.

I jumped her.

Bugger.

I screw my eyes shut to escape the embarrassment that washes over me.

Fuck. A. Duck.

I sit up, and sure enough my clothes have been tidied away. She must have emptied my jeans pockets. It seems such an intimate thing to do, rummaging through my possessions, her fingers on my clothes, my stuff.

I'd like her fingers on me.

That's not going to happen, you idiot. You frightened the poor girl.

How many houses does she clean anyway? How many pockets does she rummage through? I dislike the thought. Perhaps I should hire her full-time. Then the dull ache in my gut would never go . . . unless . . . unless . . . There's only one way I'll be rid of this ache.

Shit. That's not going to happen.

I wonder what the time is. There are no shimmers on the ceiling. Glancing out of the window, I see nothing but a wall of white.

Snow.

The predicted blizzard has arrived. A glance at my alarm clock confirms it's 1:45 p.m. She should still be here. I leap out of bed and in my dressing room pull on a pair of jeans and a long-sleeved T-shirt.

Alessia is in the drawing room, where she's cleaning the windows. All evidence of my muddy walk through the flat has disappeared.

'Hi,' I say, and wait to see how she reacts. My heart is thundering. I feel like I'm fifteen years old again.

'Hi. You sleep well?' She gives me a brief but unreadable look, then studies the cloth she's holding.

'Yes, thank you, and sorry about earlier.' Feeling ridiculous and self-conscious, I wave in the direction of the sofa where my misdemeanour took place. She nods and rewards me with a small, tight smile, and her cheeks turn a lovely shade of pink.

I look beyond her through the windows, where the view is obscured by swirling snowflakes. The snowstorm is in full force, and outside is a turbulent torrent of white.

'It doesn't often snow like this in London,' I say, moving to stand beside her at the window.

We're talking about the weather?

She steps beyond my reach, but she stares out of the windows. The snow is so dense I can hardly see the river below.

She shivers and wraps her arms around her body.

'Do you have far to go?' I ask, worried about her making her way home in this storm.

'West London.'

'How do you get home normally?'

She blinks a couple of times while she processes my words. 'Train,' she answers.

'Train? From where?'

'Um . . . Queenstown Road.'

'I'll be surprised if the trains are still running.'

I head over to my desk in the corner of the room, shuffle the mouse, and my iMac springs to life. A picture of Kit, Caroline, Maryanne and me with Kit's two Irish setters appears on my desktop, and with it I feel a wave of nostalgia and sadness. Shaking my head, I check online for the latest on local transport. 'Um . . . South Western Railway?'

She nods.

'They've suspended all services.'

'Sus-pen-ded?' Her brow creases.

Oh, she doesn't understand.

'The trains aren't running.'

'Oh.' She frowns again, and I think I hear her say 'suspended' several times under her breath, her lips forming the word.

'You can stay here,' I offer, trying not to focus on her mouth and knowing full well that she won't stay, especially given how I behaved earlier. I flinch and add, 'I promise to keep my hands off you.'

She shakes her head rather too quickly for my liking. 'No. I must go.' She twists the cloth in her hands.

'How will you get home?'

She shrugs. 'I shall walk.'

'Don't be ridiculous. You'll get hypothermia.'

Especially in those boots and that horrid excuse for a coat.

'I must return home.' She's adamant.

'I'll take you.'

What? Did that just pop out of my mouth?

'No,' she says with another emphatic shake of her head, her eyes growing wide.

'I'm not taking no for an answer. As your . . . um, employer, I insist.'

She pales.

'Yep. I'll just finish getting dressed' – I glance down at my feet – 'and then we'll go. Please.' I gesture to the piano. 'If you want to play, do.' And I turn and head back to my bedroom, wondering why I've volunteered to take her home.

Because it's the right thing to do?

Because I want to spend more time with her.

Alessia watches him pad out of the room in his bare feet. She's stunned. He's going to drive her home? She will be alone in a car with him.

Is this okay?

What would her mother say?

A vision of her mother with her arms crossed and her face etched in meek disapproval comes to her mind.

And her father?

Instinctively she cups her cheek.

No. Her father would not approve.

Her father had approved of only one man.

A cruel man.

No. Do not think of him.

The Mister is taking her home. She's glad she's memorised

the address to Magda's house. She can still see her mother's untidy handwriting scrawled on the scrap of paper that had been her lifeline. She shivers and glances outside once more. It will be cold, but if she's quick, she can leave while the Mister is changing and not inconvenience him. Yet the thought of walking all that distance does not appeal. She has done it before from much further away. Then it had taken her six or seven days with a stolen map. She shivers once more. Six or seven days she'd like to forget. Besides, he said she could play his piano. She gives the Steinway a fervent look, claps her hands with excitement, and dashes to the utility room, where she changes in seconds. Grabbing her coat, scarf and hat, she hurries back to the piano.

Leaving her coat on a chair, she sits down on the stool and takes a steadying breath. She places her hands on the keys, enjoying the cool, familiar feel of the ivory. For her the piano is grounding. It's home. Her safe place. Glancing once more out of the window, she begins *Les jeux d'eau à la Villa d'Este*, her favourite piece by Liszt, the music swirling up and around the piano, dancing in brilliant shades of white like the snowflakes outside. Her memories of her father, her six days of homelessness and her mother's disapproval are lost in the whirling, icy colours of the music.

I lean against the door frame and watch her, mesmerised. Her performance is phenomenal, each note measured and played with such precision and emotion. The music flows effortlessly through her . . . from her. Each and every nuance is there on her beautiful face and in the music as she feels her way through the piece. A piece I don't know.

She's taken off the headscarf. I've been wondering if she wears it for religious reasons, but maybe it's just for when she's cleaning. Her hair is thick and dark, almost black. As she plays, a strand comes loose from her plait and curls around her cheek. What would her hair look like loose and cascading over her bare shoulders? I close my eyes, imagining her naked as I do in my dreams, letting the music wash over me.

Would this ever get old? Listening to her?

I open my eyes.

Watching her. Her beauty. Her talent.

Playing such a complex piece from memory. The girl is a genius.

While I was away, I'd thought that I'd embellished her performance in my imagination. But no. Her technique is flawless.

She's flawless.

In every way.

She finishes the piece, her head lowered, eyes closed, and I applaud. 'That was breathtaking. Where did you learn to play so well?'

Her cheeks flush as she opens her dark eyes, but a shy smile lights up her face, and she shrugs. 'At home,' she answers.

'You can tell me more about it in the car. Are you ready?'

She stands, and it's the first time I've seen her out of that hideous nylon housecoat. My mouth dries. She's slimmer than I'd thought, but her delicate curves are all woman. She's wearing a tight green V-neck sweater; the soft swell of her breasts strains against the wool and emphasises her narrow waist, and her skin-tight jeans showcase the gentle flare of slender hips.

Fuck.

She's gorgeous.

She quickly slips out of her trainers, drops them into her plastic shopping bag, and tugs on her battered brown boots.

'Don't you wear socks?' I ask.

She shakes her head as she bends and laces each boot, but her cheeks pink once more.

Maybe no socks is an Albanian thing?

I glance out of the window, glad to be taking her home. Not only will I get to spend more time with her, but I'll find out where she lives and stop her from catching frostbite in her feet.

I hold out my hand. 'Give me your coat,' I say, and she offers me a hesitant smile when I help her into it.

This rag will never keep her warm.

When she turns to face me, I notice a little gold cross around her neck and a badge on her sweater – for a school?

Shit.

'How old are you?' I ask in a sudden panic.

'I have twenty-three years.'

Old enough. Good.

I shake my head, feeling relieved. 'Shall we go?' I ask.

She nods and, clasping her plastic bag, follows me out of the flat.

We wait in silence for the lift to take us down to the basement garage.

Once in the lift, Alessia stands as far away from me as she can. She really doesn't trust me.

After my behaviour this morning, am I surprised?

The thought depresses me, and I try to look as calm and nonchalant as possible, but I'm so acutely aware of her. All of her. Here in this small space.

Maybe it's not just me. Maybe she just doesn't like men. This thought is even more upsetting, so I brush it aside.

The basement garage is small, but because the family estate owns the building, I have parking spaces for two cars. I don't need two, but I keep them anyway, a Land Rover Discovery and an F-Type Jaguar. I'm not a petrol-head like Kit. He was an avid collector, and now his fleet of rare vintage cars is mine. I like a motor that's new and hassle-free. Christ knows what I'm going to do with Kit's collection. I'll have to ask Oliver. Maybe sell them? Give them to a museum in Kit's name?

Lost in these thoughts, I press the remote for the Discovery, and its lights flash in welcome and it unlocks. With its four-wheel drive, it'll easily tackle London's snowbound streets. Only now do I notice that the car is filthy, still covered in mud and grime from my journey to Cornwall, and when I open the passenger door for Alessia, I see the sorry mess of litter in the footwell. 'Hang on,' I say, and gather up the empty coffee cups, crisp packets and sandwich wrappers. I stuff them into a plastic bag I find on the seat and dump it all in the back.

Why am I not tidier?

A lifetime of nannies and boarding school and staff to clean up after me has taken its toll.

With what I hope is a reassuring smile, I gesture for Alessia to climb in. I'm not certain, but she looks like she's stifling a smile. Maybe the mess is amusing her.

I hope so.

She snuggles down in the seat, her eyes wide as she looks over the dashboard.

'What's the address?' I ask as I push the ignition.

'Forty-three Church Walk, Brentford.'

Brentford! Lord. In the sticks.

'Postcode?'

'TW8 8BV.'

I program the destination into the sat nav and ease the car out of its parking space. With the press of a button on the rearview-mirror console, the garage door gradually lifts, revealing the white maelstrom outside. The snow is already three or four inches deep, and it's still falling fast.

'Wow,' I say, almost to myself. 'I've never seen it like this.' I turn to Alessia. 'Does it snow in Albania?'

'Yes. There is much more snow where I am from.'

'Where is that?' I drive onto the street and head to the end of the road.

'Kukës.'

I've never heard of it.

'It is a small town. Not like London,' Alessia clarifies.

A warning beep sounds. 'Please put your seat belt on.'

'Oh.' She's surprised. 'We don't wear these where I come from.'

'Well, it's the law here, so buckle up.'

She pulls the strap across her chest and looks down for the catch, then presses the belt home. 'There,' she says, pleased with herself, and it's my turn to stifle a smile. Perhaps she doesn't travel by car very often.

'You learned to play the piano at home?' I ask.

'My mother teaches me.'

'Does she play as well as you?'

Alessia shakes her head. 'No.' And she shivers. I don't know if she's cold or if something else is spooking her. I crank up the heat, and we turn onto Chelsea Embankment. The lights from Albert Bridge wink through the swirling snow.

'It is pretty,' Alessia murmurs as we drive past.

'It is.'

Like you.

'We'll take it slow,' I add. 'We're not used to snow like this in London.' Fortunately, the roads are relatively quiet as we turn off the Embankment. 'So what brought you to London, Alessia?'

She shoots me a wide-eyed look, then frowns and looks down at her lap.

'Work?' I prompt.

She nods but seems to deflate like a balloon, withdrawing into herself.

Shit. A tingle runs down my spine. Something is off. *Way off.*

I try to reassure her. 'It's okay. We don't have to talk about that.' Hurriedly I continue, 'I wanted to ask you, how do you remember each piece so well?'

She raises her head, and it's obvious that she's more comfortable with this topic of conversation. She taps her temple. 'I see the music. Like a painting.'

'You have a photographic memory?'

'Photographic memory? I don't know. I see the music in colours. It is the colours that help me to remember.'

'Wow.' I've heard of this. 'Synaesthesia.'

'Syn-a-thee—' She stops, unable to pronounce the word.

'Synaesthesia.'

She tries again, with a little more success. 'What is this?' she asks.

'You see musical notes as colours.'

'Yes. Like that.' She nods enthusiastically.

'Well, that makes sense. I've heard that many accomplished musicians are synaesthetes. Do you see anything else in colour?'

She looks puzzled.

'Letters? Numbers?'

'No. Just music.'

'Wow. That's really something.' I give her a smile. 'I meant what I said the other day. You can use my piano anytime. I love hearing you play.'

She gives me a glorious smile that I feel in my groin. 'Okay,' she whispers. 'I like to play your piano.'

'I like to listen.' I grin back, and we fall into an easy silence.

Forty minutes later I turn into a cul-de-sac in Brentford and we arrive outside a modest semi-detached house. The light is failing, and I see a curtain pull back in the front room and a young man's face clearly visible in the light from the street lamp.

Her boyfriend?

Fuck. I have to know.

'Is that your boyfriend?' I ask, and my heart kick-starts, thumping in my ears as I wait for her answer.

She laughs, a soft, musical laugh that makes me grin. It's the first time I've heard her laugh, and I want to hear it again . . . and again.

'No. That's Michal, Magda's son. He's fourteen.'

'Oh. He's tall!'

'He is.' Her face lights up, and I feel a momentary pang of jealousy. It's obvious she's fond of him. 'This is Magda's house.'

'I see. Is she a friend?'

'Yes. She is a friend of my mother. They are . . . how do you say? Pen friends.'

'I didn't know those still existed. Do they visit each other?'

'No.' She presses her lips together and examines her fingernails. 'Thank you for taking me to my home,' she whispers, shutting down that conversation.

'It was a pleasure, Alessia. I'm sorry about this morning. I didn't mean to pounce on you.'

'Pounce?'

'Um . . . jump. Like a cat.'

She laughs again, her face shining and beautiful.

I could get used to that sound.

'You were dreaming,' she says.

Of you.

'Do you want to come in and drink a cup of tea?'

It's my turn to laugh. 'No. I'll spare you that. And I'm more of a coffee person.'

She frowns for a moment. 'We have some coffee,' she says.

'I'd better get back. It will take a while with the roads like this.'

'Thank you again for driving me here.'

'I'll see you on Friday.'

'Yes. Friday.' She gives me a radiant smile that illuminates her lovely face, and I'm smitten.

She climbs out of the car and heads to the front door. It cracks open, shedding a soft glow onto the snowy path, and the tall young man stands on the doorstep. Michal. He scowls at me as I start the car.

I laugh.

Not her boyfriend, then, and I turn the Discovery around, crank the music up, and with a ridiculous smile plastered on my face drive back into London.

Chapter Eight

'Who was that?' Michal asks, his voice clipped and frosty, as he glares at the vehicle outside. He's only fourteen, but he towers over Alessia, all shaggy black hair and skinny loose limbs.

'My boss,' she answers as she peeks through the front door to watch the car drive away. She shuts the door behind her and, unable to contain her glee, gives Michal a quick, spontaneous hug.

'All right.' Michal shrugs out of her embrace, his face flushed but his brown eyes bright with embarrassed delight. Alessia beams at him, and his answering shy smile hints at his adolescent crush on her. She steps back, careful not to be overly affectionate. She doesn't want to hurt his feelings. After all, he and his mother have been good to her.

'Where's Magda?' she asks.

'In the kitchen.' His face falls, and so does his voice. 'Something's not right. She's smoking a lot.'

'Oh, no.' Alessia's pulse quickens with a sense of foreboding. Taking off her coat, she hangs it on one of the pegs in the small hallway and goes into the kitchen. Magda is holding a cigarette, sitting at the tiny Formica table. The smoke curls above her in a hazy cloud. Though small, the kitchen is neat and tidy as usual, and the radio is burbling in Polish in the background. Magda looks up, relieved to see her.

'You got home through the snow. I was worried. Good day?' Magda asks, but Alessia notices her strained smile and the tension in her lips as she takes a long drag from her cigarette.

'Yes. Are you okay? Is your fiancé okay?'

Magda is a few years younger than Alessia's mother, though usually she looks at least ten years younger. Blond and curvy, with hazel eyes that sparkle with her wicked sense of humour, she rescued Alessia from the streets. Today, though, she looks tired, her skin pallid and her lips pinched. The kitchen stinks of cigarette smoke, which Magda normally hates – even as a smoker herself.

She blows smoke into the room. 'Yes. He's fine. It's nothing to do with him. Shut the door and sit down,' she says. A tremor runs up Alessia's spine. Perhaps Magda is going to ask her to leave. She shuts the kitchen door, pulls out the plastic chair, and sits.

'Some men from the immigration department were here today looking for you.'

Oh, no.

Alessia pales, and she hears the blood hammering in her ears.

'It was after you left for work,' Magda adds.

'Wh-wh-what . . . what did you tell them?' she stutters as she tries to still the trembling in her hands.

'I didn't speak with them. Mr Forrester from next door did. They knocked on his door because we were not here. He did not like the look of them and told them he had never heard of you. He said that Michal and I were away in Poland.'

'Did they believe him?'

'Yes. Mr Forrester thinks so. They left.'

'How did they find me?'

'I don't know.' Magda makes a face. 'Who knows how these things work?' She takes another drag from her cigarette. 'I have to write to your mother.'

'No!' Alessia grasps Magda's hand. 'Please.'

'I've already written and told her that you arrived safely. That was a lie.'

Alessia flushes. Magda does not know the full story of her journey to Brentford. 'Please,' she says. 'I don't want to worry her.'

'Alessia, if they catch you, you'll be deported to Albania—' Magda stops.

'I know,' Alessia whispers, and a trickle of sweat runs down her spine as fear tightens her throat. 'I cannot go back,' she mouths.

'You realise that Michal and I are leaving in two weeks. You have to find somewhere else to stay.'

'I know. I know. I'll find something.' Anxiety flutters in Alessia's stomach. Every night she lies in bed going through her options. So far she has saved three hundred pounds from her cleaning work. She will need the money for a deposit on a room. With Michal's help and the use of his laptop, she will try to find a place to live.

'I'll get supper started,' Magda says with a sigh as she stubs out her cigarette. The smoke swirls out of the ashtray, blending with the tension in the room.

'Let me help,' Alessia responds.

Later Alessia is huddled in her bed, staring at the ceiling. With her fingers she worries the gold cross she wears around her neck. The light from the street lamp shines through the sheer curtains across the old, peeling wallpaper. Her mind races as she tries not to panic. Earlier, after an hour searching online, she'd found a room in a house that is near Kew Bridge station. Magda says that it's not far from here. Alessia has an appointment to see it on

Friday evening when she's back from cleaning the Mister's apartment. She can barely afford it, but she needs to move, especially if the immigration department is catching up with her. She cannot be deported. She cannot go back to Albania.

She cannot.

She turns over to escape the shaft of light and snuggles up in the thin duvet to preserve as much warmth as she can. Thoughts swirl in her head, overwhelming her. She wants them to stop.

Don't think about Albania.

Don't think about this journey.

Don't think about the other girls . . . about Bleriana.

She closes her eyes, and immediately she sees the Mister asleep on the sofa, his hair a mess, his lips parted. She remembers lying on him. She remembers his swift kiss. She imagines that she's lying on him again, inhaling his scent and kissing his skin and feeling the steady beat of his heart against her breast.

I missed you.

She groans.

Every night he occupies her thoughts. He is handsome. More than handsome – he is beautiful and kind.

I love hearing you play.

He drove her home. He didn't have to do that.

You could stay here.

Stay with him?

Perhaps she could ask him for help.

No. Her situation is her problem. It's not of her making, but it's one she must deal with. She has made it this far on nothing but her ingenuity. And there's no way in hell she's going back to Kukës. Not to *him*.

He's shaking me hard. Stop this. Stop this now.

No. Don't think of him!

He's the reason she's in England. She has put as many miles as she can between them.

Think of the Mister. Only the Mister.

Her hand travels down her body.

Think only of him . . .

What had he called her? What is it called?

Synaesthesia . . . She repeats the name over and over and over while her hand moves and takes her higher and higher.

The following morning she wakes to a white wonderland. It's so quiet. Even the distant hum of traffic is muffled by the blanket of sparkling snow. As she looks out of her bedroom window, still huddled under her covers, she feels the same rush of delight she always experienced as a child when it snowed in Kukës. Then she remembers that today she is cleaning Mrs Kingsbury's house. On the plus side, it's in Brentford and only a short walk away. On the minus, it's Mrs Kingsbury, who follows her through the house criticising her cleaning methods. But Alessia suspects that Mrs Kingsbury grouses because she's a lonely old lady, and in spite of her complaining she always offers Alessia tea and biscuits when she's finished. They sit and chat, and Mrs Kingsbury tries to keep her there for as long as possible. Alessia doesn't understand why Mrs Kingsbury lives on her own. She's seen photographs of her family on her mantelpiece. Why aren't they taking care of her? After all, Nana lived with her parents after her grandfather died . . . Perhaps Mrs Kingsbury needs a lodger? Someone to look after her. She certainly has the room, and after all, Alessia is lonely, too.

Dressed only in Michal's tatty SpongeBob SquarePants pj bottoms and his old Arsenal football shirt, she gathers her clothes for the day and bolts down the stairs and through the kitchen into the bathroom.

Magda has been generous with Michal's old clothing. She often complains he's growing too fast, but it's been to Alessia's advantage. Most of the clothes she owns were once his. Except socks. Michal wears huge holes in them, so he can't hand them down. She has two pairs of her own, but that's all.

Don't you wear socks?

Alessia flushes, remembering the Mister's comment from yesterday. She couldn't bring herself to tell him she can't afford new ones. Not while she's saving for a deposit on a room.

She switches on the electric shower that is mounted over the bath and waits a few moments for the water to heat up. She strips off her clothes, climbs into the bathtub, and washes as quickly as possible beneath the trickle of water.

My hands are braced on the shower wall. I'm panting while steaming hot water cascades over me. I've been reduced to jerking off in the shower . . . again.

Fuck. What has become of my life?

Why don't I just go out and get laid?

Her eyes, the colour of a rich espresso, peek up at me through long lashes.

I groan.

This has to stop.

She's my fucking daily. Last night I tossed and turned alone in my bed again. Her laugh echoed over and over in my dreams. She was carefree and happy, playing the piano for me, wearing nothing but those pink panties, her hair falling long and lush past her breasts.

Ah . . .

Even my gruelling workout this morning has done little to get her out of my system.

There is only one way.

That's not going to happen.

But the smile she gave me when she stepped out of the car, it gives me hope, and I'll see her tomorrow. With that positive thought, I turn off the shower and grab a towel. As I shave, I check my phone. Oliver has messaged me. He's stuck in Cornwall because of the weather, which means I can spend the morning replying to condolence emails and then have lunch with Caroline and Maryanne. And this evening I'm going out with the lads.

'Finally got you out of your lair. Should I address you as "Lord Trevethick" or "milord" now, bro?' Joe says as he holds up his pint of Fuller's in salute.

'Yes. I don't know whether to address you as "Trevethick" or "Trevelyan" now,' Tom grumbles.

'I'll answer to either,' I reply with a shrug. 'Or my name – you know, Maxim.'

'I should call you Trevethick from now on . . . though it will be hard to get used to. It is your title, after all, and I know my father is bloody touchy about his!'

'Thank fuck I'm not your father.' I raise a brow.

Tom rolls his eyes.

'Won't be the same without Kit around,' Joe mutters, his ebony eyes glinting in the firelight and serious for once.

'Yes, rest in peace, Kit,' Tom adds.

Joseph Diallo and Thomas Alexander are my oldest and closest friends. After I'd been expelled from Eton, my father sent me to Bedales. There I met Joe, Tom and Caroline. We boys bonded over our love of music and, at the time, our lust for Caroline. We formed a band, and Caroline . . . well, she'd eventually chosen my brother.

'Rest in peace, Kit,' I murmur, and add under my breath, 'I miss you, you fucker.'

The three of us are ensconced in the snug at the Coopers Arms, a warm and welcoming public house not far from my flat. Nursing our pints by the blazing fire, we're two rounds in, and I'm beginning to feel the beer buzz.

'How are you holding up, mate?' Joe asks, tossing his shoulder-length dreads to one side. Joe, as well as being an excellent swordsman, has a promising career as a men's fashion designer. His father, an émigré from Senegal, is one of the most successful hedge-fund managers in the UK.

'Good, I guess. But I'm not sure I'm ready for all the responsibility.'

'I get it,' Tom says. Red-haired and amber-eyed, Tom is the third son of a baronet, who followed family tradition by joining the army. As a lieutenant in the Coldstream Guards, he did a couple of tours of duty in Afghanistan and saw too many of his comrades fall. Two years ago he was invalided out of the army from wounds inflicted two years prior by an IED in Kabul. His left leg is held together by titanium, his temper not so much. Both Joe and I have come to recognise that pugnacious gleam in Tom's eyes, and we know when it's prudent to change the subject or get him out of the room. At his request we never mention The Incident.

'When is the memorial service?' Tom enquires.

'I was discussing that at lunchtime with Caroline and Maryanne. We thought after Easter.'

'How's Caroline?'

I shift in my seat. 'Grieving.' I shrug, giving Tom a level gaze.

Tom regards me, eyes narrowed, his interest piqued. 'Something you not telling us?'

Shit.

Following The Incident, not only is Tom belligerent but he's become irritatingly insightful. 'Come on, Trevelyan, you're not playing with a straight bat. What is it?'

'No. Nothing you need to know. How's Henrietta?'

'Henry? She's great, thanks, but she keeps dropping bloody almighty hints that I need to buck up and pop the fucking question,' Tom replies with a doleful look.

Joe and I both grin. 'You're a doomed man, bro,' Joe says, and claps him on the back.

Of the three of us, Tom is the only one in a long-term relationship. Henrietta is a saint. She nursed Tom through the trauma of his injuries, and she puts up with all of his bullshit, his PTSD, his temper. He could do a lot worse.

Both Joe and I like to play the field. Well, I used to. Unbidden, a vision of the raven-haired Alessia Demachi comes to my mind.

When did I last have sex?

I frown because I can't remember. *Shit.*

'And Maryanne?' Joe asks, distracting me.

'She's okay. Grieving, too.'

'Does she need comforting?'

Comforting like I comforted Caroline?

'Mate!' I scoff in warning.

House rules. Sisters are off-limits. I shake my head. Joseph still has a not-so-soft spot for my sister. She could do a lot worse, he's a good guy, but I decide to burst his bubble. 'She met some bloke while she was skiing in Whistler. He lives in Seattle. He's a clinical psychologist or something. She plans to see him soon, I think.'

Joe gives me a quizzical look. 'Really?' He rubs his rakish goatee, his eyes full of speculation. 'Well, if he makes it over here, we'll have to see if this geezer measures up.'

'He may be coming over next month. She's pretty excited about it.'

'You know, now that you're the earl, you'll need to provide an heir and a spare,' Tom says.

'Yeah, yeah. Time enough for that yet.'

That's what I've always been. The Spare . . . Kit's nickname for me.

It turns out the title and lands needed the spare.

'Yeah. There's no way you're ready to settle down, mate. You're as much of a serial shagger as I am. And I need a wingman,' Joe says with a broad grin.

'Come on, Trevelyan, you've shagged your way through most of London,' Tom taunts, and I don't know if he's disgusted or impressed.

'Fuck off, Tom,' I say, and we all laugh.

The pub's landlady rings the bell above the bar. 'Time, gentlemen, please,' she calls.

'Back to mine?' I ask. Both Tom and Joe agree, and the three of us sink our pints. 'You okay to walk back?' I ask Tom.

'Fuck off. I got myself here, didn't I?'

'I'll take that as a yes.'

'I'm running a fucking 5K in April, you wanker.'

I hold my hands up in surrender. I keep forgetting that physically he's mended . . .

It is clear and sunny but bitterly cold, a day where her breath precedes her in a cloud of vapour as she hurries along Chelsea Embankment. There are still large patches of snow welded in icy clumps to the path, but the roads have been sanded. Traffic has returned to normal, and London is up and running again. Alessia's train was delayed this morning, and now she's a little late. But she would have happily walked from Brentford just to see *him*.

Alessia grins. She is finally at the front door to the Mister's apartment, her favourite place in the world. She slips her key in the lock and braces herself for the sound of the alarm but is relieved at the silence. Closing the door, she's surprised by the smell. The apartment reeks of stale alcohol.

Crinkling her nose at the unexpected odour, she removes her boots and pads barefoot into the kitchen. The worktops are littered with empty bottles of beer and greasy pizza boxes.

She jumps when she sees an athletic, attractive young man standing at the open fridge drinking orange juice directly from the carton. His skin is dark, he has long, knotted hair, and he's dressed only in his boxer shorts. Alessia gapes at him. He turns towards her, and his face erupts in a broad grin of perfect white teeth.

'Well, hi there,' he says, his dark eyes widening in appreciation.

Alessia blushes and mumbles, 'Hi,' then scurries into the utility room.

Who is this man?

She scrambles out of her coat, and from her plastic bag slips on her cleaning uniform: housecoat and headscarf. Lastly she slides her feet into her sneakers.

Alessia peeks around the utility-room door into the kitchen. The Mister, wearing a black T-shirt and his ripped jeans, is standing beside the fridge sharing the carton of orange juice with the stranger.

'I just frightened your barefoot help. You tapped that yet? She's hot.'

'Fuck off, Joe. And I'm not surprised you frightened her. Put some clothes on, you fucking exhibitionist.'

'Sorry, your lordship.' The stranger tugs at his hair and bows his head.

'Fuck off again,' the Mister says mildly, and he takes another swig of orange juice. 'You can use my bathroom.'

The dark-haired man laughs and, turning to go, spies Alessia watching the banter. He grins again and waves at her, causing the Mister to look in her direction. His eyes light up, and a slow smile spreads across his face, and Alessia has no choice but to come out of hiding.

'Joe, this is Alessia. Alessia, Joe.' There is a warning tone to his voice, but Alessia doesn't know if it is directed at her or at Joe.

'Good morning, Alessia. Please excuse my state of undress.' Joe gives her a theatrical bow, and when he's upright, he has a wicked, amused glint in his dark eyes. His body is toned and lean – like the Mister's. Each muscle of his abdomen is clearly defined.

'Good morning,' she whispers.

The Mister gives Joe a brooding glare. But Joe ignores him and winks at Alessia before he strolls out of the kitchen, whistling.

'Sorry about that,' the Mister says as he turns emerald eyes on her. 'How are you today?' His slow smile returns.

Her flush deepens as her heart somersaults. Any enquiry he makes about her well-being, even one so commonplace, lifts her spirits.

'I am good. Thank you.'

'I'm glad you made it here. The trains running okay?'

'They are a little late.'

'Good morning.' A man with fiery red hair limps into the kitchen wearing only his boxer shorts and a scowl.

'Good God,' the Mister mumbles under his breath, and he scrapes his hand through his tousled hair.

Alessia regards this new friend who has joined them. Tall and handsome, his limbs are fair, with shockingly livid scars that criss-cross his left leg and his left side like the tracks at a railway junction.

He notices Alessia staring at his scars.

'War wound,' he growls.

'I'm sorry,' she whispers, and she lowers her gaze to the floor, wishing it would open and swallow her whole.

'Tom, do you want some coffee?' the Mister asks, and it seems to Alessia he's trying to defuse the sudden tension in the room.

'Bloody right. I need something for this god-awful hangover.'

Alessia scuttles back into the utility room to start on the ironing. At least she's out of sight and won't offend any of the Mister's friends from in there.

I watch Alessia's hasty retreat into the scullery, her plait bouncing from side to side and brushing her waist.

'Who's the pretty girl?'

'My daily.'

Tom nods with lascivious approval. I'm glad she's gone back into her lair, away from Tom's and Joe's prying eyes. Their reaction makes me uneasy. Suddenly, surprisingly, I feel proprietary. It's an unfamiliar emotion. I don't want my friends ogling her. She's mine. Well, she's my employee.

You're the Earl of Trevethick now. She'll need to go on the payroll.

Shit.

She's *almost* my employee. I need to sort out her employment status sooner rather than later. I don't want Oliver or the Revenue breathing down my neck.

'What happened to Krystyna? I liked the old bird,' Tom says as he rubs his face.

'Krystyna's gone back to Poland. Now, will you go and put some fucking clothes on? There is a lady present, for fuck's sake,' I growl.

'Lady?'

Tom pales at the look I give him, and for once he doesn't rise to the bait. 'Sorry, old chap. I'll go and get dressed. Milk, no sugar for me.' He shuffles out of the kitchen and back to the guest room. I chide myself for inviting my friends to stay when Alessia is working here. I'm not going to make that mistake again.

Alessia has managed to avoid the men for most of the morning, and she's glad when they finally leave. She even contemplated hiding in the forbidden room, but Krystyna had been adamant. She is not to enter.

She's cleared the blankets off the sofa in the living room and has stripped and remade the bed in the spare room. *His* bedroom is now tidy, and she was surprised and delighted to note there were still no used condoms in the wastebasket. Perhaps he's disposing of them a different way. She doesn't dwell on this thought, because it depresses her. She enters his walk-in closet to put away the ironing and gather up his dirty clothes. It's only been a couple of days, but it's a mess again.

The Mister is sitting at his computer and working, doing whatever it is that he does. She still has no idea how he makes his living. She recalls the smile that lit up his face when he first saw her this morning. His dazzling smile is contagious. Grinning like an idiot, she examines the pile of clothing on the floor of his closet. Kneeling down, she picks up one shirt, then glances quickly at the half-open door. Satisfied that she's alone, she holds the shirt to her face, closes her eyes, and inhales his scent.

So good.

'There you are,' he says.

Alessia jumps and bolts upright rather too quickly, so that she stumbles backwards. Two strong hands grab her arms and save her from falling.

'Easy,' he says, and gently holds her while she finds her balance. As soon as she does, to her regret, he releases her, but his touch still echoes through her body. 'I was looking for a sweater. It's a bright day, but cold. Are you warm enough?' he asks.

She nods vigorously, trying to catch her breath. Right now, in this small space with him, she's too warm.

He surveys the pile of clothes on the floor and frowns. 'It's a mess, I know,' he mumbles with a sheepish expression on his face. 'I'm pathologically untidy.'

'Path-o-log—'

'Pathological.'

'I do not know this word.'

'Oh . . . um . . . it refers to an extreme behaviour.'

'I see,' Alessia responds, and she looks down at the clothes again and nods. 'Yes. Pathological.' She gives him a wry expression, and he laughs.

'I'll sort this out,' he says.

'No. No. I do it.' Alessia waves him away.

'You shouldn't have to.'

'It is my job.'

He grins and reaches across her for a chunky cream sweater on one of the shelves. His arm brushes her shoulder, and she freezes as her heart goes into overdrive.

'Sorry,' he says, looking a little disheartened as he leaves the closet.

Once he's gone, Alessia recovers her equilibrium.

Can he not tell the effect he has on me?

And he caught her sniffing his shirt. She covers her face. He must think she's a complete idiot. Feeling mortified and angry with herself, she sinks to her knees and sorts through the pile of clothing, folding the clothes that don't need washing and putting all his dirty stuff into the laundry basket.

I can't keep my hands off her. Any excuse.

Leave her alone, dude.

And if I touch her, she freezes. I amble back to the drawing room, feeling glum. She just doesn't like me.

Is this a first?

I think so. I've never struggled with women before. They've

always been an easy diversion for me. With a healthy bank account, a flat in Chelsea, a pretty face and an aristocratic family, I've never had a problem.

Ever.

Except now.

I should ask her out for a meal.

She looks like she could do with a decent meal.

Suppose she says no?

Then at least I'll know.

I pace the length of the windowed wall in the drawing room, stopping to gaze out at the Peace Pagoda for a few minutes and trying to summon the nerve.

Why is this so difficult? Why her?

She's beautiful. She's talented.

She's not interested.

Perhaps it's as simple as that.

The first woman who's ever said no.

She's not said no. She might give me a chance.

Ask. Her. Out.

I take a deep breath and wander back into the hallway. She is standing outside my darkroom looking at the door and holding a laundry basket.

'It's a darkroom,' I say as I stride towards her.

Her lovely brown eyes meet mine. She's curious. And I remember that I'd asked Krystyna not to clean it sometime ago. It's been a while since I've been in it myself.

'I'll show you.' I'm grateful that she doesn't back away like she normally does. 'Do you want to see?'

She nods, and as I grab the laundry basket, my fingers brush hers. My heart slams against my ribs. 'Let me have this.' My voice is gruff as I try to calm the pounding in my chest. Placing the basket on the floor behind me, I open the door, switch on the light, and stand aside to let her enter.

Alessia enters the small room. It glows with red light and smells of mysterious chemicals and the stale air of inactivity. There's a bank of short dark cabinets lining one wall, with large plastic trays on top. High above the cabinets are shelves crowded with bottles and stacks of paper and photographs. Beneath the shelves is an empty washing line from which a few pegs hang.

'It's just a darkroom,' he says, and flicks on the dim overhead light so the red glow vanishes.

'Photography?' Alessia asks.

He nods. 'It's a hobby. I thought at one time I would take it up professionally.'

'The photographs in the apartment – you take them?'

'Yes. All of them. I had a few assignments, but . . .' His voice trails off.

The landscapes and the nudes.

'My father was a photographer.' He turns to a glass cabinet filled with cameras that's behind him. He opens one of the doors and takes out a camera. Alessia catches the name 'Leica' on the front.

Holding the camera up to my eye, I study Alessia through the lens. She is all dark eyes, long lashes, high cheekbones, and full, parted lips. My groin tightens.

'You're beautiful,' I whisper, and press the shutter.

Alessia's mouth drops open, but she shakes her head and covers her face with her hands, though they don't conceal her smile. I take another shot.

'You are,' I say. 'Look.' And I hold the back of the camera out to her so that she can see the image. She stares down at her face that's been captured digitally in fine detail and then looks up at me – and I'm lost. Lost in the magic of her dark, dark gaze. 'See,'

I murmur. 'You're stunning.' Reaching forward, I tip up her chin and, leaning down, inching closer and closer so she has a chance to move away, I brush my lips against hers. She gasps, and as I pull back, she touches her fingers to her mouth, her eyes growing rounder.

'That's how I feel,' I whisper, my heart pounding.

Will she slap me? Will she flee?

She stares at me. An ethereal vision in the muted light, she tentatively raises her hand and traces my lips with her fingertips. I freeze, closing my eyes as her tender touch reverberates through my body.

I daren't breathe.

I don't want to frighten her away.

I feel her feather-light touch, everywhere.

Everywhere.

Fuck.

And before I can stop myself, I pull her into my embrace and wrap my arms around her. She melts against the length of my body, her warmth leaching into me.

Oh, man, the feel of her.

I slide my fingers under her scarf and gently slip it off her head. Clasping her plait at the base of her neck, I tug lightly, bringing her lips up to mine. 'Alessia,' I breathe, and kiss her again, softly, slowly, so as not to frighten her. She stills in my arms, then brings her hands up to clutch my biceps, closing her eyes as she accepts me.

I deepen the kiss, my tongue teasing her lips, and she opens her mouth.

Fuck.

She tastes of warmth and grace and sweet seduction. Her tongue hesitant and faltering against mine. It's captivating. It's arousing.

I have to hold myself back. I want nothing more than to bury myself in this girl – but I don't think she'll let me. I draw back. 'What's my name?' I murmur against her lips.

'Mister,' she whispers as I run my thumb down her cheek.

'Maxim. Say Maxim.'

'Maxim,' she breathes.

'Yes.' I love the sound of my name in her accent.

See, that wasn't so hard.

Suddenly there's a loud, insistent banging on the front door.

Who the hell is that? How did they get into the building?

Reluctantly I step back. 'Don't go anywhere.' I hold up my finger in warning.

'Open the door, Mr Trev . . . an!' a disembodied voice bellows from outside. 'Immigration!'

'Oh, no,' Alessia whispers, and she clutches her throat, her eyes wide with fear.

'Don't be afraid.'

The knock rattles the door once more. 'Mr Trev . . . yan!' The voice is perceptibly louder.

'I'll deal with this,' I mutter, pissed off that we've been interrupted. Leaving Alessia in the darkroom, I head down the hallway.

Through the peephole in the front door, I assess the two men outside. One is short, the other is tall, and both are dressed in cheap grey suits and black parkas. They don't look particularly official. I pause, debating whether or not to answer. But I should find out why they're here and if it's anything to do with Alessia.

I thread the sturdy security chain through the catch and open the door.

One of the men tries to burst in, but with my body pressed against the door, the chain holds. He's the short one. Thickset and balding, he oozes aggression from every pore in his body and from his sly, shrewd eyes. 'Where is she, mister?' he barks.

I recoil.

Who are these lowlifes?

Baldy's partner looms behind him: thin, silent and menacing. The hairs on the back of my neck stand to attention.

'Can I see some ID?' My voice is equally menacing.

'Open the door. We're from immigration, and we believe you have a failed asylum seeker in your apartment.' The stocky guy speaks again as his nostrils flare in anger. He has a distinct Eastern European accent.

'You need a warrant to search these premises. Where is it?' I hiss with the authority that comes from a life of privilege and several years at one of the best public schools in Britain.

The large man hesitates for a moment, and I smell a rat.

Who the fuck are these men?

'Your warrant, where is it?' I snarl.

Baldy looks uncertainly at his cohort.

'Where is the girl?' The tall, thin bloke speaks.

'There is no one here but me. Who are you looking for?'

'A girl—'

'Aren't we all?' I sneer. 'Now, can I suggest you fuck off and come back with a warrant or I'll call the police.' Taking my phone out of my back pocket, I hold it up in front of them. 'But just so we're clear. There are no girls here, let alone illegal immigrants.' I lie easily, a skill that's also a product of several years at one of the best public schools in Britain. 'Shall I call the police?'

Both of them take a step back.

At that moment Mrs Beckstrom, who lives in the neighbouring flat, opens her front door, holding Heracles, her yappy lapdog.

'Hello, Maxim,' she calls.

Bless you, Mrs Beckstrom.

'Very well, Mr Trev . . . Trev.' He can't pronounce my name.

It's Lord Trevethick to you, fucker!

'We shall be back with a warrant.' He turns on his heel, jerks his head at his colleague, and they brush past Mrs Beckstrom on their way towards the stairs. She glares at them, then smiles at me.

'Good afternoon, Mrs B,' I say with a wave, and close the door.

How the hell did those thugs find out that Alessia was here? Why are they chasing her? What has she done? There's no 'immigration' department. It's called Border Force and has been for years. I take a deep breath in an effort to damp down my anxiety and head back into the darkroom, where I suspect Alessia will be trembling in a corner.

She's not there.

She's not in the kitchen.

My concern mushrooms into full-scale panic as I race through the flat calling her name. She's not in the bedrooms or the drawing room. Finally I search the scullery. The fire-escape door is ajar, and her coat and boots are missing.

Alessia has fled.

Chapter Nine

Alessia flies down the fire escape, her heart racing as adrenaline and fear fuel her body. Once she reaches the bottom, she's in the side alley. She should be safe here. The gate to the street at the rear of the building is locked from the inside. But to be sure, she ducks between two of the bins, where the residents of Mister Maxim's block dispose of their trash. She leans against the brick wall and drags air into her lungs, trying to catch her breath.

How have they found her? *How?*

She had recognised Dante's voice immediately, and all her suppressed memories had surfaced in a terrifying rush.

The dark.

The smell.

The fear.

The cold.

The smell. Ugh. The smell.

Tears well in her eyes, and she tries to blink them away. She has led them to *him*! She knows how ruthless they are and what they are capable of doing. She lets out a loud sob and puts her fist in her mouth as she cowers on the cold ground.

He could be hurt.

No.

She has to check. She can't flee if he's hurt.

Think, Alessia. Think.

The only person who knows she is here is Magda.

Magda!

No. Did they find Magda and Michal?

What have they done to them?

Magda.

Michal.

Mister . . . *Maxim.*

Her breath comes in short, sharp bursts as panic closes her throat. She thinks she's going to faint, but suddenly her stomach roils, bile rises in her throat, and before she knows it, she's doubled over and vomiting her breakfast onto the ground. As she retches and retches, she splays her hands on the brick wall until there's nothing left in her stomach. The physical effort of throwing up leaves her wrung out but a little calmer. Wiping her mouth on the back of her hand, she stands, feeling dizzy, and peeks into the alley to see if anyone has heard her. She's still alone.

Thank God.

Think, Alessia, think.

The first thing she has to do is check that the Mister is okay. Taking a deep breath, she leaves her refuge between the bins and makes her way back up the fire escape. She moves cautiously as a sense of self-preservation kicks in. She needs to know the coast is clear, but she cannot be seen by them. It's six storeys high, so by the time she reaches the fifth storey, she's winded. She inches her way up the next staircase and peeps through the metal railings into the penthouse apartment. The glass door is closed, but she can see into the living room. There's no sign of life at first, but then, all of a sudden, the Mister barges into the living room, and she can tell he's fetching something from his desk. He's there for a moment before he bolts back out of the room.

Her body slumps against the metal balustrade. He's safe.

Thank God.

With her curiosity appeased and her conscience reassured, she staggers back down the fire escape, knowing she has to check that Magda and Michal are okay.

At ground level in the alley once more, she changes into her boots and makes her way to the gate at the rear entrance of the apartment block. It opens onto the backstreet, not onto Chelsea Embankment. She pauses for a moment Perhaps Dante and Ylli will be there waiting for her? They will be out the front, surely? With her heart beating a frantic tempo, she opens the gate and peers into the street. The only sign of life is a dark green sports car speeding to the end of the road; there's no sign of Dante and his sidekick, Ylli. Taking her woolly hat out of her bag, she tugs it on, tucks her hair inside, and sets off for the bus stop.

She walks briskly along the street, fighting the urge to run, knowing that might attract unwanted attention. She keeps her head down and her hands in her pockets, and with each step she prays to her grandmother's God to keep Magda and Michal safe. She says it over and over again, alternating between her native tongue and English.

Ruaji, Zot.

Ruaji, Zot.

God, keep them safe.

I've stood paralysed in the hallway for what seems like an age. I'm filled with dread, and my blood is thundering in my ears.

Where the fuck is she?

What the hell is she mixed up in?

What do I do?

How can she face those guys on her own?

Fuck it. I have to find her.

Where will she go?

Home.

Brentford.

Yes.

I dash down the hall to the drawing room and snatch the car keys from my desk, then run to the front door, stopping only to grab my coat.

I feel sick, my stomach churning.

There is no way those guys were from 'immigration'.

When I reach the garage, I press the electronic key, expecting the Discovery to open, but instead the Jag beeps to life.

Shit. In my haste I've picked up the wrong key.

Fuck it.

I don't have time to go back upstairs for the correct key. I clamber into the F-Type Jag and press the ignition. The engine roars to life, and I ease the car forward out of its parking space. The garage doors rise gradually, and I exit to the left onto the street and race to the end of the road, turning left again towards Chelsea Embankment. But that's as far as I get. Traffic is slow because it's Friday afternoon and the beginning of rush hour. The crowded roads exacerbate my anxiety and do nothing for my temper. I run through my interaction with the thugs repeatedly, looking for any clues as to what might have happened to Alessia. They sounded Eastern European. They looked rough. Alessia bolted – so she either knows them or believes they're from the 'immigration' department, which means she must be in the UK illegally. This doesn't surprise me. She's brought every conversation we've had about what she's doing in London to an abrupt end.

Oh, Alessia. What are you up to?

And where the hell are you?

I hope that she's gone back to Brentford, because that's where I'm headed.

Alessia sits on the train nervously fingering the small gold cross that hangs around her neck. It was her grandmother's, and it's the only possession she has that belonged to her dear nana. She treasures it. In times of stress, it brings her comfort. Though her mother and father are not religious, her grandmother was . . . She fiddles with it now and keeps repeating her mantra.

Please keep them safe.

Please keep them safe.

Her anxiety is overwhelming. They found her. How? How do they know about Magda? She needs to know that Magda and Michal are okay. Normally she likes travelling by train, but today it's too slow. As the train reaches Putney, Alessia knows that it will be another twenty minutes before it reaches Brentford.

Please hurry.

Her thoughts turn to Mister Maxim. At least he is safe, for now.

Her heart stutters.

Maxim.

He kissed me.

Twice.

Twice!

He said lovely words. About her.

You're beautiful.

You're stunning.

And he kissed her!

That's how I feel.

If circumstances were different, she would be ecstatic. She

touches her fingers to her lips. It was a bittersweet moment. Her dreams were finally realised, only to be shattered by Dante – again.

There's no way she can be involved with the Mister. *No.* Maxim. His name is Maxim.

She has brought such terrible danger to his home. She has to protect him.

Zot! My job!

She will be out of a job. Nobody wants trouble coming to their front door and criminals like Dante threatening them.

What will she do?

She needs to be careful when she returns to Magda's. She cannot let Dante find her there.

She cannot.

She must protect herself, too.

Fear grips her throat, and she shudders. She hugs herself, trying to contain her distress. All her vague hopes and dreams are lost. And in a rare moment of self-pity, she rocks to and fro, trying to find some comfort and alleviate her fear.

Why does the train have to take so long?

It pulls into Barnes station, and the doors open.

'Please. Please hurry,' Alessia whispers, and her fingers find her gold cross once more.

I speed down the A4, my mind hopping from Alessia to those men and then to Kit as I dodge through the traffic.

Kit? What would you do?

He would have known. He always knew.

I remember our Christmas holiday. Kit had been on such good form. Maryanne and I had joined him and Caroline at a jazz festival in Havana. A couple of days later, we'd all flown down to St Vincent and taken a boat to Bequia to spend Christmas together in a private villa. Maryanne had gone on to Whistler to ski and to spend New Year's Eve with friends, and Caroline, Kit and I had returned to the UK for Hogmanay.

It had been an amazing week.

And the day after New Year's Day, Kit died.

Or killed himself.

There. I thought it.

My unspoken suspicion.

Damn it, Kit. You fucker.

The A4 becomes the M4, and I spy the high-rise towers that dominate the Brentford landscape and signal that I'm near. I come off the motorway, hitting the slip road at fifty miles per hour. I slow down, but fortunately, the lights at the junction are green and I cruise through them, thankful that I'd brought her home earlier in the week and know where she lives.

Six minutes later I pull up in front of her house, leap out of the car and dash up the short pathway. There are still clumps of snow on the grass and the sad remains of a snowman. The doorbell trills somewhere inside, but there's no response. The house is empty.

Fuck.

Where is she?

Apprehension overwhelms me. Where could she be?

Of course! She'll be coming here by train.

I'd seen the sign for the station as I'd turned into Church Walk. I sprint back down the path and turn right on to the main road. The station is less than two hundred metres on my left.

Thank God it's so close.

As I dash down the station stairs, I see a train waiting on the far platform, but it's heading into London. I stop and focus my attention. There are only two platforms, and the one I'm on is for trains travelling out of London. All I have to do is wait. An electronic display hanging overhead announces that the next train arrives at 15:07. I check my watch; it's 15:03 now.

I lean against one of the white iron pillars that support the station roof and wait. There are a few other commuters waiting for the train, too. Most of them, like me, are seeking shelter from the elements. I watch as the frigid wind blows a discarded crisp packet in gusts along the station platform and across the train tracks. But it doesn't hold my attention for long. Every few seconds I glance at the empty track, praying for the London train to materialise.

Come on. Come on. I will it to arrive.

Finally the train appears around the bend, and it slowly – oh, so fucking slowly – pulls into the station and stops. I stand up straight, my stomach churning with anxiety as the doors open and a few people alight from the train.

Twelve of them.

But not Alessia.

Fucking hell.

As the train leaves the station, I check the electronic sign again. The next train is due in fifteen minutes.

That's not too long.

It's a fucking age!

Hell.

I'm glad that even in my haste to leave the flat, I remembered my coat. It's bloody cold. I cup and blow on my hands, stamp my feet, and pull up my coat collar in an effort to keep warm. Thrusting my hands into the pockets, I pace up and down the platform while I wait.

My phone buzzes, and for some insane reason I think it might be Alessia, but of course she doesn't have my number. It's Caroline. Whatever she wants can wait. I ignore the call.

After an intolerable fifteen minutes, the 15:22 from London Waterloo comes into view around the bend. It slows as it approaches the station, and after an agonising minute it stops.

Time suspends.

The doors open, and Alessia is first off the train.

Oh, thank fuck.

Relief nearly brings me to my knees, but just the sight of her calms me down.

When Alessia sees him, she stops short in complete astonishment. The other disembarking passengers stream past them as she and Maxim stare at each other, drinking each other in. The doors close with a hiss of compressed air, and the train gradually pulls out of the station leaving them on their own.

'Hello,' he says, breaking the silence between them as he approaches her. 'You left without saying goodbye.'

Her face falls, and her eyes fill with tears that spill down her cheeks.

Her anguish rips through me.

'Oh, baby,' I whisper, and open my arms. She puts her face in her hands and begins to weep. Feeling at a loss, I fold her into my embrace and hold her. 'I've got you. I've got you,' I whisper against her green woolly hat. She sniffles, and I lift her chin and plant a tender kiss on her forehead. 'I mean it. I've got you.'

Alessia's eyes widen, and she pulls away. 'Magda?' she whispers, alarmed.

'Let's go.' I take her hand, and together we hurry up the metal staircase and out onto the road. Her hand is cold in mine, and I want nothing more than to whisk her away to somewhere safe. But first of all I have to know what's going on. What trouble she's in. I only hope that she'll open up and tell me.

We walk quickly but in silence across the road and back to 43 Church Walk. At the front door, Alessia fishes out a key from her pocket, unlocks the door, and we both step inside.

The front hallway is tiny and made more crowded by the two packing boxes that stand in the corner. Alessia removes her hat and anorak, and I take them from her and hang them on one of the pegs on the wall.

'Magda,' she calls up the stairs while I shed my coat and hang it beside hers, but there's no answer. The house is empty. I follow her into the tiny kitchen.

Jesus, the place is a shoebox!

From the threshold of the dated but tidy 1980s kitchen, I watch Alessia fill the kettle. She's in her tight jeans and the green sweater that she wore the other day.

'Coffee?' she asks.

'Please.'

'Would you like milk and sugar?'

I shake my head. 'No, thank you.' I loathe instant coffee and can only tolerate it black, but now isn't the right time to tell her.

'Sit,' she says, and points to the little white table. I do as I'm told and wait, watching her while she prepares our drinks. I am not going to rush her.

She makes tea for herself – strong, with sugar and milk – and eventually hands me a mug inscribed BRENTFORD FC that bears the team logo. Taking the seat opposite me, she gazes down at the contents of her mug, which is emblazoned with the Arsenal shield, and an uncomfortable silence settles between us.

Finally I can bear it no longer. 'Are you planning to tell me what's going on? Or do I have to guess?'

She doesn't respond, but her teeth worry her upper lip. Under any normal circumstance, this would drive me crazy, but seeing her this distraught is sobering.

'Look at me.'

At last her big brown eyes meet mine.

'Tell me. I want to help.'

Her eyes widen with what I assume is fear, and she shakes her head.

I sigh. 'Okay. Let's play twenty questions.'

She looks puzzled.

'You answer each question yes or no.'

Her frown deepens, and she clutches the little gold cross that hangs at her neck.

'Are you a failed asylum seeker?'

Alessia gazes at me, then gives me the briefest shake of her head.

'Okay. Are you here legally?'

She blanches, and I have my answer. 'Not legally, then?'

After a beat she shakes her head again.

'Have you lost the power of speech?' I hope she notices the trace of humour in my voice.

Her face brightens, and she half smiles. 'No,' she says, and her cheeks colour a little.

'That's better.'

She takes a sip of her tea.

'Talk to me. Please.'

'You will tell the police?' she asks.

'No. Of course not. Is that what you're worried about?'

She nods.

'Alessia, I won't. You have my word.'

Placing her elbows on the table, she clasps her hands together and rests her chin on them. A range of conflicting emotions crosses her face as the silence expands and fills the room. I hold my tongue, silently begging her to talk. At last her dark eyes meet mine. They're full of determination. She sits up straight and places her hands in her lap. 'The man who came to your apartment, his name is Dante.' Her voice is a pained whisper. 'He brought me and some other girls from Albania to England.' She looks down at her mug of tea.

A shiver runs up my spine to my scalp, and I have a horrible sinking feeling in my stomach. Somehow I think I know what she's about to say.

'We thought we were coming here to work. For a better life. Life in Kukës is hard for some women. The men who brought us here . . . We were betrayed—' Her soft voice halts over the word, and I close my eyes as revulsion and bile rise in my throat. It's as bad as it could possibly be.

'Human trafficking?' I whisper, and I watch her reaction.

She nods once, her eyes tightly closed. 'For sex.' Her words are barely audible, but in them I hear her shame and her horror.

Fury like nothing I've felt before ignites inside me. I clench my fists trying to control my anger.

Alessia is pale.

And everything about her falls into place.

Her reticence.

Her fear.

Of me.

Of men.

Fuck. Fuck. Fuck.

'How did you escape?' I ask, trying to keep my voice even.

We're both startled by the rattle of a key in the front door. Alarmed, Alessia leaps to her feet, and I jump up, knocking my chair to the floor.

'Stay here,' I growl, pulling open the kitchen door.

A blond woman in her forties stands in the hallway. She gasps in alarm when she sees me.

'Magda!' Alessia cries. Dodging around me, she runs to embrace Magda.

'Alessia!' Magda exclaims, and hugs her. 'You're here. I thought . . . I thought . . . I'm sorry. I'm sorry,' Magda babbles, anguish in her voice, as she begins to cry. 'They were here again. Those men.'

Alessia takes Magda by the shoulders. 'Tell me. Tell me what happened.'

'Who is this?' Magda turns her tear-stained face to me with suspicion.

'This is . . . Mister Maxim. It is his apartment that I clean.'

'Did they come to his apartment?'

'Yes.'

Magda gulps and holds her hands up to her mouth. 'I'm so sorry,' she whispers.

'Perhaps Magda would like some tea, and she can tell us what happened,' I say gently.

The three of us are sitting at the table while Magda puffs on a brand of cigarette that is unfamiliar to me. I've declined her offer to try one. The last time I smoked a cigarette, it set off a chain of events that led to my expulsion from school. I was thirteen and with a local girl in the grounds at Eton.

'I don't think they were from the immigration department. They had a photograph of Michal and you,' Magda says to Alessia.

'What? How?' I ask.

'Yes. They found it on Facebook.'

'No!' Alessia exclaims, and clamps her hand over her mouth in horror. She looks at me. 'Michal has taken the selfies with me.'

'The selfies?' I ask.

'Yes. For the Facebook,' Alessia says, frowning. I quickly mask my amused expression.

Magda continues, 'They said they knew where Michal went to school. They knew all about him. All his personal information is on his Facebook page.' She takes a long drag of her cigarette, her hand trembling.

'They threatened Michal?' Alessia's face is ashen.

Magda nods. 'I had no choice. I was scared. I'm sorry.' Her voice is little more than a whisper. 'There was no way I could contact you. I gave them the address where you were working.'

Well, that clears that *mystery up.*

'What do they want with you, Alessia?' she asks.

Alessia gives me a brief, imploring look, and I realise that Magda doesn't know the full details of how Alessia came to London. I run my hand through my hair.

What to do? This is far more than I bargained for . . .

'Have you contacted the police?' I ask.

Magda and Alessia both speak at once: 'No police.' They are emphatic.

'Are you sure?' I can understand Alessia's reaction, but not Magda's. Perhaps she's here illegally, too.

'No police,' Magda says, banging her hand on the table, startling both Alessia and me.

'Okay,' I say, raising my palm to placate her. I've never met people who don't trust the police.

It's obvious that Alessia can't stay in Brentford, and neither can Magda and her son. The thugs who turned up on my doorstep were bristling with barely contained violence. 'Is it just the three of you living here?' I ask.

They both nod.

'Where is your son now?'

'At a friend's house. He's safe. I called him before I got home.'

'I don't think it's safe for Alessia to stay here, or you for that matter. These men are dangerous.'

Alessia nods. 'Very dangerous,' she whispers.

Magda's face whitens. 'But my job. My son's school. We are only here for another two weeks before I leave—'

'Magda, no!' Alessia tries to silence her.

'For Canada,' Magda continues, disregarding Alessia's objection.

'Canada?' I look to Alessia and back at Magda.

'Yes. Michal and I are emigrating. I'm getting remarried. My fiancé lives and works in Toronto.' Her brief smile is a fond one. I offer her my congratulations, then turn my attention to Alessia.

'And what are you going to do?'

She shrugs as if she's got everything under control. 'I will find another place to stay. *Zot!* I am to see a place this evening.' She glances at the kitchen clock. 'Now!' She stands up, panicked.

'I don't think that's a good idea,' I interject. 'And frankly, that's the least of your worries right now.' She's illegally in the country – how is she going to find somewhere to stay?

She sits back down.

'Those men could come back at any time. They could easily snatch you off the street.' I shudder. They want her.

Evil fuckers.

What can I do?

Think. Think.

We could all hole up in Trevelyan House in Cheyne Walk, but Caroline would ask questions, and I don't want that – it's too complicated. I could take Alessia back to my flat – but they've already been there. One of the other properties? Maryanne's place? No. Perhaps I could take her to Cornwall. No one would find us there.

And as I contemplate my options, I realise I don't want to let her out of my sight.

Ever.

The thought surprises me.

'I want you to come with me,' I say to her.

'What?' Alessia exclaims. 'But—'

'I can find you somewhere to live. Don't worry about that.' *Jesus, I have enough property at my disposal.* 'But you're not safe here. You can come with me.'

'Oh.'

I turn my attention to Magda. 'Magda, as far as I can see, you have three options since you don't want to involve the police. We can move you to a local hotel for now, or we can put you up in a house in town. Or I can organise some close-protection security for you and your son, and you can stay here.'

'I cannot afford a hotel.' Magda's voice fades, while she gapes at me.

'Don't worry about the money,' I reply.

I do the calculations in my head. It's not much in the scheme of things. And Alessia will be safe.

Worth every penny.

And maybe Tom will give me a discount. He's a mate, after all.

Magda scrutinises me, her fixed stare intense. 'Why are you doing this?' she asks, bewildered. I clear my throat and wonder why myself.

Because it's the right thing to do?

No. I'm not that altruistic.

Because I want to be alone with Alessia? *Yes. That's the real reason.* But given what she's been through, she's not going to want to be alone with me. *Is she?*

I run my hand through my hair, uncomfortable with my thoughts. I don't want to examine my motives too closely. 'Because Alessia is a valued employee,' I answer.

Yes. That sounds convincing.

Magda eyes me with suspicion.

'Will you come with me?' I ask Alessia, ignoring Magda's doubtful expression. 'You'll be safe.'

Alessia is overwhelmed. His level gaze is sincere. He's offering her a way out. This man she barely knows. Yet he came all the way from Chelsea to check that she was okay. He waited for her at the station. He held her while she cried. She can only remember her grandmother and her mother doing that for her. Apart from Magda, no one else in England has treated her with such kindness. It's a generous offer. Too generous. And Dante and Ylli are her problem, not his. She doesn't want to drag him into this mess. She wants to protect him from them. But she is illegally in England. She has no passport. Dante has it and all her belongings, so she's stuck.

And Magda is leaving soon, bound for Toronto.

Mister Maxim is waiting for her answer.

What will he want in return for his help?

Alessia knows so little about him. She doesn't even know what he does for a living. All she knows is that the life he leads is very different from hers.

'This is just to keep you safe. No strings attached,' he says.

Strings attached?

'I don't want anything from you,' he clarifies, as if he can read her mind.

No strings attached.

She likes him. She more than likes him. She's a little in love with him – but she understands it's a crush. And yet he's the only person she's told about how she came to England.

'Alessia, please answer me,' he persists. His expression is anxious, his eyes wide and open and honest. He radiates concern. Can she trust him?

Not all men are monsters, are they?

'Yes,' she whispers before she can change her mind.

'Great,' he says, and he sounds relieved.

'What?' Magda snaps, looking at Alessia in surprise. 'Do you know him?'

'She'll be safe with me,' he says. 'I'll take good care of her.'

'I want to go, Magda,' Alessia whispers.

If she goes, Magda and Michal will be safe.

Magda lights another cigarette.

'What do you want to do?' Mister Maxim turns his attention to Magda, who looks from Alessia to him, confounded.

'You haven't told me what those men want, Alessia,' Magda says. Alessia had been vague about how she came to England. She'd had to be. Her mother and Magda are the best of friends, and she didn't want Magda emailing her mother to tell her what had happened. Her mother would have been devastated.

Alessia shakes her head. 'I cannot. Please,' she pleads.

Magda huffs. 'Your mother?' she says, pulling at her cigarette.

'She cannot find out.'

'I don't know.'

'Please,' Alessia begs.

Magda sighs with resignation and turns to Maxim. 'I don't want to leave my house,' she says.

'Okay. Close protection it is.' He stands up, long, lean and impossibly handsome, and fishes his iPhone out of his jeans pocket. 'I need to make some calls.' He leaves them staring after him as he closes the kitchen door.

When Tom Alexander was invalided out of the army, he set up a security company based in central London. He deals with high-profile, high-net-worth clients. And now me. 'What have you got yourself into, Trevelyan?'

'I don't know, Tom. All I know is I need 24/7 security for a woman and her son who live in Brentford.'

'Brentford? This evening?'

'Yes.'

'You're bloody lucky I can help you.'

'I know, Tom. I know.'

'I'll come down myself and bring my best man. Dene Hamilton. I think you've met him. Served with me in Afghanistan.'

'Yes. I remember him.'

'See you in an hour.'

Alessia stands in the hallway wearing Magda's son's anorak and holding two plastic shopping bags.

'Is that everything?' I sound as bewildered as I feel.

I can't believe this is all she has.

Alessia pales and lowers her eyes.

I frown.

The girl has nothing.

'Okay,' I offer. 'I'll take those, and let's go.' She hands me both bags and still won't look me in the eye. I'm astonished at how little they weigh.

'Where are you going?' asks Magda.

'I have a place in the West Country. We'll go there for a few days while we work out what's to be done.'

'Will I see Alessia again?'

'I hope so.' But there's no way on earth she's coming back here while those bastards are on the loose.

Magda turns to Alessia. 'Goodbye, sweet girl,' she whispers.

Alessia hugs Magda and clings to her. 'Thank you,' she says as tears begin to trickle down her face. 'For saving me.'

'Hush, dear girl,' Magda murmurs. 'I would do anything for your mother. You know that.' She releases Alessia and holds her at arm's length. 'You are so strong and brave. You will make your mother proud.' She cups Alessia's face and kisses her cheek.

'Say goodbye to Michal for me.' Alessia's voice is strained and soft and full of sorrow. And my heart constricts.

Am I doing the right thing?

'We will both miss you. Maybe one day you'll come to Canada and meet my wonderful man?'

Alessia nods, but she's too choked up to say anything else, and she leaves through the front door while trying to wipe away her tears. I follow her, holding all that she has in the world.

Outside on the path, Dene Hamilton surveys the street. Tall, broad-shouldered, with close-cropped black hair, he's more menacing than his refined grey suit suggests. He's ex-army, like Tom, and it shows in his alert stance. He'll work in a shift pattern with another bodyguard who'll be arriving in the morning. Tom's people will safeguard Magda and Michal around the clock, and they'll remain until the two of them leave for Canada.

I stop to shake Hamilton's hand.

'We've got this, Lord Trevethick,' he says, his dark eyes gleaming beneath the street lamp as he scans the road and misses nothing.

'Thank you,' I reply. It still catches me off-guard when I'm addressed by my title. 'You have my number. Contact me if they need anything.'

'Will do, sir.' Hamilton gives me a gracious nod, and I follow Alessia. She averts her face when I put my arm around her, perhaps to hide the fact that she's still crying.

Am I doing the right thing?

With a brisk wave to Magda, who's standing on the doorstep, and to Hamilton, I lead Alessia to the F-Type. I unlock it and hold the passenger door open for her. She hesitates, her expression strained. I reach up to stroke her jaw with the back of my hand. 'I've got you.' My tone is gentle, to reassure her. 'You're safe.'

Alessia throws her arms around my neck and hugs me hard, totally taking me by surprise. 'Thank you,' she whispers, and before I can respond, she releases me and climbs into the car. I ignore the knot in my throat and put both her bags in the boot and climb in beside her.

'This will be an adventure,' I say, trying to lighten the mood. But Alessia gazes at me, her eyes brimming with sorrow.

I swallow.
I'm doing the right thing.
Yes.
I am.
But maybe not for the right reasons.
I exhale, push the ignition, and the engine growls into life.

Chapter Ten

I turn the Jaguar left onto the A4 and speed along the three-lane highway. Alessia is hunched down in the passenger seat with her arms wrapped around herself, but at least she's remembered to put on her seat belt. She's staring out at the passing industrial units and car showrooms, but occasionally she wipes a sleeve across her face, and I know she's still crying.

How can women cry so quietly?

'Do you want me to stop for tissues?' I ask. 'I'm sorry I don't have any.'

She shakes her head but doesn't look at me.

I understand why she's emotional. *What a day.* If I'm astounded by today's events, she must be overwhelmed. Completely overwhelmed. I think it's best if I leave her alone to gather her thoughts. Besides, it's late, and I have to make some calls.

I press the phone icon on the touch screen and find Danny's number. The sound of its ring echoes through the car via the hands-free system. Within two rings she answers.

'Tresyllian Hall,' she says in her familiar Scottish brogue.

'Danny, it's Maxim.'

'Master Maxim . . . I mean—'

'It's okay, Danny, don't worry,' I interrupt her, with a quick glance at Alessia, who's now looking at me. 'Is the Hideout or the Lookout available this weekend?'

'I think they're both available, my—'

'And next week?'

'The Lookout is booked for a weekend clay shoot.'

'I'll take the Hideout, then.'

Appropriate.

'I need' – I glance at Alessia's pale face – 'I need two of the rooms made up and some of my clothes and toiletries brought over from the Hall.'

'You'll not be staying at the Hall?'

'Not at the moment, no.'

'Two rooms, you say?'

I had hoped for one . . .

'Yes, please. And could you ask Jessie to stock the fridge for breakfast and maybe a snack tonight. And some wine and some beer. Tell her to improvise.'

'Of course, milord. When will you be arriving?'

'Late tonight.'

'Of course. Is everything all right, sir?'

'Everything's fine. Oh, and Danny, can we get the piano tuned?'

'I had all of them tuned yesterday. You mentioned you wanted them all done when you were here.'

'That's great. Thanks, Danny.'

'You're welcome, my—' I press the OFF button before she finishes.

'Would you like to listen to some music?' I ask Alessia. She turns red-rimmed eyes to me, and my chest tightens. 'Okay,' I say, not waiting for her answer. On the media screen, I find what

I hope will be a soothing album and press PLAY. The sound of acoustic guitars fills the car, and I relax a little. We have a long drive ahead.

'Who is this?' Alessia asks.

'A singer-songwriter called Ben Howard.'

She stares at the screen for a moment, then goes back to gazing out of the window.

I reflect on all my past interactions with Alessia in light of what she's told me today. Now I understand why she's been so reticent around me, and my heart is leaden. In my fantasies I'd imagined that when I was finally alone with her, she would be laughing and carefree, gazing at me with adoring doe eyes. The reality is very different.

Very. Different.

And yet . . . I don't mind. I want to be with her.

I want her safe.

I want her . . .

That's the truth.

I've never felt like this before.

Everything has happened so fast. And I still don't know if I'm doing the right thing. But I know I can't abandon her to those lowlifes. I want to protect her.

How chivalrous.

My thoughts take a darker turn as I dwell on morbid fantasies of what she might have had to endure and of what she might have seen. This young woman in the hands of those monsters.

Fuck. I grip the steering wheel tighter as anger surges like sulphuric acid in my gut.

If I ever get hold of those men . . .

My rage is murderous.

What have they done to her? I want to know.

No. I don't want to know.

I do.

I don't.

I glance at the dashboard.

Shit. I'm speeding.

Slow the fuck down, mate.

I ease my foot off the accelerator.

Steady.

I take a deep, cleansing breath.

Calm down.

I want to ask her what she's endured. What she's seen. But now is not the right time. All my plans, all my fantasies will be for nothing if she can't bear to be with a man . . . any man.

And I realise that I can't touch her.

Fuck.

Alessia tries but fails to stem her tears. She's dazed, drowning in her emotions.

Her fear.

Her hope.

Her despair.

Can she trust the man sitting beside her? She has placed herself in his hands. Willingly. And she's done that before – with Dante – and that didn't turn out so well.

She doesn't know Mister Maxim. Not really. He's shown her nothing but kindness since she met him – and what he's done for Magda is beyond what any reasonable man could be expected to do. Until she met Maxim, Magda had been the only person in England whom Alessia trusted. She had saved Alessia's life. She had taken her in, fed and clothed her, and found her work, through a network of Polish women who live in West London and help each other.

And now Alessia is travelling miles and miles from that place of refuge. Magda has reassured her that Mrs Kingsbury's and

Mrs Goode's houses would be covered by one of the other girls while Alessia is away.

How long will she be gone?

And where is the Mister taking her?

She tenses. Perhaps Dante is following them?

She tightens her arms around her body. Thinking of Dante reminds her of her nightmare journey to England. She doesn't want to think about that. She never wants to think about it again. But it haunts her in moments of quiet and in her nightmares. What's become of Bleriana, Vlora, Dorina and the other girls?

Please let them have escaped, too.

Bleriana was only seventeen, the youngest of the girls.

Alessia shudders. The song on the car stereo is about living in the confines of fear. Alessia squeezes her eyes shut. Her stomach constricts with fear, the fear she's been living with for so long, and her tears continue to fall.

We pull into the Gordano Services on the M5 just after 10:00 p.m. I'm hungry in spite of the cheese sandwich Magda made for me back in Brentford. Alessia is asleep. I wait for a moment to see if she'll wake now that the car has come to a standstill. Under the glow from the halogen lights in the car park, she looks serene and ethereal – the curve of her translucent cheek, her dark lashes splayed out above it, and the stray lock of hair from her plait that curls beneath her chin. I contemplate letting her sleep but decide I can't leave her alone in the car.

'Alessia,' I whisper, and her name is a prayer. I'm tempted to stroke her cheek, but I resist and whisper her name once more. She wakes with a gasp and a wide-eyed start, looking frantically around her. When her eyes meet mine, she stills.

'Hey. It's me. You've been asleep. I want something to eat, and I need the loo. Do you want to come with me?'

She blinks several times, her long lashes fluttering over expressive but unfocused eyes.

She is gorgeous.

Rubbing her face, she looks around the car park, and her whole body suddenly tenses and radiates anxiety. 'Please, Mister, don't leave me here,' she says quietly.

'I've no intention of leaving you here. What's wrong?'

She shakes her head, paler now.

'Let's go,' I say.

Outside, I stretch as she clambers out of the car and almost runs to my side, her eyes scanning the surroundings.

What's happened?

I offer her my hand, and she grabs it, holding tight. Then to my delight and surprise, she curls her other hand around my biceps and clings to me.

'You know, I was Maxim earlier,' I say, trying to make her smile. 'I much prefer it to Mister.'

She flashes me an anxious look. 'Maxim,' she whispers, but her eyes dart all over the car park.

'Alessia, you're safe.'

She looks doubtful.

This will never do.

Releasing her hand, I grasp her shoulders. 'Alessia, what's wrong? Please tell me.'

Her expression changes, her wide eyes haunted and bleak.

'Please,' I beg, watching the vapour from our breath mingle between us in the frosty air.

'I escaped,' she whispers.

Shit! The rest of her story – I'm going to hear it here in a service station off the M5. 'Go on,' I encourage her.

'It was a place like this.' She looks around again.

'What? A motorway services?'

She nods. 'They stopped. They wanted us to wash. To be

clean. They were being . . . um . . . kind. Or so some of the girls thought. They made it seem like it was for our . . . um . . . What is the word? Our . . . um . . . good. Benefit. Our benefit. But if we were cleaner, we would bring a higher price.'

Fuck. This is going to make me angry again.

'Before. On the journey. I heard them talking. In English. About why we were going to England. They didn't know I understood. And I knew what they were going to do.'

'Shit!'

'I told the other girls. Some of them did not believe me. But three of the girls did believe me.'

Bloody hell! There are more women!

'It was night, like now. One of the men, Dante, took three of us to the restrooms. We ran. All of us. He could not catch us all. It was dark. I ran into the woods. I ran and ran . . . I ran away. I don't know about the other girls.' Her voice is tinged with guilt.

Oh, God.

I can bear no more. Overcome by what this young woman has braved, I fold her into my arms and hold her tightly. 'I've got you,' I whisper, feeling raw and exposed and enraged on her behalf. We stand for seconds, minutes – I don't know how long – in the cold car park, and finally, tentatively, she wraps her arms around me and relaxes into my hold, hugging me back. She fits perfectly in my arms. I can rest my chin on her head, should I so choose. She looks up at me, and it's as if she's seeing me for the first time. Her dark eyes are intense. Full of questions. Full of promise.

My breath catches in my throat.

What is she thinking?

Her eyes move to my lips, and she raises her head, her objective clear.

'You want me to kiss you?' I ask.

She nods.

Fuck.

I hesitate. I've vowed not to touch her. She closes her eyes, offering herself to me. And I can't resist. I plant a soft, chaste kiss on her lips, and she melts against me with a moan.

It's a wake-up call to my libido. I groan, staring down at her parted lips.

No.

Not now.

Not here.

Not after what she's been through.

Not in a service area on the M5.

I kiss her forehead. 'Come on. Let's eat.' Surprised by my restraint and taking her hand, I lead her into the building.

Alessia trails beside Maxim, clinging to him while they cross the asphalt. She focuses on his comforting embrace and tender kiss, not what happened the last time she was in a service station. She tightens her hold on him. He makes her forget, and for that she's grateful. The doors to the concourse open, and they step into the building, but she halts, bringing them both to a stop.

The smell. *Zot.* The smell.

Fried food.

Sweet food.

Coffee.

Disinfectant.

Alessia winces as she recalls being hustled to the restrooms. Not one bystander noticed her plight.

'You okay?' Maxim asks.

'I have the memories,' she says.

He squeezes her hand. 'I've got you,' he says. 'Come on. I really need the lavatory.' He gives her a rueful smile.

Alessia swallows. 'I do, too,' she says shyly, and follows him to the restrooms.

'Unfortunately, I can't take you in there with me.' Maxim tilts his head at the entrance. 'I'll be right outside here when you come out, okay?' he says. 'You go.'

Alessia, reassured, takes a deep breath and walks into the bathroom, giving him a last glance before she turns the corner. There is no line for the stalls. Only two women, one older, one younger, are there, washing their hands at the basins. Neither of them looks as if she's been trafficked from Eastern Europe.

Alessia chides herself.

What was she expecting?

The older lady, who must be at least fifty, turns to use the hand dryer, catches Alessia's eye, and smiles. Feeling encouraged and more confident, Alessia heads into a cubicle.

When she exits, Maxim is there, leaning against the opposite wall, tall and muscular, one thumb hooked in the belt loop of his jeans. His hair is ruffled and messy, his vivid green eyes intense. He grins when he sees her, his face lighting up like a child's at New Year, and he holds out his hand. Gladly, she takes it.

The coffee shop is a Starbucks; Alessia recognises it from the many she's seen in London. Maxim orders a double espresso for himself and, at her request, a hot chocolate.

'And what would you like to eat?' he asks.

'I am not hungry,' she replies.

He raises his eyebrows. 'You didn't have anything at Magda's. I know you didn't eat anything in my flat.'

Alessia frowns. She threw up her breakfast as well, but she isn't about to tell him that. She shakes her head. She's too upset by the day's events to eat.

Maxim huffs in frustration and orders a panini.

'Actually, make that two,' he says to the barista, giving Alessia a sideways look.

'I'll bring them over,' the barista replies, directing a coquettish smile at Maxim.

'We'd like them to go.' Maxim hands her a twenty-pound note.

'Of course.' The barista bats her eyelashes at him.

'Great, thanks.' He doesn't return her smile but turns his attention to Alessia.

'I have money,' Alessia says.

Maxim rolls his eyes. 'I've got this.'

They move to the end of the counter to wait for their order. Alessia wonders what she will do about money. She has a little, but she needs what she has for a deposit on a room. Though he did say that he could find her a room.

Did he mean a room in his apartment? Or somewhere else?

She doesn't know. And she has no idea how long they will stay or where they're going or when she'll be able to earn more cash. She'd like to ask him, but it's not her place to question a man.

'Hey, don't worry about money,' Maxim says.

'I—'

'Don't. Please.' His expression is serious.

He's generous. Once again Alessia wonders what he does for a living. He has the big apartment, two cars. He organised the security for Magda. Is he a composer? Do composers make a lot of money in England? She doesn't know.

'I can see your brain working from here. What is it? Ask me? I don't bite,' Maxim says.

'I want to know what is your job.'

'What I do for a living?' Maxim smiles.

'Are you a composer?'

He laughs. 'Sometimes.'

'I thought that's what you did. I liked your pieces.'

'You did?' His smile broadens, but he looks a little embarrassed. 'You speak very good English,' he says.

'Do you think so?' Alessia flushes at the unexpected compliment.

'Yes, I do.'

'My grandmother was English.'

'Oh. Well, that explains it. What was she doing in Albania?'

'She visited in the 1960s with her friend Joan, who is Magda's mother. As children Magda and my mother sent letters and became friends. They live in different countries but have remained very good friends, though they have never met.'

'Never?'

'No. Though my mother would like to, one day.'

'Two ham-and-cheese paninis,' the barista says, interrupting them.

'Thanks.' Maxim accepts the bag. 'Let's go. You can tell me more in the car,' he says to Alessia as he picks up his coffee. 'Bring your drink.' Alessia follows him out of the Starbucks, sticking close.

In the car Maxim downs his espresso, puts the empty cup in the cup holder, and, removing half of his panini from its paper wrapper, takes an enormous bite.

Its appetising aroma fills the car.

'Hmm,' Maxim murmurs in exaggerated appreciation. As he chews, he throws Alessia a sideways look. She stares at his mouth and licks her lips.

'Want some?' he asks.

She nods.

'Here, help yourself.' He passes her the second panini, then starts the car, a smirk on his face. Alessia allows herself a cautious bite of the sandwich. A string of melted cheese sticks to her lips. She uses her fingers to scoop it into her mouth and licks her fingers. Realising how ravenous she is, she takes another bite. It's delicious.

'Better?' Maxim asks, his voice low.

Alessia grins. 'You are cunning like the wolf.'

'Cunning is my middle name,' he says, looking pleased with himself, and Alessia can't help but laugh.

Boy, that's a good sound.

At the petrol station, I pull up beside the high-octane pump. 'This won't take a minute. Eat.' I grin and get out of the car. But Alessia scrambles out after me, clutching her panini, and comes to stand beside me at the pump.

'Miss me already?' I quip, trying to lighten the mood. Her lips curl in the semblance of a smile, but her eyes scour our surroundings. She's apprehensive, and this place is making her more anxious. I fill the tank.

'It is expensive!' Alessia exclaims when she sees the cost.

'Yes, I suppose it is.' And I realise I've never paid attention to how much fuel costs. I've never had to. 'Come on, let's go pay.'

In the queue for the till, Alessia stands beside me, taking the occasional bite of her sandwich and gazing at the shelves in what looks like wonder.

'Do you want anything? Magazine? A snack? Something sweet?' I ask.

She shakes her head. 'There is so much to buy here.'

I look around. Everything seems so commonplace to me. 'Don't you have shops in Albania?' I tease.

She purses her lips. 'Of course. In Kukës there are many shops, but not like this.'

'Oh?'

'This is tidy and ordered. Very neat. Pathological.'

I grin. 'Pathologically tidy?'

'Yes. The opposite of you.'

I laugh. 'The shops aren't tidy in Albania?'

'Not in Kukës. Not like this.'

At the till I slide my credit card into the chip and PIN machine, conscious that she's watching my every move.

'Your card is magic,' Alessia says.

'Magic?' And I have to agree with her. It is magic. I've done nothing to earn the money that's paying for the petrol. My wealth is merely an accident of birth.

'Yes,' I murmur. 'Magic.'

Back at the car, we climb in, and I wait before pressing the ignition.

'What?' Alessia asks.

'Seat belt.'

'I forget. It's like the nodding and the shaking.'

What is this?

'In Albania we shake our head to say yes, and we nod to say no,' she explains.

'Wow. That must be confusing.'

'Your way is confusing. Magda and Michal had to teach me.'

Clutching the other half of my panini, I start the car and cruise down the slip road back onto the M5.

So she mixes up yes and no? I wonder if I should review any of our previous conversations, given this new information.

'Where are we going?' Alessia asks, staring ahead into the dark night.

'My family has a place in Cornwall. It's another three hours or so.'

'It is a long way.'

'From London? Yes.'

She takes a sip of her hot chocolate.

'Tell me about your home,' I say.

'Kukës? It's a small town. Nothing much happens . . . It's . . . um . . . what is the word? Alone?'

'Isolated?'

'Yes. Isolated. And . . . rural.' She shrugs and seems reluctant to say more.

'Cornwall is rural. You'll see. Earlier you were telling me about your grandmother.'

She smiles. She seems happier to talk about her grandmother. This is what I'd envisaged when I hatched our escape plan this afternoon, an easy and relaxed conversation where I find out more about her. I settle back in my seat and give her an expectant look.

'My grandmother and her friend Joan came to Albania as missionaries.'

'Missionaries? In Europe?'

'Yes. The Communists banned religion. Albania was the first atheist nation.'

'Oh. I had no idea.'

'She came to help the Catholics. She smuggled books into Albania from Kosovo. Bibles. You know. What she did, it was dangerous. She met an Albanian man and—' She pauses, and her face softens. 'They fell in love. And . . . how do you say it? The rest is history.'

'Dangerous?' I asked.

'Yes. She has many hair-stand-up stories.'

'Hair-stand-up?' I smile. 'I think you mean hair-raising.'

She grins. 'Hair-raising.'

'And Magda's mother?'

'She moved on to Poland as a missionary and married a Polish man,' she says, as if this is obvious. 'They were the best of friends. And their daughters became the best of friends.'

'And that's why you came to Magda's when you escaped.'

'Yes. She has been a good friend to me.'

'I'm glad you've had someone.'

And now you have me.

'Do you want the other half of your panini?'

'No, thank you.'

'Will you share it with me?'

Alessia eyes me for a moment. 'Okay,' she says, and fishing it out of the bag, she offers it to me.

'You take first bite.'

She smiles and does exactly that, then hands it to me.

'Thank you.' I flash her a quick grin. I'm relieved that she seems happier. 'More music?'

She nods while chewing.

'Your choice. Just press that button and scroll through the tracks.'

Alessia squints at the screen and starts exploring my playlists. She's diligently absorbed in the task. Illuminated by the screen, her face is serious and earnest. 'I do not know any of this music,' she murmurs.

I hand her back the panini. 'Choose one.'

Her finger taps the display, and I smile when I see what she's chosen.

Bhangra. Why not?

A man starts singing a cappella. 'What language is this?' Alessia asks, and takes another bite. A melted piece of mozzarella escapes out of the corner of her mouth. With her index finger, she pushes it back in and sucks her finger clean. My body comes to attention.

I grip the steering wheel. 'Punjabi. I think.'

The band kicks in on the track, and Alessia passes the panini back to me. She sways in her seat to the rhythm. 'I have not heard anything like this.'

'I sometimes use this as part of a set when I'm DJing. More?' I ask, offering her what's left of the sandwich.

She shakes her head. 'No. Thank you.'

I pop the remainder into my mouth, pleased that I managed to get her to eat more.

'DJing?' she asks.

'You know, in a club. For people to dance to. I DJ a couple of nights a month in Hoxton.'

I glance at Alessia, who is staring blankly at me.

She has no idea what I'm talking about.

'Okay, I'll have to take you to a club.'

Alessia's look is still blank, but she continues to tap her feet to the beat. I shake my head. How sheltered was this girl's upbringing?

Given what she's experienced, not so sheltered. What horror has she endured? My mind races, my thoughts depressing me.

But then I recall her confession in the car park.

She escaped.

Escaped!

'They wanted us to be clean . . . we would bring a higher price.'

I exhale.

I hope, for her sake, that she managed to avoid any horror. But somehow I doubt it. The journey alone must have been a nightmare. I try to grasp the magnitude of what she's been through and what she's achieved. She escaped. Found a place to live. A job. And she escaped again this afternoon from my flat. While she has nothing, she's one resourceful young woman: ingenious, talented, courageous and beautiful. My heart swells with unexpected pride.

'You really are something, Alessia,' I whisper, but she's lost in the music and doesn't hear me.

It's after midnight when I pull up the gravel drive and park outside the garage of the Hideout, one of the luxury holiday homes on the Trevethick estate. I don't want to overwhelm Alessia with the Hall – maybe that can happen later. The truth is, I want her to myself. There are too many staff in the great house, and I haven't figured out what I'll say about her or *to* her about the estate. Right now she doesn't know who I am, what I have, and what my birthright entails. And I like that . . . I like that a lot.

She's asleep. She must be exhausted. I study her face. Even in the harsh glare of the garage's security light, her features are soft and delicate in repose.

Sleeping beauty.

I could look at her for hours. She grimaces briefly, and I wonder what she's dreaming about.

Me?

I consider carrying her into the house but dismiss the idea. The steps down to the front door are steep and can be slippery. I could kiss her awake. She should be woken with a kiss, like a princess. I'm being ridiculous, and I remember that I've vowed not to touch her.

'Alessia,' I whisper. 'We're here.'

Opening her eyes, she regards me sleepily. 'Hello,' she says.

'Hello, beautiful. We've arrived.'

Chapter Eleven

Alessia blinks the sleep from her eyes and peers through the windscreen. All she sees is a piercing light above a large steel door and a smaller wooden door to the side. The rest of the view is shrouded in darkness, though in the distance she hears a faint rumble. With the heater off, the frigid winter air infiltrates the car. Alessia shivers.

She is here. *Alone with him.*

She shoots him an anxious glance. Now that she's sitting in the dark, with this man she hardly knows, she wonders at the wisdom of her decision. The only people who saw her leave with him were Magda and the security guard.

'Come on,' Maxim says, and, climbing out of the car, he goes to the boot to retrieve her bags, his shoes crunching on the gravel.

Dismissing her unease, she opens the car door and steps onto the gravel.

Outside, it's cold. She huddles into her anorak as the icy wind whistles in her ears. The rumble in the distance is louder. She wonders what it is. Maxim puts his arm around her, in a gesture that she suspects is to protect her from the cold. Together they walk to the grey wooden door. He unlocks it and pushes it open, ushering her ahead of him. He flips a switch inside the gatepost, and small lights embedded in the side of the flagstone steps light the path down to a stone courtyard.

'This way,' he says, and she follows him down the steep steps. An imposing contemporary house lit by uplighters in the ground stands before them. Alessia marvels at its modernity – all glass and white walls, bathed in light. Maxim unlocks the front door and guides her inside. He flips another light switch, and subtle downlighters illuminate the alabaster space with a soft glow. 'Let me have your coat,' he says, and she shrugs out of her anorak.

They are standing in an open hallway beside an impressive cloud-grey galley kitchen that's part of a vast wood-floored room. To the rear there are two turquoise sofas with a coffee table between them, and beyond that, shelving stacked with books.

Books!

She admires them and notices another door beside the shelves.

This house is so big!

The staircase next to her is enclosed in glass. The wooden steps appear to be suspended in the air, but they are anchored in a massive concrete block that runs down the centre of the stairwell and extends to the upper and lower floors.

It's the most contemporary house she's ever been in. And yet in spite of its modern design, it has a welcoming, warm feel.

Alessia begins to undo her bootlaces as Maxim marches into the kitchen and places her bags and their coats on the worktop. As she removes her boots, she's surprised by the warmth of the floor underfoot.

'This is it,' he says, gesturing at their surroundings. 'Welcome to the Hideout.'

'The Hideout?'

'It's the name of this house.'

On the other side of the kitchen is the main living area, with a white dining table that seats twelve people and two large dove-coloured sofas that stand in front of a sleek steel fireplace.

'It looks bigger than from outside,' Alessia says, intimidated by the scale and elegance of the house.

'Deceptive. I know.'

Who cleans this place? It must take hours!

'And this house, it belongs to you?'

'Yes. It's a holiday home that we rent out to the public. It's late and you must be exhausted. But would you like something to eat or a drink before bed?'

Alessia hasn't moved from her spot in the hallway.

He owns this, too? He must be a very successful composer.

She nods at his offer.

'Do you mean yes?' he asks with a grin.

She smiles.

'Wine? Beer? Something stronger?' he asks, and she steps closer. Where she's from, women generally don't drink alcohol, though she's sneaked a raki or two, but only in the last couple of years, on New Year's Eve. Her father doesn't approve of her drinking.

Her father doesn't approve of many things . . .

Her grandmother had given her wine. But Alessia had not cared for it. 'Beer,' she says, because she's only ever seen men drink it – and to spite her father.

'Good choice.' Maxim grins, and from the fridge he removes two brown bottles. 'Pale ale okay?'

She doesn't know what that means, so she nods.

'Glass?' he asks, as he pops off both tops.

'Yes. Please.'

From another cupboard he takes out a tall glass and deftly pours one of the bottles into it. 'Cheers,' he says as he hands Alessia her drink. He clinks her glass with his beer bottle and takes a swig, his lips circling the bottle's neck. He closes his eyes, savouring the taste, and for some reason she has to look away.

His lips.

'*Gëzuar*,' she whispers. He raises his eyebrows, surprised to hear her speaking her native tongue. It's a toast, mainly made by men, but he doesn't know that. She takes a sip, and the chilled amber liquid runs down her throat.

'Mmm.' She closes her eyes in appreciation and takes another, longer draught.

'Are you hungry?' His voice is husky.

'No.'

The sight of her enjoying the simple pleasure of a beer is a thrill. But now, probably for the first time ever, I'm a little lost for words. I don't know what she expects. It's strange. We have nothing in common, and the intimacy we shared in the car seems to have vanished.

'Come, I'll give you a quick tour.' I offer her my hand and show her into the larger living space. 'Drawing room. Um . . . living area, I suppose. It's all open-plan.' I wave my hand in the general direction of the room.

Now that she's further into the room, Alessia notices the gleaming white upright piano against the wall beside her.

A piano!

'You can play to your heart's content while you're here,' Maxim says.

Her heart skips a beat, and she beams at him as he releases her hand. She lifts the lid. Written on the inside is the word:

KAWAI

She doesn't recognise the name, but that doesn't bother her. She presses middle C, and it echoes in a golden yellow hue through the big room.

'E përkryer,' she breathes.

Perfect.

'Balcony over there.' Maxim points to the wall of glass at the far end of the room. 'The sea is beyond.'

'The sea?' she exclaims, and whips her head to his, wanting confirmation.

'Yes,' he says, puzzled and amused by her response.

She races to the glass. 'I've never seen the sea!' she whispers, squinting through the murky dark and flattening her nose against the cold glass in her desperation to catch a glimpse. To her disappointment there is nothing but a jet-black night beyond the balcony.

'Never?' Maxim sounds incredulous as he steps up beside her.

'No,' she says. She notices the little smudge marks her nose and breath have made on the window. Pulling her sleeve over her hand, she rubs them away.

'We'll take a walk on the beach tomorrow,' he says.

Alessia's smile becomes a yawn.

'You're tired.' Maxim glances at his watch. 'It's half past midnight. Do you want to go to bed?'

Alessia stills, gazing at him as her heartbeat soars, and his question hangs between them full of possibility.

Bed? Your bed?

'I'll show you to your room,' he murmurs, but neither of them moves. They stare at each other, and Alessia can't decide whether she's relieved or disappointed. Perhaps more disappointed than relieved – she doesn't know.

'You're frowning,' he whispers. 'Why?'

She remains mute, unable or unwilling to articulate what she's thinking or feeling. She is curious. She likes him. But she knows nothing about sex.

'No,' he utters, as if talking to himself. 'Come on, I'll take you to your room.' He collects her plastic bags from the kitchen counter, and she follows him up the staircase. At the top of the stairs is a brightly lit landing with two doors. Maxim opens the second one and switches on the light.

The off-white room is spacious and airy, with a king-size bed against the far wall and a large window to one side. The linen is off-white, too, but the bed is scattered with cushions that match the colours in the dramatic seascape that hangs above the bed.

Maxim waves her inside and places her bags on a colourful embroidered bench. As she approaches the bed, she stares at her reflection in the dark window. Maxim moves to stand behind her. Mirrored in the glass, he's tall, lean and more than handsome, and she looks wan and scruffy beside him. In every way, they are not equals, and that's never been more apparent than at this moment.

What does he see in me? I am only his cleaner.

Her mind casts back to his sister-in-law in the kitchen. She had looked elegant and stylish wearing only his oversize shirt. Alessia turns her head so she's no longer taunted by her own image while Maxim draws down the pale green blind and continues to show her around the room.

'There's an en suite here for you,' he says gently, pointing to the bathroom door and diverting her from her discouraging thoughts.

My own bathroom!

'Thank you,' she says, but the words seem woefully inadequate for the debt she owes him.

'Hey,' he says, standing in front of her, his bright eyes brimming with compassion. 'I realise that this is all very sudden, Alessia. And we hardly know each other. But I couldn't leave you at the mercy of those men. You have to understand that.' He catches a loose strand of hair that's worked its way free from her plait and gently tucks it behind her ear. 'Don't worry. You're safe here. I'm not going to touch you. Well, not unless you want me to.' Alessia catches a trace of his scent, evergreen and sandalwood. She closes her eyes, trying to keep a tight rein on her emotions. 'This is my family's holiday home,' he continues. 'Think of our time here as a holiday. A place to think, reflect, get to know each other, and get some distance from all the recent dreadful events in your life.'

A lump forms in Alessia's throat, and she bites her upper lip.

Don't cry. Don't cry. Mos qaj.

'My room's next door, if you need anything. But right now, it's really late and what we both need is some sleep.' He plants a tender kiss on her forehead. 'Good night.'

'Good night.' Her voice is hoarse and almost inaudible.

He turns and leaves the room, and she's finally alone, standing in the confines of the most glorious bedroom she has ever been invited to sleep in. She looks from the painting to the bathroom door to the magnificent bed, and slowly she sinks to the floor. Wrapping her arms around herself, she begins to weep.

I hang our coats in the cloakroom, then collect my beer from the kitchen counter and enjoy a long draught.

What a day!

That first sweet kiss, I groan thinking about it – interrupted by those fucking thugs – and then her sudden disappearance and my mad drive to that godforsaken corner of West London.

And her revelation. *Sex-trafficked.*

Fuck – that was one hell of a shock.

And now we're here. Alone.

I rub my face, trying to process everything that's happened. I should be tired after the long drive and the trials and tribulations of the day, but instead I'm wired. Glancing up at the ceiling, I pinpoint where Alessia should, I hope, be sleeping peacefully. She's the real reason I'm restless. It took every shred of self-control not to pull her into my arms and . . . And what? Even after all she's told me, I can't keep my thoughts above my waist. I'm like a fucking horny schoolboy.

Leave the woman alone.

But the truth is, I still want her and don't my blue balls know it.

Hell. After all Alessia's been through, she deserves a break.

She doesn't need my lascivious attention.

She needs a friend.

Bugger. What the hell is wrong with me?

I grab my beer and drain the bottle, then reach for Alessia's glass. She's hardly touched her drink. I take a swig and run a hand through my hair. I know damn well what's wrong with me.

I want her. Badly.

I'm infatuated.

There, I've admitted it to myself. She's invaded my thoughts and my dreams since I laid eyes on her.

I fucking burn for her.

But in all my fantasies, she shares my desire. I want her, yes. But I want her wet and willing – I want her to want me, too. I know I could seduce her, but right now if she were to say yes, she'd be doing so for all the wrong reasons.

Besides, I promised her that I wouldn't touch her unless she wanted me.

I close my eyes.

When did I acquire a conscience?

Deep down I know the answer. I am hamstrung by our inequality.

She has nothing.

I have everything.

And if I take advantage of her, what would that make me? No better than those fuckers with the Eastern European accents. I've brought her to Cornwall because I want to protect her from them – and now I have to protect her from myself.

Fuck.

This is uncharted territory.

While I down the remaining beer, I wonder what's happening at the Hall. I decide that I can find out tomorrow, and I'll also let Oliver know where I am. I doubt there's anything urgent to deal with and I'm sure he'll be in touch if there is. I can work down here. I have my phone, though I wish I'd brought my laptop.

Right now I need some sleep.

Leaving the empty glass and the beer bottle on the counter, I switch off the lights and head upstairs. I pause outside her bedroom door and listen.

Shit!

She's crying.

I've had my fill of wailing women over the last four weeks: Maryanne, Caroline, Danny, Jessie. An image of Kit's lifeless body comes to mind, and my own grief rises raw and unexpected.

Kit. Fuck. Why?

Suddenly I'm bone-tired. I contemplate leaving her to cry but hesitate outside her door as the sound pierces my mourning heart. I can't leave her sobbing. Sighing, I steel myself, then knock gently on the door and let myself in.

She's crumpled on the floor, her head in her hands, right where I'd left her. Her grief is a reflection of my own.

'Alessia. Oh, no!' I exclaim, and scoop her into my arms. 'Hush, now,' I murmur, my voice cracking. I sit down on the bed, cradle her in my lap, and bury my face in her hair. Closing my eyes, I inhale her sweet scent and tighten my arms, holding her and rocking gently.

'I've got you,' I whisper past the knot that constricts my throat. I couldn't rescue my brother from the demons that drove him out on his motorbike into an icy night, but I can help this beautiful girl, this beautiful, brave girl. Her sobbing ceases, and she splays her hand over my racing heart and holds it there, I don't know for how long. Finally she quiets and relaxes against me.

She's fallen asleep.

In my arms.

In the safety of my arms.

What a privilege this is – to hold a sleeping beauty.

I press a soft kiss in her hair and shift her onto the bed, then cover her with the throw. Her plait snakes across the pillow, and for a moment I consider untying it and freeing her hair, but she mumbles something unintelligible in her own language, and I don't want to wake her. I wonder once more if I haunt her dreams like she haunts mine. 'Sleep, beautiful,' I whisper, and switch off the light before I step onto the landing. I close her door, anxious that the glare shouldn't wake her, then turn out the hall light and stride into my bedroom, leaving my door ajar.

Just in case she needs me . . .

I press the electronic closer for the blinds, which descend over the French windows facing the sea. In the walk-in wardrobe, I strip off my clothes and find a pair of pyjamas that Danny has brought over from the main house and slip on the bottoms. In London I rarely wear pyjamas, but in Cornwall, with all the staff present, I have no choice. Leaving my clothes in a heap on the floor, I head into the bedroom and climb into bed. I turn off the bedside lamp and stare into the inky darkness.

Tomorrow will be a better day. Tomorrow I'll have the lovely Alessia Demachi to myself. I lie in bed questioning my judgement. I've taken Alessia away from all that she knows. She's destitute, friendless and totally alone. Well, she has me, and I have to behave myself. 'You're going soft in your old age,' I mutter, and fall into an exhausted, dreamless sleep.

It's the shrill sound of her scream that wakes me.

Chapter Twelve

It takes me a couple of seconds to orientate myself, and she screams again.

Fuck.

Alessia.

I fly out of bed as adrenaline fuels my body, bringing all my senses to attention. Punching the lights on in the hall, I burst into her room. Alessia is sitting up in her bed. Her head whips around at the sound and light from the hallway, her eyes wild with terror.

She opens her mouth to scream again.

'Alessia, it's me, Maxim.'

Her words rush out in a torrent: *Ndihmë. Errësirë. Shumë errësirë. Shumë errësire.*

What?

I sit down beside her on the bed, and she launches herself at me, nearly knocking me over and wrapping her arms around my neck.

'Hey,' I soothe her once I've regained my balance, and I hold her, stroking her hair.

'*Shumë errësirë. Shumë errësirë. Shumë errësirë*,' she whispers over and over as she clings to me, trembling like a newborn foal.

'English. In English.'

'The dark,' she whispers against my neck. 'I hate the dark. It is so dark here.'

Oh, thank fuck.

I'd imagined all manner of horrors and was prepared to fight any number of monsters, but I relax at her words. Keeping one arm around her, I lean over and switch on the bedside light.

'That better?' I ask, but she doesn't let go. 'It's okay. It's okay. I've got you,' I repeat several times.

After a few minutes, her trembling ceases and her body relaxes. She sits back, and her eyes meet mine.

'I am sorry,' she whispers.

'Hush. Don't worry. I'm here.'

She glances down at my chest, and a slow flush pinks her cheeks.

'Yeah, I normally sleep naked. Count yourself lucky I put these on,' I quip.

Her mouth softens. 'I know,' she says, and peeks up at me through her long lashes.

'You know?'

'Yes. You sleep naked.'

'You've seen me?'

'Yes.' Her smile is unexpected.

'Well, I'm not sure how I feel about that.' I'm grateful that she's back from whatever terror she was facing in the dark, but she continues to glance around the room anxiously.

'I am sorry. I did not mean to wake you,' she says. 'I was frightened.'

'Was it a nightmare?'

She nods. 'And when I open my eyes and it is . . . it is so dark—' She shivers. 'I did not know if I was dreaming or awake.'

'I think that would make anyone scream. It's not like London here. There's no light pollution in Trevethick. The dark here is . . . dark.'

'Yes. Like the—' She stops and cringes in revulsion.

'Like?' I whisper. The teasing amusement in her eyes has vanished, replaced by a harrowed, strained expression. Turning her face away, she stares down at her lap.

I rub her back when I'm met with her silence. 'Tell me,' I prompt.

'In the – how do you say – *kamion* . . . Truck. In the truck,' she says, suddenly inspired.

I swallow. 'Truck?'

'Yes. That brought us to England. It was metal. Like a box. And dark. And cold. And the smell . . .' Her words are barely audible.

'Fuck,' I say under my breath, and fold her in my arms again. She seems a little more reluctant to hug me this time, probably because I'm shirtless, but I'm not going to leave her to face these gruesome nightmares on her own. In one swift movement, I stand, cradling her against my chest.

She gasps in surprise.

'I think you should sleep with me.' And without waiting for a response, I carry her into my room, flick on the lights, and deposit her on the floor beside the walk-in wardrobe. Inside I find the pyjama shirt and hand it to her. I point to the en suite. 'You can go and change in there. You can't be comfortable sleeping in your jeans and that school sweater.' I grimace at her green woollen pullover.

She blinks rapidly.

Shit. Perhaps I've really overstepped the mark.

And suddenly I feel a little self-conscious. 'Unless of course you'd rather sleep alone.'

'I have never slept with a man,' she whispers.

Oh.

'I won't touch you. This is just sleep – so the next time you scream, I'll be right there.'

Of course, I'd like to make her scream in a different way.

Alessia hesitates, looking from me to the bed, and her lips purse with what I think is resolve. 'I want to sleep here, with you,' she whispers and she marches into the en suite, not shutting the door until she's found the light switch.

Feeling relieved, I stare at the closed bathroom door.

At twenty-three she's never slept with a man?

I'm not going to think about that right now. It's after three in the morning, and I'm tired.

Alessia gazes at her pale face in the mirror. Wide eyes with dark circles beneath them reflect back at her. Taking a deep breath, she shakes off the remnants of her nightmare: she'd been back in the container, but this time without the other girls.

She was alone.

In the dark.

In the cold.

With that smell.

She shivers and strips off her clothes. She'd forgotten where she was until *he* appeared.

Mister Maxim. Saving her again.

Her own Skënderbeu . . . Albania's hero.

He's making a habit of this.

And she's going to sleep with him.

He'll keep her nightmares at bay.

If her father found out, he would kill her. And her mother . . . she visualises her mother fainting at the news that Alessia is sleeping with a man. A man who is not her husband.

Don't think about Baba and Mama.

Her dear, dear mother had sent Alessia to England thinking she was saving her.

She was wrong. So wrong.

Oh, Mama.

For now she is safe with Mister Maxim. She struggles into the pj top, which is too big. She undoes her plait, shakes out her hair, then tries to tame it with her fingers but gives up. Gathering her clothes under one arm, she opens the door.

Mister Maxim's room is larger and airier than the other bedroom. It's also off-white, but here the furniture is polished wood, matching the sleigh bed that dominates the room. He is standing on the far side of the bed, and his eyes widen as he studies her. 'There you are,' he says, his voice husky. 'I was wondering if I should send a search party.'

Her gaze drifts from his startling green eyes to the tattoo on his arm. She has only glimpsed parts of it before, but even from across the room she can see the design.

A two-headed eagle.

Albania.

'What?' He follows her stare and looks down at his tattoo. 'Oh. This,' he says. 'It's a folly of youth.' He sounds a little embarrassed, and he frowns, seemingly puzzled by her keen interest. She can't take her eyes off the ink as she walks towards him. He raises his elbow so she can have a better look.

Inscribed across his biceps is a black shield bearing the image of an ivory two-headed eagle hovering over five yellow circles that are in the shape of an inverted V. Alessia places her clothes on the footstool at the end of the bed and raises her hand to touch his arm, glancing at Maxim for permission.

I hold my breath as she traces the outline of my tattoo, her finger skirting across my skin, her light touch echoing through my body, towards my groin, and I suppress a groan.

'This is the symbol for my country,' she whispers. 'The two-headed eagle is on the Albanian flag.'

What are the odds?

I grit my teeth. I'm not sure how long I can bear her touch without reciprocating.

'But not these yellow circles,' she adds.

'They're called bezants.' I sound really hoarse.

'Bezant.'

'Yes. It represents a coin.'

'In Albanian, we have the same word. Why do you have this tattoo? What does it mean?' Alluring eyes peer up at me.

What can I say?

This is the shield from my family's coat of arms.

I don't want to explain my family's heraldry at three o'clock in the morning. And the truth is, I had the tattoo done to piss off my mother. She hates them . . . but of the family coat of arms? How could she complain?

'Like I said, a youthful folly.' My eyes stray from her eyes to her lips. I swallow. 'It's too late to discuss this now. Let's sleep.' I toss back the quilt on the bed and step aside so that she can climb in. She obliges, revealing long, slender legs beneath the pyjama shirt that is way too big for her.

This is torture.

'What is this word "folly"?' she asks as I walk around the bed. She's propped herself up on her elbow, and her glorious dark hair falls in a riot of loose waves over her shoulders, past the contour of her breasts, and onto the bedding. She looks gorgeous, and I'm going to have to keep my hands off her.

'Folly in this case means a foolish action,' I say as I join her in bed. I almost snort at the irony of my word definition.

If sleeping next to this beautiful girl isn't folly, I don't know what is.

'Folly,' she whispers as she lays her head on the pillow. I dim the bedside light so it glows in the darkness, but I don't switch it off, just in case she wakes again.

'Yes. Folly.' I lie down and close my eyes. 'Go to sleep.'

'Good night,' she whispers, her voice soft and sweet. 'And thank you.'

I groan. This is going to be torture. I turn on my side, away from her, and start counting sheep.

I'm lying on the lawn near the towering stone wall that surrounds the kitchen garden at Tresyllian Hall.

The summer sun warms my skin.

The scent from the lavender that rings the lawn and the sweet fragrance of the roses that climb the wall waft over me.

I'm warm.

I'm happy.

I'm home.

A girlish laugh catches my attention.

I turn my head, drawn to the sound, but I'm blinded by the sun and can see her only in outline. Her long, raven hair blows in the breeze, and she's swathed in a translucent blue housecoat. It billows out around her slim silhouetted figure.

Alessia.

The scent of the flowers intensifies, and I close my eyes to inhale their sweet, intoxicating perfume.

When I open them, she's gone.

I wake with a start. Morning is bleeding through the cracks between the blinds. Alessia has trespassed onto my side of the bed, and she's nestled under my arm, her hand balled in a fist on my abdomen, her head on my chest. Her leg intertwined with mine.

She is all over me.

And fast asleep.

And my cock is wide awake and rock-hard.

'Oh, God,' I whisper, and brush my nose against her hair.

Lavender and roses.

Intoxicating.

My heart rate flips into overdrive as I make a mental list of all the possibilities this scenario presents: Alessia in my arms. Ready. Waiting. She is so tantalising, so close . . . too close. If I roll over, she'll be on her back, and I can finally bury myself in her. I stare up at the ceiling, praying for self-control. I know if I move, she'll wake, so I torture myself some more and lie still, enjoying the sweet, sweet agony of having her sprawled all over me. I gather a lock of her hair between my fingers, surprised by how soft and silky it feels. She stirs, her fisted hand flexes, and her fingers splay out on my belly, tickling the beginning of my pubic hair.

Fuck!

I'm so hard and want nothing more than to grab her hand and wrap it around my erection. I'll probably explode if I do.

'Mmm,' she murmurs. Her eyelids flicker open, and she looks dreamily up at me.

'Good morning, Alessia.' I'm breathless.

She gasps and scrambles to put some space between us.

'I was enjoying your visit to my side of the bed,' I tease.

She pulls the covers up to her chin, her cheeks rosy, her smile shy. 'Good morning,' she says.

'Sleep well?' I ask as I roll onto my side to face her.

'Yes. Thank you.'

'Hungry?' *I know I am. And not for food.*

She nods.

'Do you really mean yes?'

She frowns.

'You said in the car yesterday that in Albania it's the opposite.'

'You remembered.' She sounds pleased and surprised.

'I remember everything you say.' I want to tell her that she looks very lovely this morning. But I refrain. I'm behaving.

'I like sleeping with you,' she says, confounding me.

'Well, that makes two of us.'

'I did not have bad dreams.'

'Good. Me neither.'

She laughs, and I try to recall the dream that woke me. All I know is that she was part of it. As usual. 'I dreamt about you.'

'Me?'

'Yes.'

'Are you sure it was not a nightmare?' she teases.

I grin. 'Quite sure.'

She smiles. She has a bewitching smile. Perfect white teeth. Pink lips that are parted possibly in invitation. 'You look very desirable.' The words come out of my mouth in an unguarded moment. Her deep brown eyes dilate, captivating me.

'Desirable?' Her breath catches.

'Yes.'

The silence stretches between us as we gaze at each other.

'I don't know what to do,' she whispers.

I close my eyes and swallow while her words from last night echo in my head.

I have never slept with a man.

'You're a virgin?' I whisper, and open my eyes to study her face.

She blushes. 'Yes.'

Her simple affirmation is like an ice bath to my libido. I've only slept with one virgin, and that was Caroline. It was my first time, too, and it was a disaster that nearly got us expelled from school. After that my father took me to a high-class brothel in Bloomsbury.

If you're going to start fucking girls, Maxim, you'd better learn how to fuck.

I was fifteen, and Caroline moved on . . .

Until Kit's death.

Bloody hell.

Alessia's a virgin at twenty-three? Of course she is. What did I expect? She's different from every woman I've ever known. And she's looking at me all big eyes and expectation. I wonder again at the folly of bringing her here.

Alessia frowns, anxiety etched on her face.

Shit.

Reaching forward, I brush my thumb against her pouty bottom lip. She inhales sharply. 'I want you, Alessia. Very much. But I want you to want me, too. I think we need to get to know each other before we take whatever this is any further.'

There. That was the grown-up response. Yes?

'Okay,' she whispers, but she looks uncertain, and possibly a little disappointed.

What does she expect of me?

And I know I need to put some distance between us to think about this. Here in my bed she's a distraction, a pouting, soft-lipped and beautiful distraction. I sit up and cup her face in my hands. 'Let's just enjoy this holiday,' I murmur, and kiss her, and clamber out of bed.

Now is not the time.

It's not fair to her.

And it's not fair to me.

'Are you leaving?' Alessia asks as she sits up in bed. Her hair tumbles down around her small frame like a veil. Her eyes are round with concern; she looks effortlessly sexy, swamped in my pyjama shirt.

'I'm going to grab a shower, then cook us breakfast.'

'You can cook?'

I laugh at her shock. 'Yeah. Well, I can cook bacon and eggs.' I give her a sheepish smile and stride into the bathroom.

Bugger.

More self-abuse in the shower.

Water streams over my body, and with one hand spread on the marble tiles supporting me, I come quickly, thinking of her hand on my stomach and her hand wrapped around my dick.

A virgin.

I frown. Why am I making such a big deal of this? At least she hasn't been brutalised by those fuckers. Anger flares in my gut as I think of the men coming after her. She's safe here in Cornwall. So that's something.

Perhaps she's religious. She did say her grandmother was a missionary, and she wears a gold cross around her neck. Or maybe premarital sex is a taboo in Albania. I have no idea. I wash my hair and my body with the soap Danny left for me.

This is not what I had in mind when I brought her down here. Her inexperience is an issue. I like sexually adventurous women who know what they're doing, know what they want, and know their limits. Breaking in a virgin is a big responsibility. I towel-dry my hair.

It's a tough job, but someone has to do it.

Might as well be me.

I stare at the cad in the mirror.

Dude. Grow up.

Maybe she wants a long-term relationship.

I've had two relationships, but neither of them for longer than eight months. So not that long. Charlotte was socially ambitious, and she moved on to a baronet from Essex. Arabella was too into drugs for my liking. I mean, who doesn't like a bump now and then, but every day? No way. I think she's in rehab again.

A relationship with Alessia. What would that entail?

I am getting way ahead of myself here. Wrapping a towel around my waist, I head back into the bedroom. She's gone.

Fuck. My heart rate doubles.

Has she fled? Again?

I knock on the door of her room. No reply. I enter, and I'm relieved to hear the shower.

For fuck's sake, get a grip.

I leave her and go to get dressed.

Alessia doesn't think she'll ever leave this shower. At home in Kukës, the bathroom had a rudimentary shower and the floor had to be mopped after each use. At Magda's the shower was over the bath. This shower has its own enclosed space, and the hot water cascades over her from the biggest showerhead she's ever seen. Even bigger than the one in Mister Maxim's bathroom at his apartment. It's blissful and like nothing she's experienced before. She washes her hair and carefully shaves her body with the disposable razor Magda gave her.

She scrubs herself with the body wash she's brought from home. Her soapy hand moves over her breasts, and she closes her eyes.

I want you, Alessia. Very much.

He wants her.

Her hand moves down.

And in her mind it's *his* hand on her body. Touching her. Intimately.

She wants him, too.

She recalls waking up in his arms and feeling the warmth and strength of his body against her skin. Her belly flutters at the memory as her hand moves. Faster. Faster. And faster. She leans against the warmed tiles. And raises her head. Her mouth open as she gulps in air.

Maxim.

Maxim.

Ah.

Her muscles clench deep inside as she comes.

Catching her breath, she opens her eyes.

This is what she wants . . . isn't it?

Can she trust him?

Yes.

He's done nothing to shake the trust she's placed in him. Last night he rescued her from her night terrors, he was kind and gentle. He let her sleep with him to keep her nightmares away.

She feels safe with him.

She hasn't felt safe for so long. It's a novel feeling, even though she knows that Dante and Ylli are still out there somewhere looking for her.

No. Do not think about them.

She wishes she knew more about men. Men and women in Kukës don't interact like they do in England. At home men socialise with men, women with women. It has always been this way. Not having brothers and kept separate from her male cousins in social situations, her experience was limited to the few male students she met at university – and her father, of course.

She runs her hands through her hair.

Mister Maxim is not like any man she's ever known.

With the water pouring onto her face, she resolves to put all her problems out of her mind. Today, as Maxim says, it's a holiday. Her first.

Wrapping her hair in a towel and her body in a bath sheet, she pads into the bedroom. A pounding beat is coming from downstairs. She listens. The music seems at odds with what she knows about him. His compositions suggest a quieter, more introspective man than the one blasting this loud music through the house.

She lays out her clothes on the bed. All of them, with the exception of her jeans and bra, had been given to her by Magda and Michal. She frowns, wishing she had something more attractive to wear. She slips on an off-white, long-sleeved T-shirt to wear over her jeans. It's a little shapeless, but it will have to do. It's all she has.

Towel-drying, then brushing out her hair, she leaves it loose and heads downstairs. Through the glass wall surrounding the staircase, she watches Maxim in the kitchen. He's wearing a pale grey sweater and the ripped black jeans and has a tea towel draped over his shoulder while he stands at the stove. He's frying bacon – the aroma is delicious – and he's shuffling to the beat of the dance music that is thumping through the room. Alessia cannot help but grin. While cleaning his apartment, she had never seen any evidence that he could cook.

Men, where she is from, don't cook.

Or dance while cooking.

The flex of his broad shoulders, the swivel of his slim hips, and his bare feet tapping in perfect time to the music are mesmerising. She feels a delicious tightening in her belly. He rakes his fingers through his damp hair and then flips the bacon. Her mouth waters.

Mmm . . . the smell.

Mmm . . . the sight of him.

He turns suddenly, and his face lights up when he sees her on the stairs. His enormous smile mirrors hers.

'One egg or two?' he shouts above the music.

'One,' she mouths as she comes down the stairs and into the big room. She turns and gasps as she looks out through the floor-to-ceiling windows.

The sea!

'*Deti! Deti!* The sea!' she shouts, sprinting to the glass wall of doors that lead onto the balcony.

I lower the heat under the bacon and hurry to the balcony doors to join Alessia, who's jumping from foot to foot, incandescent with excitement.

'Can we go down to the sea?' Her eyes are alive with delight as she bounces up and down like a child.

'Of course. Here.' I unlock the balcony door and slide it open so that she can go outside. A gust of glacial air catches us both by surprise. It's freezing, but she rushes out, not caring about her wet hair, bare feet or thin T-shirt.

Doesn't this woman have any decent clothes?

I pick up a grey throw that's draped over the back of the sofa and walk out after her. I wrap my arms and the blanket around her, holding her as she admires the view. Her face is lit up with wonder.

The Hideout and our three other holiday homes are built along a rocky promontory. A small winding path at the end of the garden leads down to the beach. It's a bright, clear day. The sun is shining, but it's bitterly cold in the howling wind. The sea is a chilly blue, flecked with white surf, and we hear the boom of the waves as they crash against the cliffs on each side of the cove. The air smells fresh and salty. Alessia turns to me, her expression one of complete awe.

'Come on, let's eat.' I'm conscious that breakfast is on the stove. 'You'll catch your death out here. We'll go down to the beach after breakfast.' We head back inside and close the door. 'I just have to do the eggs!' I shout above the music.

'Let me help!' Alessia shouts back, following me into the kitchen area, still draped in the blanket.

I turn the Sonos volume down via the app on my phone. 'That's better.'

'Interesting music,' Alessia says in a tone that tells me that perhaps it's not her thing.

'It's Korean house. I use a few tracks when I DJ.' I retrieve the eggs from the fridge. 'Two eggs?'

'No, one.'

'You sure?'

'Yes.'

'Okay. Just one. I'm having two. You can make some toast. Bread is in the fridge, and the toaster is over there.'

Together we work in the kitchen, and I'm able to watch her. Using her long, nimble fingers, she fishes the toast out of the toaster and butters each slice.

'Here.' I take the two plates out of the warming drawer and place them on the counter, ready for toast.

She grins as I serve up the rest of our breakfast.

'I don't know about you, but I'm famished.' I abandon the frying pan in the sink, collect both plates, and usher her towards the dining table, where I've laid two places.

Alessia looks impressed.

Why does this make me feel like I've finally achieved something?

'Sit here. You can enjoy the view.'

'How was that?' Maxim asks.

They are seated at the large dining table, Alessia at the head, where she's never sat before, and she's enjoying the view of the seascape.

'Delicious. You are a man with many accomplishments.'

'You'd be amazed,' he says drily, his voice a little husky. And for some reason his tone and the way he looks at her make her breath catch.

'Do you still want to go for a walk?'

'Yes.'

'Okay.' Taking his phone, he dials a number. Alessia wonders who he's calling.

'Danny,' he says. 'No. We're fine. Can you bring a hairdryer over . . . oh, there are? Okay. Then I need a pair of wellingtons or walking boots . . .' He looks directly at Alessia. 'What size?' he asks.

She has no idea what he's talking about.

'Shoe size,' he clarifies.

'Thirty-eight.'

'That's, um . . . size five, and some socks if you have any. Yes. For a woman . . . It doesn't matter. And a decent bloody warm coat . . . Yes. For a woman . . . Slim. Small. As soon as possible.' He listens for a moment. 'Fantastic,' he says, and hangs up.

'I have a coat.'

'You won't be warm enough. And I don't know about the Albanian sock thing, but it's cold out there.'

She flushes. She has only two pairs of socks because she can't afford more – and she couldn't ask Magda for another pair. Magda had done enough for her.

Dante and Ylli had confiscated her luggage, and when she'd arrived in Brentford, Magda had burned most of the clothes she'd been wearing. They were no longer fit to be worn.

'Who is Danny?'

'She lives not far from here,' Maxim says, directing his attention to the empty plates as he stands to clear the table.

'Let me,' she says, shocked that he's clearing up. 'I will wash them, too.' She takes the plates from him and places them in the sink.

'No. I'll do this. There should be a hairdryer in the chest of drawers in the wardrobe in your room. Go dry your hair.'

'But—' *Surely he's not going to wash up! No man does that!*

'No buts. I'll do it. You've cleaned up after me often enough.'

'But it is my job.'

'Today it isn't. You're my guest. Go.' His tone is clipped. Stern. A frisson of apprehension runs up her spine. 'Please,' he adds.

'Okay,' she whispers, and hurries out of the kitchen, confused and wondering if he's angry with her.

Please don't be angry.

'Alessia,' he calls. She stops at the foot of the stairs and studies her feet. 'Are you okay?' She nods before she dashes up the stairs.

What the fuck?

What did I say? I watch her retreating figure noting that she deliberately avoids eye contact with me.

Shit.

I've upset her, but I don't know how or why. I'm tempted to go after her but decide against it and begin to load the dishwasher and clean up.

Twenty minutes later, as I'm putting away the frying pan, the entry phone rings.

Danny.

I glance up at the stairs, hoping that Alessia will appear, but she doesn't. I press the buzzer to let Danny in and turn off the music, knowing she will not approve.

The hairdryer's high-pitched wheeze rings in her ears as Alessia brushes and brushes her hair beneath its heat. With each stroke her heartbeat settles to a more even pace.

He had sounded like her father.

And she'd reacted the way she'd always reacted to her father, by getting out of his way. Baba has never forgiven her or her mother that his only child is a girl. Though it's her poor mother who bears the brunt of his anger.

But Mister Maxim is nothing like her father.

Nothing.

She finishes her hair and knows that the only way to restore her equilibrium and forget about her family for a while is to play the piano. Music is her escape. It's been her only escape.

When she comes back downstairs, Mister Maxim has disappeared. She wonders where, but her fingers are itching to play. She sits down at the little white upright, lifts the lid, and with no preamble launches into her angry Bach Prelude in C Minor. The music blazes through the room in hues of brilliant orange and red, burning away any thoughts of her father and setting her free.

When she opens her eyes, Maxim is watching her.

'That was incredible,' he whispers.

'Thank you,' she says.

He takes a step closer and strokes her cheek with the back of his finger, then tilts her chin up so she's lost in his magnetic gaze. His eyes are the most spectacular colour. Up close she notices that the irises are a darker green around the edge – the colour of a Kukës fir – while towards the dilating pupil they're lighter, like a fern in the spring. When he leans down, she thinks he's going to kiss her. But he doesn't.

'I don't know what I did to upset you,' he says.

She puts her fingers over his mouth, silencing him.

'You did nothing wrong,' she whispers. His lips purse into a kiss against her fingertips, and she removes her hand.

'Well, if I did, I'm sorry. Now, do you want to go for a walk on the beach?'

She beams at him. 'Yes.'

'Okay. You need to wrap up warm.'

Alessia is impatient. She practically pulls me down the stony path. At the bottom we step onto the beach, and Alessia can contain herself no more. She releases my hand and runs towards the raging sea, her hat flying off and her hair whipping in the wind.

'The sea, the sea!' she cries, and twirls around, her arms in the air. Her earlier pique is forgotten, her smile is wide and her face bright, lit from within by her joy. I stride across the coarse sand and rescue her discarded woolly hat. 'The sea!' she shouts again above the roar of the water, and she gesticulates wildly, her arms like a crazy windmill, welcoming each wave as it crashes to the shore.

It's impossible not to smile. Her unbridled enthusiasm for this first-time event is too appealing and too affecting. I grin as she squeals and dances back to avoid the breakers on the shoreline. She looks ridiculous, dressed in oversize wellingtons and an oversize coat. Her face is flushed, her nose pink and she is utterly breathtaking. My heart clenches.

She runs towards me with childish abandon and grabs my hand. 'The sea!' she cries once more, and drags me to the crashing waves. And I go willingly, surrendering myself to her joy.

Chapter Thirteen

They walk hand in hand along the coastal path and stop by an old ruin.

'What is this place?' Alessia asks.

'It's an abandoned tin mine.'

Alessia and Maxim lean against the chimney stack, staring out at a choppy sea that's crested with white surf as the chill wind whistles between them. 'It is so beautiful here,' she says. 'It is wild. It reminds me of my home.'

Except I'm happier here. I feel . . . safe.

That's because I am with Mister Maxim.

'I love this place, too. It's where I grew up.'

'In the house where we are staying?'

He looks away. 'No. My brother built that quite recently.' Maxim's mouth turns down, and he seems lost.

'You have a brother?'

'I did,' he whispers. 'He died.' He digs his hands deep into his coat pockets and stares out at the sea, his face bleak, carved like stone.

'I am sorry,' she says, and from his pained, raw expression she suspects that his brother's death is a recent event.

Reaching out, she places a hand on his arm. 'You miss him,' she says.

'Yes,' Maxim whispers, turning his face towards her. 'I do. I loved him.'

She is surprised by his candour. 'Do you have other family?'

'A sister. Maryanne.' His fond smile is brief. 'And then there's my mother.' His tone becomes dismissive.

'Your father?'

'My father died when I was sixteen.'

'Oh. I am sorry. Your sister and mother, do they live here?'

'They used to. They visit sometimes,' he says. 'Maryanne works and lives in London. She's a doctor.' He flashes her a proud smile.

'*Ua.*' Alessia is impressed. 'And your mother?'

'She's mostly in New York.' His answer is curt. He doesn't want to discuss his mother.

And she doesn't want to discuss her father.

'There are mines near Kukës,' she says to change the subject, and she gazes up at the grey-stoned chimney stack. It's like the chimney on the road to Kosovo.

'Really?'

'Yes.'

'What do they mine?'

'*Krom.* I don't know the word.'

'Chromium?'

She shrugs. 'I don't know the English.'

'I think I'd better invest in an English-Albanian dictionary,' Maxim mutters. 'Come on, let's walk into the village. We can have lunch.'

'Village?' Alessia has seen no sign of any dwellings on their walk.

'Trevethick. It's a small village just over the hill. Popular with tourists.'

Alessia falls into step beside him.

'The photographs in your apartment, are they from here?' she asks.

'The landscapes. Yes. Yes, they are.' Maxim beams. 'You're observant,' he adds, and from his raised brows Alessia can tell he's impressed. She gives him a shy smile, and he takes her gloved hand.

They emerge from the path onto a narrow lane. The hedgerows on either side are high but cut back from the road. The brambles and bare-twigged bushes are orderly and trimmed, and here and there they are covered in clumps of snow. They walk down and around a sweeping corner, and the village of Trevethick appears at the bottom of the lane. The stone and whitewashed houses are like nothing Alessia's seen before. They look small and old but charming nonetheless. The place is quaint – pristine – with no litter anywhere. Where she comes from, there is rubbish and construction debris in the streets, and most of the buildings are built from concrete.

At the waterfront two stone quays stretch out to embrace the harbour where three large fishing boats are moored. Around the waterfront are a few shops – a couple of boutiques, a convenience store, a small art gallery – and two pubs. One called The Watering Hole, the other, The Two-Headed Eagle. A sign hangs outside, bearing a shield Alessia recognises. 'Look!' She points at the emblem. 'Your tattoo.'

Maxim winks at her. 'You hungry?'

'Yes,' she replies. 'That was a long walk.'

'Good day, milord.' An elderly man in a black scarf, a green waxed coat and a flat cap is leaving The Two-Headed Eagle. He is followed by a shaggy dog of indeterminate breed wearing a red coat with the name BORIS embroidered in gold across the back.

'Father Trewin.' Maxim shakes his hand.

'How are you bearing up, young man?' He pats Maxim on the arm.

'Good, thank you.'

'I'm pleased to hear it. And who is this fine young lady?'

'Father Trewin, our vicar, may I introduce Alessia Demachi, my . . . friend, visiting from overseas.'

'Good afternoon, my dear.' Trewin holds out his hand.

'Good afternoon,' she says, shaking his hand, surprised and pleased that he would address her directly.

'And how are you enjoying Cornwall?'

'It is lovely here.'

Trewin gives her a benign smile and turns to Maxim. 'I suppose it's too much to hope that we'll see you at Sunday service tomorrow?'

'We'll see, Father.'

'We lead by example, my son. Remember that.'

'I know. I know.' Maxim sounds resigned.

'Brisk day!' Father Trewin exclaims, moving on from that subject.

'Indeed.'

Trewin whistles to Boris, who has sat patiently waiting for their pleasantries to cease. 'In case you've forgotten, service starts at ten sharp.' He gives them both a nod and heads on up the lane.

'Vicar is the priest, yes?' Alessia asks as Maxim opens the door to the pub and ushers her into the warmth.

'Yes. Are you religious?' he asks, surprising her.

'N—'

'Good afternoon, milord,' says a large man with red hair and a complexion to match, interrupting their conversation. He stands behind an impressive bar that is hung with decorative jugs and pint glasses. There's a burning log fire at one end of the pub and several wooden high-backed benches on either side of a line of tables, most of which are occupied by men and women who could be locals or tourists, Alessia doesn't know. From the ceiling hang fishermen's ropes, nets and tackle. The atmosphere is warm and friendly. There's even a young couple kissing at the back. Embarrassed, Alessia looks away and sticks close to Mister Maxim.

Hi, Jago,' I say to the barman. 'Table for two for lunch?'

'Megan will sort you out.' Jago points to the far corner.

'Megan?'

Shit.

'Yeah, she's working here now.'

Fuck.

I give Alessia a sideways glance and she looks puzzled. 'Are you sure you're hungry?'

'Yes,' Alessia replies.

'Doom Bar?' Jago asks, staring with overt appreciation at Alessia.

'Yes, please.' I try not to glare at him.

'And for the lady?' Jago's voice softens, his eyes still on Alessia.

'What would you like to drink?' I ask.

She peels off her hat, releasing her hair. Her cheeks are flushed from the cold. 'The beer I had yesterday?' she says. With her loose, dark curls falling almost to her waist, her shining eyes and her radiant smile, she is an exotic beauty. I'm beguiled. Totally and utterly beguiled. I can't blame Jago for staring.

'Half a pale ale for the lady,' I say without looking at him.

'What is it?' Alessia asks as she begins to unzip Maryanne's quilted Barbour jacket. And I know I've been gawking at her. I shake my head, and she gives me a shy smile.

'Hello, Maxim. Or should I say "milord" now?'

Shit.

I turn around, and Megan is standing in front of me, her

expression as dark as her clothes. 'Table for two?' she says with a saccharine tone and a smile to match.

'Please. And how are you?'

'Fine,' she snaps, and my heart sinks, my father's voice ringing in my head.

Don't fuck the local girls, boy.

I stand aside for Alessia to precede me, and we follow in Megan's dour wake. She leads us to a table in the corner by a window that overlooks the quays. It's the best table in the establishment. So that's something.

'This okay for you?' I ask Alessia, deliberately ignoring Megan.

'Yes. It is good,' Alessia responds, with a confused look at a moody Megan. I hold out her chair, and she sits. Jago arrives with our drinks, and Megan saunters off, presumably to fetch menus . . . or a cricket bat.

'Cheers.' I hold up my pint.

'Cheers,' Alessia replies. After a sip she says, 'I do not think Megan is happy with you.'

'No, I don't think so either.' I shrug, brushing off the subject. I really don't want to discuss Megan with Alessia. 'Anyway, you were saying about religion?'

She eyes me dubiously, as if pondering the Megan Situation, and then she continues, 'The Communists banned religion in my country.'

'You mentioned that in the car yesterday.'

'Yes.'

'But you wear a gold cross.'

'Menus,' Megan interrupts us, and hands us each a laminated card. 'I'll be back to take your order in a minute.' She turns abruptly and heads for the bar.

I ignore her. 'You were saying?'

Alessia watches Megan's exit through suspicious eyes but says nothing about her. She continues, 'It was my grandmother's.

She was Catholic. She used to pray in secret.' Alessia fondles her gold cross.

'So there's no religion in your country?'

'There is now. Since we became a republic when the Communists fell, but in Albania we don't make so much of it.'

'Oh, I thought religion was everything in the Balkans?'

'Not in Albania. We are a . . . what is the word? Secular state. Religion is very personal. You know, just between a person and their God. At home we are Catholics. Most people in my town are Muslim. But we do not give it much thought,' she responds with a quizzical look at me. 'And you?'

'Me? Well, I suppose I'm Church of England. But I'm not religious at all.' Father Trewin's words come back to me.

We lead by example, my son.

Bloody hell.

Maybe I should go to church tomorrow. Kit always managed to go at least one or two Sundays a month when he was down here.

Me, not so much.

That's another damn duty I have to fulfil.

'Are the English like you?' Alessia asks, pulling me back into the conversation.

'With regard to religion? Some are. Some aren't. The UK is multicultural.'

'This I know.' She smiles. 'When I travelled on the train in London, there were so many different languages spoken.'

'Do you like it? London?'

'It is noisy and crowded and very expensive. But it is exciting. I had never been to a big city before.'

'Not even Tirana?' Thanks to my expensive education, I know the capital of Albania.

'No. I have never travelled. I had never seen the sea until you brought me here.' Her glance out of the window is wistful, but it gives me an opportunity to study her profile: long lashes, pert nose, pouting lips. I shift in my seat, my blood thickening.

Steady.

Megan appears with her pinched, angry face and scraped-back hair, and my problem subsides.

Boy, she is still bitter. It was one summer seven years ago. One fucking summer.

'Are you ready to order?' she asks, glaring at me. 'Catch of the day is cod.' She makes it sound like an insult.

Alessia frowns and glances quickly at the menu.

'I'll have the fish pie, please.' And, irritated, I cock my head, daring Megan to say anything.

'For me also,' says Alessia.

'Two fish pies. Any wine?'

'I'm fine with the beer. Alessia?'

Megan turns to the lovely Alessia Demachi. 'For you?' she snaps.

'The beer is good for me, too.'

'Thank you, Megan,' I grunt in warning, and she shoots me a look.

She'll probably spit in my food – or, worse, in Alessia's.

'Shit,' I murmur under my breath as I watch her march back to the kitchen.

Alessia studies my reaction.

'That goes back several years,' I say, and tug at my sweater collar, embarrassed.

'What does?'

'Megan and I.'

'Oh,' Alessia says, her tone flat.

'She's ancient history. Tell me about your family. Do you have any siblings?' I ask, desperately trying to move on.

'No,' she says abruptly, and it's obvious she's still considering Megan and me.

'Parents?'

'I have a mother and a father. Like all people.' She raises a beautiful, arched eyebrow.

Oh. The delectable Demachi has teeth.

'And what are they like?' I ask, stifling my amusement.

'My mother is . . . brave.' Her voice becomes soft and wistful.

'Brave?'

'Yes.' Her expression turns sombre, and she glances out of the window once more.

Okay. This subject is definitely off-limits.

'And your father?'

She shakes her head and shrugs. 'He is an Albanian man.'

'And that means?'

'Well, my father is old-fashioned, and I do not . . . how do you say? We do not see eye for eye.' Her face falls a little, and her troubled expression tells me this, too, is off-limits.

'Eye to eye,' I correct her. 'Tell me about Albania, then.'

Her face brightens. 'What do you want to know?' She looks up at me through those long dark lashes, and my groin tightens again.

'Everything,' I whisper.

I watch and listen to her, enthralled. She is passionate and eloquent, painting a vivid picture of her country and her home. She tells me Albania is a special place where family is at the centre of everything. It's an ancient country, influenced over the centuries by several cultures with differing ideologies. She explains that it's both Western and Eastern facing, but more and more her country looks to Europe for inspiration. She's proud of her hometown. Kukës is a small place in the north near the border with Kosovo, and she enthuses about its spectacular lakes, rivers and gorges, but most of all the mountains that surround it. She comes alive talking about the landscape, and it's clear this is what she misses about her homeland.

'And that is why I like it here,' she says. 'From what I have seen, the landscape in Cornwall is also beautiful.'

We are interrupted by Megan and fish pie. Megan plonks the plates down on the table and leaves without a word. Her face is sour, but the fish pie is warming and delicious, and there's no sign that anyone spat in it.

'What does your father do?' I ask cautiously.

'He has a garage.'

'Does he sell petrol?'

'No. He fixes cars. Tyres. Mechanical things.'

'And your mother?'

'She is at home.'

I want to ask Alessia why she left Albania, but I know it will remind her of her harrowing journey to the UK.

'And what did you do in Kukës?'

'Well, I was studying, but my university closed, and so sometimes I work in a school with the little children. And sometimes I play the piano . . .' Her voice tails off, and I don't know if it's because she's feeling nostalgic or if it's for another reason. 'Tell me about your work.' It's clear she wants to change the subject, and because I don't want to tell her what I do yet, I fill her in on my DJing career.

'And I've done a couple of summers in San Antonio in Ibiza. Now, that's a real party place.'

'This is why you have so many records?'

'Yes,' I answer.

'And what is your favourite music?'

'All music. I don't have a favourite genre. What about you? How old were you when you started playing?'

'I was four.'

Wow. Early.

'Did you study music? I mean, music theory?'

'No.'

That's even more impressive.

It's gratifying to see Alessia eat. Her cheeks are rosy, her eyes aglow, and I suspect that after two beers she's a little tipsy.

'Would you like anything else?' I ask.

She shakes her head.

'Let's go.'

It's Jago who brings over our bill. I suspect Megan has refused or she's on a break. I settle up and take Alessia's hand as we leave the pub.

'I just want to make a quick detour to the shop,' I say.

'Okay.' Alessia's lopsided smile makes me grin.

The shops in Trevethick are owned by the estate and leased to the locals. They do good business from Easter right through to the New Year. The only one that's actually useful is the general store. We're miles from the nearest big town, and it carries a huge range of items. A dulcet bell rings as we enter.

'If there's anything you need, let me know,' I tell Alessia, who is looking at the magazine display, swaying slightly. I head to the counter.

'Can I help you?' asks the sales assistant, a tall young woman I don't recognise.

'Do you stock night-lights? For kids?'

She leaves the counter and searches the shelves in a nearby aisle. 'These are the only night-lights we have.' She holds up a box with a small plastic dragon inside.

'I'll take one.'

'It'll need batteries,' the assistant informs me.

'I'll take batteries, too.'

She takes the package and returns to the counter, where I spy condoms.

Well, I might get lucky.

I glance around at Alessia, who is leafing through one of the magazines.

'I'll have a packet of condoms, too.'

The young woman blushes, and I'm glad I don't know her.

'Which would you prefer?' she asks.

'Those.' I point to my brand of choice. Hastily she puts the packet into a plastic bag with the night-light.

Once I've paid, I join Alessia at the front of the shop, where she's now checking out the small display of lipsticks.

'Is there anything you want?' I ask.

'No. Thank you.'

Her refusal doesn't surprise me. I've never seen her wear makeup.

'Shall we go?'

She takes my hand, and we walk back to the lane.

'What is that place?' Alessia points at a distant chimney only partly visible as we walk up the lane towards the old mine. I know it, of course; it stands atop of the west wing of the great house that is Tresyllian Hall. My ancestral home.

Bugger.

'That place? It belongs to the Earl of Trevethick.'

'Oh.' Her brow creases for a moment, and we continue on in silence while I wage an inner war with myself.

Tell her you're the fucking Earl of Trevethick.

No.

Why not?

I will. Not yet.

Why not?

I want her to know me first.

Know you?

Spend time with me.

'Can we go down to the beach again?' Alessia's eyes are alight with excitement once more.

'Of course.'

Alessia is entranced by the sea. She runs with the same uninhibited joy into the shallow surf. The wellingtons keep her feet dry from the crashing waves.

She is . . . effervescent.

Mister Maxim has given her the sea.

Overcome with giddy delight, she closes her eyes, stretches out her arms, and breathes in the chilly, salted air. She can't remember ever feeling this . . . full. For the first time in a long time, she's enjoying a small slice of happiness. She has a keen sense of connection to the cold, wild landscape that somehow reminds her of her homeland.

She feels like she belongs.

She is complete.

Turning around, she regards Maxim as he stands on the shoreline with his hands deep in his coat pockets, watching her. The wind ripples his hair, the traces of gold glinting in the sun. His eyes are full of mirth and shine a burning emerald green.

He is breathtaking.

And her heart is full. Full to the brim.

She loves him.

Yes. She loves him.

She is giddy. Excited. And in love. This is what it should feel like. Joyful. Filling. Free. The realisation surges through her like the bracing Cornish wind that whips her hair across her face.

She is in love with Mister Maxim.

All her unarticulated feelings bubble to the surface, and her face erupts into a megawatt smile. His answering smile is dazzling, and for a moment she dares to hope.

Perhaps one day he will feel the same way, too?

She dances over to him and in an unguarded moment launches herself at him, flinging her arms around his neck.

'Thank you for bringing me here,' she exclaims, breathless.

He grins down at her as he holds her close. 'It's my pleasure,' he says.

'It will be!' she quips, and laughs as his eyes widen and his mouth drops open.

She wants him. All of him.

She whirls out of his arms and back into the shallows.

Good God, she's tipsy, maybe even a little drunk. And beautiful. I'm infatuated.

Suddenly she slips and falls as a wave crashes over her.

Shit.

Panicked, I race to help. She tries to scramble to her feet and slips again, but when I reach her, she's laughing. And soaked. I help her up. 'I think that's enough swimming for one day,' I mutter. 'It's freezing. Let's get you home.' And I take her hand. Alessia gives me a crooked grin and trails after me across the sand towards the path back to the house. Pausing every few steps, she seems reluctant to leave the beach, but she's still giggling and appears happy enough. I don't want her catching a chill.

Back in the warmth of the Hideout, I pull her into my arms. 'Your giggling is irresistible.' I kiss her quickly, and slip off her soaking coat. Her jeans are sodden, but thankfully the rest of her clothes underneath seem dry. I rub her arms briskly to warm her. 'You should go and change.'

'Okay.' Alessia grins and heads to the stairs. Taking her coat – well, Maryanne's coat – I hang it up in the hallway over the radiator, where it will dry. I remove my boots and socks, which are also wet, then head into the guest cloakroom.

When I come out, she's disappeared and I assume she's gone upstairs to find a dry pair of jeans. I sit down on one of the kitchen barstools and call Danny to arrange supper.

Next I call Tom Alexander.

'Trevethick. How the devil are you?'

'Good, thanks. Anything to report from Brentford?'

'No. It's all quiet on the western front. How's Cornwall?'

'Cold.'

'You know, old boy, I've been thinking. This is an awful lot of trouble to go to for your daily. She's a pretty girl and all that, but I hope she's worth it.'

'She is.'

'I've never known you to be a sucker for a damsel in distress.'

'She's not a dam—'

'I hope you've sealed the deal.'

'Tom, that's none of your fucking business.'

'Okay. Okay. I'll take that as a no.' He laughs.

'Tom,' I warn.

'Yes, yes, Trevethick. Keep your bloody hair on. It's all good here. That's all you need to know.'

'Thank you. Keep me updated.'

'Will do. Farewell.' He hangs up.

I stare down at the phone.

Fucker.

I email Oliver.

To: Oliver Macmillan

Date: 2 February 2019

From: Maxim Trevelyan

Re: Whereabouts

Oliver

I'm in Cornwall attending to a private matter and staying at the Hideout. I'm not sure how long I'm going to be here.

Tom Alexander will be invoicing me for his services via his security company, payment for which should come out of my personal allowances.

If you need to reach me, email is better, as phone reception down here, as you know, is spotty.

Thanks.
MT

Then I text Caroline.

In Cornwall. Will be
here a while.
Hope all well with you. Mx

She texts back immediately.

**Do you want me to
come down?**

No. Things to do.
Thanks for the offer.

Are you avoiding me?

Don't be silly.

**☹ I don't believe you.
I'll call you at the Hall.**

I'm not at the Hall.

Where are you, then?
And what the fuck are you doing down there?

Caro. Leave it.
I'll call next week.

What are you up to?
I'm intrigued and I miss you.
I have to see the Stepsow again this evening. Cxxxx

Good luck. Mx

How the fuck am I going to explain to Caroline what's happening down here? I run my hands through my hair, hoping to find inspiration. Nothing comes to me, so I go looking for Alessia. She isn't in either of the upstairs bedrooms.

'Alessia!' I call as I come back into the main living area, but she doesn't reply. I dash down to the lower floor and quickly check the three ground-level guest bedrooms, the games and cinema rooms.

No Alessia.

Fuck.

I try to quell my rising panic and run back upstairs and through to the spa to see if she's in the Jacuzzi or the sauna.

No sign.

Where the fuck is she?

I check the scullery.

And there she is, sitting bare-legged on the floor, reading a book while the tumble dryer rumbles away.

'Here you are.' I conceal my exasperation, feeling ridiculous for my concern. She stares up at me with warm brown eyes as I sink down onto the floor beside her.

'What are you doing?' I'm breathless as I lean against the wall. She draws her knees up and stretches her white top over them, concealing her legs. She rests her chin on her knees, her face an endearing shade of embarrassed pink.

'I'm reading, and I am waiting for my jeans to dry.'

'I can see that. Why didn't you change?'

'Change?'

'Into another pair.'

She blushes a deeper shade of pink. 'I do not have another pair.' Her tone is hushed and tinged with shame.

Bloody hell.

And I recall the two pathetic plastic bags that I packed into the boot of my car. They held everything she owns.

Closing my eyes, I lean my head back against the wall, feeling utterly stupid.

She has nothing.

Not even clothes. Or socks.

Shit.

Checking my watch, I realise it's too late to go shopping. And I've had two pints, so I can't – I don't drink and drive. 'It's late now. Tomorrow I'll take you to Padstow, and we can get you some new clothes.'

'I cannot afford new clothes. My jeans will be dry soon.'

Without acknowledging her comment, I glance down at her book. 'What are you reading?'

'I found this on the bookshelves.' She holds up *Jamaica Inn* by Daphne du Maurier.

'Do you like it? It's set in Cornwall.'

'I've just started it.'

'From what I remember, I enjoyed it. Look, I'm sure I have something you can wear.' I rise and hold out my hand. Clutching the book, she's a little wobbly as she stands, and the hem of her top is wet.

Shit. She'll catch a cold.

I try not to look at her long, naked legs. I try not to imagine them wrapped around my waist. I fail.

And she's wearing the Pink Panties.

Torture.

My need is a slow, dull ache.

I'll have to shower. Again.

'Come on.' My voice is thick with desire, but fortunately she doesn't seem to notice. We head upstairs, and she ducks into the guest room while I explore the walk-in wardrobe to see what other clothes Danny has brought to the house.

Alessia appears by the door a few moments later wearing SpongeBob pyjama bottoms and an Arsenal FC shirt.

'I have these,' she says with an apologetic and still half-tipsy smile.

I stop rummaging.

Even in ridiculous, faded pyjamas and a football shirt, she is stunning. 'They'll do.' I smirk as I imagine slipping those trousers off her hips and down her legs.

'These were Michal's,' she says.

'I guessed.'

'They were too small for him.'

'They look a little big for you. We'll get you some clothes tomorrow.'

She opens her mouth to protest, but I raise my finger to her lips. 'Hush.' Her lips are soft to my touch.

I want this woman.

She pouts and forms a kiss against my skin, and her eyes stray to my mouth and darken. My breath catches in my throat. 'Please don't look at me like that,' I whisper, taking my finger off her lips.

'Like . . . what?' Her voice is barely audible.

'You know. Like you want me.'

She flushes and stares down at her feet.

'I am sorry,' she whispers.

Shit. I've upset her. 'Alessia.' I close the space between us so I'm almost touching her. The enchanting scent of lavender and roses mixed with the salty air of the sea invades and intoxicates my senses. I stroke her cheek, and she leans her lovely face into my palm.

'I do want you,' she murmurs, raising alluring eyes to mine. 'But I don't know what to do.'

I brush her bottom lip with my thumb. 'I think you've had too much to drink, beautiful.'

She blinks, and her eyes cloud with a look I don't understand. And with a lift of her chin she turns and walks out of the room.

What the hell?

'Alessia!' I call, and follow her, but she ignores me and descends the stairs.

I sigh and sit down on the top step and rub my face. I'm confused. I am trying – really fucking trying – to be noble here.

I snort at the irony.

I know the look she was giving me.

Hell. I've seen it often enough.

A fuck-me, fuck-me-now look.

Isn't that why I brought her here?

But she's tipsy, and she has no one, and she has nothing. Nothing at all.

She has me.

Hook. Line. And sinker.

If I fuck her, I'll be taking advantage.

Simple.

So I can't.

But I've offended her.

Shit.

The mournful strains of the piano suddenly fill the house. It's a melancholic Bach prelude in E-flat minor. I know it well because I studied it for my grade four or five music examination as a teen. She plays exquisitely, teasing out all the emotion and revealing the depths of the piece. Her skill is phenomenal. And she's articulating everything she feels through the music. She's pissed off. At me.

Bloody hell.

Maybe I should take her up on her offer – fuck her and take her back to London. But even as the thought enters my head, I know I can't do that.

I have to find somewhere for her to live.

I rub my face again.

She could live with me.

What? No.

I've never lived with anyone.

Would it be so bad?

The truth is, I don't want any harm coming to Alessia Demachi. I want to protect her.

I sigh.

What's happening to me?

Alessia pours her confusion into the Bach prelude she's playing. She wants to forget everything. His look. His doubt. His rejection. The music slowly moves through her and out into the room, filling it with the sombre colours of regret. And as she plays, she surrenders herself to the melody and forgets. Everything.

When the final notes die, she opens her eyes, and Mister Maxim is standing by the kitchen counter, watching her.

'Hey,' he says.

'Hey,' she responds.

'I'm sorry. I didn't mean to upset you. That's twice today.'

'You are very contrary,' Alessia says, trying to voice her confusion. As an afterthought she adds, 'Is it my clothes?'

'What?'

'That you do not like.' After all, he's insisted he wants to buy her new clothes. She stands, and in an uncharacteristic, brave moment she gives him a quick twirl. She hopes she will make him smile.

Walking towards her, he eyes her football shirt and her cartoon pj's and rubs his chin as if considering her hypothesis. 'I love that you're dressed like a thirteen-year-old boy.' His tone is dry, but amused, too.

Alessia giggles. Loudly. Infectiously. And he laughs with her.

'That's better,' he whispers. He grasps her chin and kisses her. 'You are a very desirable woman, Alessia, whatever you're wearing. Don't let me or anyone else make you feel otherwise. You're also very, very talented. Play something else. For me. Please.'

'Okay,' she says, mollified by his kind words, and she sits down at the piano once more. She gives him a quick, knowing smile and starts to play.

It's my song.

The song I finished after I met her.

She knows it. By heart. And she plays it a damned sight better than I do. I started this song when Kit was alive . . . and now I hear my own sorrow and regret in the harmonies that fill the room. Grief hits me like a tidal wave, crashing over me. Drowning me. A knot forms in my throat, and I try to contain my emotion, but it expands, constricting my ability to breathe. I watch her, spellbound but aching as the music punctures my heart and touches the yawning void that is Kit's absence. Her eyes are closed. She's concentrating and losing herself in the sad, solemn melody.

I've tried to ignore my grief. But it's there. It's been there since the day he died. I told Alessia that I loved him. I did. I really did love him. My big brother.

But I never told him.

Not once.

And now I miss him more than he'll ever know.

Kit.

Why?

Tears burn behind my eyes as I lean against the wall, trying to fight my anguish and loss. I cover my face with my hands.

I hear her gasp, and she stops. 'I'm sorry,' she whispers. I shake my head, unable to speak or look at her. Hearing the scrape of the stool, I know that she's stepped away from the piano. Then I feel her near me, and she touches my arm. It's a compassionate gesture. And it's my undoing.

'That reminded me of my brother.' I squeeze the words past the lump in my throat. 'We buried him here, three weeks ago.'

'Oh, no.' She sounds crestfallen, and she wraps her arms around me, surprising me, and whispers, 'I am so sorry.'

I bury my face in her hair and inhale her soothing scent. And I cannot stop the tears sliding down my face.

Shit.

She's unmanned me.

I didn't cry at the hospital. I didn't cry at the funeral. I haven't cried since my father died when I was sixteen years old. Yet here. Now. With her I let go. And I sob in her arms.

Chapter Fourteen

Alessia's heart rate accelerates as she panics. Confused, she holds him, her mind in a whirl.

What has she done?

Mister Maxim. Mister Maxim. Maxim.

She thought he'd find it amusing that she knew his piece.

But no, she's reminded him of his grief. Her remorse is swift and merciless and flutters staccato in her belly. How could she have been so insensitive? He tightens his hold on her as he weeps, making no sound. Three weeks is no time. No wonder he's still grieving. She draws him closer and strokes his back. She remembers how she felt when her grandmother passed away. Nana had been the only one who understood her. The only person she could really talk to. She's been gone a year.

She swallows the burning sensation in her throat. Maxim is vulnerable and sad, and she wants nothing but to make him smile again. He has done so much for her. She runs her hands up his shoulders and to the nape of his neck and, clasping his head, turns his face to hers. His gaze holds no expectations; all she sees in his luminous green eyes is his sorrow. Slowly she pulls his mouth to hers and kisses him.

I groan when her lips brush mine. Her kiss is timid but so unexpected and oh, so sweet. I screw my eyes shut as I fight the outpouring of my grief. 'Alessia.' Her name is a blessing. My hands cradle her head, my fingers threading through her soft, silky hair as I accept her hesitant, unschooled kiss. She kisses me once, twice, three times.

'I've got you,' she whispers.

And her words draw all the air from my lungs. I want to crush her to me and never let her go. I can't remember the last person who consoled me in my hour of need.

Alessia kisses my neck. My jaw. And my lips once more.

And I let her.

Gradually, my grief recedes, leaving only hunger in its wake. My hunger for her. I've been fighting my attraction to her since I saw her standing in my hallway holding that broom. But she's broken through all my defences. She's exposed my grief. My need. My lust. And I'm powerless to resist.

She moves to hold and stroke my face, which is still damp with tears, and her caress spirals like a tornado through my body. I'm lost. Lost to her compassion, her courage, and her innocence. I'm lost to her touch.

My body responds.

Fuck.

I want her. I want her now. I've wanted her forever.

I tilt her head back and move one hand to hold the nape of her neck, my fingers still in her hair. With the other hand, I circle her waist and pull her against the length of my body. I deepen the kiss, my lips more insistent. Alessia lets out a little gasp, and

I seize the moment and tease her tongue with the tip of mine. She tastes as sweet as she looks, and she moans.

I light up like Piccadilly Circus.

She pushes at my chest, suddenly breaking our kiss, and stares up at me with a dazed, astonished look.

Shit. What's this?

She's breathless, flushed, and her pupils are dilated . . .

Man, she's exquisite. I don't want to let her go. 'You okay?'

A shy smile pulls at the corners of her mouth, and she nods.

Does she mean yes or no?

'Yes?' I want clarification.

'Yes,' she whispers.

'Have you ever been kissed?'

'Only by you.'

I don't know what to say to this.

'Again,' she beseeches me, and I need no further prompting. My grief is a distant memory. I'm firmly in the now with this beautiful, innocent young woman. My fingers tighten in her hair, and I ease her head back so that her mouth is once more raised to mine. I kiss her again, tempting her lips apart with my tongue, and this time I'm met with the tip of hers.

I growl deep in my throat, my arousal complete, straining against black denim.

Her hands slide up my biceps, and she clings to me as our tongues stroke and tease and taste each other. Over and over.

I could kiss her all day.

Every day.

I slide my hand down her back to her perfect behind.

Oh. God.

Placing my palm on her backside, I push her against my erection.

She gasps and frees her lips from our kiss but doesn't let me go. She's breathing hard, eyes the colour of night, wide and shocked.

Fuck.

I hold her startled gaze and, summoning every ounce of my self-control, I ask, 'Do you want to stop?'

'No,' she says quickly.

Thank fuck.

'What's wrong?' I ask.

She shakes her head.

'This?' I ask, and press my hips against her.

She gasps.

'Yes, beautiful. I want you.'

Her lips part as she inhales.

'I want to touch you. Everywhere,' I whisper. 'With my hands. With my fingers. With my lips. And with my tongue.'

Her eyes darken.

'And I want you to touch me,' I add in a husky tone.

Her mouth forms a perfect, soundless O. But her gaze shifts from my eyes to my mouth to my chest and back to my eyes.

'Too fast?' I ask.

She shakes her head. And fists her fingers in my hair and tugs, drawing my lips back to hers.

'Ah,' I murmur against the corner of her mouth as pleasure rushes down my spine to my groin. 'That's right, Alessia. Touch me. I want you to touch me.' I crave her touch.

She kisses me and hesitantly pushes her tongue between my lips. And I take all that she's got to give.

Oh, Alessia.

We kiss. And kiss until I think I'm going to burst. I skirt the waistband of her pyjamas and slip my hand inside against the warm, soft skin of her behind. She stills for a second, then grips my hair firmly, tugging hard, and kisses me with ardour – greedy and feverish.

'Easy,' I breathe. 'Let's take this slow.'

She swallows and places her hands on my arms, looking a little abashed.

'I like your hands in my hair,' I reassure her, and to make amends I run my teeth along her jawline up to her ear. Her moan is soft and husky as her head falls into the palm of my hand.

It's music to my dick.

'You're so beautiful,' I whisper, and my fingers clench in her hair, tugging gently. Her chin lifts, and I anoint the underside of her throat with feather-light kisses until I reach her ear. With my other hand, I squeeze her behind, as my lips seek hers once more, my tongue teasing and exploring her mouth, giving and taking as her lips learn mine and I learn hers. I trail kisses down her neck to where her pulse beats fast and furious beneath her skin.

'I want to make love to you,' I whisper.

Alessia stills.

I cradle her face with both hands and brush her lips with my thumb. 'Talk to me. Do you want to stop?' She bites her top lip, and her eyes dart towards the window, where the sky is colour-washed with a splash of pink from the coming dusk. 'No one can see us,' I assure her.

Her smile is hesitant, but she whispers, 'Do not stop.'

I stroke her cheek with the backs of my fingers and lose myself in her dark, dark gaze. 'Are you sure you want to do this?'

She nods.

'Tell me, Alessia. I need to hear you say it.' I kiss the corner of her mouth once more, and she closes her eyes.

'Yes,' she breathes.

'Oh, baby,' I murmur. 'Wrap your legs around me.' I clasp her waist and lift her, easily. She puts her hands on my shoulders. 'Legs. Round me.' Face shining with what I hope is lust and excitement, she hooks her legs around my waist, and her arms circle my neck.

'Hold on.'

I take the stairs while she kisses my throat.

'You smell good,' she says, as if to herself.

'Oh, sweetheart, so do you.'

I set her down beside the bed and kiss her again.

'I want to see you.' My hands find the hem of her football shirt. Gently I pull it up and over her head. Even though she's wearing a bra, she crosses her arms in front of her breasts as her hair falls in a dusky, curling cascade to her waist.

She's shy.

She's innocent.

She's stunning.

I'm aroused and touched at once, but I want her to feel comfortable.

'Do you want to do this in the dark?'

'No,' she says immediately. 'Not the dark.'

Of course. She hates the dark.

'Okay. Okay. I get it,' I reassure her. 'You're gorgeous.' My voice is filled with breathless wonder as I discard her shirt on the floor. I smooth her hair off her face, my hands finding her chin. I gently kiss her again and again until she relaxes, splaying her hands on my chest and kissing me back. Her fingers bunch in my sweater, and she tugs.

I peer down at her. 'You want me to take this off?'

She nods with enthusiasm.

'For you, beautiful, anything.' I drag my sweater and T-shirt off and drop them beside her Arsenal FC top. She glances from my eyes to my naked chest, and I stay still . . . letting her look. 'Touch me,' I whisper.

She gasps.

'I want you to. I don't bite.'

Not unless you ask me to . . .

Her eyes light up, and carefully she places her hand over my heart.

Fuck.

I'm sure it somersaults beneath her fingers.

I close my eyes, enjoying the searing sensation.

She leans forward and kisses my skin where my heart is thundering.

Yes.

I sweep her hair off her neck and skim my lips down her throat and across her shoulder to her bra strap. I smile against her fragrant skin. Her bra is pink. With my thumb and finger, I ease her strap off her shoulder as her ragged breathing fills my ears.

'Turn around,' I murmur. Alessia raises heated eyes to mine and turns so her back is against my front. She crosses her arms, covering herself once more. I scoop her hair from her other shoulder and kiss her neck while slipping my other arm around her and across her belly and grasping her hip. I pull her against me so my erection is cradled at the top of her behind.

I groan in her ear and she squirms against me.

Fuck. Me.

With great care I ease down her remaining strap, skimming my fingers across her shoulder and pressing tender, wet kisses in their wake on her skin.

Her skin is soft. And fair. And almost flawless.

She has a little mole at the base of her neck beneath the chain that holds her gold cross. I kiss it. Her scent is clean and wholesome. 'You smell wonderful,' I murmur between kisses as I undo her bra. Moving my arm up her body, I feel the weight of her breasts on my forearm. She sucks in a breath and holds her bra against her body with crossed arms.

'Easy,' I murmur, and while I hold her close, I skim my fingers down her stomach and between her hips. Then dip my thumb into the waistband of her pyjamas and glide it along her belly as I tease her earlobe with my teeth.

'*Zot*,' she moans.

'I want you,' I whisper, and nip her again. 'And I do bite.'

'*Edhe unë të dëshiroj*.'

'English.' I kiss that spot behind her ear and slip my hand inside her pyjamas and slide my fingers over her sex.

She's shaved!

She stiffens against me, but I graze my thumb over her clitoris. Once. Twice. Three times. Four, and she throws her head back against my shoulder and whimpers.

'Yes,' I whisper, and continue stroking her. Teasing her. Arousing her. With my fingers.

She drops her arms, her bra sliding to the floor, and she grabs my legs, pulling at my jeans and clenching her hands around the material. Her mouth drops open, her eyes are screwed shut, and she's panting.

'Yes, baby. Feel it.' I tease her ear with my teeth. And she bites her upper lip as my fingers continue to tantalise her.

'*Të lutem. Të lutem. Të lutem*.'

'English.'

'Please. Please,' she rasps.

And I continue to give her what she wants. What she needs.

Her legs start to tremble. And I tighten my arm around her. She's close.

Does she know?

'I've got you,' I whisper, and her grasp on me tightens so she's almost cutting off the circulation to my legs. She whimpers and suddenly cries out as her body slowly convulses, and she comes apart in my arms.

I hold her through her orgasm, and she sags against me.

'Oh, Alessia,' I whisper at her ear, and, lifting her into my arms, I draw back the quilt and lay her down on the bed. Her hair fans out like a wild mane over the pillows and down over her breasts, concealing all but her dark pink nipples from me.

Fuck.

Bathed in the soft, rosy light from the gathering dusk, she's exquisite – even in SpongeBob pyjama trousers. 'Do you have any idea how beautiful you look right now?' I ask, and she turns astonished eyes to mine.

'*Ua*,' she whispers. 'No. English. Wow.'

'Wow. Yes.' My jeans feel several sizes too small, and I want to rip off her pyjamas and bury myself in her. But she needs time. I know this. I wish my cock understood. Not taking my eyes off hers, I undo the top button and unzip the flies of my jeans to give my erection some much-needed room.

Maybe I should remove them.

Leaving on my underwear, I slip my jeans off and drop them on the floor. I take a deep breath and try to bring my breathing under control.

'May I join you?' I ask.

Eyes wide, she nods, and I need no further encouragement. I lie down beside her, propped up on my elbow. I take a strand of her hair, marvelling at its softness, and wind and unwind it around my fingers.

'You like?' I ask.

She smiles, a shy but carnal smile. 'Yes. I like.' And her tongue quickly skims her top lip. I stifle my groan, and, reaching up, I run the back of my index finger down her cheek, along her chin and down her neck. My fingers stop at her little gold cross.

The sight of it makes me pause.

'Are you sure you want to do this?' I ask.

Her fathomless eyes stare into mine, and I feel exposed, like she's scrutinising my soul. It's sobering. I feel far more naked than I am.

She swallows. 'Yes.'

'If there's anything you don't like. Or you don't want to do. Tell me. Yes?'

She nods and reaches up to caress my face. 'Maxim,' she whispers, and I lean down and brush her lips with mine. She groans, and she threads her hands through my hair, and her tongue tentatively touches and moistens my top lip. Desire scorches through me like wildfire. I hold her chin and deepen our first horizontal kiss. I want her. All of her. Now. Here.

I revel in her response and her kiss. Exploring. Tasting. Wanting.

Abandoning her mouth, I trail my lips down her chin, down her throat, and along her sternum. With my hand I sweep her hair aside, revealing my goal. She gasps, her fingers pressed to my scalp as I gently lave her nipple and pull it into my mouth. And suck. Hard.

'Ah,' she cries.

I blow gently on it, and she writhes beside me. I skim my hand over her hip and up to her other breast. Cupping it gently, I fondle and squeeze and marvel at how responsive she is when I brush the peak with my thumb. In a split second, her nipple is tall and rigid, matching its twin. She moans, and her hips start to move to a rhythm I know so well. I skate my hand down her body, caressing her as I go and continuing to tease her breasts with my lips.

My fingers slip under her waistband and she pushes her sex into my hand. I have her. In the palm of my hand. I groan. She's wet.

She's ready.

Fuck.

Slowly, slowly, I ease my finger inside her.

She's tight. And wet.

Yes.

I withdraw my finger and ease it into her once more. 'Ah,' she mewls, and she tenses and fists the sheets.

'Oh, baby, I want you so much.' My lips are between her breasts. 'I've burned for you since I first saw you.'

Her body rises to meet my hand, and she tips her head back against the pillow. I kiss her stomach and leave a wet trail of possession down her skin, to her navel. I circle it with my nose while my fingers move in and out of her. I kiss her belly and run my tongue from hip to hip.

'*Zot* . . .'

'Time to say goodbye to these,' I murmur against her belly. Removing my hand from inside her, I sit up.

'I never thought . . .' she says, but her voice fades as I ease her pyjamas down her legs, then toss them on top of my jeans.

'Wow,' I whisper. She's finally naked in my bed and she's sexy as hell. 'You've seen me naked before.'

'Yes,' she whispers. 'But you were lying down on your front.'

'Okay.' *Well, this might be an education.*

I yank my underwear off, finally freeing my straining cock. And before the sight of my erection can shock or alarm her, I lean over and kiss her. Really kiss her, pouring all my want and need into her first fully naked kiss. She responds, her lips greedy, kissing me back. I caress her waist, and my hand slides down to her hip, pulling her soft, sweet body against me. With my knee I ease her legs apart. Her body rises to meet mine as her hands grasp my head once more. Tasting her skin, I skim my lips down her throat to her gold cross. I twirl it with my tongue, enjoying the taste, while my hand moves once more to capture her perfect, shapely breast.

She moans when my thumb brushes over her nipple and it rises to a sweet bud beneath my touch. My lips follow, kissing and tugging gently.

'Oh *Zot*,' she whines, tightening her fingers in my hair.

I don't stop. Restless and eager, my mouth moves from one nipple to the other, tugging, licking, kissing . . . sucking. She squirms and whimpers beneath me, and my hand travels south to my ultimate goal. Alessia stills as my fingers brush over her sex, her breathing broken and rapid.

Yes.

She's wet. Still.

My thumb finds the ultimate prize, and I circle her clitoris, again and again, and gradually I ease one finger inside her once more. Her hands stray from my head, stroking my back, and then she runs her fingernails over my shoulders and digs in. But I persist, moving my finger in and out, building the rhythm while my thumb grazes and circles her clitoris over and over.

Her hips are flexing in that age-old beat, and her legs stiffen beneath me. She's close. Abandoning her breasts, I kiss her mouth and tug her lower lip with my teeth. She clenches her fists against my shoulders as her head rolls back.

'Alessia,' I whisper as she cries out, her orgasm ripping through her. I hold her close as her body quivers with aftershocks, and then I kneel between her legs. She opens dark eyes that gaze up at me in clouded wonder.

Reaching for a condom, trying to keep my body in check, I whisper, 'Are you ready? It'll be quick.'

Might as well be truthful.

She nods.

I reach for her chin. 'Tell me.'

'Yes,' she breathes.

Thank. Fuck.

I rip the packet with my teeth and roll on the condom, and for a horrible moment I think I'm going to come here and now.

Fuck.

I bring my cock under control and cover her body with mine, keeping my weight on my elbows.

She closes her eyes and tenses beneath me.

'Hey,' I whisper, and kiss her eyelids in turn. Her arms circle my neck, and she whimpers.

'Alessia.' Her lips find mine, and she kisses me hungrily. Feverishly. Desperately. And I can hold off no more.

Slowly. Slowly. Slowly, I sink into her.

Oh. Good. God.

Tight. Wet. Heaven.

She cries out, and I still. 'Okay?' I rasp as I let her adjust to my intrusion.

'Yes,' she breathes after a beat.

I'm not sure whether or not to believe her, but I take her at her word and begin to move. Into her. Once. Twice. Thrice. Again. And again. I rock against her.

Don't come. Don't come. Don't come.

I want to prolong this forever.

She groans, and her hips begin to move in a fitful, fledgling counterpoint.

'Yes, move with me, beautiful,' I encourage her as her short, breathy gasps of pleasure spur me on.

'Please,' she whispers, begging for more, and I willingly oblige. Sweat beads on my back as my body fights my restraint. I push and push until finally she stiffens beneath me and her fingernails dig into my flesh.

I move once, twice . . . a third time, and she screams as she lets go, her cry and her climax my undoing.

I come. Forcefully. Loudly. And calling out her name.

Chapter Fifteen

Maxim is heavy on top of her, his breathing forced and urgent, while Alessia lies panting beneath him. She's overwhelmed with sensation and a bone-deep fatigue, but most of all by his . . . invasion. She feels consumed. He shakes his head, leans up on his elbows, taking his weight off her, and clear, concerned eyes burn into hers. 'Are you okay?' he says.

She makes a mental inventory of her body. In truth she's a little sore. She had no idea that the act of love was so physical. Her mother had told her it would hurt the first time.

And she was right.

But then, once her body got used to his presence, she'd enjoyed it. More than enjoyed it. At the end she'd lost all sense of self and shattered into tiny little pieces, exploding inside – and it had been . . . incredible.

He eases out of her, the alien feeling making her wince. He covers them both with the duvet and, leaning on his elbow, stares down at her with concern. 'You haven't answered me. Are you okay?'

She nods, but the narrowing of his eyes tells her that he's not convinced.

'Did I hurt you?'

She bites her lip, still unsure what to say, and he flops down on the bed beside her and closes his eyes.

Shit. I hurt her.

I'd been transported from the depths of despair to an earth-shattering climax, but my rosy, post-coital, best-fuck-ever glow vanishes like a magician's rabbit. I reach down and yank the condom off my dick, disgusted with myself. When I drop it on the floor, I'm shocked to see my hand smeared with blood.

Her blood.

Fuck.

I rub my hand on my thigh and turn back to face the recrimination in her lovely face. But she stares at me, looking apprehensive and vulnerable.

Bloody hell.

'I'm sorry I hurt you.' I kiss her forehead.

'My mother said to me it would hurt. But only the first time.' She pulls the quilt up to her chin.

'Only the first time?'

She nods, and hope blossoms in my chest. I caress her cheek. 'So you'd be willing to give it a second try?'

'Yes, I think so,' she says, giving me a coy smile, and my cock thickens in approval.

Again? Already?

'Only . . . only if you want to,' she adds.

'Only if I want to?' I can't keep the incredulity out of my voice. I laugh and swoop down and kiss her. Hard. 'Sweet, sweet Alessia,' I whisper against her lips. She grins up at me, and suddenly my heart thunders. I need to know. 'Was it good . . . for you?'

She blushes her not-so-innocent shade of pink. 'Yes,' she whispers. 'Especially at the end when I—'

When you came!

I grin, and elation radiates through my chest.

Thank fuck!

Her attention turns to her hands, which are still clutching the quilt, and her brow creases.

'What is it?' I ask.

'For you,' she says quietly. 'Was it good for you?'

I laugh. 'Good?' I laugh again, head held back, and I'm deliriously happy, and it's been a while since I felt that way. 'Alessia, it was exceptional. That was the best fuck . . . um . . . sex I've had in years.'

Why is that?

Her eyes widen, and she gasps in horror. 'That is a bad word, Mister Maxim.' She tries to feign disapproval, but her eyes twinkle with mirth. I beam down at her and run my thumb over her bottom lip.

'Say "Maxim".' I want to hear my name in her provocative accent again.

Her cheeks redden once more.

'Say it. Say my name.'

'Maxim,' she whispers.

'Again.'

'Maxim.'

'That's better. I think we should get you cleaned up, beautiful. I'll run us a bath.'

I throw off the covers and climb out of bed, and, collecting the condom from the floor, I stride into the bathroom.

Fuck.

I feel . . .

Giddy.

I'm a grown man, and I'm giddy!

Sex with her is better than being amped on coke . . . any drug. Any day.

I dispose of the contraceptive and turn on the taps over the bath, then add some bubble bath and watch the water turn to sweet-smelling foam. Taking one of the facecloths, I put it on the side.

Gushing water fills the tub, and I marvel at the day's events. I've finally laid my daily. Normally, once I've bedded a woman, I can't wait to be alone. But that's not how I feel today. Not with Alessia. I'm still enchanted by whatever spell she's cast over me. And, what's more, I get to spend this week and maybe next week with her . . . The prospect is exciting.

My cock stirs in agreement.

I glance at myself in the mirror and catch my euphoric grin, and for a moment I don't recognise myself.

What the fuck is happening to me?

I run my hand through my hair in an effort to tame it and remember her blood on my hand.

A virgin.

I'll have to marry her now. I snort at my ridiculous thought as I wash my hands, but I wonder if any of my ancestors found themselves in that position. Two of my forebears were involved in well-documented, scandalous liaisons, but my knowledge of my family history is sketchy at best. Kit was thoroughly versed in the family's history and lineage. He paid attention. My father made sure of that. My mother made sure of that. It was all part of Kit's duties as heir. He knew that keeping the earldom intact meant everything to our family.

But he's no longer here.

Fuck. Why didn't I pay attention?

The bath is full, and I wander back into the bedroom, feeling a little despondent. But the sight of Alessia staring at the ceiling lifts my spirits.

My daily.

Her expression is completely unreadable. She turns and sees me and immediately shuts her eyes.

What?

Oh, I'm naked.

I want to laugh but decide that it's probably not a good idea, so I lean against the door frame, cross my arms, and patiently wait for her to open her eyes again.

After a few moments, she pulls the bedding over her nose and peeps above it, with only one eye open.

I grin. 'Take a good look.' I spread my arms wide.

She blinks, and her eyes shine with a combination of embarrassment, amusement, curiosity and, I think, a little admiration. She giggles and pulls the covers over her head. 'You are teasing me.' Her voice is muffled.

'Yes, I am.' Unable to contain myself, I saunter to the bed, and her knuckles whiten as she tightens her hold on the quilt. I lean over and brush her fingers with my lips. 'Let go,' I whisper, and I'm surprised when she does. I whisk off the bedding, and she squeals, but I scoop her up into my arms and stand tall. 'Now we're both naked,' I say as I nuzzle her ear. She folds her arms around my neck, and I carry her, giggling, into the bathroom and set her down beside the tub. Immediately she covers her breasts.

'You don't have to be shy.' I tease a strand of her hair and wind it around my index finger. 'You have great hair. And a great body, too.'

Her half smile and timid glance tell me this is what she needs to hear. I tug gently on the strand, and she leans towards me so that I'm able to kiss her forehead. 'Besides, look.' With my chin I point to the picture window behind the bath. She turns, and her sharp intake of breath lets me know she loves the view. The window looks out over the cove, and at the horizon the sun is kissing the sea in a spectacular symphony of colour: gold, opal, pink and orange burst through the purple cloudscape and over the darkening water. It's splendid.

'*Sa bukur.*' Her voice is full of wonder. 'So beautiful.' And she loosens her arms.

'Like you,' I say, and kiss her hair. Her delicious fragrance – lavender and roses mixed with the scent of fresh sex – fills my nostrils. I close my eyes. She's more than beautiful. She's the whole package. Bright. Talented. Funny. And courageous. Yes, above all, courageous. My heart stutters, and suddenly I'm overwhelmed with emotion.

Fuck.

Swallowing hard to contain my feelings, I offer her my hand and bring her fingers to my lips. I kiss each in turn before she steps into the bath.

'Sit.'

She quickly twists her hair into a gravity-defying knot that perches on her head and sinks beneath the bubbles. She winces, and I feel a stab of guilt, but her face relaxes as she looks out at the mesmerising sunset.

I have an idea. 'I'll just be a minute.' I duck out of the bathroom.

The water is deep, hot, and soothing, and the bubbles have an exotic fragrance that Alessia doesn't recognise. She examines the bottle. It reads:

JO MALONE
LONDON
ENGLISH PEAR & FREESIA

It smells expensive.

She leans back and stares out of the window, and her body gradually unwinds.

The view.

Ua!

It's a picturesque scene. The sunset in Kukës is spectacular, but it sets behind the mountains. Here the sun is sinking languidly into the sea, illuminating a golden path on the water.

Remembering how she stumbled in the waves earlier, she smiles. How foolish she'd been. Foolish and free for a few hours at least, and now here she is in Mister Maxim's bathroom. It's bigger than the en suite in the guest room – and has two basins beneath ornate mirrors. She feels a momentary pang that Maxim's brother, who had built the property, could no longer enjoy it. It's a fine house.

Catching sight of the facecloth, Alessia grabs it and gently washes between her thighs. The area is a little tender.

She'd done it.

It.

On her own terms, with someone of her own choosing, someone she desires. Her mother would be shocked. Her father . . . She shudders to think what he might do if he knew. And she'd done it with Mister Maxim, an Englishman, he of the startling green eyes and the face of an angel. She hugs herself, recalling how gentle and considerate he'd been, and her heart beats a little faster. He'd made her body come alive. She closes her eyes and remembers his clean scent, his fingers on her skin, the softness of his hair . . . his kiss. His blazing eyes, full of desire. She sucks in a breath . . . And he wants to do it again. Her muscles tighten deep in her belly. 'Ah,' she whispers. It's a delicious feeling.

Yes. She wants to do it again, too.

She chuckles and hugs herself harder, trying to contain her

dizzying elation. She feels no shame. This is how she's supposed to feel. This is love, isn't it? She grins and feels a little smug.

Maxim reappears carrying a bottle and two glasses. He's still naked.

'Champagne?' he offers.

Champagne!

She has read about champagne. But never thought she'd experience the taste.

'Yes, please,' she says, as she sets the facecloth aside and tries to look anywhere but at his penis.

She's fascinated and embarrassed at the same time.

Large. Hooded. Flexible. Not how it was earlier.

Her experience of male genitalia has been limited to works of art. It's the first time she's ever seen any in the flesh.

'Here, hold these.' Maxim interrupts her thoughts, and a blush steals across her face. He hands her the champagne glasses and smiles down at her. 'You'll get used to it,' he says, and his eyes sparkle with humour. Alessia wonders if he was referring to the champagne . . . or his penis, which makes her blush even more. Tearing off the copper-coloured foil, he twists the wire cage and pops off the cork with ease. He pours the bubbling liquid into the glasses. Alessia is surprised and delighted to see that it's pink. Putting the bottle down on the windowsill, he clambers into the opposite end of the bath and carefully sinks into the water. The foam rises to the brim. He grins, waiting for the water to spill over the side of the bath – but it doesn't. She draws up her knees as he slides his feet on either side of her.

He takes a glass from her and clinks the one she holds. 'To the bravest, most beautiful woman I know. Thank you, Alessia Demachi,' he says, and he's no longer playful but deadly serious, gazing intently at her, his eyes darker, no longer sparkling.

Alessia swallows in response to the pulsing deep in her belly.

'*Gëzuar*, Maxim.' Her voice is husky as she raises the glass to her lips and takes a sip of the chilled liquid. It's light and bubbly and tastes of fine summers and rich harvests. It's delicious. 'Mmm,' she murmurs in appreciation.

'Better than beer?'

'Yes. Much better.'

'I thought we should celebrate. To first times.' He holds up his glass, and she does the same.

'First times,' she says, and turns to stare out of the window at the setting sun. 'The champagne is the same colour as the sky,' she says in wonder, and she knows that Maxim is watching her, but he, too, turns to enjoy the magnificent view.

'So decadent,' she says, almost to herself. She's bathing with a man, a man who is not her husband, a man she's just had sex with for the first time ever, and she's drinking pink champagne.

She doesn't even know his full name.

A shocked giggle bubbles up from her happy place.

'What?' he asks.

'Your family name, is it Milord?'

Maxim's mouth drops open, and then he chuckles. Alessia pales a little and takes another sip.

'I'm sorry.' He seems chastened. 'That's just a . . . um . . . No. My surname is Trevelyan.'

'Trev-el-ee-an.' Alessia repeats it a couple of times. It's a complicated name, for a complicated man? Alessia doesn't know. He doesn't seem complicated – just very different from any man she knows.

'Hey,' Maxim says. Placing his glass on the windowsill, he grabs the soap and lathers it between his hands. 'Let me wash your feet.' He holds out his hand.

Wash my feet!

'Let me,' he whispers when she hesitates. Setting her glass on the sill, she tentatively places her foot in his hand, and he begins to massage the soap into her skin.

Oh.

She closes her eyes as his strong fingers work methodically over her instep, up her heel, and around her ankle. He rubs the sole with just the right amount of pressure.

'Ah . . .' she moans.

When he reaches her toes, he washes each individually, then rinses them off, gently tugging and twisting each one. She squirms beneath the water and opens her eyes. His steady gaze holds hers and leaves her breathless.

'Good?' he asks.

'Yes. More than good.' She sounds hoarse.

'Where do you feel it?'

'Everywhere.'

When he squeezes her little toe, all her muscles clench deep inside her. She gasps, and he raises her foot and, with a wicked smile, kisses her big toe.

'Now the other one,' he orders in a soft voice. This time she doesn't hesitate. His fingers work their magic once more, and by the time he's finished, her entire body has turned to liquid. He kisses each toe in turn, except the smallest, which he puts into his mouth and sucks. Hard.

'Ah!' Her belly flutters. She opens her eyes to the same intense look, though now his lips are curled in a private smile. He kisses the ball of her foot.

'Better?'

'Mmm . . .' She can manage only an incoherent mumble.

A strange need claws at her belly.

'Good. I think we should get out before the water goes cold.' He stands and with long legs steps out of the bath. Alessia shuts her eyes. She doesn't think she'll ever get used to seeing him naked or get used to the aching, hungry sensation lingering deep, deep within her.

'Come on,' he says. He has wrapped a towel around his waist

and is offering her a navy robe. Feeling a little less shy, she stands and takes his hand as he helps her out of the bath. He envelops her in the robe, which is soft but far too big for her. She turns to face him, and he kisses her, properly, fully, his tongue exploring her mouth. His fingers at her nape, holding her, guiding her. When he releases her, she's breathless.

'I could kiss you all day,' he murmurs. Tiny drops of water cling to his body like dew. In her dazed state, Alessia wonders what they would taste like if she licked them off.

What!

She inhales sharply at her wayward thoughts.

How wanton.

She smiles. Perhaps she'll get used to seeing him naked.

'Okay?' he asks. She nods, and, taking her hand, he walks her back into the bedroom, where he releases her. He picks up his jeans from the floor and drags them on. She watches wide-eyed while he towel-dries his back.

'Enjoying the view?' He's smirking at her.

Her face is suddenly warm, but she holds his gaze. 'I like looking at you,' she whispers.

His smirk transforms into a charming, sincere smile. 'Well, I like looking at you, too, and I'm all yours,' he says, but his brow creases with uncertainty and he looks away. He recovers quickly and pulls on his T-shirt and sweater, then swaggers towards her and caresses her cheek, his thumb brushing the line of her jaw. 'You don't have to get dressed if you don't want to. I'm expecting Danny with our supper.'

'Oh?'

Danny again? Who is she? Why won't he talk about her?

Leaning down, he kisses Alessia. 'More champagne?'

'No, thank you. I will get dressed.'

Oh. From her tone I think she wants me to leave her alone while she dresses. 'You okay?' I ask. Her small smile and nod confirm that she's fine. 'Good,' I mumble, and return to the bathroom to collect our glasses and the Laurent-Perrier.

The sun has finally disappeared, shrouding the horizon in darkness. Downstairs in the kitchen, I switch on the lights and put the champagne in the fridge while I consider Alessia Demachi.

Man, she's unexpected.

She seems happier and more relaxed, but I'm not sure if it was the foot massage, the bath, the champagne, or the sex. Watching her response in the bath had been a carnal treat. When she closed her eyes and moaned as I massaged her feet, she was breathtaking, her sexuality innate.

The possibilities . . .

For fuck's sake.

I shake my head at my lascivious thoughts.

I was determined to leave her alone.

Determined.

But when I finally surrendered to my grief, she distracted and comforted me. And I succumbed . . . to a woman wearing SpongeBob pyjamas and an old Arsenal FC shirt. I can scarcely believe it.

I wonder what Kit would have made of Alessia.

You're not fucking the staff, are you, Spare?

No. Kit probably would not have approved of what I've done, though he would have liked Alessia. He always had an eye for a pretty girl.

'This house is so warm,' Alessia says, interrupting my thoughts. She stands in front of the kitchen counter wearing those pyjama bottoms and the white top.

'Too warm?' I ask.

'No.'

'Good. More fizz?'

'Fizz?'

'Champagne?'

'Yes. Please.'

I retrieve the bottle from the fridge and charge our glasses once more.

'What would you like to do?' I ask once she's taken a sip. I know what I want to do, but given she's sore, it's probably not a good idea.

Maybe later tonight.

Taking her glass, Alessia sits down on one of the sofas in the reading area and eyes the chess set on the coffee table. The entry phone buzzes.

'That will be Danny,' I say, and release the latch at the entry phone.

Alessia leaps up from the sofa.

'It's okay. There's nothing to worry about,' I reassure her.

Through the glass wall, I watch Danny take hesitant steps down the steep, illuminated stone stairway carrying a white plastic crate. It looks heavy.

I open the door and trot out in my bare feet to meet her halfway up the steps.

Fuck. The ground's freezing.

'Danny. Let me take that.'

'I've got it. Maxim, you'll catch your death of cold out here,' she scolds, her expression disapproving. 'I mean, my lord,' she adds as an afterthought.

'Danny. Give me the crate.' I'm not taking no for an answer.

Pursing her lips, she hands it to me, and I grin at her. 'Thank you for this.'

'I'll come and put it on for you.'

'It's fine. I'm sure I can work it out.'

'It would be much easier if you were up at the house, sir.'

'I know. I'm sorry. And thank Jessie for me.'

'It's your favourite. Oh, and Jessie put a spud jack in the crate for the potatoes. They've already been in the microwave, so they shouldn't take long to crisp up. Now, get inside with you. You're not wearing shoes.' She scowls while shooing me into the house. And because it's freezing, I do as I'm told. Through the full-height windows, she spies Alessia on the sofa and gives her a wave, which Alessia returns.

'Thank you,' I call from the shelter of the doorway with its cosy under-floor heating. I don't introduce her to Alessia. I know it's rude. But I really want to remain in our bubble for a little longer. Introductions can happen later.

Danny shakes her head, her white hair ruffled by the chilly wind, and turns to go back up the steps. I watch her ascend. She hasn't changed in all the years I've known her. This woman has tended my grazed knees, bandaged my cuts and scrapes, and iced my bruises since I was old enough to walk – always in her plaid skirt and stout shoes, never in trousers. No. I smile, it's Jessie, her partner for twelve years, who wears the trousers in that relationship. Briefly I wonder if they're ever going to marry. It's been legal for long enough. They have no excuse.

'Who is that?' Alessia asks, and peeks into the crate.

'That's Danny. I told you, she lives near here, and she's brought our supper.' I retrieve the casserole dish from inside the crate. There are four large potatoes, and my mouth waters when I spot the banoffee pie.

Man, Jessie can cook.

'The stew needs heating, and we can have it with baked potatoes. Sound okay?'

'Yes. It is very okay.'

'Very okay?'

'Yes.' She blinks. 'My English?'

'Is great,' I answer, and, grinning, I brandish the spiked potato baker from the crate.

'I can do that,' she says, though she looks a little doubtful.

'No. I'll do it.' I rub my hands together. 'I'm feeling domestic this evening, and trust me – it doesn't happen often. So take advantage.'

Alessia arches a brow, amused, as if she's seeing me in an entirely new light. I hope it's a good thing.

'Here.' In one of the cupboards, I find an ice bucket. 'You can fill this with ice. The fridge in the scullery dispenses ice. It's for the champagne.'

A glass or two later, Alessia is curled up on one of the turquoise sofas, her feet tucked beneath her, watching me while I finish putting the stew in the oven.

'Do you play?' I ask, as I come and sit beside her. Alessia's eyes flick to the marble chess set and back to me, her expression unreadable.

'A little,' she says, and takes a sip of her drink.

'A little, eh?' It's my turn to raise an eyebrow. *What does she mean?* Without taking my eyes off her, I grab a white pawn and a grey one and shuffle them between my cupped hands and offer them to her in my fists. She licks her top lip and deliberately traces her index finger over the back of one hand. A tremor runs from my hand up my arm and directly to my dick.

Wow.

'This one,' she says, looking up at me through inky lashes. I shift in my seat, trying to bring my body under control, and turn up my palm. It's the grey pawn. 'Black.' I turn the board so that the grey chess pieces are in front of her. 'Okay. I'll start.'

Four moves in and I'm dragging my hands through my hair. 'As usual, you've been holding out on me, haven't you?' My tone is wry. Alessia bites her top lip in an effort to suppress her smile and look serious. But her eyes are alive with amusement as she watches me struggle to outmanoeuvre her.

Of course she can play like an ace.

Man, she is full of surprises.

I scowl in the hope that it'll intimidate her into making a mistake. Her smile broadens, lighting up her beautiful face, and I can't help my answering grin.

She is stunning.

'You're rather good at this,' I observe.

She shrugs. 'There is not much to do in Kukës. At home we have an old computer but no games consoles and clever phones. Piano, chess and books, and some TV, that is what we have.' She glances at the bookshelf at the end of the room, her eyes full of appreciation.

'Books?'

'Oh, yes. Many, many books. In Albanian and English. I wanted to be an English teacher.' She studies the board for a moment, all humour gone.

Now she's a cleaner on the run from sex-trafficking thugs.

'But you enjoy reading?'

'Yes.' She brightens. 'Especially in English. My grandmother smuggled books into the country.'

'You mentioned that. Sounds risky.'

'Yes. It was dangerous for her. Books in English were banned by the Communists.'

Banned!

Once again I realise that I know very little about her homeland.

Dude, concentrate.

I take her knight, feeling smug. But one glance at her face tells me she's hiding her smirk. She slides her rook left three squares and chuckles. '*Shah* . . . no. Check.'

Shit!

'Okay, our first and last game of chess,' I grumble as I shake my head in self-disgust.

This is like playing Maryanne. She always beats me.

Alessia tucks her hair behind her ear, takes another sip of champagne, and twirls her gold cross with her fingers. She's thoroughly enjoying herself – thrashing me.

It's a humbling moment.

Concentrate.

Three moves later she has me.

'Checkmate,' she says, assessing me intently, and her solemn expression steals my breath away.

'Well played, Alessia Demachi,' I whisper as desire heats my blood. 'You're very good at this.'

She glances at the board, breaking the spell. When she raises her head, she gives me a coy smile. 'I played chess with my grandfather since I am six years. He was – how do you say? – a demon player. And he wanted to win. Even against a child.'

'He taught you well,' I murmur, recovering my equilibrium. What I really want to do is take her right here on the sofa. I consider pouncing on her – but concede that we should eat first.

'Is he still alive?' I ask.

'No, he died when I am twelve years.'

'I'm sorry.'

'He had a good life.'

'You say you wanted to be an English teacher. What happened?'

'My university closed. They had no money. And my courses stopped.'

'Well, that sucks.'

She giggles. 'Yes. It sucks. But I like working with little children. And I teach them music and read English to them. But only for two days each week, as I am not . . . what is the word? Qualified. And I help my mother at home. Another game?' she asks.

I shake my head. 'I think my ego might need some time to recover before we do that again. Are you hungry?'

She nods.

'Good. That stew smells amazing, and I'm starving.' Beef stew with prunes is my favourite of all Jessie's dishes. She used to cook it for winter shoots on the estate when Kit, Maryanne and I were pressed into service as beaters, driving the birds towards the guns. The aroma is tantalising. After all our activities today, I'm famished.

Alessia insists on dishing up, and I let her do that while I set the table. Surreptitiously I watch her as she busies herself in the kitchen. Her movements are neat and elegant. She has an intrinsic, sensuous grace, and I wonder if she's ever been a dancer. When she turns, her glorious hair spills down around her elfin face, and with a delicate flick of her wrist she flips it out of the way. Her long, slender fingers hold the knife as she slices open the baked potatoes, releasing wisps of steam. With her brow fixed in concentration, she spreads butter on them, and she stops to lick some melted butter from her index finger.

My groin tightens.

Oh, sweet Lord.

She glances up and catches me watching her.

'What is it?' she asks.

'Nothing.' My voice is gruff. I clear my throat. 'I just like looking at you. You're so lovely.' I move quickly and fold her in my arms, taking her by surprise. 'I'm glad you're here with me.' My lips meet hers in a quick, loving kiss.

'I am glad, too,' she says with a shy smile. 'Maxim.' My face splits in two. I love hearing my name in her accent. I grab our plates.

'Let's eat.'

The beef-and-prune stew is aromatic, sweet and tender. 'Mmm,' Alessia murmurs, closing her eyes in appreciation. '*I shijshëm.*'

'Is that Albanian for "I hate this"?' Maxim asks.

She giggles. 'No. It's delicious. Tomorrow I will cook for you.'

'Do you?' he asks.

'Cook?' Alessia places her hand on her heart, affronted. 'Of course. I am an Albanian woman. All Albanian women cook.'

'Okay. We'll go shopping tomorrow for ingredients.' His grin is infectious, but as he regards her, his face grows more serious.

'One day,' he says, 'will you tell me the whole story?'

'Story?' Her heart begins to thud.

'Of how and why you came to England.'

'Yes. One day,' she says.

One day. One day! ONE DAY!

Her heart skips a beat. Those two words imply a tangible future with this man.

Don't they?

But as what?

Alessia is confused about how men and women interact in England. It's different in Kukës. She's seen enough American TV shows – when her mother wasn't monitoring what she was watching – and in London she's seen how free and easy men and women are in public together. Kissing. Talking. Holding hands. And she knows that these couples are not married. They are lovers.

Maxim holds her hand.

They talk.

He makes love to her . . .

Lovers.

Surely that's what she and Mister Maxim are now.

Lovers.

Hope stirs in her heart, and it's a rousing but scary sensation.

She loves him. She should tell him. But she's too shy to declare herself. And she doesn't know how he feels about her. But she knows she would walk to the end of the earth for him.

'Would you like dessert?' he asks.

Alessia pats her stomach. 'I am full.'

'It's banoffee pie.'

'Banoffee?'

'Bananas, toffee and cream.'

She shakes her head. 'No, thank you.'

He takes their empty plates to the kitchen counter and returns with a slice of banoffee pie. Sitting down, he places the plate on the table and takes a bite. 'Mmm . . .' he says with exaggerated appreciation.

'You are teasing me. You want me to want your dessert?' she says.

'I want you to want a great many things. Right now it's dessert.' Maxim smirks and licks his lips. With his fork he scoops up a small piece smothered in cream and offers it to her. 'Eat,' he whispers, his voice seductive and his heated stare mesmerising. In response, she parts her lips and accepts the mouthful.

Oh, Zot i madh!

She closes her eyes and savours the confection as it dissolves. It's a sweet slice of heaven. When she focuses on him again, he's smiling with an I-told-you-so grin. He presents her with another, larger piece. This time she opens her mouth without hesitating. But he pops it into his own mouth, grinning with mischief as he chews. She laughs. He is so playful. She pouts, and he rewards her with a wicked grin and another bite of pie. His eyes stray to her lips as he gently wipes the corner of her mouth with his index finger.

'You missed this,' he murmurs, holding up his cream-smeared finger. Gone is his humour. It's replaced by a darker, simmering look. Alessia's pulse thrums faster. And she doesn't know if it's the champagne that's making her bolder or his scorching gaze, but she surrenders to her instincts. Leaning in towards his finger and with her eyes on his, she licks the cream off with the tip of her tongue. Maxim closes his eyes, and a low hum of appreciation rumbles in his throat. Emboldened by his reaction, she licks again, then kisses the tip before gently teasing it with her teeth. Maxim's eyes fly open, and she closes her lips around his finger and sucks. Hard.

Mmm . . . He tastes clean. Male.

Maxim's mouth drops open. Alessia continues to suck, watching his pupils dilate as his eyes linger on her mouth. His response is arousing. Who knew she had the power to stir him? It's a revelation. She scrapes her teeth against the pad of his finger, and he groans.

'Screw the pie,' he says, almost to himself, and he withdraws his finger slowly from her mouth. He clasps her head and kisses her, his tongue going the way of his finger. Wet. Hot. Exploring and claiming her. Alessia responds immediately, her fingers twisting in his hair and hungrily kissing him back. He tastes of banoffee pie and Maxim. It's a heady mix.

'Bed or chess?' he murmurs against her lips.

Again? Yes! A thrill travels at light speed through her body. 'Bed.'

'Good answer.' He caresses her cheek, brushing his thumb across her bottom lip, and smiles, his eyes alight with sensual promise. Taking each other's hand, they walk upstairs. On the threshold of the bedroom, he flips the wall switch so that only the bedside lamps illuminate the room. He turns unexpectedly and kisses her, his hands on each side of her face as he backs her against the wall. Her heart begins to pound as he presses his body along the length of hers. He wants her. She can feel him.

'Touch me,' he breathes. 'Everywhere.' And his lips are on hers again, possessive and needy, coaxing a moan from deep in her throat. 'Yes. Let me hear you.' His hands slide down to her waist. She splays her hands on his chest while his lips continue to savour her mouth. When he releases her, they are both panting. He rests his forehead against hers, their breath mingling, both of them straining for air.

'What you do to me.' His voice is as scft as a spring breeze. He looks down at her, the longing in his eyes burning into her soul. He grips the hem of her top and pulls it over her head. She's naked beneath, and her natural inclination is to cover her breasts. But he catches her hands and grips them, keeping his eyes on hers. 'You're stunning. Don't hide.' He kisses her again while interlacing his fingers with hers so they are palm to palm. Holding her still, he continues the sweet invasion of her mouth. When she pulls away for air, he kisses her throat, her jaw, and his teeth skim her chin before he plants large wet kisses on the pulse point at her neck.

Her blood drums through her body with a reckless beat. Inside, she's melting. Everywhere. She flexes her fingers, but he doesn't let them go.

'Do you want to touch me?' he asks against her throat.

She groans.

'Tell me.'

'Yes,' she whispers, and he tugs her earlobe gently with his teeth. Squirming against him, she moans and flexes her fingers again. This time he releases her and his hands grab her hips and tug her against his erection.

'Feel me,' he murmurs.

She does. All of him.

Ready. Waiting. For her.

Her heart stutters, and she gasps.

He wants her. And she wants him.

'Undress me,' he coaxes, and her fingers find the hem of his T-shirt. Hesitating for only a moment, she drags it up and over his head. Once she's dropped it on the floor, he puts his hands on his head.

'Now what are you going to do with me?' he asks, and a pleased, sexy smile curls his lips.

Alessia inhales, overwhelmed by his bold invitation as her eyes flit over his body. Her fingers are itching to touch him. To feel his skin beneath hers.

'Go on,' he whispers, a seductive challenge in his voice. She wants to touch his chest, his stomach, his belly. She wants to kiss him there, too. The thought elicits a strange, delicious tightening deep inside her. Hesitantly, she raises her hand, and with her index finger she traces a line from his chest down between his abdominal muscles to his navel. His eyes never leave hers, his breath hitches, and she continues skating her finger down over his belly through the hair to the top button of his jeans. Her courage deserts her, and she hesitates.

Maxim grins and grabs her hand, raising it to his lips and kissing her fingertips. He turns it over and places his lips and the tip of his tongue on the inside of her wrist where her blood is pumping. He circles his tongue deliberately over her pulse, and Alessia gasps. With a smile he releases her and clasps her head. His lips find hers once more, and he explores her mouth.

She's panting when he lets her go. 'My turn,' he says. And with infinite care and a feather-light touch, he trails his index finger between her breasts, down her stomach, to her navel, which he rings twice before proceeding to the waistband of her pj's. Alessia's heart starts thumping, echoing in an insane rhythm in her head.

Suddenly he kneels down in front of her.

What?

She grabs his shoulders to stay upright. His hands move around to her behind as he kisses the underside of each breast and trails soft, sweet kisses to her navel.

'Ah,' she groans as his tongue rims and dips into her belly button. She runs her fingers through his hair, and he looks up at her and gives her a wicked grin. With his hands on her behind, he sits back on his haunches and pulls her forward, holding her in place, and runs his nose up her sex.

'Wha—!' Alessia exclaims in shock. She tightens her fingers in his hair, and he groans.

'You smell good,' he whispers, and she gasps. His hands slip into the waistband of her pj's and cup her bare backside, kneading her flesh as he rubs his nose over her clitoris, on and on.

This is not what she was expecting. The sight of him on his knees at her feet, doing what he's doing to her body, is too stimulating. She closes her eyes, tips her head back, and moans. His hands shift, and she feels her pj's gliding down her legs.

Zot.

His nose stays at the apex of her legs.

'Maxim!' she cries, scandalised, and she tries to pull his head away.

'Hush,' he murmurs. 'It's okay.' And his tongue replaces his nose as he resists her feeble attempts to stop him.

'Ah,' Alessia moans as he continues to tease her, his tongue circling around and around and around. She stops fighting him. Losing herself to the sensation and revelling in the carnal delight of his touch. Her legs begin to tremble, and Maxim grasps her hips and persists in his delicious torment.

'Please,' she begs, and he stands in one fluid movement. She clutches his hips, and he kisses her again, his hands in her hair pulling her head back, and she opens up for him, relishing his tongue. He tastes different – salty, slick, and she realises he tastes of her!

O perëndi!

His mouth on hers, his hand skims down her body, his thumb brushing over her nipple, tracing the line of her waist, then down to the junction of her thighs. His fingers tease her where moments before his tongue had been, and he slips a finger inside her. Quivering and driven by instinct, she presses her hips towards him, trying to find relief against his hand.

'Yes,' he hisses with obvious pleasure as he circles his finger inside her, pushing in and out. When she tips her head back and closes her eyes, he withdraws his hand and tugs at his jeans. The zipper obliges, and out of his back pocket he produces a condom. He makes short work of removing his jeans, and Alessia watches dazed but fascinated as he rips open the packet and rolls the condom over his erection. She's breathing hard and fast . . . but she wants to touch him. There. Except she doesn't have the nerve. Yet.

And they're not even in bed . . . What is he going to do? He kisses her again and puts his hands around her waist.

'Hold on,' he whispers, and he lifts her. 'Wrap your legs and arms around me.'

What? Again?

She does as he asks, surprised once more by her own agility while he puts his hands under her behind and leans her back against the wall.

He's panting. 'You okay?' he asks.

She nods, wide-eyed and needy. Her body aches for him. She wants him . . . badly. He kisses her and eases his hips forward and slowly sinks into her.

She groans and winces as he stretches and fills her.

He stops. 'Too much?' he asks, and she hears his concern. 'Tell me.' His voice is urgent. 'If you want to stop. Just say.'

She flexes her thighs. This is okay. She can do this. She wants this. She lays her forehead against his. 'More. Please.'

He groans, and he begins to move, flexing his hips. Slow at first, but as Alessia pants and moans, he increases his rhythm. She tightens her hold around his neck as he picks up speed. The feeling is intense as the sensation spirals through her body. And she starts to build as he moves and moves.

Oh. No. This is too much. It's too overwhelming. She digs her nails into his shoulders.

'Maxim, Maxim,' she whimpers. 'I can't.'

Immediately he stops moving, his breathing ragged. He kisses her and takes a deep breath, and without breaking their intimate contact he turns and walks to the bed. He sits down on the bed, then eases her gently onto her back and gazes at her with eyes the colour of a forest in spring, his pupils large, betraying his need. Reaching up, she caresses his cheek, marvelling at his athleticism.

'Better?' he asks as he nestles between her legs and holds his weight on his forearms.

'Yes,' she whispers, and her fingers thread through his soft hair. His teeth nip at her lips, and he begins to move again. Gradually at first, but increasing his speed. This is easier, not quite as deep, and before she's aware of it, her body is no longer her own but moving to Maxim's rhythm, matching his pace as he moves back and forth into her time and again. She's lost in him, with him . . . building and building, stiffening and stiffening.

'Yes,' Maxim hisses, and he pushes once more and suddenly stills with a growl. Alessia cries out as she explodes around him once, twice, again, spiralling out of control beneath his tense body.

When she opens her eyes, his forehead is against hers, his eyes screwed shut.

'Oh, Alessia,' he breathes.

After a moment he opens his eyes, and she strokes his cheek as they gaze at each other. He is so dear. So, so dear.

'*Të dua*,' she whispers.

'What does that mean?'

She smiles, and he responds in kind, his face full of wonder and . . . reverence, maybe. He bends and kisses her lips, her eyelids, her cheeks, her jaw, and slowly eases himself out of her. Alessia whimpers feeling the loss, then she drifts, replete but exhausted, and falls asleep in his arms.

She lies curled up beside me, swaddled in the quilt.

Small. Vulnerable. Beautiful.

This young woman who has been through so much is now here beside me, where I can protect her. I stretch out, watching the steady rise and fall of her chest: her lips parted as she breathes, her dark lashes fanned out over her cheeks. Her skin is fair, her lips rosy. She's gorgeous, and I know that I will never tire of looking at her. I'm enthralled and spellbound by her. She's magical, in every way.

I've had sex too many times to count, but I've never felt this connected. It's a foreign and unsettling feeling, as is my yearning for more.

I brush a stray lock of hair off her forehead simply as an excuse to touch her. Alessia stirs and mumbles something in Albanian, and I freeze, afraid that I've woken her. But she settles once more into a peaceful sleep and I remember that she'll fear the dark should she wake. Careful not to disturb her, I climb out of bed and hurry downstairs to retrieve the night-light I purchased earlier. I fit the batteries, switch it on, and place it on the bedside table next to Alessia. Should she wake, she won't be in darkness.

Slipping back under the covers, I lie down and study her. She's lovely – the curve of her cheek, of her chin, the way that tiny gold cross nestles in the hollow at the base of her throat – she's exquisite. She looks young but serene as she sleeps. Taking a strand of her hair, I wind it around my finger. I hope to God she's feeling safer now. And that her dreams aren't the nightmares she endured yesterday. She sighs, and her lips curl in a smile. Her expression is encouraging. I gaze at her until I can no longer keep my eyes open. And before I drift off to sleep, I murmur her name.

Alessia.

Chapter Sixteen

I sense her before I'm fully awake. The warmth of her body seeps into mine. Enjoying the feel of her skin on my skin, I open my eyes to greet the misty morning and the lovely Alessia. She's fast asleep and curled around me like a fern, her hand on my belly, her head on my chest. My arm is wrapped possessively around her shoulders, holding her close, and she's naked. I grin as my body rouses.

What a difference a day makes.

I lie for a moment cherishing her heat and the fragrance of her hair. She shifts and mumbles something unintelligible, and her eyelids flutter open.

'Good morning, beautiful,' I whisper. 'This is your early-morning wake-up call.' And I ease her onto her back. She blinks a couple of times as I kiss the tip of her nose and nuzzle the pulse point beneath her ear, and she beams and throws her arms around my neck as my hand travels down to her breast.

* * *

The sun is shining. The air is crisp and cold. 'No Diggity' blares over the sound system as I drive up the A39 towards Padstow. I've ruled out going to Sunday service. There'll be too many people at the local parish church who know me. Once I've told Alessia who I am and what I do . . . then maybe. I glance at her as her heels bounce in time to the music. She flashes me a quick crotch-tightening grin.

Man, she is captivating.

Her smile lights up the Jag's interior – and me.

I give her a wicked smile in return, remembering this morning. And last night. She tucks her wild hair behind her ear, and an innocent blush steals across her cheeks. Perhaps she's thinking about this morning, too. I hope so. I see her, a vision in my bed, head tipped back in ecstasy, her mouth open as she cries out and comes, her hair spilling over the edge of the bed. My blood heads south at the thought. *Yeah.* She seemed to enjoy it. She seemed to enjoy it very much. Shifting in my seat at the memory, I reach across to squeeze her knee.

'You okay?' I ask.

She nods, her deep brown eyes sparkling.

'Me, too.' I take her hand, bring it to my lips, and give her a grateful kiss on her palm.

I feel buoyant – more than buoyant, I'm elated. I'm happier than I've been . . . since . . . since Kit died. No. Since before Kit's death. And I know it's because I'm with Alessia.

I'm intoxicated with her.

But I don't dwell on my feelings. I don't want to. They are new and raw and a little unsettling. I've never felt like this. Truth is, I'm excited. I'm going shopping with a woman, and I'm looking forward to it – is this a first?

But I suspect it will be a battle with Alessia. She's proud. Maybe it's an Albanian characteristic. At breakfast she was adamant that

I couldn't buy her any new clothes. But she's sitting beside me in her only pair of jeans, the thin, greying white top, her leaky boots, and my sister's old jacket. This is a fight she's not going to win.

I park in the spacious car park by the quay. She's curious, peering through the windscreen at our surroundings.

'Want to look around?' I ask, and we climb out of the car.

It's a picture-postcard scene: antiquated houses and cottages built of grey Cornish stone line the small harbour where a few fishing boats are moored up, idle, because it's a Sunday.

'This is a good view,' Alessia says. She's huddled in her coat, and I stretch my arm around her shoulders and hold her to me.

'Let's go and get you some warm clothes,' I offer with a smile, but she immediately steps out of my embrace.

'Maxim, I cannot pay for new clothes.'

'It's my treat.'

'Treat?' She frowns.

'Alessia, you have nothing. This is very easy for me to put right. Please. Let me. I want to.'

'It is not right.'

'Says who?'

She taps her finger to her lips, and it appears that this is not an argument she's considered. 'Me. *I* say,' she answers eventually.

I sigh. 'They are a gift for all your hard work—'

'They are a gift because I have sexual intercourse with you.'

'What? No!' I laugh, appalled and amused in equal measure. I quickly scan the quay to check no one can hear us. 'I offered to buy you clothes before the sex, Alessia. Come on. Look at you. You're freezing. And I know your boots leak. I've seen your wet footprints in my hallway.'

She opens her mouth to speak.

I hold up my hand to stop her. 'Please,' I insist. 'It would give me great pleasure.'

She purses her lips, unimpressed. I try a different tack. 'I'm going to buy them for you anyway, whether you're there or not. So you can come with me and choose something you like or leave it to me.'

She folds her arms.

Fuck. Alessia Demachi has a stubborn streak.

'Please. For me,' I beseech her, holding out my hand. She glares at me, and I give her my very best smile. Then she sighs – resigned, I think – and puts her hand in mine.

Yes.

Mister Maxim is right. She needs clothes. Why is she being so obstinate about his generous offer? It's because he's done so much for her already. She trots beside him along the quay, trying to ignore the scandalised voice of her mother that rings in her head.

He is not your husband. He is not your husband.

She shakes her head.

Enough!

She's not going to let her absent mother make her feel guilty. She is in England now. She is free. Like an English girl. Like her grandmother. And Mister Maxim said that she is on holiday, and if it gives him pleasure . . . After the pleasure he's given her, how can she refuse? She blushes recalling his . . . what did he call it?

Early-morning wake-up call.

Alessia fights back her smile. He could wake her up like that any day.

And he cooked her breakfast again.

He is spoiling her.

She hasn't been spoiled in a very long time.

Ever?

She glances up at him as they walk into the centre of Padstow, and her heart lurches. He looks down at her, his eyes lively, and his handsome face erupts into a wide grin. He looks roguish this morning. It must be the stubble on his face. She likes the feel of it beneath her tongue. She loves the feel of it against her skin.

Alessia!

She had no idea she could be so wanton. Mister Maxim has woken a monster. She laughs to herself.

Who knew?

Her thoughts take a sombre turn. What is she going to do when they go back to London and the holiday comes to an end? She wraps one hand around his biceps and squeezes his hand with the other. She doesn't want to think about that. Not now. Not today.

This is a holiday.

As they walk, the words became her mantra.

This is a holiday.

Ky është pushim!

Padstow is bigger than Trevethick, but the old, cramped houses and narrow lanes are the same. It's a picturesque little town. The place is bustling with people, tourists and locals out enjoying the sunshine in spite of the cold. There are children eating ice cream. Young people holding hands, like Maxim and her. And older people happily arm in arm. Alessia is amazed that people can express their affection so freely on the streets. It is not the same in Kukës.

I turn into the first shop that sells women's clothing. It's a local chain store, and I stand in the middle of the shop staring at all that's on offer. Everything looks pleasant enough, but frankly I'm a little overwhelmed. Alessia is hanging on my arm like a limpet. And I have no idea where to start. I'd had the vague idea that I'd have her cooperation, her enthusiasm, even – but she doesn't seem interested in the merchandise.

A young sales assistant approaches us. Blond and breezy, with a bright, girl-next-door smile and a bouncing ponytail to match, she asks, 'Can I help you, sir?'

'My . . . um, girlfriend needs everything. She's left all her stuff in London, and we're here for a week.'

Girlfriend? Yes. That works.

Alessia looks up at me, surprised.

'Sure. What do you need?' the assistant asks with a cheery glance at Alessia.

Alessia shrugs.

'Let's start with jeans,' I interject.

'What size?'

'I do not know,' Alessia replies.

The assistant looks puzzled, and then stands back appraising her. 'You're not from around here, are you?' she says pleasantly.

'No.' Alessia flushes.

'I think you're a small, either a size eight or ten.' She gives us an expectant look, waiting for confirmation.

Alessia nods, though I think it's because she doesn't want to be rude.

'Why don't you go into the changing room, and I'll find some jeans in those sizes, and we'll go from there?'

'Okay,' Alessia mumbles, and with an inscrutable look at me, she follows the assistant to the changing rooms.

I hear the assistant inform Alessia, 'My name's Sarah, by the way.' I breathe a sigh of relief and watch Sarah retrieve a couple of pairs of jeans from the shelves.

'Dark and light denim and a pair in black,' I prompt. Her ponytail bobs merrily as she flashes me a smile and gathers several pairs.

Wandering around the shop, I rifle through some clothes racks trying to decide what would look good on Alessia. I've been shopping with women before, but they've always known what they wanted. I am dragged along on these trips either to pay or to give an opinion that will be ignored. The women I know all have confidence in their own style. I wonder if I should send her shopping with Caroline.

What?

Back in London?

No. That's probably not a good idea.

Not yet.

I frown. *What am I doing?*

I'm fucking my daily. That's what I'm doing.

In my mind I hear her cry as she orgasms. My dick hardens at the memory.

Bugger.

Yes. I'm fucking her, and I want to do it again.

That's why I'm here.

I like her. Really like her. And I want to protect her from all the shit she's endured . . . And I have so much, and she has nothing.

I snort. It's a redistribution of wealth. Yes. How altruistic and socialist of me. My mother would not be thrilled. That thought makes me smile.

I find a couple of dresses I like, one in black and one in emerald green, and hand them to the assistant.

Will Alessia like these?

I sit down in a convenient chair outside the dressing-room area and wait, trying to put aside my disquieting thoughts.

Alessia appears wearing the green dress.

Wow.

I feel a little light-headed.

I've never seen her in a dress.

Her hair cascades down below her breasts, which are swathed in a soft fabric that clings.

Everywhere.

Breasts. Flat stomach. Hips. The dress stops short at her knees, and she's barefoot. She looks sensational – a little older, maybe, but more womanly and sophisticated.

'It is not too low?' Alessia asks, tugging at the neckline.

'No.' My voice is hoarse, and I cough to clear it. 'No, it's fine.'

'Do you like it?'

'Yes. Yes. I like it a lot. You look lovely.'

She gives me a shy smile. I hold up my finger and motion for her to turn around. She does quickly and giggles.

The fabric clings to her arse, too.

Yep. She's gorgeous.

'I approve,' I say, and she heads back into the dressing room.

Forty-five minutes later, Alessia has a new wardrobe: three pairs of jeans, four long-sleeved tops in various colours, two skirts, two plain shirts, two cardigans, two dresses, two sweaters, a coat, socks, tights and underwear.

'That's one thousand three hundred and fifty-five pounds, please.' Sarah beams at Maxim.

'What!' Alessia squeaks.

Maxim hands over his credit card, pulls Alessia into his arms, and kisses her long and hard. She is breathless when he releases her, and she stares down at the floor, mortified. She cannot face Sarah. In Alessia's town, holding hands in public is considered forward. Kissing. No. Never. Never in public.

'Hey,' Maxim murmurs, putting his hand beneath her chin to pull her face up.

'You spend too much,' she whispers.

'Not for you. Please. Don't be angry with me.'

Her gaze lingers on my face, but I have no idea what she's thinking.

'Thank you,' she says finally.

'You are most welcome,' I reply, relieved. 'Now we're going to get you some decent shoes.'

Alessia's face lights up like a summer's day.

Ah. Shoes . . . the way to every woman's heart.

In a nearby shoe shop, she chooses a pair of stout ankle boots in black.

'You'll need more than one pair of shoes,' I say.

'These are all I need.'

'Here, these are nice.' I hold up a pair of ballet flats. I wish they stocked high-heeled fuck-me shoes, but alas – everything in the store is practical.

Alessia hesitates.

'I like these,' I say, hoping my opinion will influence her decision.

'Okay. If you like them. They are nice.'

I grin. 'And I like these.' I hold up a brown leather knee-high boot with a heel.

'Maxim,' Alessia objects.

'Please.'

She gives me a reluctant smile. 'Okay.'

'We can leave your boots for recycling here,' Maxim says as they stand at the sales counter. Alessia looks down at the new boots she's wearing and then at her old pair. They are all she has left of her clothes from home.

'I would like to keep them,' she says.

'Why?'

'They are from Albania.'

'Oh.' He looks surprised. 'Well, perhaps we can get them resoled.'

'Resoled? What is this?'

'Repaired. The bottom of the shoe replaced. Understand?'

'Yes. Yes,' she replies, excited. 'Resoled.'

She watches as Maxim hands over his credit card once more.

How can she ever repay him?

One day she'll earn enough money to pay him back. In the meantime she has to think of something she could do for him. 'Remember, I want to cook,' she says.

This is one way.

'Today?' Maxim asks as he picks up her bags.

'Yes. I want to cook for you. To say thank you. Tonight.'

'Okay. Let's take these bags back to the car, and we can shop for food after we've had some lunch.'

They dump the bags in the small trunk of the car, and as they walk hand in hand to a restaurant, Alessia tries not to dwell on Maxim's generosity. It is rude in her culture to reject a gift, but she knows what her father would call her if he knew what she was doing. He would either kill her or have a heart attack. Probably both. She's already dishonoured him, and until recently she had the bruises to prove it. Once again she wishes he were more open-minded – and less violent.

Baba.

Her mood nosedives.

We lunch at Rick Stein's Café. Alessia's quiet, and when we order our food, she's a little subdued. I wonder if it's because I've spent money on her clothes. Once the waitress has taken our order, I reach over and take Alessia's hand, giving it a reassuring squeeze. 'Alessia, don't worry about the money. For the clothes. Please.' She gives me a tight smile and takes a sip of her sparkling water.

'What's wrong?'

She shakes her head.

'Tell me,' I insist.

She shakes her head again, turning away to stare out of the window.

Something is off.

Shit. Have I upset her?

'Alessia?'

She turns back to face me, and she looks distraught.

Fuck.

'What is it?'

She gazes at me, dark eyes clouded with misery, and it's like a knife to my gut.

'Tell me.'

'I cannot pretend I am on holiday,' she says softly. 'You buy me all these things, and I can never pay you the money. And I don't know what will happen to me when we go back to London. And I am thinking about my father and what he would do to me' – she pauses and swallows – 'and to you, if he knew what we had done. I know what he would call me. And I'm tired. I'm tired of being afraid.' Her voice is a raw whisper, and tears shine in her eyes. She looks directly at me. 'That is what I am thinking.'

I stare back. Paralysed, but empty and aching. For her.

'That's a lot to think about,' I murmur.

The waitress returns with our food and cheerily places my Californian chicken sandwich in front of me and the butternut squash soup in front of Alessia. 'Everything okay?' she asks.

'Yes. Fine. Thanks.' I dismiss her.

Alessia picks up her spoon and stirs her soup while I'm helpless and floundering for something to say. Her voice barely audible, she says, 'I am not your problem, Maxim.'

'I never said you were.'

'That is not what I mean.'

'I know what you mean, Alessia. Whatever happens between us, I want to be sure you're okay.'

She gives me a sad smile. 'I am grateful. Thank you.'

Her response angers me. I don't want her gratitude. I think she's got some old-fashioned notion about being my mistress. And what her father has to do with us, I don't know. It's 2019. Not 1819.

What the hell does she want?

Fuck. What do I want?

I watch as she lifts her soup spoon to her lips, her face pale and sad.

At least she's eating.

What do I want? From her?

I've had her beautiful body.

And it's not enough.

It hits me. Like a sledgehammer. Right between the eyes.

I want her heart.

Fuck.

Chapter Seventeen

Love. Confusing. Irrational. Frustrating . . . Exhilarating. This is what it feels like. I am madly, crazily, ridiculously in love with the woman sitting opposite me.

My daily. Alessia Demachi.

I've felt like this since I first laid eyes on her standing in my hallway clutching a broom. I remember how disconcerted I was . . . How angry. How the walls closed in on me and I had to escape because I didn't understand the depth of my feelings. This is what I was running from. I thought I was just wildly attracted to her. But no. It's not just her body I crave. It's never been just that. I'm drawn to her in a way I've never been to any other woman. I love her. That's why I went after her when she fled to Brentford. That's why I brought her here. I want to protect her. I want her happy. I want her with me.

Fuck.

It's a revelation.

And she has no idea who I am or what I do. And I know so little about her. In fact, I have no idea how she feels about me.

Yet she's here with me, so surely that means something. I think she likes me. But then again what choice does she have? I'm her only option. She was afraid, and she had nowhere to run. And on some level I knew that, and I tried to stay away from her, but I couldn't, because she's carved her way into my heart.

I've fallen in love with my cleaner.

Well, this is a fine fucking mess.

And now she's finally opening up to me – but in spite of all I've done, she's still afraid. I've not done enough. My appetite evaporates.

'I am sorry. I did not want to be the kill buzz,' she says, interrupting my thoughts.

'Kill buzz?'

She frowns. 'My English?'

'I think you mean buzzkill.'

Her smile is half-hearted.

'You're not,' I reassure her. 'We'll figure this out, Alessia. You'll see.'

She nods, but she doesn't look convinced. 'You are not hungry?'

I eye my chicken sandwich, and my stomach rumbles. She giggles, and it's the most wonderful sound in the world.

'That's better.' I delight in her amusement, relieved that she's recovered her sense of humour, and I turn my attention back to my meal.

Alessia relaxes. She can't remember talking about her feelings to him before, and he doesn't seem angry with her. When he glances at her, his eyes are warm, his expression reassuring.

We'll figure this out, Alessia. You'll see.

She looks down at her butternut squash soup, her appetite returning. She marvels at the chain of events that has brought her here. When her mother put her into the minibus on the freezing backroad in Kukës, she knew that her life would change beyond all recognition. She had such hope for a new life in England. She didn't expect the journey to be so hard, or so dangerous. And the irony was that she had been trying to run from danger.

And yet it brought her to him.

Mister Maxim.

He of the handsome face and easy laugh and brilliant smile. She watches him as he eats. He has impeccable table manners. He's neat and tidy and chews with his mouth closed. Her English grandmother, who was a stickler for manners, would have approved.

When he looks across at her, his eyes are a luminous green. The most extraordinary colour. The colour of the Drin. The colour of her home.

She could watch him all day.

He gives her a reassuring smile. 'Okay?' he asks.

Alessia nods. She loves the warmth of his smile when he looks at her, and she loves the heat in his eyes . . . when he wants her. She blushes and looks down at her soup. She never expected to fall in love.

Love is for fools, her mother used to say.

Maybe she is a fool, but she loves him. And she's told him. But of course he doesn't understand her native tongue.

'Hey,' he says.

She looks up. He's eaten his food.

'How's your soup?'

'It is good.'

'Well, eat up. I'd like to get you home.'

'Okay,' she says, and she likes the idea of 'home'. She'd like to make her home with him. Permanently. But she knows it's not possible.

A girl can dream.

* * *

The drive back to Trevethick is more muted than their earlier journey. Maxim is preoccupied and listening to strange music playing over the sound system. Their stop at a supermarket called Tesco on the way out of Padstow has yielded all the ingredients Alessia needs to make *tavë kosi*, her father's favourite dish. She hopes Maxim will like it. She gazes out at the passing countryside. Still cloaked in winter, the landscape reminds her of home. Though here the trees are cropped short and warped by the bitter Cornish wind.

She wonders how Magda and Michal are getting on in Brentford. It's Sunday, so Michal will probably be doing his school homework or online gaming, and Magda will be cooking or talking to her fiancé, Logan, via Skype, or maybe she's packing for their move to Canada. Alessia hopes they are safe. She glances at Maxim, who seems lost in his own thoughts; he would know how Magda and Michal are if he's been in touch with his friend. Maybe he'll let her use his phone later, and she can catch up with the news from home.

No, Brentford is not her home.

She doesn't know where her next home will be.

Determined to keep her spirits up, she lets go of that thought and listens once more to the extraordinary sounds coming from the sound system. The colours are clashing: purples, reds, turquoise . . . it's like nothing she's heard before.

'What is this music?' she asks.

'It's from the soundtrack of *Arrival*.'

'Arrival?'

'The film.'

'Oh.'

'Have you seen it?'

'No.'

'It's great. A real headfuck. About time and language and the difficulties of communication. We can watch it at home. Do you like the music?'

'Yes. It's strange. Expressive. And colourful.'

His smile is brief. Too brief. He has been brooding. She wonders if he's dwelling on their earlier conversation. She has to know. 'Are you angry with me?'

'No. Of course not! Why would I be angry with you?'

She shrugs. 'I don't know. You are quiet.'

'You've given me a lot to think about.'

'I am sorry.'

'There's no need to apologise. You haven't done anything wrong. If anything . . .' He trails off.

'You have not done anything wrong,' she says.

'I'm glad you think that.' He gives her a quick, sincere smile that dispels her doubts.

'Is there any food you don't eat?' she asks, and wishes she'd found out before they went shopping.

'No. I eat pretty much anything. I went to boarding school,' he answers, as if this explains his entire ethos on food. But Alessia's knowledge of boarding schools is limited to Enid Blyton's Malory Towers, a favourite book series of her grandmother.

'Did you like it?' she asks.

'First one, no. I was expelled. The second one, yes. It's a good school. I made good friends there. You met them.'

'Oh, yes.' Alessia blushes as she remembers the two men in their underwear.

They settle into an easier conversation, and by the time they arrive home, she's more cheerful.

We carry the bags into the house, and while Alessia unpacks the groceries, I take her clothes upstairs. I put them in the spare bedroom, then change my mind and place the bags in the walk-in wardrobe in my room. I want her in here with me.

It's presumptuous.

Fuck.

I'm tangling myself in knots. I don't know how to behave with her.

Sitting down on the bed, I put my head in my hands. Did I have a game plan before we got here?

No.

I was thinking with my dick. And now . . . well, I hope I'm thinking with my head and following my heart. During the drive home, I contemplated what to do. Should I tell her that I love her? Should I not? She's given me no indication of how she feels about me, but then she's reticent about most things.

She's here with me.

That means something, surely?

She could have stayed with her friend, but that would have meant those gangsters returning and finding her. My blood turns to ice. I shudder to think what they would do to her if they did. No. I was her only option. She has nothing. How could she go on the run?

Yet she arrived in the UK with nothing, and she survived. She's resourceful, but at what cost to herself? The thought weighs heavily on me. What did she do during the time between her arrival and finding Magda?

The anguish in her eyes in the restaurant. It was . . . affecting.

I'm tired of being afraid.

I wonder how long she's felt this way. Since she got here? I don't even know how long she's been in the UK. There's so much I don't know about her.

But I want her to be happy.

Think. What to do?

First. We have to make her legal here. And I have no idea how to do that. My solicitors should know the answer. I can only imagine Rajah's face when I tell him I'm harbouring an illegal immigrant.

Her grandmother was English. Maybe that will help.

Fuck. I don't know.

What else could I do?

I could marry her.

What?

Marriage?

I laugh out loud, because the idea is so absurd.

Why not?

It would freak my mother out. For that reason alone, it's worth popping the question. Tom's words from our night at the pub come back to me: *You know, now that you're the earl, you'll need to provide an heir and a spare.*

I could make Alessia my countess.

My heart starts hammering. That would be a bold move.

And maybe a little sudden.

I don't even know if she has feelings for me.

I could ask her.

I roll my eyes. I am going round and round in circles. The truth is, I need to find out more about her. How could I ask her to be my wife? I know where Albania is on the map, but that's about it. Well, I can put that right, now.

I drag my phone out of my pocket and open Google.

It's dark when my phone starts to complain about its remaining battery life. I'm sprawled across the bed, reading everything I can about Albania. It's a fascinating place, part modern, part ancient, with a turbulent history. I've found Alessia's hometown. It's in the northeast, nestled among mountain ranges and a few hours' drive from the capital. From all I've read, it does appear that life is more traditional in that region.

This explains a great deal.

Alessia is cooking downstairs. Whatever she's making, its savoury aroma is enticing. I get up and stretch and head downstairs to see her.

She's still dressed in her white top and jeans, and she has her back to me at the stove, mixing something in a pan. My mouth waters; it smells delicious.

'Hi,' I greet her, and sit down on one of the barstools at the counter.

'Hi.' She gives me a quick smile, and I notice she's plaited her hair. I plug my phone into one of the charging sockets beneath the counter and fire up the Sonos.

'Is there any music you'd like to hear?' I ask.

'You choose.'

I select a mellow playlist and hit PLAY. RY X blasts out of the speakers overhead, making us both jump. I turn it down. 'Sorry about that. What are you cooking?'

'A surprise,' she says with a coquettish glance over her shoulder.

'I love surprises. It smells good. Can I do anything to help?'

'No. This is my thank-you. Would you like to drink?'

I laugh. 'Yes. I would like a drink. Do you mind if I correct your English?'

'No. I want to learn.'

'"Would you like *a* drink?" is what we say.'

'Okay.' She flashes me another smile

'And yes, I would. Thank you.'

She sets the pan aside and from the counter takes an open bottle of red wine and pours me a glass.

'I've been reading about Albania.'

She whips her eyes to mine, her face lighting up like the early dawn. 'Home,' she whispers.

'Tell me more about life in Kukës.'

Maybe it's because she's distracted while cooking supper, but she finally opens up and starts to describe the house she lived in with her father and mother. It's beside a vast lake, surrounded by fir trees . . . And while she's telling me, I watch and marvel at how she moves about behind the counter with such ease and grace, as if she's been cooking in this kitchen for years. Whether it's grating nutmeg or adjusting the timing on the oven. She's like a professional. And as she cooks, she tops up my wine, washes dishes, and gives me insights into her claustrophobic life in Kukës.

'So you don't drive?'

'No,' she answers as she lays the table for us.

'Does your mother drive?'

'Yes. But not often.' She smiles when she sees my consternation. 'You know that most Albanians did not drive until the mid-1990s. Before the fall of the Communists. We had no cars.'

'Wow. I had no idea.'

'I would like to learn.'

'To drive? I'll teach you.'

She's taken aback. 'In your fast car? I do not think so!' She laughs as if I've suggested flying to the moon for lunch.

'I could teach you.' We have enough land here, we don't need to be on the public highway. We'll be safe. A vision of her driving one of Kit's cars, maybe his Morgan, comes to mind. Yes. That would be suitable for a countess.

Countess?

'This will take another fifteen minutes or so to cook,' she says, and she taps her lips with her finger. There's something on her mind.

'What would you like to do?'

Alessia chews her bottom lip.

'What is it?' I ask.

'I'd like to talk to Magda.'

Of course she wants to talk to her. Magda's probably her *only* bloody friend. Why didn't I think of that?

'Sure. Here.' I unplug my phone and find Magda's contact details. When the call connects, I hand the phone to Alessia, who gives me a grateful smile.

'Magda . . . Yes, it's me.' Alessia moves to sit down on the sofa while I try and fail not to eavesdrop. I imagine that Magda is relieved to hear that Alessia is still in one piece. 'No. Fine.' Alessia glances up at me, her eyes shining. 'Very fine,' she says with a wide grin, and I find myself reciprocating.

I'll take 'very fine' any day.

She laughs at something Magda says, and my heart swells. It's so good to hear her laugh; she doesn't do it often enough.

As she talks, I try not to watch her, but I can't resist. Unconsciously she winds a lock of hair that's escaped from her plait around her fingers as she tells Magda about the sea and her impromptu dip in it yesterday.

'No. It's beautiful here. It reminds me of home.' She looks up at me again, and I'm caught in her all-consuming gaze.

Home.

I could make this her home . . .

My mouth dries.

Mate! You are getting way ahead of yourself!

I look away, breaking the spell of Alessia's stare. I'm troubled by where my thoughts are heading and take a sip of wine. My reaction is all too new and too presumptuous.

'How is Michal? And Logan?' she asks, hungry for news, and she's soon lost in a lively conversation about packing and Canada – and weddings.

Alessia laughs again, and her voice changes, becoming softer . . . sweeter. She's talking to Michal, and I know from her tone that she's exceptionally fond of him. I shouldn't be jealous – he's a kid – but maybe I am? I'm not sure I appreciate this new and unwelcome feeling.

'Be good, Michal . . . I miss you . . . Bye.'

She glances at me once more. 'Okay. I will . . . Goodbye, Magda.' She hangs up and wanders back to me to hand me my phone. She looks happy. I'm glad she made the call.

'All good?' I ask.

'Yes. Thank you.'

'And with Magda?'

'She is packing. She's happy and sad to be leaving England. And she is relieved to have the security man near.'

'Great. She must be excited to start a new life.'

'She is. Her fiancé is a good man.'

'What does he do?'

'Something to do with computers.'

'I should get you a phone, and then you can speak to her when you want.'

She looks appalled. 'No. No. That is too much. You cannot do that.'

I raise a brow, knowing full well that I can.

She arches a brow in return, displeased, but I'm saved by the ping of the oven timer.

'Dinner is cooked.'

Alessia places the casserole dish on the table beside the salad she's made. She's pleased that the yogurt crust has risen into a crisp, golden brown dome. Maxim is impressed. 'It looks good,' he says, and Alessia suspects he's being over-effusive.

She serves him a portion and sits down. 'It is lamb, rice and yogurt with a few secret . . . um . . . ingredients. We say *tavë kosi*.'

'We don't bake our yogurt here. We put it on our muesli.'

She laughs.

He takes a bite and closes his eyes as he savours the food. 'Mmm.' He opens his eyes and nods enthusiastically. He swallows. 'This is delicious. You weren't lying when you said you could cook!'

Alessia blushes under his warm gaze.

'You can cook for me anytime.'

'I would like that,' she murmurs. She would like that very much.

We talk and drink and eat. I ply her with wine and questions. Many questions. About her childhood. School. Friends. Family. Reading about Albania has inspired me. Sitting across from Alessia is inspiring, too; she's so full of life. Her eyes are shining and expressive as she talks. And she's animated, using her hands to demonstrate a point.

She's captivating.

Occasionally she will tuck that stray strand of hair away, her fingers skimming around the shell of her ear.

I'd like her fingers on me.

I anticipate unravelling her plait later and running my fingers through her soft, luscious hair. It's heartwarming to see her so carefree and talkative for a change. From the sweet flush on her cheeks, I suspect it might be the wine. I take a sip of the tasty Italian Barolo that's working its magic.

Replete, I push my plate away and refill her glass. 'Tell me about a typical day in Albania.'

'For me?'

'Yes.'

'There is not much to tell. If I am working, my father will drive me to the school. And when I am home, I help my mother. Washing. Cleaning. Like I do for you.' Espresso eyes peek up, unmasking me with her knowing look. It's sexy as hell. 'And that is all I do,' she adds.

'Sounds rather dull.' Too dull for bright Alessia. And I suspect a little lonely.

'It is.' She laughs.

'From what I've read, northern Albania is quite conservative.'

'Conservative.' She frowns and takes a quick sip of her wine. 'Do you mean traditional?'

'Yes.'

'Where I am from, we are traditional.' She stands to clear the crockery from the table. 'But Albania is changing. In Tiranë—'

'Tirana?'

'Yes. It's a modern city. It is not so traditional or conservative there.' She puts the plates in the sink.

'Have you been?'

'No.'

'Would you like to go?'

She takes her seat once more and tilts her head to the side, brushing her index finger across her lips. Her look is wistful for a brief moment. 'Yes. One day.'

'Have you travelled at all?'

'No. Only in books.' Her smile brightens the room. 'I have travelled all over the world in books. And I've been to America watching TV.'

'American TV?'

'Yes. Netflix. HBO.'

'In Albania?'

She grins at my surprise. 'Yes. We have television!'

'So, back home, what did you do for kicks?' I ask.

'Kicks?'

'Fun. You know. Fun.'

She looks a little puzzled. 'I read. Watch TV. Practise my

music. Sometimes I listen to the radio with my mother. The BBC World Service.'

'Do you go out?'

'No.'

'Never?'

'Sometimes. In the summer we will walk in the town in the evening. But it is with my family. And sometimes I play the piano.'

'A recital? For the public?'

'Yes. At the school and weddings.'

'Your parents must be proud.'

A shadow crosses her face. 'Yes. They were. Are,' she corrects herself, and her voice falters and dips, becoming soft and sad. 'My father, he likes the attention.' Her demeanour changes, and she seems to fold in on herself.

Shit. 'You must miss them.'

'My mother. I miss my mother,' she answers quietly, and takes another sip of wine.

Not her dad? I don't push her on that. Her mood has shifted. I should change the subject, but if she misses her mother so much, perhaps she wants to return. I remember what she told me:

We thought we were coming here to work. For a better life. Life in Kukës is hard for some women. We were betrayed—

Maybe that's what she wants. To go home. And though I dread what her answer might be, I ask her anyway. 'Would you like to go back?'

'Back?'

'Home.'

Her eyes widen with fear. 'No. I cannot. I cannot.' Her tone is a hushed, rushed whisper, and the fine hairs on my neck stand on end.

'Why?'

She remains mute, but I want to know. I press her. 'Is it because you don't have a passport?'

'No.'

'Then why? Was it that bad?'

She screws her eyes shut and bows her head as if ashamed. 'No,' she whispers. 'It's because . . . it's because I am betrothed.'

Chapter Eighteen

My chest constricts as if I've been kicked in the solar plexus.

Betrothed?

What medieval claptrap is this?

She looks up at me. Her eyes wide, exposing her distress. Adrenaline pumps through my body; I'm ready for a fight. 'Betrothed?' I whisper, knowing full well what it means.

She's fucking promised to another.

She bows her head again. 'Yes.' Her voice is barely audible.

I have a rival. *Shit.*

'And you were going to tell me this . . . when?'

Her eyes are scrunched shut as if she's in pain.

'Alessia, look at me.'

She lifts her hand to her mouth – to suppress a sob? I don't know. She swallows, then raises her eyes to meet mine. Her expression is raw, her despair palpable. My anger dissolves in a second, leaving me in turmoil.

'I am telling you now,' she says.

She's unavailable.

The pain is instant. Visceral. Shocking. I'm in free fall.

What the hell?

My world has shifted. My ideas. My vague plans. Being with her . . . marrying her . . .

I can't.

'Do you love him?'

She draws back and gapes at me in shock. 'No!' It's a breathless, passionate denial. 'I do not want to marry him. That is why I left Albania.'

'To get away from him?'

'Yes. I was to be married in January. After my birthday.'

It was her birthday?

I stare blankly at her. And suddenly the walls are closing in on me. I need space. Like when I first met her. I'm suffocating in a whirlwind of doubt and confusion. I need to think. I stand, and in one deliberate move, raise my hand to sweep my hair aside and gather my thoughts. Alessia recoils beside me. She cowers and clasps her head in her hands as if she's waiting—

What?

'Fuck. Alessia! Did you think I was going to hit you?' I exclaim, and step back, horrified by her reaction. Another piece of the puzzle that is Alessia Demachi falls into place. No wonder she always stood out of my reach. And I'm ready to kill the motherfucker. 'Did he hit you? Did he?'

She looks down at her lap. Ashamed, I think.

Or maybe she has some misplaced loyalty to the fucking arsehole from Buttfuck, Nowhere, who has a spurious claim on my girl.

Fucking hell.

I clench my fists, my rage murderous. She's so still. Head bowed. Folding in on herself.

Calm down, mate. Calm yourself.

I take a deep cleansing breath, my hands on my hips. 'I'm sorry.'

Her head whips up. Her look direct and earnest. 'You have done nothing wrong.'

Even now she's trying to pour oil on my troubled waters.

The few steps between us are too great a distance. She watches me warily as I approach, and cautiously I crouch down beside her. 'I'm sorry. I didn't mean to frighten you. I'm just shocked that somewhere out there you have a . . . suitor, and I have a rival for your affections.'

She blinks rapidly, and her face softens as a rosy tinge marks her cheeks.

'You have no rivals,' she whispers.

My breath catches, and warmth spreads in my chest, chasing the last of the adrenaline away. These are the sweetest words that she has said to me.

There's hope.

'This man, he's not your choice?'

'No. He is my father's choice.'

I reach for her hand and bring it to my lips, planting one soft kiss on her knuckles.

'I cannot go back,' she whispers. 'I have dishonoured my father. And if I return, I will be forced into marriage.'

'Your . . . betrothed. Do you know him?'

'Yes.'

'You don't love him?'

'No.' Her vehement, monosyllabic response tells me all I need to know. Perhaps he's old. Or unattractive. Or both.

Or he hits her.

Fuck.

Standing, I pull her into my arms, and she comes willingly, putting her hands on my chest. I fold her against my body and hold her. And I don't know if I'm comforting her or myself. The thought of her with someone else, someone who mistreats her, is horrifying. I bury my face in her fragrant hair, grateful that she's here. With me. 'I'm sorry that you've had to put up with so much shit,' I murmur.

Looking up at me, she brushes her index finger over my lips. 'That is a bad word.'

'It is. It's a bad word for a bad situation. But you're safe now. I've got you.' Leaning down, I brush my lips against hers and it's like a spark to dry kindling, my body comes alive. It takes my breath away. She closes her eyes and tilts her head back, offering her mouth to me. I cannot resist. In the background, RY X is still singing in his husky, melancholy falsetto about only falling in love. It's soulful. And rousing. And relevant.

'Dance with me.' My voice is hoarse. Alessia gasps as I tighten my hold on her and start to sway with her in my arms. She splays her hands on my chest and glides them over my shirt, feeling me. Touching me. Reassuring me. And curling her fingers around my upper arms as she moves with me.

Slowly.

We shuffle from side to side to the unhurried and seductive rhythm of the ethereal song. Her hands slide up my arms and over my shoulders and into my hair. She nuzzles my chest.

'I have never danced like this,' she murmurs.

My hand skims down her body to the base of her spine, holding her to me. 'I've never danced with you.'

With my other hand, I gently tug on her plait, lifting her lips to mine. I kiss her. Long. Slow. Tasting her. Rediscovering her sweet mouth with my tongue while we sway together. I unfasten the elastic tethering her hair and slide it off. I groan as she shakes her head, and her hair falls wild and free down her back. Cradling her face, I kiss her again. I want more. So much more. I need to reclaim her. She's with me. Not with some violent bastard from a godforsaken town a world away.

'Come to bed,' I whisper, my voice low.

'I have to wash the dishes.'

What?

'Fuck the dishes, baby.'

Her brow furrows. 'But—'

'No, you don't. Leave them.'

And the thought pops into my head. *If I married her – she'd never have to do another dish again.*

'Make love with me, Alessia.'

She sucks in a breath, and an inviting, shy smile curls her lips.

We flow together. My hands cocoon her head as I move, slowly savouring every delectable inch of her. She is soft and strong and beautiful beneath me. I kiss her, pouring my heart and soul into her mouth. It's never felt like this. Each stroke is bringing me closer to her. Her legs hold me in place, and her hands run over my back. Her nails etching her passion on my skin. I lean up and study her dazed face. Her eyes are wide and her pupils the darkest, most carnal espresso. I want to see her. All of her. I stop and press my forehead against hers.

'I need to see you.' I ease out of her and roll us over so that she's on top of me. She's breathless and unsure. With my arm under her behind, I slide her up my body so her legs are on either side of my hips. And I sit up so she's astride me, her arms on my shoulders. I clasp her face and kiss her. Moving my hand down to caress her breast, I deliberately tease her nipple between my thumb and finger as my lips skim from her mouth along her jaw to her throat. She tips her head back and lets out a husky moan of pure pleasure. My erection throbs in response.

Yes.

'Let's try this,' I murmur against the fragrant skin of her shoulder. I wrap my arm around her waist and lift her, my eyes on hers as I lower her slowly onto me.

Fuck.

She's tight. And wet. And exquisite.

Her mouth drops open as she gasps, her eyes large with want. 'Ah,' she breathes, and my lips seize hers, my fingers in her hair as I claim her mouth again.

She's panting and gripping my shoulders when I pull back.

'Okay?' I ask.

She gives me a frantic shake of her head. 'Yes,' she breathes, and it takes me a moment to realise she's reverted to the Albanian form of yes. I take her hands and lean back until I'm lying on the bed, staring at the woman astride me. The woman I love.

Her hair spills down over her shoulders and breasts in a riotous, sensual tumble. She leans forward and spreads her hands on my chest.

Yes. Touch me.

She sweeps her fingers and palms over my skin. Feeling me. Through my chest hair and over my nipples, which pucker in delight.

'Ah,' I breathe.

She bites her lower lip, stifling her wanton, victorious smile.

'That's right, beautiful, I love your touch.'

I love you.

She leans down and kisses me. 'I like touching you,' she says softly. Shyly. And my cock strains for more.

'Take me,' I murmur.

She pauses, not understanding, and I lift my hips to give her a clue. Alessia cries out, and it's a loud, guttural sound of pleasure that almost pushes me over the edge. She splays her hands on my chest, trying to keep her balance. I grasp her hips. 'Move. Like this,' I hiss through my teeth. I ease her up and back down. And she gasps, but, placing her hands on my arms, she rises up and back down.

'That's it.' I close my eyes and enjoy the sensual feel of her.

'Ah,' she calls out.

Shit.

Make this last.

She moves. Slowly and hesitantly at first. But as her confidence builds, she finds her rhythm. I open my eyes as she rises once more, and this time I flex my hips, meeting her. Her cry is visceral and wakes every sense in my body.

Fuck. I grab her hips, moving her faster and faster. She's panting. Short, sharp gasps for air. Gripping my arms. Her head lolling from side to side with each thrust of mine.

Head tipped back. Calling to the gods, she's every inch a goddess. Her hold on my arms tightens, and she cries out and stills on top of me as she comes.

It's enough to trigger my release, and I cry out, holding her to me as I come and come and come.

Alessia lies in the afterglow of their lovemaking. Maxim has his head on her stomach, his arms around her, as she runs her fingers idly through his hair. She loves the feel of his hair beneath her fingers. Her mother never gave any indication that the sexual act could be so pleasurable. Perhaps this is not the relationship she has with Baba. Alessia frowns. She doesn't want to think about her parents having sex, but her mind wanders, and she remembers her grandmother, Virginia. Now, *she* married for love. They were happy. Even when they were older, her grandparents would exchange looks that made Alessia blush. Her nana's was a marriage that she hoped to emulate. Not her parents' marriage. They were never demonstrative with each other.

Maxim never hesitates to hold her hand or kiss her in public. And he talks to her. When has she ever sat for an evening and had a proper conversation with a man? Where she comes from, if a man talks to a woman for any length of time, it is considered by some to be a sign of weakness.

She glances at the little light-up dragon on the nightstand, a beacon in the darkness. He bought this for her because he knows she's scared of the dark. He brought her here to protect her. He cooked for her. He bought her clothes. He made love to her . . .

Tears prick the corners of her eyes, and her heart overflows with uncertainty and longing, burning her throat with unspoken emotion. She loves him. Her fingers tighten in his hair as she's overwhelmed by her feelings for him. He wasn't angry with her when she told him she was betrothed. If anything, he was anxious that her heart might belong to another.

No. My heart is yours, Maxim.

And he was shocked that she thought he might beat her. Her hand goes automatically and instinctively to her cheek; her father is less of a talker, more of a man of action . . .

She runs her fingers over Maxim's shoulder and traces the outline of his tattoo. She wants to know him better. Perhaps she should ask him more questions. He is evasive about his job. Maybe he has many? She shakes her head. It is not her place to question him. What would her mother say if she did? For now she will enjoy the little bubble that they share together in Cornwall.

Maxim nuzzles her belly and kisses it, distracting Alessia from her unsettling thoughts of home. He looks up at her, his eyes a vibrant emerald in the soft glow from the little dragon. 'Stay with me,' he says.

She smooths his hair off his forehead and frowns. 'I am staying with you.'

'Good,' he says, and he kisses her belly again, but his time his mouth moves lower . . . and lower.

I open my eyes as early-morning light seeps through the gaps in the blinds. I'm wrapped around Alessia. My head on her chest, my arm around her waist. The warmth and sweet smell of her skin invades my senses, and my body rises to greet her. Gently I nuzzle her neck, leaving drowsy kisses at her throat.

She rouses, her eyelids fluttering open.

'Good morning, princess,' I whisper.

She smiles, a sleepy, sated look on her face. 'Good morning . . . Maxim.' Her tone is tender, and I think I hear her love in the way she says my name. Or maybe I'm imagining it because I want to hear it.

There. I want her love.

All of it.

I'm prepared to admit it to myself.

But can I admit it to her?

The whole day extends before us, open and free – and I'm with her. 'Let's spend the day in bed.' My voice is husky with sleep.

Her fingers skim my chin. 'Are you tired?'

I grin. 'No . . .'

'Oh,' she says, and her smile mirrors mine.

His tongue. His mouth. What he does to her. Alessia is lost in a storm of sensation. Her hands tighten around his wrists as she hangs on a precipice. She's close. So close. He teases her again and again with his able tongue and gradually eases a finger inside her, and she falls, her orgasm ripping through her as she cries out.

Maxim kisses her belly, her breasts, as he inches up her body and stills above her.

'That is a fantastic sound,' he whispers, and he rolls on a condom and oh, so slowly sinks into her.

When I return from the bathroom, her side of the bed is empty.

Oh.

The disappointment is real. I'm ready for more. I don't ever think I'll have enough of Alessia.

Judging by the grey light seeping into the room, it must be mid-morning. And it's raining. I raise the blinds, and then I hear her, so I scramble back into bed. Crockery rattling, she enters the bedroom. She's wearing my pyjama top and carrying breakfast on a tray. 'Good morning again,' she says with a radiant smile, her hair flowing down over her shoulders.

'Well, hello, coffee!' The aroma is mouth-watering. I love proper coffee. I sit up, and she places the tray on my lap. Eggs. Coffee. Toast. 'This is a treat.'

'You said you wanted to stay in bed.' She climbs in beside me and steals a piece of buttered toast.

'Here.' I scoop up some scrambled eggs on a fork and offer it to her. She opens her mouth, and I feed her.

'Mmm . . .' she says, and closes her eyes in appreciation.

My dick rouses at the sight.

Steady. Let's eat first.

The eggs are amazing. She's added feta cheese, I think.

'This is heaven on a plate, Alessia!'

Her cheeks pink, and she takes a sip of coffee.

'I wanted to play some music.'

'On the piano?'

'No – I mean, to listen.'

'Oh. You need a phone. Here.' I reach over and grab my iPhone.

I really must get her a phone.

'This is the code.' I punch in my security code to unlock it. 'And I use this app. Sonos. You can have music anywhere in the house.' I hand it to her.

She starts flicking through the app. 'You have so much music.'

'I like music.'

She shoots me a quick smile. 'Me, too.'

I take a sip of coffee.

Ugh!

'How much sugar did you put in this?' I splutter.

'Oh, I'm sorry. I forget you don't have the sugar.' And she screws up her face, and I think it's because she cannot contemplate coffee without sugar.

'Is this how you drink it?'

'In Albania? Yes.'

'I'm amazed you have any teeth left.'

She grins, showing me she has perfect teeth. 'I have never tried coffee without sugar. I will make you some more.' She hops out of bed, all long naked legs and flowing raven hair.

'It's okay. Don't go.'

'I want to.' And she disappears once more, taking my phone with her. A few moments later, I hear Dua Lipa singing 'One Kiss' over the sound system downstairs. Alessia doesn't just like classical music. I smile . . . I think the artist might be Albanian, too.

Alessia dances around the kitchen, preparing another coffee for Maxim. She cannot remember a time when she felt this content. She came close at times when she was dancing and singing with her mother in the kitchen in Kukës. But here there is more room to dance, and with the lights on she can see her image reflected in the glass wall that leads to the balcony. She grins; she looks so happy. It's such a contrast to when she arrived in Cornwall.

Outside, it's a cold and wet morning. She shimmies over to the window and stares out at the scene. The sky and sea are a dismal grey, and the wind is battering and sculpting the silvery trees that line the path to the beach, but it's still a sight she finds magical. The surf is crashing on the shore, white-whipped and foamy, yet she can only hear the faint roar of the waves and cannot feel a draught through the glass doors. She's impressed. The house is well built, and she's grateful that she's here, warm and cosy with Maxim.

The espresso machine burbles, and she sashays back across the room to make his coffee.

Maxim is still in bed, but he's finished his breakfast and placed the tray on the floor. 'There you are. I missed you,' he says when Alessia returns with fresh, unsweetened coffee. She hands him the cup, and he drains the entire contents as she gets back into bed.

'That's better,' he says.

'You like it?'

'Very much.' He puts the coffee cup aside. 'But I like you more.' He hooks his index finger over the first button of the oversized pj top that she's wearing and tugs. The button opens, revealing the soft swell of her breast, and with his eyes burning into hers he runs his finger gently over her skin and across her nipple. Her breath catches as her nipple peaks and hardens beneath his touch.

Her lips part in a silent gasp, and her gaze is intense and inviting. My dick stirs.

'Again?' I whisper.

Will I ever have my fill of this woman?

Alessia's coy smile is encouragement enough. Leaning forward, I press my lips against hers and undo the rest of her buttons, and slip the pyjama shirt off her shoulders. 'You're so beautiful.' My words are an invocation.

Her eyes on mine, she raises her hand hesitantly, and her finger traces the line of my jaw, brushing my stubble. Through her parted lips, I watch as she runs her tongue across the underside of her top teeth. 'Hmm . . .' Her voice rumbles in her throat.

'You like it, or do you want me to shave?' I whisper.

She shakes her head. 'I like this.' Her fingertips stroke my chin.

'You do?'

She nods and, leaning in, plants a soft kiss at the corner of my mouth and runs her tongue over my stubble, following the line her finger took earlier. I feel it in my groin.

'Oh, Alessia.' I grasp her face and lower us both onto the bed, kissing her as we recline. My lips are on hers, my tongue is on hers, and she's as greedy as ever, taking all I have to give. My hand travels down her body, over her breast, her waist, and her hip, and I cup her backside and squeeze. My lips follow, worshipping her breasts in turn until she's squirming beneath me. And when I gaze at her to catch my breath, she's panting.

'I want to try something new,' I murmur.

Her mouth forms the letter O.

'Okay?' I ask.

'Yes . . .' she says, but her wide-eyed look tells me she's uncertain.

'Don't worry. I think you'll like it. But if you don't, just tell me to stop.'

She caresses my face. 'Okay,' she whispers.

I kiss her once more. 'Turn over.'

She looks puzzled.

'Onto your front.'

'Oh.' She giggles and does as she's told. I prop myself up on my elbow and sweep her hair aside and off her back. She has a beautiful back and an even lovelier backside. I glide my hand down the curve of her spine to her behind, enjoying the soft, smooth planes of her skin. Leaning over her, I kiss the little mole at the base of her neck.

'You're so lovely,' I murmur in her ear, and plant soft kisses from there down her neck and along her shoulder as my hand continues to descend and move between her buttocks. She wiggles her arse beneath my palm as I slip my hand further between her legs and begin to circle her clitoris with my fingers. Her head is lying on the bed, her cheek to the sheet so I can easily observe her. Alessia's eyes are closed, her mouth open as she inhales, absorbing the pleasure elicited by my fingers.

'That's right,' I whisper, and slip my thumb into her. She whimpers. She's wet and warm and wonderful. She pushes her behind against my hand, and I circle my thumb inside her. She gasps, and it's a call to my bursting dick. I keep up the rhythm. Round and round. She tightens her hold on the sheets and screws up her eyes as she moans. She's close. So close. And I withdraw my thumb and reach for a condom.

She blinks up at me. Wanting. Ready.

'Don't move,' I murmur, and shift between her legs, parting them with my knee. I pull her up onto my lap so she's sitting astride me facing the wall. My dick snuggles in the line between her buttocks.

One day . . .

'We're going to do this from behind,' I murmur.

Her head whips around to me, her eyebrows raised in alarm.

I laugh. 'No. Not like that. Like this.' Lifting her, I ease her slowly down on my erection. Her fingernails dig into my thighs, and her head drops back on my shoulder while I graze her earlobe with my teeth. She's panting, but she tenses her legs and haltingly rises up and down again.

Fuck. Yes.

'That's right,' I whisper, and I shift my hands to her breasts, cupping them both and teasing each nipple between my thumb and forefinger.

'Ah!' she cries, and it's a primeval, sexy sound.

Fuck.

'You okay?'

'Yes!'

Slowly I lift her up and over, and she places her hands on the bed. I ease back and then forward into her. She cries out and, bending down, places her head and shoulders on the bed.

She looks amazing. Her hair sprawled across the sheets, her eyes tight shut, her mouth open, and her arse in the air. The mere sight of her makes me want to come.

She also feels amazing.

Every. Single. Fucking. Inch of her.

I grasp her hips and move into and out of her again.

'Yeah . . .' she groans, and I start to move. Harder. Really move. Harder still.

This is heaven.

She cries out. And I stop.

'No!' Her voice is hoarse. 'Please. Don't stop.'

Oh, baby!

And I'm unleashed. I take her. Over and over, sweat beading on my brow and trickling down my body, as I hold back my release until, finally, she cries out and climaxes around me again and again and again. I thrust once more and join her, loving her, filling her, and collapsing on top of her while calling out her name.

Alessia lies on her front, breathless, spiralling down from her climax, as he lies on top of her. His weight is . . . agreeable. She never knew her body had such capacity for pleasure. She's sweaty and languid and satisfied, wrung out from her incredible orgasm.

But as she recovers her composure, truth be told, she feels a little guilty at this indolence. She has never spent the whole morning in bed.

He nuzzles her ear.

'You're incredible,' he whispers as he moves to her side and gathers her in his arms.

She closes her eyes. 'No, you are,' she says. 'I never knew . . . I mean . . .' She stops and looks up at him.

'That it could be so intense?'

'Yes.'

His brow crinkles. 'Yes. I know what you mean.' He gazes through the window at the grey, rain-soaked vista. 'Do you want to go out?'

She snuggles closer, filling her senses with him. The smell of his skin. His warmth. 'No. I like being here with you.'

'I like it, too.' He kisses the top of her head and closes his eyes.

I wake alone from my doze only to hear the strains of Rachmaninov – my favourite of his concertos – coming from downstairs. It sounds odd . . . and then I realise, it's just the piano. Of course there's no orchestra.

Oh, this I have to see.

I jump out of bed and drag on my jeans, but I can't find my sweater, so I grab the throw from the end of the bed, wrap it around my shoulders, and head downstairs.

Alessia is playing the piano wearing nothing but my cream sweater. She's found some earbuds and is listening to my iPhone with her eyes closed, and she's playing. Without the sheet music. Without an orchestra. Is she listening to the concerto?

She must be.

Her fingers fly over the keys, and the music surges through the room with so much feeling and finesse it leaves me breathless. She leaves me breathless. I can almost hear the orchestra in my imagination.

How does she do this?

She truly is a prodigy.

I watch her. Transfixed as the music soars.

It's . . . emotional.

She reaches the crescendo at the end of the movement, her head bobbing in time to the music, her hair rippling down her back . . . and she stops. She sits for a moment. Her hands in her lap as the notes fade into the ether. I feel I'm intruding, watching her like she's an exotic species in her own unique habitat. But I can't help it, I break the spell and raise my hands and applaud.

She opens her eyes, surprised, I think, to see me there.

'That was sensational.'

She takes the earbuds out of her ears and gives me a shy smile. 'I'm sorry. I didn't mean to wake you.'

'You didn't.'

'I've only played this a few times. I was learning it before I left . . .' She stops.

'Well, you play it very well. I could hear the orchestra.'

'From the phone?'

'No. In my imagination. You were that good. Were you listening to the piece?'

She flushes. 'Thank you. Yes. I was.'

'You should be on the stage. I would pay to see you.'

She grins.

'What colours did you see?' I ask.

'In the music?'

I nod.

'Oh . . . this is a rainbow,' she says with such raw enthusiasm. 'So many different colours.' She opens up her arms to try to convey the complexity of what she sees . . . but it's something I'll never know.

'It's . . . it's . . .'

'Like a kaleidoscope?'

'Yes. Yes.' She nods vigorously with a huge smile, and I realise that the word must be the same in Albanian.

'As it should be. I love this piece.'

I love you.

I step towards her and kiss her on the lips. 'I am in awe of your talent, Miss Demachi.'

She stands and places her arms around my neck. I wrap us both in the throw that I'm wearing.

'I am in awe of yours, Mister Maxim,' she says, and she laces her fingers around my neck and pulls my lips towards hers.

What? Again!

She moves up and down. More graceful this time. Tall and proud. She looks amazing as her breasts bounce with her. Her eyes are intent on me. She's embracing her power, and it's so fucking sexy. Her tempo is perfect, and she takes me higher and higher. She leans down and threads her fingers through mine, squeezing them, then kisses me. An open-mouthed, wet and warm, demanding kiss.

'Oh, beautiful,' I moan . . . I'm close.

And she leans up and tilts her head back and cries out my name as she comes.

Fuck! I'm lost. And I let go and join her.

When I open my eyes, she's gazing down at me in wonder.

Alessia is sprawled on Maxim's chest, and they're lying on the floor of the living room, by the piano. Her heart is slowing and her breathing subsiding, but she shivers. She's a little cold.

'Here.' Maxim drapes the throw over her. 'You are going to wear me out.' He flinches as he pulls the condom off but smiles up at her.

'I like wearing you out. And I like looking down at you,' she whispers.

'I like looking up at you.'

Watching him come when she's on top of him gives her a sense of power. A power she never thought she'd have – it's heady. Now if she could just pluck up the courage to touch all of him . . .

His glowing green eyes burn into hers. 'You really are something, Alessia,' he says, and he smooths her hair from her face. For a moment she thinks he's going to say something else. But he smiles up at her, a glorious smile. Then he adds, 'I'm hungry.'

She gasps. 'I must feed you.'

She tries to move, but he holds her in place. 'Don't go. You're keeping me warm. I should light a fire.' He kisses her jaw, and she snuggles into him, feeling a peace she didn't know was possible.

'We should go out to eat,' Maxim says. 'It must be after four o'clock.' The rain is still hammering down outside.

'I want to cook for you.'

'You do?'

'Yes. I like cooking,' Alessia replies. 'Especially for you.'

'Okay.'

Alessia winces as she sits up on me.

'What is it?' I ask, and I sit up in one swift move so we're nose to nose. The throw falls to her waist, and I pull it up to keep her warm.

She blushes. 'I am a little sore.'

Fuck! 'Why didn't you tell me?'

'Because you probably wouldn't have done that . . .' she says, averting her eyes and her voice low.

'Damned right!' I close my eyes and place my forehead on hers. 'I'm sorry,' I whisper.

I'm an idiot.

She places her fingers on my lips. 'No. No. Don't be sorry.'

'We don't have to do this.'

What am I saying?

'I want to do this. I mean it. I really like it,' she insists.

'Alessia, you have to talk to me. Tell me. Frankly, I could do this all day with you. But enough. We're going out. First, though, let's have a shower and get cleaned up.' I lift her off me, stand up, collect our clothes from the floor, and together we head back upstairs.

I turn on the water in the shower as Alessia watches me, huddled in the throw, her eyes dark and mysterious. The afternoon sun is beginning to fade. I switch on the lights and test the water. It's toasty.

'Ready?' I ask her.

She nods and lets the throw fall to her feet, and she dashes past me into the piping-hot stream of water. I join her, and we both stand under the cascading shower as it warms us. I grab the shower gel, pleased that she's becoming more comfortable about revealing her gorgeous body.

That's what happens when you spend the day fucking . . .

I grin and begin to lather some soap in my hands.

She has never showered with anyone. She can feel him move about behind her, his body brushing against her . . . *that* part of his body brushing against her as she stands beneath the shower. The part she hasn't dared touch yet. She wants to – she just needs to find the self-confidence.

The water is deliciously hot. She closes her eyes and enjoys the soothing feel of it bouncing off her skin, making it a little pink.

He moves her hair from her back and places a wet kiss on her shoulder.

'You're so beautiful,' he says.

She feels his hands at her neck, and with circular strokes he starts to massage the soap into her skin. His strong fingers knead her muscles.

'Ah,' she groans.

'You like?'

'Yes, muchly.'

'Muchly?'

'My English?'

Alessia senses Maxim's grin.

'Is much better than my Albanian.'

She giggles. 'This is true. It is funny – I say the wrong word, and it sounds right to me, but when you say it, it does sound wrong.'

'It must be my accent. Do you want me to wash you all over?' His voice is husky.

'All over?' Alessia's breath hitches.

'Mmm-hmm,' Maxim confirms, the sound a low, sexy rumble near her ear. He puts his arms around her and soaps his hands and begins to knead the soap into her skin. He washes her neck, her breasts, her belly, and gently between her thighs. Her head rolls back on his chest as she surrenders to his touch, feeling his excitement against the top of her backside. She moans, and his breathing deepens, becoming harsher in her ear.

Suddenly he stops. 'There, you're done. And I think we should get out.'

'What?' She feels bereft without his hands on her.

'Enough.' He opens the shower door and exits the shower.

'But,' she protests.

He grabs a towel and puts it around his waist, covering his erection. 'I only have so much willpower, and, amazingly, my body is ready for action again.'

She pouts, and he laughs. 'Don't tempt me.' He holds up the

blue robe and waits for her. She shuts off the water and steps out of the shower, where he wraps her in the robe and holds her. 'You are irresistible. But as much as I want you . . . enough. And I'm hungry.' He kisses the top of her head and releases her. She watches him leave the bathroom, feeling her heart swell with her love for him.

Should I tell him?

But as she follows him into the bedroom, her courage fails her. She likes how they are at the moment. She has no idea how he'll react, and she doesn't want to burst their bubble.

'I will get dressed and cook for you.'

He cocks an eyebrow. 'You don't have to get dressed.'

She feels her cheeks pink. *He has no shame.* But he beams, his smile so dazzling that it takes her breath away.

It's almost midnight, and I lie gazing at Alessia, who is fast asleep beside me.

What a wonderful, lazy, falling-in-love Monday.

It's been a perfect day.

Making love. Eating. Making love. Drinking. Making love. And listening to Alessia play the piano . . . and watching her cook.

She shifts and mumbles something in her sleep. Her skin is translucent in the light from the little dragon, her breathing soft and even. She must be exhausted after all we've done . . . yet she's still a little shy. One of these days, I want her to touch me. Everywhere.

I stiffen at the thought.

Enough!

She will. In her own time, I'm sure. We didn't even leave the house today. All day. And she cooked for me once more, another delicious and wholesome meal. Tomorrow I'd like to do something special with her – something outdoors, provided the weather improves.

Show her where you grew up.

No. Not yet. I shake my head.

Tell her.

An idea comes to mind, and if the weather is better tomorrow, it will be fun, and it may give me the opportunity to tell her who I am . . . We'll see.

I plant a tender kiss on her temple, inhaling her sweet fragrance. She stirs and mumbles something unintelligible, but she settles and sleeps on.

I've fallen in love with you, Alessia.

I close my eyes.

Chapter Nineteen

Alessia wakes listening to the low rumble of Maxim's voice. She opens her eyes to see him sitting up next to her, on the phone. He smiles down at her and continues his conversation. 'I'm glad Miss Chenoweth agreed,' he says. 'I think a twenty-bore for the lady. I'll have the Purdeys.'

She wonders what he's talking about. Whatever it is, his eyes shine with excitement.

'Let's use the easy birds. The teals.' Maxim winks at her. 'About ten? Great. I'll see Jenkins then. Thanks, Michael.' He ends the call and snuggles back down into bed, his head on the pillow facing her. 'Good morning, Alessia.' He leans across and gives her a swift kiss. 'Sleep well?'

'Yes. Thank you.'

'You look lovely. Hungry?'

She stretches out beside him, and his eyes darken. 'Hmm . . .' she says.

'You look very tempting.'

She smiles.

'But you said you were sore.' He kisses her on her nose. 'And I have a surprise for you today. After breakfast we're going out. Dress warm. And you might want to plait your hair.'

He climbs out of bed.

Alessia pouts. She was sore yesterday. She feels fine this morning, but before she can cajole him into a little more time in bed, he waltzes naked into the bathroom. All she can do is admire his fine physique, the muscles in his back rippling as he walks, his long legs . . . his backside. He turns and gives her a wicked smile, then closes the door.

She grins.

What does he have planned?

'Where are we going?' Alessia asks. She's wearing her green hat, her new coat, and I know she's wearing layers beneath. I think she'll be warm enough.

'It's a surprise.' I give her a sideways look, then ease the car into gear.

Before she woke this morning, I called the Hall and spoke to Michael, the estate manager. It's a crisp, bright day, perfect for what I've arranged. After all our rigorous activity yesterday, we need a break and some fresh air.

Rosperran Farm has been part of the Trevethick estate since Georgian times. The Chenoweth family have been tenant farmers there for more than a hundred years. The present incumbent, Abigail Chenoweth, has given us permission to set up in one of the fallow southerly fields. As we get nearer, I wish I were in the Discovery. My Jag isn't good with fields, but we can park on the road. When we pull up, the gate is already open, and inside I spy Jenkins and his Land Rover Defender. He gives me a cheery wave.

I flash an enthusiastic grin at Alessia. 'We're going to shoot clays.'

Alessia looks bemused. 'Clays?'

'Clay pigeons?'

She appears to be none the wiser.

I'm now less certain that this is a good idea. 'It'll be fun.'

She gives me a worried smile, and I get out of the car. It's a cold day, but not so cold that I can see the condensation of my breath.

'Good morning, my lord,' Jenkins says.

'Hi.' I check to see if Alessia has overheard, but she's climbing out on her side of the car. '"Sir" will do, Jenkins,' I mutter as she approaches us. 'This is Alessia Demachi.' She takes his outstretched hand.

'Good morning, miss.'

'Good morning.' She gives him a charming smile, and Jenkins flushes. His family has served the Trevelyans for three generations, though mainly at Angwin, our Oxfordshire estate. Jenkins flew the family coop four years ago and has been working at Tresyllian Hall as an assistant gamekeeper. He's a little younger than me and a keen surfer. I've seen him on a board – he put Kit and me to shame. He's also an excellent shot and an expert gamekeeper. He runs many of the shoots on the estate. Beneath his flat cap and shock of sun-bleached hair, he has a good brain and a cheerful, easy smile.

Alessia looks up at me with a puzzled expression. 'We are hunting birds?'

'No. We're shooting clays.'

She looks nonplussed.

'They're discs made of clay.'

'Oh.'

'I've brought a couple of shotgun choices for the lady. I have your Purdeys, and Ms Campbell insisted I bring your shooting jacket, sir.'

'Great.'

'And coffee. And sausage rolls. And hand warmers.' Jenkins smiles.

Trust Danny.

'The traps are set. Teals,' he says.

'Excellent.' I turn to Alessia. 'Good surprise?' I ask her, feeling doubtful.

'Yes,' she says, but she doesn't sound certain.

'Have you shot a gun before?'

She shakes her head. 'My father has guns.'

'He does?'

'He hunts.'

'Hunts?'

She shrugs. 'Well, he will go out with his gun. He will go out overnight. To shoot wolves.'

'Wolves!'

She laughs at my expression. 'Yes. We have wolves in Albania. But I have never seen one. I'm not sure my father has either.' She smiles at me. 'I would like to shoot.'

Jenkins gives her a warm smile and directs her to the back of the Defender, where he has our guns and all the necessary equipment.

She listens intently to what he has to say. He takes her through a safety briefing and shows her how the gun works and what she needs to do. While he does, I change quickly into my waistcoat and jacket. It's chilly, but I'm warm enough in these old clothes. I open my gun case and remove one of the Purdey twelve-bore shotguns. It's a rare vintage piece that belonged to my grandfather. He commissioned a matching pair of Purdey Over-and-Under shotguns in 1948. The silver engravings are exquisite and bear the charges from the Trevethick coat of arms intricately interwoven, with Tresyllian Hall in the background; the stock is a rich, gleaming walnut. The pair of guns were handed down to my father on my grandfather's death, and when Kit turned eighteen, my father gave him one of the guns as a birthday gift. When my father died, Kit gave me this one – the one that belonged to my dad.

And now, with Kit gone, I own both of them.

I'm hit by a sudden wave of sadness. A vision of the three of us in the gun room, my father cleaning this gun, my brother cleaning his then twenty-bore, and me looking on, as an excited eight-year-old finally allowed in the gun room. My father calmly explained how to dismantle the gun, how to oil the stock, grease the steels, clean the barrel and the action. He was meticulous. And so was Kit. I remember watching them with wide-eyed fascination.

'All set, sir?' Jenkins pulls me out of my reverie.

'Yes. Great.'

Alessia is wearing protective glasses and ear defenders. She still manages to look lovely. She cocks her head to one side.

'What?' I ask.

'I like this jacket.'

I laugh. 'This old thing? It's just Harris tweed.' I grab some cartridges, protective glasses and some ear defenders and break open the barrel of my gun.

'Ready?' I ask Alessia.

She nods, and with her Browning shotgun open, we all walk over to the makeshift shooting area that Jenkins has set up with some hay bales.

'I have the traps set just beyond that ridge for a low driven target,' Jenkins says.

'Can I see a bird?'

'Sure.' Jenkins presses his remote, and a clay flies into the air about one hundred metres in front of us.

Alessia gasps. 'I will never hit that!'

'Yes you will. Watch. Stand back.'

And I feel like showing off. She's a better pianist than me, she can cook better than me, and she beat me at chess . . .

'Give me two birds, Jenkins.'

'Yes, sir.'

I put on my glasses and ear protection. Then open and load the barrel with two cartridges and mount my gun. Ready. 'Pull!'

Jenkins releases two clays that soar up in front of us. I squeeze the trigger and pop off the top barrel, then the second, hitting both clays so that they shatter, the shards falling to the ground like hail.

'Shot, sir,' Jenkins says.

'You hit them!' Alessia exclaims.

'I did!' I can't help my smug grin. 'Okay, your turn.' I open the barrel and stand aside for her.

'Feet apart. Your weight on your back foot. Good. Look at the trap. You've seen the trajectory of the clay, you'll want to follow it up in a smooth movement.' She nods vigorously. 'Mount the stock as hard against your shoulder as you can. You don't want any recoil.'

'Okay.'

I'm amazed that she's following what I'm saying.

'Right foot back a bit, miss,' Jenkins adds.

'Okay.'

'Here are your cartridges.' I hand her two, and she loads them into the chamber and charges the gun. I stand back.

'When you're ready, shout "Pull". Jenkins will send up one clay, and you have two chances to hit it.'

She gives me an anxious glance and mounts her gun. She looks every bit the countrywoman, even in her woolly hat, her cheeks rosy and her plait hanging down her back.

'Pull!' she shouts, and Jenkins releases a bird.

It sails up before us, and she fires first one, then the second shot.

And misses.

Both times.

She pouts as the clay smashes on the ground several feet away from us.

'You'll get the hang of it. Have another go.'

A steely glint appears in her eye, and Jenkins steps forward to give her some pointers.

On the fourth clay, she hits it.

'Yes!' I shout in encouragement. She dances over to me.

'Whoa! Whoa! Barrel down!' both Jenkins and I exclaim simultaneously.

'Sorry.' She giggles and opens the gun. 'Can I have another shoot?'

'Of course. We have all morning. And it's "shot".'

She beams at me. Her nose is pink, but her eyes are bright and lively with the thrill of a new experience. Her smile could melt the hardest of hearts, and mine fills with elation. It's so gratifying to see her enjoying herself after all she's been through.

Alessia and Maxim sit in the trunk of Mr Jenkins's car, their legs hanging over the back, sipping coffee from a thermos and eating pastries with some kind of meat inside. Alessia thinks it's pork.

'You did well,' Maxim says. 'Twenty out of forty clays isn't bad going for a first time.'

'You did much better.'

'I've done this before. Many times.' He takes a sip of coffee. 'Did you enjoy it?'

'Yes. I'd like to do it again. Maybe when it is not so cold.'

'I would like that.'

She smiles as her heart skips a beat. He wants to do this again, too. That's a good sign, surely. She takes a sip of coffee.

'Ay!' She grimaces.

'What is it?'

'No sugar.'

'Is it that bad?'

She takes another cautious sip and swallows. 'No. It's not that bad.'

'Your teeth will thank you. What would you like to do now?'

'Can we walk by the sea again?'

'Sure. And then we can go for lunch.'

Jenkins returns. 'The trap's all packed, sir.'

'Great. Thanks for this morning, Jenkins.'

'It's a pleasure, my – sir.'

'I'd like to take my guns back to the Hideout and give them a clean there.'

'Of course. You'll find all you need in the case.'

'Excellent.'

'Good day, sir.' We shake hands. 'Miss,' he says, and he touches his fingers to his cap as a slow flush spreads across his cheeks.

'Thank you, Jenkins,' Alessia says, and when she gives him a brilliant smile, his cheeks redden more. I think she has a new conquest.

'Shall we go?' I ask her.

'It is your gun?'

'Yes.'

She frowns.

'Jenkins keeps it for me. By law, it has to be locked up. We have a gun cabinet at the Hideout.'

'Oh,' she says, her confusion obvious.

'Ready?' I ask to distract her.

She nods.

'I'll have to take this home.' I hold up the gun case. 'And we can go for a walk on the beach, then somewhere nice for lunch.'

'Okay.'

I open the car door for her, and she gives me a fleeting smile as she climbs in.

That was close.

Just tell her.

Every day I don't tell her who I am, I'm lying to her.

Fuck.

It's as simple as that. I open the boot and place the gun case inside.

Just fucking tell her.

I get in beside her, close the car door, and glance across at her.

'Alessia—'

'Look!' she exclaims, and points through the windscreen. Before us stands a magnificent buck deer, its coat grey and long, appropriate for the winter months, its usual white spots hidden in among its fur. Where the hell did it come from? It's less than four years old, judging by its size, but it sports an impressive set of antlers, which I know it'll shed over the next couple of months. I wonder if it's from the fallow deer herd we have at the Hall or if it's wild. If it's from the Hall, how did it get out? It peers down its imperious nose, fixing us with black eyes.

'*Ua*,' Alessia whispers.

'Have you ever seen a deer?' I ask.

'No.'

We stare at the beast as it flares its nostrils and sniffs the air.

'Maybe the wolves ate them all,' I whisper.

She turns to me and laughs, head back and free. It's such an endearing sound.

I made her laugh!

In the nearby field, Jenkins starts his Land Rover, spooking the buck. It rears back, turns and bolts over the drystone wall into some scrubland.

'I didn't know there were wild animals in this country,' Alessia says.

'We have a few.' I start the car, feeling that the moment to tell her is lost.

Bollocks.

I'll tell her later.

And deep down I know the longer I wait, the worse it's going to be when I finally spill the beans.

My phone buzzes in my jacket. It's a text, and I know it's from Caroline.

That's another issue I have to deal with at some point. But right now I'm going to take my lady for another walk on the beach.

Alessia holds up the little dragon, a lantern in the darkness as they lie in bed. 'Thank you,' she whispers. 'For today. For yesterday. For this.'

'It's my pleasure, Alessia,' Maxim responds. 'I've had a wonderful day.'

'I did, too. I don't want it to end. This has been the very best day.'

Maxim strokes her cheek with his index finger. 'The very best day. I'm glad I got to spend it with you. You really are lovely.'

She swallows, glad that the fading light will hide her blush. 'I'm not sore any more,' she whispers.

Maxim stills, his eyes searching hers.

'Oh, baby,' he says and suddenly his mouth swoops down on hers.

It's after midnight, and Alessia dozes beside me. I must tell her about who I am.

Earl of Trevethick.

Fuck.

She deserves to know. I rub my face.

Why am I so reluctant to come clean?

Because I don't know how she feels about me.

And also, apart from my title, there's the small matter of my wealth.

Bugger.

My mother's suspicious nature has left its mark.

Women will only want you for your wealth, Maxim. Remember that.

God. Rowena can be such a bitch.

Gently, in order not to wake her, I lift a strand of Alessia's hair and wind it around my finger. She was reluctant to let me buy her clothes, reluctant when she has nothing. She doesn't want me to buy her a phone, and she always chooses the cheapest item on the menu. This is not the modus operandi of a gold-digger.

Is it?

And the other day she said that I have no rivals. I think she cares for me. If she does, I wish she'd tell me. It would make this so much easier. She's talented, bright and brave – and eager. I smile thinking about her carnal appreciation. Yes. Eager. I lean over and kiss her hair.

And she can cook.

'I love you, Alessia Demachi,' I whisper, and I lay my head on my pillow and gaze at her . . . this beguiling woman. My beautiful, precious girl.

I'm woken by my phone. It's morning, and too bloody early judging by the dim light seeping through the space between the blinds. Alessia is wrapped around me as I reach across and pick up my phone. It's Mrs Beckstrom, my neighbour in London.

Why the hell is she calling me?

'Hello, Mrs Beckstrom. Is everything all right?' My voice is low so I don't wake Alessia.

'Ah, Maxim. There you are. I am sorry to call you so early, but I think you've been burgled.'

Chapter Twenty

'What?' A chill sweeps across my skin as every hair on my body stands to attention, and suddenly I'm fully awake. I run my fingernails over my scalp.

Burgled? How? When?

My mind and heart are racing.

'Yes. I was taking Heracles for a morning walk. I do so love a walk beside the river early in the morning, whatever the weather. It's so quiet and restful.'

I roll my eyes. Get on with it, Mrs B.

'Your front door is open. It may have been open for a few days. I don't know. But I thought it odd. So today I had a peek inside, and of course you're not there.'

Did I lock the flat in my panic to leave and go search for Alessia?

I can't remember.

'I'm afraid the place is a frightful mess.'

Fuck.

'I was going to call the police, but I thought I'd call you instead, dear.'

'Well. Thank you. I appreciate it. I'll deal with this.'

'I am so sorry to be the bearer of bad news.'

'It's okay, Mrs B. Thank you.' I hang up.

Shit! Fuck! Bollocks!

What have the fuckers stolen? I don't have much – all the important stuff is in the safe. I hope they haven't found that.

Bugger. Bugger. Bugger.

What a fucking nuisance. I may have to go back to London, and I don't want to go. I'm having way too much fun with Alessia. I sit up in bed and look down at her. She's blinking up at me sleepily, and I give her a reassuring smile.

'I've got to make a call.' I don't want to worry her with these details, so I get up, wrap the throw around my waist, and head into the spare room with my phone. I call Oliver as I pace the floor.

Why didn't the alarm go off?

Did I set it? Shit! I left in such a rush. I don't know.

'Maxim.' He's surprised to hear from me. 'Everything okay?'

'Good morning. My neighbour's just called me. She says I've been burgled.'

'Oh, shit.'

'Precisely.'

'I'll get around there right away. Shouldn't take me more than fifteen minutes at this time.'

'Great. I'll ring you back in about twenty.'

I hang up. My mood has nosedived, and I start to think about what I'd really miss if it was taken. My cameras. My decks. My computer . . .

Shit! My father's cameras!

What a fucking pain in the arse this is – some fucking low-life addict or maybe some feral teenage kids wrecking my place.

Fuck. A. Duck.

I had plans to spend the day with Alessia, maybe go down to

the Eden Project. Well, I might still be able to do so, but I need to assess the damage – and I don't want to do it from my phone. If I FaceTime Oliver from the iMac up at the great house, I'll get a better view; he can show me via his phone what's happened.

Feeling fucked off and with a heavy heart, I head back into the bedroom, where Alessia is still in bed.

'What is wrong?' she asks, sitting up, her hair falling over her breasts. She looks rumpled and sexy and eminently fuckable. The sight of her is a balm that immediately makes me feel better. But, sadly, I'll have to leave her for a short while. I don't want to burden her with this news. She's had enough to deal with over the last few weeks.

'I've got to pop out and take care of something. We may even have to go back to London. But you stay in bed. Sleep. I know you're tired. I'll be back soon.' She pulls the quilt up, her brow furrowed in concern. I give her a swift kiss and go grab a shower.

When I come out of the bathroom, she's gone. I dress quickly in jeans and a white shirt. I find her downstairs in the kitchen, wearing only my pyjama shirt and clearing up our dishes from the night before. She hands me a cup of espresso. 'To wake you up,' she says with an adoring smile, though her eyes are wide, wary. She's anxious.

I swallow it down. It's hot, strong and delicious. A little like Alessia.

'Don't worry, I'll be back before you know it.' I kiss her once more, grab my coat, and I'm out the door, dodging the raindrops and bolting up the steps. I climb into the car and speed off along the lane.

Alessia watches Maxim vault up the steps and close the gate behind him. He looks worried, and she wonders where he's going. Something bad has happened. A frisson skitters up her spine, but she's not sure why. She sighs. There's so much she doesn't know about him.

And he said they might have to return to London. She will have to face the reality of her situation.

Homelessness.

Zot.

She's pushed it all aside for the last few days, but so much is unresolved in her life. Where will she live? Will Dante have given up looking for her? How does Maxim feel about her? She sucks in a breath as she tries to shake off her concerns and hopes that he can deal with whatever the problem is quickly and return. Even now the house feels empty without him. The last few days have been blissful, and she hopes they don't have to go back to London. She's not ready to return to reality yet. She's never been happier than she is here, with him. In the meantime she'll finish loading the dishwasher. Then she'll shower.

I take a shortcut along the back roads to the great house that is Tresyllian Hall because it's faster than going up the main drive. The rain is growing heavier, drumming on the car windscreen and roof as I slice through the narrow lanes. Passing the gatehouse at the southern entrance to the estate, I slow as the car rattles over the cattle grid, then accelerate up the driveway through the south pasture. In this winter rain, the landscape is dreary and damp and dotted with the occasional sheep. Come spring, the cattle will be out to graze again. Through the leafless trees, I catch sight of the house. Nestled in the wide dale, slate grey and Gothic, it dominates the landscape as if plucked from a novel by one of the Brontë sisters. The original house was built on the site of an old Benedictine priory. But the land and the abbey were seized by Henry VIII during the dissolution of the monasteries. Over a century later, in 1661, following the restoration of the monarchy, the estate was bestowed, along with the title Earl of Trevethick, to Edward Trevelyan for his services to Charles II. The great house he built was all but destroyed by fire in 1862, and this neo-Gothic monstrosity, with all its finials and fake moulded battlements, was built in its place. It's the seat of the earls of Trevethick, a huge rambling pile, and I've always loved it.

And now it's mine.

I am the custodian.

The car rocks over a second cattle grid as I drive around the back of the great house and pull up outside the old stables where Kit's car collection is housed. Abandoning the Jag, I dash up to the kitchen door, and I'm pleased to find it open.

Jessie is in the kitchen cooking breakfast, with Kit's dogs at her feet. 'Good morning, Jessie,' I call as I dash through. Jensen and Healey both jump up and scramble after me.

Jessie's voice follows me out into the corridor. 'Maxim! I mean, my lord!'

I ignore her and head into Kit's study. Fuck. *My* study. The room feels and smells as if my big brother is still in residence, and I halt as an intense pang of grief bubbles up from nowhere.

Damn you, Kit. I miss you.

The truth is, the office looks as though my father is still in residence. Kit had not changed a thing apart from installing an iMac. This was my father's refuge. The walls are painted blood-red and covered with his photographs, landscapes and portraits, even a couple of my mother. The furniture dates back to before the war, the 1930s, I think. With canine enthusiasm – tails wagging and tongues licking – the dogs jump up at me while I make my way to the desk.

'Hello, boys. Hi. There. Hi. There. Steady.' I pet them both.

'Sir, it's great to see you, but is everything okay?' Jessie asks as she enters behind me.

'The Chelsea flat has been burgled. I'm going to sort it out from here.'

'Oh, no!' Jessie's hand flies to her mouth.

'No one's hurt,' I reassure her. 'Oliver's there and assessing the damage.'

'That's terrible.' She wrings her hands.

'It's a pain in the arse, is what it is.'

'Can I get you anything?'

'I'd love some coffee.'

'I'll fetch some straightaway.' She bustles out of the room, and Jensen and Healey, with mournful looks at me, follow her out. I sit down at Kit's – no, my desk.

Firing up the iMac, I log in and open FaceTime, then click on Oliver's contact link.

Alessia stands under the powerful shower enjoying the hot water streaming over her. She will miss this when they leave to go back to London. As she washes her hair, the thought depresses her. She's loved this magical time in Cornwall, just the two of them. She will always treasure the memory of her stay in this extraordinary house with him.

Maxim.

As she soaps her hair, she opens one eye, unable to shake her anxiety. Even though she's locked the bathroom door, she's nervous. She's not used to being alone, and she's missing him. She's become accustomed to his presence. Everywhere. She blushes and smiles.

Yes. Everywhere.

Now, if she could just work up the courage to touch him . . . everywhere.

Much of my flat is unaffected by the burglary. The darkroom is undisturbed, so my camera gear is intact, and more important from a sentimental point of view, I still have my father's cameras. And I'm lucky the thieves didn't find the safe. They've stolen some of my shoes and some jackets from my wardrobe, though it's difficult to tell, as there are clothes thrown around my bedroom.

The drawing room, on the other hand, is a mess. All my photography has been ripped off the walls. My iMac is smashed on the floor. My laptop and mixing consoles are gone, and my vinyl is all over the floor. Fortunately, the piano is untouched.

'That appears to be the extent of it,' Oliver says. He's holding up his phone and using the camera so I can inspect the damage on my computer screen.

'Fuckers. Any idea when they broke in?' I ask.

'No. Your neighbour didn't see anything. But it could have been anytime over the weekend.'

'It could have been after I left on Friday. How did they get in?'

'You saw the state of the front door.'

'Yeah. They must have forced it with something heavy. The fuckers. I must have forgotten to set the alarm in my haste to leave.'

'It didn't go off. I think you probably did forget. But I don't think that would have deterred them.'

'Hello . . . ?' A disembodied voice from somewhere else in the flat interrupts us.

'That will be the police,' Oliver says.

'You called them? That was quick. Good. Let me know what they say. Call me back.'

'Will do, sir.' He rings off.

I stare despondently at the screen. I don't want to go back to London. I want to stay here, with Alessia.

There's a knock on the door, and Danny appears in the doorway. 'Good morning, sir. I hear you've been robbed.'

'Morning, Danny. Yes. Though it doesn't look like I've lost anything irreplaceable. It's just a mess.'

'Mrs Blake will be able to tidy up any mess. What a nuisance this is.'

'Indeed.'

'Where would you like your breakfast?'

'Breakfast?'

'Sir, Jessie's made you breakfast. French toast. Your favourite.'

Oh. I wanted to get back to Alessia.

Danny, sensing my hesitancy, gives me The Look over her glasses. The Look that made me, Kit and Maryanne quail as young kids.

You settle down now, children, and eat your supper. Or I will tell your mother.

She always played the Mothership card.

'I'll take it in the kitchen with you and the rest of the staff, but I have to be quick.'

'Very good, sir.'

Alessia's wrapped in towels to dry off after her shower. In the walk-in closet, she rummages through the clothes that Maxim bought her a few days ago. She cannot seem to shake her apprehension. She jumps at every strange noise she hears. It's rare for her to be on her own. At home in Kukës, her mother was always around, and in the evenings her father, too. Even in the Brentford house, when she lived with Magda, Alessia was seldom alone; either Magda or Michal was there.

She wills herself to concentrate on the task at hand. After all, she has her new clothes. She decides on the black jeans with a grey top and a pretty pink cardigan. She hopes that Maxim will like what she's chosen.

Finally dressed, she picks up the hairdryer and switches it on, its high-pitched whir filling the silence.

When I enter the kitchen, it's crowded and humming with the early-morning banter of some of the staff, Jenkins among them. Seeing me, they all stand as one, a frankly feudal display of deference, which I find irritating. But I let it go. 'Good morning, all. Please. Sit. Enjoy your breakfast.'

There are various pleasant mutterings of 'my lord'.

During its heyday, Tresyllian Hall would have employed well over three hundred and fifty staff, but now we manage with twelve full-time and about twenty part-time employees. We also have eight tenant farmers, whom I met on my recent trip. They raise livestock and various arable crops across ten thousand acres. All organic. Thanks to my father.

By Trevethick tradition the outdoor and household staff eat at separate sittings. At this moment the assistant estate managers, the gamekeeper, assistant gamekeeper and the gardeners are enjoying Jessie's cooked breakfast. I note that mine is the only plate with French toast.

'I hear you've had a break-in, sir,' Jenkins says.

'Sadly, yes. It's a massive pain in the arse.'

'I'm sorry to hear that, milord.'

'Michael about?'

'Dentist this morning. He says he'll be in around eleven.'

I bite into my breakfast. The melt-in-the-mouth goodness of Jessie's French toast takes me back to my childhood. Kit and I talking cricket scores or bickering about who was kicking who under the table, Maryanne's nose in a book . . . and Jessie's French toast served up with stewed fruits. Today it's apple with cinnamon.

'It's nice to have you here, my lord,' Danny says. 'I hope you don't have to rush back to London.'

'Police just arrived. I'll find out a bit later.'

'I've let Mrs Blake know about the burglary. She and Alice can pop round from the house to your flat and clear up.'

'Thanks. I'll ask Oliver to liaise with her.'

'Are you enjoying the Hideout?'

I give her a swift grin. 'Very much. Thank you. It's very comfortable.'

'I hear you had a successful day yesterday.'

'It was fun. Thank you again, Jenkins.'

He gives me a nod, and Danny smiles. 'That reminds me,' she says. 'There were two very unsavoury characters who came calling for you yesterday.'

'What?' She has my immediate attention, and everyone else's in the room. She pales.

'They were asking after you. I told them to bugger off, sir.'

'Unsavoury?'

'Rough-looking, sir. Aggressive. From Eastern Europe, I think. Anyway—'

'Fuck!' *Alessia!*

Alessia pulls the brush through her hair. It's finally dry enough. She switches off the hair dryer, feeling ill at ease and wondering if she heard something. But it's only the sound of the crashing waves in the cove below. She stands staring out of the window down at the sea.

Mister Maxim gave her the sea.

She smiles remembering her antics on the beach. The rain is easing off. Perhaps they could go for another walk on the shore today. And back to that pub for lunch. That was a good day. Every day here with him has been a good day.

From downstairs she hears the scrape of furniture on the wooden floor and hushed male voices.

What?

Has Maxim brought someone back to the house?

'*Urte!*' someone grates in a strangled whisper. It's her mother tongue! Fear and adrenaline sweep through her body as she stands frozen in the bedroom.

It's Dante and Ylli.

They've found her.

Chapter Twenty-One

I tear down the lane, clattering over the cattle grid and pushing the Jag to go faster. I have to get back to the house. I'm finding it hard to breathe. My anxiety is a weight pressing on my chest.

Alessia.

Why did I leave her at the house? If something has happened to her . . . I will never forgive myself.

My brain works feverishly.

Is it them? The bastards who trafficked her? I feel sick to my stomach. How the hell did they find us? How? Maybe they were the fuckers who burgled my flat. They found information on the Trevethick estate and Tresyllian Hall. And now they're here. Asking questions. The fucking nerve of them, coming to my house. I grip the steering wheel.

Hurry. Hurry. Hurry.

If they locate her at the Hideout . . . I'll never see her again.

My panic mushrooms.

She'll be dragged into a horrific underworld, and I'll never be able to find her.

No. Fuck. No.

I swerve down the lane towards the Hideout, spraying gravel into the hedgerows.

Alessia's heart is pounding, her pulse thumping in her ears even as the blood drains from her head. The room spins once, twice, and her legs start to shake.

She's in her worst nightmare.

The bedroom door is open, and she hears their whispers downstairs. How did they get in? A creak on the stair galvanises her into action. She sprints into the bathroom and quietly shuts the door. With shaking, clammy hands, she locks it behind her while she gasps for air.

How did they find her?

How?

She's dizzy with fear. Feeling powerless, she quickly scans the room looking for something to use to defend herself. *Anything.* His razor? Her toothbrush? She picks up both and slips them into her back pocket.

But the drawers are empty . . . there's nothing there.

All she can do is hide. She can only hope that the door will hold until Maxim returns.

No. Maxim!

He is no match for them. He is one man – and they are two. They will harm him. Tears well in her eyes, and she sinks to the floor as her legs give out under her. She leans against the door as human ballast in case they try to break it down.

'I heard something.' It's Ylli. He's in the bedroom. When did her own language become so terrifying? 'Check that door.'

'You in here, you fucking bitch?' Dante calls out, and rattles the bathroom door, testing the handle. Alessia puts her fist in her mouth to stop from screaming, and tears trickle down her cheeks. Her body starts shaking. Her terror is overwhelming. And she pants, taking in shallow breaths. She's never felt so frightened. Not even in the truck that brought her to England. She's completely impotent. She doesn't know how to fight, and there's no escape from this room. And she has no way to warn Maxim.

'Come out!' Dante's voice makes her jump. It's inches from her ear on the other side of the door. 'It will only be worse for you if we have to break the door down.'

Alessia screws her eyes up tight and stifles her sobs. Suddenly there's a horrific thud, like a sack of grain falling to the floor, followed by loud cursing, and Alessia is jolted backwards.

Zot. Zot. Zot.

He's trying to break down the door. But it holds. Alessia stands and puts her foot against the door, silently cursing that she's not wearing shoes and socks. Her feet grip the limestone floor, and she presses her full weight against the door in the hope that it might help hold him back.

'When I get in there, I'm going to kill you. You fucking bitch. Do you know how much you cost me? Do you?'

He slams into the door again.

And Alessia knows it's only a matter of time. She sucks in a sob as her despair takes hold. She never found the courage to tell Maxim she loves him.

The Jag hurtles down the lane towards the Hideout, and I spot an old BMW encrusted with at least a year's worth of dirt, and it's abandoned haphazardly outside the garage.

Fuck. They're here.

No. No. No.

My fear and rage race into overdrive, threatening to overcome me.

Alessia!

Calm down, mate. Calm the fuck down. Think. Think. Think.

I pull up and park the car hard against the gate. They won't get out that way. If I go down the entry steps, they'll see me, and I'll lose the element of surprise. I fling open the car door and run to the little-used and hidden side gate and down to the scullery-room door. My breath is coming in short, sharp bursts as adrenaline pumps into my bloodstream, doubling my heart rate.

Calm down, mate. Calm down.

The scullery door's ajar.

Fuck. Maybe this is how they got into the house. I gulp down a steadying breath, my heart hammering, and gently push open the door and creep in. The adrenaline has sharpened my senses. My breathing is deafening.

Quiet. Be fucking quiet.

There's shouting. Upstairs.

No. No. No.

If they touch one hair of her head, I will murder them. I turn to the gun cabinet high on the wall and unlock it. I'd stashed my shotguns there yesterday before Alessia and I went for a walk on the beach. Trying to remain calm, I concentrate on removing one of the Purdeys as quietly as I can. With smooth and deliberate movements, I lift it out, open up the barrel, and load two cartridges. I put four more into my coat pocket. I have never been so grateful as I am right now that my father taught me how to shoot.

Keep calm. You will only have a chance to save her if you keep calm.

I repeat this mantra in my head. Releasing the safety, I brace the gun against my shoulder and sneak into the main room. There's no sign of anyone downstairs, but I hear an almighty crash from upstairs, followed by shouting in a foreign tongue.

Alessia screams.

Alessia shrieks as the door gives way, and she's flung across the bathroom floor. Dante almost falls into the room. She curls up into a ball, sobbing, as fear paralyses her body. Her bladder fails, and the tell-tale wetness seeps down her legs and into her new jeans.

Her fate is sealed.

She's breathing in short, shallow gasps as her throat constricts. She's dizzy. Dizzy with fear.

'There you are, you fucking bitch.' He grabs her hair, pulling her head up.

Alessia cries out, and he slaps her hard across her face.

'Do you know how much you've cost me, you fucking whore? You're going to pay every fucking penny back to me with your body.' His face is inches from hers. His eyes dark and feral and full of rage. Alessia gags. His breath is rank, as if something died on his tongue, and his body odour washes over her in a haze of squalor.

He slaps her hard again and drags her to her feet by her hair. The pain is indescribable – as though her scalp is being torn from her head.

'Dante! No! No!' she wails.

'Stop fucking snivelling, you filthy whore, and move!' He shakes her hard and throws her into the bedroom, where Ylli is waiting. She lands on the floor, sprawling out like a starfish. She curls up quickly.

This can't be happening.

She screws her eyes shut, waiting for the inevitable blows.

Just kill me. Just kill me. She wants to die.

'And you've pissed yourself. You dirty *piçka*. I'm going to fuck you up.' Dante swaggers around her and kicks her hard in her belly.

She screams as pain shoots through her body, leaving her gasping for air.

'Step away from her, you fucking piece of shit!' Maxim's voice bellows through the room.

What?

Alessia opens bleary eyes. *He's here.*

Maxim is standing on the threshold, shrouded in his dark coat like an avenging archangel, his eyes flashing a deadly green, and he's brandishing his double-barrelled shotgun.

He's here. With his gun.

The evil fucker whirls around to face me. He blanches in shock and jumps back, gaping at me, sweat beading on his pale bald pate. His thin-faced friend also steps back and holds up his hands, his lips twitching. He looks like a fucking rodent, drowning in his oversized parka. The urge to pull the trigger is overwhelming. I have to fight every instinct to stop myself. Baldy is watching me, his eyes focused, weighing me up. Will I shoot? Do I have the balls?

'Don't fucking tempt me!' I roar. 'Keep your hands up or I'll fucking end you. Step away from the girl. Now!'

He takes another cautious step back, his eyes flying from me to Alessia as he considers his options.

He has none.

Fucker.

'Alessia. Get up. Now. Move!' I bark, as she's still within his reach. She scrambles to her feet. Her face is red on one side where the cunt must have hit her. I fight the compulsion to blast his head off. 'Get behind me,' I say through gritted teeth.

She slips around me, and I hear her panting with fear. 'Both of you. On the floor, on your knees!' I shout. 'NOW! And not a fucking word from either of you.'

They exchange a quick look.

And I brace my finger on the trigger. 'Two barrels. Both primed.

I can take you both down. I will blow your fucking balls off.' And I aim for Baldy's crotch.

His eyebrows shoot up his ashen forehead, and both men sink to their knees.

'Hands behind your heads.'

They do as they're told. But I have nothing to restrain them with.

Bollocks.

'Alessia, are you okay?'

'Yes.'

My phone starts buzzing in my pocket. *Shit.* I bet it's Oliver.

'Can you take the phone out of the back pocket of my jeans?' I ask Alessia while keeping my aim on the two gangsters. Deftly, she does. 'Answer it.' I can't see what she's doing, but after a moment I hear her.

'Hello?' she says, and there's a pause before she speaks again, in a hushed voice choked with fear. 'I am Mister Maxim's cleaner.'

Jesus. She's so much more than that.

Baldy spits words at his rat-faced colleague. *'Është pastruesja e tij. Nëse me pastruese do të thuash konkubinë.'*

'Ajo nuk vlen asgjë. Grueja asht shakull për me bajt,' Ratface replies.

'Shut the fuck up!' I roar at the two of them. 'Who is it?' I ask Alessia.

'He says his name is Oliver.'

'Tell him we've captured two intruders at the Hideout and to call the police. Now. Tell him to call Danny and ask her to send Jenkins here right away.'

Haltingly, she does.

'Tell him I will explain later.'

She repeats what I've said. 'Mr Oliver says he is doing it . . . Goodbye.' She hangs up.

'Lie down, both of you. On your front. Hands behind your back.' Baldy gives Ratface a quick look. Is he going to try something? I step forward and lower the barrel, aiming for his head.

'Hello!' A voice from downstairs calls up. It's Danny. Already? That makes no sense.

'Upstairs, Danny!' I shout, not taking my eyes off the two low-lifes. I motion with the gun. *Fucking lie down.* They comply, and I approach the two prone figures on the bedroom floor. 'Don't move a muscle.' I press the muzzle of the gun into Baldy's back. 'Try me. The shot will break your spine and enter your stomach, and you'll die a slow, agonising death – which is more than you deserve, you fucking animal.'

'No. No. Please,' he whimpers like a beaten dog in his thick accent.

'Shut up and keep still. Do you understand? Nod if you do.'

Both men give me quick, furious nods, and I chance a glance at Alessia who is wide-eyed, pale and hugging herself in the doorway. Behind her, Danny appears – and Jenkins behind Danny.

'Oh, my God.' Danny's hand goes to her mouth. 'What's happening here?'

'Did Oliver reach you?'

'No, milord. We followed you after you leapt up from the breakfast table. We knew something was wrong . . .'

Jenkins hovers in the background.

'These two kidnappers broke into the house. They were after Alessia.' I press the barrel into Baldy's back.

'Do you have anything I can restrain them with?' I ask Jenkins, keeping my eyes trained on the men on the floor.

'I've some baling twine in the back of the Land Rover.' He turns and hurries back down the stairs.

'Danny, take Alessia back to the Hall, please.'

'No,' Alessia protests.

'Go. You cannot be here when the police arrive. I'll be with you as soon as I can. You'll be safe with Danny.'

'Come on, child,' Danny says.

'I need a change of clothes,' Alessia mumbles.

I frown. *Why?*

Alessia dashes into the walk-in wardrobe and comes out a few moments later carrying one of the bags from our shopping the other day. With one unreadable glance at me, she follows Danny down the stairs.

Alessia stares, unseeing, out of the windscreen, her hands wrapped around her body as the old woman named Danny drives the large, rattling car down a country lane.

Where are we going?

Her head aches, her scalp and face are throbbing. It also hurts her side when she takes a breath. She tries to keep her breathing shallow.

Danny has wrapped her in a blanket that she took from the sofa in the holiday house.

'We don't want you catching cold, dear,' she'd said.

She has a kind, gentle voice with an accent that Alessia cannot place. She must be a good friend to Mister Maxim to take such care of her.

Maxim.

She would never forget how he looked when he saved her, in his long coat, brandishing a shotgun like a hero from an old American movie.

And she had thought he would be at their mercy.

Her stomach roils.

She's going to be sick.

'Please stop the car.'

Danny pulls to a stop, and Alessia almost falls out of the vehicle. She doubles over, retching on the side of the road, losing her breakfast.

Danny comes to her aid, holding her hair back as Alessia heaves and heaves until her stomach's empty. Finally she straightens up, trembling.

'Oh, child.' Danny offers her a handkerchief. 'Let's get you back to the Hall.'

As they continue on their journey, Alessia hears sirens in the distance and imagines that the police are arriving at the Hide-out. She trembles, knotting the handkerchief in her fingers.

'It's okay, dear,' the old woman says. 'You're safe now.'

Alessia shakes her head, trying to process all that has just happened.

He's saved her. Again.

How could she ever thank him?

Jenkins makes short work of tying the two thugs' hands behind their backs. He lashes their ankles together for good measure. 'My lord,' he says, and points to the butt of a pistol that shows above the waistband of Ratface's trousers, visible now that his parka has ridden up.

'Armed breaking and entering. This gets better and better.' I'm grateful he didn't try to use the weapon on me – or Alessia. I pass Jenkins the shotgun, and after a moment's hesitation, because he deserves it, I give Baldy a fast, forceful kick in his ribs. 'That's for Alessia, you fucking scumbag.' He grunts in pain as Jenkins looks on, and I kick him again, harder this time. 'And all the other women you've sold into slavery.'

Jenkins gasps. 'Traffickers?'

'Yes. Him, too! After Alessia.' I nod towards Ratface, who's glaring at me with hatred. Jenkins gives him a swift kick.

I kneel beside Baldy and grab his ear, wrenching his head back. 'You are a blight on humanity. You're going to rot in jail, and I'll make sure they throw away the fucking key.' He puckers his lips and tries to spit in my face, but he misses, his spit drizzling down his chin. I slam his head onto the floor with a loud thud. Hopefully he'll have a cracking headache. I stand up, fighting the renewed urge to kick him to a pulp.

'We could finish them off and dispose of the bodies, my lord,' Jenkins offers, placing the barrel of the gun against Ratface's head. 'No one would ever find them on the estate.' For a moment I'm not sure if Jenkins is joking or not – but Ratface believes him, screwing his eyes up, his expression riddled with dread.

Good. Now you know how Alessia felt, you piece of shit.

'Tempting though that idea is, it would make an awful mess in here, and I don't think the cleaning crew would thank us.'

We all look up when we hear the sirens.

'And there's the small matter of the law,' I add.

Danny turns into a smaller lane, by a charming old-fashioned house, and the antiquated car shakes as they go over some metal rods in the road. The land here is green and lush even though it's winter. They drive through an open and rolling pasture. It looks . . . groomed, not wild like the countryside she's seen since she got here. It's dotted with well-fed sheep. As the car rattles down the road, a large grey house looms before them. It's imposing. The biggest house Alessia has ever seen. She recognises the chimney. It's the one she saw from the road when she was walking with Maxim. He said it belonged to someone, but she can't remember who. Perhaps this is where Danny lives.

Why is she cooking for Mister Maxim when she lives here?

Danny drives around to the rear of the house and pulls up by the back door.

'We're here,' she says. 'Welcome to Tresyllian Hall.'

Alessia tries but fails to give her a smile and climbs out of the car. Still feeling unsteady on her feet, she follows Danny through the door and into what looks like the kitchen. It's a large, airy room, the most spacious kitchen Alessia has ever seen. Wooden cupboards. Tiled floor. It's spotlessly tidy. Old and modern at the same time. There are two stoves. Two! And a massive table that seats at least fourteen people. Two tall dogs with auburn coats come bounding towards them. Alessia recoils.

'Down, Jensen. Down, Healey!' Danny's command stops the dogs in their tracks. They lie down, gazing up at both women with big expressive eyes. Alessia regards them suspiciously. They are handsome hounds . . . but where she comes from, dogs do not live in the house.

'They are harmless, my dear. Just pleased to meet you. Come with me,' she says. 'Would you like a bath?' Her tone is solicitous and kind, but Alessia blushes, mortified.

'Yes,' she whispers. *She knows!* She knows that she's wet herself.

'You must have had a terrible fright.'

Alessia nods and blinks back the tears that well in her eyes.

'Ah, lassie, don't you be crying. His lordship wouldn't want that. We'll get you sorted.'

Lordship?

She follows Danny along a wood-panelled corridor hung on both sides with old paintings of landscapes, horses, buildings, religious scenes, and a couple of portraits. They pass many closed doors and ascend a narrow wooden staircase to yet another long, panelled corridor. Eventually Danny stops and opens a door into a pleasant room with a white bed, white furniture and pale blue walls. She walks through the room to an en suite bathroom and turns on the taps. Alessia stands behind her, pulling the blanket around herself and watching as water thunders into the bath and steam rises. Danny adds some aromatic bubble bath that Alessia recognises as Jo Malone, like in the Hideout.

'I'll bring some towels for you. If you put your clothes by the bed, I'll have them laundered in no time.' She gives Alessia a sympathetic smile and slips out, leaving her alone.

Alessia stares at the water cascading into the bath, a foam forming and spreading over the surface. The bath is old. A tub with claw feet. Her body starts to shiver, and she clutches the blanket and pulls it tighter around her.

She is still standing there when Danny returns with fresh towels. Draping them over a white wicker chair, she shuts off the water, then turns her attention to Alessia, her sharp blue eyes shining with compassion. 'Do you still want a bath, dear?'

Alessia nods.

'Would you like me to leave?'

Alessia shakes her head. She doesn't want to be alone. Danny lets out a sigh of sympathy.

'Okay, then. Would you like me to help you undress? Is that what you want?'

Alessia nods.

'And we'll need to interview your fiancée,' PC Nicholls says. She's around the same age as me, tall and willowy, bright-eyed and keen, scribbling down every word I utter. I drum my fingers on the dining-room table. How much longer are we going to be? I'm anxious to get to Alessia, *my fiancée . . .*

Both Nicholls and her boss, Sergeant Nancarrow, have patiently sat through the sorry tale of Alessia's attempted kidnapping. Naturally, I've been economical with the truth, but I've kept as close to it as I can. 'Of course,' I respond. 'Once she's recovered. Those bastards really roughed her up. If I hadn't arrived back here when I did . . .' Briefly I close my eyes as a tremor runs down my spine.

I might never have seen her again.

'You've both been through a terrible experience.' Nancarrow shakes his head in disgust. 'Will you have her checked over by a doctor?'

'Yes.' I hope Danny's had the foresight to organise one.

'I hope she makes a quick recovery,' he says.

I'm glad Nancarrow's here. I've known him since I was a child. We've had the odd run-in over noisy, late-night parties and drinking on the beach. But he has always been fair. And of course it was he who came to the house to inform us of Kit's tragic accident.

'If these men have form, they'll be on our database. Petty crime, more serious offences, they'll all show up, Lord Trevethick,' Nancarrow continues. 'Got everything you need, Nicholls?' he asks his eager colleague.

'Yes, sir. Thank you, my lord,' she says to me. She looks thrilled, and I suspect she's never had to deal with an attempted kidnapping before.

'Good.' Nancarrow gives her an approving smile. 'Lovely place you have here, my lord.'

'Thank you.'

'And how have you been keeping? Since your brother passed away?'

'Holding up.'

'Sad business.'

'Indeed.'

'He was a good man.'

I nod. 'He was.' My phone buzzes, and I check my screen. It's Oliver. I ignore the call.

'We'll be on our way, sir. I'll let you know how the investigation proceeds.'

'I bet these arseholes were the ones who broke into my flat in Chelsea.'

'We'll be sure to check on it, sir.'

I escort them to the front door.

'Oh, and congratulations on your impending nuptials.' Nancarrow offers me his hand.

'Thank you. I'll pass your well wishes on to my fiancée.'

I just have to ask her to marry me first . . .

The water is hot and soothing. Danny has left to wash Alessia's dirty laundry. She's promised to be back in a *wee* minute. She's going to fetch the rest of Alessia's clothes from the car and bring her some painkillers for her head. It's throbbing because Dante pulled her upright by her hair. Alessia's trembling has subsided, but her anxiety remains. She closes her eyes and all she can see is Dante's snarling face in front of hers. She opens them again immediately and shudders, remembering the smell.

Zot. The stink of him. Fetid. Stale sweat. Unwashed. And his breath.

She gags. And splashes her face to rinse away the memory, but the hot water stings where he hit her.

Ylli's words sound in her head.

Nëse me pastruese do të thuash konkubinë.

If by cleaner you mean concubine.

Concubine.

The word is apt. She doesn't want to acknowledge it, but it's the truth. She is Maxim's concubine – and his cleaner. Her mood grows bleaker still. What did she expect? The moment she defied her father, her fate was sealed. But she'd had no choice. If she had stayed in Kukës, she would be married to a volatile and violent man. Alessia shudders. She had begged her father to stop the betrothal. But he ignored her and her mother's pleas. He had given that man his word of honour.

His *besa*.

And there was nothing either of them could do. Baba would not go back on his word. He would bring great dishonour to the family name if he did. Her mother's solution was to unwittingly put her in the hands of those gangsters. But now that they are in police custody, they are no longer a threat to her, and she has to accept the reality of her situation. While she's been in Cornwall, laughing on the beach, drinking in the pub, eating in fine restaurants, having sexual intercourse and falling in love with Mister Maxim, she has lost sight of that reality. Being with him has filled her head with illusions. Just as her grandmother had done – giving her crazy ideas about independence and liberation. Alessia had left her homeland to escape her betrothed but also, in good faith, expecting to find work. That's what she needed to do. To work, to be independent – not a kept woman.

She stares into the dissipating bubbles in the bath.

She hadn't expected to fall in love . . .

Danny comes bustling back into the bathroom holding a large navy-blue bathrobe. 'Come now. Let's get you out of there. We don't want you turning into a prune,' she says.

Prune?

Alessia rises. On automatic. And Danny drapes the bathrobe around her and helps her step out of the bath. 'Is that better?' she asks.

Alessia nods. 'Thank you, missus.'

'My name's Danny. I know we haven't been formally introduced. But that's what everyone calls me here. I've brought a glass of water, some tablets, and an ice pack for your head and some arnica cream for your cheek. It will help with the bruising, and I've called the doctor to come look at that nasty bruise on your side. Let's get you into bed. You must be exhausted.' She ushers Alessia into the bedroom.

'Maxim?'

'His lordship will be along as soon as he's dealt with the police. Come now.'

'His lordship?'

'Yes, dear.'

Alessia frowns, and Danny's expression echoes hers.

'Did you not know? Maxim is the Earl of Trevethick.'

Chapter Twenty-Two

Earl of Trevethick?

'This is his house,' Danny says gently, as if talking to a child. 'All the land surrounding the house. The village—' She stops. 'He didn't tell you?'

Alessia shakes her head.

'I see.' Danny's white brows knit together, but she shrugs. 'Well, I'm sure he had his reasons. Now, shall I leave you to get dressed? Your bag of clothes is on the chair.'

Alessia nods, and Danny takes her leave, shutting the door behind her. Stunned, Alessia stares at the closed door, her mind imploding. Her knowledge of the English peerage is limited to two Georgette Heyer books her grandmother had smuggled into Albania. As far as Alessia knows, there is no aristocracy in her country. In ancient times, yes, but since the Communists had seized all land after the Second World War, the nobles that lived there had fled.

But here . . . Mister Maxim is an earl.

No. Not Mister. He's *Lord Maxim.*

Milord.

Why didn't he tell her?

And the answer echoes loudly and painfully through her head.

Because she is his cleaner.

Nëse me pastruese do të thuash konkubinë.

If by cleaner you mean concubine.

She sucks in a breath, wrapping the bathrobe tighter around herself against the winter chill and this distressing news.

Why did he keep this from her?

Because she is not good enough for him, of course.

She is only good for one thing . . .

Her stomach lurches at his betrayal. How could she be so gullible? Feeling raw and wounded by his dishonesty, she wipes away the tears that spring to her eyes. She's been in denial.

Her relationship with him has been too good to be true.

Deep down she suspected this. And now she knows the truth.

But he never made any promises to her. Those were all in her head. He's never told her he loves her . . . He's never pretended to love her. Yet in the short time she's known him, she's fallen for him. Fallen from a great height.

I am a fool. A misguided fool in love.

She closes her eyes in anguish as hot tears of shame and regret course down her cheeks. Furious, she dashes them away and begins to dry herself briskly.

This is her wake-up call.

She takes a long breath – she's cried enough. Her deepening anger gives her momentum. She's not going to cry over him. She's mad at him, and at herself for being so stupid.

In her heart she knows that her fury is masking her hurt, and she's grateful for it. It's less painful than his betrayal.

She drops the robe on the floor, grabs the bag of clothes off the blue chair, and empties the contents onto the bed. Thankful that she had acted on impulse to bring her old clothes, too, she tugs on her pink panties, bra, her own jeans, her Arsenal FC top, and her trainers. That's the extent of her own stuff. She's not brought her coat, but she grabs one of the sweaters that Mister Maxim – Lord Maxim – bought her, and the blanket that Danny had grabbed from the Hideout.

Dante and Ylli will be arrested, and surely once the police establish the extent of their crimes, they'll be incarcerated and those brutes will no longer be a threat to her.

She can leave.

She's not going to stay here.

She doesn't want to be with a man who has deceived her. A man who will cast her aside when he tires of her. She would rather leave than be sent away.

She has to get out. Now.

Swiftly she downs the two tablets Danny has left for her. Then, with one last glance around the elegant bedroom, she opens the door a crack. There's no one on the landing. She slips out of the room, closing the door behind her. Somehow she needs to find her way back to the Hideout to retrieve her money and her belongings. She cannot leave the house the way she came in – Danny might be in the kitchen. She turns right and heads down the long corridor.

The Jag skids to a halt by the old stables. I fling open the door and abandon the car, flying into the house. I'm desperate to see Alessia.

Danny, Jessie and the dogs are in the kitchen. 'Not now, boys,' I instruct the dogs as they leap up to greet me and be petted.

'Welcome back, my lord. The police gone?' Danny asks.

'Yes. Where is she?'

'In the blue room.'

'Thanks.' In haste I make for the door.

'Oh, my lord . . .' Danny calls after me and there's a waver in her voice that brings me to a halt.

'What? How is she?'

'Shaken, sir. She threw up on the way over here.'

'Is she okay now?'

'She's had a bath. And she's changing into fresh clothes. And . . .' Danny glances with uncertainty at Jessie, who goes back to peeling spuds.

'What is it?' I demand.

Danny pales. 'I mentioned that you're the Earl of Trevethick.'

What?

'Shit!' I race out of the kitchen, along the west hallway, and bound up the back stairs towards the blue room with Jensen and Healey at my heels. My heart is pounding.

Bugger. Bugger. Bugger. I wanted to tell her. What must she be thinking?

Outside the blue-room door, I stop and take a deep breath, ignoring the dogs, who have chased after me convinced some new game is afoot.

Alessia's had a horrific scare today. Now she's in a place she doesn't know, with people she doesn't know. She's probably utterly overwhelmed.

And she's going to be really fucking angry I didn't tell her . . .

I knock on the door, briskly.

And wait.

I knock again. 'Alessia!'

There's no answer.

Fuck. She's really pissed off with me.

With caution I open the door. Her clothes are scattered on the bed, her robe discarded on the floor, but there's no sign of her. I check the bathroom. It's empty except for the trace of her scent. Lavender and roses. For an instant I close my eyes and inhale. It's soothing.

Where the hell is she?

She's probably gone off to explore the house.

Or she's left.

Shit.

I storm out of the room and bellow her name down the corridor. My voice echoes off the walls hung with portraits of my ancestors, but it's met with a resounding silence. Dread seeps into my bones. Where is she? Has she passed out somewhere?

She's fled.

This is all too much for her. Or maybe she thinks I don't care . . .

Fuck.

I pace down the hallway, throwing open each door, with Jensen and Healey as my wingmen.

Alessia is lost. She's trying to find a way out. On tiptoe, she walks past door after door, painting after painting, along yet another wood-panelled corridor, until she eventually reaches a pair of double doors. She pushes through and finds herself at the top of a grand, wide staircase carpeted in scarlet and blue, which leads to a cavernous dark hallway below. On the landing there's a mullioned bay window, beside which stand two suits of armour holding what look like pikes. On the wall over the staircase is a massive faded tapestry, bigger than the kitchen table she saw earlier, that depicts a man on bended knee to his sovereign. Well, Alessia *assumes* he must be the sovereign, judging by the crown he's wearing. On the opposing walls above the staircase, there are two portraits. Huge. Both men. One is from an ancient time, the other far more recent. She sees the family resemblance in their faces and has a flash of recognition. They each stare at her with the same imperious green eyes. *His* green eyes.

This is Maxim's family. His heritage. She finds it almost impossible to grasp.

But then her gaze falls on the carved twin-headed eagles that sit on the newel posts at the top, the turns and the bottom of the staircase.

The symbol of Albania.

Suddenly she hears him shout out her name. It startles her.

No.

He's back.

He shouts again. He sounds panicked. Desperate. Alessia freezes at the top of the impressive staircase, staring at the history that surrounds her. She's torn. From far off beneath her, a clock with a booming chime signals the hour, making her jump. Once, twice, three times . . .

'Alessia!' Maxim calls again, nearer this time, and she can hear his footsteps. He's running – running towards her.

The clock is still chiming. Loud and clear.

What should she do?

She grips the ornate eagle at the corner of the staircase as Maxim and the two dogs burst through the double doors. He stops when he sees her. His eyes sweep from her face to her feet, and he frowns.

I've found her. But my relief is tempered by her aloof yet inscrutable expression and the fact that she's wearing her old clothes and carrying a sweater and a blanket.

Shit. This does not look good.

Her stance reminds me of the first time I encountered her in my hallway, all those weeks ago. She's clutching the newel post like she clutched that broom. My senses are on high alert.

Tread warily, dude.

'There you are. Where are you going?' I ask.

She tosses her hair over her shoulder with that careless grace she has and tilts her chin in my direction. 'I'm leaving.'

No! It's like she's kicked me in the stomach.

'What? Why?'

'You know why.' She sounds haughty, her expression etched with righteous indignation.

'Alessia. I'm sorry, I should have told you.'

'But you did not.'

I can't argue with that. I stare at her while the hurt in her dark eyes burns a hole in my conscience.

'I understand.' She lifts one of her shoulders. 'I am only your cleaner.'

'No. No. No!' I stalk towards her. 'That's not the reason.'

'Sir. Is everything okay?' Danny's voice echoes off the stone walls and up the staircase from beneath us. I lean over the balustrade, and she appears with Jessie and Brody, one of the estate hands, in the hallway below. The three of them gape up at us open-mouthed, like curious carp from the fish pond.

'Go. Now. All of you. Go!' I wave them away. Danny and Jessie exchange anxious glances, but they scatter.

Thank fuck.

I turn my attention back to Alessia. 'This is why I didn't bring you here. There are just too many people in this house.'

She tears her gaze away from me, her brow furrowed, her mouth a tight line.

'This morning I had breakfast with nine staff, and that was just the first sitting. I didn't want to intimidate you with all . . . this.' I wave at the portraits of my father and the first earl while she traces the intricate carvings on the eagle with one finger. She remains mute.

'And I wanted you to myself,' I whisper.

A tear slides down her cheek.

Fuck.

'Do you know what he said?' she whispers.

'Who?'

'Ylli.'

One of those fucking intruders at the Hideout. 'No.' *Where is she going with this?*

'He said that I am your concubine.' Her voice is hushed, full of shame.

No!

'That's . . . absurd. It's the twenty-first century . . .' It takes all my self-restraint not to pull her into my arms, but I inch closer, so close that the warmth from her body seeps into mine. Somehow I manage not to touch her. 'I would say that you're my girlfriend. That's what we say here. Though I don't want to presume. We've not discussed our relationship, as this has all happened so quickly. But that's what I want to call you. Girlfriend. My girlfriend. Which means that we are together in a relationship. But that's only if you'll have me.'

Her eyelashes flutter over her dark, dark eyes, but she gives nothing away.

Shit.

'You're a bright, talented woman, Alessia. And you're free. Free to make your own choices.'

'But I'm not.'

'You are *here*. I know you're from a different culture, and I know we're not economic equals, but that's just an accident of birth . . . We are equals in every other way. I've fucked up. I should have told you, and I'm sorry, deeply sorry. But I don't want you to go, I want you to stay. Please.'

Her fathomless eyes strip me bare as she studies my face, and then she turns her attention to the carved eagle.

Why is she avoiding me? What is she thinking?

Is it the trauma she's just been through?

Or is it because those fuckers are out of the picture, so she no longer needs me?

Shit. Maybe that's the reason.

'Look, I can't keep you here if you want to leave. Magda is moving to Canada. So where you'll go, I don't know. If nothing else, stay until you know where. But please don't go. Stay. With me.'

She can't run . . . she can't.

Forgive me! Please.

I hold my breath. Waiting.

It's excruciating. I'm the defendant in the dock waiting for the verdict.

She turns her tear-stained face to me. 'You are not ashamed of me?'

Ashamed? *No!*

I can bear it no longer. I skim the back of my index finger across her cheek, capturing a tear. 'No. No. Of course not. I . . . I . . . I've fallen in love with you.'

Her lips part, and I hear her just-audible gasp.

Shit. Am I too late?

Her eyes glisten with fresh tears, and my heart clenches with a new and intimidating sensation. Perhaps she'll reject me. My anxiety level ratchets up several notches, and I've never felt as vulnerable as I do now.

What's the verdict, Alessia?

I open my arms, and she looks from my hands to my face. Her expression uncertain. It's killing me. She bites her lower lip and takes one small hesitant step, and she's in my embrace. I wrap my arms around her and press her to my chest. I never want to let her go. Closing my eyes, I bury my nose in her hair and inhale her sweet scent. 'My love,' I whisper.

She shudders and starts to sob.

'I know. I know. I've got you. You've had a terrible fright. I'm sorry I left you on your own. It was a stupid thing to do. Forgive me. But those arseholes are in police custody. They're gone. They won't harm you again. I've got you.' Her arms slide around me, and she grabs my coat at the back. She holds me as she weeps.

'I should have told you, Alessia. I'm sorry.'

We stand for seconds, minutes, I don't know. Jensen and Healey give up on us and wander down the stairs.

'You can cry on me anytime,' I tease. She sniffles, and I tip her chin up and stare down into beautiful, red-rimmed eyes. 'I thought . . . oh, God, I thought if they got their hands on you . . . I'd never see you again.'

Swallowing, she gives me a weak smile.

'And you must know,' I continue, 'I'd be honoured to call you mine. I need you.' And loosening my hold, I gently caress her face, avoiding the slight red mark on her right cheek. The sight of her bruise fills me with anger, but, taking great care not to touch it, I smooth away her tears with my thumbs. She places her hand on my chest. Through my shirt I feel the warmth. It spreads. Everywhere.

Alessia clears her throat. 'I was so scared. I thought I'd never see you again. But my biggest . . . um, sorrow . . . um, regret,' she whispers, 'was that . . . was that I never told you that I love you.'

Chapter Twenty-Three

Joy bursts like a million fireworks within me from head to foot. Its intensity leaves me breathless. I can't quite believe it. 'You do?'

'Yes,' Alessia whispers with a timid smile.

'Since when?'

She pauses and lifts a shoulder in a coy shrug. 'Since you gave me the umbrella.'

I beam at her. 'I felt so good about that. Your wet footprints were all over my hall. So . . . are you saying you'll stay?'

'Yes.'

'Here?'

'Yes.'

'I'm so very glad to hear that, my love.' I brush her bottom lip with my thumb and lean down to kiss her. I place my lips on hers, gently, but she ignites around me, her fervour taking me by surprise. Her lips and tongue are greedy, urgent, her hands are in my hair, tugging and twisting. She wants more. So much more. I groan as my body comes alive, and I deepen the kiss, taking everything she has to offer. There's a desperate quality to her demanding mouth. She's needy. And I want to be the one to fulfil her need. My hands move into her hair, holding her still, steadying her, slowing our pace. I want to take her, here, now, on the landing.

Alessia.

My arousal is instant.

I want her.

I need her.

I love her.

But . . . she's been through hell. She winces when I run my hand down her side. And her reaction brings me to my senses.

'No . . .' I whisper, and she pulls back, giving me a carnal but bewildered and disappointed look.

'You're hurt,' I explain.

'I'm okay.' She's breathless, and she cranes her neck to kiss me again.

'Let's just take a moment,' I whisper, and I rest my forehead on hers. 'You've had a horrible morning.' She's extremely emotional, and her ardour may be a direct reaction to being roughed up by those arseholes.

The thought is sobering.

Or maybe it's because she loves me.

I like that idea better.

We stand forehead to forehead as we each catch our breath.

She strokes my cheek, then tilts her head to one side, and a hint of a smile plays on her lips. '*You* are the Earl of Trevethick?' she teases. 'When were you going to tell me?' There's a mischievous twinkle in her eye, and I laugh out loud, knowing that she's echoing my question from the other night.

'I'm telling you now.'

She grins and taps her lip with her finger. I turn and wave theatrically to the portrait that dates from 1667. 'May I introduce Edward, the first Earl of Trevethick. And that gentleman' – I point to the other painting with my thumb – 'that's my father, the eleventh earl. He was a farmer and a photographer, too. And he was an ardent Chelsea supporter, so I'm not sure what he would have made of your Arsenal top.'

Alessia gives me a puzzled look.

'They are rival London football teams.'

'Oh, no.' She laughs. 'Where is your portrait?'

'I don't have one. I haven't been the earl for very long. My older brother, Kit. He was the real earl. But he never got around to having his portrait painted.'

'Your brother who died?'

'Yes. The title and everything that comes with it were his responsibility until a few weeks ago. I wasn't meant for the role, for all . . . this.' I tilt my head towards the suits of armour. 'Running this place – this museum – it's all new to me.'

'Is that why you didn't tell me?' Alessia asks.

'It's one of the reasons. I think part of me is in denial. All this, and the other estates, it's a lot of responsibility, and I've not been trained for it.'

Whereas Kit was . . .

This conversation is getting too deep and too close to home. I continue with a slight smile. 'I'm very lucky. I've never really had to work before, and now all this is mine. And I have to maintain it for the next generation. It's my duty.' I give her an apologetic shrug. 'This is who I am. And now you know. And I'm glad you've decided to stay.'

'My lord?' Danny calls up from below.

Maxim's shoulders sag a little. Alessia senses that he wants to be left alone. 'Yes, Danny?' he answers.

'The doctor is here to see Alessia.'

Maxim turns an anxious gaze to her. 'Doctor?'

'I'm okay,' Alessia says, hesitantly.

He frowns. 'Send her up to the blue room.'

'It's not Dr Carter, it's Dr Conway, sir. I'll send *him* up right away, my lord.'

'Thank you,' Maxim calls down to Danny, and he takes Alessia's hand. 'What did that bastard do to you?'

Alessia can't look him in the eye. She feels ashamed, ashamed that she's brought this horror into Maxim's life. 'He kicked me,' she whispers. 'Danny wanted the doctor to see this.' She lifts the side of her Arsenal shirt to reveal a vivid red mark that's the size of a woman's fist.

'Fuck.' Maxim's expression hardens, his mouth pressing into a thin line. 'I should have killed that scum,' he hisses. He takes her hand, and they walk back to the blue room, where an elderly man with a large leather bag is waiting. Alessia is surprised to see that the clothes she'd left on the bed and the floor have been tidied away.

'Dr Conway. It's been a while.' Maxim shakes hands with him. The doctor has wild white hair, a wispy moustache and a beard to match. His keen blue eyes are the same colour as his crooked bow tie. 'Have we brought you out of retirement?'

'My lord, you have. But only for today. Dr Carter is on holiday. It's good to see you looking so well.' He places a hand on Maxim's shoulder, and a look passes between them.

'And you, Doctor,' Maxim answers, his voice gruff, and Alessia suspects the doctor is checking on Maxim's well-being following the death of his brother.

'How's your mother?'

'The same.' Maxim's lips quirk up.

Dr Conway's laugh is deep and gravelly. He turns his attention to Alessia, who tightens her hold on Maxim's hand. 'Good day, my dear. Ernest Conway at your service.' He gives her a little bow.

'Dr Conway, this is my girlfriend, Alessia Demachi.'

Maxim looks at her, his shining eyes full of pride. As he turns back to the doctor, his expression hardens. 'She's been assaulted and was kicked in the side by someone who is now in police custody. Miss Campbell thought it best that a doctor examine her.'

Miss Campbell?

'Danny,' he answers her unspoken question. He gives her hand a quick squeeze. 'I'll leave you to it,' he adds.

'No. Please don't go,' Alessia blurts out. She does not want to be alone with this strange man.

Maxim nods in understanding. 'Of course, if you'd like me to stay.' He sits down in a small blue armchair, stretching out his long legs. Reassured, Alessia turns her attention to the doctor.

His expression is serious. 'Assaulted?'

Alessia nods and feels her face flush with mortification.

'Would you like me to take a look?' Dr Conway asks.

'Okay.'

'Please sit.'

The doctor is kind and patient. He runs through several questions before he asks her to lift her shirt, and keeps up a steady stream of chatter while he examines her. His kind manner helps her relax, and she learns that he brought Maxim and his siblings into the world. Alessia glances at Maxim, who gives her a comforting smile.

Her heart expands.

Mister Maxim loves her.

She smiles back at him.

And he grins.

The doctor prods Alessia around her stomach and ribs, and the spell between her and Maxim is broken. She winces at Dr Conway's touch.

'There's no permanent damage. And you're lucky not to have

any cracked ribs. Just take it easy. And try some paracetamol if it's painful. Miss Campbell will have some.' Dr Conway gives her a gentle pat on the arm. 'You'll live,' he says.

'Thank you,' Alessia says.

'I should just take a quick photograph of the bruise. The police might need it for their records.'

'What?' Alessia's eyes widen.

'Good idea,' says Maxim.

'Lord Trevethick, would you mind?' He hands Maxim his phone. 'Just the bruise.'

'Darling, I'll only photograph the bruise. Nothing else.'

She nods and lifts her shirt once more, and Maxim takes a few quick snaps.

'Done.' He hands the phone back to the old man.

'Thank you,' Dr Conway replies.

With a look of relief, Maxim says, 'I'll show you out, Doctor.'

Alessia quickly rises to her feet and takes Maxim's hand. He smiles down at her and laces his fingers through hers. 'We'll both see you out.' Maxim gestures to the door, and they follow Dr Conway into the corridor.

They watch as the doctor drives off in his old car. Maxim has his arm around Alessia's shoulders, and she's nestled into his side. It feels . . . natural. They are standing in the wide hallway at the front of the house. 'You know, you can hold me, too,' Maxim says, his tone warm and encouraging. Shyly she snakes an arm around his waist. He grins. 'See how well we fit together?' And he kisses the top of her head. 'I'll give you the tour later. Right now I want to show you something.' They turn around, but Alessia stops when she notices the large sculpture above the stone fireplace that dominates the hall. It's the shield that Maxim has tattooed on his biceps, but it's more decorative. There are two stags on each side, a knight's helmet above it, and above that, in a swirl of yellow and black, a small coronet bearing a lion. Beneath the shield there's a scrolled caption: FIDES VIGILANTIA.

'My family's coat of arms,' Maxim explains.

'And on your arm,' she asks. 'What do the words mean?'

'It's Latin. "Loyalty in vigilance".'

She looks puzzled, and Maxim shrugs. 'Something to do with the first earl and King Charles II. Come.' It seems he doesn't wish to say any more. He's buoyant, eager to show her something, and his excitement is infectious. From somewhere deep in the house, the clock that Alessia heard earlier announces the hour, one chime echoing through the Hall. He grins, looking boyish and adorable. She can't quite believe he's fallen for her; he's talented, handsome, kind, wealthy, and he's saved her from Dante and Ylli once more.

Hand in hand they walk through a lengthy hallway that's lined with paintings and the occasional ornate console table laden with statues, busts and ceramics. They ascend the great staircase where they had their conversation earlier and cross to the other side of the landing from the double doors.

'I think you might like this,' Maxim says, and he opens the door with a flourish. Alessia walks into a large chamber with wood-panelled walls and an elaborate plaster ceiling. At one end is a bookcase that covers the entire wall, but at the other, bathed in light from a huge mullioned window, is a full-size grand piano, the most ornate piano Alessia has ever seen.

She gasps and whips her head around to Maxim.

'Please. Play,' he says.

Alessia claps her hands and bolts across the wooden floor, the sound of her quick footsteps echoing off the walls.

She stops a pace away from the piano to take in its majesty. It's made of a highly polished wood with a rich grain that gleams in the light. The legs are solid and intricately carved with leaves and grapes, the sides inlaid with a complex marquetry of golden ivy leaves. She runs her finger along the cartouche. It's splendid.

'She's old,' Maxim says over Alessia's shoulder. Lost in wonder, she hadn't heard him approach. She doesn't understand why he sounds apologetic.

'It's magnificent. I have never seen a piano like this,' she whispers in admiration.

'It's American. From the 1870s. My great-great-grandfather married a railroad heiress from New York. This came here with her.'

'It's beautiful. How does it sound?'

'Let's find out. Here.' Maxim makes quick work of lifting the top board and using the longer prop to hold it open. 'I don't think you'll need this, but I thought you might like to see it.' Raising the music rack, he sets it in place. It's etched in a fine filigree. 'Cool, huh?'

Alessia nods in awe.

'Sit. Play.'

Alessia flashes him a delighted grin and pulls the carved piano stool forward. Maxim steps out of her sight line, and she closes her eyes to collect herself. She places her hands on the keys, relishing the feel of the cool ivory beneath her fingertips. She presses down, and the D-flat major chord sings into the room, resonating off the wooden panelling. The tone is rich, like the dark green of a forest fir, but the action is light – surprisingly light for such an old piano. Opening her eyes, she stares down at the keys, wondering how this instrument could have survived for so long and made it through such an epic journey from America. Maxim and his family must cherish their possessions. Shaking her head with incredulity, she places her hands on the keys once more and, not bothering with her warm-up piece, begins to play her favourite Chopin prelude. The notes of the first four bars dance across the room in a verdant spring green – the colour of Maxim's eyes. But as she plays, the colours become darker and more ominous, filling the room with portent and mystery. Consumed by the music, she surrenders herself to each precious note. It drives away her anxiety and her fear. All the horror of the morning fades and then disappears in the dark and emerald greens of Chopin's remarkable, stirring masterpiece.

I watch, enthralled, as Alessia plays the 'Raindrop' Prelude. With her eyes closed, she's lost in the music, her face expressing every thought and feeling that Chopin evokes in the piece. Her hair flows down her back, glinting like a raven's wing in the light of the winter sun that streams through the window. She's captivating. Even in that football shirt.

The notes swell and fill the room . . . and my heart.

She loves me.

She said so.

I'll have to get to the bottom of why she thought she'd be better off leaving. But for the moment I'll listen and watch her play. Hearing a muffled cough from outside the room, I look up. Danny and Jessie are poised on the threshold, listening. I wave them in . . .

I want to show Alessia off.

This is what my girl can do.

They tiptoe into the room and stand watching Alessia with the same look of amazement that I'm sure I had when I first heard her play. And they can see she doesn't have the sheet music – she's performing this from memory.

Yeah. This is what she does best.

Alessia plays the final two bars, and the notes fade into the air . . . leaving us entranced. As she opens her eyes, Danny and Jessie burst into applause, as do I. She smiles shyly at them.

'Brava, Miss Demachi! That was exceptional,' I exclaim as I walk over and bend to kiss her, my lips grazing hers. When I look up, Danny and Jessie have gone, as discreetly as they appeared.

'Thank you,' Alessia whispers.

'What for?'

'Saving me. Again.'

'It is you who has saved me.'

She frowns as if she doesn't believe me, and I sit down beside her on the piano stool. 'Trust me, Alessia, you've saved me in ways I can't even begin to fathom, and I don't know what I would have done if they'd taken you.' I kiss her once more.

'But I've brought such trouble into your life.'

'You have done nothing of the kind. This is not your fault. For God's sake. Never think that.'

Her lips thin for a moment, and I know she doesn't share my point of view, but she reaches up and strokes my chin.

'And for this,' she whispers, and glances at the piano. 'Thank you.' She leans up and kisses me. 'Can I play some more?'

'All you want. Always. I'm going to make some calls. My flat was burgled over the weekend.'

'No!'

'I suspect it was the same two bastards who are now in the custody of the Devon and Cornwall Police. I think that's how they found us. I need to talk to Oliver.'

'The man I spoke to on the phone?'

'Yes. He works for me.'

'I hope they did not take much.'

I caress her face with one hand 'Nothing that can't be replaced – unlike you.' Dark eyes shine at me, and she leans her face into my hand. I brush my thumb over her bottom lip and ignore the fire that lights low in my belly.

Time for that later.

'I won't be long.' I give her a swift kiss and head towards the door. Alessia launches into Louis-Claude Daquin's piece 'Le Coucou', which I learned when doing my grade six, and the bright and breezy notes follow me out of the room.

From *my* study – not Kit's – I call Oliver. Our conversation is all business. He's handling the fallout from the burglary. Mrs Blake and one of her assistants are at the flat clearing up, two members of the construction crew in Mayfair have been dispatched to repair the front door, and a locksmith will change the locks on the entry to the street. The alarm is untouched and working fine, but we decide to change the code. I choose Kit's birth year as the new number. Oliver is keen for me to return to London; he has documents that I need to sign for the Crown Office to register my succession to the earldom and entry onto the Roll of the Peerage. With Alessia's assailants under arrest and in custody, there's no reason for us to stay in Cornwall. When I finish with Oliver, I call Tom to see how Magda and her son are faring. I tell him about the attempted kidnapping.

'Well, that's fucking audacious,' Tom splutters. 'How's your young lady? Is she okay?'

'She's tougher than all of us.'

'Good to hear. I think I should keep an eye on Mrs Janeczek and her son for a couple of days. Until we find out what the police are going to do with those scumbags.'

'Agreed.'

'I'll report anything suspicious.'

'Thanks.'

'You okay?'

'Peachy.'

Tom laughs. 'Good to hear. Over and out.' Moments after I hang up on Tom, my phone buzzes. It's Caroline.

Damn. I told her I'd call next week.

Shit – it is *next week.*

I've lost track of time.

Sighing, I answer the phone with a terse 'Hey'.

'There you are,' she snaps. 'What the hell are you playing at?'

'Hello, Caroline, it's nice to talk to you, too. Yes, thanks, I've had a great weekend.'

'Don't start with your bullshit, Maxim. Why haven't you called me?' Her voice cracks, and I know she's hurt.

'I'm sorry. Events have been a little beyond my control down here. Please let me explain when I see you. I'll be back in London tomorrow or the day after.'

'What events? The burglary?'

'Yes and no.'

'Why all this subterfuge, Maxim?' she whispers. 'What's going on?' Her voice drops lower. 'I've missed you.' Her grief echoes through each syllable of her response. And I feel like shit.

'I'll tell you when I see you. Please.'

She sniffs, and I know she's crying.

Fuck.

'Caro. Please.'

'You promise?'

'I promise. As soon as I'm back. I'll come see you.'

'Okay.'

'Bye for now.' I hang up and ignore the sinking feeling in my stomach. I have no idea how she'll react to what's been happening here.

Yes, I do. It's going to get ugly.

I sigh once more. My life has been complicated beyond recognition by Alessia Demachi, but even as the thought pops into my head, I smile.

My love.

We could head back to London tomorrow. I can see for myself the damage done to my flat.

There's a knock on the door.

'Come in.'

Danny enters. 'Sir, Jessie's prepared some lunch for you and Alessia. Where would you like us to serve it?'

'In the library. Thank you, Danny.' I think the formal dining room might be a little overwhelming just for the two of us, and the breakfast room is a little dull. She likes books, so . . .

'If it suits your lordship, we'll be set up in five minutes.'

'Great.' I realise how hungry I am. A quick glance at the Georgian wall clock above the door tells me it's two fifteen. Its steady tick reminds me of the times I waited in this office for the bollocking my father administered whenever I'd transgressed – which was often. Right now the clock says . . . way past lunchtime.

'Oh, Danny,' I call her back.

'My lord?'

'After lunch can you go to the Hideout and retrieve all our belongings and bring them here? Put everything in my room, including the dragon night-light that's beside the bed.'

'Will do, sir.' With a nod she departs.

As I approach the bottom of the staircase, I hear the music. Alessia is deep into another complex piece – one I don't know. Even down here it sounds amazing. I quickly head up the stairs and stand just inside the room watching her from afar. I think this composition is by Beethoven. I haven't heard her play any of his work before. A sonata, maybe? The music is rousing and passionate one moment and then quieter and softer the next. Such a lyrical piece. And she plays it exquisitely. She should be filling concert halls.

The music spirals down to its close, and Alessia sits for a second, her head lowered, eyes closed. When she looks up, she's surprised to see me.

'Another great performance. What was it?' I ask as I stroll across the floor towards her.

'It is Beethoven. "Tempest",' she says.

'I could watch and listen to you play all day. But lunch is served. Rather late. You must be hungry.'

'Yes. I am.' She jumps up off the stool and accepts my outstretched hand. 'I love this piano. It has a rich . . . um . . . tone.'

'Tone. That's the correct word.'

'You have so many instruments here. I only had the eyes for the piano at first.'

I grin. 'Only had eyes for. No "the". You really don't mind me correcting you?'

'No. I like to learn.'

'Cello is my sister Maryanne's instrument. My father played the double bass. The guitars are mine. The drums over there were Kit's.'

'Your brother's?' she asks.

'Yes.'

'It is an unusual name.'

'Kit is short for Christopher. He was a demon on drums.' I stop by the crash cymbal and run my fingers over the polished bronze. 'Kit. Drum kit. Get it?' I flash her a smile. Alessia gives me a puzzled look.

'We used to joke about it.' I shake my head, remembering Kit's shenanigans on the drums. 'Come on. I'm hungry.'

Maxim's eyes gleam a brilliant green as he looks at her, but she can see from the tension across his forehead that his grief is still raw and he misses his brother.

'So that's the music room,' he says as they leave and head back down the great staircase, stopping at the bottom. 'The main drawing room is through those double doors, but today we're having lunch in the library.'

'You have a library?' Alessia asks, excited.

He smiles. 'Yes, we have a few books. Some of them are quite old.' They head back towards the kitchen, but Maxim stops outside one of the doors in the corridor. 'I should warn you, my grandfather was keen on all things Egyptian.' He opens the door, standing aside for Alessia to enter. She pauses a few steps into the room. It's like she's entered another world – a treasure trove of literature and antiquities. On every available wall, there are floor-to-ceiling bookshelves stuffed with books. At each corner is either a plinth or a cabinet holding treasures from Egypt: canopic jars, statues of pharaohs, sphinxes, a full-size sarcophagus!

A fire rages in the grate beneath an ornate marble fireplace that's set between two tall but narrow windows overlooking a courtyard. Hanging above the mantelpiece is an old painting of the pyramids.

'Oh, boy, the staff have gone all-out,' Maxim says, as if to himself. Alessia follows his gaze. Before the fire a small table covered in a fine linen cloth is elaborately set for two: silver cutlery, cut glasses, and delicate china plates decorated with small thistles. He holds out a chair for her. 'Sit.' He nods at her seat. Alessia feels like the noblewoman Donika Kastrioti, the wife of Skënderbeu, Albania's fifteenth-century hero. She gives him a gracious smile and sits down at the table facing the fire. Maxim sits at the head.

'As a young man in the early 1920s, my grandfather worked with Lord Carnarvon and Howard Carter, excavating various sites in Egypt and stealing all these antiquities. Maybe I should send them back.' He pauses. 'Until very recently that was Kit's dilemma.'

'You have so much history here.'

'Yes, we do. Rather too much of it, perhaps. It's my family's legacy.'

Alessia cannot imagine the responsibility of dealing with such a heritage.

There's a knock at the door, and without waiting for an answer, Danny enters, followed by a young woman carrying a tray.

Maxim reaches for his linen napkin and drapes it on his lap. Watching him, Alessia follows suit. Danny takes two plates from the tray and serves each of them what looks like a salad with meat and avocado and pomegranate seeds.

'Pulled pork from one of the local farms, with a salad of fresh leaves, finished with a pomegranate jus,' Danny says.

'Thanks,' Maxim responds, and gives Danny a quizzical look.

'Would you like me to pour the wine, my lord?'

'I've got this. Thanks, Danny.'

She gives him a little nod and discreetly ushers the young woman out of the door.

'A glass of wine?' Maxim picks up the bottle and studies the label. 'It's a good Chablis.'

'Yes. Please.' She watches as he half fills her glass. 'I have never been . . . waitered on, except when I am with you.'

'Waited on,' he says. 'While we're here, you might as well get used to it.' He winks at her.

'You do not have staff in London.'

'No. Though that may have to change.' His brow furrows for a moment, and then he raises his glass. 'To narrow escapes.'

She raises hers. '*Gëzuar*, Maxim. My lord.'

He laughs. 'I'm still not used to the title. Eat up. You've had a horrible morning.'

'I think the afternoon will be much better.'

Maxim's look is heated – and Alessia smiles and takes a cautious sip of her wine.

'Mmm . . .' It is so much better than the wine she tasted with her grandmother.

'You like?' Maxim asks.

She nods and studies her cutlery. She has an array of knives and forks to choose from. Glancing at Maxim, she sees him smile and pick up the outermost knife and fork. 'Always start from the outside and work inwards with each course.'

Chapter Twenty-Four

After lunch we head outside. Alessia's hand is warm in mine. The day is crisp and cold, and the sun is low in the sky as we walk together down the beech-lined avenue that leads to the front gates. Jensen and Healey scamper along behind, beside and in front of us, grateful to be outdoors. After the trauma of this morning, I think we're both enjoying this quiet and peaceful walk in the late-afternoon sunshine.

'Look!' Alessia exclaims as she points to the herd of fallow deer grazing on the horizon of the north pasture.

'We've had deer here for centuries.'

'The one we saw yesterday. It was from here?'

'No. I think it was wild.'

'The dogs do not bother them?'

'No. But we keep the dogs out of the south pasture near lambing time. We don't want them worrying the sheep.'

'There are no goats here?'

'No. We're more sheep and cattle people.'

'We are goat people.' She grins at me. Her nose is pink from the cold, but she's bundled up in her coat, hat and scarf. She looks adorable. And I find it hard to believe that she was the victim of an attempted kidnapping this morning.

My girl is stoic.

But there's one thing that's been bugging me. I have to know. 'Why did you want to leave? Why didn't you want to stay and have it out with me?' I hope she doesn't hear the apprehension in my voice.

'Have it out with you?'

'Talk to me. Argue with me,' I explain.

She stops beneath one of the beech trees and looks down at her boots, and I don't know if she's going to answer me.

'I was hurt,' she says after an age.

'I know. I'm sorry. I didn't mean to hurt you. I never want to hurt you. But where would you have gone?'

'I don't know.' She turns to face me. 'I think it was . . . how do you say? Instinct. You know, Ylli and Dante . . . I've been running for so long. I was a little crazy.'

'I can't imagine how terrifying that was for you.' I cringe and close my eyes, thanking all the gods that I got to her in time. 'But you can't run every time we have a problem. Talk to me. Ask me questions. About anything. I'm here. I'll listen. Argue with me. Shout at me. I'll argue with you. I'll shout at you. I'll get it wrong. You'll get it wrong. That's all okay. But to resolve our differences, we have to communicate.'

A fleeting look of anxiety crosses her face.

'Hey.' I tilt her chin up and draw her closer to me. 'Don't look worried. If . . . if you're going to live with me . . . you know. You need to tell me how you feel.'

'Live with you?' she whispers.

'Yeah.'

'Here?'

'Here. And in London. Yes. I want you to live with me.'

'As your cleaner?'

I laugh and shake my head. 'No. As my girlfriend. I meant what I said on the landing. Let's do this.' I hold my breath. My heart is racing. And deep down, I don't know what choice she has – but I love her. I want her with me. Marriage seems too big a step to throw at her right now. I don't want her to run again.

Bro, it's also a big step for you!

'Yes,' she whispers.

'Yes?'

'Yes!'

With a shout of joy, I scoop her up and swing her around. The dogs start barking and jump up at us with tails wagging, eager to join in the fun. She's giggling, but suddenly she winces.

Shit.

I set her down immediately.

'Did I hurt you?'

'No,' she says, and I take her face between my palms, and she sobers, her eyes shining with love and maybe desire.

Alessia.

Leaning down, I kiss her. And what's meant to be a gentle I-love-you kiss becomes something . . . other. She opens up like an exotic flower, kissing me back with a passion that's staggering and I revel in all she has to give.

Her tongue in my mouth.

Her hands moving over my back and clutching at the material of my coat.

All the stress of this morning – the sight of her with those lowlifes, the fact that I might never have seen her again – all of that vanishes, and I pour my fears and my gratitude that she's still with me into our kiss. When we come up for air, our breath mingles in a steamy fog in the cold around us, and her fingers are wrapped around the lapels of my coat.

Jensen sticks his muzzle into my thigh. Ignoring him, I lean back to look at Alessia's dazed expression. 'I think Jensen wants to join in.'

Her giggle is breathy, and it speaks directly to my groin.

'I also think we're wearing too many clothes.' I rest my forehead on hers.

'Do you want to take them off?' She chews on her lip.

'Always.'

'I am warm. Too warm,' she whispers.

What?

I look down at her once more. My remark was flippant and meant to be amusing – not a come-on.

What is she saying?

'Oh, *sweetheart*, you've just been through a terrible ordeal.'

She lifts one shoulder in a 'so what?' manner and averts her eyes.

'What are you telling me?' I ask.

'I think you know.'

'You want to go to bed?'

Her broad grin is all the encouragement I need, and against my better judgement I grab her hand. Beaming and giddy, we trot back to the house with the dogs in hot pursuit.

'This is my room.' Maxim stands aside for Alessia to enter. It's a few doors down from the blue room where Danny had brought her earlier.

A magnificent four-poster dominates the dark green room. Made of the same highly polished wood as the piano, the bed is just as intricately carved. The flames in the fireplace cast flickering shadows over the carvings. Above the mantelpiece there's a painting of the house and the surrounding countryside, and at the far end of the room stands an immense wardrobe in the same wood as the bed. On every wall are shelves covered in books and curios, but Alessia's gaze is drawn to the bedside table where the little dragon night-light sits.

Maxim throws several more logs on the fire until it blazes. 'Good. I'm glad someone had the foresight to light the fire.' Returning to stand in front of her, he points to a wicker basket perched on the ottoman at the end of the bed. 'I've had your stuff brought here from the Hideout. I hope that's okay.' His voice is low and soft, and his eyes glow. Intense. Growing larger and darker . . . full of his desire.

A tingle runs down Alessia's spine.

'It's okay,' she whispers.

'You've had a rough day.'

'I want to go to bed.' She remembers their kiss on the stairs. She would have taken his clothes off then and there if she'd had the nerve.

He strokes her face. 'Maybe you're still in shock.'

'I am,' she whispers. 'I am shocked that you love me.'

'With all my heart,' Maxim says with real sincerity, but then he smiles and puts his arm around her. 'And with this.' He tilts his pelvis forward so she can feel his erection against her hip. His eyes alive with carnal humour. She returns his smile as the fire in her belly ignites. She's been longing to touch him – after all, he's touched her everywhere, with his hands . . . with his lips . . . with his tongue, just as he promised. Her gaze moves to his mouth, his skilled and sensual mouth, and the flames in her belly lick higher.

'What do you want, beautiful?' The backs of his fingers stroke her face, and his eyes sear her soul. She's wanted him since he said he loved her.

'I want you.' The words are barely audible.

He groans. 'You never cease to surprise me.'

'Do you like surprises?'

'From you, very much.'

Alessia tugs at his white shirt until it slips out of the waistband of his jeans. 'Are you going to undress me?' Maxim's voice is hoarse, like he's stopped breathing.

She eyes him from beneath her lashes. 'Yes.' She can do this. And with brave but trembling fingers, she undoes the lowest of his shirt buttons. She glances up at him.

'Go on,' he coaxes, his tone soft and seductive.

Alessia hears the burgeoning excitement in his voice. It feeds her desire. She undoes the next one up, revealing the top button of his jeans and the line of hair that points to his lean abdomen. The next button reveals his navel and his honed stomach muscles. Maxim's breathing alters. Rising. More rapid. The sound excites her, and her fingers fly up his shirt, unfastening it until it's hanging loose and open, revealing his sun-kissed chest. She longs to lean forward and place her lips against his flesh.

'What now, Alessia?' He's waiting. 'Whatever you want,' he says, arousing her. She leans forward and presses her lips against the warmth of his chest, where his heart thunders beneath his skin.

I am itching to touch her. But I can't. This is the most audacious she's been with me since we first made love. My body is straining. How can her innocent touch be so erotic? She's driving me wild. She eases my shirt over my shoulders and tugs it down to my elbows. I present her with my wrists. 'Cuffs.'

She flashes me a grin and undoes each one in turn, then drags my shirt off and drapes it over the armchair in front of the fire.

'Now what are you going to do?' he says. Alessia steps back to admire his fine, toned physique in the dancing light of the fire. The gold in his hair glints, and his eyes are a luminous green. They watch her, full of promise as he stares.

Emboldened by his gaze, she reaches down and peels off her sweater, then tugs her football shirt over her head and shakes her hair loose. But her courage fails at the last minute, and she hesitates, holding the top to her breasts. Maxim steps forward and gently takes it from her. 'You're lovely. I like looking at you. You won't be needing this.' He tosses it on top of his shirt, then takes a strand of her hair and winds it around his finger. Bringing it to his lips, he kisses it. 'You are so brave. In so many ways. And I've fallen for you. All of you. Madly. Passionately.' His words heat her blood, and he tugs the lock, drawing her into his arms. He angles her head and kisses her like his life depends on it. 'I could have lost you,' he whispers.

His skin is warm against hers, and the desire within her burns brighter. She wants him. All of him. Greedily, she kisses him, her tongue twisting with his. Her hands rest on the back of his head, drawing him closer. His lips move to her jaw, her throat. And her hands travel down his body to the waistband of his jeans.

She wants to touch him. Every inch of him. But she stops. She doesn't know what to do. Maxim holds her chin tenderly between his fingers. 'Alessia,' he growls against her ear. 'I want you to touch me.' The need in his voice is arousing.

'I want to.'

He grazes her earlobe with his teeth.

'Ah,' she groans as the muscles tighten deep in her belly.

'Undo my jeans.' He kisses a trail of butterfly kisses down her neck. Hastily her fingers scramble to his waistband, brushing against his hardened penis. She stops, fascinated by his body, and in a really bold move places her hand over his erection.

'Oh, God,' he whispers.

Tentatively her fingers trace around him.

He gasps, and she stops. 'I am hurting you?'

'No. No. No. This is good. Yeah.' He's breathless. 'Really good. Don't stop.'

She grins, feeling more confident. With deft fingers she undoes his top button. He stands stock-still as she moves to the zipper.

I take a deep breath. She is going to unman me. Her delight is contagious, and I love that she's finally plucking up the courage to undress me. In the firelight her skin is radiant, and the deep red and blue highlights glimmer in her hair. I want to throw her onto the bed and make easy, sweet love to her. But I need to slow down. Let her discover things at her own pace. While she undoes my flies, she seems less self-conscious. She's even forgotten she's not wearing her bra. She has beautiful, full breasts. I want to worship each one until her nipples are rock-hard and she's squirming beneath me. But I restrain myself and muffle my groan. She tugs my jeans down my legs, and I step out of them, so I'm standing before her in just my underwear.

'Your turn,' I whisper, and make quick work of her flies and peel off her jeans. She steps out of them, and I cup her face gently and kiss her. 'It's cold. Let's get into bed.'

'Okay.' She slides under the covers, her eyes on me.

'Oh – the bed is cold!' she squeaks.

'We'll warm it up.'

Alessia's eyes flit to his straining shorts.

He grins. 'What?' he asks.

She flushes.

'What?' Maxim insists.

'Take them off.'

'My underwear?' Maxim's smile is lopsided.

'Yes.'

He smirks – and removes one sock. Then the other. 'There!'

'That is not what I was talking about.' She giggles, marvelling at how boyish he can be. He laughs and with one swift move slides off his shorts, freeing his erection – then tosses the underpants at her.

'Hey!' she cries out, playfully. She deflects them, but he leaps onto the bed, landing beside her.

'Brrr . . . move over.' Maxim snuggles in beside her under the sheets, putting his arm around her and pulling her close. 'I want to hold you for a moment. I can't believe I almost lost you today.' He plants a soft kiss in her hair and squeezes her tight. She sees he's closed his eyes – as if he's in pain.

'You didn't. I am here. I would have fought them to stay with you,' she whispers.

'They would have hurt you.'

Sitting up suddenly, he lifts her hand to inspect the bruise on her side. His demeanour hardens. 'Look at what they did to you.' He hesitates, concerned.

'It's okay.' She's suffered worse . . .

'Maybe we should just nap.' Maxim looks doubtful.

'What? No.'

'I don't think—'

'Maxim! Don't think.'

'Alessia—'

She reaches up and places a finger on his lips. 'Please . . .' she says.

'Oh, baby.' Taking her hand, he kisses each knuckle. Then he bends down and rings her bruise with tender kisses. Her fingers find his hair, and she tugs hard, so that he has to look up at her.

'Does it hurt?'

'No,' she says hurriedly. 'I want this. I want you.' He sighs, and his mouth travels up to her breast and its nipple, teasing and sucking as he goes. She groans and writhes beneath him, closing her eyes and surrendering to the pleasure of his touch and his lips. Her fingers dig into his back, and she feels his erection against her hip. She's yearning to explore his body. All of his body.

He looks up at her. 'What is it?'

'I . . . I . . .' She blushes.

'Tell me.'

She laughs, embarrassed, and shuts her eyes.

'Tell me.'

She opens one eye and squints at him.

'You're driving me crazy. What is it?'

'I want to touch you,' she says, and hides her face with her hands.

Peeking through her fingers, she watches Maxim's eyes soften – amused, she thinks. He lies down beside her. 'I'm all yours,' he says. She leans up on one elbow, and they gaze at each other. 'You're so lovely,' he whispers.

She strokes his cheek, enjoying the feel of his rough stubble.

'Here, let me help you . . .' Taking hold of her hand, he plants a kiss in her palm. He moves it to his chest, and she splays it out against his skin, feeling his warmth. His lips part as he takes a sharp breath. 'I like you touching me.'

Encouraged, she moves her hand down, her fingers tickling the fine hair that's sprinkled across his chest. She skims over one of his nipples, and it puckers under her touch.

'Oh,' she breathes in delight.

'Oh,' he responds, his voice hoarse, his eyes hooded and a dark, mossy green. He's watching her like a hawk. She bites her upper lip, and he groans. 'Don't stop,' he whispers. Feeling more wanton and enjoying the fact that she's turning him on, she moves her hand south over his smooth skin, over the bluffs and dips of his abdominal muscles. He tenses beneath her touch, and his breathing accelerates. She reaches the line of hair that leads down to her destination, and her courage falters.

'Here,' he says, and, taking her hand, wraps it around his erection. She gasps, both shocked and thrilled in equal measure. It's big and hard and velvet smooth at once. Her thumb brushes the tip, and he closes his eyes, inhaling sharply. She tightens her hold, enjoying the feel of him beneath her fingers, feeling the pulse within him. He turns blazing eyes to her. 'Like this,' he whispers, and, guiding her hand, moves it slowly a fraction down and then up.

I've never had to show a woman what to do. It's possibly the most erotic thing I've ever done. Alessia's brow is furrowed as she concentrates, but her eyes are alive with wonder and desire, her mouth a little slack as she moves her hand, finally finding her rhythm and driving me wild. When she licks her lips, I want to come in her hand.

'Alessia, enough. I'm going to come.'

She immediately removes her hand as if she's been burned, and I regret saying anything. I want to swoop over and into her – but she's got that damned bruise, and I can't. I don't want to hurt her. She takes matters into her own hands, climbing onto me, her lips finding mine as she kisses me, pushing her tongue into my mouth. Tasting me. Her hair forms a lush curtain around us. And for a split second, we stare at each other in the firelight. Rich brown eyes to green. She's so bewitching. And giving. And sensual. And she's here with me.

She leans down and kisses me once more, and I reach over to the bedside table to grab a condom.

'Here.' I show her the packet, and for a moment I wonder if she's going to take it and put it on me – but she blinks, uncertain. 'Move down. I'll show you what to do.' I rip open the packet, take out the rubber, and, pinching the end, quickly roll it over my eager dick. 'There. All done. We just have to get your knickers off.'

She laughs as I roll her onto the mattress and hook my thumbs into her pink panties. *The* pink panties. I sweep them down her long legs and pitch them onto the floor. I'm kneeling between her thighs, but I sit back on my heels and pull her onto my lap with my arm around her waist, careful to avoid that bruise. 'Is this okay?' She has her hands on my shoulders, and I lift her and position her over my straining cock. I'm waiting for her answer. She leans forward, her lips eager on mine, and I take that as my cue, and slowly . . . oh, so fucking slowly . . . I lower her onto me. Her teeth close around my bottom lip, and for a moment I think she's going to bite me.

When I'm fully inside her, she gasps and releases my lip.

'Okay?' I breathe.

'Yes.' She nods. Enthusiastically. Her fingers are once more knotted in my hair, and she yanks hard, bringing my lips to hers. She's ravenous. Devouring me. Needy. Kissing me with the same intensity that she showed on the stairs. And I don't know if it's because of what happened to her earlier or if it's because I've told her that I love her, but she's on fire. She moves. Up and down. Again and again. Taking me . . . taking me . . .

It's heady. It's hot. But it's frantic.

This is going to end too soon!

'Hey.' I tighten my hold around her, stilling her, and I smooth her hair from her face. 'Easy, baby. Easy. We have the rest of the evening and all night. And tomorrow. And the day after that.' Dark, dazed eyes blink at me. And my heart swells with a new and intoxicating feeling that consumes me. 'I've got you,' I whisper. 'I love you.'

'Maxim,' she breathes, leaning forward and kissing me once more, her arms clasped around my neck. She starts to move again, more slowly, letting me savour her. Inch by inch. Steadier . . . easier . . . It's heaven.

Fuck.

And she rises and falls. Rises and falls. Taking me with her . . . climbing and climbing, until she stalls and cries out her orgasm, her mouth raised to the heavens and triggering my own shattering release.

'Oh, Alessia . . . !'

We lie still and quiet, facing each other. Not speaking. Just looking. Eyes. Noses. Cheeks. Lips. Faces. We gaze at each other. Absorbing each other. The only light is from the flickering flames of the fire, and all I hear is the spit and crackle of the burning logs and the thud of my heartbeat as it slows. Alessia raises her hand and traces my lips with her fingers. 'I love you, Maxim,' she whispers.

And I lean forward and kiss her once more. Her body rises to meet mine and we make sweet, sweet love again.

We are cocooned beneath the sheets in our own makeshift camp in my bedroom. Both of us are sitting cross-legged, knees touching, eyes intent on each other, and lit by the light of the little dragon that joins us in our secret, tented hideout.

She's talking.

And talking.

And I'm listening.

She's naked, her hair is loose and flowing down to her waist, preserving her modesty, and she's explaining how she learns a new piece for the piano.

'I will read the music for the first time, and I will see the colours. They . . . how do you say? Match a key.'

'A colour for each key?'

'Yes. D-flat major is a green. Like a fir tree. From Kukës. The "Raindrop" Prelude. All greens. But some darker greens as the piece changes. Other keys are different colours. And sometimes a piece may have many colours. Like the Rachmaninov. And they . . . um . . . print in my head. And I remember the piece.' She shrugs and gives me an impish smile. 'For a long time, I thought everyone sees all the colours in music.'

'If only we were so lucky.' I run a finger down her soft cheek. 'You're special. Very special to me.'

She blushes her lovely shade of pink.

'And who's your favourite composer? Bach?' I ask.

'Bach.' She breathes his name with such veneration. 'His music is . . .' She gestures and waves with her hands seeking inspiration, trying to capture the magnitude of what she wants to say, and she closes her eyes as if she's experiencing an ecstatic, religious moment . . .

'Awe-inspiring?' I offer.

She laughs. 'Yes.' She sobers and lowers her lashes, then peeks up at me through them. 'But my favourite composer is you.'

I inhale sharply. I'm not used to her compliments.

'My composition? Wow. You flatter me. What colours do you see with that?'

'That was sad and solemn. Blues and greys.'

'Fitting,' I murmur, and my thoughts turn to Kit. She reaches up and caresses my cheek, bringing me back to her.

'I watched you play it at your apartment. I was supposed to be cleaning. But I had to watch you. And listen. It's beautiful music.' Her voice softens to a barely audible whisper. 'I fell more in love with you then . . .'

'You did?'

She nods, and my heart swells at her words.

'I wish I'd known you were listening. I'm glad you liked it. You played it so well at the Hideout.'

'I loved it. You are a talented composer.'

I take her hand and trace a pattern on her palm. 'You're a very accomplished pianist.'

She grins and flushes once more.

Surely she should be used to compliments.

'You're so talented. And beautiful. And brave.' My fingers stroke her face and I draw her lips to mine. And beneath the sheet, we lose ourselves in a kiss. When Alessia pulls away to catch her breath, she gazes at me with longing once more. 'Shall we . . . make love . . . again?' She leans forward and places her lips on my chest above my heart.

Oh, boy.

Alessia is lying across me, head on my chest, her fingers tapping out a melody over my stomach. I don't know what it is – but I'm enjoying it. I call the kitchen via the internal phone system. 'Danny, I'd like some supper in my room. Can we have some sandwiches and a bottle of wine?'

'Very good, my lord. Beef?'

'Great. And a bottle of the Château Haut-Brion.'

'I'll leave a tray outside the door, sir.'

'Thank you.' I smile at the blatant glee in her voice and hang up the phone. I don't know why, but Danny knows that Alessia is different. I've brought women here before, but Danny's never been as solicitous as she's been today. She must know that I'm in love. Head over heels. Completely. Utterly. Wholly. In love.

'You have a phone for inside the house?' Alessia looks up at me.

'It's a big house.' I grin.

She laughs. 'It is.' She glances at the window; it's pitch-black outside. Is it seven o'clock? Ten o'clock? I've lost all track of time.

Alessia's curled up in one of the armchairs facing the fire, wrapped in a green throw, enjoying a roast beef and salad sandwich and drinking red wine. Her hair is a wonderful mess, spilling over her shoulders down to her waist. She's luminous. And lovely. And mine.

I throw another log on the fire, sit down in the armchair opposite her, and take a sip of the delicious wine. I've not felt this degree of peace since Kit died . . . In fact, I can't remember ever feeling this way.

Maxim puts down his glass and picks up a sandwich. He looks glorious. Rumpled hair, stubble, wicked green eyes that glow with desire and love in the firelight. He's wearing his bulky cream sweater and his black jeans with a rip at the knee, and she spies his skin beneath . . . Alessia drinks him in.

'Happy?' he asks.

'Yes. Very. . . muchly.'

He grins. 'I feel the same. I don't think I've ever been happier. I know you'd like to stay here, and so would I, but I think we should go back to London tomorrow. If that's all right. I have stuff I need to do.'

'Okay.' Alessia nibbles at her lip.

'What?'

'I like being in Cornwall. It is not as busy as London. There are less people. Less noise.'

'I know. But I should get back to London and check on my flat.'

Alessia examines her glass of wine. 'Back to reality,' she whispers.

'Hey. It's going to be okay.'

She stares into the fire, watching one of the logs spit embers onto the hearth.

'Darling, what's wrong?' Maxim is concerned.

'I . . . I want to work.'

'Work? Doing what?'

'I don't know. Cleaning?'

His brow creases. 'Alessia, I don't think so. You don't need to clean any more. You're a talented woman. Is that really what you want to do? We need to find something more interesting for you. And we need to make sure that it's legal for you to work here. I'll look into it. I have people who can help.' His smile is sincere and encouraging.

'But . . . I want to earn my own money.'

'I understand. If you're caught, though, you'll be deported.'

'I don't want that!' Alessia's heartbeat spikes. She cannot go back.

'Neither of us wants that,' Maxim reassures her. 'Don't worry about this. We'll figure it out. Maybe you can do something with your music, eventually.'

She studies him. 'I will be your kept woman.' Her voice is low. This is what she wanted to avoid.

His answering smile is rueful. 'Only until it's legal for you to work here. Think of this as a redistribution of wealth.'

'How socialist you are, Lord Trevethick,' she teases.

'Who knew?' He raises his glass to her. She reciprocates, and as she takes a sip of wine, an idea forms in her head. But will he agree?

'What is it?' he asks.

Alessia draws a deep breath. 'I will clean for you. And you will pay me.'

Maxim frowns, taken aback. 'Alessia. You don't need—'

'Please . . . I want this.' She stares at him, silently begging for him to agree.

'Ales—'

'Please.'

He rolls his eyes in exasperation. 'Okay. If that's what you want. But on one condition.'

'What?'

'Can I veto the housecoat and scarf?'

'I will think about it.' She smirks, feeling more light-hearted.

He laughs, and she breathes a sigh of relief. She will have something to do while *his people* resolve her immigration status.

A warmth spreads through her body. This is not where she thought her life might lead, here in this old, grand house with this handsome, gentle, kind man. Of course she had fantasised about it – in a vague way. But she thought it was impossible.

She had challenged her destiny and taken a huge risk when she left Albania, and fate had not let go without a fight.

Yet her Mister had intervened, and now she's here with him.

Safe.

He loves her, and she loves him. And the future stretches before her, full of possibility. Perhaps, after all this time, fortune has turned its benign smile on her.

Chapter Twenty-Five

A primal wail disturbs my dream, waking me in an instant.

Alessia.

In the soft light from the little dragon, I see that she's asleep beside me, but utterly still, her hands clenched into fists beneath her chin. She's like a statue petrified by some natural disaster. She parts her lips and cries out again, the most eerie and unearthly of sounds. I prop myself up on my elbow and gently shake her awake.

'Alessia. Sweetheart. Wake up.'

Her eyelids fly open. She looks around wildly and immediately starts fighting me off.

'Alessia. It's me. Maxim.' I grab her hands before she does either of us any harm.

'M . . . M . . . Maxim,' she whispers, and stops struggling.

'You're having a bad dream. I'm here. I've got you.' I gather her in my arms and pull her on top of me, kissing the crown of her head. She's trembling.

'I . . . I thought . . . I thought . . .' she stutters.

'It's okay. It's just a bad dream. You're safe.' I hold her and tenderly stroke her back, wishing I could take all her fear and pain away. She shivers but seems to settle, and before long she's asleep again.

I close my eyes, one hand in her hair and the other on her back, enjoying her weight and her skin against mine. I could get used to this.

Alessia wakes in the grey light of early morning. She's nestled under Maxim's arm, her hand splayed on his belly. He's fast asleep, with his face turned towards her. His hair is tousled, his lips slightly parted, and his cheeks and jawline shaded with stubble. He looks relaxed and quite irresistible. She stretches out beside him, enjoying the pull of her muscles. Her side is a little sore, and her bruise is still tender, but she feels . . . good.

No. More than good.

Hopeful. Calm. Powerful. Safe.

Because of this wonderful man asleep beside her.

She loves him. With all her heart.

And what's more remarkable, he loves her, too. She can scarcely believe it.

He's given her hope.

Maxim stirs, and his eyelids blink open.

'Good morning,' she whispers.

'It is now,' he answers with a mischievous gleam in his eye. 'You look lovely. Sleep well?'

'Yes.'

'You had a nightmare.'

'Me? Last night?'

'You don't remember?'

Alessia shakes her head. He skims her cheek with the backs of his fingers. 'I'm glad you don't. How are you feeling?'

'Good.'

'Good or *good*?' His tone is sultry.

'Very good.' She grins.

Maxim rolls over, pinning her to the mattress, and stares down at her, his green eyes glowing. 'God, I love waking up next to you,' he whispers, and kisses her throat. She throws her arms around his neck and surrenders gladly to his skilled mouth.

'I suppose we should get up and go back to London,' Maxim murmurs against her belly. Alessia's fingers play with his hair, but she's too relaxed to move. She's relishing the few moments of quiet after their passionate storm. Finally he interrupts her reverie. 'Shower with me.' He turns his head to look up at her with the broadest of smiles.

How can she resist?

Alessia towel-dries her hair while I shave. The bruise on her side looks smaller, but it's still a livid purple. A wave of guilt washes through me – she certainly gave me no indication last night or this morning that she was in any pain. She gives me a dazzling smile over her shoulder, and like a sea mist in the breeze, my guilt fades into the ether.

Part of me wants to stay here with her forever. But I'm also anxious to leave. I don't want Sergeant Nancarrow or his colleague coming to the Hall to interview Alessia. I need to keep her away from the police. If necessary, I'll inform him that business has taken me back to London.

It will be a shame to go. I'm enjoying our comfortable familiarity, and I marvel at the change in her. She seems far more confident, and it's been only a few days. Tossing her hair to the side, with a glance at me, she strolls out of the bathroom, naked as the day she was born. I peek around the door frame; the view is too tantalising not to enjoy, her hair swinging almost to her waist in a gentle counterpoint to her walk. She stops at the bed and rummages through the wicker basket on the ottoman, looking for some clothes. When she glances up and catches me gawking, she smirks. And I move back to stare at my reflection in the mirror with a smug grin. Her new-found confidence is sexy as hell.

A few moments later, she appears in the doorway and leans on the frame. She's wearing the clothes I bought her, and I know it's going to be a good day. 'In the bottom of the armoire, there should be a bag you can use for your clothes. Or I can ask Danny to pack them for you.'

'I can do it.' She folds her arms, studying me. 'I like to watch you shave.'

'I like you watching me,' I murmur as I finish up. Turning, I brush her lips with a kiss, then wipe my face of the remaining foam. 'Let's have some breakfast and get on the road.'

Alessia is animated on our drive back to London. We talk and laugh and talk some more – she has the most infectious giggle. When we hit the M4, she takes command of the music, and we listen to the Rachmaninov. As the first bars of the piano concerto begin to play, I'm reminded of when she played this piece at the Hideout – the memory is stirring. I watched her lose herself in the music, and she took me with her. From the corner of my eye, I notice Alessia's fingers pressing imaginary keys through the cadenza. I'd love to see her play this again, but this time as a performance with a full orchestra.

'Have you seen *Brief Encounter*?'

'No.'

'It's a classic British film. The director uses this piece throughout the movie. It's cool. It's one of my mother's favourite films.'

'I'd like to see it. I love this music.'

'And you play it so well.'

'Thank you.' She gives me a shy smile. 'What is she like?'

'My mother? She's . . . ambitious. Clever. Funny. Not very maternal.' As I say it, I feel a stab of disloyalty, but the truth is, Rowena always seemed bored or inconvenienced by her young children. She happily handed us over to our various nannies and sent us off to boarding school. It was only after our father died that we became more interesting to her.

Though she was always interested in Kit.

'Oh,' says Alessia.

'My relationship with my mother is a little . . . strained. I suppose I never forgave her for leaving my father.'

'She left him?' She sounds shocked.

'She left all of us. I was twelve.'

'I'm sorry.'

'She met someone younger – and broke my father's heart.'

'Oh.'

'It's okay. It was a long time ago. We have an uneasy truce now. Well, ever since Kit died.' Talking about this is grim. 'Choose another song,' I prompt when the Rachmaninov finishes. 'Something cheerful.'

She smiles and scrolls through the list. '"Melody"?'

I laugh. 'Rolling Stones? Yes. Play that.' She taps the screen, and the countdown begins: *Two. One, two, three,* followed by the blues piano. Alessia grins. She likes it. Lord, I have so much music I'd like to share with her.

The roads are quiet and we make good time. We fly past the junction for Swindon, with a further eighty miles to go until we reach Chelsea. But I have to stop for petrol, so I take the slip road for Membury Services. Alessia's demeanour suddenly changes. Her hand grips the door handle and she casts large, apprehensive eyes at me.

'I know that service stations make you anxious. We'll just get petrol. Okay?' Reaching over, I give her knee a reassuring squeeze. She nods but looks unconvinced. I pull up by a petrol pump, and she hops out to stand beside me while I fill up. 'You going to keep me company?'

She nods and dances from foot to foot to stay warm, her breath a gauzy cloud around her. Her eyes survey the locale and fix on the parked trucks. She's watchful. Wary. It's painful to see her this way, especially when she'd been so relaxed this morning.

'You know you're safe now. The police have them,' I say to reassure her, but then the pump stops with a loud metallic clunk, startling us both. The tank is full. 'Let's pay.' Hooking the nozzle back in its holder, I slip my arm around her shoulders, and we head into the shop. She walks beside me, subdued.

'You okay?' We're in the queue, and she's radiating anxiety, taking furtive glances at everyone in the shop.

'It was my mother's idea,' she blurts, quickly, quietly. 'She thought she was helping me.' It takes me a couple of seconds to realise what she's referring to.

Bloody hell. She's telling me *this story* now? A frisson runs up my spine. Why now? I have to pay for my petrol. 'Hold that thought.' I raise my index finger and hand the shop assistant my credit card. His eyes shift to Alessia, several times.

Man, she is so out of your league.

'Please enter your PIN,' he says, smiling at Alessia, who barely gives him a glance. She's watching the forecourt, checking who's out there.

When I'm done, I take her hand. 'Shall we continue talking in the car?'

She nods.

As we climb back into the Jag, I wonder why she picks service stations and car parks for her revelations. I drive away from the pumps, park the car facing woodland, and the engine idles off. 'Okay. Do you still want to talk?'

Alessia stares out at the leafless trees in front of us and nods. 'My betrothed. He is a violent man. One day . . .' Her voice falters.

My heart sinks. It is as I feared.

What the fuck did he do to her?

'He does not like me playing the piano. He does not like the . . . um . . . attention that I get.'

I despise him even more.

'He is angry. He wants me to stop . . .'

My hands tighten on the steering wheel.

Alessia's voice is practically inaudible. 'He hits me. And he wants to break my fingers.'

'What?'

She looks down at her hands. Her precious hands. She cups one with the other, holding it tenderly.

The piece of shit hurt her.

'I had to get away.'

'Of course you did.'

And I have to touch her, so that she knows I'm on her side. Folding both her hands in one of mine, I squeeze gently. The temptation to haul her into my lap and just hold her is overwhelming, but I resist. She needs to talk. She gives me a hesitant look, and I let go. 'I went in a small bus to Shkodër, and there we move into the big truck. Dante and Ylli are there with five other girls. One of them has . . . I mean – is only seventeen years.'

I gasp. Shocked. *So young.*

'Her name is Bleriana. On the truck. We talked. A lot. She lives in the north of Albania, too. In Fierza. We became friends. We made plans to find work together.' She stops – lost in the horror of her story, or maybe she's wondering what became of her friend.

'And they take everything from us. Except the clothes we are wearing and our shoes. There is only one bucket in the back . . . You know.' Her voice fades.

'That's awful.'

'Yes. The smell.' She shudders. 'And all we have is a bottle of water. One bottle for each of us.' Her leg starts jiggling, and her face pales – I'm reminded of how she looked when I first met her.

'It's okay. I'm here. I've got you. I want to know.'

She turns dark, devastated eyes to me. 'Do you?'

'Yes. But only if you want to tell me.'

Her eyes move over my face, scrutinising me. Exposing me, like that first time in my hallway.

Why do I want to know?

Because I love her.

Because she's the sum of all her experiences, and this, sadly, is one of them.

She takes a deep breath and continues, 'We were in the truck for three, four days maybe. I don't know how long. We stopped before the truck went on a – what is the word? – ferry. For carrying cars and trucks. We were given bread. And black plastic bags. We had to put them over our heads.'

'What?'

'It is to do with the immigration. They measure the, um . . . *dioksidin e karbonit*?' She flounders for the words.

'Carbon dioxide?'

'Yes. That is it.'

'In the cab?'

She shrugs. 'I don't know, but if there is too much, the authorities know there are people in the truck. They measure it. Somehow.

'We drove onto the ferry. The noise was loud. Too loud. The engines. The other trucks . . . and we were in the dark. My head in the plastic bag. And then the truck stopped. The engine was off, and all we could hear was the creaking and groaning of the metal and the tyres. The sea was rough. So rough. We were all lying down.' Her fingers move to the little cross at her neck, and she starts to fiddle with it. 'It was hard to breathe. I thought I was going to die.'

A lump forms in my throat. My voice is hoarse. 'No wonder you don't like the dark. That must have been terrifying.'

'One of the girls was sick. The smell.' She stops and gags.

'Alessia . . .'

But she continues. She seems compelled. 'Before we went on the ferry, when we are eating the bread, I heard Dante say in English – he did not know that I understood the language – he said that we would be earning our money on our backs. And I knew our fate.'

My fury is swift, burning through my blood. I wish I'd killed the fucker when I had the chance and dumped his body the way Jenkins suggested. I have never felt as inadequate as I do in this moment. Alessia drops her head, and I lift her chin gently with my fingers. 'I'm so sorry.'

She turns to face me, and there's a fire in her eyes. It's not sorrow reflected back at me, or self-pity – she's angry. Really angry. 'I heard rumours, before. Girls missing from our town and from neighbouring villages. And from Kosovo. It was in the back of my mind when I boarded the bus – but you always hope.' She swallows, and beneath her anger I see the anguish in her eyes. She feels like a fool.

'Alessia, you are not to blame, and neither is your mother. She acted in good faith.'

'She did. And I had to get away.'

'I understand.'

'I told the girls what Dante said. And three of them believed me. Bleriana, she believed me. And when we had the chance to escape, we did. We ran. I don't know if the others succeeded. I don't know if Bleriana got away.' There's a trace of guilt in her voice. 'I had Magda's address on a piece of paper. People here were celebrating Christmas. I walked for days . . . I think it was six or seven days. I don't know. Until I reached her house. And she looked after me.'

'Thank God for Magda.'

'Yes.'

'Where did you sleep while you were walking?'

'I didn't sleep. Not really. It was too cold. I found a shop, and I stole a map.' She lowers her gaze.

'I can't begin to imagine this horror that you've been through, and I'm sorry.'

'You do not have to be sorry.' She gives me a slight smile. 'This was before I met you. Now you know. Everything.'

'Thank you for telling me.' I lean over and kiss her forehead. 'You brave, brave woman.'

'Thank you for listening.'

'I'll always listen, Alessia. Always. Shall we go home now?'

Seemingly relieved, she gives me a nod, and I restart the engine and reverse out of the space. I head for the slip road back to the motorway.

'There's one thing I want to know,' I add, reflecting on the horrid tale she's just shared.

'What?'

'Does he have a name?'

'Who?'

'Your . . . betrothed.' I spit the word out. I loathe him.

She shakes her head. 'I never say his name.'

'Like Voldemort,' I mutter under my breath.

'Harry Potter?'

'You know Harry Potter?'

'Oh, yes. My grandmother—'

'Don't tell me, she smuggled the books into Albania?'

Alessia laughs. 'No. She had them sent to her. By Magda. My mother read them to me as a child. In English.'

'Ah, another reason you speak such good English. Is she fluent as well?'

'Mama? Yes. My father . . . he does not like it when we speak to each other in English.'

'I bet.' The more I hear about her father, the more I dislike him, too. But I keep that to myself. 'Why don't you find another song?'

She scrolls through the screen, and her eyes light up when she finds RY X. 'We danced to this song.'

'Our first dance.' I smile at the memory. It seems like a lifetime ago.

We settle into a comfortable silence, both of us listening to the music. She seems preoccupied by the rhythm, swaying gently to and fro. And I'm happy to see that she's recovered her equilibrium after telling her harrowing story.

While she chooses another song, I brood. This man, this fucker who harmed her, her *betrothed*, I want to know everything about him if I am to protect her from him. I need to sort out Alessia's legal status, urgently – but I have no idea how. Marrying her would help, but I think she needs to be here legally for me to do that. I resolve to call Rajah as soon as possible.

I smirk as we pass the junction for Maidenhead, and shake my head, amused by my own idiocy. I'm embracing my inner twelve-year-old boy. I glance at Alessia, but she hasn't noticed. She's deep in thought, tapping her finger against her lips.

'His name is Anatoli. Anatoli Thaçi,' she says.

What? 'He who must not be named?'

'Yes.'

Mentally I file the arsehole's name away. 'You decided to tell me?'

'Yes.'

'Why?'

'Because he has more power without a name.'

'Like Voldemort?'

She nods.

'What does he do?'

'I am not sure. My father owes him a big debt, something to do with his business, I think. But I don't know what. Anatoli is a powerful man. Rich.'

'Really?' My voice is dry. I hope to God that my bank balance is bigger than his.

'I don't think his business is . . . um . . . legal. Yes?'

'Yep. That's how we'd say it. He's a crook.'

'A gangster.'

'What is it with you and gangsters?' I scowl. She chuckles, and it's the most disarming and unexpected sound. 'What's so funny?'

'Your face.'

'Ah.' I grin. 'That's reason enough.'

'I love your face.'

'I'm rather attached to it as well.'

She laughs once more and then sobers. 'You are right. He is not funny.'

'He's not. But he's far away. He can't hurt you here. We'll be home soon. Can we listen to the Rachmaninov again?'

'Sure,' she says, scrolling through the screen once more.

I pull the F-Type up outside the office, and Oliver comes out to greet me and hand over new keys for my flat.

'This is my girlfriend, Alessia Demachi.' I lean back, and Oliver reaches through the car window to shake Alessia's hand.

'How do you do,' he says. 'I'm sorry we're not meeting under better circumstances.' He gives her a warm smile.

Her answering smile is dazzling.

'I hope you've recovered from your ordeal.'

Alessia nods.

'Thanks for sorting all this out,' I say. 'I'll see you in the office tomorrow.' He gives me a wave, and I ease the Jag into the traffic.

Maxim carries the bags from the car to the elevator. It's odd to be back here, knowing that she'll now be staying. The doors open, and they step in, and Maxim drops her bag and pulls her into his arms. 'Welcome home,' he whispers, and her heart skips a beat. She strains upward to kiss him. And his lips find hers, kissing her hard and long until she forgets her name.

When the doors open, they are both breathless.

An old lady is standing at the entrance to the elevator. She's wearing large dark sunglasses, a garish red hat, with earrings and a coat to match, and she's clutching a diminutive hairball of a dog. Maxim releases Alessia. 'Good afternoon, Mrs Beckstrom.'

'Oh, Maxim. How lovely to see you,' she replies in a high-pitched voice. 'Or should I address you by your title now?'

'Maxim is fine, Mrs B.' He manoeuvres Alessia out of the elevator and holds the door back for the old lady. 'This is my girlfriend, Alessia Demachi.'

'How do you do?' Mrs Beckstrom beams at Alessia but continues talking before Alessia can reply. 'I see you've had the front door repaired. I hope you didn't lose much during the burglary.'

'Nothing that can't be replaced.'

'I hope they don't come back.'

'I think the police have them already.'

'Good. I hope they hang them.'

Hang? They hang people here?

'I'm off to walk Heracles now it's finally stopped raining.'

'Enjoy your walk.'

'I'll do just that. You, too!' And she looks sideways at Alessia, who cannot help but blush. The doors close, and Mrs Beckstrom disappears.

'She's been my neighbour forever. She's about a thousand years old, and she's batty.'

'Batty?'

'Crazy,' he explains. 'And don't be fooled by that dog. He's a vicious little bastard.'

Alessia smiles. 'How long have you lived here?'

'Since I was nineteen.'

'I don't know how old you are.'

He laughs. 'Old enough to know better.'

She frowns while Maxim unlocks the front door.

'I'm twenty-eight.'

Alessia grins. 'You are an old man!'

'Old. I'll give you old!' He bends suddenly, surprising her, and scoops her up over his shoulder, avoiding her bruised side. She squeals and laughs as he waltzes into the apartment.

The alarm bleeps, and Maxim turns around until Alessia is facing the alarm panel. Breathless, she enters the new code that he gives her, and when the beeping stops, Maxim slides her down his front so that she's once more in his arms.

'I'm glad you're here with me,' he says.

'I am glad, too.'

From his pocket he draws the keys that Oliver gave him earlier. 'For you.'

Alessia takes them. They're on a key chain with a blue leather fob that reads ANGWIN HOUSE.

'The keys to the kingdom,' she says.

Maxim grins. 'Welcome home.' He bends to kiss her, his lips

coaxing hers. She groans as she responds, and they lose themselves in each other.

Alessia screams as she climaxes. It's a cock-hardening sound. Her fingers are clenched around the sheets. Her head tossed back. Her mouth open. I kiss her clitoris as she writhes beneath me, then her belly, her navel, her stomach and her sternum as she mewls, and taking her cries into my mouth, I ease into her.

My phone buzzes. And without looking at the caller ID, I know it's Caroline. I'd promised to see her. Ignoring the phone, I gaze down at Alessia, who is dozing beside me. She's becoming quite demanding in bed – and I like it. Leaning down, I kiss her shoulder, and she stirs.

'I have to go out,' I murmur.

'Where are you going?'

'I have to see my sister-in-law.'

'Oh.'

'I haven't seen her for days, and I need to talk some things through with her. I won't be long.'

Alessia sits up. 'Okay.' She glances out of the window. It's dark.

'It's six p.m.,' I tell her.

'Shall I make something for us to eat?'

'If you can find something. Please.'

She smiles. 'I'll do that.'

'If you can't find anything, we'll go out. I'll be about an hour.' Reluctantly I throw the quilt aside, get out of bed, and start to dress under Alessia's appreciative gaze.

I don't tell her that I'm dreading this meeting.

Chapter Twenty-Six

'Good evening, my lord,' Blake says as he opens the front door to Trevelyan House.

'Hello, Blake.' I don't correct him. After all, as much as it pains me, I am the earl. 'Is Lady Trevethick at home?'

'I believe she's in the morning room.'

'Great. I'll see myself up. Oh, and thank Mrs Blake for clearing up after the burglary. She's done a great job.'

'Will do, sir. Very unfortunate business. May I take your overcoat?'

'Thanks.' I slip out of my coat, and he folds it over his arm.

'Something to drink?'

'No. I'm good. Thanks, Blake.'

I vault up the stairs, turn left, take a deep, steadying breath, and open the morning-room door.

Alessia examines the chaos that is the walk-in closet off Maxim's bedroom. The drawers, the rails – they are all bursting with his clothes, leaving no room to store hers. She takes her duffel bag through to the spare room and proceeds to unpack, hanging her new clothes in the small armoire.

Placing her bag of toiletries on the bed, she wanders through the apartment. Everything is achingly familiar, but now she's viewing the place from a new perspective. She'd always thought of Maxim's home as a place of work. She had never dared to imagine that one day she might be living *here*, with *him*. She'd never aspired to live in a place as grand as this. She does a twirl in the doorway of the kitchen, feeling giddy and grateful – and happy. It's a precious and rare feeling. She still has so much to figure out in her life, but for the first time in a long time she's hopeful. With Maxim at her side, she feels that no obstacle is insurmountable. She wonders if he'll only be an hour . . . She's missing him.

She runs her fingers along the wall of the hallway. The photographs that had been hanging there have disappeared. Maybe they were stolen during the burglary.

The piano!

She races into the living room. It's still there, unscathed. Breathing a sigh of relief, she switches on the lights. The room looks fresh and clean, his record collection in place. But the desk is bare – the computer and the sound gear gone. Here, too, the photographs that used to hang on the walls are missing. She walks with trepidation towards the piano, scrutinising all its parts. Under the glow of the chandelier, it's glossy and gleaming – newly polished, she thinks. Placing her hand on the ebony, she walks around it, stroking its sweeping curves. When she gets to the business end, she notices that his compositions are gone. Perhaps they've been tidied away. She lifts the lid and presses middle C: it's a golden sound that rings through the empty room, seducing her, calming her . . . centring her. She sits down on the stool, shakes off her feelings of solitude, and begins to play Bach's Prelude No. 23 in B Major.

Caroline is sitting by the fire, staring into the flames, huddled in a tartan throw. She doesn't look around when I walk in.

'Hi.' My subdued greeting competes with the crackle of the fire. Caroline angles her head towards me, her expression forlorn, her mouth turned down in sorrow.

'Oh, it's you,' she says.

'Who were you expecting?' She hasn't risen to greet me and I'm beginning to feel a little unwelcome.

She sighs. 'I'm sorry. I was just thinking about what Kit would be doing now if he were here.' From nowhere my grief emerges and smothers me like an itchy woollen blanket. I shrug it off, swallowing the lump that's sticking in my throat. When I get closer to her, I see she's been crying.

'Oh, Caro . . .' I murmur, and squat beside her chair.

'Maxim, I'm a widow. I'm twenty-eight, and I'm a widow. This wasn't part of the plan.'

I take her hand in mine. 'I know. It wasn't in any of our plans. Even Kit's.'

Pained blue eyes meet mine. 'I don't know,' she says.

'What do you mean?'

She leans forward so she's facing me and in a conspiratorial whisper says, 'I think he meant to kill himself.'

I squeeze her fingers. 'Caro. That's not true. Don't think that. It was just a horrid accident.' My eyes meet hers, and I'm trying for my most earnest look, but the truth is – I've had the same thought. I can't let her know that, though, and I don't want to believe it either. Suicide is too painful for those of us left behind.

'I keep going over that day,' she says, searching my face for answers. 'But I have no idea why . . .'

Alas, neither have I.

'It was an accident,' I reiterate. 'Let me sit.' Releasing her, I slump into the chair opposite hers, facing the fireplace.

'Do you want a drink? After all, this is your house.' Her words have a bitter edge that I ignore. I don't want a fight.

'Blake already offered, and I declined.'

She exhales and turns back to stare at the flames. We both do, each of us lost in the pain of losing Kit. I had expected the third degree from her, but she's not forthcoming at all, and we sit in an uneasy silence. After a while the fire dies down. I get up and place another couple of logs in the grate and stoke the flames.

'Do you want me to go?' I ask.

She shakes her head.

Okay, then.

I sit back down, and she tilts her head to the side, her hair falling across her face until she tucks it behind her ear. 'I heard about the burglary. Did you lose anything important?'

'No. Just my laptop and my decks. I think they smashed my iMac.'

'People are shitty.'

'They are.'

'What were you doing in Cornwall?'

'This and that . . .' I'm trying for humour.

'Well, that's illuminating.' She rolls her eyes, and I glimpse a flash of the spirited Caroline I know. 'What were you doing in Cornwall?'

'Escaping from gangsters, if you must know.'

'Gangsters?'

'Yes . . . And falling in love.'

Alessia explores the kitchen cupboards and drawers, looking for something to cook for supper. She's not examined their contents in any comprehensive way before. But as she goes through them, she notes that the utensils are all clean and the pots and pans are pristine. She suspects they've never been used. Two of the pans still have the price stickers attached. She finds a few groceries in the larder: pasta, pesto, sun-dried tomatoes, some jars of herbs and spices. Enough to make a meal, but these ingredients don't inspire her. She eyes the kitchen clock. Maxim will be a while yet. She has time to go to the local store to find something a little more enticing for her man.

A silly grin spreads over her face.

Her man.

Her Mister.

At the bottom of the armoire, she finds the Ziploc bag that she'd stuffed in Michal's old rugby sock – the bag that holds her precious savings. Taking out two twenty-pound notes, she slips them into the back pocket of her jeans, grabs her coat, sets the alarm, and leaves.

'What?' splutters Caroline. 'You? In love?'

'And why would that be so improbable?' I note that she doesn't continue her line of questioning about 'gangsters'.

'Maxim, the only thing you love is your dick.'

'That's not true!'

She cackles. And it's good to hear her laugh, but not so good that it's at my expense. Noticing my less-than-enthusiastic reaction, she tries to bring her amusement under control. 'Okay, so who's been on the sharp end of it?' she says indulgently.

'You don't have to be quite so crude.'

'That's not an answer.'

I gaze at her, and the warmth and humour slowly fade from her face.

'Who?' she presses me.

'Alessia.'

She frowns for a split second, and then her eyebrows shoot up. 'No!' She gasps. 'Your daily?'

'What do you mean, no?'

'Maxim. She's your fucking daily – literally!' And a dark cloud crosses her face; a storm is brewing.

I shift in my seat, irritated by her response. 'Well, she isn't my daily any more.'

'I knew it! That time when I met her. In your kitchen. You were so weird and attentive towards her.' She spits each word out like venom. She's horrified.

'Don't be so dramatic. That's not like you.'

'It *is* like me.'

'Since when?'

'Since my bloody husband upped and killed himself,' she hisses, her eyes glassy with animosity.

Shit.

She went there. She's using Kit's death in an argument.

I gulp down my shock and grief as we glare at each other, the air between us ripe with our unspoken thoughts.

Abruptly she turns her attention back to the fire, her contempt evident in the stubborn line of her chin. 'You should just fuck her out of your system,' she grumbles.

'I don't think I'll ever get her out of my system. I don't want to. I'm in love with her.' My words are softly spoken, and they hang in the air as I wait for Caroline's reaction.

'You're crazy.'

'Why?'

'You know why! She's your fucking *cleaner.*'

'Does that matter?'

'Yes, it matters!'

'No, it doesn't.'

'QED. You're crazy if you don't think it matters.'

'Crazy in love.' I shrug. It's the truth.

'With the help!'

'Caro, don't be such a snob. You can't choose who you love. Love chooses you.'

'Bloody hell!' She stands suddenly, looming over me. 'Don't give me some bullshit clichéd homily. She's just a grimy little freeloader, Maxim. Can't you see that?'

'Fuck off, Caroline!' I stand up, bristling with a sense of injustice, and we're practically nose to nose. 'You know nothing about her—'

'I know her type.'

'From where? From where do you Know. Her. Type. Lady Trevethick?' I enunciate each syllable, my words echoing off the blue-painted walls and framed artwork of this small drawing room.

I'm furious.

How dare she judge Alessia? Caroline, like me, has led a life of utter fucking privilege.

She blanches and steps back, looking at me as if I've just slapped her.

Fuck.

Mate! This is getting out of hand.

I run my fingers through my hair.

'Caroline, it's not the end of the world.'

'It is to me.'

'Why?'

She glares at me with a look that's both wounded and enraged. I shake my head. 'I don't understand. Why is this such a big deal to you?'

'What about *us*?' she asks, her voice wavering, her eyes wide.

'There is no "us".' God, she's so annoying. 'We fucked. We were grieving. We're still grieving. I've finally met someone who makes me step up and think about the life I lead, and—'

'But I thought—' She interrupts me, though her words dry up at the look I give her.

'What did you think? Us? Together? We had that! We tried that! And you chose my brother.' I'm shouting.

'We were young,' she whispers. 'And after Kit died . . .'

'No. No. No. You do not get to do that. Don't try to make me feel guilty – it takes two, Caroline. You made the first move when we were both empty and aching with grief. Maybe it was just an excuse. I don't know. But we're not a good combination. We never have been. We had our chance but you went off and fucked my brother. You claimed him and his title. I am not your fucking consolation prize.'

She gapes at me with horror writ large on her face.

Fuck.

'Get out!' she whispers.

'You're throwing me out of my own house?'

'You bastard! Get the fuck out. Go!' she screeches. Picking up an empty wine glass, she hurls it at me. It hits my thigh and falls to the wooden floor, where it shatters. We glare at each other in the ensuing and oppressive silence.

Tears pool in her eyes.

And I can bear it no more. I turn on my heel and exit, slamming the door behind me.

Alessia walks briskly down a side street towards the convenience store that she knows on Royal Hospital Road. It's a cold, dark night, and she pushes her hands deeper into her pockets, grateful for the warm coat that Maxim bought for her. A tingle runs up her spine, raising all the fine hairs on the back of her neck.

She glances behind her, suddenly uneasy. But under the street lamps all is quiet; she is alone, except for a woman walking a large dog on the other side of the road. Alessia shakes her head, chiding herself for overreacting. In Albania, at night, she would be wary of the djinn – the demons that roam the earth after sundown. But she knows that this is superstition. She's still jumpy after her encounter with Dante and Ylli. All the same, she picks up her pace and trots to the end of the street and around the corner to the Tesco Express.

The store is busier than usual, and she's grateful that there are many customers milling through the aisles. Grabbing a shopping basket, she walks to the fresh produce section and begins to browse through the vegetables on sale.

'Hello, Alessia. How have you been?' It takes a fraction of a second for her to realise that the calm, familiar voice is speaking in Albanian. It takes another fraction of a second for fear to grip her heart and her soul.

No! He's here!

I stand outside Trevelyan House trying to get a hold of my temper. Furious, I button up my coat against the February chill.

That did not go well.

Fisting my hands, I thrust them into my pockets.

I am so fucking angry right now. Too angry to go home to Alessia. I need to walk off my temper. Consumed by my thoughts and beyond pissed off, I turn right and stride up Chelsea Embankment.

How could Caroline think she and I had a chance?

We know each other too well. We're supposed to be friends. She *is* my best friend. And she's my brother's widow, for fuck's sake.

This is one fine bloody mess, dude.

But truth be told, I had no idea that she had designs on me beyond the occasional fuck.

Shit.

She's jealous.

Of Alessia.

Fuck.

My mind's a mess. I scowl as I cross Oakley Street and stalk past the Mercedes-Benz garage. Even the familiar grace and beauty of the *Boy with a Dolphin* statue on the corner cannot lift my mood. My anger is as dark as the night.

Alessia turns, her heart pounding, fear streaking like lightning through her veins. She's suddenly dizzy, her mouth dry. Anatoli is standing over her, invading her space. He's close. Too close. 'I have been looking for you,' he continues in their mother tongue. His full lips are twisted in a seemingly casual smile that doesn't touch his piercing, pale blue eyes. He scrutinises her, looking for answers. His chiselled face is thinner and his fair hair longer than she remembers. He looms over her, bundled up in what looks like an expensive Italian coat, intimidating her even now.

She starts to tremble as she wonders how the hell he found her. 'H-h-h-hello, Anatoli,' she stutters, her voice shaky and full of fear.

'Surely you can do better than that, *carissima*. No smile for the man you are going to marry?'

No. No. No.

Alessia's feet seem frozen to the shop floor as despair rises through her body. Her mind races – how can she escape? She is surrounded by shoppers going about their business, but she's never felt so stranded and alone. They are oblivious to what is happening in front of them.

Gently Anatoli strokes her cheek with a gloved finger, and her stomach recoils.

Don't touch me.

'I've come to take you home,' he says casually, as if they'd been talking only yesterday. Alessia stares at him, unable to speak. 'No kind words? You are not pleased to see me?' His eyes flash with a spark of irritation – and something more, something darker. Speculation? Admiration? A challenge accepted?

Bile rises in Alessia's throat, but she swallows it down. He grasps her arm at her elbow and squeezes. 'You are coming with me. I have spent a small fortune tracking you down. Your parents are devastated by your disappearance, and your father says you sent no word back to them that you were safe and well.'

Alessia is confused. This is not what happened. Does he know that her mother helped her? Is her mother okay? What did her mother say?

He tightens his hold on her arm. 'You should be ashamed of yourself. But we'll deal with that later. Right now let's go and collect your things, I'm taking you home.'

Chapter Twenty-Seven

I storm down Cheyne Walk.

Fuck it. I need a drink to help me calm the fuck down. I snatch a look at my watch. Alessia's not expecting me back until seven. I have time. I do an about-face and head back to Oakley Street, with the Coopers Arms firmly set in my mind as my destination.

The wind whips around me, but I don't feel the cold. I'm too angry. I cannot believe Caroline's reaction.

Or maybe I knew it would be bad.

Did I? That bad? Throwing-me-out-of-the-house bad?

Bollocks to that.

Usually the only person who makes me this angry is my mother.

Both of them are appalling snobs.

As am I.

Fuck.

I'm not! No.

What will Caroline say when I tell her I want to marry Alessia?

What will my mother say?

Marry someone with money, darling.

Kit chose wisely.

My dark mood grows darker still as I stomp into the night.

'I am not going with you,' Alessia says, her voice shaking and betraying her fear.

'Let's discuss this outside.' Anatoli tightens his grip on her elbow to the point of pain.

'No!' Alessia cries, and she wrenches her arm free from his hold. 'Don't touch me!'

He glares at her, his neck reddening and his eyes narrowing to icy pinpricks. 'Why are you behaving like this?'

'You know why.'

His mouth presses into a hard line. 'I came a long way for you. I am not leaving without you. You are promised to me by your father. Why are you dishonouring him?'

Alessia flushes.

'Is it the man?'

'Man?'

Alessia's heart beats faster. *Does he know about Maxim?*

'If it is, I'll kill him.'

'There is no man,' she whispers quickly, her fear spiralling out of control, sucking her down deeper into her despair.

'That friend of your mother. She sent an email. She said there was a man.'

Alessia is dumbfounded.

Magda?

Anatoli takes the basket from her and clasps her arm once more at the elbow.

'Let's go,' he says, and he leads her towards the automatic door, dumping the shopping basket on the nearby stack. Alessia, still reeling from his sudden appearance, allows him to lead her out into the street.

I stand at the bar nursing a Jameson. The amber liquid sears my throat, but it calms the violent storm as it pools in my stomach.

I'm a fool.

A priapic fool.

I knew that bedding Caroline was going to come back and bite me on the arse.

Fuck.

She's right, though. I've never thought beyond my dick. Until Alessia. And then that all changed.

Changed for the better.

I've never met anyone like her, someone possessing nothing – except her talent, her resourcefulness, and her beautiful face. I wonder what I would have made of my life if I'd been born in lowlier circumstances. Maybe I'd be a struggling musician – if I'd even learned to play. *Shit.* There's so much that I take for granted. I've been coasting through my life, everything handed to me on a plate, nothing affecting me, and doing exactly as I pleased. Now I have to work for a living, and several hundred people depend on me and my decisions. It's a daunting task and a huge responsibility that I have to accept if I want to maintain my lifestyle.

In the midst of this turmoil, I found Alessia, and in an indecently short time I've come to care for her more than I've ever cared for anyone. More than I've ever cared for myself. I love her, and she loves me and cares for me. She's a rare gift, a wonderful woman who needs me. And I need her. She's a woman who makes me step up my game.

A woman who makes me want to be a better man.

Isn't that what one wishes for in a life partner?

And then there's Caroline. As I stare despondently into my glass, I have to admit that I hate arguing with Caroline. She *is* my best friend. She has been forever. My world feels out of kilter if we're at loggerheads. It happened occasionally, when Kit was here to mediate, but she's never thrown me out of the house before.

What's worse is that I had meant to ask for her help sorting out Alessia's legal status in the UK. Caroline's father is a senior mandarin in the Home Office. If anyone can help, he can.

But that's out of the question for the moment.

I drain my glass. Caroline will come around.

I hope she'll come around.

I slam the glass on the counter and nod to the barman. It's 7:15, time to go. I need to get back to my girl.

Anatoli keeps a firm grip on Alessia's elbow as he marches her back up the street towards Maxim's building. 'You are his housekeeper?'

'Yes.' Her answer is clipped. She's trying not to panic, thinking through her options.

What if Maxim is home?

Anatoli threatened to kill him.

The thought of what Anatoli might do to Maxim is terrifying.

Magda must have written to her mother. *Why?* Alessia had begged her not to.

She has to get away, but Alessia knows she cannot outrun him.

Think, Alessia, think.

'So he is your employer?'

'Yes.'

'That is all?'

Alessia turns her head sharply. 'Of course!' Her tone is vehement.

He stops, pulling her roughly, and regards her through hooded eyes that gleam with suspicion in the muted glow of the street lamps. 'He's not had what's mine?'

It takes a moment for Alessia to realise what he's referring to. 'No,' she says quickly, breathlessly, blushing so that her cheeks heat up in spite of the frigid February air. Anatoli nods once, as if accepting her answer, and she feels a momentary pang of relief.

He follows her into the apartment. The alarm beeps, and Alessia is thankful that Maxim has not returned. Anatoli looks around the hallway. Out of the corner of her eye, she watches his brows rise. He's impressed.

'He has money, this man?' he mutters. She doesn't know if he's directing a question at her or not. 'And you live here?'

'Yes.'

'Where do you sleep?'

'In that room.' Alessia points to the door of the spare bedroom.

'Where does he sleep?'

She nods towards the master-bedroom door. Anatoli opens the door and marches inside. Alessia stands in the hallway, frozen with panic. Can she escape? But he returns moments later holding the small wastebasket. 'And this?' he growls.

Alessia manages to mobilise her features and screws her nose up in disgust at the condom in the bin. She shrugs, trying desperately for nonchalance. 'He has a girlfriend. They are out at the moment.'

He puts the basket down, seemingly satisfied with her answer. 'Get your things. I am parked outside.'

She stands motionless, her heart racing.

'Go. Now. I don't want to wait for him to return. I don't want a scene.' He undoes his coat, slips his hand inside his jacket, and pulls out a pistol. 'I am serious.'

Alessia blanches at the sight of the gun, and her breathing shallows with panic. He'll kill Maxim, of that she has no doubt. Her head begins to swim. Silently she begs her grandmother's God to keep Maxim away.

'I came here to rescue you. I don't know why you are here. We can talk about that later. But right now I want you to pack your things. We are leaving.'

Her fate is sealed. She will go with Anatoli. She must, to protect the man she loves. She has no choice. How did she think she could escape her father's *besa*?

Tears of helpless anger pool in Alessia's eyes as she heads into the spare bedroom. She packs quietly and efficiently, her hands shaking as rage and terror war within her. She wants to go before Maxim returns. She has to – to protect him.

Anatoli appears on the threshold. His eyes sweep over her and the empty room. 'You look very . . . different. Western. I like it.'

Alessia says nothing as she zips up the duffel bag, but for some reason she's grateful she's still wearing her coat.

'I don't know why you are crying.' He sounds genuinely perplexed.

'I like England. I would like to stay. I have been happy here.'

'You have had your fun. It is time to come home and accept your responsibilities, *carissima*.' Slipping the gun into his overcoat pocket, he grabs her bag.

'I have to leave a note,' she blurts.

'Why?'

'Because it is the right thing to do. My employer will worry. He has been good to me.' She almost chokes on her words.

Anatoli gazes at her, and she has no idea what he's thinking. Perhaps he's weighing what she's said. 'Okay,' he says eventually. He follows her into the kitchen, where a notepad and pen lie beside the phone. Alessia scribbles quickly, careful with her choice of words, hoping desperately that Maxim will read between them. She doesn't know how well – or if – Anatoli speaks or reads English. She cannot take the chance – she cannot write what she really wants to say.

Thank you for protecting me.

Thank you for showing me what love means.

But I cannot escape my destiny.

I love you. I will always love you. Until the day I die.

Maxim. My love.

'What does it say?'

She shows him and watches as his eyes scan the words. He nods. 'Good. Let's go.' She lays her new keys on top of the note. They'd been hers for only a few precious hours.

It's a still, cold night, and frost is beginning to form, sparkling ice-white under the light from the street lamps. When I turn the corner, the road is quiet except in the distance a man is closing the door of a black Mercedes S-Class that's parked in front of my building.

'Maxim!'

I turn to see Caroline running down the street towards me.

Caroline? What on earth?

But something about the man with the Mercedes pulls my attention back. The scene is odd, because he's walking around to the near side of the car. It's wrong. I'm missing something. My senses are suddenly on high alert: I can hear the crisp clip of Caroline's heels as she gets closer, I can smell winter and the Thames on the chilly breeze, and I strain my eyes to stare at the number plate of the car. Even from this distance, I can tell that it has foreign plates.

The man opens what must be the driver's door.

'Maxim!' Caroline calls again. I turn, and she runs up to me and throws her arms around my neck with such force that I have to put my arms around her to balance us both and stop us from falling to the ground. 'I'm so sorry,' she sobs.

I say nothing as my focus is drawn back to the car. The driver climbs in and slams the door while Caroline offers more apologies, but I ignore her as the indicator light starts blinking and the car pulls away from the curb into the light of a street lamp.

And then I see it. The small red-and-black flag of Albania on the number plate.

Alessia hears Maxim's name shouted down the street. She turns around in the passenger seat as Anatoli opens his door. Maxim is standing at the end of the block – and a fair-haired woman runs into his arms, hugging him.

Who is she?

He cradles her head.

No!

He holds her waist.

And she remembers – the woman wearing his shirt, standing in his kitchen.

Alessia, this is my friend and sister-in-law, Caroline.

Anatoli slams the door shut, making Alessia jump and forcing her to look ahead.

His sister-in-law? His married sister-in-law – and his brother is dead.

Caroline is his widow.

Alessia chokes back a sob.

This is where he has been. With Caroline. And now they are hugging in the street and he's holding her. The betrayal is swift and cruel, slicing Alessia into tiny pieces and shattering her faith in herself – and in him.

Him. Her Mister.

A tear oozes down her cheek as Anatoli starts the engine.

Smoothly he manoeuvres the car out of the parking space and drives away from the only happiness Alessia has ever known.

'Fuck!' I shout as dread spawns dark and deadly in my gut.

Caroline startles. 'What is it?'

'Alessia!' Abandoning Caroline, I race up the street, only to see the car disappear into the distance.

'Shit. Shit. Shit. Not again!' I grab my hair with both hands, helpless. Completely helpless.

'Maxim, what is it?' Caroline is now standing beside me outside the entrance to my building.

'They've got her!' I fumble for my keys to open the front door.

'Who? What are you talking about?'

'Alessia.' I crash through the front door and don't bother with the lift. Leaving Caroline at the foot of the stairs, I race up all six flights to my flat. When I unlock the door, the alarm starts beeping, confirming the worst of my fears.

Alessia is not here.

I silence the alarm and listen, hoping beyond hope that I have this wrong. Of course I hear nothing except the wind rattling the skylight in the hallway and my blood pulsing through my ears.

Frantically I start running through each room, my imagination shifting into overdrive. They have her. They have her again. My sweet, brave woman. What will those monsters do to her? Her clothes are not in my bedroom. Nor the spare room . . .

In the kitchen I find her keys and the note.

Mister Maxim
My betrothed is here and he is
taking me to my home in Albania.
Thank you for everything.
Alessia

'No!' I scream, overwhelmed by my despair. Picking up the phone, I hurl it at the wall. It shatters into pieces as I sink to the floor, my head in my hands.

For the second time in less than a week, I want to cry.

Chapter Twenty-Eight

'Maxim, what the fuck is going on?'

I take my head out of my hands, and Caroline is standing at the doorway. She looks windswept and unkempt, but calmer than she did a few minutes ago.

'He's taken her.' My voice is hoarse as I struggle to control my rage and despair.

'Who has?'

'Her fiancé.'

'Alessia has a fiancé?'

'It's complicated.'

She folds her arms and frowns, with what seems like genuine concern. 'You look shattered.'

I turn blazing eyes at her. 'I am.' Slowly I get to my feet. 'I think the woman I want to marry has just been kidnapped.'

'Marry?' Caroline blanches.

'Yes. Fucking marry!' My voice booms off the walls, and we glare at each other, the words hanging between us, ripe with regret and recrimination. Caroline closes her eyes and tucks her hair behind her ear. When she opens them, they are steely blue with resolve.

'Well, you'd better go after her, then,' she says.

Alessia stares unseeing out of the car window, drowning in tears she cannot stop. They flow freely as grief shrouds her misery.

Maxim and Caroline.

Caroline and Maxim.

Was what she experienced with him all a lie?

No! She can't bring herself to think that. He said he loved her – and she had believed him. She still wants to believe him, but of course it doesn't matter any more. She'll never see him again.

'Why are you crying?' Anatoli asks, but she ignores him. She doesn't care what he does to her now. Her heart is in shreds, and she knows that it will never heal. He switches on the radio, and an upbeat pop song blasts over the speakers, jarring Alessia's nerves. She suspects he's done it to distract himself from her silent sobbing. Anatoli turns the volume down and hands her a box of tissues. 'Here. Dry your eyes. Enough of this nonsense, or I'll give you something to cry about.'

She takes out a wad of tissues and continues to stare listlessly out of the window. She can't even bring herself to look at him.

She knows that she will die at his hands.

And there's nothing she can do.

Maybe she can escape. In Europe. Maybe she can choose how she dies . . . She closes her eyes and drifts into her own version of hell.

'Go after her?' I ask, my mind racing.

'Yes.' Caroline is emphatic. 'But I have to ask, what makes you think she's been kidnapped?'

'Her note.'

'Note?'

'Here.' I hand her the crumpled piece of paper and turn away, rubbing my face, trying to gather my splintered thoughts.

Where will he take her?

Did she go willingly?

No. She only had revulsion for him.

He tried to break her fucking fingers!

He must have forced her to go.

How the hell did he find her?

'Maxim, this note doesn't read like she's been kidnapped. Have you thought that maybe she's decided to go home?'

'Caro, she did not leave of her own free will. Trust me.'

I have to get her back.

Fuck.

I storm past Caroline and head into my drawing room.

'Fucking hell!'

'What now?'

'I don't have a working fucking computer!'

I need your passport,' Anatoli says as they speed through London's streets.

'What?'

'We are driving to the Eurotunnel train. I need your passport.'

Eurotunnel. No!

Alessia swallows. This is real. It's happening. He's taking her back to Albania.

'I don't have a passport.'

'What do you mean you don't have a passport?'

Alessia stares at him.

'Why, Alessia? Tell me! Did you forget to pack it?'

'No.'

'I don't understand.' He frowns.

'I was smuggled into this country by some men who took my passport.'

'Smuggled? Men?' His jaw clenches, and a muscle twitches in his cheek. 'What is going on?'

She's too tired and too broken to explain. 'I don't have a passport.'

'Fucking hell.' Anatoli smacks the steering wheel with his palm. Alessia flinches at the sound.

'Alessia, wake up.'

Something has changed. Alessia is confused.

Maxim?

She opens her eyes, and her heart sinks further into hell. She's with Anatoli, and the car is at a standstill, parked on the side of the road. It's dark, but by the glow of the headlights she can tell they are on a country road surrounded by frosted fields.

'Get out of the car,' he says. Alessia stares at him, and a small blossom of hope flowers in her chest.

He's going to leave her here. She can walk back. She's done it once before.

'Out,' he says more forcefully.

He opens his car door, climbs out and comes around to her door, opening it wide. Taking her hand, he hauls her out of her seat and leads her to the back of the car, where he opens the boot. It's empty but for a small rolling suitcase and her bag.

'You'll have to get in here.'

'What? No!'

'We have no choice. You don't have a passport. Get in.'

'Please, Anatoli. I hate the dark. Please.'

He frowns. 'Get in or I'll put you in.'

'Anatoli. Please. No. I don't like the dark!' He moves quickly, picking her up, dumping her in the boot, and slamming the lid shut before Alessia can fight back.

'No!' she shouts. It's pitch-dark inside. She starts to kick and scream as the darkness bleeds into her lungs, suffocating her like the black plastic bag from the last time she crossed the Channel.

She can't breathe. She can't breathe. She screams.

Not the dark. No. Not the dark. I hate the dark.

Seconds later the lid pops open and a blinding light shines in her face. She blinks. 'Here. Take this.' Anatoli hands her a torch. 'I don't know how long the battery will last. But we have no choice. Once we are on the train, I can open the boot.'

Stunned, Alessia takes the torch and holds it protectively to her chest. He moves her bag so that she can use it as a pillow, then shuffles out of his overcoat and lays it over her. 'You may get cold. I don't know if the heating works in here. Go back to sleep. And be quiet.' He gives her a stern look and shuts the boot once more.

Alessia clutches the torch and scrunches up her eyes, trying to regulate her breathing as the car starts to move. In her head she begins to play Bach's Prelude No. 6 in D Minor on repeat – the colours flashing brilliant hues of bright blue and turquoise in her mind – her fingers flexing, tapping out each note on the torch.

Alessia is shaken awake. She looks sleepily up at Anatoli, who towers over her as he holds open the lid of the boot. His breath is a foggy cloud around him, lit by a solitary light from the parking lot. His face is stark and ashen. 'What took you so long to wake up? I thought you were unconscious!' He sounds relieved.

Relieved?

'We're going to stay the night here,' he says.

Alessia blinks, huddling down into the coat. It's cold. Her head is fuzzy from crying. Her eyes are swollen. And she doesn't want to spend the night with him.

'Out,' he snaps, and extends his hand. Sighing, Alessia sits up. The cold wind whips around her, blowing her hair across her face. Stiffly she clambers out of the car, refusing Anatoli's help. She doesn't want his hands on her. He reaches past her for his coat, which he shuffles on. He grabs his case and hands her the bag containing her clothes before shutting the boot. The parking lot is deserted except for two other cars. Not far away stands a squat, nondescript building that Alessia assumes is a hotel.

'Follow me.' He walks briskly towards the entrance. Alessia quietly sets her bag on the ground, turns and runs.

I stare at the ceiling, my mind churning through all the plans I've put in place since Alessia was taken. Tomorrow I'll fly to Albania, and Tom Alexander will accompany me. Annoyingly, it's too short notice for a private jet, so we're flying scheduled. Thanks to Magda, we have the address of Alessia's parents. It's also thanks to Magda that Alessia's fiancé found her. I don't dwell on this titbit of information, because it makes me incandescent with fury.

Calm down, mate.

We'll pick up a car, drive to Tirana and overnight there at the Plaza hotel. Tom has arranged for us to meet up with a translator who will come with us to Kukës the following day.

And we'll stay there for however long it takes. We'll wait for Alessia and her kidnapper.

Not for the first time this evening, I wish I'd bought her that phone. It's so frustrating not being able to contact her.

I hope she's okay.

I close my eyes, imagining horrible scenarios.

My sweet girl.

My sweet, sweet Alessia.

I'm coming to get you. I've got you.

I love you.

Alessia flees blindly into the dark, fuelled by her adrenaline rush. She's running over the asphalt, then onto rough grass. Behind her she hears a shout. It's him. She hears his footsteps pounding on the frozen ground. Getting closer.

Closer still.

Then silence.

He's on the grass.

No.

She pushes herself harder, hoping that her feet will carry her away from him. But he grabs her, and she's falling. *Falling.* Tackled to the ground so forcefully that she scrapes her face on the frosted grass. Anatoli lies on top of her back, panting heavily. 'You stupid bitch. Where the hell do you think you're going to go at this time?' he hisses in her ear. He kneels up and drags her over until she's lying on her back, then sits astride her. He slaps her hard across her face snapping her head to the side. He leans down over her, puts his hand on her throat, and squeezes.

He's going to kill her.

She doesn't struggle.

She stares at him. Her eyes on his. In their frigid blue, she sees the darkness of his heart. His hate. His anger. His inadequacy. His hand tightens, and he's choking the life from her. Her head begins to swim. She reaches up and clutches his arm.

This is how I am going to die . . .

She sees her end. Here. Somewhere in France at the hands of this violent man. She wants it. She welcomes it. She doesn't want to live a life in fear, like her mother. 'Kill me,' she mouths.

Anatoli growls something incomprehensible – and lets go.

Alessia takes a huge breath and puts her hands up to her

throat, coughing and spluttering, her body overruling her, fighting for life, sucking in precious air, and reviving her.

She gasps. 'This is why I don't want to marry you.' Her voice is husky and small, forcing sound through her bruised larynx.

Anatoli grabs her jaw and looms over her, his face close enough for her to feel his warm breath on her cheek. '"A woman is a sack, made to endure",' he snarls, with a cruel glint in his eye.

Alessia gazes at him as hot tears scald the sides of her face and pool in her ears. She hadn't been aware that she was crying. He is quoting from the ancient Kanun of Lek Dukagjini, the primitive feudal code that governed the mountain tribes in the north and east of her country for centuries. Its legacy lingers. Anatoli sits back.

'I would be better off dead than with you.' Her voice is emotionless.

He frowns, nonplussed. 'Don't be ridiculous.' He slowly rises, standing over her. 'Get up.'

Alessia coughs once more and staggers painfully to her feet. He clasps her elbow and marches her back to where her abandoned bag sits in the parking lot. He picks it up and grabs his own suitcase several steps further on.

He makes short work of checking in. Alessia hangs back while he hands over his passport and credit card. Anatoli speaks fluent French. She's too weary and too sore to be surprised.

Their spartan suite has two main rooms. The living room has dark grey furniture and a small kitchenette to the side. The wall behind the sofa is painted in cheerful mismatched stripes. Through the open door beyond, Alessia spies two double beds. She breathes a sigh of relief. Two beds. Not one. Two.

Anatoli dumps her bag on the floor, shoves off his coat, and throws it on the sofa. Alessia watches him, listening to the thud of her pulse thrumming in her ears. In the silence of the room, it's deafening.

What now? What will he do?

'Your face is a mess. Go and clean yourself up.' Anatoli points to the bathroom.

'And whose fault is that?' Alessia snaps.

He glowers at her, and for the first time she notices his red-rimmed eyes and his pale complexion. He looks exhausted. 'Just do it.' He even sounds exhausted. She heads into the bedroom, then the bathroom, slamming the door with such force that the loud bang makes her jump.

The bathroom is small and dingy, but in the insipid glow of the light above the mirror Alessia sees her reflection and gasps. One side of her face is red from his slap, and on the other there's a graze on her cheekbone from where she hit the ground. Around her throat there are vivid red marks in the shape of his fingers. Tomorrow they will be bruises. But what shocks her most is the lifeless eyes staring back at her from beneath swollen lids.

She is dead already.

With swift, automatic movements, she washes her face, wincing as the soapy water touches the scrape. She pats herself dry with a towel.

When she re-enters the living room, Anatoli has hung up his jacket and is searching through the minibar.

'Are you hungry?' he asks.

She shakes her head.

He pours himself a drink – Scotch, she thinks – and downs the entire glass in one gulp, closing his eyes to savour the taste. When he opens them again, he seems calmer. 'Take off your coat.'

Alessia doesn't move.

He pinches the bridge of his nose. 'Alessia, I do not want to fight with you. I am tired. It's warm in here. Tomorrow we will go back out into the cold. Please take your coat off.'

Reluctantly she removes her coat as Anatoli stares at her, making her feel self-conscious. 'I like you in jeans,' he says, but

Alessia can't look at him. She feels like a prize sheep on the auction block as he appraises her. She hears the rattle of bottles, but this time Anatoli produces a Perrier out of the fridge. 'Here, you must be thirsty.' He pours it into a glass and offers it to her. After a moment's hesitation, she takes it and drinks.

'It's almost midnight. We should sleep.'

Her eyes meet his, and he smirks. 'Ah, *carissima*, I should make you mine after the stunt you pulled outside.' He reaches for her chin, and she flinches as his fingers graze her skin.

Don't touch me.

'You are so beautiful,' he murmurs, as if he's speaking only to himself. 'But I don't have the energy to fight you. And I think it would be a fight. Yes?'

She closes her eyes, battling a wave of revulsion that unsettles her stomach. Anatoli chuckles, and his lips caress her forehead in a soft kiss. 'You will grow to love me,' he whispers. He picks up their bags and takes them into the bedroom.

Never.

The man is delusional.

Her heart belongs to another. It will always belong to Maxim.

'Go and change into your nightclothes,' he says.

She shakes her head. 'I will sleep like this.' She doesn't trust him.

Anatoli cocks his head, his expression severe. 'No. Take your clothes off. You won't run if you're naked.'

'No.' She crosses her arms.

'No you won't run, or no you won't take your clothes off?'

'Both.'

He exhales, frustrated and tired. 'I don't believe you. But I also don't understand why you are running.'

'Because you are an angry, violent man, Anatoli. Why would I want to spend my life with you?' Her voice holds no emotion.

He shrugs. 'I don't have the energy for this conversation. Get into bed.' Seizing the moment, in case he changes his mind, she scuttles into the bedroom. There she slips off her boots and huddles on top of the bed further away, turning her back on him.

She listens as he moves around the room, undressing and folding his clothes. Her anxiety mounts with each movement and with each sound. After an eternity the soft slap of his footsteps pad on the floor as he approaches her bed. He stands beside her, his breathing shallow, and she feels his eyes on her. Everywhere. She squeezes hers shut, pretending to sleep.

He tuts, and she hears the rustle of sheets and blankets, and to her surprise he drapes a blanket over her. He switches off the light, plunging the room into darkness, and the bed dips as he lies down.

No! He should be in the other bed.

She stiffens, but he's beneath the covers while she's on top. He puts his arm around her and shuffles closer. 'I will know if you leave the bed,' he says, and he kisses her hair.

She recoils and clutches her little gold cross.

Soon his even breathing tells her that he's asleep.

Alessia stares into the darkness she fears and wishes it would swallow her up. Her tears refuse to fall. She's all cried out.

What is Maxim doing?

Is he missing me?

Is he with Caroline?

She sees Caroline in his arms as Maxim holds her close, and Alessia wants to scream.

Alessia is too warm, and someone is murmuring in the background. She cracks one eye open momentarily, bewildered as to where she might be.

No. No. No.

A wash of fear and despair fills her with anguish when she remembers.

Anatoli.

He's on the phone in the other room. Alessia sits up and listens.

'She's okay . . . No. Far from it . . . She's reluctant to return home. I don't understand it.' He's talking to someone in Albanian, and he sounds confused and upset. 'I don't know . . . Maybe . . . There was a man. Her employer. The one who was mentioned in the email.'

He's talking about Maxim!

'She says she is just his cleaner, but I don't know, Jak.'

Jak! He's talking to my father!

'I love her so much. She's so beautiful.'

What? He doesn't know the meaning of the word 'love'!

'She hasn't told me yet. But I want to know, too. Why would she leave?' His voice cracks. He's emotional.

I left because of you!

She left to get as far away from him as she could.

'Yes. I will bring her back to you. I will make sure she's unharmed.'

Alessia places her hands on her still-tender throat. What the hell? *Unharmed?*

He's a liar.

'She's safe with me.'

Ha! Alessia almost wants to laugh at the supreme irony of that statement.

'Tomorrow night . . . Yes . . . Goodbye.' She hears him move about the room, and suddenly he appears at the door wearing only his trousers and an undershirt.

'You're awake?' he says.

'Sadly, it would appear so.'

He gives her an odd look and chooses to ignore her comment. 'There is some breakfast for you out here.'

'I'm not hungry.' Alessia feels reckless and bold. She doesn't care any more. Now that Maxim is out of harm's way, she can behave as she wishes.

Anatoli rubs his chin and regards her thoughtfully. 'Suit yourself,' he says. 'We leave in twenty minutes. We have a long way to go.'

'I'm not going with you.'

He rolls his eyes. '*Carissima*, you have no choice. Don't make this painful for both of us. Don't you want to see your father and mother?'

Mama.

His eyebrows rise a fraction. He's noticed the chink in her armour and, sensing victory, swoops in for the kill. 'She misses you.'

She rises out of bed and sullenly grabs her bag and, skirting him as widely as she can, heads into the bathroom to wash and change.

Under the shower an idea begins to form in her head.

She has her money. Maybe she *should* return to Albania. She can get a new passport – and a visa – and return to England.

Maybe I should stay alive.

And as she briskly towel-dries her hair, she feels a new sense of purpose.

She will get back to Maxim. And see for herself. See if everything they shared was a lie.

Chapter Twenty-Nine

Alessia dozes in the front seat. They are on an autobahn travelling way too fast. They've been driving for hours, through France, through Belgium, and she thinks they're now somewhere in Germany. It's a cold, wet, winter day, and the landscape is flat and bleak, reflecting Alessia's mood. No. She feels more than bleak – she's desolate.

Anatoli seems grimly determined to get to Albania as fast as possible. At the moment he's listening to a German talk show on the radio, which Alessia doesn't understand. The monotony of the voices, the constant rumble of road noise and the dreary countryside are all dulling her senses. Sleep is what she wants. When she's asleep, her anguish is a low hum, like static on the radio. It's not the searing pain that tears at her heart when she's conscious.

She turns her mind to Maxim.

And the pain amplifies.

Stop. It's too much.

She looks through tired eyes at her 'betrothed', studying him.

His face is hardened in concentration as the Mercedes eats up the miles. His complexion is fair, betraying his northern Italian roots, his nose straight, his lips full, and his blond hair, uncommon in her town, is long and unkempt. Alessia can look at him dispassionately and judge him to be a handsome man. But those lips have a cruel twist to them, and those eyes are piercing and cold when he's glaring at her.

She remembers when she first met him. How charming he'd been. Her father had told her that Anatoli was an international businessman. During that first meeting, he'd seemed so dashing and knowledgeable. He was well travelled, and she'd listened rapt to his stories of Croatia, Italy and Greece – these faraway places. She'd been shy, but pleased that her father had selected such an erudite man for her.

Little had she known.

After she had met him a few times, she started to see flashes of the man he really was. His irrational anger at the local children who'd surrounded his car out of curious wonder when he came to visit, his temper when arguing with her father about politics, and his sly admiration when her father scolded her mother for spilling some raki. The signs were there, and he'd rebuked Alessia a few times, too, but his true nature had been constrained by social etiquette.

It was at a local dignitary's wedding, where Alessia was playing the piano, that Anatoli had finally revealed his dark side. Two young men, whom she had known at school, lingered when she finished playing. They flirted with her until Anatoli managed to usher her into a side room, away from them and the festivities. Alessia, secretly thrilled, had thought he wanted to steal a kiss, since it was the first time they'd been alone together. But no – Anatoli was furious. He slapped her hard across her face, twice. It was a shock, even though living with her father had prepared her for physical anger.

The second time it happened, she was at the school. A young man came to ask her a couple of questions after her recital. Anatoli chased him away and dragged her into the cloakroom. There he hit her a couple of times and grabbed her hands and pulled back her fingers and threatened to break them if he ever caught her flirting again. She'd begged him to stop, and mercifully he had, but he'd pushed her to the floor and left her sobbing in that room, alone.

That first time, she kept his attack a secret. She excused it. It was a one-off. She had misbehaved. She had encouraged the young men by smiling at them.

The second time Alessia was devastated.

She'd thought that maybe she could break the cycle of violence that beset her mother, but it was her mother who'd found her while she lay curled up, sobbing and trembling, on the floor.

I don't want you to go through your life with a violent man.

They'd wept together.

And her mother had taken action.

But it was all for naught.

Now here she is – with *him*.

Anatoli gives her a sideways look. 'What is it?'

Alessia averts her eyes, ignoring him, and stares out of the window.

'We should stop. I'm hungry, and you've not eaten,' he says.

She continues to ignore him, though hunger claws at her stomach, reminding her of her six-day walk to Brentford.

'Alessia!' he barks, making her jump.

She turns to him. 'What?'

'I'm talking to you.'

She shrugs. 'You've kidnapped me. I don't want to be with you, and you expect conversation?'

'I didn't know you could be this disagreeable,' Anatoli mutters.

'I'm just getting started.'

Anatoli's mouth twitches – and to her surprise he seems

amused. 'I can say this about you, *carissima*, you are not boring.' He flicks the indicator, and they pull off the autobahn into a service area. 'There's a café here. Let's get something to eat.'

Anatoli places a tray bearing a black coffee, several sachets of sugar, a bottle of water and a cheese baguette in front of her. 'I cannot believe *I* am serving *you*,' he utters as he sits. 'Eat.'

'Welcome to the twenty-first century,' Alessia retorts, folding her arms in an act of defiance.

His jaw hardens. 'I will not tell you again.'

'Oh, do your worst, Anatoli. I'm not eating. You bought it, you eat it,' she snaps, ignoring her growling stomach. His eyes flare in surprise, but he presses his full lips together, and Alessia suspects he's trying not to smile. He sighs, reaches over, picks up her baguette, and takes a theatrically large bite out of it. With his mouth full, he looks both absurd and ridiculously pleased with himself, so much so that an involuntary snicker escapes from Alessia.

Anatoli smiles – a proper smile that travels all the way to his eyes. They regard her warmly, and he no longer tries to hide his amusement. 'Here,' he says, and he hands her the remaining part of the baguette. Her stomach chooses this moment to rumble, and when he hears it, his smile broadens. She eyes the baguette and him and sighs. She's so hungry. Against her better judgement, she takes it from him and begins to eat.

'That's better,' he says, and starts on his own meal.

'Where are we?' Alessia asks after a few bites.

'We've just passed Frankfurt.'

'When will we reach Albania?'

'Tomorrow. I hope to be home by tomorrow afternoon.'

They eat the rest of their food in silence.

'Finish up. I want to get going. Do you need to use the restroom?' Anatoli stands over her, keen to move on. Alessia takes her coffee without adding sugar.

Like Maxim.

It's bitter but she downs it anyway and grabs her water bottle. The service station, with its large parking lot and smell of diesel fumes, is hauntingly familiar and reminiscent of the journey she made with Maxim – but the difference is, she wanted to be with Maxim. Alessia's heart aches. She is getting further and further away from him.

I'm sitting in the British Airways business-class lounge at Gatwick Airport, waiting for the afternoon flight to Tirana. Tom is leafing through *The Times* and sipping a glass of champagne while I'm brooding. I've been in a state of high anxiety since Alessia was taken from me.

Maybe she went with him willingly.

Maybe she's changed her mind about us.

I don't want to believe that, but doubt is creeping into my mind.

It's insidious.

If that's what's happened, at least I'll get to confront her about her change of heart. To distract myself from my unsettling thoughts, I snap and upload a few photos to my Instagram. Once that's done, I think back over the morning's events.

First I'd bought Alessia a phone, which is now in my backpack. I'd met with Oliver and gone through a quick agenda of all estate business; to my relief everything seemed to be running just fine. I'd signed the papers required by the Crown Office for my inclusion onto the Roll of the Peerage, with Mr Rajah, my solicitor, acting as my witness. I'd given both men a redacted version of the weekend's events with Alessia and asked Rajah to recommend a lawyer specialising in immigration services, so we could begin the process of securing some kind of visa for Alessia to be in the UK.

Afterwards, on a whim, I'd visited my bank in Belgravia,

where the Trevethick Collection is secured. If I find Alessia and all is not lost, I will ask her to marry me. Over the centuries my ancestors have amassed quite a haul of fine jewellery crafted by the most prominent artisans of their day. When the collection is not on loan to museums around the world, it is safely stored in the bowels of Belgravia.

I needed a ring, one that would do justice to Alessia's beauty and talent. There were two in the collection that might have been suitable, but I chose the 1930s Cartier platinum-and-diamond ring that my grandfather, Hugh Trevelyan, bestowed on my grandmother, Allegra, in 1935. It's an exquisite, simple and elegant ring: 2.79 carats and currently valued at forty-five thousand pounds.

I hope Alessia likes it. If all goes to plan, she'll return to the UK wearing it – as my fiancée.

I pat my pocket yet again, checking that the ring is safe, and scowl at Tom, who's stuffing his face with nuts. He looks up. 'Hang in there, Trevethick. I can tell you're fretting. She'll be fine. We'll rescue the girl.' He'd insisted on accompanying me when I called him and told him what had happened. He's left one of his guys to keep watch on Magda, and he's here with me. Tom loves an adventure. It's why, back in the day, he joined the army. He's up on his metaphorical white charger, ready for the fray.

'I hope so,' I answer. Will Alessia see us that way – as rescuers, not as an inconvenience? I don't know. I'm itching to get on the plane and get to her parents' home. I have no idea what I'll find there, but I hope I find my girl.

'Why did you leave Albania?' Anatoli asks when they're back on the autobahn. His voice is soft, and Alessia wonders if he's trying to lull her into a false sense of security. She's not that stupid.

'You know why. I've told you.' Though as the words leave her mouth, she realises she doesn't know what story he's been told. Perhaps she can embellish the truth. It might make it easier on her and on her mother. But it depends on what Magda said. 'What did my mother's friend say?'

'Your father intercepted the email. He saw your name and asked me to read it for him.'

'What did it say?'

'That you were alive and well and were going away to work for a man.'

'Is that all?'

'More or less.'

So Magda had not mentioned Dante and Ylli. 'What did my father say?'

'He asked me to come and get you.'

'And my mother?'

'I didn't speak to your mother. This does not concern her.'

'Of course it concerns her! Stop being prehistoric!'

He gives her a sideways look, taken aback by her outburst. 'Prehistoric?'

'Yes. You are a dinosaur. She deserves to be consulted.'

Anatoli's puzzled frown speaks volumes; he has no idea what she's talking about. Alessia continues, warming to her subject, 'You are a man from another century. From another time. You and all the men like you. In other countries your Neanderthal attitude to women would be unacceptable.'

He shakes his head. 'You have been in the West too long, *carissima*.'

'I like the West. My grandmother was from England.'

'Is that why you went to London?'

'No.'

'Why, then?'

'Anatoli, you know why. I want to make it clear to you. I don't want to marry you.'

'You will come around, Alessia.' He waves his hand as if to brush off her rejection as trivial.

Alessia huffs, feeling aggrieved but feeling brave, too. After all, what can he do while he's driving? 'I want to choose who I marry. It's a simple enough request.'

'You would dishonour your father?'

Alessia flushes. Of course her attitude – her defiance, her *wilfulness* – brings great shame to her family.

She turns back to the window, but in her mind this conversation is not over. Perhaps she can appeal to her father once more.

She allows herself a moment to think about Maxim, and her grief rises, raw and real. Her bravado evaporates, and her mood plummets once more into despair. Her heart is beating but empty.

Will she ever see *him* again?

Somewhere in Austria, Anatoli stops at the services again, but this time only for diesel. He insists Alessia accompany him into the store. Reluctantly she trails after him, oblivious to her surroundings.

Back on the autobahn, he announces, 'We'll be in Slovenia soon. When we get to Croatia, you'll need to go into the boot.'

'Why?'

'Because Croatia is not part of the Schengen Agreement, and there's a border.'

Alessia blanches. She hates being in the boot. She loathes the dark.

'When we stopped for petrol, I bought more batteries for the torch.'

She glances at Anatoli, and he catches her eye. 'I know you

don't like it. But it can't be helped.' He turns his attention back to the road. 'And it shouldn't be for so long this time. When we stopped in Dunkirk, I thought you were unconscious from carbon monoxide poisoning or something.' He frowns, and if Alessia is not mistaken, she would swear he's concerned. This afternoon at the restaurant, he had regarded her with warmth.

'What is it?' he asks, snapping her out of her reverie.

'I'm not used to concern from you,' she states. 'Only violence.'

Anatoli's hands tighten on the steering wheel. 'Alessia, if you don't do as you're told, there are consequences. I expect you to be a traditional Gheg wife. That's all you need to know. I think you have become too opinionated while you've been in London.'

She doesn't answer him but turns away and stares out at the passing countryside, nursing her misery as they drive on into the afternoon.

Our flight lands in Tirana at 20:45 local time in pouring, icy rain. Tom and I are travelling with hand baggage only, so we go straight through customs and emerge into a modern, well-lit airport terminal. I don't know what I'd been expecting, but the place looks like any small airport in Europe, with all the facilities one might need.

Our rental car, on the other hand, is a revelation. My travel agent had warned me that there were no prestige cars for hire, so I find myself at the wheel of a car whose make I have never heard of: a Dacia. It's the most basic and analogue car I've ever driven, though it does have a USB port in the radio so we can plug in my iPhone and use Google Maps. I'm surprised to find myself liking the car; it's practical and sturdy. Tom christens it *Dacy*, and after some negotiation at the exit to the car park and a small bribe to the parking attendant, we are off.

Driving at night – in torrential rain, on the wrong side of the road, in a country where private car ownership was unheard of until the mid-1990s – is a challenge. But forty minutes later, Dacy and Google Maps get us in one piece to the Plaza hotel in the centre of Tirana.

'Fuck, that was hairy,' Tom announces as we pull up in front of the hotel.

'Damn right.'

'Though I've driven in worse conditions,' he mutters. I turn off the ignition, knowing that he's making an oblique reference to his time in Afghanistan. 'How far did you say this girl's hometown is?'

'Her name's Alessia,' I growl, for what feels like the tenth time, and wonder about the wisdom of agreeing to let Tom accompany me. 'I think it's about a three-hour drive.' He's a good man in a pinch, but diplomacy has never been his strong point.

'Sorry, old man. Alessia.' He taps his forehead. 'I've got it. I hope the rain holds off tomorrow. Let's check in and find somewhere to have a drink.'

In the boot of the Mercedes, Alessia clutches the flashlight torch as the car lurches to a stop. They must have reached the border with Croatia. She closes her eyes, pulls Anatoli's coat over her head, and switches off the torch. She doesn't want to get caught. She just wants to get home. She hears voices – they are quiet and in control. And the car starts to move. She breathes a sigh of relief and flicks on the bright beam once more. She's reminded of the makeshift hideaway beneath the sheets that she shared with Maxim and the little dragon. They were sitting and talking on his vast, baronial bed, their knees touching and . . . Her pain is swift and sudden. She aches to the bottom of her soul.

Before long the Mercedes slows and stops. The engine idles, and moments later Anatoli opens the boot. Alessia switches off the torch and sits up, blinking in the darkness.

They are on a deserted rural road; a small bungalow squats darkly opposite them. Anatoli is lit by the car's tail lights, his face cast in demonic red, his breath an ominous cloud around him. He offers his hand to help her out, and because she's tired and stiff, she accepts. She stumbles as she steps out of the boot, and he yanks her forward, into his arms.

'Why are you so hostile?' he breathes against her temple. Tightening his hold around her waist, he grasps the back of her head with his hand and grips her hair. In spite of the cold, his breath is hot and heavy between them. As Alessia registers what's happening, his lips swoop down hard on hers. He tries to force his tongue into her mouth, and she struggles, fear and loathing careening through her body in a potent mix. She pushes ineffectually at his arms and frantically twists, trying to struggle out of his hold. He leans back to look down at her, and before she can stop herself, she slaps him across his face, her palm ringing from the blow, and he retreats. Shocked. She's breathing gulps of air, adrenaline coursing through her veins, chasing away her fear and leaving anger in its stead. Anatoli glares at her, rubbing his cheek, and before she can blink, he slaps her hard across her face. Once. Twice. Her head jerks from the right to the left, and she staggers at the force of each blow. With little care he picks her up and drops her back into the boot so that she hits her shoulder, her backside and her head. And before she can protest, he slams the lid shut.

'Until you learn to behave and be civil, you can stay in there!' he shouts. Alessia clutches her throbbing head as anger burns in her throat and behind her eyes.

This is her life now.

I take a sip of Negroni. Tom and I are in a bar next door to the hotel. It's contemporary, sleek and comfortable, and the staff are friendly and attentive, but not overly so. What's more, they serve a bloody good Negroni.

'I think we fell on our feet with this place,' Tom says as he takes another slug of his drink. 'I don't know what I was expecting. Goats and wattle-and-daub shacks, I think.'

'Yes. I had the same idea. This place exceeds all expectations.'

He eyes me speculatively. 'Forgive me, Trevethick. But I have to know. Why are you doing this?'

'What?'

'Chasing this girl all over Europe? Why?'

'Love,' I state, as if it's the most understandable reason in the world.

Why doesn't he get this?

'Love?'

'Yep. It's that simple.'

'For your daily?'

I roll my eyes. What is it about the fact that Alessia used to clean for me? *And still wants to clean for me!* 'Just deal with it, Tom. I'm going to marry her.'

He splutters into his drink, spitting red liquid over the table, and I wonder again at the wisdom of bringing him on this journey. 'Steady on, Trevethick. She's a pretty girl, from what I remember, but is that wise?'

I shrug. 'I love her.'

He shakes his head, bemused.

'Tom, just because you haven't got the nerve to do the decent thing and pop the fucking question to Henrietta – who is a saint to put up with you – don't judge.'

He frowns, and a pugnacious gleam lights up his eyes. 'Listen, old boy, I wouldn't be doing my duty as a friend if I didn't state the fucking obvious.'

'The fucking obvious?'

'You're in mourning, Maxim.' His voice is surprisingly gentle. 'Have you considered that this sudden infatuation is part of your way of dealing with your brother's death?'

'This has nothing to do with Kit, and I'm not fucking infatuated. You don't know her like I do. She's an exceptional woman. And I've known countless women. She's different. She's not bothered by trivial shit . . . She's smart. Funny. Courageous. And you should hear her play the piano. She's a fucking genius.'

'Really?'

'Yes. This is the real deal. I'm seeing the world in a whole different light since I met her. And questioning my place in it.'

'Steady on.'

'No, Tom. You steady on. She needs me. It's good to be needed, and I need her.'

'But that's no basis for a relationship.'

I grit my teeth. 'It's not just that. You've fought for your country. You now run a successful business. What the fuck have I ever done?'

'Well, you're about to take your place in the history of the Trevethick family, and preserve that legacy for generations to come.'

'I know.' I sigh. 'It's daunting, and I want someone I trust beside me. Someone who loves me. Someone who appreciates me for more than my wealth and title. Is that too much to ask?'

He frowns.

'You've found that person,' I add. 'And you take Henrietta for granted.'

He exhales and stares down at the remains of his drink.

'You're right,' he mumbles. 'I love Henry. I should do the decent thing.'

'You should.'

He nods. 'Okay. Let's order another.' He signals to the waiter for another round of drinks, and I wonder if I'll have to deal with this level of doubt about Alessia from all my friends . . . from my family.

'Make them doubles,' I call.

Alessia wakes and realises the car has stopped. The engine is off. The lid of the boot lifts, and Anatoli is standing over her once more. 'Maybe you have learned some manners?'

Alessia gives him a venomous look and sits up, rubbing her fists in her eyes.

'Get out. We'll spend the night here.' He doesn't offer her his hand this time but reaches in and grabs his coat from her and slips it on. The biting wind wraps around her, and she shivers. She aches everywhere, but she climbs out of the boot and, feeling gloomy, stands to one side, waiting for his next move.

Anatoli's gaze follows her, and his lips press into a thin, angry line. 'Feeling a little more docile now?' he sneers.

Alessia says nothing.

He snorts and reaches for their luggage. Alessia glances around. They are in a parking lot in the centre of a city. An imposing hotel looms in the near distance. It's several storeys high and lit up like a Hollywood movie with the word WESTIN crowning its facade. Abruptly Anatoli grabs her hand and tugs her towards the entrance. He doesn't break his stride, so she has to scurry to keep up.

The foyer is all marble, mirrors and modernity, and Alessia spots the discreet sign: they are in the Westin Zagreb. Anatoli checks them into the hotel in what sounds like flawless Croatian, and a few minutes later they are riding up to the fifteenth floor in the elevator.

Anatoli has booked them a luxurious suite that is furnished in creams and browns. There's a couch, a desk and a small table, and through the sliding doors Alessia can see one bed.

One.

No!

She remains standing, tired and helpless, just within the threshold.

Anatoli shrugs off his coat and throws it onto the couch. 'Are you hungry?' he asks, opening the doors of the dresser beneath the TV. Eventually he finds the minibar. 'Well?' he snaps.

Alessia nods.

Anatoli motions with his head towards a leather-bound book on the desk. 'We'll get room service. Choose something. And take off your coat.' Alessia picks up the book and leafs through the pages to the in-room-dining section. The entries are in Croatian and English; she scans the selections and immediately chooses the most expensive item on the menu. She has no compunction about having Anatoli spend his money. She frowns, remembering how she resisted Maxim's attempts to pay . . . Anatoli has retrieved two small bottles of Scotch and is unscrewing the top from each in turn. Yes, Alessia has no compunction at all. She's a kidnap victim, and he's meted out enough physical abuse on her body already. He owes her. But with Maxim . . . the balance was all wrong. She had owed him. So much. Her Mister. She lets him slip quietly from her mind, to be mourned later.

'I'll have the New York steak,' she declares. 'With an extra salad. And fries. And a glass of red wine.' Anatoli turns to regard her with surprise.

'Wine?'

'Yes. Wine.'

He considers her for a moment. 'You have become very Western.'

She stands taller. 'I would like a glass of French red wine.'

'French now?' He raises a brow.

'Yes.' And as an afterthought she adds, 'Please.'

'Okay, we'll get a bottle.' He lifts his shoulder in a nonchalant shrug, and he sounds *so reasonable.*

But he's not. He's a monster.

He pours both whiskies into a glass and watches her as he reaches for the phone. 'You know, you're a very attractive woman, Alessia.'

She freezes. *What now?*

'Are you still a virgin?' His voice is soft, cajoling.

She gasps and feels a little faint. 'Of course,' she breathes, attempting to look outraged and embarrassed at once.

He cannot know the truth.

His gaze hardens. 'You seem different.'

'I am. I've had my eyes opened.'

'By someone?'

'Just . . . by my experiences,' she whispers, wishing she had never responded. She's antagonising a snake.

Anatoli dials room service and orders their meal while Alessia removes her coat and sits down on the couch to watch him warily. When he finishes his call, he grabs the TV remote, switches on the local news, and sits at the desk with his drink. For a while he watches the news, ignoring her, occasionally sipping his whisky. Alessia is relieved that his attention is elsewhere. She watches the TV as well, trying to understand the newsreader, and she catches a few words. She concentrates; she doesn't want her mind to wander. It will only wander back to Maxim, and she refuses to grieve his loss in front of Anatoli.

When the programme is over, he turns his attention back to Alessia. 'So you ran away from me?' he says.

Is he talking about yesterday?

'When you left Albania.' He takes a last swig of Scotch.

'You threatened to break my fingers.'

He rubs his chin, thoughtful for a moment. 'Alessia . . . I—' He stops.

'I don't want excuses, Anatoli. There's no excuse for treating another human being the way you have treated me. Look at my neck.' She pulls down her sweater, revealing the bruises he left yesterday, and raises her chin, making them conspicuous.

He flushes.

There's a discreet knock on the door, and with a frustrated glance at Alessia, Anatoli retreats to open it. A young man dressed in Westin livery is outside with a dining cart. Anatoli beckons him in and stands back as the server transforms the cart into a table. It's covered in a white linen tablecloth and plush place settings for two. There's a jaunty single yellow rose in a ceramic vase, striving to represent a little romance.

Ironic.

Alessia's sorrow surfaces, eating at her insides, and she has to fight back tears while the waiter opens the wine. Placing the cork in a ceramic dish, he pulls several plates from a warming drawer beneath the cart and removes their metallic covers with a flourish. The aroma is tantalising. Anatoli says something in Croatian and slips the waiter what looks like a ten-euro note, for which he seems extremely grateful. Once the young man has left the room, Anatoli summons Alessia to the table. 'Come and eat.' He sounds like he's sulking.

Because she's hungry and tired of fighting, Alessia sits down at the makeshift table. This is how it will be, a slow, grinding erosion of her will, so that in time she will submit to this man.

'This is most Western, yes?' he says as he sits opposite her and picks up the bottle of wine. He pours her a glass.

Alessia mulls over his earlier statement. If Anatoli wants a traditional Albanian wife, then that's what he will have. She will not eat with him. Or sleep with him, except when he wants sex. Surely that's not really what he wants. She stares down at her dinner as the walls of the room close in, suffocating her.

'*Gëzuar*, Alessia,' he says, and she looks up. Anatoli has raised his glass in a quiet salute to her, his eyes wide, his expression warm. Her scalp tingles. She wasn't expecting this . . . honour! Picking up her glass, she offers it in a reluctant toast to him and takes a sip.

'Mmm,' she says, closing her eyes, seduced by the taste of the wine. When she reopens them, Anatoli is watching her, his eyes darkening, and in his gaze she sees a promise of something she doesn't want.

Her appetite vanishes.

'You won't run from me again, Alessia. You will be my wife,' he murmurs. 'Now, eat.'

She stares down at the steak on her plate.

Chapter Thirty

Anatoli refills her glass again. 'You've hardly touched your food.'

'I'm not hungry.'

'In that case I think it's time we went to bed.' The tone of his voice makes her look up sharply. He's sitting back in his chair, watchful. Waiting. Like a predator. He taps his bottom lip with his index finger as if deep in thought, his eyes gleaming. He's had at least three glasses of wine. And the whisky. He tosses the remaining contents of his glass down his throat and rises from his seat, slowly. His eyes on her, intense, darker. She's paralysed by his stare.

No.

'I don't see why I should wait for our wedding night.' He steps closer.

'No. Anatoli,' she breathes. 'Please. No.' She clutches the table.

He runs a finger down her cheek. 'Beautiful,' he whispers. 'Get up. Don't make this hard for both of us.'

'We should wait,' Alessia whispers, her brain churning through her options.

'I don't want to wait. And if I have to fight you, so be it.' He moves suddenly, grabbing her by her shoulders and yanking her upright and out of her seat so forcefully that she knocks her chair to the floor. Fear and anger surge through her body. She twists and kicks, her foot striking his shin and then the table, rattling the crockery and cutlery and knocking over her glass so that it spills the remaining wine.

'Ow. Fuck,' he whines.

'No!' she shouts, lashing out with both her feet, her fists flailing, hoping to strike him. He lunges at her and grabs her around the waist, jerking her into his arms. He lifts her off her feet while she kicks out at anything and everything in their path in an effort to strike him.

'No!' she screams. 'Please, Anatoli!'

Ignoring her cries, he tightens his arms around her and half drags, half carries her into the bedroom.

'No. No. Stop!'

'Quiet!' he shouts as he shakes her and throws her face-down onto the bed. He sits beside her, holding her still, pressing down on her back with one hand while the other starts tugging at her boots.

'No!' she screams again. She twists, kicking him, once, twice, trying to struggle out of his hold as she pummels him with her fists.

'For fuck's sake, Alessia!'

She's wild, her anger and loathing giving her a strength she didn't know she possessed. She fights, consumed by her rage and directing it at the man she hates.

'Fucking hell.' Anatoli throws himself on top of her, crushing her into the mattress and knocking the breath from her body. She tries to buck him off, but he's too heavy.

'Calm down,' he pants in her ear. 'Calm down.'

She stills, marshalling her resources and struggling to gulp air into her lungs. Anatoli shifts his weight and flips her over so that they're nose to nose. Keeping his leg over her thighs, he grabs her hands and pulls them above her head, pinning them there with one hand.

'I want you. You are my wife.'

'Please. No,' she whispers, staring into his wild, wide eyes. In them she sees his excitement – his lean body vibrates with it. She feels it against her hip. He stares down at her, breathing hard, and one of his hands moves over her body, over her breast and belly to her flies.

'No. Anatoli, please. I'm bleeding. Please. I'm bleeding.' She's lying, but it's a last desperate attempt to stop him. He frowns, as if not understanding, and then his expression changes from lust to distaste.

'Oh,' he says.

Releasing her hands, he rolls off her and stares up at the ceiling. 'Maybe we should wait,' he grumbles.

Alessia twists onto her side, drawing up her knees and curling into a ball, making herself as small as possible. Despair, revulsion, fear – these are her bedfellows now. Her tears start to choke her, and she feels the bed move as Anatoli rises and walks back into the living room.

How long can she cry before her tears dry up?

Moments. Seconds. Hours.

Later Anatoli drapes a blanket over her. She feels the bed dip as he climbs in, beneath the covers. He shuffles over, wraps his arm around her, and tugs her unyielding body closer. 'You will suit me well, *carissima*,' he murmurs, and his lips brush her cheek in a surprisingly gentle kiss.

Alessia puts her fist to her mouth, stifling her silent scream.

She wakes suddenly. The room is in semi-darkness, lit only by the grey light of the coming dawn. Beside her, Anatoli is fast asleep. His face is relaxed and less stern in repose. Alessia stares at the ceiling, her mind on full alert. She's still dressed and wearing her boots. She could run.

Go. Now. She wills herself.

Slowly, stealthily, she rolls off the bed and tiptoes out of the room.

The detritus of their meal from the previous night is still on the table. Alessia eyes the cold fries, hastily grabs a few and stuffs them into her mouth. While she eats, she rummages through her bag and finds her money. She slips the notes into her back pocket.

She stops and listens.

He's still asleep.

Beside her bag she spies Anatoli's suitcase. Maybe he keeps his money in there . . . If he does, it could help her escape. Carefully she unzips it, not knowing what she'll find inside.

It's neatly packed. There are some clothes – and his gun.

The gun.

She fishes it out.

She could kill him.

Before he kills her.

Her heart starts pounding, and her head begins to spin.

She has the power. The means. The pistol is weighty in her hand.

Standing up, she sidles towards the bedroom door and watches Anatoli sleep. He hasn't moved. A tremor runs up her spine, and her breathing shallows. He's kidnapped her. Beaten her. Choked her. Nearly raped her. She despises him and everything he stands for. She's terrified of him. She raises her trembling hand and takes aim. Quietly she releases the safety. Her head is throbbing, sweat beading on her brow.

This is it.

Her moment.

Her hand wobbles, and her vision blurs with her tears.

No. No. No. No.

She dashes them away and drops her hand.

She's not a murderer.

She turns the gun around. And stares down the barrel. She's seen enough American television to know what to do.

She doesn't want to blindly accept her fate. This is one way out.

She could end it all, now. Her misery would be over.

She will feel nothing. Ever again.

Her mother's anguished face comes to her mind.

Mama.

How devastated would she be . . . ?

She thinks of Maxim. And dismisses the thought of him immediately.

She'll never see him again.

Her throat is closing. Choked with emotion. She screws up her eyes. Panting.

She can die at her own hand. Not Anatoli's . . .

And someone will have to clean up afterwards.

No. No. No.

She crumples to the floor. Defeated. A failure. She cannot take her own life. She doesn't have the gumption. And deep down she wants to stay alive in the vague hope of seeing Maxim again. She can't run. She needs to get home. Zagreb is not five days' walk from London, it's so much further. She's helpless. She rocks quietly to and fro, holding herself and cradling the gun, while she silently surrenders to her grief. She's never been so distraught. She's never wept this many tears. Ever. Even after her traumatic escape and on her long walk to Magda's. She'd mourned her grandmother and felt her loss – but she never felt this desolate. This sorrow is overwhelming. She cannot kill him, and she cannot kill herself. She's lost the man she loves, and she's bound to a man she loathes.

Her heart is broken. *No.* Her heart has disappeared.

As the sun peeks over the horizon, she stifles her sobs and through her tears she examines the gun. It's similar to one of her father's.

There is something she *can* do; she's seen her father do it often enough. She unclips the magazine and is surprised to find only four bullets in it. She removes them and then sharply pulls the slide back and catches the remaining round as it's ejected from the chamber. She reloads the magazine into the gun and pockets the bullets. Then she places the pistol back in Anatoli's case and zips it up.

Standing, she wipes away her tears. *Enough with the crying,* she scolds herself. She glances towards the window as the skyline of Zagreb materialises in the early-morning light. From the fifteenth floor of the Westin hotel, the city is spread out beneath like a terracotta patchwork quilt. It's an arresting vista, and in a distracted moment she wonders if Tiranë is similar.

'You're awake.' Anatoli's voice startles her.

'I was hungry.' She glances at the table of leftover food. 'Now I'm going to have a shower.'

Grabbing her bag, she scuttles into the bathroom and locks the door.

When she emerges, Anatoli is up and dressed. Their crockery and the leftover food have been cleared away, and there's fresh linen on the table, with a continental breakfast laid out for them.

'You stayed,' Anatoli says quietly. He seems subdued, though he's as watchful as ever.

'Where would I go?' Alessia replies wearily.

He shrugs. 'You left once before.'

Alessia stares at him. Mute. Despondent. Exhausted.

'Is it because you care for me?' he whispers.

'Don't flatter yourself,' she says, and, sitting down, picks out a pain au chocolat from the bread basket.

He takes his seat opposite her, and she can tell he's hiding a slight and hopeful smile.

Tom and I wander across the vast Skanderbeg Square, which is close to the hotel. It's a clear, chill morning, with the sun reflecting off the multicoloured marble tiles that pave the gargantuan space. It's dominated on one side by a bronze statue of Albania's fifteenth-century hero on horseback, and on the other by the National History Museum. Although I'm anxious to get to Alessia's town and find her home, we have to wait to meet our interpreter.

I'm unsettled and jittery and unable to keep still, so to kill time Tom and I take a quick walk through the museum. I distract myself by snapping numerous photographs and posting the odd one online. I get told off twice, but I ignore the officials and continue to take photographs surreptitiously. It's hardly the British Museum, but I'm fascinated by the Illyrian artefacts. Tom, of course, is preoccupied with the displays of medieval weaponry; Albania has a rich and bloody history.

At ten we stroll down one of the tree-lined boulevards towards the coffee-house where we've arranged to meet our translator. I am struck by how many men are sitting around drinking coffee outside, even though it's cold.

Where are the women?

Thanas Ceka is dark-haired and dark-eyed, a postgrad student at the University of Tirana doing his doctorate in English literature. His English is excellent, he has a ready smile and an easy-going nature – and he's brought his girlfriend. Her name is Drita, and she's an undergraduate studying history. She's petite and pretty, and her spoken English is not as good as Thanas's. She wants to come with us.

Well, this could get complicated.

Tom glances at me and shrugs. I haven't got time to argue. 'I'm not sure how long we're going to be,' I state as I finish my coffee. It could double as paint stripper – I don't think I've ever drunk coffee this strong.

'It's cool. I've cleared my schedule for the week,' Thanas responds. 'I've never been to Kukës myself, but Drita has.'

'What do you know of Kukës?' I ask Drita directly.

She gives Thanas a nervous glance.

'That bad?' I eye them both.

'It has a reputation. When the Communists fell, Albania was . . .' Thanas pauses. 'It went through a difficult time.'

Tom rubs his hands. 'I love a challenge,' he says, and Thanas and Drita have the grace to laugh.

'We shall be okay with the weather,' Thanas says. 'The motorway is open, and it hasn't snowed for a couple of weeks.'

'Shall we get going?' I ask, eager to leave.

The landscape has changed. Gone are the dreary, fallow fields of Northern Europe; the terrain is stark, rocky and barren in the winter sunshine. Under any other circumstances, Alessia might have enjoyed this journey. She's had a lightning tour of Europe's highways. But she's with Anatoli, the man she'll be forced to marry – and she still has to face her father when they reach Kukës. She is not looking forward to the inevitable confrontation, and deep down she knows it's because her mother will bear the brunt of his anger.

They tear across another bridge at an alarming speed. Below

them is a vast body of water, reminding Alessia of the Drin – and reminding her of the sea.

The sea.

And Maxim.

He gave me the sea.

Will she ever see him again?

'The coastline in Croatia is very picturesque. I do a lot of business here,' says Anatoli, breaking the silence that's hung between them since they left Zagreb.

Alessia glances at him. She doesn't care about his business. She doesn't want to know what he does. There was a time when she was curious, but that time has passed. Besides, as his wife – a *good* Albanian wife – she will ask no questions.

'I have several properties here.' He gives her a wolfish grin, and she realises he's trying to impress her, like he did when she first met him.

She turns away, staring out at the sea, and her mind spirals back to Cornwall.

The drive out of Tirana is frankly terrifying. Pedestrians have an unnerving habit of just stepping out into the road, and the roundabouts are free-for-alls – cars, trucks, buses all jostling for priority. It's like a giant game of chicken, and at this rate my nerves will be in shreds by the time we reach Kukës. Tom is constantly slamming his hand on the dashboard, yelling at pedestrians and drivers alike. It's bloody annoying.

'For fuck's sake, Tom, shut the fuck up! I'm trying to concentrate.'

'Sorry, Trevethick.'

By some miracle we make it out of the city centre unscathed. Once we reach the main road, I start to relax a little, but I drive slowly; drivers here are unpredictable.

There are several car dealerships and countless petrol stations on the roadside. As we leave Tirana behind, we pass a grand, imposing neoclassical building that looks rather like a wedding cake.

'What's that place?' I ask.

'It's a hotel,' Thanas says. 'It's been under construction for many years.' He shrugs when our eyes meet in the rear-view mirror.

'Oh.'

The lowlands look fertile and green considering it's February. There are squat, red-roofed houses dotted among the fields. While I drive, Thanas gives us a potted history of Albania and shares more information about himself. His parents lived through the fall of Communism, and both of them learned English via the BBC World Service, even though it was banned under Communist rule. It transpires that the BBC, and most things British, are held in high regard by Albanians. The UK is where they all want to go. There or America.

Tom and I exchange a glance.

Drita speaks quietly to Thanas, and he translates. Kukës was nominated for the Nobel Peace Prize in 2000, after the town accepted hundreds of thousands of refugees during the Kosovan conflict.

This I knew. I remember Alessia's look of pride when she regaled me about Kukës and all things Albanian in the pub in Trevethick.

It's been two days since she left, and I feel like I'm missing a limb.

Where are you, my love?

We join the main motorway to Kukës, and soon we are flying into the chilliest of blue skies, steadily climbing higher and higher towards the majestic, snow-capped peaks of the Albanian

Alps, and the Shar and Korab mountain ranges that dominate the landscape. There are gorges with clear white-water rivers, craggy canyons, and steep, jagged cliffs. It's stunning, and apart from this modern motorway the land around us seems untouched by time. There's an occasional hamlet with terracotta-tiled houses, smoke rising from chimneys, stooks of hay flecked with snow, washing on lines, goats free, goats tethered – this is Alessia's country.

My sweet girl.

I hope you're okay.

I'm coming to get you.

The temperature drops the higher we go. Tom has taken the wheel so that I can play DJ and take photographs with my phone. Thanas and Drita are quiet, enjoying the views and listening to Hustle and Drone, who are streaming through the car stereo system from my iPhone. We emerge from a long mountain tunnel to find we're right among the peaks. They're covered with snow but are surprisingly bare, with very few trees. Thanas explains that after the Communist regime fell, there were fuel shortages, and in some places the locals cut down all the trees for firewood.

'I thought we were high enough to be above the treeline,' Tom says.

In the middle of this rocky wilderness, we encounter a tollbooth, and while we queue up behind a few battered cars and trucks, my phone buzzes. I'm amazed I can get a signal in these mountains on top of Eastern Europe.

'Oliver, what's up?'

'I'm sorry to interrupt your day, Maxim, but the police have been in touch. They were rather hoping to interview your . . . um . . . fiancée, Miss Demachi.'

Ah . . . so now he knows. I ignore the fiancée part of his statement. 'As you know, Alessia has returned to Albania, so they'll have to wait until she comes back to London.'

'I thought as much.'

'Did they say anything else?'

'They have recovered your laptop and some sound equipment.'

'That's good news!'

'And the case is now in the hands of the Metropolitan Police. It appears that Miss Demachi's assailants are known to the police and wanted in connection with other crimes.'

'The Met? Good. Sergeant Nancarrow said those arseholes might have form.'

Tom gives me a sideways glance.

'Have they been charged?'

'As far as I know, not as yet, sir.'

'Keep me up to date with these proceedings if you can. I want to know if they're charged and if they make bail.'

'Will do.'

'Just relay my message to the police about Miss Demachi. Say she's had to return to Albania for a family matter. Everything else okay?'

'Tickety-boo, sir.'

'Tickety-boo?' I laugh. 'Great.' I hang up and pass Tom five euros to pay for the toll.

If Dante and his accomplice are still in custody, the police must be treating this seriously. Maybe they've got them for trafficking; I hope so. I hope they lock the fuckers up and throw away the key.

A short while later, we see a sign for Kukës and my spirits lift. We're nearly there. Soon we're driving alongside a huge lake, which, when I consult my Google Maps, turns out to be a river – the Drin which feeds Fierza Lake. I remember Alessia talking with such passion about the landscape around her town. My anticipation is growing exponentially. I urge Tom to drive faster. I am going to see her. I am going to save her. I hope.

She might not need saving.

She might want to be here.

Don't think that!

As we round a sweeping curve of the motorway, Kukës finally comes into view. It's nestled in the valley, with a wide, blue-green river-lake in front of it and ringed by dramatic mountains. The vista is spectacular.

Wow.

This was Alessia's view, every day.

We cross a sturdy bridge over the water. On a bluff above, a ghostly abandoned building stands sentinel, and I wonder if it's another unfinished hotel.

On the outskirts of Nikšić, in Montenegro, Anatoli pulls into the parking lot of a roadside café. Alessia stares listlessly out of the window.

'I'm hungry. You must be, too. Let's go,' he says. Alessia doesn't bother to argue but follows him into the pleasant, clean space. It's relatively new and decorated with a fun theme – automobiles – a cherry-red hot rod is painted above the bar. It's an inviting place. But not for Anatoli; he's irritable. He's slapped the steering wheel several times and sworn loudly in the last couple of hours, infuriated by other drivers. He is not a patient man.

'Order something for both of us. I'm going to the restroom. Don't run. I'll find you.' He scowls at Alessia and leaves her to choose a table.

She's now keen to make it home. Given how Anatoli behaved yesterday evening, she doesn't want to spend another night with him. She'd rather face her father. She skims the menu, trying to find common words that she might recognise in either English or Albanian, but she's tired and can't seem to concentrate.

Anatoli returns. He looks tired. Of course, he's been driving constantly for several days now, but Alessia refuses to feel any sympathy for him.

'What did you order?' he snaps.

'I haven't. Here's the menu.' She hands it to him before he can gripe. A waiter joins them, and Anatoli orders without asking her what she wants. She's amazed that Montenegrin seems to be yet another language he speaks fluently. The waiter scuttles away, and Anatoli pulls out his mobile phone.

Cool blue eyes meet hers. 'Keep quiet,' he says, and he dials a number. 'Good afternoon, Shpresa, is Jak there?'

Mama!

Alessia sits up. Fully engaged. He's talking to her mother.

'Oh . . . Well, tell him we'll be home around eight this evening . . .' Anatoli's eyes slide to Alessia. 'Yes, she's with me. She's well . . . No . . . She's in the restroom.'

'What!'

Anatoli puts his index finger to his lips.

'Anatoli, let me talk to my mother,' Alessia insists, holding out her hand for the phone.

'We'll see you then. Goodbye.' He hangs up.

'Anatoli!' Tears of anger threaten as a lump swells in her throat. She's never felt as homesick as she does now.

Mama.

How could he begrudge her a few words to her mother?

'If you were a little more docile and grateful, I would have let you talk to her,' he says. 'I have come a long way for you.'

Alessia glares at him, then drops her eyes. She doesn't want to meet the challenge in his; she cannot bear to look at him after this latest outrage. He's cruel and vindictive and petulant and childish. Fury quietly seeps into every vein in her body.

For all that he's done, she will never forgive him.

Ever.

Her only hope is to plead with her father and beg him not to force their marriage.

Close up, Kukës is not what I thought it would be. It's a nondescript town of weathered Soviet-style apartments built in blocks. Drita informs us via Thanas that it was constructed during the 1970s. The original old town of Kukës is now at the bottom of the lake; the valley was flooded to feed the hydroelectric dam that provides power to the surrounding region. The roads are lined with fir trees, there's a blanket of snow on the ground, and the streets are quiet. There are a few shops, selling household goods, clothes and farm equipment, and a couple of supermarkets. There's a bank, a pharmacy and many cafés, where, as is customary, men sit outside in the afternoon sunshine wrapped up against the chill, drinking coffee.

Again, where are all the women?

The most distinctive feature of the town is that at the end of each street, wherever I look, the mountains stand tall and proud in a dramatic backdrop. We are surrounded by their majestic beauty, and I find myself wishing I'd brought my Leica.

My travel agent has booked us into a hotel called, of all things, Amerika. Google Maps guides us through the backstreets to the hotel itself. It's a curious mix of old and modern, with an entrance that looks like a Christmas grotto, especially now, as it's dusted with snow.

Inside, it has to be one of the kitschiest places I've ever seen, crammed with touristy knick-knacks procured from the USA, including several plastic Statues of Liberty. The decor is impossible to define, a mishmash of styles, but the overall effect is . . . cheery and friendly. The host, a wiry, bearded man in his thirties, is warm and welcoming and greets us in a broken version of English before ushering us upstairs to our rooms via a tiny lift. Tom and I take the twin room, leaving the double for Thanas and Drita.

'Will you ask him for directions to this place?' I hand Thanas a crumpled piece of paper with Alessia's parents' address.

'Yes. What time would you like to go?'

'Five minutes. Just give us time to unpack.'

'Steady on, Trevethick,' butts in Tom. 'Can't we have a drink first?'

Hmm . . . As my father would say, some Dutch courage always helps.

'A quick one. And just one. Okay? I'm going to meet my future wife's parents – I don't want to be stocious.' Tom nods enthusiastically and claims the bed nearer the door. 'I hope to God you don't snore,' I say as I unpack.

An hour later we are parked in a small lay-by that leads to two open, rusty metal gates. Beyond, down a concrete driveway, is a solitary, terracotta-roofed house on the banks of the Drin. Only the roof is visible.

'Thanas, you'd better come with me,' I say, and we leave Drita and Tom in the car. The glow of the setting sun casts tall shadows across the driveway. We're on a large plot, surrounded by naked trees, though there are a few firs and a sizable, well-kept vegetable patch. The house is painted a pale green and has three storeys and two balconies that face the water, from what I can see. It's larger than the other houses we saw on our way here. Perhaps Alessia's folks are affluent. I have no idea. The lake looks magnificent, lit up with the hues of a fading winter sunset.

On the outside of the house, there's a satellite dish, and it reminds me of a conversation I had with Alessia.

And I've been to America by watching TV.

American TV?

Yes. Netflix. HBO.

I knock on what I assume is the front door. It's made of a good solid wood, so I knock again, harder this time, to be sure to be heard. My heart is pounding, and in spite of the cold a trickle of sweat runs down my back.

This is it.

Game face on, dude.

I'm about to meet my new in-laws – though they don't know that yet.

The door half opens, and a chink of light behind her reveals a slight, middle-aged woman in a headscarf. In the fading evening light, I see that she's giving me a quizzical look, a little like Alessia.

'Mrs Demachi?'

'Yes.' She looks bewildered.

'My name's Maxim Trevelyan, and I've come about your daughter.'

She gapes at me, blinking furiously, then opens the door a little wider. She's trim with slight shoulders, and she's rather dowdily dressed in a voluminous skirt and blouse. Her hair is hidden beneath her headscarf, reminding me of the moment when I first saw her daughter standing like a frightened rabbit in my hallway.

'Alessia?' she whispers.

'Yes.'

She frowns. 'My husband . . . is not here.' Her English sounds rusty and her accent much thicker than her daughter's. She peers anxiously past me, scanning the driveway – for what, I don't know – and then she looks directly at me. 'You cannot be here.'

'Why?' I ask.

'My husband is not at home.'

'But I need to talk to you about Alessia. I think she's on her way back here.'

She tilts her head, suddenly alert. 'We are expecting her soon. You have heard she is returning?'

My heart leaps in response.

She's coming home. I was right.

'Yes. And I've come to ask you and your husband for . . .' I swallow. 'For . . . permission to marry your daughter.'

'Our final border crossing, *carissima*,' Anatoli says. 'Back to your home country. Shame on you for leaving it and skulking away like a thief and dishonouring your family. When we return, you can apologise to your parents for the worry you have caused them.'

Alessia averts her eyes, inwardly cursing him for making her feel guilty for running away. She was running from him! She knows that many Albanian men leave their country to work abroad – for women it's not so easy.

'This is the last time you have to go in the boot. But wait, I need to retrieve something first.' She stands back and looks west to where the sun has finally disappeared behind the hills. The chill in the air reaches through her clothes and entwines around her heart. And she knows it's because she's pining for the only man she'll ever love. Tears rise unexpectedly into her eyes, and she blinks them back.

Not now.

She doesn't want to give Anatoli the satisfaction.

She will cry tonight.

With her mother.

She inhales deeply. This is what freedom smells like – chilly, foreign. When she next takes a deep breath, she'll be in her homeland, and her adventures will become a . . . what did Maxim call it? A *folly* from the past.

'Get in. It will be night soon,' Anatoli snaps as he holds open the boot.

The night belongs to the djinn.

And she's staring at one now. That's what he is. The djinn personified. She climbs in without complaint and without touching him. She's getting closer to home, and for the first time, she's looking forward to seeing her mother.

'Soon, *carissima*,' he says, and there's a troubling glint in his eye.

'Shut the lid,' she responds as she clutches the torch.

His lips lift in a sardonic smile, and he slams it down, leaving her in darkness.

Mrs Demachi gasps, and with another quick and anxious glance past me, she steps aside. 'Come in.'

'Wait in the car,' I say to Thanas, and I follow her into a confined vestibule, where she points to a shoe rack.

Oh. Quickly I slip off my boots, relieved that I'm wearing matching socks.

And that would be because of Alessia . . .

The hall is painted white, its shiny tiled floor topped by a brightly coloured kilim rug. She waves me on into an adjoining room, where two old sofas covered in bold and colourful patterned blankets face each other across a small table that's also covered in a rich printed cloth. Beyond is a fireplace, its mantelpiece peppered with old photographs. I squint, hoping to see one of Alessia. There's one of a young girl with large, serious eyes, seated at a piano.

My girl!

The grate is piled with logs, but they remain unlit in spite of the cold, and I suspect that this is the drawing room used to receive company. Pride of place is given to the old upright piano that sits against the wall. It's plain and shabby, but I bet it's tuned to perfection. This is where she plays.

My talented girl.

Beside the piano is a tall shelf stacked with well-thumbed books.

Alessia's mother has not asked me to remove my coat. I don't think I'm going to be here for long.

'Please. Sit,' she instructs.

I take a seat on one of the sofas, and she perches on the edge of the one opposite, radiating tension. Clasping her hands together, she stares at me expectantly. Her eyes are the same dark shade as Alessia's – but whereas Alessia's are full of mystery, her mother's hold only sadness. I guess it's because she's anxious about her daughter. But from her lined face and the sprinkling of grey in her hair, it's obvious she's not led an easy life.

Life in Kukës is hard for some women.

Alessia's quietly spoken words come back to me.

Her mother blinks a couple of times. I suspect I'm making her nervous or uncomfortable, and for that I feel a little guilty.

'My friend Magda, she writes to me about a man who helps my Alessia and also Magda herself. Is that you?' Her voice is hesitant and soft.

'Yes.'

'How is my daughter?' she whispers. She's studying me intensely, clearly desperate for news of Alessia.

'When I last saw her, she was fine. More than fine, she was happy. I met her when she worked for me. She came to my house to clean.' I simplify my English, hoping Alessia's mother can keep up.

'You have come all the way from England?'

'Yes.'

'For Alessia?'

'Yes. I've fallen in love with your daughter, and I believe she loves me, too.'

Her eyes widen. 'She does?' She looks alarmed.

Okay . . . this is not the reaction I'd been expecting.

'Yes. She told me she does.'

'And you want to marry her?'

'Yes.'

'How do you know that she wants to marry you?'

Ah!

'In truth, Mrs Demachi, I don't know. I haven't had the chance to ask her. I believe that she's been kidnapped and is being brought to Albania against her will.'

She leans her head back, her eyes intense, assessing me.

Shit.

'My friend Magda speaks well of you,' she says. 'But I don't know you. Why would my husband let you marry our daughter?'

'Well, I know she doesn't want to marry the man her father has chosen for her.'

'She says this to you?'

'She's told me everything. And what's more, I listened. I love her.'

Mrs Demachi bites her upper lip, and the mannerism is so reminiscent of her daughter that I have to hide my smile. 'My husband will return soon. And it is for him to decide what will become of Alessia. His mind is set on her betrothed. He has given his word.' She looks down at her clasped hands. 'I let her go once, and it broke my heart. I don't think I can let her go again.'

'Do you want her to be trapped in a violent, abusive marriage?'

Her eyes whip to mine, and in them I see a glimpse of her pain and her insight, swiftly followed by her shock that I know – this is her life.

Everything that Alessia ever said about her father comes back to me.

Mrs Demachi whispers, 'You must go. Go now.' She stands up.

Fuck.

I've offended her.

'I'm sorry,' I say as I stand, too.

She frowns, looking momentarily confused and undecided. Then, suddenly, she blurts out, 'Alessia will return here at eight o'clock this evening, with her betrothed.' She averts her eyes from mine for a moment, probably wondering if it was a good idea to impart this state secret.

Reaching out, I want to squeeze her clasped hands in gratitude, but I stop myself, as my touch may not be welcome. Instead I give her my most sincere and grateful smile. 'Thank you. Your daughter means the world to me.'

She thaws briefly, rewarding me with a hesitant smile of her own, and again I see a little of Alessia in her.

She shows me to the door, where I slip on my boots and she ushers me out. 'Goodbye,' she says.

'Are you going to tell your husband that I've been here?'

'No.'

'Okay. I understand.' I offer what I hope is a reassuring smile, and I head back to the car.

Back at the hotel, I'm restless. We've tried watching TV. Neither Tom nor I understand what we're watching. We've tried reading, and now we're in the bar. It's on the roof and would offer an impressive daytime view of Kukës, the lake and the surrounding mountains. But it's dark and the vista offers no solace for me.

She's on her way home.

With him.

I hope she's okay.

'Sit down. Maybe have a drink,' Tom says. I give him a sideways look. It's at times like this that I wish I smoked. The anticipation and the tension are almost unbearable. After one slug of whisky, I can bear no more.

'We're going.'

'It's too early!'

'I don't care. I can't stay cooped up here waiting. I'd rather wait with her folks.'

At 7:40 we return to the Demachi house.

Time to be a grown-up.

Tom waits in the car once more with Drita while Thanas and I walk down the driveway. 'And remember, I've not been here before. I don't want to get Mrs Demachi into trouble?' I say to Thanas.

'Trouble?'

'With her husband.'

'Oh. I understand.' Thanas rolls his eyes.

'You understand?'

'Yes. Life is different in Tiranë. Here it's much more traditional. Men. Women.' He grimaces.

I wipe my sweaty palms on my coat. I haven't felt this nervous since my interview for Eton. I have to make a favourable impression on Alessia's father. I need to persuade him that I'm a better option for his daughter than the arsehole he's chosen.

That's if she wants me.

Shit.

I knock on the door and wait.

Mrs Demachi answers the door. Her eyes flit from Thanas to me.

'Mrs Demachi?' I ask.

And she nods.

'Is your husband at home?'

She nods once more, and in case we're overheard, I replay the introduction I made to her earlier in the day as if it hadn't happened. 'Come in,' she says. 'You must speak to my husband.' Once we've removed our shoes, she takes our coats and hangs them in the hall.

Mr Demachi stands when we enter a larger room at the back of the house. It's an airy, spotless kitchen-cum-living room, the two areas separated by an arch. A pump-action shotgun hangs ominously on the wall above Mr Demachi's head. I note that it's within easy reach.

Demachi is older than his wife; his face is weather-beaten, his hair more grey than black. He wears a sombre dark suit that lends him the air of a Mafia don. His eyes give nothing away. I'm glad he's half a head shorter than me.

As Mrs Demachi quietly explains who we are, his expression becomes more and more mistrustful.

Shit. What is she saying?

Thanas whispers a running commentary. 'She's telling him that you wish to speak to him about his daughter.'

'Okay.'

Demachi gives us both an uncertain smile as he shakes our hands in turn, then waves at an old pine sofa, inviting us to sit. He appraises me with shrewd eyes the same shade as Alessia's, while Mrs Demachi wanders through the arch into the kitchen.

Demachi looks from me to Thanas and starts to speak. His voice has a rich, deep timbre that's almost soothing to listen to. Thanas immediately starts to translate for both of us.

'My wife tells me you are here because of my daughter.'

'Yes, Mr Demachi. Alessia worked for me, back in London.'

'London?' He looks impressed for a moment, but the shutters come down quickly. 'What did she do, exactly?'

'She was my cleaner.'

He closes his eyes for a moment, as if this news is too painful to hear, which surprises me. Or perhaps he thinks this is beneath her . . . or maybe he misses her, I don't know. I take a deep breath to calm my spiralling nerves and continue. 'I have come to ask for her hand in marriage.'

His eyes pop open in surprise, and he scowls. It's an exaggerated expression. But I don't know to what end. 'She's already promised to another,' he says.

'She does not wish to marry that man. He is the reason that she left here.'

Demachi's eyes widen at my outspoken candour, and I hear a small gasp from the kitchen.

'Did she tell you this?'

'Yes.'

Demachi's expression is inscrutable.

What the hell is he thinking?

The creases in her father's forehead deepen. 'Why do you wish to marry her?' He seems perplexed.

'Because I love her.'

Kukës is achingly familiar. Even in the dark. Alessia is both excited and apprehensive about seeing her parents. Her father will beat her. Her mother will hold her in her arms, and they will cry together.

Like they always do.

Anatoli drives over the bridge to the Kukës peninsula and turns left. Alessia sits up, straining to catch a first glimpse of home. Less than a minute later, she sees the lights of her parents' house and frowns. There's a car parked near the end of the drive with two people leaning against it, facing the river and smoking. Alessia thinks it's odd but dismisses the thought, too preoccupied by her imminent reunion with her parents. Anatoli steers the Mercedes around the parked car and down the driveway.

Before the car has come to a complete stop, Alessia flings open the passenger door and flies up the path and through the front door. Without taking off her shoes, she races down the main hallway.

'Mama!' she calls, and she bursts into the living room, expecting to see her mother.

Maxim and another man she barely notices stand. They had been sitting with her father, who is now staring up at her.

Alessia's world stops, and she freezes as she tries to process what she's seeing.

She blinks a couple of times as her empty, aching heart kick-starts back into life. She has eyes for only one man.

He's here.

Chapter Thirty-One

My heart is beating a frantic tattoo. Alessia stands in the middle of the room. Astounded.

She's here.

She's finally here. Dark, dark wide eyes stare back at me in disbelief.

Yes. I came to get you.

I've got you. Always.

She looks stunning. Slender. Sweet. Her hair wild. But her skin is pale. Paler than I've ever seen her before, and she has a graze on one cheek and a bruise on the other. There are dark circles beneath her eyes that are shining with unshed tears.

A lump forms in my throat.

What have you been through, sweetheart?

'Hello,' I whisper. 'You left without saying goodbye.'

Maxim is here. For her. Everyone else in the room disappears. She can see only him. His hair is tousled. He looks pale and tired, but relieved. His startling green eyes drink her in, and his words touch her soul. The same words he used when he came to find her in Brentford. But there's a question on his face, beseeching her. It's asking why she left. He doesn't know how she feels about him. But he came anyway.

He's here.

He's not with Caroline.

How could she doubt him? How could he doubt her?

She lets out a small, sharp cry and races into his waiting arms. Maxim cradles her against his chest, holding her tightly. She inhales his scent. It's clean and warm and familiar.

Maxim.

Never let me go.

A movement at the periphery of her vision catches her attention. Her father has risen from his seat, and he's gaping at the two of them. He opens his mouth to say something—

'We're home!' calls Anatoli from the hall, and he swaggers into the room carrying her duffel bag, expecting a hero's welcome.

'Trust me,' Alessia whispers to Maxim.

He stares into her eyes, his face full of love, and he kisses the top of her head. 'Always.'

Anatoli halts at the doorway. Stunned into silence.

Alessia turns to her father, who's looking from us to the arsehole who kidnapped her. Anthony? Antonio? I don't remember his name, but he's a good-looking bastard. His glacial blue eyes are wide with bewilderment at first, but they narrow, coolly assessing me and the woman in my arms. I tuck Alessia under my arm, protecting her from him and her father.

'Babë,' she says to her dad, *'më duket se jam shtatzënë dhe ai është i ati.'*

There is a collective gasp of shock that rattles through the room.

What the fuck did she say?

'What?' roars the arsehole in English, and he drops her bag as his face contorts with anger.

Her father glowers dumbfounded at her and me, his complexion becoming more florid.

Thanas leans towards me and whispers. 'She's just told her father she thinks she's pregnant and that you're the father.'

'What?'

I feel a little dizzy. But wait . . . She can't possibly . . . We only . . . We used . . .

She's lying.

Her father reaches for his shotgun.

Fuck.

You told me you were bleeding!' Anatoli screams at Alessia, and a vein in his forehead pulses with wrath.

Mama starts crying.

'I lied! I didn't want you to touch me!' She turns to her father. 'Babë, please. Don't make me marry him. He is an angry, violent man. He will kill me.'

Baba stares at her, both bemused and angry, while beside Maxim a man Alessia doesn't know quietly translates everything she's just said into English. But she has no time for this stranger now. 'See,' she says to Baba, and opening her coat, she yanks down the neck of her sweater, revealing the dark bruises around her throat.

Mama sobs out loud.

'What the fuck!' Maxim bellows, and he lunges at Anatoli, grabbing him by the neck and throwing them both onto the floor.

He's fucking dead.

Adrenaline coursing through my body, I take the fucker

by surprise, knocking the breath out of him as he hits the floor with me on top of him.

'You fucking arsehole!' I roar, and punch his face, smacking his head to one side as I sit astride him. I hit him again as he struggles, taking a swipe at my face, which I dodge. But he's strong, and he writhes beneath me, so I close my fingers around his throat and squeeze. He grabs my hands, trying to shake me off. He puckers his lips and spits at my face, but I dodge that, too, and his spittle falls back onto his cheek, so he's covered in his own slime. This only enrages him more. And he bucks and bucks. He's shouting at me in his own language. Words I don't understand – but I don't fucking care.

I squeeze harder.

Die, you fucker.

His face reddens. His eyes bulge.

I lift my hands, bringing his head up, and then slam it down on the kitchen tiles. Grateful to hear the loud thud.

Somewhere behind me I hear a scream.

Alessia.

'Get. Off. Me!' the arsehole gasps in broken English.

And suddenly there are hands on me, trying to pull me away. Fighting them off, I lean in close, close enough to smell his stale breath. 'You touch her again and I'll fucking kill you!' I snarl.

'Trevethick! Trevethick! Maxim! Max!' It's Tom. He's grabbing my shoulders, hauling me off. I drag air into my lungs as I stand, my whole body vibrating with fury and a lust for revenge. The arsehole glares up at me, and I find Alessia's father standing between us holding his shotgun. With a venomous look, he waves the barrel, motioning for me to back off.

Reluctantly I oblige.

'Calm down, Maxim. You don't want to cause an international incident,' Tom says as he and Thanas tug me back. The arsehole scrambles to his feet, pure loathing in his scowl.

'You're like all Englishmen,' the arsehole snarls. 'You're soft and weak, and your women are hard.'

'Soft enough to beat the shit out of you, you piece of crap,' I snap.

As the red mist clears, I can hear Alessia fretting behind me.

Shit.

Alessia's father stands between the two men, looking at each of them in consternation.

'You come into my house bringing violence? In front of my wife and my daughter?' he addresses Maxim and his friend Tom.

Where did Tom appear from? Alessia wonders. She remembers meeting him in Brentford and recalls him in Maxim's kitchen with the scars down his leg. Tom runs a hand through his rust-red hair as he gazes at her father.

The translator leans forward and murmurs her father's words to Maxim in English. Maxim holds up his hands and steps back. 'I apologise to you, Mr Demachi. I love your daughter, and I don't wish to see any harm come to her. Especially at the hands of a man.' Maxim gives Baba a pointed look. Baba frowns and turns his attention to Anatoli.

'And you. You bring her back to me covered in bruises?'

'You know how spirited she is, Jak. She needs to be broken.'

'Broken? Like this?' Baba points to her neck.

Anatoli shrugs. 'She's a woman.' His tone implies that she's of no consequence.

As the words are translated for Maxim, his jaw tightens and his fists clench. He bristles with tension and anger.

'No,' Alessia murmurs, reaching out and touching Maxim's arm to calm him.

'Quiet, you!' her father snaps, whirling around to face her. 'You brought this shame on us. You run. And you return a whore. Spreading your legs for this Englishman.'

Alessia hangs her head, her cheeks ashen.

'Babë, Anatoli will kill me,' she whispers. 'And if you want me dead, I'd rather you shot me with that gun you're holding, so I might die at the hands of someone who is supposed to love me.'

She glances at Baba, who blanches at her words while Thanas quietly translates them.

'No,' Maxim says, with such heartfelt conviction that all eyes turn to him. He moves quickly, ushering Alessia behind him. 'Don't touch her. Either of you.'

Baba stares at him, but Alessia doesn't know whether her father is outraged or impressed.

'Your daughter is soiled goods, Demachi,' Anatoli says. 'Why would I want another man's leftovers and her bastard? You can keep her, and kiss goodbye to the loan I promised you.'

Baba scowls at him. 'You would do this to me?'

'Your word is worthless,' Anatoli growls.

The translator quietly relays the words in English. 'Loan?' Maxim says. He turns his head slightly and speaks so that only Alessia can hear him. 'This arsehole *paid* for you?'

Alessia flushes.

Maxim faces her father. 'I will match any loan,' he says.

'No!' Alessia exclaims.

Her father glares at Maxim, furious.

'You dishonour him,' Alessia whispers.

'*Carissima*,' Anatoli declares from the doorway. 'I should have fucked you when I had the chance.' He uses English so that Maxim can understand.

Maxim lurches at him, bristling with anger once more, but Anatoli is ready this time. From his coat pocket, he whisks out his pistol and takes aim at Maxim's face.

'No!' Alessia shrieks, and she darts quickly in front of Maxim, shielding him.

'I don't know whether to shoot you or him,' Anatoli snarls

at her in his mother tongue, and he looks to her father for permission.

Baba stares back at Anatoli and then at Alessia.

Everyone quiets. The tension is a thick blanket over the whole room. Alessia leans forward. 'What are you going to do, Anatoli?' She jabs her index finger at him. 'Shoot him or me?' Thanas translates.

Maxim grabs her arms, but she shakes him off.

'Who hides behind a woman?' Anatoli sneers in English. 'I have enough bullets for both of you.' His look of triumph makes her nauseated.

'No, you don't,' Alessia retorts.

Anatoli frowns. 'What?' And he measures the weight of the gun in his hand.

'This morning in Zagreb, I took the bullets out while you were sleeping.'

Aiming the gun at Alessia, Anatoli tightens his finger on the trigger.

'No!' roars her father, and he rams Anatoli with the butt of the shotgun so hard that he falls to the floor. Seething, Anatoli takes aim again, this time at her father, and pulls the trigger.

'No!' Alessia and her mother shout in unison. But nothing happens. The hammer clicks and echoes against an empty chamber.

'Fuck!' Anatoli shouts, and he glares up at Alessia, a bizarre combination of admiration and contempt on his face. 'You are one fucking annoying woman,' he mutters, and he staggers to his feet.

'Go!' Baba bellows. 'Go now, Anatoli, before I shoot you myself. You want to start a blood feud?'

'Over your whore?'

'She is my daughter, and these people are guests in my house. Go. Now. You are no longer welcome here.'

Anatoli gazes at her father, his fury and impotence written in every tense muscle on his face. 'You've not heard the last of this,' he snarls at Baba and Maxim. Turning on his heel, he pushes past Tom and heads out of the room. Moments later they hear a loud bang as he slams the front door.

When Demachi slowly turns to face Alessia, his eyes are blazing. Ignoring me, he concentrates his menacing look on his daughter. 'You have dishonoured me,' Thanas translates. 'Your family. Your town. And you return here in this state?' Her father waves a hand up and down her body. 'You have dishonoured yourself.'

And I watch Alessia hang her head with shame, and a tear slides down her cheek. 'Look at me,' he growls. When she looks up, he pulls back his arm to backhand her face, but I grab her and tug her out of his reach. She's shaking.

'Don't you dare touch a hair on her head,' I snarl, towering over him. 'This woman has been through hell. And all because of you and your shit choice of a husband for her. She's been kidnapped by sex traffickers. She's escaped. She's gone without food. She's walked for days with nothing. And after all that, she was resilient enough to get herself a job and hold body and soul together with barely any help. How can you treat her this way? What kind of father are you? Where is *your* honour?'

'Maxim! This is my father.' Alessia grabs my arm, a look of horror on her face, as I lay into her so-called father. But I'm on a roll, and Thanas sounds like he's keeping up with me.

'How can you speak of honour if this is the way you treat her? And, what's more, she may be carrying your grandchild – and you threaten her with violence?'

Out of the corner of my eye, I spot Alessia's mother, who is clutching her apron, her expression full of horror. It's chastening.

Demachi is staring at me as if I'm completely crazy. He looks to

Alessia and then back to me, his fury and disgust clear in his dark eyes. 'How dare you come into my house and tell me how to behave? You. You who should have kept his pecker zipped in his pants. Don't talk to me of honour.' Thanas blanches as he translates. 'You dishonour us all. You dishonour my daughter. But there's one thing you can do,' he growls through gritted teeth, and in one swift move he cocks his shotgun with a loud click.

Shit.

I've gone too far.

He's going to kill me.

I feel rather than see Tom tense in the doorway.

Demachi points the gun at me and shouts, *'Do të martohesh me time bijë!'*

The Albanians look flabbergasted. Tom is ready to pounce. And all eyes are on me: Mrs Demachi's. Alessia's. Thanas's. They all gape in shock. And Thanas quietly translates, 'You're going to marry my daughter.'

Chapter Thirty-Two

Oh, Babë, no!

Alessia realises that she hadn't thought through her lie about the pregnancy. In a panic she whirls away from her shotgun-wielding father, desperate to explain the truth to Maxim. She doesn't want to force him into marriage!

But Maxim is sporting the biggest grin.

Joy shines in his eyes, evident for all to see.

His expression takes her breath away.

Slowly he sinks onto one knee, and from the inside pocket of his jacket he produces . . . a ring. A beautiful diamond ring. Alessia gasps, and her hands fly to her face in utter amazement.

'Alessia Demachi,' Maxim says, 'please do me the honour of becoming my countess. I love you. I want to be with you always. Spend your life with me. At my side. Always. Marry me.'

Alessia's eyes fill with tears.

He brought a ring.

This is what he came here to do.

To marry her.

She's breathless with shock.

And then it hits her. Like a freight train. Her elation. He really does love her. He wants to be with her. Not Caroline. He wants her with him, always.

'Yes,' she whispers, tears of joy running down her face. All watch, speechless and as amazed as Alessia, while Maxim slides the ring onto her finger and kisses her hand. Then, with a whoop of happiness, he springs up and sweeps her into his arms.

I love you, Alessia Demachi,' I whisper. Setting her down, I kiss her. Hard. Closing my eyes. I don't care that we have an audience. I don't care that her father is still holding his shotgun pointed in my direction or that her mother is still in the kitchen wide-eyed and weeping. I don't care that one of my closest friends is looking at me in shock and alarm as if I'm crazy.

Right now. Here. In Kukës, Albania, I'm the happiest I've ever been.

She said yes.

Her mouth is soft and yielding. Her tongue caressing mine. It's been only days, but I've missed her so much.

Her tears rub off on my face. Wet and cooling.

Fuck. I love this woman.

Mr Demachi coughs loudly, and Alessia and I surface, winded and giddy from our kiss. He waves the muzzle of his shotgun between us, and we both step back, but I grasp her hand firmly. I'm never letting her go. Alessia is grinning and blushing, and I'm light-headed with love.

'*Konteshë?*' her father, his brow creased, asks Thanas. Thanas looks to me, but I have no idea what Demachi said.

'Countess?' Thanas clarifies.

'Oh. Yes. Countess. Alessia will be Lady Trevethick, Countess of Trevethick.'

'Konteshë?' her father says again, and it seems like he's feeling his way around the word and its meaning.

I nod.

'Babë, zoti Maksim është Kont.'

Three Albanians turn to stare at me and Alessia as if we've each grown an extra head.

'Like Lord Byron?' Thanas asks.

Byron?

'He was a baron, I think. But he was a peer. Yes.'

Mr Demachi lowers his gun, continuing to gape at me. No one else in the room moves or says anything.

Well, this is awkward.

Tom shuffles forward. 'Congratulations, Trevethick. Didn't expect you to propose on the spot.' He puts his arms around me and claps me on the back.

'Thanks, Tom,' I reply.

'This'll make a great story for the grandchildren.'

I laugh.

'Congratulations, Alessia,' Tom adds, giving her a little bow, and she rewards him with a glorious smile.

Mr Demachi turns to his wife and barks an instruction. She heads deeper into the kitchen and returns with a bottle of clear spirits and four glasses. I glance at Alessia – she's radiant. Gone is the harrowed woman who walked into this room earlier.

She shines. Her smile. Her eyes. She takes my breath away.

I'm a lucky guy.

Mrs Demachi fills the glasses and distributes them – only to the men. Alessia's father lifts his glass. *'Gëzuar,'* he says, and there's a look of relief in his shrewd, dark eyes.

This time I know what that means. I raise my own glass.

'Gëzuar,' I repeat, and Thanas and Tom echo the toast. We all upend our glasses and down our drinks. It's the fieriest, most lethal liquid that I've ever poured into my throat.

I try not to cough. And fail.

'That's great,' I lie.

'Raki,' Alessia whispers, and she's trying to hide her smile.

Demachi sets down his glass and refills it, then refills the rest.

Another? Shit. I mentally prepare myself.

Alessia's father raises his raki once more. *'Bija ime tani është problem yt dhe do të martoheni, këtu, brenda javës.'* He downs his shot and brandishes his gun with a look of glee.

Thanas quietly translates. 'My daughter is your problem now. And you'll be married, here, within a week.'

What?

Fuck.

Chapter Thirty-Three

A week!

I give Alessia a bemused smile, and she grins and releases my hand.

'Mama!' she blurts, and I watch her run to her mother, who's been standing patiently in the kitchen. They embrace and cling to each other as if they'll never let go, and both begin to silently weep in that way that women do.

It's . . . affecting.

It's obvious they've missed each other. More than missed each other.

Her mother wipes away her daughter's tears, speaking rapidly in her native tongue, and I have no idea what they are saying. Alessia's laugh is more of a gurgle, and they hug each other again.

Her father watches them and turns to me.

'Women. They are so emotional.' Thanas translates his words, but Demachi looks relieved, I think.

'Yes,' I answer, my voice gruff, and I hope I sound manly. 'She's missed her mother.'

But not you.

Alessia's mother relinquishes her, and Alessia steps towards her father. 'Babë,' she murmurs, her eyes wide once more.

I hold my breath, poised to intervene if he so much as lays a finger on her.

Demachi raises his hand and gently holds her chin. '*Mos u largo përsëri. Nuk është mirë për nënën tënde.*'

Alessia gives him a timid smile, and he leans down and kisses her forehead, closing his eyes as he does. '*Nuk është mirë as për mua,*' he whispers.

I look at Thanas, waiting for his translation, but he's turned away, giving them this moment – and I think maybe I should, too.

It's late, I'm exhausted but I can't sleep. Too much has happened, and my mind is racing. I lie awake staring at the dancing, watery reflections on the ceiling. The patterns that form are so comforting in their familiarity that I grin. They mirror my ecstatic mood. I'm not in London, I'm at my soon-to-be-in-laws', and the reflections are from the full moon, skipping over the deep, dark waters of Fierza Lake.

I didn't have a choice about where I stayed – Demachi insisted it should be here. My room is on the ground floor, and though sparsely furnished, it's comfortable and warm enough and has a splendid view of the lake.

There's a rustle at the door, and Alessia sneaks in and closes it behind her. All my senses come alive, and my heart starts pounding. She tiptoes towards the bed, her body swathed in the most virginal, all-covering, Victorian-style nightdress I have ever seen. Suddenly I feel that I'm in a gothic novel, and I want to laugh at the ridiculousness of this situation. But she places her finger to her lips and then in one swift move draws her nightgown over her head and drops it onto the floor.

I stop breathing.

Her beautiful body is bathed in the pale light of the moon.

She's perfect.

In every way.

My mouth dries, and my body stirs.

I toss back the covers, and she slides into bed beside me, gloriously naked.

'Hello, Alessia,' I whisper, and my lips find hers.

And without words we embrace our reunion, her passion taking me by surprise. She's unleashed; her fingers, hands, tongue and lips are on me. And mine on her.

I'm lost.

And found.

Oh, the feel of her.

And when she throws her head back in ecstasy, I cover her mouth to stifle her cries and bury my face in her soft, lush hair and join her.

When we're quiet once more, she nestles in my arms, her body entwined with mine as she dozes. She must be exhausted.

I let my contentment seep into my bones.

I've got her back. The love of my life is with me, where she belongs. Although if her father knew she was here, he'd shoot us both, I'm sure.

Watching her with her parents these last few hours, I've learned so much about her. Her emotional reunion with her mother – and her father – was affecting. I think he does love her. Very much.

But it seems like she's been fighting against her upbringing since before I met her, fighting to be her own person. And she's succeeded. Plus, she's taken me on an epic journey of self-discovery with her. I want to spend the rest of my life with this woman. I love her so much, and I want to give her the world. She deserves nothing less.

She stirs, and her eyes open. She beams up at me, her smile illuminating the room.

'I love you,' I whisper.

'I love you,' she responds, reaching up to caress my cheek, her fingers tickling my stubble. 'Thank you for not giving up on me.' Her voice is as soft as a summer breeze.

'Never. I've got you. Always.'

'And I've got you.'

'I think your dad will shoot me if he finds you here.'

'No, he'll shoot *me*. I think he likes you.'

'He likes my title.'

'Maybe.'

'Are you okay?' I'm serious now, my voice dropping as I search her face for clues of what she's endured for the past couple of days.

'Now that I'm with you, I am.'

'I'll kill him if he ever comes near you again.'

She puts her finger on my lips. 'Let's not speak of him.'

'Okay.'

'I am sorry. For the lie.'

'Lie? About the pregnancy?'

She nods.

'Alessia, it was genius. Besides, I wouldn't mind some kids.'

An heir and a spare.

She smiles and, leaning up, kisses me, tempting and teasing my lips with her tongue, and I'm hungry for more.

I ease her onto her back to make love to her once again.

Mindful. Beautiful. Fulfilling. Love.

As it should be.

Later this week we'll be married.

I can't wait.

I just have to tell my mother . . .

Alessia's Music

Chapter Two

'Le Coucou' by Louis-Claude Daquin (Alessia's warm-up piece)
Prelude No. 2 in C Minor BWV847 by J. S. Bach (Alessia's angry Bach prelude)

Chapter Four

Prelude No. 3 in C-sharp Major BWV848 by J. S. Bach

Chapter Six

Prelude and Fugue No. 15 in G Major BWV884 by J. S. Bach
Prelude No. 3 in C-sharp Major BWV872 by J. S. Bach

Chapter Seven

'Années de Pèlerinage, 3ème année', S. 163 IV, *Les jeux d'eaux à la Villa d'Este* by Franz Liszt

Chapter Twelve

Prelude No. 2 in C Minor BWV847 by J. S. Bach

Chapter Thirteen

Prelude No. 8 in E-flat Minor BWV853 by J. S. Bach

Chapter Eighteen

Piano Concerto No. 2 in C Minor, Op. 18-1 by Sergei Rachmaninov

Chapter Twenty-Three
Prelude No. 15 in D-flat ('Raindrop') by Frédéric Chopin
'Le Coucou' by Louis-Claude Daquin
Piano Sonata No. 17 in D Minor, Op. 31, No. 2 ('Tempest' III) by Ludwig van Beethoven

Chapter Twenty-Six
Prelude No. 23 in B Major BWV868 by J. S. Bach

Chapter Twenty-Eight
Prelude No. 6 in D Minor BWV851 by J. S. Bach

Acknowledgements

To my publisher, editor and dear friend Anne Messitte, thank you. For Everything.

I am indebted to all the team at Knopf and Vintage. In your attention to detail, your dedication and your support, you go above and beyond. You do a fantastic job. Special thanks to Tony Chirico, Lydia Buechler, Paul Bogaards, Russell Perreault, Amy Brosey, Jessica Deitcher, Katherine Hourigan, Andy Hughes, Beth Lamb, Annie Lock, Maureen Sugden, Irena Vukov-Kendes, Megan Wilson and Chris Zucker.

To Selina Walker, Susan Sandon and all the team at Cornerstone, thank you for all your excellent work, enthusiasm and good humour. It is much appreciated.

Thank you to Manushaqe Bako for the Albanian translations.

Thank you to my husband and my rock, Niall Leonard, for first edits and countless cups of tea.

Thank you to Valerie Hoskins, my unprecedented agent, for your mindful counsel and all the jokes.

Thank you to Nicki Kennedy and the crew at ILA.

Thank you to Julie McQueen for having my back.

Thank you to Grant Bavister from the Crown Office, Chris Eccles from Griffiths Eccles LLP, Chris Schofield and Anne Filkins for advice on earldoms, heraldry, trusts and property matters.

Huge thanks to James Leonard for his tuition in the language of posh young Englishmen.

For all the advice on clay pigeon shooting, thank you Daniel Mitchell and Jack Leonard.

To my beta readers Kathleen Blandino and Kelly Beckstrom, and to my pre-readers Ruth Clampett, Liv Morris and Jenn Watson – thank you all for the feedback, and for being there.

To the Bunker – it's been nearly ten years now – thank you for joining me on this journey. My author friends – you know who you are. Thank you for inspiring me every day. And to the residents of Bunker 3.0, thank you for your constant support.

Major and Minor, thank you, for the help with the music, and for being exceptional young men. Shine bright, you beautiful boys. You make me so proud.

And finally, I will forever be grateful to everyone who has read my books, watched the movies, and enjoyed my stories. Without you this amazing adventure would not have been possible.

ABOUT E L JAMES

E L James is an incurable romantic and a self-confessed fangirl. After twenty-five years of working in television, she decided to pursue a childhood dream and write stories that readers could take to their hearts. The result was the controversial and sensuous romance *Fifty Shades of Grey* and its two sequels, *Fifty Shades Darker* and *Fifty Shades Freed*. In 2015, she published the no. 1 bestseller *Grey*, the story of *Fifty Shades of Grey* from the perspective of Christian Grey, and in 2017, the chart-topping *Darker*, the second part of the Fifty Shades story from Christian's point of view. Her books have been published in fifty languages and have sold more than 150 million copies worldwide.

E L James has been recognised as one of *Time* magazine's 'Most Influential People in the World' and *Publishers Weekly*'s 'Person of the Year'. *Fifty Shades of Grey* stayed on the *New York Times* Best Seller List for 133 consecutive weeks. *Fifty Shades Freed* won the Goodreads Choice Award (2012), and *Fifty Shades of Grey* was selected as one of the 100 Great Reads, as voted by readers, in PBS's *The Great American Read* (2018). *Darker* has been longlisted for the 2019 International DUBLIN Literary Award.

She co-produced for Universal Studios the Fifty Shades movies, which made more than a billion dollars at the box office. The third instalment, *Fifty Shades Freed*, won the People's Choice Award for Drama in 2018.

E L James is blessed with two wonderful sons and lives with her husband, the novelist and screenwriter Niall Leonard, and their West Highland terriers in the leafy suburbs of West London.

THE FIFTY SHADES TRILOGY

Romantic, liberating and totally addictive, the Fifty Shades Trilogy will obsess you, possess you and stay with you forever.

Daunted by the dark secrets of the tormented young entrepreneur Christian Grey, Ana Steele has broken off their relationship to start a new career with a US publishing house.

But desire for Grey still dominates her every waking thought, and when he proposes a new arrangement, she cannot resist. Soon she is learning more about the harrowing past of her damaged, driven and demanding Fifty Shades than she ever thought possible.

But while Grey wrestles with his inner demons, Ana must make the most important decision of her life.

A decision she can only make on her own . . .

THE FIFTY SHADES TRILOGY

Romantic, liberating and totally addictive, the Fifty Shades Trilogy will obsess you, possess you and stay with you forever.

When Ana Steele first encountered the driven, damaged entrepreneur Christian Grey, it sparked a sensual affair that changed both their lives irrevocably.

Ana always knew that loving her Fifty Shades would not be easy, and being together poses challenges neither of them had anticipated. Ana must learn to share Grey's opulent lifestyle without sacrificing her own integrity or independence; and Grey must overcome his compulsion to control and lay to rest the horrors that still haunt him.

Now, finally together, they have love, passion, intimacy, wealth, and a world of infinite possibilities.

But just when it seems that they really do have it all, tragedy and fate combine to make Ana's worst nightmares come true . . .

SEE THE WORLD OF *FIFTY SHADES OF GREY* THROUGH THE EYES OF CHRISTIAN GREY.

Their scorching, sensual affair ended in heartbreak and recrimination, but Christian Grey cannot get Anastasia Steele out of his mind, or his blood. Determined to win her back, he tries to suppress his darkest desires and his need for complete control, and to love Ana on her own terms.

But the horrors of his childhood still haunt him, and Ana's scheming boss, Jack Hyde, clearly wants her for himself. Can Christian's confidant and therapist, Dr. Flynn, help him face down his demons? Or will the possessiveness of Elena, his seducer, and the deranged devotion of Leila, his former submissive, drag Christian down into the past?

And if Christian does win Ana back, can a man so dark and damaged ever hope to keep her?

arrow books